THE YAWNING HEIGHTS

ALEXANDER ZINOVIEV

THE YAWNING HEIGHTS

Translated from the Russian
by Gordon Clough

THE BODLEY HEAD
LONDON   SYDNEY
TORONTO

British Library Cataloguing
in Publication Data
Zinoviev, Aleksandr
The Yawning Heights.
I. Title
891.7'3'4F   PG3490.I/
ISBN 0-370-30039-4

Originally published in Switzerland as
Ziyayushchie Vysoty
by Editions L'Age d'Homme, Lausanne
Copyright © Editions L'Age d'Homme 1976
Translation © The Bodley Head Ltd
and Random House Inc. 1978, 1979
Printed in Great Britain for
The Bodley Head Ltd
9 Bow Street, London WC2E 7AL
by W & J Mackay Limited, Chatham
Filmset in 11 on 12pt Plantin
First published in Great Britain 1979

CONTENTS

Translator's Preface

To render a pun from one language to another in such a way that both the meaning and the joke are conveyed is one of the hardest tasks an author can set his translator. Yet Alexander Zinoviev, a man for whom I have conceived a considerable admiration and respect as I have grappled with this book, has set me that problem constantly, right from the title page. 'The Yawning Heights' is an accurate, but wholly inadequate rendering of two Russian words—'Ziyayushchie Vysoty'. The verb 'ziyat'' means to gape or to yawn, as an abyss. But in the jargon of Soviet speechmakers and leader-writers the word which often prefaces 'vysoty' (heights) is 'siyayushchie' (with an s, not a z): 'gleaming' or 'radiant', as in phrases like 'the gleaming heights of socialism'—the radiant future towards which the Communist Party of the Soviet Union claims to be leading the progressive forces of mankind. So the title *The Yawning Heights* both encapsulates the paradox and snipes accurately at the jargon of the Soviet gospel.

And where are these 'yawning heights' to be observed? Zinoviev has placed them in the invented city or country of Ibansk. This too is a double pun, deriving partly from the commonest Russian forename Ivan, and partly from the coarse verb 'yebat''—to fuck. So Ibansk means, broadly speaking, a fucktown or fuckland for the Ivans.

These two examples give a taste of the translation problems which Zinoviev sets, and also, incidentally, of his attitude to the society which he is savaging. And his targets are very specific. So are some of his characters. In Ibansk all the inhabitants are called Ibanov. (The Russian man in the street, the John Doe, is Ivan Ivanovich Ivanov.) They are identified by descriptive names which have a touch of *The Pilgrim's Progress* about them—Leader, Teacher, Sociologist, Journalist, Artist, Writer. There are scores of characters in the book whom it is possible to identify fairly accurately with real figures from the Soviet intellectual and political scene. Truth-teller, for instance, clearly represents Solzhenitsyn, and Dauber the sculptor Neizvestniy, who at one time was a close associate of Zinoviev. The Boss is just as clearly Stalin, and Hog is Khrushchev. Which of the characters is Zinoviev himself? I think there are parts of him in a large number, but if I had to go for one, it would be Bawler. There are too many similarities between Bawler's biography and Zinoviev's own life for it to be purely coincidental. And I have no doubt that other characters would be clearly identifiable by anyone who had lived in the Soviet intellectual milieu which Zinoviev is writing about. But many of them are plainly archetypes as well, and I doubt whether the Western reader is losing very much by the lack of positive identification.

Alexander Zinoviev, his wife and daughter, are now in the West. The fact that they at least are no longer prisoners of the Ibanskian regime does not in any way invalidate his attacks on it. This year's trials of dissenters like Orlov, Shcharansky, Podrabinek and the rest show that Ibansk—the centre of population inhabited by no-one—is still very much a reality.

In an autobiographical note, which reached the West in the spring of 1978, Alexander Zinoviev says he wrote this enormous book in a period of six months. Unfortunately, it took far longer than that to translate, and it would have taken longer still had I not had the help of a band of long-suffering typists—Juliet Aylward, Lois Hill, Carole Lacey and, above all, Lalage Waldman, to all of whom my thanks.

G.C.
London, 1978

Author's Note

This book is made up of fragments of a manuscript which were found accidentally—i.e. without the leadership's knowledge—on a newly opened rubbish dump which was soon abandoned thereafter. The ceremonial opening of the dump took place in the presence of the Leader and his Deputies arranged in alphabetical order. The Leader delivered an historic speech in which he said that the age-old dream of mankind would soon be realised, as on the horizon we could already see the yawning heights of soc-ism. Soc-ism is an imaginary social order which would come into being if individuals were to behave to one another within society in complete accordance with the social laws. It can in fact never be attained because of the falsity of the premises on which it is based. Like every extra-historical absurdity, soc-ism has its own erroneous theory and incorrect practice, but it is almost impossible to establish either in theory or in practice what the theory and practice of soc-ism actually are, and to distinguish between them. Ibansk is a populated area inhabited by no-one, and which has no existence in reality. And if by sheer chance it did exist, it would be a pure figment of the imagination. At all events, if its existence were possible anywhere, it is anywhere but here, in Ibansk. Although the events and ideas described in the manuscript are, all things considered, imaginary, they have a certain interest as evidence of the erroneous ideas of mankind and human society held by the remote ancestors of the people of Ibansk.

Ibansk 1974

I

THE

YAWNING

HEIGHTS

I

STACMLFTC

All our scientists claim, and many foreign scientists accept, that the inhabitants of Ibansk are a whole head taller than everybody else, with the exception of those who have followed their example. They are taller, not by reason of any reactionary biological superiority (from that point of view they are identical to everyone else), but because of the progressive historic conditions in which they live and the correctness of the theory for which they have been the guinea pigs; and thanks too to the wisdom of the leadership which has guided them so brilliantly. For this reason the people of Ibansk do not live in the old-fashioned and commonplace sense of the word as it is applied to other people in other places. The Ibanskians do not live, but carry out epoch-making experiments. They carry out these experiments even when they know nothing about them and take no part in them, and even when the experiments are not taking place at all. This book is devoted to the examination of one such experiment.

The experiment under consideration is called STACMLFTC, from the initial letters of the names of its principal participants. The name was composed by Colleague and was first used in the scientific literature by Thinker, who took this opportunity to publish a series of articles on another and more compelling theme. The articles were written on a high dialectical level, with the result that no-one read them, but everyone applauded them. After this, the term STACMLFTC became generally accepted and no longer used.

The experiment was dreamt up by the Institute for the Prophylaxis of Stupid Intentions, and carried out under the supervision of the Brainwashing Laboratory, written up in the Fundamental Journal and was supported by an initiative from below. The experiment was approved by the Leader, his Deputies, his Assistants and by everybody else—except for a few holding mistaken opinions. The aim of the experiment was to detect those who did not approve of its being carried out and to take appropriate steps.

Methodological principles

Two groups of people took part in the experiment; the experimenter group and the guinea-pig group. These groups were composed of one and the same people. The guinea-pigs knew that they were guinea-pigs. The experimenters knew that the guinea-pigs knew this. The guinea-pigs knew that the experimenters knew that they knew. And so on. Moreover, the experimenter group and the guinea-pig group were autonomous and had no influence on one another. There were no informational links between them, and as a result complete mutual understanding was achieved. The guinea-pigs were guided by the following principles: (1) well, what can you do about it? (2) what would change if . . . ? (3) the hell with it! Colleague proved that from these basic principles there logically followed a string of derivative principles: (4) whatever you do there's no avoiding it; (5) there's got to be a limit; (6) why don't they just fuck off? The experimenters, on the other hand, were guided by the following principles: (1) whatever happens they won't get anywhere; (2) all will be revealed; (3) it'll all sort itself out. The aforementioned Colleague extrapolated from these bases the derivative principle (4) they will all plead guilty to everything.

The question as to whether or not this system proves the principle 'they will think up everything for themselves' has so far remained unresolved. But that in principle is not of principal concern, since everything thinks itself up, as there is nothing to be invented, since everything already exists. Thanks to the principles which have been set out there was an increase in the flow of useless information and a reduction in man-hours. The experiment became the reverse of autonomous and, like every well thought out and logically conducted experiment, it ended in nothing. The achievements of Science and Technology had their parts to play in the experiment. In particular, Instructor used a synchrophasocyclobetraton laser beam to sweep the area of Schizophrenic's lavatory and to register his intention of writing a quasi-scientific sociological thesis, an idea

(14)

which came into his mind at the very moment when, after severe constipation, he achieved the desired result and submitted the existing structure to severe criticism. This outstanding discovery was completely passed over in the Journal, and so we have no need to dwell on it here.

Time and place

After historic experiments the village of Ibansk was transformed. The former school building was redesignated The Associate Department of the Institute. The lavatory was rebuilt and clad in steel and glass. Now, from an observation platform, the tourists who flow into Ibansk in a never-ending stream can convince themselves with their own eyes that the false rumours that have reached them are the purest slander. A new Leader was appointed, and the old one was hidden somewhere because he was no longer of use. The new one was just as old as the old one, but no less progressive and erudite. Next door to the lavatory was built a new hotel in which the Laboratory was housed. So the tourists should have something to look at during the time they had free from visits to model factories, around the hotel ten new picturesque churches of the 10th century and earlier were built. Their walls were adorned with ancient frescoes by Artist himself, who painted a portrait of the Leader in the foreground. He was awarded prizes, decorations and titles for his work. Artist depicted the industrious heroism and the military prowess of our freedom-loving ancestors, and outstanding cult figures of that far-off but not wholly forgotten age. In the main fresco Artist painted the Leader and his Deputies, who for this were awarded prizes, while the Leader himself got two: one for the one thing, the other for the other. As a result food prices were lowered, which meant that they merely doubled, instead of rising by five per cent as they did outside Ibansk. The Ibanuchka River was dammed. It overflowed, flooded a potato field (the former pride of the Ibanskians) and swelled into a lake (the present pride of the Ibanskians). And for this all the inhabitants, with one or two exceptions, were decorated. The Leader made a long speech about it in which he analysed everything and outlined everything. In conclusion he said with confidence: 'Just you wait and see—we've hardly started.' The speech was prepared by

Claimant with a large group of helpers. This fact was kept somewhat secret, in the sense that everyone knew about it except the Leader, who was decorated for it and was then given a further decoration because he had been decorated.

On the far bank of the river there was a new development of apartment blocks all identical outside, but indistinguishable inside. Chatterer, who by chance had obtained a self-contained unself-contained room in an apartment in this area, used to say that everything there was so much alike that he was never wholly confident that he was in his home or that in fact he was himself and not somebody else. Member took him up on this and argued that this was a sign of progress, challenged only by madmen and enemies, since variety inevitably produces inequality. 'Just you wait,' he said, 'when they've built the food stores and other cultural and educational establishments, you'll like it so much that wild horses won't drag you away.'

In the centre of the new development there was a vacant lot which remained vacant for a long time. Initially the intention was to build a Pantheon there, then that was changed to the idea of an artificial lake stocked with pressed caviare. In the end they built a Bar—known as the Milk Bar. The Bar became enormously popular. There was always a great crowd around it whether the Bar was selling beer (which rarely happened) or not (which also rarely happened). People brought their own drinks with them. They sat around in groups on barrels, boxes and rubbish heaps. Groups formed for greater or shorter intervals. Some kept going for months and even years. Fairly recently one of them celebrated its 50th anniversary. To mark this occasion, all the customers were given decorations, while the Leader himself got two: one of them for not taking part, the other for taking part. A long-standing group seldom assembled its full complement. Normally two or three or four members of the group would meet in various combinations. But the meeting place of the group always remained the same.

The beginning

Once, Colleague, who had set himself the task of exposing and eliminating obstacles, turned up at the Bar. Although he had a complete right to jump any queue to get everything that there was to be had and even what was not to be had, to the surprise of the assembled company he took his place in a long queue and listened. The people who were talking had every appearance of being intellectuals, but for some reason or other, they addressed each other formally and did not use unprintable (in the old sense) words when they were talking about an unprintable (in the new sense) subject. Member said that it was senseless to deny the existence of queues, food shortages, fiddling, and boorishness. They were all facts. But they were also nothing more than the small change of life which did not derive from the essence of our 'Ism'. When the 'Ism' came to its full flower, they would no longer exist. Indeed, had not the 'Ism' been created by our best people to ensure that nothing like that *could* exist? 'You're right,' said Chatterer. But the 'Ism' means more than ceremonial meetings and processions. It is a specific form of organisation and production. Everything else is just talking points for blind deaf-mute idiots. Colleague said that he agreed with both of them, and produced the familiar saying that the full 'Ism' could be built in one town but it would be better to live in another. Member said that in his day you didn't exactly get a pat on the head for telling stories like that. Colleague told Member that it wasn't his day now, but ours. Chatterer said that he could see no difference in principle.

They found a place to drink at the edge of the vacant lot in a cosy garbage pit. Member delivered a diatribe and began to tidy up. Colleague rolled a barrel over from the Bar after he'd chatted-up the sales girl and made a date with her. Chatterer nicked a crate from someone. Careerist said that it was his crate and he'd only left it to get a fifth glass of beer, but Colleague just laughed at him and so he joined the group. Member took a hip flask from his pocket. Chatterer dashed a tear from his eye and said that he had never lost his faith in man. After the third round they reached that state of euphoria which makes men prepared to risk the hazards of the drunk-tank. Chatterer poured out all the criticisms he felt about his work. 'Your complaints are childish,' Colleague replied. 'You say you've got ten parasites, five trouble-makers, three informers and two paranoiacs. I think you're bloody lucky. There are two hundred people in my department. Two of them work half-way decently—one from stupidity, the other from habit. For the rest—well, great parasites have little parasites upon their backs to bite 'em; little parasites have lesser parasites, and so ad infinitum. They're scandalously untalented. They moan all the time and tell tales. They're always scheming. All they can think about is how best to waste more time. Look, do you see that stupid-looking sod over there knocking it back? He's one of ours. He's an Instructor, and I can tell you he's a first-class bastard and distinguished cretin. Even in the simplest situations he can't tell who's for us and who's against us.' Chatterer said that it wasn't altogether bad if people worked badly in his outfit, because if they worked well there, then it really would be bad for the rest of us. Careerist said that it couldn't be any worse. This prompted Colleague to recall the well-worn old story about optimists and pessimists, (Pessimist: 'Things are as bad as they could be.' Optimist: 'Oh, no. Don't worry, they'll get worse.') and he accused Careerist of being a pessimist. 'You might think,' Careerist said, 'that you spend all your time collecting anecdotes.'

After a few more pints Chatterer said that there was a sense in which it wasn't good that people worked badly, and it would be better if things improved. 'But generally speaking'—he completed his thought a few pints later—'that's of no consequence. No-one knows what is good and what is bad. Except perhaps for Writer.' Careerist said it was the same everywhere. 'Say that a vital part of a machine is broken, and we've got a very urgent, very important job to do, and we've got the go-ahead. So I ring the boss and tell him. He says, "Not to worry, I'll just ring the right department and they'll fix it for you." That evening I ring the department. They say it's the first they've heard about it. Next morning I ring the boss again. He's in a meeting and that's that. Next day I go and see him. Wait two hours. He says not to worry. Since it's so important and urgent we'll get it sorted out straightaway. He calls in the department head and tells him in my presence to get it done straightaway. Two days go by. Still nothing. A week after they've had a written order, they've got the drawings out, studied the technicalities and done the costing. Two weeks later they have it ready. Only it's the wrong part and not properly made. So I go back to the boss. "Nothing I can do about it," he says, "you can see for yourself." And he shrugs his shoulders."Sort it out for yourself." So I buy a bottle of vodka and I go and see the fitters and I say, "Look lads, there's another one like this once I get the part." Half an hour later there it is and a few spares as well. And the boss of the department gets a bonus.' Chatterer asked how they managed to get anything done at all with such a marvellous organisation. Careerist just shrugged. Colleague said it was all trivial. Unlimited resources. Unlimited powers. Concern for the job. Business-like people. Altogether a non-standard situation. Thereafter it became the normal kind of business where parasites and rogues flourish. Member said that in his time nothing like that ever happened. Chatterer said that in those days there simply wasn't anything comparable so the question didn't arise. Colleague said that it was always the same. Things only work out well when we aren't around. Chatterer agreed, things are always better without people like you. Colleague said he had to go, spat into an unfinished glass of beer, said he didn't understand how people could drink such filthy muck, and went his way. He's a great man, thought Member, and decided to start passing on via Colleague certain denunciatory documents and his proposals for setting things right.

Schizophrenic

In the time he had free from enforced idleness Schizophrenic was writing a sociological thesis. He was doing this work with all its predictable consequences at the request of his old friend Dauber. He didn't like writing and didn't want to write. He had to go to incredible and exhausting lengths to grab hold of his thoughts as they disappeared at lightning speed, and pin them to the paper. Apart from that, he was convinced that sooner or later everybody would find out what he was doing and he would be sent back to the Laboratory. And that made him feel gloomy. But he couldn't not write. He had a vague feeling of awareness of a secret known only to him or at all events to a very few, and he could not face ending his useless life without having made every effort to communicate that secret to the world. He knew that the world was deeply uninterested in this secret, but that was of no consequence. He felt a moral duty not to other people —for he owed absolutely nothing to other people—but to himself. Mankind consisted of himself alone. And it was before the eyes of this mankind that his primitively transparent life flowed by. It was before this mankind that he would have to answer at his last hour. But as far as Schizophrenic was concerned the most unpleasant aspect of the work of writing was the lack of a table and a decent fountain pen. Once Sociologist had brought him a beautiful pen back from abroad but it had got lost somewhere.

The idea of writing this thesis came from a conversation he'd had with Dauber. Dauber had said: 'Your forecasts and appraisals are coming quite strikingly true. How do you do it?' 'It's very simple,' replied Schizophrenic. 'All you have to do is to forecast what is forecastable, and to evaluate things which there is some sense in evaluating.' 'But how do you distinguish the predictable from the unpredictable and the assessable from the unassessable?' asked Dauber. 'I have my own theory for that,' said Schizophrenic. 'Tell me,' Dauber said. 'I'll try,' said Schizophrenic, 'but I warn you that it's a long way from being scientific theory.' 'Not to worry,' said Dauber, 'as long as it's true.' 'The other thing,' Schizophrenic continued, 'is that to use my theory you need patience more than thinking power. Let's say for instance, that you've been commissioned to do a painting and there's a hint of more work to come, and there've been a couple of lines in the press about your work without your name being mentioned. It might look as if there's a good wind blowing your way. But according to my theory there can't be any new winds for you. Just wait a bit longer and you'll see for yourself.' 'I've seen that for myself many times,' said Dauber. 'That's true enough,' said Schizophrenic. 'But every time it happens, you regard it as a chance fact, and not as something that is inevitable and theoretically predictable. Finally, my theory, like any other theory, is simple to the point of triviality, but learning how to use it is extremely complicated. It's rather like trying to teach an Ibanskian to eat rice with chopsticks— and you know how hard that is.' Dauber said, 'Your theory interests me as a purely intellectual manifestation, and not as an aid to the formulation of a code of sensible conduct. I rely on intuition to guide me in that. When I was in the Army I used to play dice, and I played rather well. Once I won the wages of nearly all the flying crew of my squadron. I had a whole heap of cash. Then we all went on the piss for three days. My method was very simple. First I'd stake ten roubles which I could afford to lose. If I lost I jacked it in. If I won I'd put twenty in the pot. If I lost I stopped, if I won, the stake went up to forty. As long as I kept on winning I went on doubling up. When the win was big enough I went for the jackpot. Sometimes the game went on long enough and I won.' 'Great,' said Schizophrenic. 'You've got the mind of a true scientist, not of an artist. Your method, like my theory, only works on one condition: you have to find people prepared to gamble regularly for a long enough time. And we haven't got very much time left.'

And Schizophrenic began to write. He wrote everything straight on to the paper without corrections. When he'd written a passage he handed it to Dauber, and never gave it a further thought. Dauber handed it on to somebody else to be typed, and the thesis spread all over Ibansk by unfathomable routes, getting into every institution and especially into those where it wasn't intended it should go. Finally it reached the Institute where Colleague discovered it by chance in the desk of a careless instructor. Schizophrenic called his thesis *Socio-Mechanics*, for reasons which he set out in the text.

Socio-mechanics

Scientific sociology has been in existence for more than a century. The number of professional sociologists in the world has swollen to an improbably colossal horde. Even here in Ibansk, where sociology has been permitted for only a comparatively short time, where it's been practised only temporarily and only on a scale and in directions which are acceptable to the leadership, even here, in a very few years, the number of sociologists has risen beyond the thousand mark and their researches have begun to take on a menacingly scientific character. Suffice it to say by way of example, that one of our best sociologists worked out a method permitting him to demonstrate a fact which struck the imagination of the Ibansk intelligentsia like a bolt from the blue. He showed that only 99.9999999999 per cent of the leaders of Ibansk are loyal to the other leaders of Ibansk, a statement which came into violent conflict with the official point of view, according to which 105.371 per cent of the total number of leaders are loyal. As a result of this it became necessary somewhat to restrict the development of sociological research in Ibansk and the above mentioned lately-eminent sociologist, despite his grandiose field studies on behalf of the Laboratory, found himself unable to establish how important a role in Ibansk and its surroundings was played by non-existent public opinion. For this reason instead of producing the three-volume work of scientific generalisations which he had intended, he was obliged to produce five volumes and to publish in the Journal a series of articles about the importance of the role of public opinion.

Bearing in mind the situation which has developed, I have decided not to hazard an entry into the disciplines of scientific sociology, but to set down my thoughts instead in the form of a new and particular discipline—Socio-Mechanics. The choice of title was dictated by the fact that I intend to take a non-historical view of the social qualities and relationships of people. According to this view, where there exist agglomerations of individuals sufficiently large for us to be able to speak about a society, social laws are always the same. These laws are simple and in a certain sense well known. Their recognition as laws which govern people's social life is hindered by the social law according to which the harder they strive to be officially recognised as better, the worse they in practice become.

From the very beginning I have been prepared to accept that my concept may be mistaken, but I still retain some little hope, since, as is well known, he errs well, who errs first. But if even this hope should turn out to be illusory, I will be glad of the fact that I was not as solitary in this world as has seemed to me hitherto.

Sociologist's observation

Later Sociologist, who was carrying out an analysis of Schizophrenic's thesis at the request of Doctor, underlined the last paragraph in red and wrote in the margin: Yes, he is mistaken; no, he's not the first.

Instructor

When the Institute learned that Schizophrenic was getting up to his tricks again, his old thesis was brought out of the archives and given to Instructor for closer study. The thesis had the strange title CORFTUO. The meaning of the title is explained in the text. But Doctor didn't bother to read the text and reached a faultless diagnosis on the basis of the title alone. Instructor studied the author's explanation, but decided to dig down to the concealed essence. The thesis began with a dedication.

Dedication

When he is explaining the meaning of his work to visitors to his studio, Dauber usually speaks about the problems of the inter-relation between the Spiritual and the Corporeal, the Human and the Animal, the Natural and the Urban, the Terrestrial and the Cosmic, the Great and the Small, and so on. When they hear these phrases which are clearly intended to be an indication of a high intellectual level, the visitors begin to nod their heads and to say 'da', 'ja', 'oui', 'yes', and so on according to which language they hope will provide them with a verbal equivalent for this unfamiliar material. Of course the use of such high flown language is in every way justified by Dauber's work, and of themselves, the words do not diminish the sensation of excellence which the works inspire. But there is in them another and less apparent level of content, to describe which demands the use of other linguistic resources. I have tried to formulate them. As a result I have produced a thesis which was just as much a surprise for me as for anybody else. It could perhaps be presented as an illustration to the works of Dauber, but as an out-of-the-ordinary illustration. It is an illustration of thoughts. And an illustration of thoughts should be very different from the generally familiar illustration of images. The illustration of an image is itself an image. The illustration of a thought should be a thought set out by those means which are available to the illustrator. I wrote this thesis at the request of Dauber himself, for he wanted to know one of the possible direct reactions of an interested observer of his work. I therefore wrote it straight down and made only the most trifling corrections to the text. So if you take what I have said about an illustration as a joke, then this thesis can be regarded simply as an experimental fact relating to the problem of the perception of works of art by their contemporaries.

2

CORFTUO

Treatise on fate, freedom, truth, morality and so on
In this treatise which aims to be both exhaustively incomplete
and rigorously unsystematic, it is my intention to set down
everything which I do not know on good authority about the
emergence of the guardhouse in the Ibansk School of Military
Aviation (ISMA) and about its early period of development
which was omitted from the official history because it had no
consequences.

Terminology
In place of the generally accepted guardhousological term
'guardhouse' I am going to use the word 'cooler', primarily
because it is shorter and more easily pronounced not only in
Ibanskian but in any other language. But there are also other
more cogent reasons. The term 'guardhouse' has a suspiciously
intellectual ring. The term 'cooler' has deep roots in folk culture. The term 'guardhouse' conveys a feeling of alienation but
'cooler' has about it a pleasant suggestion of spiritual refresh-
ment. It is closer to the as yet unrevealed mysteries of the
Ibanskian soul and is therefore a more accurate usage from the
scientific point of view. And as the Ibanskian soul becomes
increasingly an irresistible example to all nations, save for the
temporary absence of a few, the term 'cooler' has incomparably
greater perspective perespectives than its West European competitor. The term 'perespectives' means exactly the same as the
term 'perspectives' but is to be distinguished from it by the
higher social rank of those who use it. The term 'prespectives'
has acquired a still higher social rating. This term may only be
used by special permission of the highest authorities.

On one false hypothesis
Recently there appeared an unpublished book by the structuralist Ibanov, a native structuralist, but one better known

abroad, called *The Roots of the Contemporary Ibanskian Language from Time Immemorial*. This book alleges that the word 'cooler' arose quite independently from the West European word 'guardhouse'. Its basic derivation is the Tatar-Mongol word 'kule' (to kill). This root also developed into the word 'colony'. When the expression 'the spread of colonialism' was analysed by the computers in the Institute of Applied Coolotherapy, it was shown that the word 'colony' meant initially a number of literate persons in whom the 'cooler' had a particular interest. It was only later, when all other aspects of people's social existence came under the control of the 'cooler' that the 'colony' became a territorial unit. It was on this basis that the foreign, and therefore by definition reactionary, sociologist Ibanov produced his original but far from new hypothesis on the overthrow of the Tatar-Mongol yoke and the liquidation of its results. According to this theory, far from our destroying the Tatar-Mongol hordes and driving them from our territories, the very opposite happened; they destroyed us, drove us out and stayed behind in our place for ever. Administering a well deserved rebuke to the author of this hypothesis, if it can so be described, our colleague Ibanov confirmed yet again that the cooler appeared contemporaneously with the family and private property.

Chronology

Various points of view have been expressed about the time of the establishment of the cooler in ISMA. And as is usual in serious modern science, none of those theories corresponds to reality. Thus, in the five-volume work by our most distinguished coolerologist Ibanov, *The Genesis of the Cooler and its Influence on the Subsequent Democratisation of Society*, it is claimed that the cooler in ISMA was established only at the end of January. But one Fellow-worker who has survived for the moment, personally spent ten days in this cooler in December. Moreover when he arrived he found that there was already a group of men under arrest who had had time to acquire all the signs of a spontaneous prime social cell. As has been established by our applied sociology—recently authorised within reasonable limits (see for example the book by Ibanov and Ibanov, *A Tentative and Officially-approved Introduction to So-Called*

Applied Sociology)—the formation of such a social cell begins with the emergence of a leader, a process which needs at least a week to accomplish, and is completed by an initially unsuspected cell member becoming an informer. This transformation, which takes place unnoticed by the other members of the cell, and by the member himself, brings a social cell of this kind into the social organism as a whole. This takes at least another week. Thus at the time of arrival of our Fellow-worker in the cooler it had been in operation for no less than two weeks. Here we must disagree with Ibanov who, in his prize-winning monograph, *Informers in the Service of Social Cybernetics*, reduces this period to one week on the basis that the official informer Writer had been planted in the cooler, where he could not have failed to pursue his normal calling.

The fact of the matter is that the emergence of an individual as an informer in official and spontaneous social groupings follows laws whose principles differ in each case. In particular, as Ibanov proved in his article *Mathematical Models in the Theory of the Classification of Informers*, in official social cells the informer is appointed and in spontaneously-formed cells he simply emerges. Moreover the fact that Writer was an official informer was known from the beginning in the cooler and therefore he could not have been the immanent informer in the given social cell. It is perhaps worth remarking that the identity of this latter has not yet been completely established. Ibanov's opinion that the immanent informer was Patriot is not without foundation but it cannot be considered proven. Patriot himself in a major article published in the collection *Victims* hints at Dauber and even at Deviationist. Finally during his time in the cooler as an official informer, Writer specialised in reporting on such matters as stolen property, absence without leave, malicious gossip and so on, while the immanent informer would clearly have specialised in thoughts and intentions, as the following facts show. The theft by the prisoners of the largest cooking pot (Ferdinand) full of porridge remained undiscovered while a guard who took part in a discussion about objective truth and revealed his views on guard-duty, was very soon removed from the school and dispatched to an undisclosed destination. We may presume that the confusion over the precise date of the establishment of the cooler in ISMA is also connected with the fact that in January it was transferred from the room next to the kitchen to the cellar beneath the guardroom. Written evidence about the existence of the cooler before this transfer has not been preserved as a result of the walls being whitewashed, and historians have erroneously accepted the date of the transfer as the date of establishment. Incidentally this mistake illustrates one of the great merits of the general principle of historicism in our approach to problem-solving.

The school building

It is generally acknowledged that the ISMA building is the most beautiful and majestic of all those within the urban confines of Ibansk. Stamps depicting it can be found even in the countries of Latin America and Black Africa. It was built shortly before the War from a half-ruined stately home, an unfinished house belonging to a merchant, and a synagogue, and it has passed firmly into our golden architectural heritage. As a result, more than five hundred administrators, military leaders and visiting writers were given prizes, and comrade Ibanov himself was given two (the first for forbidding it, the second for authorising it). The bourgeois modernist Le Corbusier, when he saw the building with his own eyes, said that there now was nothing left for him to do here, and returned home. The leading art critic Ibanov, writing about this in his article *Why I am not a Modernist*, pointed out that that was the best place for him. The main feature of the ISMA building is that it has two façades: the main one in the rear, and a spare one at the front. The façades are built in so many varied styles that foreign tourists and guests—and even old inhabitants—still believe that they are different buildings. Because of this, before the war the municipal government handed the building over simultaneously to two organisations—the Aero Club and the Meat and Dairy Combine. A conflict situation developed. The bosses of each organisation prepared dossiers highly critical of each other and the leaders of both groups were arrested. Soon the supply of raw material for one of the conflicting organisations ran out, and the conflict was resolved with complete theoretical correctness. In his book *The Unity and Conflict of Opposites in the Town of Ibansk and its Surroundings*, the philosopher Ibanov quoted this case as a characteristic example of the fact that in our country, as distinct from others, contradictions do not grow into antagonisms but are resolved through being overtaken by events.

If you stand facing the main façade of the ISMA building, with your back to the town's main waterway, the River Ibanuchka, and the planned hydro-electric station, you will immediately understand how right Leader Ibanov was when he said, at the official opening ceremony, that in the radiant future which had recently dawned, every worker would live in splendid palaces like this. The façade of the building is decorated with nine hundred columns of every order known to world architecture, and on the roof a multitude of towers reaches towards the sky, blending into a unified whole, a perfect reproduction of the inimitable domes of the church of Iban the Blessed. Overcome by so much beauty, Ibanov, the world-famous engineer of human souls, produced this high-flown sentence in the editorial of the bi-annual journal *Dawn of the North-East*: 'In the presence of such unearthly beauty one can only stand to attention and bare one's head.' His namesake Ibanov, an officer-cadet, happened to glance at the aesthetic aspect of the building—which in his erroneous opinion was completely unsuited to normal human life—and, warily examining the three-storey-high statue of the Leader, whispered to his old friend, cadet Ibanov: 'As far as the number of columns per head of population goes, we have overtaken even the Greeks. Now we are the leading columnial power in the world.' His friend reported this conversation to the appropriate authorities, and the fate of the slanderer was decided before taps was sounded that evening. As it is put in The Ballad:

And cursing his fate, not a word of farewell,
He was carted away to a nasty cold cell.

The cell he was put into was one in the barracks, because the cells at ISMA hadn't yet been built. This gave the Command of the school a shadowy notion. As a result, Colleague was sent off on a Qualification Advancement Course where he went back to his study of the Prime Sources.

The shithouse

The designers of the ISMA building made one minor omission which was later to play an important part in the development of the literature of lavatorial realism. The architects made no provision for the shithouse. It later became clear that this was a deliberate and malicious omission, as they supported Ibanov's erroneous theory which states that shithouses should be eradicated at the initial stage. The writer Ibanov then produced another memorable sentence: 'If anyone gets caught, he is to be eliminated.' The omission was noticed only when the building was taken over exclusively by the Aero Club. They had to find a spot in the courtyard a long way from the building, and less cluttered with rubbish than the rest, and build a latrine-type shithouse. Two hours had to be allocated in the cadets' working day for trips to the lavatory, calculated on the basis of three ten-minute visits per head, and fifteen hazard-free seats. Of course there was not calculation in the real sense. The figure was initially arrived at purely empirically, and only given a theoretical basis *ex post facto* by the use of the powerful instrument of modern multiplication tables. Our local philosopher Ibanov used this in his book *The Dialectics of the General and the Particular in the Town of Ibansk and its Environs* as a brilliant example of the theoretical prediction of an empirical fact, comparable in its consequences for the development of science with the discovery of the positron. After dark there was a considerable risk that a visit to the shithouse would result in your getting a soiled uniform, and so the cadets began to avoid using it even during the day. A path was built, but it was too late—the cadets had become accustomed to using any convenient crannies of the rubbish tip in the yard, and the shithouse itself came to be used only by suspicious and solitary intellectuals seeking to display their ego. They were put under close observation.

On the non-use of information

On the way to the Bar Chatterer was joined by Schizophrenic. Colleague and Member were already there. Member was pressing Colleague to take an exercise book in which he'd set out his thoughts on reconstruction. He kept on pleading with the inflexible Colleague that it was stupid to try to cover up things like floods and earthquakes, things for which the Government had no responsibility. They are natural disasters or statistical facts which are unavoidable in any complex process. And rumours are bound to spread anyway. Colleague tried to change the subject by telling anecdotes. But, like any typical survivor of that epoch, Member had undergone a total amputation of his sense of humour and was totally immune to laughter. As Colleague gloomily eyed this fiendish fighter for truth, he said to himself, 'This is exactly what you deserve, you miserable cretin. I should have given up these stinking ideas long ago and taken up currency speculation. The pay is better and there's less responsibility. And the people are nicer.' Member refused to give up: 'Just take this latest price-drop. Why couldn't you honestly and directly tell people that the harvest was too good, that productivity had increased more than expected and commodity prices had fallen below the norm? Then people would understand and show some initiative themselves.' At this point Chatterer and Schizophrenic joined in the discussion. Colleague tried to change the subject, with a wink to show that Instructor was listening, but Chatterer said he didn't give a damn, just let him go on eavesdropping—after all, that was what he was paid for. And if Colleague didn't like it, he could go f—— himself—no one was keeping him. Schizophrenic said Member was talking nonsense, as information, by definition, could never be truthful and complete. No information at all was needed for the normal functioning of society, and the leadership's instinct was correct: to inflate worthless trivia, hush up important events and do all our rethinking for us. Perhaps it's not so much a correct instinct as a natural way of behaving. Perhaps the leadership would gladly have acted differently, but could not. Chatterer said that a healthy society, like a healthy man, didn't need information about the state of its health, and such information was totally useless to a dying man or to a dying society. Member began to sound off about disease and diagnosis. Chatterer objected that sickness is the normal condition of society; societies cannot be cured for the doctors do not exist, and those who do make diagnoses and write out prescriptions must be crushed like bed-bugs. 'That's not the heart of the matter,' said Colleague. 'You must lie to speak the truth, and speak the truth so as to lie.' And Colleague told the well-known anecdote about how one of our athletes was beaten by one of theirs, and the way it was reported in our papers was that our man came second and that theirs was next to the last. In the final analysis, radio, television and the newspapers don't derive from the essential essence of the 'Ism'. Schizophrenic said that when truth was permitted because it was unavoidable, it was generally known already and there was no need to reveal it. So people prefer to wander about aimlessly, leaping from one magnificent lie to another. A lie is always a revelation. And afterwards it can always be justified on the grounds that existence is complicated and that anyone can make an honest error.

Chatterer said that there are certain objective laws of disinformation like the laws of gravity, and that Schizophrenic almost certainly had some thoughts on that subject. Schizophrenic said that such laws do indeed exist. For example there is a tendency to minimise bad news and play up good news as much as possible. And if there is no good news, it has to be invented. People do not lie from evil intent, nor from stupidity, but because deception is the most acceptable form of social intercourse. This law works strictly formally and on any material. So people lie even when there is no need to do so and even when it may be harmful, because that is the only thing they know how to do. Member said that this theory did not explain the distortion of history. 'On the contrary,' said Colleague. 'People need to be told that everything was always worse before. For even a verifiable triviality may disclose a higher standard of living in the present.' Member said that the truth about the past cannot be hidden. There is incontrovertible material evidence. Chatterer said that only idiots would let themselves be consoled like that. Initially people hide the truth deliberately, and then cannot recognise it even when they want to. The only reliable props of memory are mammoths' broken skulls and the remnants of their last meal. And you can hardly call that history! History leaves no traces. It only leaves consequences which have nothing in common with the circumstances which gave rise to them.

The monument to the leader
In front of the main façade of the ISMA building, read Instructor, a larger than life-size statue to the Leader was erected on a granite pedestal with massive chains which for a long time were thought to be decorative. The foundations subsided unexpectedly, causing the statue to lean forward beyond the maximum permitted by the highest authorities, and it looked as though

sooner or later the Leader would plunge his mighty nose into the River Ibanuchka, reducing the hydro-electric station, which was planned to be built close by, into fragments. The sculptor was dealt with appropriately. Colleague came from the capital and discovered that in this position the statue had become even more stable. And the Very Important Person, who had come to present the development with a medal, observed that the statue inspired a feeling of guilt and a fear that this very guilt was about to crush you, which fully coincided with the Leader's world-renowned humanism. But it was too late to resurrect the sculptor, for science discovered how to do this only a great deal later. And even if he had been resurrected, there would have remained some doubt whether he was actually the same person. The statue was so oriented that wherever a cadet was going, he was bound to come face to face with it. This had an irresistible effect. On one occasion, Fellow-worker was setting off on French leave and when he saw the familiar profile outlined against the gloomy sky, he turned back in horror. Then he tried to slip away by climbing over the fence by the shithouse although this route was more dangerous. When the cult of personality was unmasked, and all its consequences were liquidated, the statue was hidden somewhere for the time being, and replaced by a naked torso by Ibanov which everyone ignored. Ten years before this event, Colleague had dreamed a prophetic dream in which he saw the statue totter and begin to fall. At first Colleague rejoiced and cried 'at last!' but then he saw that the statue was falling directly on top of him and he trembled. He tried to hold it up, but he wasn't strong enough and it crashed in quite a different direction—to this day, no-one knows in precisely which. For this, Colleague was elected to the Academy.

The ballad

The Ballad of the Unknown Officer-Cadet was published for the first and last time on the walls of the old shithouse at ISMA. Its supposed author, cadet Ibanov, was in consequence removed from the school, sent to the front, and soon became unknown. The Ballad began like this:

> I, my lads, am not a poet.
> I've no talent and I know it.

I don't write for publication
And get no remuneration.
What is more if truth be told,
Writing really leaves me cold.
But if I'm very bored, why then
I take a pencil or a pen.
When on guard I'm bored indeed
That's when I tried to write this screed.
There's no need to read right through it,
But I'd best get on and do it.

In January the old shithouse was destroyed. In its place a new one was built with a higher coefficient of utility and a lower cost price per unit. After this the staff and reservists of the school recognised the existence of two separate epochs: the epoch of the old shithouse and that of the new. The earlier period became a legend which enshrined all the best qualities of civilisation. The walls of the new shithouse were covered in no time with sketches, verses and aphorisms, largely of a certain erotic content. But there was nothing to equal The Ballad. And Deviationist was moved to prophecy: The time of the masterpieces was over, and the epoch of mass production of mediocrity was upon us. Since The Ballad was never published in any other form and since the memory of man is short-lived and fragmentary, this outstanding production of wall art must in all probability be considered to be lost forever. But the degradation of art was compensated for by the progress of scientific thought. Patriot, who took part in the building of the new shithouse, discovered two qualitatively differing strata of excrement and formulated the idea of measuring the calorific value of food by the calorific value of what remained as a result of its consumption by the average cadet. These two strata also differ sharply from the point of view of their emotional relationship to the world. It is perhaps enough to compare such lines from The Ballad as:

When they served us herring soused
We got some liquor and caroused

with the best lines from the new lavatory era, for example these:

I sat weeping on the pot,
Ate a little, crapped a lot

in order to see the change from the joyous themes—in the spirit

(33)

of the High Renaissance—to a gloomy decadence. The Deputy Political Instructor, who just happened to look into this new shithouse, deduced from this the need to strengthen political education. The results soon became apparent. Alongside the lines quoted above appeared these new ones:

> For one long hour I sat and writhed
> And laughed until I split my sides,
> I only had one bowl of kasha
> But filled the bog up, what a smasher.

But it's hard to say whether this was a manifestation of optimism, or just skilled apologetics.

Deviationist

In December, cadet Ibanov, who was on a training flight, parachuted out of his plane. His explanation was that his engine had caught fire. But when the aircraft crashed, it did not burst into flame. The expert commission which examined the engine discovered the charred fragments of cloth but attached no significance to it. Their argument ran as follows:

Since the plane did not catch fire even when it hit the ground, then it is clear that there was no danger of fire in the air. To this cadet Ibanov replied that judgements about the past which seemed true in the present were not necessarily true in the past, and that he would have liked to have seen what conclusion the experts would have reached when they saw flames coming from the engine if they had been at that moment in the aircraft. Colleague, who had done research on this subject before the War and had come very close to getting the Degree of Candidate of Humane Sciences, unmasked this statement as an attempt to distort dialectics by means of bourgeois formal logic. Cadet Ibanov's action was construed as an attempt to deviate by means of the deliberate destruction of valuable war material. And cadet Ibanov (hereafter known as Deviationist) was sent off to join Slanderer.

> My God! My God! Oh, what a fall!
> They've sent me to a tribunal.

(from The Ballad)

Murderer
Because I am so weak and human

I was tempted by a woman.
I stroked her tits and pinched her fanny;
I'm not a very fussy man—I
Should have looked more at her face
I wouldn't be in such disgrace.

(from The Ballad)

In December cadet Ibanov, who'd grabbed himself a bit of French leave, wounded the female citizen Ibanova in her left buttock with a home-made knife. At the inquiry cadet Ibanov testified that he was passionately in love with female citizen Ibanova and was going to marry her but that she had capriciously deceived him, lured by the gift of food offered to her by Quarter-master Rat Face, and had begun to co-habit with him as well. Colleague examined the weapon, experimented with it on female citizen Ibanova's right buttock, and failed to understand how cadet Ibanov had managed with such a blunt knife to penetrate the thick hide of female citizen Ibanova; his suspicions were aroused. When they were drawing up the indictment none of those present could think of a scientific, or indeed any literary, term for a woman's arse. It was cadet Ibanov who proposed that the word buttock should be used here, to which Colleague replied that now it was all clear to him. Cadet Ibanov (from now on known as Murderer) was put into the cells together with Deviationist and Slanderer to await transfer to the garrison prison. Female citizen Ibanova came to visit Murderer, and when he saw her through the window, he was horrified. As The Ballad puts it:

Never in my life, I trow,
Have I seen so plain a cow.
I look again and feel all woosey—
Could that really be my floosey?

Slanderer asked Murderer whether he had really meant to marry her. He answered that it was perfectly possible. Firstly, he'd only seen her in the dark. Secondly she was the first (and perhaps the last) woman in his life, and thirdly there was something about her.

A report for the leader

'Why haven't we seen you for such a long time?' asked Member. 'I've been very busy,' said Chatterer. 'We're writing a

(35)

report for the Leader, who wants to deliver this report specially for us.' 'What's the report about?' asked Member curiously. 'I don't know,' said Chatterer. 'We'll find out when we hear it.' Member said that in his time Himself wrote all his own speeches. Chatterer said that Himself couldn't write at all. It was simply that there were fewer reports and, for one reason or another, the people who wrote them never survived. Usually for the other reason. 'OK,' said Member, 'now stop pulling my leg.' 'I'm not,' said Chatterer, 'that's the way it is. We noticed ourselves that we were in need of correction and re-orientation. So we reported this through channels. So the decision was taken that we be corrected and re-orientated, and the decision was communicated to the proper quarters. The matter went right up to the Deputies. Since the Leader had decided that it was time for him to interfere in something personally, he was steered in this direction. He told the Deputies to prepare a report four hours long. The Deputies told the Assistants, the Assistants told the Bosses and the Directors, and so it came down to your humble servants. We of course, as aristocrats of the spirit, wouldn't get involved in this sort of thing. So we passed the job of preparing the report to the most mediocre, coarse, and hamfisted Executives who were desperate for advancement by any means, for any kind of advancement. They write down a load of mush, with inflated figures, absurd references and distorted notions, all plagiarised, and this flow of completely inconsequential nonsense is set moving upwards. At every stage it is polished by the rejection of sentences which could be interpreted in more than one way, by the addition of sentences which totally defy interpretation of any kind, by substituting woolly formulae for precise ones, by rounding off figures and so on. The huge army of miscellaneous officials, high-grade and low-grade, spend a great deal of time on visits to official retreats and luxury sanatoria and on study trips abroad. For at least half a year, the report goes up and down for re-writing and re-re-writing. Finally the text is typed out in bold letters and with the stressed syllables underlined, and it lands on the Leader's desk. Advisers indicate the comments that the Leader should make on the report, and after the Leader has given his approval, the text goes back down again for another rewrite. It's true that this time nothing is done about it, because the final version of the report taking into account the Leader's observations, has already been prepared for reading and has long been waiting in the adjacent office which belongs to the Assistant directly concerned.

At the proper occasion, the Leader has several rehearsals and then delivers the speech, getting all the stresses wrong and distorting all the foreign words. And the report becomes a document of the greatest historical importance. It will be published in three volumes with illustrations and commentaries. The Journal will print explanatory articles, reactions, praise, promises, and of course, criticism of those who are in error and who don't understand. Claimant will write a leading article with references to the Leader, the Deputies and the Assistants in a proportion of 50–10–1 on every page. We shall be obliged to study the report in special meetings organised for the purpose. And only then will we understand what we have done, what we should have done, and what we should on no account have done. Member said that that of course was a parody. Even he wrote his own works himself. Chatterer said that that's why Member was always having his knuckles rapped. If he were to follow the example of the Leader, his pamphlets could be found in massive editions in every lavatory. Schizophrenic asserted that Chatterer's outline was perfectly straight-faced: since where mass exploitation is concerned, the greatest wisdom coincides with the greatest stupidity. So, from the point of view of the final result, it is a matter of complete indifference whether a report is prepared by first-class intellectuals, or by first-class fools. And as the latter are, for many familiar reasons, preferable to the former, it is they who write the reports and so the reports turn out a good deal wiser than if they had been composed by geniuses.

Scientific laws

Initially, this is what I planned, wrote Schizophrenic. To draw up a list of clear intuitive statements about the rules governing social behaviour, and then, basing myself on this, to construct a theory, observing all the rules for the construction of theories, i.e. setting out the basic concepts and postulates and going on to the derivative concepts, theorems and so on. But later, after discussions with people of various classes and educational levels, I came to realise that this was only a secondary technicality. The man in the street is interested not in science as such but only in the forewords, explanations, and digressions which relate to it. In the present case, the theory which I was preparing to construct is devoid of meaning unless we first establish to what category of objects it relates. This must be done if only because even tentative clarity has been lost amid the welter of literature produced here on the subject. In particular, even among professional sociologists, I have met no-one who could define what is meant by the concept of the social individual, far less agree with anybody else about it. Moreover, the whole concept of scientific laws and the methodology of science is subject to such confusion and ambiguity among the specialists that I am obliged to descend to an even more fundamental linguistic base and define what I mean by the scientific law. As a result, the theory I had originally hoped to propound will have to be postponed indefinitely.

A scientific law is a statement (an assertion, a judgement, or a proposition) which possesses certain characteristics: (1) it is true only under specific conditions; (2) under these conditions it is true at all times and in all cases without any exceptions whatsoever (the exception which proves the rule is a dialectical nonsense); (3) the conditions under which such a statement is true are never fully realised in reality but only partially and approximately. So it cannot be asserted literally that scientific laws are detectable in the reality under study (*discovered*); they are thought up (*invented*) on the basis of the study of experimental data calculated in such a way that they can afterwards be used to derive new judgments from the given judgments about reality (including use for prediction) by the route of pure logic. The laws of science of themselves can neither be refuted nor confirmed empirically. They can be justified or not depending on how well or how badly they fulfil the role indicated above.

Let us take for example this assertion: 'If in one firm a man is paid more for his work than in another firm, then the man will choose to work in the former on condition that for him the work in both these firms differs only in the scale of payment.' That part of the sentence after the words 'on condition' determines the condition of the law. It is clear that two jobs identical in everything save the pay do not exist. There is at best a certain approximation to this ideal from the point of view of one individual or another. If we find cases where the man chooses to work in the firm where the pay is less, these cases do not negate the assertion under consideration. It will be clear in such cases that the condition of the law has not been fulfilled. It may even happen that in observed reality, people always choose work in firms which pay less. Nor can this be interpreted as a demonstration of the falsity of our assertion. This may arise for the reason that in such firms, other conditions of labour are more acceptable (for example a shorter working day, lighter duties, or a chance of doing some of one's own work in the firm's time). In such a situation the assertion under consideration may be excluded from the number of scientific laws as non-operative and unnecessary.

It should be clear from the above that one cannot regard as a scientific law an assertion which merely generalises from the results of observation. For example, a man who is obliged to go round Government departments and observe an assortment of departmental heads might reach a conclusion: 'All departmental heads are scroungers and careerists.' This assertion may be true or false. But it is not a scientific law since it is qualified by no conditions. If there are conditions which make no difference, then it is a special case and should be so indicated. But if the conditions make no difference, then they are fulfilled by any situation and the concept of a scientific law becomes necessarily inapplicable.

Normally the kind of conditions that are determinant do not fall into the category above but apply to concrete manifestations which are subject to observation. Take for example this assertion: 'In mass production the quality of the product diminishes so long as the enterprise is being run by inept management, and so long as there is no personal responsibility for quality and no personal interest in the maintenance of quality.' Here the condition is so formulated that examples can be adduced of such conditions in reality. And it does not exclude the possibility of cases where mass production may be linked with an improvement in quality since there may be other powerful factors in operation which the assertion overlooks. This kind of assertion is not a scientific law. It is merely a general assertion which may be true or false and which actual instances may confirm or refute.

If we speak of scientific laws, we must distinguish between what are described as the laws of things themselves, and the assertions people make about these laws. The delicacy of this distinction lies in the fact that we know about the laws of things only by formulating certain assertions, and we accept the laws of science as a description of the laws of things. However, this distinction can be drawn sufficiently clearly and simply. The laws of things can be described by the most varied linguistic means including assertions of the type, 'All men are deceivers', 'If you flick a mare on the nose she will wag her tail' and so on, which are not scientific laws. If, in a scientific law its basic part is separated from the description of the conditions, then this basic part can be interpreted as a determination of the law of things. And in this sense scientific laws are essentially an assertion of the laws of things. But the isolation of scientific laws as special linguistic forms involves our directing our attention in quite a different direction from that of the question of the laws of things and their corollaries. The similarity of phraseology and the apparent coincidence of the problems create complications here which are out of all proportion with the essential banality of the matter under scrutiny.

To distinguish scientific laws from the laws of things, it is clear that we must distinguish between the consequences of the former and the latter. The consequences of the former consist of the assertions derived from them by general rules or rules relating to the science in question. And they are also scientific laws (although derivative in relation to the laws engendering them). For example, one can construct a sociological theory in which, from a given postulate, namely that the individual strives to evade responsibility for his behaviour to other individuals who are in some sort of common relationship with him, there will be derived a given assertion, namely that the individual tends to social failure (not to keep his word, not to keep secrets, to waste other people's time, and so on). Moreover, the derived assertions are governed by the same conditions as the original postulates. The difficulty of normal deduction here lies in the fact that all the postulates underlying the conclusion should contain a fixed element defining the conditions, or else this element should itself be a conclusion. The general scheme of deduction is this: from the postulates 'A on condition B' and 'C on condition that D' is derived 'X on condition that Y' if Y is derived from B and from D simultaneously.

The consequence of laws of things fixed by scientific laws is not more laws of things but certain facts of reality itself to which the scientific laws are related. Take for example a law according to which there exists a tendency to appoint to senior posts not the wisest and the most talented people but the most mediocre and dim-witted—who are acceptable to management on other grounds and have the right connections. The consequence of this law is that in a given sphere of activity (for example in research institutes, in schools and universities, in cultural organisations and so on), senior posts are usually (or at any rate frequently) occupied by people who are stupid and inept from the point of view of the business they are involved in but cunning and resourceful in terms of their career interests. At every step people come up against the effects of social laws. Some of these laws are subjectively dismissed as coincidences (although in strict logic the word 'coincidence' is totally inappropriate), and others cause surprise, although they occur regularly. Who has never heard someone say, or never said himself, about the appointment of a certain person to a senior post, 'how could they appoint such a fool to such a responsible job, how could they give such a cretin such work to do and so on'? But it is not this kind of thing that should cause surprise but rather when senior posts are given to wise, honest and talented people. That is truly a deviation from the law. But that too is no accident. It is no accident not in the sense that it conforms with the law, but in the sense that the concept of coincidence is here once again unsuitable. Incidentally the expression 'responsible post' is stupid since all posts are irresponsible—the expression has sense only as an indication of the high grade of the post.

Chatterer

At this point Schizophrenic remembered Chatterer. In order to understand what society is made up of, he thought, mere emotion and a good grasp of facts are quite inadequate no matter how many facts there are and how terrifying they may seem to the man in the street. An advanced system of methodological principles of understanding is also required. These principles are simple and accessible to all. But in preparation someone must formulate them in a rigorously professional manner. Chatterer could do it, but evidently he has dropped out after all this business. What a pity that such a brilliant mind should be wasted like that.

The doubts of Dauber

Dauber said that the question of the relationship between scientific laws and the laws of things still remained unclear to him. Was reflection appropriate here or not? Schizophrenic said that he was getting deeply bored by the number of examples which confirmed the correctness of his theory. One of the consequences of the action of social laws was a tendency to a single-plane orientation of consciousness. A certain pattern of lines of force developed, turning the minds of men in one and the same direction. Everyone had to think according to the plan: scientific laws either reflected the laws of life or they did not. At the present time it was considered progressive to acknowledge both propositions in part. But that does not change the general orientation. 'And even you,' said Dauber, 'you do not see the possibility of any other position. But logically there can be no other position.' 'What has logic got to do with this?' asked Schizophrenic. 'How about this position: "I don't give a damn what you think or say on this subject"? That is a position of indifference to the given orientation; it is a preference for a different orientation in which this kind of question does not even arise. You would call me a cretin if I were to start talking about your work in terms of "reflecting", "expressing" and so on.' Dauber said that now he understood. But he took the opportunity to ask Sociologist for his professional opinion about Schizophrenic's manuscript. Sociologist leafed through the manuscript, admiring himself in the mirror, and pronounced it a load of rubbish, a pale imitation of obsolete ideas from abroad; he cited a few dozen foreigners and six of our people (three times his own, twice that of his wife, and once that of Thinker). But Schizophrenic's manuscript disturbed him: it was beyond a joke! Just think, here we are, doing an important job, slaving away, putting in time on trips abroad and at meetings, defending theses, writing articles and books summing up the situation and prospects, practically turning ourselves inside out, and along comes a twopenny-halfpenny junior research worker without a degree, who has the nerve to form his own judgements on questions on which we and only we are the acknowledged experts! No, that really made him spit. After he'd admired his features for another half hour in the mirror, Sociologist telephoned Colleague.

A dinner at Claimant's

One evening Claimant, who had played an outstanding if unnoticed role in the experiment we are considering, gave a dinner party. The guests were Sociologist and his Wife, and Thinker without his wife, whom he'd left as soon as he realised the worry and wastefulness of family life. Claimant took succulent pieces of almost raw, bloody meat, (which he got from the special 'closed' shop for top people, where the ordinary public could not buy), flung them into his gaping mouth, and chewed them with evident enjoyment. And Claimant held forth. He held forth, in a voice which could be heard by all those who wanted to hear or overhear, and one which could not fail to be heard by those who did not want to, and even by those who positively wanted not to hear. He lubricated his words with foreign wines acquired during his many trips abroad and brought back as gifts because he liked the bottles, unfamiliar to the Ibanskian eye in shape and colour, for all that these contained a filthy liquid that Claimant found loathsome, and which, when he was alone with his ghastly wife and his grimy conscience, he rejected in favour of his more usual hooch. 'It's high time we got rid of all these rogues and scoundrels,' trumpeted Claimant, 'for if we do not, soon they will take over. Our duty. . . . We must. . . . To lead the workers and the intellectuals along the right road.' Sociologist took succulent, well cooked chunks of meat bought from the special 'closed' shop, crammed them into his gaping mouth, getting them tangled up in his beard, and masticated with evident disdain. He adored airing his views on avant-garde topics, and hated it when he was prevented from doing so. He was now suffering therefore from an enforced mutism, for Claimant never let his interlocutors get in a single word. He held the exotic bottles up to the light with the air of a connoisseur, clicked his tongue, and drank incredible amounts of every possible blend. This lad'll go far, he thought, watching Claimant. He's got a devilish grasp of things. I know what he's after! And he's got a good chance, too. If we were to help him, then the cause of our left-wing intellectuals would be greatly advanced. And Sociologist nodded his head in agreement with what Claimant was saying. Wife fastidiously took morsels of medium-rare meat from the special 'closed' shop with her stubby little sharp-nailed fingers, placed them neatly in her gaping mouth, munched them quickly, and coquettishly hitched her leather miniskirt a little higher to reveal her thighs—the fat thighs of a forty-year-old bluestocking. She was even fonder of holding forth than Sociologist and Claimant, and had a complete right to, for she was intellectually far more able than anyone present except Thinker, a fact of which she had become increasingly doubtful recently, since she had defended her thesis. And so she suffered more than anyone else from the effrontery of Claimant, who completely ignored her as a stupid cow. Claimant, she thought, is a boor and a lout. But he is determined and he does understand the situation. And he's got connections. He's well read, of course. And anyway he's a head taller than all these Neanderthals. They are all just common criminals. There's no one around with a better claim than Claimant. And above all, he's one of US.

Thinker took almost raw pieces of meat from the special 'closed' shop in his great hairy paw with its dirty nails, steered them in the direction of his gaping mouth, and chewed them leisurely with the air of a man doing everyone a favour. Thinker was an incredibly wise man and he understood that it was better not to interrupt Sociologist and his Wife, as what they said was almost always rubbish; and that as far as Claimant was concerned, one had to speak with gestures. His mighty bald dome radiated total understanding and agreement with Claimant's views. This scum's really got it made, he thought. Ah well, that's life. In this world it's only the nonentities and the rogues who prosper. Incidentally, I mustn't forget to touch him for a couple of hundred. Thinker had long owed Claimant a massive sum of money, but today he was desperately short. He had to find a hundred roubles to pay for an ikon he was giving to an Italian girl who had brought him some velvet trousers as a present, and with whom he planned to sleep, and another hundred for an ikon to give to a French girl who had brought him some socks and who planned to sleep with him. This is first-rate meat, said Thinker, when Claimant paused for a second to shove his forefinger in his mouth and search the crannies of his teeth for an errant fragment. Claimant said he was entitled to it. Incidentally, he'd had a word with Assistant, and they'd take Thinker on part-time. They'd got a good closed shop, too. Just ignore what it looks like outside. 'They've got some very bright people. You can get away with saying things there that'd get you into big trouble anywhere else. And they're training people not for us, but for their own uses. And of course the standard's got to be higher. So there'll be lots of travelling. They send all their staff who've got foreign languages abroad to lecture.'

'I think,' said Claimant, reverting to his earlier theme, 'I think we've got to attract the cissies for the good of the cause. Especially Slanderer. He'd bring a whole flock with him. He thinks a lot of himself of course, but he's certainly a figure-head. We'll have to get him made an Academician.' Wife said that of course Slanderer deserved it, but we mustn't forget that there are others who are no worse—and perhaps even bet-ter—and younger. 'One of Thinker's articles has just been translated, and I'm just about to publish my pamphlet. It might be thought of as being too popular, but all the same I've managed to include a lot of interesting thoughts on the dialec-tics of the general and the particular, and to have a good go at Secretary.' Sociologist interrupted his Wife. 'What's supposed to be so special about Slanderer? If he'd done anything remark-able, he'd have made sure that everyone knew about it and talked about it. But no-one knows anything or understands anything. And you don't come across many references to him, either. They're fewer and fewer.' Thinker said that Slanderer was far from naive and uninterested in day-to-day matters. 'He gets paid in foreign currency for the translations of his books.' 'Oh, they're like sheep; they're all pretence,' said Claimant, 'but they pick up what they can where they can. I heard quite by chance that he's trying to sneak his latest book into the Pub-lishers—for a fee, of course. But for an accident, he would have got away with it.' Although they all knew that these particular publishers never paid fees, they all began to calculate the fee that Slanderer might have picked up for his unnecessary and incomprehensible book.

Before he left, Thinker casually asked Claimant to lend him three hundred roubles until payday. 'We all know about your paydays,' Claimant thought, but he gave him the money and got another three hundred roubles' worth of leverage over Thinker. As he lay in bed, Claimant thought about Wife's thighs (he's a lucky chap, the old windbag!) and told his own scrawny bitch that he'd been too hasty in proposing Slanderer for the Academy. Slanderer's well known and, the times being what they are, he might just make it. If he does, he won't stand on ceremony with us. He'll have our guts for garters. He thinks we're all fools and rascals. We can't be led by the nose like that. I'll have to speak to Academician. That wily old bastard's as jealous as hell of Slanderer, and he'll shoot him down in two shakes. And Claimant fell asleep, pacified. In his last waking moment there flashed across his mind the notion of taking on a housekeeper, of acceptable age—there, he thought, was something he ought to consider. On the way back to their state-owned villa, Wife said to Sociologist that if she had to choose between two evils, she would choose Claimant and not Slanderer.

Artist's statement

Artist wrote a long letter to the Institute about the activities of that so-called 'artist' Dauber, drawing very serious attention to them. He wrote that no-one understands Dauber's work. Foreigners often visited him and put out slanderous rumours that Dauber is a genius. And there are some of our own so-called intellectuals who support these rumours which have not been approved by the Commission. It is no accident that those who do *not* think Dauber is a genius do not visit him. And they are the overwhelming majority. It is widely known that Dauber is a drunk, a drug-addict, a womaniser, a homosexual, a lesbian, a currency speculator, every other kind of speculator, an egoist and a shark. Artist laid special stress on the fact that Dauber is not a genius by any means, and requested that urgent steps be taken in this connection.

Colleague's report

At the Bar everyone knows who I am and what my aims are. As a result, they all speak to me so openly that it is impossible to establish the truth. It seems that they consider that if a colleague does not conceal who he is, then he must be off duty, and you can say anything you like to him. Moreover, there is this strongly established tradition among the Ibansk intelligentsia: they are at their most open and frank with those to whom they should not be talking at all. Our problem is not in gathering evidence, but in extracting anything of value from this avalanche of words. Added to that is the difficulty that they talk and talk nineteen to the dozen, but only to come out with the same stale truisms repeated ad nauseam. And since in our business truth is only that which is novel and elicited with much effort, the study of the problem which interests us is coming up against great difficulties. To overcome these difficulties, we shall have to see that the subjects of the experiment learn to hold their tongues and hide their evil thoughts.

On foresight

The laws of science are a means of observing conformity with the law in a real sense and not merely in the apparent chaos of events, wrote Schizophrenic. In its application to social manifestations, this notion is associated with two questions: (1) What is going on? (2) What will come to pass? The former leads on to the latter. In posing this problem, the last thing we want is to hear yet again about the facts which we already know and which underlie the problem, or about similar facts. We want to know whether this will actually come to pass or not, will it get worse or not, will it ever end or not, will it spread or not, and in particular, will it affect us or not, will it affect others or not—in other words, we want to know what is going to happen. So the question of whether events conform to a law really boils down to the question whether it is possible to forecast events.

But no two forecasts are alike. It is one thing to forecast, for example, that on such and such a date such and such an aircraft will crash in such and such a place. It is impossible to predict such an event by the application of scientific laws. Indeed, if it were possible so to predict, then we must assume that people would take steps to see that it did not happen, thus making it

(47)

even more impossible to predict. Such an event can, of course, be predicted, say, by people who have planted a bomb in the aircraft. But that is not a scientific prediction. It is quite another matter to predict, say, that the number of aircraft accidents will increase. Here we are talking not about a single empirical instance, but about a certain tendency in a complex chain of events. Now not every individual flight of an aircraft is subject to this prediction, and it is not so easy to take steps to eliminate this tendency. Social laws are also among those which make it possible to predict something of the tendencies of events *en masse*, and to conceive something of the future of individual events only from this standpoint. Knowledge of events enables us to work out a more or less effective orientation in the flow of the events of life, and to work out a strategy of life or at least the makings of such a strategy. The manifestation we refer to as the ability to get on in the world really amounts to a certain skill in orienting oneself in life, which is based on an intuitive and fragmentary comprehension of the social laws. The sociological theory of which I speak is merely a manifestation of intuition.

Writer

In the beginning Writer produced mediocre slanderous verses. His series *Freedom-loving themes* had a good deal of popularity:

> Where you are not,
> Life is tedious and harsh,
> An iron grey sky
> O'er the swamp and the marsh.

But he caught himself in time and turned over a new leaf. He began to write truthful talented compositions of a high literary level. After the removal of the old Leader, Writer published his *Confession of a True Artist* which became the manifesto of Ibansk prose writers of the new era:

> We have all made our mistakes,
> Some time, some place,
> And even I, leaving the highway,
> I may have taken the wrong turning.
> But basically I've been proved right,
> And count myself now every man's equal,
> Now, like everyone, I shall sing the praises,

Of the role of personality. Oh, pardon me—
the role of the masses.

Writer was paid a large fee, and then he was assigned the task of travelling around the world at the state's expense to preach the real truth. Recently he returned, and rang round everyone he knew and did not know. He telephoned Dauber. 'I say, old man,' he said, 'I'm dying to see you. I want to ask your advice on a matter of great importance to me.' Dauber said come round, and Writer turned up at the studio with two chicks, three lasses and four women.

'Hello, old man,' he said, and sniffed Dauber three times. 'I'm glad to see you. You're looking good. Well, how are things here? You've heard, of course, that I'm just back from Over There. They really live it up, those bastards. All the gear you want. Just look at me. Quite something, isn't it? And dirt cheap. You can see any film you want, write what you like. Nothing like here. They're saying over there that you're thinking of leaving. You should have done it long ago. They want you over there. Let's see what you've been doing lately.' Writer glanced swiftly at Dauber's works, yawned, and said that he'd seen enough of that sort of stuff Over There. 'I don't understand what our leaders are so afraid of, whatever daft things we do. We're all so untalented. Including you. Don't get up-tight, I'm saying that as a friend. And mediocrity always comes to their support. It might give out the odd spark or two, but in the end it always sides with them. Real talent is neither pro nor anti—it just doesn't give a damn about their silly games. It's got its own affairs that concern no one else. And what's more, its friends always destroy it sooner or later. You can't imagine what happened here when I published my *Poem on Duty*. That band of mediocrities was ready to tear me into shreds out of sheer black envy. I had no end of trouble getting it nominated for a prize. And they won't give it me, the bastards. Sorry, old man, but I can't give you any more time. Things to do.' And, leaving behind the latest number of the Journal, Writer vanished from the studio, along with the two chicks, the three lasses, and the four women.

'What do you make of that?' Dauber asked Slanderer, when Writer had gone. 'What did he come here for?' 'You know perfectly well why,' said Slanderer, 'but if you want a formal

(49)

scientific analysis, here it is. First, so he could tell you and anyone else who happened to be in the studio that he'd been Over There, and to parade all his finery. Secondly, to remind you that he's a success. Thirdly, to hint that no-one would object if you were to emigrate over there. And finally, to let you and anyone else around know that the last number of the Journal has a big article over Thinker's signature analysing the philosophical sense and the social significance of his *Poem on Duty*.'

The poem on duty

The *Poem on Duty* created a great stir in all circles and raised Writer into the ranks of the most talented thinkers of Ibansk and its neighbouring territories. In the final version, as is well known, the poem was published in two parts:

I

I am proud of the midden in which I sit up to my ears.

II

I devotedly lick the leaders' arses.

There were contradictory rumours that there had been other versions of the poem, that they had been rejected by the censors, that the poem had only been published with massive cuts and even then only as a result of public pressure above and to the right. Thinker's bold article put an end to this tittle-tattle. Probing into Writer's creative laboratory, which Writer composed especially for this purpose after the publication of the Poem, Thinker was able to show convincingly that the author had undergone a prolonged creative evolution. Thinker isolated three stages in this evolution. In the first, civil-lyrical stage, the poem had first been conceived in this form:

I lie in bed, nude as they come,

And contemplate your mighty bum.

The word 'mighty' was struck out and replaced by 'enormous', and in its turn 'enormous' was struck out and replaced by 'mighty'. 'Nude as they come' was stricken out and replaced by 'nuder than some'. Finally, the last line was taken out altogether, and at the conclusion of the first stage the poem appeared thus:

I lie in bed, nuder than some,

And in my hands clutch your fat bum.

Then a further line was added:

A pleasure which just strikes me dumb.

But this line was crossed out in red pencil, and the author was never to return to it. The first stage lasted from January to December. In the second, civil-personality, stage running from another January to another December, the author composed a whole series of variant versions:

1. I piss the pool of pee in which I lie,
   And lick my own arse. What a guy am I.
2. I adore the arse I lick,
   And shit the shit in which I sit.
3. I sit to my ears in my own,
   And the thing that I lick is my own.
4. I sit.
   I lick.

According to Thinker, this fourth variation, however much of a paradox it may seem at first sight, leads to the final version.

The third, civil-state, stage which lasted five years after the first two stages, was a period of an agonising creative search for the best of the variations. It was only after the historic experiments that the author summoned up the courage of a true artist, and chose the version he should have chosen.

When Fellow-worker had read the poem, he said:

The law has always been the same,
To our days from antiquity,
The poet's mind is maimed, and lame
But this one's in totality.

Ravings

Schizophrenic locked his door so that the drunken owner of the flat in which he rented a tiny room should not come bursting in, set on his knees the board which served him as a writing desk, and fell to thinking. What a good thing I'm alone, he thought. I wish that everything could remain as it is. If only for a while. I must somehow manage to communicate even one thousandth part of what I've thought, even if it's only to one person. Otherwise, what's the use? Then there came into his mind a sort of confusion, of which Instructor later said that it had come from his subconscious: typical Freudian ravings. Schizophrenic came first in the mathematical Olympiad. Academician himself came and shook him by the hand, remarking that he was a sloven who couldn't even square up the corners when he made his bed. Schizophrenic kept on making and remaking his bed, and all the time Academician kept on tearing it apart. On the far bank he could hear enemy officers issuing their orders. Schizophrenic could not understand why they were shouting the precise co-ordinates of their headquarters so loudly. The war was going to start tomorrow morning, and they were still on a staff exercise. The officers were being taught how to write reports about the deaths and burials of their men. The manoeuvres went on and on, and they were running out of names. Schizophrenic invented a simple and effective method for the creation of a practically speaking unlimited number of names. Academician praised him, saying that he would make an officer one day. But when Academician had studied Schizophrenic's method, he told Instructor that it had no scientific value. Then Schizophrenic began to write his treatise.

Social laws
It is widely accepted, wrote Schizophrenic, that human society is one of the most complex of manifestations, and that as a result, the study of human society is beset with unusual difficulties. That is a delusion. In fact, from a purely cognitive point of view, society is the easiest manifestation to study, and its laws are primitive and accessible to all. If it were not so, social life would be totally impossible, since in society people live by these laws and must necessarily realise what they are. There are of course difficulties inherent in the study of society. But they are far from being of an academic nature. In order to understand society, the main thing to grasp is that it is simple in detail, and complex only in the huge accumulation of detail; one has also to resolve to speak the truth on the matter, to acknowledge the banality of one's ideas, to discount the established system of prejudices, and to have the ability to give one's thoughts wide publicity. There is one difficulty of a cognitive nature. This is that deduction is impossible owing to the excess of data, the multiplicity of initial concepts and assumptions, the paucity of deducible consequences, and the practical uselessness of what is deduced.

All this has a dispiriting effect on the modern scientist, whose mind has been stuffed full of mathematicisation, formalisation, model-making and so on. And the most primitive of the laws of society are social laws.

When we speak of social laws, we are usually referring to the state, the law, ethics, religion, ideology and other social institutions which govern people's behaviour and which make them coalesce into a homogeneous society. But social laws do not originally depend on such institutions and affect neither their inter-relationship nor their functioning. They lie in quite a different sector of social life. It is of absolutely no concern to them what it is that unites people in a particular society. They operate somehow or other, since over an adequate period of time people come together in sufficiently large groups. The institutions referred to above exist themselves in accordance with social laws, and not the other way round.

Social laws are the definitive rules (of actions, of conduct) determining how people behave to one another. Their basis is the historically established and constantly developing impetus of people and groups of people towards self-preservation and the improvement of their conditions of existence in a social situation. Examples of such rules are: less give and more take; less risk, more profit; less responsibility, more kudos; less dependence on others, greater dependence of others on oneself, and so on.

Social laws are clearly not fixed in the same way as the rules of morality, law and so on, for reasons which can easily be divined, and about which I will write specifically later. But despite this, they are known by all and are accessible to all. People discover them and assimilate them with striking ease. This is explained by the fact that they are natural, that they respond to the historically established nature of human beings and human groups. It needs exceptional conditions for a particular man to develop within himself an ability to depart from their authority and to act despite them. And it needs a long and bloody period of history for a group of human society to develop the ability to resist the social laws to any perceptible degree.

People learn the rules of social behaviour. They learn them on the basis of their own experience, by observing others, by their upbringing, through education and experiment, and so on. The rules are self-evident. People have the mental capacity to learn the rules for themselves, and society offers enormous opportunities to put them into practice. In most cases people are not even aware of the fact that they are going through a systematic training for their role as social individuals as they carry out what they consider to be entirely normal day-to-day activities. Inevitably so, for if they do not learn the rules of society, they are incapable of living.

Although the rules of society are natural in that they correspond to the nature of man, people prefer to keep silent about them or even to conceal them (in the same way that they hide dirty linen or lock themselves in the lavatory as they perform their natural functions). Why is this? Because society has progressed largely by inventing devices which limit or regulate the action of social laws. Morality, law, art, religion, the press, publicity, advertising, public opinion and so on, have in great measure (although not of course entirely) been invented as such devices. And while all these, as they have developed into massive organisations, have themselves been influenced by the rules of society, they have in various ways fulfilled and (where they exist) fulfil an anti-social role. The social progress of society has been by and large an anti-social progress. For centuries people have been taught to channel their conduct in forms acceptable from the point of view of morality, of religion, of law, of tradition and so on, or to conceal their behaviour from outside observation as something reprehensible. And it is hardly surprising if the rules of social behaviour seem to them to be improper if not actually criminal. Moreover, individually people develop in such a way that they regard social rules merely as possibilities which might just as well not exist. If a man behaves according to these rules and recognises the fact, then very frequently he experiences psychological conflicts and doubts; he experiences what is happening as a spiritual drama. Examples of people who have demonstrated their ability to defy social laws and who have as a result become objects of the greatest veneration corroborate the idea that these laws are repugnant, or, more precisely, that they are not laws at all, but something unlawful. Finally, examples of societies in which social laws, by virtue of the authority of morality, religion, the code of law, public opinion and so on, have acquired a terrifying

(54)

role, tend ultimately to embroil the real situation and erect an insurmountable barrier to truth—a striking example of the evil created by men from the best motives. Incidentally, the best motives as a rule provide cover for the most repulsive people.

Social laws are always visible, and in this field it is useless to expect discoveries like the discovery of micro-particles, chromosomes and so on. In this context the only discovery can be to establish what is visible and well known in a certain system of concepts and assertions, and to demonstrate how such trivialities can fulfil the role of laws which govern human existence, and how our social life is directed not by benevolent titans but by vile nonentities. Herein lies the basic difficulty in understanding social life.

When, nevertheless, people talk about given social laws, they usually deprive them of the status of general human laws and regard them as inhuman laws of some 'ism' or other. It is supposed by that that in another, better 'ism' there would be no place for them. But that is erroneous. First, there is absolutely nothing *in*human about them. They are simply what they are. They are in no way more *in*human than the laws of companionship, of mutual help, of respect, and so on. The contrasting of the conception of evil and good social laws has, from the scientific point of view, absolutely no sense at all, since they are merely mirror images one of another, isomorphous in structure and equivalent in their consequences. Let us, for example, take the principle of the conception of bad social laws: 'Every man A tries to undermine the social positions of another man B' (all other conditions being constant). Equivalent to this is the principle of the conception of good social laws: 'Every man B tries to bolster the social positions of another man A'. Only on condition that the concepts are mixed can this effect be avoided. But here mixed concepts exclude the possibility of a scientific approach and the construction of a theory. In other words if we take a concept according to which evil is inevitable and good accidental, or the opposite concept whereby good is inevitable and evil accidental, by this we do not resolve the question as to which occurs more frequently, good or evil, and the concepts in question do not of themselves explain either the one thing or the other, which means that they may be equally well used to demonstrate either.

And, secondly, a humane or *in*human 'ism' is formed in a given country, and depends not on the social laws as such, but on the complex coincidence of historical circumstances, including whether or not the people of the said country have the ability to develop institutions opposed to the social laws— (moral principles, legal institutions, public opinion, publicity, press, opposition parties and so on). Only in cases where nothing of this kind exists, or where it has reached only an early stage of development, can the social laws acquire great strength and determine the entire physiognomy of the society, including the capacity to define the nature of the organisations intended to protect people from such laws. And then a special kind of society is brought into being, in which hypocrisy, oppression, corruption, waste, irresponsibility (individual and collective), shoddy work, boorishness, idleness, disinformation, deceitfulness, drabness, bureaucratic privilege, all flourish. These societies betray a distorted evaluation of personality—nonentities are elevated to great heights, exceptional people are debased. The most moral citizens are subjected to persecution, the most talented and efficient are reduced to the lowest common denominator of mediocrity and muddle. It is not necessarily the authorities who achieve this. A person's own colleagues, friends, work-mates and neighbours bend all their efforts to deny a man of talent the possibility of developing his own individuality, or an industrious man the chance of advancement. All this takes on a universal character embracing every sphere of activity, and particularly the spheres of government and of creative activity. Society is threatened with being turned into a barracks. This threat determines the psychological state of the citizens. Boredom and anxiety prevail, and a constant fear of worse to come. A society of this kind is condemned to stagnation and to a chronic putrefaction if it cannot find within itself the strength to resist these tendencies. And this condition can last for centuries. I know a ninety-year-old man who suffers from tuberculosis and an ulcer: he cannot be called a healthy man on the grounds that he has reached the age of ninety and seen all his vigorous contemporaries into their graves. And if I am to die without having reached even half the age of that old man, I shall still not envy him.

Sociologist's opinion

When he had read this extract from Schizophrenic's manuscript, Sociologist said to Dauber that Schizophrenic would get into really hot water for it. 'Whatever for?' asked Dauber in surprise. 'What do you mean, what for?' replied Sociologist, no less surprised. 'This is all about us and our society.' 'There isn't a word here that says it's all about us,' observed Dauber. 'Our bosses are no fools,' said Sociologist. 'Hypocrisy, oppression, disinformation, waste and so on—a babe in arms would recognise who all that's about.' And Sociologist told a story of a man who shouted 'Arrogant blockhead!' and was arrested for insulting the Leader, even though he protested that it was his workmate he had in mind. 'Come off it—you and your work-mate!' he was told; 'everyone knows who the arrogant blockhead must be.' 'But that's not legal,' cried Dauber, 'to charge a man with slandering us, just because someone decided that his words could be applied to us.' 'What's legality got to do with it?' exclaimed Sociologist. 'I'm talking about an established system of evaluation which provides the raw material for legality. This manuscript will be assessed by an expert. And only a man who will produce the desired conclusion will be nominated as an expert. A lawyer? He's not a specialist, and can't be an expert in this sort of case. Another expert? Name me one. I know by heart the name of every single person who has the right to be an expert in this kind of matter.' 'What about you?' asked Dauber. 'I'm his best hope,' said Sociologist. 'But what can I do? And what's more I want to stay out of it. The work isn't so strong in the scientific sense that it's worth going to the scaffold over. And as the basis for a denunciation it's nothing compared to what we already know.' 'Slanderer thinks,' said Dauber, 'that Schizophrenic is a genius.' 'Certainly,' said Sociologist, 'he has an idea or two. But there are plenty of people who are thought of as geniuses . . . But we've got our own criteria to go by.'

Deviations from the norm

'I have read your treatise,' Member said to Schizophrenic, 'and I cannot agree with you on a whole number of points. For example, what you have to say about the role of the state. Have you read today's papers? No? Well, they prove my point. They've discovered a bunch of bribe-takers and condemned them. One of them was a professor, another a university lecturer. The others were all in the same line of business. As you can see, we're not afraid of exposing such matters. So you see, young man, that the main question for us isn't the presence of shortcomings—everyone's got faults—but the struggle against them by the forces of the state.' 'But did the papers mention that the biggest crook was the director of their ideologically top-grade establishment?' put in Chatterer. 'And his chief henchman was head of the Department of Ethics, incidentally. And they didn't mention the fact that not long ago the entire local government of a district was pulled in on far graver charges than mere penny bribes such as they're writing about here. And have you heard about the case of the lawyers? No? Pity!' 'How do you know all this?' asked Member. 'All Ibansk knows about it,' said Chatterer. 'But there haven't been any reports about it,' said Member. 'Does that mean that it never happened?' asked Chatterer. 'And do you know what happened to the main crooks in the affair you know about and which therefore actually happened? They were let off with a warning and a slight demotion. They didn't even have their villas confiscated.' 'These facts must be checked,' said Member, 'and steps taken.' 'Just you try,' said Chatterer, 'and see what'll happen to you. We're concerned with a more serious matter than central heating radiators that don't heat, or minor fiddling with the apple crop.'

'It's silly to deny that the state fights against breaches of the law,' said Schizophrenic. 'But I want to draw your attention to the purely social aspect of the state's activity. Let's examine a case like this. The administrative manager of an enterprise you know well acquired power vastly greater than that of the managing director. He handled all matters relating to apartments, villas, motor cars, salaries and so on. And he took bribes on such a scale that in comparison these heroes in the papers are mere third-rate fiddlers. Now, do you think that no-one knew about all this? Everybody knew. But that didn't matter. Tacit knowledge is one thing, formal acknowledgement something quite different. What was going on suited the people at the top, and the people at the bottom kept quiet either out of fear or in the hope of a percentage. Anyway, when the manager finally overreached himself, and there was a threat of scandal, he was actually taken in hand. But how? They rapped him gently over the knuckles, warned him, reproved him. He trimmed his appetite a little. The state fights faults all right, but not in the name of any high idealism—it does the least it can get away with, and then only if it has something to gain. In doing so the state acts fully in accordance with social laws, as an organ of social justice, and not as a protection for the oppressed and the injured. It's worth noting here that (apart from the fact of the state itself being a collection of social individuals), different social laws have mutually opposing consequences. The manager I was talking about was trying, in accordance with one social law, to get as much as he could for himself out of his position and, as a result, was strengthening his position as much as he could. The other officials, according to different social laws, were seeing to it that his real position (in terms of wealth and power, in the first instance) should not too far exceed his official position. The combined effect of differing social laws is a tendency towards a middle-of-the-road position. Social law is the result, and also the means of this tendency towards the middle. As far as degrees of punishment are concerned, they, as everyone knows, are determined by the social position of the person being punished (with the rare exception of a totally extreme situation).' 'I wholly agree with you,' said Chatterer. 'I can add just one further thought which might be useful for Member. In our country there are not and cannot be any shortcomings. And those shortcomings which are sometimes acknowledged to exist here are so rare and unusual a deviation from our healthy fault-free norm that to all intents and purposes they do not and cannot exist, and they are therefore openly combated with the very aim of showing everyone that to all intents and purposes they cannot and do not exist.' Member said that he would certainly establish whether the facts mentioned above were true, and would see that justice was done. When Member had gone, Chatterer said to Schizophrenic that Member was a striking example of an individual completely incapable of understanding a general rule in specific events. Schizophrenic said that according to his observations, people everywhere lacked an intuitive feeling for legality, and its place within them was filled with a banal capacity for simple generalisations. It is easy to generalise. But it is just as easy to refute a generalisation, since one constantly observes examples which contradict them. I have just conceived the idea of examining to what extent certain cognitive operations respond to social demands. I can say at once that a simple generalisation as applied to events in the life of society will wholly conform to them, but any attempt to grasp their underlying laws is anti-social.'

Elections to the Academy

The Academy had one vacancy for a full Academician, and two for corresponding members. About a hundred candidates were proposed for full membership, and for the two corresponding memberships there were proposed almost everyone who wanted to be proposed, could be proposed, could not be proposed or could not be not proposed. Lists of candidates appeared in the newspaper for two weeks. The Institute proposed the Leader and his Deputies. The Laboratory proposed the Assistants and the Deputy Assistants. The Journal proposed the Assistants to the Deputy Assistants, the senior Colleagues, and the junior Counsellors. Three scientists were also proposed who from their youth had no connection of any kind with science, but who had since gone on to more responsible work. The first wrote a confidential letter about the second, in which he demonstrated convincingly that the latter was not at all the person he made himself out to be. The second wrote an open letter about the first, proving just as conclusively that he himself was indeed who he made himself out to be, while the former was truly not the person he was taken for. The third broadcast the real facts about the first two. The first two published a joint statement about the deviations of the third when they were all Over There together. Then they elected a fourth who had not been proposed at all, but who had been of great help to a certain man who was very close to the Leader, and a fifth who happened to be that certain man, but who remained incognito as required by high considerations of state. One Deputy was also elected (the Leader had been elected at the previous election, but was proposed each time as a sign of love and respect), and five Assistants, thirty-three Deputy Assistants, and about a dozen assorted Colleagues and Counsellors. These latter were immediately sent away on foreign assignments.

Slanderer was also proposed. At the Council, he was personally proposed by Claimant and seconded by Academician. The hall burst into applause. Everyone went about looking delighted, and saying that new times had come at last. 'Yes,' some of them said, 'the tide of history cannot be turned back.' 'You can't turn back the clock of history,' said others. Yet others said that time carried forward with irreversible momentum. They all shook Claimant warmly by the hand and praised his courage. In the past, anyone who had proposed Slanderer would have found himself up against a wall looking down the muzzles of the firing squad. As little as two years ago no-one would have dared even consider the possibility. Everyone was bitchy about Slanderer's having agreed to submit himself to the ballot. 'That's real academic disinterestedness for you,' junior and senior lecturers with and without degrees whispered to each other as they idled in the corridors. 'I could just do with a villa like his,' said one bearded youth. 'Or a flat like his,' said a girl with an over-developed figure who had just defended her dissertation on the latest trendy topic. 'His lectures were appalling,' said a third being of indeterminate sex. 'And what's more he's hopelessly out of date. The lead's been taken over by the Newfoundland school. Read my article in the Journal.'

Slanderer never believed he would be elected. But he submitted the necessary forms every time to augment his collection of rejections. He had already collected several dozen letters of refusal to his applications for permission to attend conferences, symposiums, colloquiums and lectures, for election as a corresponding member, for prizes and so on. 'Now,' he said, 'my collection will be embellished by yet another valuable exhibit.' At the meeting of the selection committee, Academician delivered a two-hour speech on Slanderer's work. 'Of course,' he said, 'Slanderer is unguarded in what he says, he is rude to the bosses, and he is a hopeless organiser. Of course, he is not quite one of US. Not to the point where he is altogether not one of US: but not not one of US to such a degree that we should consider him not one of US at all. And at all events he is not to such a degree not one of US that we cannot consider him not one of US. They publish him Over There, and invite him over, and he doesn't rebuff them. We have told him more than once that he should deliver a rebuke to them. And he has refused. Take, for example, his recent election Over There. I personally asked him to turn it down. There were more worthy candidates. But he refused to refuse. But I,' Academician said in conclusion, 'I am for him.' And Slanderer was not included in the list of candidates. In the evening Academician telephoned him and told him in detail how he had stood up for him, but that these reactionaries had done their own dirty work. 'But we'll show them yet. We'll certainly get you in at the next election.' At all the elections which followed there was no mention of Slanderer's name, and worthier and younger candidates were put forward, as on each occasion the winds shifted.

The beginning

A group of men under arrest, read Instructor, consisting of Slanderer, Deviationist and Murderer, led by Sergeant and escorted by two troopers armed with training rifles with holes drilled in them so that they couldn't be fired, was moving off to the garrison cooler. The route lay by the Square of the Leader, along the streets named after his closest associates, then along the streets named after his great predecessors, and finally along the street named after the Leader himself, which led straight to the cooler. As they were on their way, a conversation took place which serves as a reminder of the spiritual life of the intellectuals of that epoch. Slanderer said that he had only been joking, and Deviationist said that for jokes like that they take you out and stick you up against a wall. Murderer said that we'll all fetch up there sooner or later and who's to say which of the two is better. One of the troopers said that one would do better to think before sounding off. Deviationist said that there was no point in thinking first, because if a man thinks, he's sure to sound off. The other trooper said that there were all manner of people who shoot off their mouths, and then other people get into trouble. Murderer said it was always other people who got into trouble, but that the trooper shouldn't worry, because he wasn't 'other people', he was exactly where he belonged. On reaching the cooler, it turned out there were no vacancies. Owing to force of circumstances, the vague idea of creating a cooler specifically for ISMA became a real and immediate problem—which yet again confirms the old philosophical truth: even in our country nothing happens without sufficient

(62)

basis. It is now impossible to establish who first gave public voice to this idea, since, like every truly great idea which reflects the maturing demands of society, it floated on the wind. The Commandant of the School said we had as much right to it as anyone else. Colleague gave the idea a secure scientific basis. The Sergeant was given the job of translating the idea into reality. On this subject, he delivered a long speech which consisted in the main of highly idiomatic expressions, such as where the f— did anyone think he was going to find a f—ing building and f—ing people to run it. Deviationist said that Sergeant's speech was pure rhetoric, since there was adequate room inside the School building to set up a dozen coolers with a full complement of prisoners and guards. Murderer added that mankind, as history teaches us, never experiences any difficulty in principle in the establishment of prisons. The entire School staff joined in discussing the problem of where to put the new cooler. The School split into two main groups of opinion—the Reformers and the Retributionists. The Reformers insisted that the cells should be in a warm, dry, light room near the kitchen. The Retributionists held the diametrically opposite view, favouring a flooded cellar beneath the guardroom. Murderer produced the argument which swayed the debate in favour of the Reformers. Since a prison is part of the super-structure of society, to establish one in a cellar is a crude ideological error. Sergeant joined the ranks of the Reformers, for the first and last time in his life falling a prey to the corrupt bourgeois humanism of the great French educators of the eighteenth century. When he realised his error he tried to recant, but in our country it is easier (while still not easy) to do something from scratch than to redo something which has already been done (usually badly done), so the prison was organised in accordance with the wishes of the Reformers. The room had to be cleared of new engines for old planes which had been withdrawn from service ten years before they got to the School, but which were still on the secret list, plank beds installed and little stoves put in. The formal opening of the cooler was attended by officers of the School and the Garrison, and also by the civilian workers from the kitchens. The Commander of the Garrison Bath house delivered a speech which no-one listened to but everyone remembered. Then they sat

(63)

down on the beds as if they were about to set off on a long journey. With a stool and a file of newspapers they'd taken from the reading room, Slanderer, Deviationist and Murderer set off for the newly opened prison. Colleague wished them a good house-warming. The cooler was about to begin its historic existence. When the bosses had left, Murderer wedged the door shut with the leg from the stool, the remainder of which, together with the newspapers, they burnt in the stove.

Angles A and Angles B,
We've had all that shit now, you see!

(From The Ballad)

Patriot

The new cooler, having started as a manifestation of historical necessity, soon began to have a feedback effect on the life of the school. It became a powerful weapon in the education of the new man. Hardly had Murderer got the door jammed shut with the leg of the stool, than there was a knock at the door, which turned out to be Patriot, an outstanding cadet, both in his military and political education. From the threshold he informed them that he had been sentenced to ten days for requesting to be sent to the front, but that he could see no logic in this, since fifty cadets were being despatched to the front without having the slightest desire to go. Deviationist observed that this merely demonstrated the iron logic of the social laws since, according to these laws, Patriot's destiny was at the whim of his superiors and not under his own control, and by putting in a request for transfer to the front, he had offended against the social laws by evincing a wish to control his own fate by his own will—so he had got everything he deserved. 'But,' Deviationist continued, 'Patriot has not carried out this sacrifice in vain. In the eyes of his officers he has now shown himself to be a true patriot. Now he can stay peacefully behind the lines. His conscience is clear—he has, after all, as good as been to the front. Now he will be sent to the front only in the extreme case when there is no-one else left to send.' Patriot listened to what Deviationist had to say with the total scorn of the front-line warrior for the Rats of the Rearguard, and within five minutes he was kipping on his bunk, poisoning the atmosphere to such

(64)

putrid effect that without a doubt he must have just been transferred from kitchen duty. As the Ballad has it:

> Woe to any guardhouse dwellers
> Who sleep beside our kitchen fellers.
> The noxious farting from their asses
> Will make them choke, like poison gases.

Defeatist

The next to arrive after Patriot was Defeatist—Cadet Ibanov, who on the way to the airfield had picked up a leaflet dropped by God knows what enemy aircraft who for some reason had penetrated so far behind the lines. Defeatist was in an irresponsible state of mind and firmly believed that he had picked up the leaflet purely mechanically and hadn't read it. To this Murderer pointed out that thoughtless impulsive actions reveal a hidden factor of personality, as the Special Department and the Tribunal were well aware. At this, Defeatist shot himself and fell unconscious next to Patriot. Slanderer said that trying to grab everything was a primal and fundamental human characteristic. This lad clearly had a very high grabbing coefficient. Had it not been for this idiotic accident with the leaflet, he would probably have had a long and enviable career ahead of him. 'Hardly,' said Deviationist. 'In any career conformity to the norm is always more highly valued than exceeding the norm. Our platoon commander was a great soldier, always beautifully turned out. But deep in their hearts the high command decided he was a bit of a dandy and nicknamed him Dancer. So he was never appointed company commander.'

Panicker

The next arrival was Panicker—Cadet Ibanov, famed throughout the School because he spoke first and didn't think afterwards. During a political instruction lesson, when the instructor was telling the class that our forces, having inflicted great losses on the enemy, had withdrawn from towns A, B, C, D . . . he came out with a particularly brainless remark 'Hurray! The enemy is in panic and is fleeing behind us!' No-one grasped the sense of these words, although everyone burst out laughing. When the political instructor had wiped the tears of laughter from his eyes, and spluttered 'What a joker!' he packed

Panicker off to the newly opened cooler as a matter of course. The Sergeant posted three men to guard the cooler. They and Panicker all flaked out on the bunks. The door was wedged shut again, but this time with a bayonet, because the stool leg had been carelessly burnt in the stove.

Sociologist

Like other representatives of the intelligentsia, Sociologist visited the Bar, but he paid no attention to groups of drinkers, and deep in his heart regarded them with scorn, while acknowledging to his intimates that there might be something to them. 'At all events,' he said, 'these gatherings disturb the official structures.' Recently Sociologist had been abroad (he hadn't been back long enough even to report to Academician and Instructor), where he'd loudly propagandised our greater achievements, while quietly studying Their methods. And Sociologist thought that there were great changes just around the corner. And he was not wrong. Methods were permitted to the extent that they produced the desired results without disturbing the basis of society. But even that was sufficient inducement for Sociologist to look at the gatherings at the Bar through different eyes. It suddenly occurred to him that he'd found a vein of gold. There, before him, in a pure state, without any extraneous admixtures, unclouded by economic, political, juridical, family and suchlike similar factors, the social laws lay, stood, fidgetted and grimaced—as they pursued their inevitable business.

These people, thought Sociologist, gather here and form groups as they like, quite freely, without any compulsion. They aren't connected by any economic, political, bureaucratic, family or other inter-relationships. 'Here, in a pure state, with no extraneous admixtures, we can observe the laws of the formation and functioning of primary social cells, we can see sociality as it is, study the social laws as they naturally are.' Now he would be able to tweak Their (the foreign sociologists') noses, and twist Our sociologists round his little finger. He just had to ensure that no-one could trip him up, and indeed that no-one should notice anything.

Carefully combing his beard and rehearsing some suitable phrases and postures as he stood in front of his mirror, Sociologist put on a foreign suede jacket and foreign corduroy

trousers, picked up his foreign rectangular briefcase, telephoned Instructor and set off for the Bar. He jumped the queue
to buy himself a beer, and tried to infiltrate one of the drinking
groups and start his concrete research by means of a professionally prepared interrogation . . . oh, pardon, these old habits die
hard! . . . questionnaire. But he didn't have much luck. He was
taken for an informer, and no group would let him in. Finally
on the outskirts of the crowd he spotted a group of three men,
one of them wearing a hat, another glasses, and the third a
moustache. Judging by that, thought Sociologist, they must be
intellectuals, and he set off in their direction. They cleared a
space for him on the crate to put his beer-mug and continued
their conversation without paying any attention to him. 'You
haven't convinced me of anything,' said Member. 'I considered
and still consider that a man should have a correct view of the
society he lives in.' 'Why "should"?' objected Chatterer. 'That
is the psychology of oppression. Let a man decide for himself
whether he should or not. And why should your view be
accepted as correct? That's oppression again. Let a man choose
for himself.' 'But I have a right to set out my own view on
society if I think it's right,' retorted Member. 'Considering that
you've had your knuckles rapped,' said Chatterer, 'you've no
such right. Who d'you think you are anyway? An Old Member
—big deal! Judgements on society don't belong in the field
of law, they belong in the field of prerogatives. They're not
the prerogatives of an individual—they're the prerogative of the
authorities, and then only in special cases. An individual has the
right only to subscribe to what is established, and even then
only in established forms and within established limits.'
'What's more,' added Schizophrenic, 'your assertions don't
stand up to any kind of criticism. For example, you say that our
trade union organisation is parasitical and that the unions ought
to be liquidated and their useful functions handed over to the
authorities and the boards of directors. What would you
achieve by that? D'you really think that you would actually
release a million people to divert on to Great Construction
Projects? Rubbish! First of all, you wouldn't get these people to
go voluntarily. Secondly, relying on the connexions and opportunities of their own whose existence you aren't even aware of,
this entire workforce would infiltrate and inflate the existing

(67)

organisations and spawn a whole lot of new ones no whit less parasitical than the old. And thirdly, their place would immediately be filled by another organised group performing the identical functions.'

Sociologist asked if he might join in the discussion which he found extremely interesting. He said that he was a sociologist working on this very problem, that he'd recently been abroad, where things of course were quite different from here, and that he agreed with the last speaker. Striking an appropriate attitude, he began to orate in a voice that could be heard all over the waste lot. 'Recently we finished a sociological study of manufacturing costs in the Factory. We spent almost a year on it. We came up with the conclusion that the work force should be reduced by five hundred, and presented the Director with our results. And what do you think? He just laughed at us. He said he knew that perfectly well without our help, except that it wasn't five hundred but at least a thousand he ought to get rid of. But he wasn't allowed to dismiss one person. They would never authorise him. Quite right too. Where would they go? They've got families to feed. Redirection of labour? Where to? Conditions would first have to be created to tempt people of their own free will, and that costs a lot of money, which we haven't got yet. So it's not as easy as it seems to solve apparently trivial problems. You don't need to be very bright to see what's wrong. And it's pretty simple to come up with wise suggestions. But to find a real solution—that's another matter.' Chatterer observed that nothing real could be found here, since there was nothing real in nature; he drank his beer and said goodbye. Sociologist suggested another round and more conversation.

The advantages of the cooler

Instructor locked his office door. 'Let's have a rest from all this rubbish,' he said, and hurriedly took Schizophrenic's manuscript from the safe.

> At last your sleepy eyelids close,
> But look, it's time to don your clothes,
> Lights go out—and Corporal's here
> Bawling to be sure we hear:
> Reveille!

(From The Ballad)

When the prisoners heard the racket of the corporal of the reserve regiment bawling 'Reveille!' they woke up but, aware of their privileged position, remained in bed. The advantages of the cooler regime were becoming apparent. The philosophical truth regarding the pros and cons of freedom was confirmed. A period of non-freedom, as it should be in a genuine historical drama, began with a feeling of relief and temptation. First, there was no need to fold your blankets, since there were no blankets to fold. Secondly, no-one was going to turn you out in all weathers for P.T. And the attitude to P.T. of the cadet at liberty is expressed in these terms by the author of The Ballad:

> Then according to the rota,
> Of P.T. we do our quota.
> Bloody stupid, you'll agree,
> To have to go and do P.T.
> Your back is breaking,
> Arms feel rough,
> We cry out aching
> 'That's enough'
> 'Silence, fellers!' Sergeant cries,
> 'Now for the next exercise.'

Thirdly, there is no need to go to the Flying School to study theory. The author of the Ballad sums up the average free cadet's attitude to education thus:

> Mornings when it's barely light,
> We're marched off to the School of Flight.
> To sit in class is simply torture,
> Trying to master what they've taught yer.
> Learning how to fly a plane
> Means sitting at school desks again.
> Ailerons, flaps and elevators,
> Higher maths for navigators.
> Learn the functions of controls
> Learn the stresses during rolls,
> And the same again tomorrow—
> A trainee's life is toil and sorrow.
> I can't stomach all this crap,
> And so in class I take a nap.

The drawbacks of the cooler

Even the cooler has its drawbacks. First of all, the food. Secondly, the work. Inasmuch as expenditure of energy is inversely proportional to the degree of non-freedom, work on jankers is as good as a holiday. But inasmuch as the degree of unpleasantness of work is inversely proportional to the degree of freedom, work on jankers is roughly equivalent to penal hard labour. Prisoners in the cooler are allocated work which is distasteful to society. Early one morning a rumour started that it had been decided to demolish the old shithouse and build a new one. The cooler was plunged in gloom. The rumour was confirmed. It was at about this time that the officers, who had their own centrally-heated lavatory, reached the conclusion that the old shithouse could no longer satisfy the increasing demands of society, and was now actually retarding the Irresistible Forward March. In philosophical terms, content no longer corresponded with form. A staff committee was formed. The Deputy delivered a speech. It was only on this occasion that the mainstay of martial oratory was revealed to be a prompt-sheet, and this produced a great impression on the cadets. The Deputy cited many examples of heroism at the front and in the rear, and called for these examples to be followed. The C.O. ordered: 'Volunteers, two paces forward, march!' But then the unexpected happened. There were no volunteers. For three hours after that, the cadets were kept standing outside in the frost. All the high-ranking officers of the School made speeches, even those whose existence had never been suspected. The prospect of gaining the title of 'privy-emptier' was so appalling, that not even the offer of five packs of tobacco and a three-day pass was of any help. There is no knowing how this episode would have ended if someone hadn't remembered the existence of the cooler. The C.O. conceived the idea of using the prisoners, and he ordered the platoon commanders to secure an additional two prisoners each. By lunchtime, the cooler was full to bursting. After this, Colleague produced and validated the theory that the cooler was a form of organisation of labour which in no way contradicted the glorious ideals of the state. The shithouse detail (as it was dubbed by Patriot, who had quickly settled in to the cooler and now felt quite at home there) included Writer, Intellectual, Gelding, Leadswinger,

Dauber and Fellow-worker. History has not preserved the names of the rest.

Fellow-worker and others

Fellow-worker got into the cooler as a result of a misunderstanding. When he signed on for yet another loan, he overdid it and subscribed his entire annual salary. He was much praised, and for a whole month he was held up to everyone as a shining example. After a month a new loan was floated, and Fellow-worker had nothing left to contribute. The School therefore could not raise a one hundred per cent subscription. Leadswinger, who had a professional aptitude for avoiding duties and parades, got in by a pure accident. After making his bed he had managed to slip in again beneath the mattress. But an inspection took place just then, which took note of this excellently made bed, and decided to examine the method employed. Gelding and Dauber had been guarding an aircraft which had crash landed. First, they swapped the petrol which remained in the tanks for milk. Then for the price of a half litre of raw alcohol they sold one of the wings to be made into saucepans and spoons by a demobilised war veteran. When they had drunk the alcohol on empty stomachs, they landed first in the sick bay, and then in the cooler. The unnamed members of the squad had been caught passing the time with an aged cook. Although she had no intention of complaining, they were assumed to have evil intentions.

Writer

Writer found himself inside because he had written an article in the local paper under the pseudonym of 'Corporal', although he had never held that rank. Leadswinger said that Writer had fallen victim to his boundless vanity. But Fellow-worker did not agree, asserting that Writer had fallen victim to the black jealousy of his worthless competitors. The fact that Writer was an offical informer was well known even to the local dogs. He didn't even try to hide the fact himself, but made open use of it to get off work details and to go into town without leave on the pretext of a summons to see the Bosses. But once he was caught in the act of writing a fair copy of a routine denunciation with a pen borrowed from one of its victims on paper borrowed from another. There was some suggestion of setting up a kangaroo court, but on Intellectual's advice a wiser course was chosen: henceforth Writer was to prepare his denunciations under supervision. Intellectual read him a fine lecture on the theory of information. If we purge the lecture of all the incomprehensible foreign words, of specialist terminology and, principally, of terms which would not pass the censor, it would have come out roughly like this. The main thing in a report is not the meatiness of its content, but its literary style. 'Art for art's sake' is never more appropriate than here, since here it takes on the sense of 'denunciation for the sake of denunciation'. A report should be so composed that it leaves the Bosses themselves a little scope for intellectual activity. It should be so drafted that the Bosses get the drift without any difficulty, but also to reassure them that their source is too big an ass to make any use of his findings. For instance, a report might say 'Cadet Ibanov on the night of such and such stole Cadet Ibanov's gaiters and sold them to Cadet Ibanov for half a loaf of bread.' There's no getting away from the fact that the report contains weighty matter. But is that what the Bosses need? In fact, that is the very sort they do *not* need, since a report like that allows them no room for their own thoughts. Do you know what they'd say about a report like that? 'Ah, we've got a bright one here. We must keep an eye on him. Get Ibanov to take care of him.' Secondly, the Bosses aren't concerned with the discovery of crime, but with creating the impression that crimes won't remain undiscovered if they are committed. They need to harmonise two contradictions—first, that no crime should be committed within the unit, and secondly, that it is demonstrable to their superiors that any crime actually committed is discovered. So you would do better to rewrite your report like this: 'On the night of such and such Cadet Ibanov lost his gaiters. The following day Cadet Ibanov swapped a pair of gaiters with Cadet Ibanov for half a loaf of bread.' Everything is clear. And furthermore, what fertile ground you've left them for reflection and decision. You don't even need to write a report about who stole the loaf of bread from the canteen.

Intellectual

Intellectual was apprehended for some offence, but no-one knew what. Some said that he was linked with the 'Black Cat' gang. Others hinted at much worse. Fellow-worker claimed to have heard from one of the cadets that he'd heard Intellectual telling the story of the boilerman from the Japanese consulate who was cohabiting with the consul's sow, and who, on the consul's denunciation, was shot as a Japanese spy. But Writer claimed that Intellectual had got in a mess for something completely different. Once Intellectual had given Writer a splendid subject for a short story. In a certain undertaking workers suddenly and unaccountably began to disappear. As the staff was too large anyway, no-one paid much attention to this. But then one day the boss disappeared and an inquiry was instituted. A hatch was discovered which led directly to a mincing machine in the kitchen, and it turned out that the canteen manageress had been mincing up the missing workers and turning them into sausage-meat. The inquiry revealed that the manageress had been a White Guard Colonel. Writer wrote the story and took it along to a publishing house where he was well respected. There he was taken off into a secluded office and interrogated for a long time to discover his source of information. Writer reckoned that Intellectual had behaved in an uncomradely fashion, as he had not warned him that his information was confidential. As a matter of record, Intellectual had been sent to the cooler because one night he was too idle to go into the yard, and instead pissed into the sergeant's boot. The sergeant was so affronted that he floored the culprit with the foulest term of abuse he could muster: 'Intellectual!' he shouted and dispatched him to the cooler without more ado.

Slanderer, Claimant, Thinker

After Slanderer refused to write an article for the Journal criticising Secretary, which Claimant had asked him to prepare, Claimant ordered Thinker to drop this man who had betrayed their common interests. We proposed him for the Academy, but he . . . We were thinking of recommending him for a prize, and he . . . We were about to publish a review of his book, and he . . . And Claimant ordered that the review should be dropped from the next number of the Journal, and from every following number. If it hadn't been for Thinker (what a good job he was around!) things would have gone a lot worse for Slanderer. When he looked through the list of publications prepared for the Journal, Thinker found five of Slanderer's. He struck out four, so as not to attract unnecessary attention to Slanderer, and to preserve a reference to at least one work. So as not to irritate the Instructors, Thinker removed all textual references to Slanderer. Just let him go on working in peace, he thought. What's the point of all this fuss about his work? It just puts him off. In the next number there appeared an article with minor critical references to Slanderer. That's not bad, thought Thinker. To be forgotten is the worst kind of pogrom. We'd better leave that in. Everyone said that it was only thanks to Thinker that Slanderer was able to go on living and working in peace. There was even a rumour that Sociologist and Claimant were pulling strings to get a flat for Slanderer. In the following number of the Journal, there was a critical but benevolent article about Slanderer. Everyone shook Thinker by the hand and remarked on his courage in removing from the article about Slanderer the kind of observations that in the past would have been enough to get him shot. But this demolition job was strictly among professionals—it was not to be taken seriously. The less so since any fool could see that the criticism was a put-up job. Slanderer stood only to gain by it. Finally, a totally destructive article about Slanderer turned up in the offices of the Journal. 'Illiterate rubbish,' said Thinker. 'It'll take at least a fortnight's work to get it ready for the press.'

More about laws

Dauber met Schizophrenic near the pedestal of the former Leader. The inscription on the pedestal was so carefully obliterated that it could be read easily even from the far bank of the River Ibanuchka. 'Where's Chatterer got to?' asked Dauber. 'He's gone to welcome the supreme commander of a recently liberated country who's known as "the Corporal",' said Schizophrenic. 'What's got into him?' asked Dauber. 'Nothing, he was sent,' said Schizophrenic. 'His entire establishment was carted off to specially reserved seats.' 'Why couldn't they just tell this Corporal to go to hell?' asked Dauber. 'No way,' said Schizophrenic. 'Their seats are paid for.' 'How crazy!' remarked Dauber. 'Not a bit of it,' said Schizophrenic. 'It's a typical manifestation of the social laws. Society as a whole is an individual, whose body is the population of the country, and whose brain and will are the leadership. The brain all on its own can't feel joy at the Corporal's visit, since joy is a function of the body as well.' 'And where's Member?' asked Dauber. 'He's lobbying some Councillor or other,' said Schizophrenic.

The Bar was closed because of the visit of the Corporal. Dauber swore and suggested they went back to his studio. On the way there, he said, 'Strange changes come over people. Take Artist, for instance. He used to be a decent lad, but now he's a first-class bastard. Member was a typical pen-pusher, but now he's become a fighter for justice.' 'That may seem strange in individual cases,' said Schizophrenic, 'but in the mass people just play out logically calculated variants of behaviour according to some formula or other. In the simplest instance, the probability that a certain N. will perform actions of a type x is equal to the quotient of the division of the degree of danger for the individual in the said type of action by the number of logically conceivable variants of behaviour. The number of people who choose the type of behaviour x is equal to the product of the total number of people obliged to select a type of behaviour from all the possible variants by the probability referred to.' 'I can't contradict that,' said Dauber. 'But your judgments seem to me to be too relentless. There are no illusions left. Surely not everything can be reduced to figures and formulae?' Schizophrenic said, 'Yes, everything could, if you so desired. People don't do so, partly because they don't feel the need. And partly because they are satisfied with comparative evaluations—wiser, more stupid, more talented, more important, and so on. You see, it's a question of habit. The usual way is to guess. Partly, too, because social measurements are too fraught with consequences objectionable to the leadership. Imagine the fuss if it were to turn out that the Leader is more stupid than his Deputy, although the theory implies the reverse!' Dauber said that there was still something which bothered him about the social laws, and tried to put his finger on what it was. Schizophrenic eventually guessed what his problem was. 'The thing is,' he said, 'that people assimilate the social laws as skills in behaving in a defined way in defined circumstances towards other people. These skills are of course modified by the influence of various circumstances, and can only be recognised as general laws if all instances are regarded in the mass. So we have to formulate them in such a way as to exclude all those circumstances which cloud the essence of the matter and which invariably leave fingerholds for doubts and criticism. A convenient approach might be to formulate assertions about the social laws in the same way as we formulate assertions about the tendencies, the preferences, about the propensities of people to carry out actions of a particular kind in given situations. Expressions of the kind "N. prefers x^i, (or strives towards x^i)" here mean the following: if it were possible to establish n similar situations, differing only in the consequences which would follow from carrying out actions $x^1, x^2, x^3 --- x^n$, then N. would choose x^i, (where i is a particular one of $^1, ^2 --- ^n$). The main thing here is to understand that to say "N. prefers x^i" is not the same as saying "N. always accomplishes x^i if he is obliged to choose between $x^1, x^2 --- x^n$". The first is irrefutable, even if N. accomplishes not x^i, but some other choice of $x^1, x^2 --- x^n$, while the second factor can be refuted. Finally, to say "N. prefers x^i" cannot be construed as meaning "N. more often (in more cases, with greater probability) accomplishes x^i if he has to choose from $x^1, x^2 --- x^n$", as the second expression may be false, which in no way detracts from the truth of the first. I know one womaniser who prefers plump blondes, but who spends almost all his time with slim brunettes.' 'That's clear enough,' said Dauber. 'I prefer the company of people like Michelangelo, Picasso, Rodin, Dostoevsky, Bulgakov and so on, but I spend most of my time in the company of people like Artist, Writer, Colleague, Sociologist, Claimant and Thinker.' 'It's not quite the same thing,' said Schizophrenic; 'but similar.'

A discussion about freedom
The prisoners stuck their crowbars and spades in the snow and crowded into the shithouse, read the Instructor. It soon became almost impossible to breathe because of the tobacco smoke, which did, however, have the advantage of making the place a little warmer and a great deal more comfortable. A bitching session developed. This gradually turned into a discussion about the nature of freedom—a problem of utmost topicality for the prisoners. The discussion followed all the rules of scientific debate—everybody shouted at the top of his voice

and didn't listen to a word anyone else said. Total mutual incomprehension was achieved. Slanderer's conception was this: 'Freedom is the knowledge of the inevitable, as the classic writers have taught us, and although here we are sitting in the shithouse we must not forget it. We all have at least secondary education, and some of us higher, or partial higher, education.' Murderer's conception: 'Slanderer is talking rubbish. Suppose you were locked up in the cooler—if you recognised the inevitability of that, then you would claim that you were free. Freedom is quite the opposite—not an inevitability, but an evitability; as for whether you recognise it as such, what's the difference! It's sometimes better when it is not recognised; for instance, until the brass discover that one can by-pass the official exit and leave camp without permission, we are, sometimes, free.' Patriot's conception: 'We are the freest people who have ever lived.' Panicker's conception: 'Freedom is the freedom to perform certain actions; a man can be said to be free to perform a certain action if and only if the performance of that action by him depends exclusively on his own will, i.e. nothing except his own will obliges him to carry out the action or hinders him from so doing; for instance, if Patriot wants to leave the shithouse immediately and no-one interferes with his so doing, then he is free to leave the shithouse; if, on the other hand, Murderer shoves Patriot into the cess-pit, then Patriot is not free to leave. All the rest is mere philosophical verbiage.'

Deviationist's conception was the most developed: 'A man is free to perform or not to perform a certain action only if that depends entirely on his own free will. But that is not all. That is only the beginning. For example, is Cadet Ibanov free or not today to go and see his girl-friend after work? If he were simply to put his best uniform on and go, the problem would be solved. But Ibanov knows that that is forbidden. And if he goes off without permission and gets caught, he's for the cooler. Or even worse. So when we speak about the freedom of people as regards one action or another, we have to take into account the presence or absence of any official ban on this activity. We have to consider the nature of the punishment consequent on a breaking of the ban: if the punishment is too weak, then it can be disregarded. But if there is an official ban on actions of the given type, and the punishment for the breaking of the ban is sufficiently severe, then a man is officially not free as far as these actions are concerned. But if, despite that, the man is able, thanks to exceptional circumstances, to avoid the punishment, then to all intents and purposes he is free as far as the given actions are concerned, while remaining officially un-free. So Writer was in practice free to slip off into town without permission, and the fact that he now finds himself here in the cooler is a pure accident. If they hadn't had the problem of finding people to rebuild the bog everything would have turned out fine. There are occasions when a man officially is free but in practice is not. And there are cases, too, when it is not enough to have no ban on an action, but official permission has to be sought as well. Sometimes even that is not enough, and a rule is needed to prevent the obstruction of acts which are permitted or at any rate not prohibited. Up to this point I have been talking about the relationship between one individual man and one individual action. But in social life we find the problem of the relationship between a given group of people to a given range of actions. For example, we could take the problem of the relationship of the cadets Ibanov (not one individual cadet) to a number of acts, including chasing skirts and getting drunk. Are the cadets free to engage in such pursuits as womanising or getting drunk? We cannot for the moment answer this question. First we must introduce the concept of degrees of freedom and indicate methods of measuring them. In particular, the degree of freedom can be stated as a value defining the relationship of free man/actions to the total number of man/actions of the given type. This value will lie between zero and one. The degree of freedom is equivalent to zero if for all people comprised in the total all actions of the given type are un-free, and equivalent to one if for all people comprised in the total all such actions are free. Other cases lie between these two values. Nevertheless, this schema greatly simplifies the real situation, since in it all man/actions are taken to be equally indicative, and there is a sufficiently large number of them. But in reality this is not the case. In reality people have differing social values. Sometimes the freedom to publish one's works for thousands of people to read is not an indication of press freedom, while the lack of freedom to disseminate a single copy is an indication of the absence of freedom of the press. Sometimes people never try to perform certain actions although such actions are not officially forbidden, or they attempt to perform them so rarely that there can be no basis for judging the presence or absence of actual freedom, since there is no way of measuring the degree of freedom. But let us assume that there is a means of measuring degrees of freedom and the conditions in which that means can be used. Now we must agree on what values are appropriate to determine the presence or absence of freedom. Here certain variants are possible. For instance, in some cases we may be able to agree that the presence of freedom may be acknowledged when the value of the degree of freedom is greater than 0.5. So it is quite possible that a group of people may have a high degree of freedom relative to actions of a given type, while a certain Ibanov may in similar circumstances be un-free. Add to this the fact that in relation to various numbers of actions there may be a variety of degrees of freedom. I have dealt with only a few aspects of the problem. But it should be clear from this that any general discussion of this subject without a terminology determined with sufficient accuracy and without strictly established facts is meaningless. Here, finally, is a little problem for you to ponder over. Take two countries, A and B. In both, the people are allowed to go on tourist trips abroad. You want to determine whether this implies that a genuine freedom to travel does exist in these countries. You have the following data at your disposal. In country A, 100 people applied for visas, and 99 were granted them, 1 was not. In country B over the same period there were 5,000 applications of which 4,500 were granted, and five hundred not. Which country, A or B, is the freer in relation to tourist trips abroad?' A bitter argument broke out, in the course of which it became clear that more than half the prisoners had never heard of tourist trips abroad or exit visas. Their position can be accurately determined by their shouts of, 'You've eaten yourself into a stupor!', 'Whatever next!', 'Send them to work on the farm!', 'Why not to the moon, while you're at it!', 'That's nothing to do with us', and so on. Panicker summed up: The discussion was over and truth had been throttled in the struggle. Intellectual said to Deviationist that he, Deviationist, was essentially right, but that he'd omitted two important aspects—the moral and the civic. For a state which was highly developed in the civic sense, the problem of freedom had quite a different meaning than for a state with an under-developed civic spirit. In the former the degree of freedom is determined by the extent to which society is able to allow a *de facto* freedom of action to people who are considered to be in opposition. Then lunch time came round, and the prisoners filed back into the cooler, awaking the guard, who had slept on his toilet-seat through the entire discussion.

Congress

After the rehabilitation and resumption in Ibansk of what had formerly been the bourgeois reactionary pseudo-science of logic, within two months there had grown up a friendly and closely knit family of avant-garde logicians who surpassed all others. At the international congress held that summer in a seaside resort, Ibansk was able to provide the biggest delegation, one thousand strong, a clear proof of the advantages of our system. Writer produced some enthusiastic verses on the subject for the Newspaper.

From Ibansk roared the express
Heading for the great Congress.
Crammed with savants of renown
As with grafters is our town.

Slanderer was invited to be the delegation chairman. After many discussions he was provisionally included in the delegation, but at the last moment he was dropped, as owing to a certain aggravation of the situation, Academician decided to write the report himself. Apart from Academician, Claimant, Sociologist, Thinker, Wife, Writer, Artist, Colleague, Instructor and their close relatives, distant acquaintances and young female research assistants, the delegation included colleagues who knew foreign languages and colleagues whose function was to keep an eye on the conduct of the others. When they reached their destination it transpired that Thinker was the only one who knew any foreign languages, and not the ones which were needed, in fact precisely the reverse. To do him justice, those he knew he knew perfectly adequately. Before the trip everyone had had an X-ray and an inoculation. They were instructed to buy vodka to ensure a friendly atmosphere. Then the delegation was split in two, each half being instructed to keep an eye on the other. 'The main thing to remember,' said the Assistant in his final briefing, 'is to hold your knife and fork in your left hand and your chop in your right. Don't talk to anyone without permission. Don't get into conversations which haven't been previously authorised. Always give tit for tat. Remember who you are, whence you are, where you are, and why you're there.' The success of the delegation exceeded all expectations. It produced five hundred denunciations, eight hundred devastating speeches, five thousand critical observations, and twenty thousand disparaging rejoinders. The enemy was thrown into complete confusion, his ranks demolished, and, riddled by irreconcilable internal contradictions, he withdrew to reexamine his basic positions. By economising on what they ate, the delegates were able to buy five hundred imitation suede jackets, skirts and coats and fifteen hundred pairs of trousers with leather trimmings and the incomprehensible tag 'Made abroad'. Thinker, by virtue of his special rights as a very important person, visited a number of dubious establishments, and brought back two packs of playing cards with pictures of naked women of all nationalities except our own. On the return journey he showed these cards to the young female research assistants and asked them, as he stroked their thighs with his kindly soft hand and gazed straight at them with his wise sad eyes, where at home was all this notorious pornography to be found then? The impression he produced was devastating, and Thinker's authority as an outstanding philosopher was greatly enhanced. Later Thinker gave one pack to Claimant's wife. Slanderer just received greetings from his foreign colleagues, and their regrets that once again the state of his health and family commitments had prevented his attending the congress.

Social and official

I distinguish, wrote Schizophrenic, between the official and the social. Officialdom is an historical form in which a recognition of socialness exists. The official is the antithesis of the social, growing from its roots and continuously linked with it. The official is the *doppelgänger* of the social; they are irreconcilable enemies and inseparable friends. The official does not coincide with the state, with the law, with morality, with ideology and so on. To isolate it demands a totally different viewpoint on society. The anti-social is that which sets a limit to social laws, hinders them and in general strives towards the liquidation of their authority. The anti-official is that which is hostile to the official as a recognition of the social. The functions of the anti-social can be fulfilled by the state, morality, religion and so on. But they can both perform the functions of the anti-social while at the same time being at the service of both the social and the official. An extreme manifestation of the social is total amorality, while an extreme manifestation of the anti-social is a moral conscience; an extreme manifestation of the official is formal bureaucracy, and the extreme manifestation of the anti-official is criminality. But all that, of course, is just a sketchy outline. And I am writing about this more with the intention of reorienting our familiar views of society to one which I consider to be more interesting.

I shall give a number of examples which illustrate the distinctions I have drawn. Socially, N. is a demagogue, a fool, a careerist, but officially he is a serious scholar, a fine orator and a splendid administrator. When N. was elected to the Academy, everyone on the sidelines spat and clawed at each other. But on the platform itself, everyone praised N. to the skies, shook his hand, congratulated him on his much deserved election and so on. If N. goes abroad on a visit, that means socially that he's wheedled, schemed, pulled strings and so on, while officially it means that he has completed some great work, pulled his weight, done his part. I shall revert to this from a slightly different angle. Socially an individual is no better (and in extreme cases worse) than his actions, officially an individual is on a par with his actions, anti-socially an individual may be (extreme case, is always) better than his actions, and anti-officially an individual is not on a par with his actions. Even in cases where there may appear to be a coincidence, one can detect shades of difference. For example, socially there is a tendency to make people completely independent of the social groups to which they belong, while officially the tendency is to make individuals wholly controlled not only by social groups they belong to, but also by the authorities.

The basic law of the relationship between the social and the

(82)

official is a striving towards their correspondence and even to their coincidence. This gives rise to certain specific tendencies in reality which are detectable by the naked eye. For example, socially a boss cannot be more intelligent than his subordinates as a group (the intellectual index of the boss cannot exceed that of the subordinates as a group) while officially the boss cannot be more stupid than his subordinates as a group. Inasmuch as there is a tendency to bring the official into correspondence with the social and vice versa, then the realisation of this tendency in the given case is a tendency to lower the intellectual potential of the group (a tendency towards making it more stupid).

The mutual interaction of the social and the official strengthens the social in those cases where their correspondence is achieved. For example, the more the state has invested resources in a given individual (degrees, titles, prizes, an apartment, a villa, trips abroad at the state's expense and so on) the higher his social position becomes. And the higher his social position, the more he is able to grab, i.e. to force the state to invest even more resources in him.

The evolution of Sociologist
When he had read this extract from Schizophrenic's manuscript, Sociologist added to his article which had been accepted for publication in the Journal a long passage in which he proved that in addition to the articulations of society established within our 'ism' there is a possibility for others, more secondary, to exist. For example, he could suggest as follows: Slanderer told Dauber that there was no point in letting Sociologist read Schizophrenic's treatise, because that jackal would merely steal the ideas, distort them, and what's more write a denunciation. Dauber bore the advice in mind, but it was already too late. Sociologist had begun to study Schizophrenic's manuscript without any help from Dauber.

Directions in art
Artist and Dauber had been students together, and had been close friends. Once Dauber said jokingly that there was really only one rule in art: the higher placed the arse you licked, the better artist you were. 'You can't be a great artist if you are not

painter to the King.' Artist took the joke seriously and soon their paths in art and life divided, although they remained on friendly terms. His outstanding successes led to Artist being awarded prizes, elected to Academies, and finally given an appointment. His portrait of Adviser brought him a flat. His villa came from his portrait of Assistant. His portrait of Deputy's wife yielded him a car. When he painted Deputy he got a trip abroad. When he painted his first portrait of the Leader he was awarded the top prize and won Ibansk-wide fame. He was given a permanent pass to the Institute, and was told that they'd be glad to see him any time of day or night. For his second portrait of the Leader he was awarded the entire three-year allocation of studio funds for his own studio alone. For his portrait of Assistant, he was given his own exhibition, open round the clock with no admission charge. And yet Artist would have felt happier had it not been for the existence of Dauber.

At his own expense and after great difficulty Dauber found himself a tiny attic to use as a studio. And from time to time, working in complete anonymity, he turned something out, but not without scandals and rows. Artist got to hear some stupid rumours, which he didn't want to believe. He well knew what our art was about, and who our true artists were. Finally, some dubious intellectuals began to agitate for an exhibition of Dauber's work. A commission was set up under the chairman-ship of Artist. The commission ruled against a one-man show. But since the winds of change were beginning to blow even through the spheres of cultural control, they decided to set up a new commission to examine the possibility of showing one of Dauber's more suitable works at a general exhibition of the works of amateur old-age pensioners and folk-art clubs. The head of the new commission, Artist, paid a personal visit to Dauber's studio and was flabbergasted, although he showed no sign of it. 'What d'you take yourself for—a genius?' he said. 'That's just laughable. We have no geniuses and never will have. You know that perfectly well. Won't you acknowledge, old man, that you're just turning out this stuff to confuse everybody?' Then Artist suggested to Dauber that they should put on a joint exhibition. 'I'll tell you the subject and show you how to do it so it all comes out right,' he said. Dauber was touched by this kind attention, but turned down the idea of a joint exhibition. At the meeting of the commission, Artist said that Dauber did too much work, which was a sure sign that he was producing rubbish. In technique his paintings did not fit our ideology, and in content they were of a low level of achievement. Moreover, Dauber was a drunkard, a lecher, a homosexual, a speculator, a shark, an internal émigré; he didn't support his family, had abandoned his parents and so they had died long ago, he didn't pay his union dues, paid no attention to the views of his colleagues, and systematically ignored jubilee exhibitions. And so Dauber's works were not allowed into the exhibition. One of Artist's friends brought Dauber the transcript of the meeting of the commission. At first Dauber was very angry, and then he laughed for a long time, and rang Slanderer and they set off to the Bar.

Recently, Slanderer hadn't been doing any work at all. 'The less you work,' he used to say, 'the more stable your situation is. Work only exasperates idlers. And as nearly everyone is idle, the conclusion is self-evident.' Dauber told Slanderer about the exhibition. 'It's not worth doing anything about,' said Slanderer; 'there's nothing to be done about it. It's the same everywhere. In our society slander, envy and oppression are the inevitable companions of any outstanding man.' 'Yet he used to be a good painter,' said Dauber. 'Able people who haven't the courage or the means to realise their abilities are the most dangerous,' said Slanderer. 'Basically they're able to stoop to any dirty tricks. There are a lot of them. They lash out in despair, in anger and in boredom. And they destroy everything that can prick their consciences.' At the Bar Schizophrenic wrapped up what had happened in dispassionate but concise formulae. 'Every concrete event,' he said, 'is the product of the action of many social, psychological and other laws, and so it appears to be a complete accident. Artist was angry that you didn't want to follow his advice, wasn't he? Right. If the victim resists, then the oppressor always flies into a rage and sees the resistance as a breach of justice. The usual formula is "We try to do this for them (you, him) and they (you, he)!!!" Collegial solidarity? True. It exists, but only among the muck-peddlers. If you had agreed to a joint exhibition with Artist, everything would have been arranged in a flash. However, in

(85)

this spirit of fraternal solidarity he would have made you paint and exhibit rubbish, not your best work. Collegial solidarity only operates when the colleague feels that you are weaker than he is or at any rate not so much stronger than he is that anyone would notice. And then only if the solidarity is going to be useful, or at any rate harmless, to him. The control your colleagues exercise is always the most watchful. I'm sure they won't let you anywhere near a general exhibition, because you'd spoil their game. What matters to them is that there should be no discord in the established harmony. All this talk about ideology, inhumanity, formalism and so on is just a convenient way of getting on with their own thing in their own way.' 'You break the rules of the game,' said Chatterer. 'Instead of going through all the prescribed stages and doing everything to the prescribed norms and producing the same old crap, you are doing something totally different, you do it all too much, and you want to get away without playing their games.' 'Yes,' said Dauber. 'But Artist put himself at their head.' 'True, but at what a price,' said Schizophrenic. 'I once went to his studio and observed him in the travails of creation. He'd been working for the last three months on a lousy portrait of the Director's Wife, and the portrait really hadn't begun to work. Artist talked long and boringly about his ambitions and his view of the world, which he wanted to convey in the smile of this old woman who had grown gaga through dwelling on her own exclusivity; mankind thereafter, he reckoned, would never be able to guess its meaning.' 'The more insignificant the work being created,' said Slanderer, 'the greater are the pains of creation. There isn't anything to get hold of. Things flow of their own accord from a true artist, and all he's got to do is to catch them and set them down. But you've got to wring it out drop by drop if you're just a nonentity like Artist.' 'The aim's the important thing,' said Dauber. 'Try to write a brilliant leading article for the News-paper, it never comes off. A supergenius and the dreariest little hack journalist will come up with much the same thing. It's rather like painting a portrait of the Leader.'

Problems of power
'Something strange is happening to our friends,' said Dauber. 'Nothing special,' said Slanderer; 'they're just coming to

power.' 'But they already *are* in power,' said Dauber. 'They've obtained high posts, which is not exactly the same thing as achieving power,' said Slanderer. 'That is just the possibility of achieving power. They've still got to confirm themselves in office. And to do that they have to raise themselves a step higher, increase the number of lackeys and move them on to power, discredit and remove their competitors, sever any dubious connections they may have and dissociate themselves from any dubious acts they may have committed in the past, remove or neutralise anyone who knows what they're really like, save society from danger (whether the danger's real or imaginary makes no difference, though it's better if it's imaginary but looks real) so that they can demonstrate their usefulness and indispensability, and finally, place the seal of their individuality on the lot.' 'What's the point of all that?' asked Dauber. 'They're not fools, and they look as if they're more educated and cultured than everybody else.' 'When it comes to the point,' said Slanderer, 'their education and culture are their trump cards, nothing more than that. And what I've been talking about isn't an individual aim or demand. It's simply a formal mechanism of power which is equally inevitable for boors and educated men, progressives and reactionaries, moralists and cynics. For example, the higher the rank attained by the careerist, the larger the group he drags in his train and which boosts him upwards. And by the same token such a group is more greedy and more pitiless. Now to some small degree all able people are careerists. It takes very great abilities and an exceptional chain of circumstances to get a man to give up a career. The subordinate power-structure has to be changed. That's laid down in the mechanics of the business. You have to change it even when there's no need to do so. To change it even for the worse. Even if it makes fresh enemies. Nothing short of a clean sweep will assure you of loyal subordinates. For instance, Claimant fired A and replaced him with B. Do you think B is better? No. His work is distinctly inferior. At the moment he's fawning on Claimant, but, given the chance, he'll betray him lock, stock and barrel. And Claimant knows that perfectly well. But he can't do anything else. For the time being B is his man, and the ritual of exchanging the A he did not appoint for the B he did appoint must be observed.

(87)

Schizophrenic is absolutely right. Society can be regarded as a huge number of cells connected one with another and performing certain actions whether or not the cells contain a man. And people simply get into these cells (which cell depends on their individual fate) and do everything that the cells oblige them to. And moreover, people who are removed from a post have to be discredited, even if you damage yourself in the process. There are two ways of advancing: one is to make yourself bigger, the other is to make others smaller. The first course is out of the question for the masses, and difficult and dangerous for the careerist. So the latter remains. Claimant is always flinging mud at Secretary. Do you think that's because in his time Secretary played such a dismal role and took a hand in all those crimes? Rubbish! Claimant couldn't care less about that. He's not above the worst skullduggery himself. In fact he does go in for it, too, although in a rather different style. Times have changed. Secretary has one foot in the grave. He's prepared to advance Claimant to any post he wants. But that doesn't matter in the slightest. Claimant abuses Secretary to show that he is wiser, more talented, more moral, more progressive and so on, than Secretary. Incidentally, Claimant is stupid. I'm afraid that he's overdone it, and people will actually come to believe that he *is* wise, talented and progressive. And when that happens, it will put a brake on his career. Moreover, the technique of taking power requires that power be taken in a battle of good against evil. If the battle doesn't occur of its own accord, it has to be provoked or simply invented. Now Secretary has got genuinely angry with Claimant and will start abusing him in his turn. According to the technique of career-building there is no harm in that. It is in fact even necessary. You need to have an obsolete enemy. And if possible one who seems strong but is actually weak. And Secretary is a cretin as well. It never enters his head that if he wants to bring Claimant down, instead of abusing him he should praise him, or else ignore him altogether. But this he cannot do, since he is an ordinary social individual and part of the mechanism of power. And that is still not all. He still has to save society from a serious threat, and not a familiar one that's over and done with, but a new one, something that threatens to throw us right off course. This threat should be socially conceivable and significant, and at the same time one which is not too easily unmasked. It should be one which certain circles believe in. It should be a threat which evidently only they could detect and forestall, in other words one which will demonstrate their usefulness and their indispensability. And at this moment they are still looking for this threat. Which is why that abusive article about me, the attacks on N. and so on, are no accident.'

'But they were your students,' said Dauber. 'Not my students,' said Slanderer, 'just a rabble. Sociologist and his Wife and many others from that crowd used at one time to hang around my coat tails. Now that compromises them, since I haven't gone through the same evolutionary process that they have. And moreover I have the measure of them. I am a dangerous witness and a sore point in their consciences. All these are ordinary banal truths which we know perfectly well from literature, but which horrify us when they affect us personally. And then again, these literary stereotypes come out into the open too plainly. It's as if you'd taken the skin off society and exposed its entire anatomy. The curious thing here is something else—the linguistic form their claims take. They speak out in the role of forward-looking, educated, creative and progressive personalities, saving mankind from the threat posed by the supporters of the old Chairman. They are the representatives and pioneers of the highest achievements of world culture. For example, in the past here, decent people were beaten up on the grounds that their approval of E. made them supporters of the other side's reactionary ideology. The same crowd now beat up decent people on the grounds that their disapproval of E. makes them opponents of their progressive science.' 'There has to be some way of fighting against all this,' said Dauber. 'You have a reputation, you've got pupils.' 'A reputation means nothing to them,' said Slanderer. 'And I have no pupils. They vanished like a puff of smoke. There's no way out—they are unassailable. At the Publishing House, they dropped my article from the collection. Why? It didn't suit the theme of the book. Proving that it was the *only* article on the theme of the collection (which I put together myself) would cost incredible effort with no guarantee of success. And time is passing. If I do get my own way, it'll be too late. The next collection of articles won't come out at all. They don't do any work themselves, so there's nothing for them to print. And the collection has not even been planned. They invited me to be the delegation chairman at the Congress, and then dropped me from the delegation at the last moment. Academician said that there was an unhealthy interest in me, but that he was backing me to the hilt. All right, so it was a nice gesture, not to be sniffed at. But to be on the safe side they threw me out of the delegation. And so on in the same spirit. They sit in judgment on the works of my diploma and postgraduate students—delays, niggling complaints, inordinate claims and so on. Officially, they say we must sort it all out—it's a serious subject, an unsupported concept. But in fact they only have one aim—to isolate me. Should I leave? But where to? Everywhere's the same. And anyway, there isn't even a territorial choice.' Dauber agreed that of course all this was depressing. 'But you mustn't give in. You must work, work, work. As for them—let them get lost.' 'In our business,' Slanderer said, 'we need people, an organisation, access to print. On my own all I can do is produce ideas which will either be filched, destroyed and distorted, or ignored altogether. So the best thing is to do nothing. But even that won't satisfy them completely, since the past is still alive. What they need beyond that is that the past should cease to exist.'

The abduction of 'Ferdinand'
For Instructor, life took on a new meaning. He got through his tedious duties as fast as he could, locked himself in his office and read and re-read Schizophrenic's manuscript. He understood nothing in it, and so read it with great interest. After dinner, he read, we were hungry. Then Leadswinger proposed that they should steal the biggest cooking pot of all, which was known as 'Ferdinand'. The plan of the robbery was simple to the point of genius. Two prisoners would go into the kitchen, take the pot from the stove and carry it out. If anyone noticed them, which was to be ruled out by the laws of psychology, they would pretend it was a joke. The guard could be bribed with porridge, but it would be better to distract him. So that is what they did. Dauber, Writer and Patriot proposed throwing dice for food. The guard rose to the bait; they let him win some stewed fruit, and he threw himself wholeheartedly into the

game, and went on to forfeit all his meals for the next three days. Murderer and Panicker calmly lifted 'Ferdinand' from the stove and no-one paid the slightest attention. When the disappearance was discovered, the School was thrown into an incredible upheaval. Colleague came straight away. When he smelt the vile aromas that hung around the cooler, and gazed deeply into all our eyes, he understood that he had come too late. Operation 'Ferdinand' became one of the most celebrated and glorious pages in the history of the School. When, several decades later, Fellow-worker met a former cadet, the only thing the latter could remember about the School was the story of 'Ferdinand'.

A conversation about The Glorious Future

When they had eaten their fill of kasha, the prisoners sat for a time in silence, intoxicated by the unfamiliar feeling of repletion, and then went on to tell obscene and unfunny stories, which made them fall about with laughter. ('A soldier went into town on an evening pass and, just in case, he fastened his cock to his leg. The result was that he spent the entire evening standing on one leg at a crossroads.') Then there were true stories which no one believed. ('We had one soldier on guard duty who took a stiff out of the morgue and propped it up at his guard post, and sneaked out of camp the back way.') They ended with an inspiring conversation about the glorious future. Defeatist said that then everything would be fine—you'd always eat your bellyful, there wouldn't be any cooler, and they'd let you go a-whoring every week. Panicker said that Defeatist was taking a purely consumeristic approach, and that in fact the 'Ism' was mainly a high consciousness which should inhibit people from helping themselves to double rations and put Leadswinger firmly in his place. Intellectual said that scientifically devised norms of demand would be introduced. 'You'll go to the Office for the Rationalisation of Demand with ten forms signed and rubber-stamped, fill in a questionnaire and hey presto, they'll give you coupons or enter you on a special list. For example, Defeatist's needs would be something like this: uniform—cotton, other ranks, for the use of (CORFTUO); footwear—boots, or rather shoes, with puttees, Broad army-style (BAS); food, a bowl of kasha three times a day.' Defeatist started to protest, but the others laughed him down; 'Get on and eat what you're given.' Gelding took Intellectual's idea a stage further. The norms for people like Colleague, Deputy and so on would be set at a higher level: blue serge trousers, chrome leather shoes, half a kilo of sausage and two bowls of buckwheat kasha per day. Leadswinger said that in time they would put a great cauldron of mashed potato on every street corner, so you could have as much as you wanted. Gelding said that for this to be achieved, the people's consciousness would have to reach a state of development hitherto unheard of. Deviationist added that to achieve this we would need an even higher level of productive capacity—atomic energy, the conquest of space, the Ibansk Hydro-Electric station. Defeatist said that everyone would be happy and that we would all be able to choose jobs to suit ourselves. Panicker said that initially they would combine obligatory work with voluntary. Defeatist, for instance, would spend eight hours a day as lavatory cleaner, and the rest of his time as an amateur general. What was yet to be decided was whether there would be any amateur lavatory cleaners, and whether the amateur generals would be allocated troops by the professional generals. Or whether the professional generals would be allocated amateur troops. Patriot said that the army would atrophy and there would be no more generals. Nor soldiers. Panicker said that the state would be ruled by kitchen maids. Gelding said 'What's so funny about that? In the first place, the business of government would be so devised that even kitchen maids (if so authorised, of course) would be capable of assuming any task of government. And secondly, it was questionable whether certain statesmen in fact possessed an intellectual capability superior to that of a kitchen maid. Just you try to make ends meet when you've got hardly any money coming in and two kids to bring up, and you'll find that you really have to use your brain.' To this Patriot said that the state would perish away and belched in the face of Deviationist, who in response fastidiously observed that the distinguishing feature of patriots was that they ate oats and reeked as if they had been stuffing themselves with shashlik and pressed caviar, whereupon the conversation died of inanition.

A discussion about mind

On the way to the shithouse Intellectual set out his method for the measurement of intellectual potential in individuals and entire social groups. This involved the division of mental activity into elementary operations of roughly equal strength, and calculating the average number of such operations per unit of time. 'I am prepared to bet,' said Intellectual, 'that using this criterion, we shall see that the mental potential of Sergeant, whom we unjustly consider to be a degenerate, is many times higher than that of the Chief of the General Staff, whom everyone regards as a genius.' Gelding said that the positions allocated to people on the social ladder bore no relation to their intellectual capabilities. He had noticed this when he was a child. His father was a very big wheel indeed. It's true that he was taken down a peg for something, but this didn't make him any more intelligent. Even Gelding's mother used to express her surprise that a fool like that could be trusted with responsibilities. To this his father would say, 'So I'm not as bright as they come, but just look at Ibanov, who's after my job and probably will give me the shove in the end—he really is a dope of the first water.' But Dauber had doubts about the effectiveness of Intellectual's method. Just try to compare such mental operations as the decision whether or not to open the second front, or to build a new shithouse at the Flying School. Intellectual said that those were complex operations which could easily be broken down into their elements. Moreover, a great many people take part in them, so each of them has a very simple task to perform. Moreover, the degree of complexity of the task from the intellectual point of view is inversely proportional to the degree of responsibility of the people taking the decisions. Dauber asked how this would affect the work of a writer or a painter. Intellectual replied that his method did not cover creative activity, which was a deviation from the norm. Deviationist said there was no need to bring creative work into consideration since, the way things were going, the creative element in the work of writers, artists and other representatives of the creative professions (who proliferated like undoctored dogs) was diminishing catastrophically and would soon be immeasurably smaller than the creative element in the work of sergeants and kitchen maids. Dauber sighed and remembered what delicious food his mother had been able to concoct from any old rubbish. Intellectual recalled the stroke of genius recently shown by Sergeant, who had gone round the market buying in worn out old boots at five roubles a pair; he had then exchanged them in the commissary for new ones, which he was selling at about eighty. Deviationist said that didn't show intelligence but cunning. Intellectual said that wisdom and cunning were one and the same thing from the point of view under discussion. They are distinguishable only by shades of morality, intention, choice of means, and other extremely relative indicators. Dauber asked how Intellectual's method could be used to determine the intellectual potential of a whole group. Intellectual suggested a number of variants. The first variant was the ratio of members of the group with intellectual potential of an average, above average and below average level. The second variant was the relation of the sum of the indicators of the intellectual levels of the members of the group to the total number of members. The third variant was the influence on the behaviour of the group by those members who had a certain potential level. The fourth variant was the degree of punishability of those members of the group with the highest potential. The fifth variant was the degree of un-punishability of those with the highest potential in the group. The list of variants could be extended. That wasn't the problem. The problem was that people have no interest in measuring their intellectual potential. Or rather, only very few people were interested, and only then because they were convinced of their own intellectual superiority. The rest were more concerned to conceal their intellectual poverty. Deviationist said there was no need to measure, since everything was quite clear without measurement. But measurement would never be allowed anyway, the result of scientifically calculated measurements would be figures which would have the force of an official document. Panicker said that in fact intelligence never plays the part ascribed to it by all those intellectuals. He didn't mean Intellectual, of course, who clearly knew what he was talking about. Statistics clearly showed, for example, that for every two dumb cadets you produce one intelligent general. Try explaining that by Intellectual's method. Slanderer said that the application of the word 'intelligence' to generals came more into the category of animal-psychology, and Panicker was behaving like a typical sophist by playing with words.

The social individual

The social individual, wrote Schizophrenic, can be an individual person, a group of people, an association of groups, or even an entire nation. The elementary social individual (for the sake of brevity I shall now omit the word 'social') cannot be dismembered into two or more separate individual persons. The complex consists of two or more individuals. A normal individual has an organ with which he reflects and evaluates a situation, establishes what is best for himself and for others, foresees the immediate consequences of his actions and the actions of others. In man that organ is the brain, and in a group it is those persons and organisations who control the group. The task of this organ is to ensure the best possible conditions of existence for the individual.

I start from the assumption that the normal individual (and they are in the overwhelming majority) correctly evaluates his position in society, his possibilities, exterior circumstances, the most immediate consequences of his own actions and so on. I say 'most immediate' since that is enough for the operation of the social laws. To foresee the consequences of events far ahead into the future is impossible, not so much because of the complexity of situations but because of circumstances which are in principle unpredictable. For ordinary social existence it is enough to know the most immediate consequences of people's actions, and individuals are capable of doing so. For example, A knows that if he denounces B, then B will run into trouble (he may be fired, for instance, passed over for an award, find his trip abroad cancelled, and so on) and that is all A needs to know. As a result of their actions individuals may find themselves in a bad position, but this cannot be regarded as resulting from errors in social behaviour. From a social point of view, individuals do not make errors. The concept of 'error' in this sense is quite simply inapplicable. For example, if A denounces B and the eventual result is unpleasant consequences for A, that does not mean that A's denunciation was an error. Here A has acted in full accord with certain social laws, and only that. And the outcome has no connection with the law as such. It is similar to the case of a glass falling to the floor and breaking. That is not the glass's fault. It is the result of the action of certain physical laws, and only that.

The social individual also has the capacity to make volitional decisions—he has freedom of will and choice, at least as far as some actions are concerned. For example, an individual is free to vote for or against the publication of a given article. When I speak about freedom of will with regard to this action, I mean that the performance or non-performance of this action depends entirely on the consciousness and the will of the individual in question. The social individual also, within certain limits sufficient to regard him as an entity, has power over his own body. If the individual comprises a group of people, then the above means that the ruling people or organisations have authority over those they rule. Finally, the social individual tends towards self-preservation, avoids worsening his own position, tries to achieve better conditions of existence and so on, and takes certain actions to these ends. The task of sociology lies primarily in identifying the rules by which these principles are realised in social life. In other words, the social individual carries out his actions according to the following principles: 1) He does nothing voluntarily and knowingly which contradicts his own interests. 2) If without fear of retribution (and minor retribution does not come into this) he can take advantage of his social situation in his own interests, he will do so to the limit. Thus bribes, enforced seduction, the compelling of subordinates to co-operate in various machinations, bluffing for the sake of profit, the diversion of public funds into one's own pocket or to one's own benefit, all these (not to mention officially established privileges such as special shops, cars, villas, the free availability of all kinds of services, etc.) are natural manifestations of man's social life. And only the fear of discovery and punishment to a certain extent (and even then sometimes to only a very small degree) prevents the possibility of catastrophic consequences.

The characteristics I have indicated come into the very definition of the term 'social individual'. But the social individual has other characteristics as well. These are: position in society, strength of influence, degree of immunity, degree of power to hurt others, effectiveness at grabbing power, strength of patronage, strength of intellect, level of morality, degree of self-reliance, and so on. All these characteristics can be precisely defined, so much so that some of them may be inferred from others. All these signs are in principle measurable.

What the individual thinks about himself and what others think about him more or less coincide (or at least there is a tendency towards coincidence). For himself an individual can be as complex and spiritually rich as he wishes. From the social point of view, if this spiritual wealth exceeds the limits of the normal or professional mean, its effect on the individual is more negative. From the social point of view the individual is a kind of mould with no internal structure with clearly defined forms and functions. Social progress consists in part in forming individuals to carry out more complex functions while retaining a simpler internal (spiritual) structure. What the individual thinks is of no relevance. What is important is how he acts. And he acts according to social rules.

The social individual is neither evil nor good. He simply has these two characteristics to a greater or lesser degree. The measurement of these qualities is not of principal interest. The values of these qualities in individuals are contained within specific socially acceptable limits (these latter are subject to historical variation, but are sufficiently well defined within each epoch). A departure from this framework is dangerous both to the individual himself and also to those with whom he has to deal. Excessive intelligence, for instance, is as dangerous from the social point of view as excessive stupidity.

Any social individual has a social situation and an official situation. The social situation of the individual is a function of many parameters—the position he occupies, the prestige of his profession, his access to various kinds of privileges, connections, influence and so on. The official situation is defined by the post occupied and by the official status of the said post. There is never a complete identity of social and official situation, and in a sufficiently large and diverse society it can never be achieved in practice. However in view of the broad tendency for the social and the official to coincide, a correspondence tends to be established even in this case. This can be observed in the attempt to establish norms of life in such a way that income, honour, fame and so on should be determined exclusively by the official situation of the individual (the director of a firm should have a higher income, a better apartment, a more attractive villa, than his subordinates; a full member of the Academy should be considered a more important scientist than a corresponding member, and a corresponding member more highly regarded than a simple doctor and so on). The social individual tries to improve his social position. From this point of view all individuals are careerists, ambitious, greedy and so on, but not all are able to achieve their desired objectives, and the majority from the very beginning are aware of the hopelessness of their efforts and resign themselves, which gives them an appearance of virtue. And rare are those who have the capacity to succeed but find it in themselves to choose another path at the dictates of their conscience. Though even there, they reckon to achieve success on a chosen course.

We must distinguish between the actual and nominal social significance of the individual. The actual side includes the social characteristics of the individual, and the nominal side is a way of expressing those characteristics where the case involves the official utilisation of the individual. The relationship between the actual and the nominal can be illustrated by the relationship between the actual characteristics of a man and the kind of testimonial he is given when he is seeking a new post, an award or a trip abroad. For instance, A is a careerist, a shark, a lecher, a boor, a plagiarist and so on. Everyone who needs to know, knows that this is his actual character. But his nominal characteristics may turn out like this: morally sound, a highly qualified specialist, has excellent students, and so on. Now, when people give such nominal characteristics to A, they are not lying, but doing something rather different. They are following the accepted usage in that particular sphere to indicate that A is suitable and useful for the affair in question—and nothing more than that. If A's actual characteristics were to be recognised in his nominal ones, this would imply not an objective evaluation of him, but evidence that A had taken the wrong turning, that he was about to be dropped, that he was thought unsuitable, and so on. But when A really *does* compromise himself, and people begin to say, well, we didn't know what he was really like, or we overlooked it, then those people *are* lying, for the real face of a social individual is, as a rule, accurately and thoroughly known by all the people about him.

Cause and guilt

Half an hour before the Bar opened, Chatterer and Member were already standing in line. Member was saying that he had written a new work on the excessively high standard of living of the people of Ibansk, putting forward proposals for lowering it. He had called the work 'Slanderous reflections about . . .' 'Why only the Ibansk people?' asked Chatterer. 'Because they live better than anyone else,' said Member, 'and I have precise facts to prove it.' 'Facts are falsehoods,' replied Chatterer. 'And what's more, you don't need facts at all, because your whole conception is officially fallacious and scientifically harmful. First, the people of Ibansk live no worse and no better than anyone else. They live the same. That is the official line. Principles can be neither proved nor disproved. Secondly, you are confusing the scientific and the official consciousness. . . .'

At this moment Sociologist came up. He shook Member by the hand, and said 'Hi friend!'. Then he shook Chatterer by the hand, and said 'Hi friend!'. Member was indignant at this informal approach. Chatterer said that it was of no importance, since Sociologist regarded them as experimental rabbits, ants, rats and similar vermin. 'So he wants to show that he's a true democrat and uses informality as a device.' If Sociologist wants to be informal, then they should respond informally. But when talking to each other they will continue to maintain a certain formality of address: between them there should be a certain distance without which good relations are unthinkable. Each taking a couple of glasses of beer, Sociologist, Chatterer and Member headed for their usual spot. Sociologist led the way, demonstrating by his whole appearance that he knew the way better than the others. On the way he said that what Chatterer had just said was rubbish. He was democratic by nature, even though his grandfather had been a member of the First Guild of Merchants, his father had been a diplomat, and he himself had been brought up abroad. After the first glass, Member referred to his interrupted conversation with Chatterer and asked what it was that he was supposed to have been confusing. 'From the scientific point of view,' said Chatterer, after cursing

(99)

the barmaid for having watered the beer beyond the accepted norm, 'one must talk of the causes of certain manifestations. But from the official point of view, such a statement of the problem is unacceptable. In any situation, the official consciousness always poses the question: "Where does the fault lie?" And as for the official consciousness, guilt must be personified, since only conscious beings can be accused, and not inanimate nature or dumb beasts, the problem is posed even more sharply: "Who is responsible for this?" From the official point of view, even natural disasters like earthquakes, droughts and floods, must be the responsibility of specific people. And the keepers of the official conscience, the bureaucrats, take this guilt on themselves and so try to hide such disasters from the population. They think themselves responsible (or rather fear that they will be blamed) even for the consequences which derive from the nature of man in society, and so they try to distort this nature and lay the blame on throwbacks, noxious influences and so on.'

Schizophrenic came along and asked what formula Member had used to calculate demand per head of population. Member said he'd done it the usual way—taken the total income and divided it by total number of people. Schizophrenic said that this was propaganda and not science. 'First, you have to allow for the coefficient of eye-wash, which basically reduces the official tally of consumption. Secondly, you have to consider the hierarchy of consumption, the distribution of people between different levels of consumption, and the coefficient of levelling. Thirdly, you have to take into account the coefficient of the relationship of a group at a given level to a given product. So you come up with a far more complex formula which is just as useless as Member's very simple formula, since everything is clear without resort to either. If it's potatoes and artificial beaver lamb you're distributing, you'll get one result, and if it's black caviar and mink, you'll get quite another.' Dauber and Slanderer came up and joined in the general attack on Member. Schizophrenic summed up the discussion, saying that they had witnessed a typical example of the social law which he had brought to light, 'One for all and all for one', and suggested they should drink to the health of this outstanding seeker after non-existent justice. 'I hear you're going abroad,' said

Member. 'Not abroad, to B,' said Slanderer. 'Do you think they'll let you?' asked Member. 'I'm about seventy per cent certain that there's not much chance,' said Slanderer, 'and thirty per cent certain there's no chance at all.' 'So why all the effort of applying?' asked Member. 'Because if you don't go through the rigmarole of applying, then you can't say that they wouldn't let you go,' said Slanderer.

On stupidity, baseness
and other characteristics of the individual

The qualities of the social individual, wrote Schizophrenic, can be divided into the positive and the negative. An example of the former is intelligence. An example of the latter is stupidity. I wish to demonstrate that the former cannot be regarded as the absence of the latter, nor the latter as the absence of the former. Intelligence is not the absence of stupidity, nor is stupidity the absence of intelligence. This does not contradict the fact that these two qualities, beyond a certain value, are mutually exclusive. When in common speech we say that a man is stupid (or intelligent), that is an intuitive indication that the man has the attribute of stupidity (or intelligence) to a fairly high degree. When we say that a man is not stupid (not intelligent), then we mean that he does not possess the attribute of stupidity (or intelligence) in sufficient measure. Everyone knows that people can gain in intelligence. But for some reason one seems to pay little attention to the fact that people can also gain in stupidity. In life, we often meet stupid people of whom one can say that they are outstandingly stupid. Here we can distinguish between talented and untalented imbeciles. Stupidity must be learnt, just as intelligence is. People can attain to a really high degree of stupidity only after a long life and a great deal of practice. Absolutely the same is true of such attributes as cynicism, baseness, guile, jobbery, trouble-making and so on. The ability to be really vile doesn't come instantly. To become an egregious bastard, you require not only a natural talent for it, but also a long and single-minded apprenticeship. So it is not surprising that the really outstanding bastards are to be found more often among the ranks of the elderly and well educated. Moreover, where society plays a dominant role, negative qualities are not regarded as shortcomings. Quite the opposite, they are regarded as virtues, and encouraged by every means. Here they are normal. An outstanding intelligence is regarded here as an abnormality, and outstanding stupidity as outstanding intelligence. Highly moral people are regarded as amoral villains, and the most abject nonentities as models of virtue. What is in question here is not the absence of one quality, but the presence of another. As a result a strangely negative type of personality is formed which reacts to the positive in the same way as the electron to the positron (or vice versa). Just as the presence of a negative charge is not the absence of a positive, and of a positive charge is not the absence of a negative, so in the given case, I repeat, a negative type of personality is a personality which has certain specific attributes. When I use the terms 'positive' and 'negative' I am making no value-judgments about them. If we reverse the terms, the essence of the matter is not affected, in the same way that the relationship between an electron and a positron would remain exactly the same even if they swapped names.

Negative and positive characteristics are to a certain extent so similar that for a long time (and perhaps indefinitely) people fail to notice the differences between them. It sometimes happens that two people live and work together, read the same books, meet the same people, but at the same time develop in totally incompatible directions. And when one day it is suddenly noticed that they are opposites—for example, one is an outstanding fool, and the other an outstandingly intelligent man—this produces a spiritual drama and sharp conflicts. Incidentally, it is comparatively rare to come across individuals with highly developed positive characteristics. Individuals with highly developed negative characteristics turn up in huge numbers. But in the great majority of cases negative and positive qualities do not reach a level where it is possible to say of an individual with any precision that he is intelligent, stupid, mean, noble, or what have you. The normal individual has, in a more or less developed form, both positive and negative characteristics (he is averagely intelligent, averagely stupid, averagely noble, averagely mean and so on). Only in a few strong manifestations does the positive characteristic exclude its opposite (negative) *doppelgänger*. For example, a person with highly developed intelligence totally lacks stupidity, or at least his stupidity is wholly under-developed, and a highly developed crook either has a total lack of nobility, or possesses it only in embryonic form. From the point of view of the human type we can distinguish civilisation and anti-civilisation. The latter is just as capable of development as the former. Highly developed anti-civilisation destroys civilisation (and vice versa) but in the interim they live side by side and are even hard to tell apart. They grow into each other and anti-civilisation becomes the dominant partner: civilisation is merely anti-civilisation's more or less recognisable companion.

Logic and language

An article in the Newspaper against AS made a great impression on everyone. This time everyone except Chatterer attacked AS. 'I have great respect for AS, in fact I'd go on my knees to him,' said Dauber, 'but this time I cannot agree with him. He seems to have lost his sense of moderation.' 'That's a strange position to take up,' said Careerist. 'What possible justification can there be for these scoundrels!' Member attacked AS in the crudest language, calling him a speculator, a man capable of every betrayal to serve his own ends. Chatterer said that he totally supported AS if for no other reason than that he was alone. 'And if a man is alone against every one else, he is always right. Later on you'll realise for yourselves that he is right. And then how could you possibly believe official reports? You know perfectly well that not one line of our official reports can be believed, and yet here you are suddenly believing everything. What's up with you? Why don't you accept the possibility that someone might have been tampering with the facts? It's a very serious matter, better not to jump to conclusions and condemnations. AS has put his finger on something which forces us all (those who are pro and those who are anti) to re-examine our consciences. And we don't like the idea. We are angry with him for his invasion of our souls and consciences. He asks a direct question—"what sort of people are we?" The scoundrels know perfectly well what sort of people they are, and so they hate AS. Decent people begin to realise that they are accessories to the scoundrels, which makes them scoundrels themselves. Hence their venom. But leave the content of the problem and come back to the purely textual aspect. Here is one of AS's sentences which has provoked your anger, noble and honest though that anger doubtless is: "If you . . . (and AS is speaking to those who carry out the pogroms) . . . If you really want to establish democratic freedoms, then do not do this, that or the other, since they would interfere with the realisation of such a programme." You have interpreted this sentence to mean that AS approves of the actions of the pogrom-makers and believes that they really do want to establish democratic freedoms. Now that is a common mistake in logic. If a man accepts an assertion such as "If X, then Y", it in no way follows that he accepts X. And if you educated and exceptional people manage to commit that childish error so easily, then what do you suppose others will do? If people want to confuse themselves, they'll trample over far more serious things than the laws of logic. The appalling thing here is not your total incomprehension but your total refusal to understand anything about a situation which you find so painful. Of course, it's unpleasant suddenly to feel oneself a cretin and a creep.'

After an awkward silence, they began to argue about the laws of logic. Eventually Chatterer was able to persuade them all that these laws deal with linguistic operations, and not with real things. So they began to talk about language. Member said that language was given to man for the purpose of expressing his thoughts. Chatterer remarked that Member said this rather as if language were handed out by the government in the same way as they hand out work, accommodation, bread and trousers. Dauber said that language was given to men so that they could conceal their thoughts. Slanderer refined this idea, and said that language was given to man to hide his own intentions and distort the intentions of others. Then attention turned again to Chatterer, who at one time had been considered a great expert in this field, but who had been banished from it by the more progressive Ibanskian representatives of world science, which was not even aware of their existence.

'You recall,' said Chatterer, 'what happened when Slanderer was proposed for the Academy? Slanderer had said previously that he didn't want to submit himself to the ballot, but he was proposed, and he signed the papers. And he was accused of inconsistency. Now was he inconsistent? When I came here today, I didn't want a drink. You offered me one, and I took it.

Inconsistent? No. We merely have to distinguish between the absence of desire to do something, and the presence of a positive disinclination to do it. Those aren't the same thing. One can be indifferent to something—i.e. one can lack both the inclination and the disinclination to do it. Slanderer didn't wish to be elected, but neither did he wish to refuse election. Everyone interpreted that as hypocrisy, although they themselves had been behaving hypocritically all along. Now this is why I mentioned this trivial instance. It is usually believed that people act according to the laws of logic, and depart from them only in exceptional circumstances—and then they are allegedly unaware of what they are doing. That is rubbish. To act according to the laws of logic while remaining unaware of doing so is in principle impossible because of the very nature of these laws. And secondly the percentage of linguistic operations which take place according to the laws of logic, compared with the total number of linguistic operations, is so infinitely small that to talk about some logical stage of thought is just laughable. In fact, people hardly use the laws of logic at all, and it's far from the case that people use them all the time without being aware of the fact. Just try to analyse the speeches of politicians and lawyers from a logical point of view, and you will be surprised to find yourself detecting in them an almost complete absence of logic, although logic should be the basis of their considerations. Science? One of the severest scientific disciplines—physics, is full of underhand linguistic tricks. From the logical point of view, people's linguistic activities are completely chaotic, and the introduction of logic is, in effect, a wholly insignificant attempt to bring a little order into that chaos.' Schizophrenic said that he fully agreed. Linguistic chaos is an accurate reflection of social chaos. Human linguistic usage is essentially illogical. Logic is one of the weapons of the anti-social. A weapon of the social, on the other hand, is anti-logic, which for camouflage is called dialectical logic. So logic is not all that inoffensive after all. One of these days it will get people into just as much trouble as politics. Incidentally, the coefficient of logicality does not in practice depend on level of education, and is inversely proportional to social grading.

Member said that all the same he still regarded AS's behaviour as dictated by purely personal motives. Chatterer said that AS did indeed have such a shortcoming, but Member's behaviour was dictated not by his own but by other people's personal motives. Member protested, but by this time no-one was listening to him.

A discussion of denunciations

We were marched off to work, read Instructor. Panicker began to sing, and the rest joined in jauntily:

> Where the infantry don't go,
> Where the armoured trains don't show,
> Where the tanks don't penetrate,
> There we go to defecate.

When the prisoners had crushed into the lavatory and relieved themselves of the weighty consequences of yesterday's blow-out, Patriot let fall a tear: 'We behaved badly. Look, we left our comrades with no supper, and got the bosses into trouble.' Writer proposed gagging Patriot with his own gaiters. Defeatist supported that proposal, but at the same time said that on the whole he agreed with Patriot. Gelding urged that they should not be so quick to draw conclusions, and set out the modern concept of the role of denunciation in social systems of a homogeneous type. In order to control the conduct of a collective, one needs to know the actual situation. And for that purpose, as has been established by the bourgeois pseudo-science of cybernetics which has recently come to our service, we need a feedback. Official accounts, summaries and reports are either empty and commonplace, or they are downright falsehoods and eyewash—but the leadership needs to know the real truth. Here the vital role of feedback is supplied by denunciations. Intellectual said that the leadership needed the real truth in Gelding's sense only to such a degree and with such an orientation as would best help them to secure the maximum tenure in power, and the best chances for their future careers. Apart from that, Gelding was confusing two types of information which were different in principle—denunciation, and if you like, information. A denunciation is always personalised—information is impersonal. As a matter of information there is no value in knowing who went absent without leave today, yesterday, or the day before. The only important thing as far as information is concerned is the fact itself and its frequency (either in percentages or probability). Denunciation is negative, since it is a report on deeds, words and thoughts allegedly directed against . . . or allegedly damaging to . . . Information is for the most part positive or at least neutral. Put more precisely, it does not evaluate. Denunciation is intended for the forces of repression, who do not of themselves have the prerogative of government. Information is intended primarily for the organs of government which are not directly concerned with repression. The aim of a denunciation is to know with the purpose of excising, punishing, destroying. The aim of information is to know with the purpose of correcting, improving, preserving. They are on different planes. The peculiarity of the situation lies in the fact that information, where it is public and official, is false, and, where it is secret, it rapidly tends towards denunciation.

Deviationist said that to speak of any kind of genuine truth in social life is just rubbish. First, to say 'genuine truth' is like saying 'salty salt'. Secondly, the concept of truth in the academic sense is totally irrelevant. For example, what is a man really like? A man can think one thing and say another, say one thing and do another. He can have mutually contradictory thoughts on one and the same subject. He can carry out actions leading to mutually contradictory results. A normal man of himself is anything you like. And that means nothing. A normal man comprises every imaginable characteristic regardless of how such characteristics inter-relate. Which is why there is nothing in him, for the concept of 'a man as such', or 'a real man' is just an abstraction. Only as an official being, a citizen, reacting in a defined way to official indicators, is a man something defined. In a normal society there are such indicators, i.e. officially established and recognised cases in which the words, deeds and thoughts of a man are characteristic: his behaviour at work, his speeches at meetings, his published articles, his testimony in court, his church attendance and so on. And what lies beyond that is of no concern to anyone, for it does not constitute a socially significant fact and therefore does not exist. For example, if from the rostrum you vote 'yes' and then go home and tell your wife and your friend that your real opinion is 'no', officially you are 'pro' and not 'anti'. As an 'anti' person you simply do not exist at all, imagine what you like on that score. I have

known people in the security services whose talk was all anti
—but they were profoundly pro in conviction. A man who is
exactly the same person both officially and unofficially is either
an unrealisable dream of the leadership, or he is a liar, a
hypocrite, wastrel, cretin, louse. When people begin to distinguish what in a man transcends the official, this simply characterises the sort of society which sanctions such a distinction.
The inevitable consequence of this sanction is the moral decay
of people (such traits begin to develop as servility, obsequious-
ness, double-dealing, civic cowardice, dishonesty etc., which
are subject to neither official nor moral retribution.) But the
main thing is that the special organisations of the society begin
to seek in man what does not exist there. Hence people's
behaviour is subject to a false interpretation and we get
official deception. If in society a search begins for the real truth,
that means one thing only—a call for people to start writing
denunciations.

Patriot said that in such circumstances, denunciations would
produce good. Panicker said that so far no-one had calculated
the percentage of cases in which denunciations had caused
harm and the percentage which had had good results.
Deviationist said that that wasn't the point. In this case to
quantify was erroneous. There are more basic reasons to consider denunciation immoral, regardless of whether it is useful or
not. Even if it is useful in a hundred per cent of cases, it remains
a sign of degradation. At this point, everyone got confused and
lost the thread completely. Gelding said to Intellectual that a
man's secret conscience and its official expression were still not
in complete rapport. Intellectual said that this was of no consequence, since the secret has a tendency to coincide with the
official, and the coincidence is achieved the quicker the less the
pressure experienced by the individual. 'The way you look at
it,' said Gelding, 'people turn into swine voluntarily.' Intellectual said that that was so even in cases where there was coercion.
Gelding said that that was dialectics, and from his childhood
he'd liked dialectics about as much as he liked cod liver oil.
Patriot said that cod liver oil had its uses. Gelding told him to
get stuffed. Then dinnertime came around, and the debate was
adjourned.

Thinker

Thinker knew that he was the most intelligent and educated person in Ibansk. He had a job on the Journal and was pleased about that since most people weren't as well placed as he was. But at the same time he was dissatisfied, for there were other people with better jobs. Insofar as everyone who didn't have a job as good as his was more stupid than he was, he thought his position perfectly justified. But insofar as all those who had jobs superior to his were also more stupid than he was, he felt himself unjustly passed over. He knew perfectly well that if he were more stupid, he would have a better job. And because of this he was filled with rending self-pity, and came to the point of despising even more the inhabitants of Ibansk, who fully deserved this scorn because of all their former history. In the eyes of the avant-garde thinking and creative intelligentsia of Ibansk Thinker was a man to be taken out and shot, and shot on the one hand unjustly (or rather, unlawfully), but on the other hand justly, because he nurtured deviant ideas.

Thinker did not live so much as fulfil a Mission and pursue an Aim. What the Mission was, and what the Aims were, no-one knew. But everyone was aware that they existed. Everyone said what a good job that we've got Thinker There. What would go on There if he wasn't There? If it weren't for him, things would be even worse.

Unlike all the other inhabitants of Ibansk, Thinker was a worldly man. He only sat at his desk to work out at whose expense he would consume today's shashlik and bottle of vodka, from whom to borrow a large sum of money in the form of an irredeemable debt, and with whose wives and in what order to spend the rest of the day. Incidentally he always intended to repay his debts some time, just as he was preparing to write a book in exchange for a fat fee.

Sometimes Thinker wrote orthodox but inept articles. The occasions when they appeared became high days and holidays for the thinking part of the Ibansk population. Everyone could see with their own eyes how outstandingly courageous Thinker was, Thinker who was the first to refer to the historic speeches of the new Leader, and who raised to a record number his total of references to them. He even dared to refer to an as yet unwritten speech of the Leader, which brought him an undeserved rebuke for indiscretion and excessive progressiveness. There were rumours that he would soon be removed. It was Thinker himself who started these rumours in the form of a gloomy supposition. And when they came back to him in the form of authentic questions from his female fans, he shrugged his shoulders ironically—you know perfectly well that there's no place here for an intelligent and able man like me. And he went off on a special mission abroad to deliver a lecture and then to take stock of the situation.

Juridical trivia

Member came up extremely agitated. 'Just think,' he said, 'I'm being accused that my writings—that's what they've called them—my writings are prejudicial to our society. May I ask who decides whether or not damage has been caused, and if so in what form and how much?' 'Your naïvety astonishes me,' said Chatterer. 'There are experts for that, of course.' 'Excuse me,' yelled Member, 'but what criteria do they follow? Where have they been drawn up? Who's confirmed them? Just you show me these criteria!' Chatterer calmly answered that the experts were guided by their sense of duty, by their general grasp of the situation, by their correct and proven intuition. 'That's all just sophistry,' said Member. 'And can writing the truth cause damage as well?' 'That depends on what and how you write,' said Chatterer. 'You claim that we have a caste system, and that this leads to corruption, to careerism, to indifference and all the rest. But everybody knows that those are just isolated facts which we can cope with successfully ourselves. Broadly speaking, nothing of the kind exists at all. So your statements are simply slander.' 'But do you know,' asked Member, 'what percentage is needed to distinguish between truth and slander? How many cases? A hundred? A thousand? A million? Who's going to keep the count? I'm not generalising. I'm only giving the facts. Facts, facts and only facts.' 'This argument's pointless,' said Slanderer. 'For it to make sense, you'd need full juridical clarity on these facts, and you haven't got it.' 'This problem,' said Schizophrenic, 'is essentially insoluble for it is a purely juridical problem. What's needed here are specialists in these matters, with a personal interest in the observation of established juridical norms. And finally, you need complete information, public opinion, a chance of exposing violations of those norms and so on, that's to say, society should have at its disposal means to enforce respect for the juridical norms. And a last thing: the juridical norms themselves should be established with all this in mind, as otherwise nothing will come of them whatever you do. Left to its own devices and the operation of social laws, jurisprudence has a tendency to develop systems of juridical norms wherein imprecision is enshrined as a principle. Every article is balanced by its contradictory opposite, and a system of exceptions and provisos originates which makes the conduct of jurisprudence here an entirely arbitrary matter.' 'But something must be done,' said Member. 'A start must be made. If all we do is to pass by looking indifferent, as you youngsters are doing, we'll never get anywhere.' You're right,' said Chatterer. 'But action must go beyond a certain threshold, below which it is meaningless.' 'There I can't agree with you,' said Schizophrenic. 'What you choose to describe as meaningless actions do have a meaning, as a preparation, as an accumulation of experience of action in general.'

On justice
'It is monstrously unjust,' said Dauber. 'I am an artist. It is my legal right to visit museums in France and Italy. I am constantly being invited to go there. They've held exhibitions of my work. I want to travel at my own expense. I haven't committed any crimes. I don't dabble in politics. And yet they won't let me go. Claimant's been to France twice, and for a holiday in Italy. Sociologist spends most of his time abroad. Thinker's been round all the galleries in Paris and Rome. Even Instructor's been to Paris. But they won't let *me* go. What's it all about? Only Slanderer was invited to be the chairman of our delegates to the congress. Hundreds of people went—all the riff-raff. But anyway he wasn't allowed to go.' 'The only thing that's unjust,' said Chatterer, 'is what doesn't fit in with the rules of a given social formation. You and Slanderer have received a great deal—your independence, fame, a reputation as great artists. What more do you want? You want on top of that to travel at others' expense (or at your own, it makes no difference) to a foreign country? In our country a trip abroad is the highest

reward for the outstandingly distinguished, for the most reliable. Or it is a duty. Or follows from the exploitation of one's official function and connections. In our conditions it would be precisely an injustice to let you go. You have become famous against the will of the leadership, not in accordance with the laws of our society. You should be punished for that, not allowed to go abroad.' 'But that's silly even from the point of view of the state,' said Dauber. 'The state's interests are an empty abstraction,' said Chatterer. 'There are interests of specific categories of people which they camouflage as being the interests of the state. In fact these people don't give a rap for the state. They only think of themselves. Do you think they feel proud of their country when they're over there and they hear what people say about you and Slanderer? Not at all. All they feel is anger and envy. They feel deeply and unwarrantably insulted by what they hear. And when they come back they seek their revenge on you.' 'But at all events it's the state that suffers, whether materially or morally,' said Dauber. 'It does,' agreed Chatterer. 'But the state belongs to no-one, and no-one's hurt therefore, except for people like you. And as far as you're concerned the general view is that you think only of yourselves. The only people who think about the state are they—its true representatives and defenders.' 'You turn everything upside down,' said Dauber. 'What I'm doing,' said Chatterer, 'is restoring to things which in our view have been turned upside down their genuine appearance.'

Puss appears in the arena of history

The facts about Puss were known in Ibansk only to a handful of highly refined intellectuals like Thinker, Claimant and Sociologist and to a few old veterans of the Laboratory where he appeared once, in the dawn of his misty youth, so terrified that he'd soiled his pants and bore a circumstantial letter of confession adducing a great many names and facts. I'll revert later to this notable event in Puss's irreproachable biography. And yet despite his almost complete obscurity, the role that Puss played in the spiritual life of Ibansk was so insignificant that to pass over it would be a grave distortion of the historical truth. Puss had everything which in the conditions of Ibansk a decent, intelligent and educated man could dream of. He was completely independent, i.e. he could do nothing and be rewarded for it, he could sometimes go on foreign trips and regularly voted on a variety of councils, committees and commissions. Moreover, he always openly expressed his own opinion against dubious ideas of novice authors, which deservedly won him the reputation of an austere and incorruptible champion of the interests of world science. He had a good apartment and decent income. His former wife had deserted him to return with his former son to her parents, scornfully refusing the maintenance she was entitled to by law, and this admirably suited Puss, who was as parsimonious as they come. It suited him even more so because in the room that she had vacated, he was able to assemble a library which even Thinker and Sociologist might have envied. One of his articles in some journal or other was translated into some Western language. And although no-one paid the slightest attention to the article, Puss was very proud of it. And when he complained about the difficult position of the creative intelligentsia of Ibansk, he used to say, 'Look how I, a man with a world reputation, can't even get permission to enlarge the garden round my villa.'

Puss was 105 per cent certain that he was a decent, intelligent and educated man. And as beyond any doubt he was more decent, more intelligent and better educated than all the others including Thinker (a ventriloquist!) and Sociologist (a babbler!), he assumed that his own confident assessment of himself was shared by everybody else, which indeed more or less corresponded to the truth. (Everyone knows the kind of scum we're obliged to live among!) With the exception of certain insignificant peccadilloes which wouldn't be worth recalling were they not so insignificant. Once, back in the old days, his friend, an active party worker, publicly accused Puss that as a sign of protest against the just steps being taken against the poison-plot doctors, he'd had himself circumcised. Slanderer advised Puss to go to the appropriate authorities and to produce his most powerful argument rejecting this accusation. Puss came out in red spots and stammered that unfortunately he was actually in no position to use this argument. Slanderer said that in that case, he should prepare for the worst. And that was when Puss did it in his pants and wrote a long letter in which he betrayed everybody including Slanderer.

But despite his outstanding successes in science, and his good position in life, Puss was in a constant state of irritation and of justified anger. The trouble was that in the circles in which they moved people gradually, almost imperceptibly began to talk about certain ideas and articles of Slanderer. Of course Puss never read Slanderer's articles. Why waste precious time on rubbish! Slanderer studied and worked in the same places as Puss (apart from a brief ten-year interval) and in such places, as Puss knew very well, the appearance of anything significant was *a priori* ruled out. If Puss himself wasn't able to produce anything to attract the attention of the people Over There (anything significant can occur only Over There, and whatever takes place Over There must needs be significant!) then clearly Slanderer could do nothing at all in that respect. And if Over There people were translating his writings and talking about him, then this was an unhealthy manifestation which clearly had an ideological or a political connotation. Surely the leadership couldn't fail to understand that? It was someone's duty to speak out about this honestly, directly and openly. So Puss wrote a secret denunciation.

Unexpectedly something happened which dotted the i's, as Thinker later elegantly expressed it. Puss and a group of colleagues went to a symposium Over There to which Slanderer had been invited but, because of Puss's letter, to which he had not been allowed to go. And for this reason, Puss and his group ran into some unpleasantness. The scandal was hushed up. But the decision to dot the i's began to assume a more positive form. 'It's time to finish with all of this,' said Puss. Everyone was in agreement that it was time to take appropriate steps about Slanderer. But no-one was prepared to take the initiative. Now this problem was resolved. When he came back from the symposium, Puss wrote a report in which he gave all credit to the great work done by our delegation, and mentioned in passing the name of Slanderer, describing his conduct as unpatriotic and uncomradely. Claimant suggested that the report should be polished and sent to the Journal. Inspired by this success, Puss began to gather material together. And for the first time for many years, he felt that although he was useless to society, he was nevertheless indispensable.

On the abstraction of the individual

'For you,' said Dauber, 'the elemental social individual is an unstructured sphere. But in fact, a real individual is nothing of the kind. He has extensions into the past (his ancestors, previous events in his life), into the future (his children, his ambitions) and spatially (his links with other people). Try for example to tear me out of my social milieu, and I will trail behind me thousands of threads of all kinds.' 'Well, what about it?' said Schizophrenic. 'If you try to construct a science you'll see for yourself that unless you accept my abstraction, there's nothing you can do. How are you going to take stock of your threads? Clearly you're going to have to introduce certain terms and examine what they mean in terms of characteristics of the individual. So it's of no consequence whether you now regard individuals as smooth spheres or as formless constructions with a multiplicity of extensions. The amalgam of characteristics will be exactly the same. The essence of the matter doesn't lie in figurative representations (a solid sphere, something rooted in a solid medium, a plastic body with extensions and so on) but in the choice of initial characteristics and their correlations.' 'The theory according to which people are just cogs, cells and so on of the complex mechanism of society is officially condemned here,' said Dauber. 'That's not a theory, it's ideology,' said Schizophrenic. 'It's condemned officially, but in practice it's a commonplace fact. And by that very fact, the possibility of a scientific approach to the problems of society is excluded before you start. It's enough to hint at that for you to be plunged deep into the quagmire of ideology and held there until you snuff out as a scientist. And on top of that there is popular prejudice. I can see that even for you my arguments are just a more or less amusing diversion. But imagine how all our mutual friends react to that. It doesn't bear thinking about.'

The normality of absurdity
and the absurdity of the norm

'Just look at that,' said Slanderer, showing Dauber his book published in English. 'Look at the price and then multiply that by the number of copies printed. Quite a sum isn't it? And the state needs hard currency. There was a time when it was possible to publish a book in English here and sell it abroad.

Then that sum would come into our pockets. But they refused. My colleagues rejected the book because it didn't come up to the right level. After all, they could hardly accept that Slanderer's popularity was growing Over There! And what's more he might be paid royalties, which is equally inadmissable. All right, so be it. Then a publishing house Over There tried to make a contract with one of our publishers for an edition Over There. The state would have got some hard currency. True, less than they would have got in the first case, but all the same, there would have been something. And I might have got something too. Our publishers asked advice from my university. My friends wrote a savage appraisal of my book, and the deal fell through. Well, the book's been published just the same but the state doesn't get a penny out of it.'

'I'll tell you an even funnier story,' said Dauber. 'There was this foreigner who wanted to buy my etchings openly and above board. He offered a hundred roubles each. But our people refused. They asked him to pay twenty-five. The foreigner didn't want to buy them cheap because he was making a capital investment: the dearer he buys, the dearer he sells. Now do you understand why our people insisted on twenty-five roubles?' 'No,' said Slanderer. 'It's very simple,' said Dauber. 'Our most expensive academicians never sell for more than twenty-five roubles, and so they could never admit that any old Dauber, who had no letters after his name, might sell his work for more than they could.' 'How did it all end?' asked Slanderer. 'The deal fell through,' said Dauber. 'I once worked out how much the state could earn from me. Although Schizophrenic explained it all to me with exhaustive clarity, I still can't understand the monstrous stupidity of this kind of thing.'

They began to talk about the position of the creative intelligentsia and, naturally, to make comparisons. Slanderer said that he earns less than a shorthand-typist Over There, and a professor of his rank would earn something like twenty times more. Dauber said that everyone's very happy to accept his drawings as gifts, but no-one's prepared to buy them even for halfpennies. Chatterer said that after they'd had a drink or two their conversation always degenerated into woolliness and he appealed for greater clarity. 'Are there many professors of the same rank as Slanderer in our circles? Just one. There are no others. And what about the rest? The rest, who have degrees and diplomas, don't live at all badly. And if you take into account that they are trash for all their titles, they don't live too badly. Do we have many artists like Dauber? Just the one. And how do the others live?' 'That's all very well,' said Dauber. 'I'm not talking about that.' 'Well, what are you talking about?' asked Chatterer. 'The fact that people don't buy? The people who appreciate you haven't any money and can't buy. Those who have money either don't appreciate you, or prefer as a matter of course to get things free, or they prefer three-piece suites and antique chandeliers or wine glasses with the monograms of Napoleon I, or Nicholas II. In a word there's nothing stupid about that. What is stupid is the pair of you and your pretentions.' 'We haven't any pretentions,' said Dauber. 'We're merely surprised.' 'Well, it's your surprise that's stupid,' said Chatterer. 'You live in one kind of society, and try to live off the culture of a different kind. It's within that culture that you're working, and it's from Over There that you take your criteria for the evaluation of your position. Over here you're the exception and not the rule. And so everything that is normal looks absurd when applied to you. You're alien and yet you want people to regard you as if you represented the virtue of this society. Why should Slanderer live better than Sociologist or Claimant? Because he is an outstanding scientist and they are insignificant nobodies? Rubbish. Who decides on their merits as scientists? By our criteria Sociologist and Claimant are outstanding scientists, and Slanderer is an able, serious etc. scientist at a lower level. Apart from that Sociologist and Claimant travel abroad and sit on commissions, councils and presidiums. They have the ear of the Assistant and even of the Deputies. In other words they have a function, and Slanderer just sits hunched over papers which nobody here needs. It's an act of charity merely to tolerate Slanderer here—that's the highest reward he can expect. And the same goes for Dauber. In the end you must accept that there is nothing exceptional in what has happened to you. It doesn't generally happen, since there aren't many of you, and so there aren't many such cases. It is a natural phenomenon. A phenomenon can be natural, i.e. can be the result of the action of the laws of a given society, even if in general it is unprecedented. Moreover, the law of a given type of society tends to eliminate completely such exceptional phenomena as Slanderer and Dauber. Let me point out, too, that AS is a normal manifestation of the vitality of this society even though he is treated as an enemy. And *you* are a deviation from the norm, whether you be regarded as one of us or simply ignored. Facts of this kind confuse the overall picture of our life: they lump together qualitatively heterogeneous manifestations.'

Social action

A social action is the action of an individual which has certain characteristics, wrote Schizophrenic. It is an action directed towards another individual or to other individuals which, in some way or another, affects their interests. Secondly, it is a conscious action. The individual takes account of the predicted effect of his action on specified or unspecified individuals. Thirdly, it is a free action, i.e. the individual can choose to carry it out or not to carry it out. And finally, the individual carries out his action in his own interests.

The evasion of an action can also be a social action in itself. The action of an individual towards himself is either a concealed action which concerns other people (be they unspecified, potential, or interchangeable persons) in which case it is a social action (for example, self-immolation); or it can be an action whose aim is to show people the nature of the individual, to define the individual's face in the eyes of people in whom the individual is interested. In this case too, it is an action which relates to other people, i.e. it is a social action. Such actions include frequent examples of the type 'I am willing to do anything you want', 'You can count on me', 'I don't want anything to do with you', and so on.

Usually a social action produces an immediate result and then ceases to exist. Where the action seems to aim at a fulfilment in the long term (sometimes years ahead), it is either not a social action at all, or its aim is assessed *a posteriori*, or it achieves latent results which render it obsolete. Incidentally this question is of no interest to sociology.

What forces individuals to carry out social actions of one kind or another? Usually in such cases we speak of the aims and the motives of the actions. But in principle I reject this approach as meaningless. People carry out social actions because of social laws. And there can be no deeper basis for social action. Insofar as aims and motives are concerned they relate to people's actions on quite a different non-sociological plane, and particularly on the psychological plane. From the sociological point of view they merely camouflage the social laws for their own and for others' eyes. Let us take an example. A speaks at a meeting and criticises B. As far as he is concerned this action is motivated by his concern for B, his desire to help him back on to the true path. But someone else assesses A's action as sheer self-interest (promoting himself in the eyes of the leadership). A third assesses A's action as motivated by a desire to harm B. But what has happened in reality? There is no such thing here as 'reality' since all three aspects are equally present. All that remains is a unanimity of judgment, and the absence of controversy, indifference and so on. Here the whole concept of an aim is meaningless. The aim of a social action is simply the wish of the individual who carries it out. But a man often sees himself as a casual observer sees him and deceives himself just as he deceives others. Moreover, even when he is conscious that he wishes to cause other people harm, he is unaware that he is acting towards them according to the social law which obliges the individual to do everything he can to weaken the social position of his peers. And it is in principle impossible to establish what is his actual aim.

If an individual, in undertaking a given social action towards certain other individuals, uses a third individual as an intermediary or a means towards this action, then this latter individual is acting for him, not as a social individual, but as any other instrument (as a knife, a rifle, a club and so on). His action in relation to him is not a social action (if of course this individual is only a means). Cases of this kind constitute one of the uncontrollable directions which can be taken by the unexpected consequences of social actions. In particular, in wishing to cause someone harm, an individual may benefit another individual, by using him as an intermediary, for in this case the action is carried out not according to social laws.

People carry out a great number of social actions. These are categorised according to how important they are for the people towards whom they are directed. People become accustomed to many of them, fail to notice them, attach no great importance to them. Actions of this kind for example include insults exchanged in crowded places (in queues, on public transport), the rudeness of shop assistants, the deliberate slowness of officials dealing with visitors to firms or institutions, and all manner of discourtesy from people at the top who are certain of their impunity, and so on. Other actions play a more significant role in people's lives because they have a determining influence on their fate. Such for example are betrayal, a false denunciation, a stab in the back, and so on. Each individual has a predisposition, more or less firmly established in the course of his development, to carry out actions of a particular type, in such a way that it is sometimes possible to characterise his behaviour: two-faced, cowardly, trustworthy, sincere, vindictive, and so on. But not every characteristic of this kind is a social characteristic. Inasmuch as individuals all obey the same social laws, the characteristics of an individual's social behaviour can contain only the purely quantitative and structural qualities of actions (when I speak of structural qualities I have in mind, for example, a predisposition to actions via intermediaries or without intermediaries). For this reason there are not and in principle cannot be any objectively stable social evaluations of individuals other than purely quantitative ones. And those cases we often meet in which one person pronounces differing and often contradictory judgements on another are not evidence of any depravity in people, but merely of the fact that they are people and nothing more. They act in accordance with social laws, and the reproaches of their conscience do not as a rule trouble them.

Two or more people can find themselves in a social situation if and only if each of these individuals carries out social actions in relation to the others, or if he himself is the object of the actions of the other (or both one and the other) and all individuals are aware of their situation in these actions and the situation of the other individuals in this group.

When he had read this extract from Schizophrenic's manuscript, Sociologist absently stuffed it in his pocket to take home.

Room wanted

For many years, autumn, for Slanderer, began with his buying small ad forms and filling them in thus: 'Single Ibanskian, scientific worker, seeks separate room in quiet flat.' People with rooms to let knew from experience that this kind of tenant was the most desirable from every point of view and within a few days Slanderer would find a room completely adequate for his extremely humble needs. Having studied for many years the established but entirely unofficial system for sub-letting rooms, Slanderer was struck by the following facts. The tenants paid huge sums of money for their rooms and their flats. The number of tenants was colossal. As a result literally hundreds of millions of roubles circulated, bypassing the official financial system. Slanderer carried out a few straightforward calculations and established that a few dozen simple residential hotels charging slightly higher rates would recover their cost within a few years, would provide the state with an enormous income and would simplify people's lives. He mentioned this at the Bar. Member became extremely agitated. Chatterer as usual was quick to destroy the illusion and spread disappointment. 'Firstly,' he said, 'to whom and how would the rooms be let? To anyone you like? You wouldn't get away with that here for a start. The rooms would be let to people who already enjoy privileges where it comes to accommodation: people on business trips and people who can afford bribes. And people who wanted to rent privately in most cases would never get into the hotels. Say for example a man and his wife have split up. Their apartment has enough living space. So why should the husband be offered a room in a hotel? Get a divorce and share your living space so people who rent rooms now would go on doing so as before. Secondly, such a system of hotels would contradict the principle of tying people to places (let's call it passport control) and also the principle of making living conditions depend on the social position of the individual. A hotel system would increase the degree of independence of the individual in society (or it would be better to say would weaken the degree of dependence as it is laughable here to talk about any degree of independence) and this would contradict the social laws of this society. Finally, were your plans to be put into practice they would bring virtually no economic benefit. In your calculation you haven't taken social factors into account: if we read that a building has cost a million, then you must take it that at least two million have been squandered. Then there's the staffing. Multiply your figures by three. Repairs—the buildings would have to be repaired even before they came into use. You can multiply your amortisation figures by three or, better, by five. Finally, management. Your hotel chain would be so top-heavy with managers, bookkeepers, clerks and so on, that nothing would be left of your super profits; and your system will live by the general laws of our society, so much so that you'd never even begin to regard it as a realisation of your Utopian dream.' Slanderer raised his hands in surrender. 'With a brilliant mind like yours,' he said to Chatterer, 'you should be running something really big.' 'Rubbish,' said Chatterer. 'You need quite different qualities to run anything. Just ask Schizophrenic: he has a few notions on the subject.' Member said that, all the same, he was going to look into the problem.

The problem of truth

Instructor read on. 'Life,' said Writer, 'is given to man only once. We don't know what will happen to us tomorrow. All will pass away—our cigarette holders, our knives, our sugar stocks. You know what? I vote we have ourselves a piss-up. There's a bird I know in town who can fix it all.' They discussed it for half an hour, then all chipped in what they could and one of the guard went off with Writer to find his girlfriend. For good measure she threw in a bag of homemade buns. The party was a wow—never again were they to see quite such a get-together. Patriot, who was swinging the lead with impunity, on the excuse of his evening's cultural activites, recited the 'Ballad' with great expression. His rendering of the passages dealing with guard duty was particularly successful.

> Every other day or so
> It's our turn for sentry go.
> Clean our boots and stand in line,
> Same old orders every time.
> First the corporal has his say,
> Then the sergeant, come what may.
> That's not all. There's much, much more
> The poor sentry must endure.
> He must like a ramrod stand
> With his rifle in his hand,
> Never blinking—that's quite hard.
> Now it's time to change the guard.

'All O.K.?' asks the relief,
Shaking hands with the old chief.
They roll a fag and have a puff,
And joke about the general staff.
The old one says, 'Now then, don't you
Do anything I wouldn't do!'

When Patriot reached the description of the guard-changing scene, the orderly came tearing in and called for silence. As he left he said, 'Some of us have got better things to do, you know!'

Then through the trees the new guard stroll
To the place of their patrol.
In the sky stars 'gin to peep;
In the guardhouse, peaceful sleep,
Everyone's asleep but you—
I mean the guard commander, too.
Far away, a twinkling light,
And close, dogs howling in the night.
At their posts the sentries curse,
The racket makes things even worse.
The heavens above are clear as glass.
Then comes a piercing whistle blast.
The sentries jump—alas, alack,
Someone's coming up the track.
The guard commander wakes confused
And shakes the sergeant, quite bemused.
'Get up you fool, don't take all day,
The duty officer's on his way!'

There followed a picturesque scene in which the guard of honour prepared to receive the inspecting officer, and the passage ended thus:

But when the officer walks in,
All's in order. So he then
Signs the routine guard report:
'Guards at their posts and all alert.
Guardroom clean. All well turned out.'
That's what guard duty's all about.

Deviationist said that that was a typical example of the stratification of society into informationally autonomous groups. Representatives of such different groups appear to live together. They even eat in the same canteen and shit in the same shithouse.

But they do not know and cannot know what each other understands by concepts like truth. In such circumstances, knowledge of the truth is socially punishable, and so everyone hides the truth. The inspecting officer has no interest in declaring that a State of Emergency exists in the platoon because a certain Ibanov has been caught napping at his post at the gasoline store, and Ibanov has no interest in being reported because of this. In such cases the truth comes to light only as an exception when there is no concealing it. And it is evaluated not as a normal state of affairs, but as an extremely abnormal exception. Normal social life is wholly made up of such concealments of the truth. Sentries almost invariably sleep at their posts, said Sentry, to judge by his own observations. He at all events had begun to sleep at his post from his very first stint on guard duty. He was even asleep when the regimental flag was run up. Not that it was very comfortable—your knees were always giving way and your rifle had a distinct tendency to fall out of your hands. But he had managed to sleep all the same, and he'd never been nicked for it. It must be assumed that the genes and chromosomes are programmed in some way: no-one is ever taught how to sleep on guard, but everyone knows how to do it. Before the war he had served on the frontier. The man in the next position to him on sentry go was a vigilant ass who kept awake through everything. The man was cut to pieces by saboteurs. For his part, he hid himself carefully and slept like a log. As a result the saboteurs didn't find him and he remained alive. Someone asked why he hadn't woken. The sentry said that the inbuilt programme which he had mentioned was activated solely in response to certain specific people on our own side—the sergeant of the guard for instance, the duty officer, the inspecting officer and so on. Dauber said that if you put some kind of spy-equipment like a television camera at every post, no-one could fall asleep. Deviationist said that that would change nothing: as a covert weapon, a television camera would not constitute solid proof and would be scarcely different from a denunciation, while if it were used officially, it would be discovered and therefore outwitted. And anyway, the technical means of surveillance was not the real problem. The situation we were considering here was in some ways the antithesis of the situation in quantum mechanics. In quantum mechanics there is no knowing what is actually going on, but assertions about this unknown quantity can be proved by officially recognised methods. But in this case everyone knows what is actually happening, but no assertion is capable of proof by officially recognised methods. You must surely know how much more the men in power in this world consume than we do? But just you try and prove it. Dauber said that he'd once come across this case: they'd been on a parachute course and one cadet had died from terror in mid-air. When they buried him, the wreath on his coffin bore a quotation from Gorki: 'Let us sing the glory of the foolhardiness of the bold!' Intellectual said that we had to take into account the conversion of truth into falsehood, which was probably also inherent in our genetic pattern. For example, in his next novel Writer would say: 'There were spades and crowbars leaning up against the shithouse wall, which was evidence that people were working there', but he will pass over the fact that people were working badly. In fact, there is no certainty that work was being done—the only certainty is that it was being done badly. Gelding added that there was one further aspect about the problem under discussion—the evaluative aspect. For example, the sergeant is a wild beast from Leadswinger's point of view, but from his own point of view he's a tame donkey. Leadswinger from the sergeant's point of view is a parasite, but he sees himself as a victim of persecution and injustice. When people talk about the living truth they have in mind not some objective and dispassionate truth, but a kind of justice and one which is, moreover, in their own strictly personal interests. Intellectual, speaking as the only sober man among them (he had drunk nothing), said that they were never going to reach any clear conclusion by going on like this, and suggested that they dropped the conversation. 'All things considered,' he said to Leadswinger, 'it's an empty argument and a basic problem. Truth is what people take to be true.'

A party at Sociologist's house

When he got back from his latest trip abroad and he'd written his reports for the Laboratory and the Institute, Sociologist held a magnificent party. He invited Claimant, Thinker, Colleague, Writer, Artist, Schizophrenic, Slanderer, Careerist and many others. There were a number of reasons for the party.

First, Sociologist had been on a trip of a kind that none of his guests had ever undertaken or ever would. Apart from a great variety of mind-boggling goods (jeans, pornographic postcards, books by writers who were banned over here, and so on) Sociologist had brought back many impressions and wanted others to profit from them. Secondly, he had finally completed the furnishing of his new apartment which he, unlike the majority of representatives of the creative and progressive intelligentsia (with the exception of Claimant, Thinker, Writer, Artist and one or two others), had received as a reward for services rendered and had not bought as part of the co-operative. An enormous amount of money had gone into the apartment. There were two complete suites that had cost four thousand each, one which had cost fifteen hundred, other furniture bought separately from antique shops, three crystal chandeliers, about forty antique candelabra, several crucifixes, a couple of dozen ikons, more than ten sets of bookshelves stuffed full of foreign books, and so on and so on. Sociologist had wanted to buy an etching from Dauber for twenty-five roubles but it turned out by chance he didn't have any money with him, and so Dauber gave him two etchings worth a hundred and fifty each as a housewarming present. Clearly all this magnificence had to be put on show. It's true that it was almost impossible to work one's way through all this magnificence to get to the bedroom, which was almost always empty. But this was of little concern to Sociologist and Wife, as they normally lived and worked at the rent-free villa provided for them by the Institute for their use when they were writing reports and for the short intervals between reports. But the most remarkable thing about Sociologist's apartment was the building in which it was located. When Sociologist, caressing his beard and preening himself, carelessly let slip where his new apartment was, everyone opened their eyes wide and said 'Oh ho'. The apartment above Sociologist belonged to Champion, and Test-pilot lived below him. Every night there was such a fortissimo sound of music and dancing from Champion's apartment that Sociologist's crystal chandeliers swayed and jangled, while Test-pilot yelled abuse at anything and everything and particularly at our own innocent little ways, so loudly that the multitudinous candelabra rattled and vibrated, and the ikons and the crucifixes on the walls swung about alarmingly. This in no way disturbed Sociologist and his Wife but filled them with an awareness of their own importance and of the fact that they had reached a most elevated sphere. The third reason for the party was that Sociologist's Wife had ordered a fabulous dress designed by the foremost fashion-designer of Ibansk. The pattern had cost her a thousand roubles, she'd paid five hundred roubles for the making-up, the material (the dress was made of a gossamer-like chiffon) had cost her another five hundred, and she had paid yet another five hundred for the chiffon to be painted in oil colours. Many and varied rumours had been circulating in Ibansk about the dress, and to resolve the gossip once and for all it had been decided to put the dress on public exhibition. The table was piled high with food from the special shop reserved to the exclusive use of the topmost people. When Schizophrenic saw the enormous quantity of red and black caviare, sturgeon, pike, salami and other things whose names he didn't even know, he asked whether it was all real. Chatterer said that he thought that this kind of food was only ever seen these days in fossil form. The evening went by in a relaxed, and cheerful way, and as Wife put it, was most interesting.

Sociologist compared life here and There. Everything There was several degrees better than here, and we looked pretty down-at-heel in comparison with Them. His Wife said that We must together . . . , together we must . . . They must be . . . Claimant said that They were boors, reactionaries, careerists and scoundrels; he cited instances and made his proposals. He made a clear and convincing case that if Claimant did not become Director, Thinker—Editor, Sociologist—Correspondent, Wife—Dean of Studies, and all the others present—under-secretaries, deputies, assistants and sympathisers with Us, then all our achievements and successes would turn to dust, and civilisation would be unable to progress to a higher level. Thinker sat, one velvet-clad leg crossed negligently over the other, smoothing his hair with his chubby dirty-nailed hand and smiled ironically. The wine flowed, there were many stories, jokes, much backbiting and rumours. There was talk of foreign clothes, antique furniture, domestic and foreign policy. Those not present were roundly abused. Writer told stories about the Leader 'Once,' he said, when the laughter and shouting had died down a little, 'there was a knock on the Leader's door. He went to the door, put on his glasses, took a scrap of paper from his pocket and read out the words "Who is it?".' Colleague began to talk about unknown facts and known measures. Sociologist said that despite everything, We stood a whole head higher than Them on the spiritual plane. We were experiencing a spiritual drama, not They. Materially They were living off the fat of the land, while We lived in poverty, and yet in terms of inner spiritual culture We could give Them a hundred points start. Wife said that it had recently occurred to her that the Ibanskian soul, a mystery for Them (but not, of course, for Us), was a mystery for Them because of Their complete incomprehension of the conflict between our rich spiritual life and our poor material conditions, and not because of any confusion between East and West. Schizophrenic and Slanderer quietly slipped away. 'What a nightmare!' said Schizophrenic. 'They include you and me in their We. And there's that fool of a woman and her vapid ideas. Where the hell are they supposed to lead? Surely she doesn't seriously take her idiotic rambling for genuine thoughts?' 'Of course she does,' said Slanderer. 'Whether you like it or not, those people are our intellectual élite, the spiritual leaders of our society. And as far as the mysterious Ibanskian soul is concerned, she isn't far from the truth.' 'Just with one small correction,' said Schizophrenic. 'Imagine that the brain cells are little people with all their social attributes, connections and relationships. And these little people behave in the same way as you and I. So the mysterious Ibanskian soul is nothing more than the notorious Ibanskian whore-house carried to the nth degree and transferred into the Ibanskian head but not transformed within it.' 'The hardest thing of all,' said Slanderer, 'is to unravel a mystery which does not exist. God, what a bore!'

Social groups

A social group is an agglomeration of two or more social units, wrote Schizophrenic. But not every such agglomeration is a social group. In the first place it is an agglomeration of units enforced by the more or less constant conditions of their existence. So this agglomeration is sufficiently stable and durable and is not a social accident for the units. From this point of view an agglomeration of people in a bus or of the drunks in the Bar is not of itself a social group. In the second place, it may be an agglomeration of units which can in its turn be a social unit itself. Within it there is a division of functions; firstly the division of units into the part which forms the body of the group, and into the part which forms its controlling (or dominant) organ. Unlike the elementary social unit, here the body of the unit and its controlling organ themselves consist of units. This is the source from which the entire study of sociology derives.

Social groups are divided into simple (primary) and complex (derivative) groups. The primary group as a rule is small. In most cases groups of this kind contain no more than ten people. The controlling organ consists of one individual—the Director. I shall consider below cases which deviate from this norm. All the members of the group are socially equal (equal in their social situation). No one of them is superior to another. And they are all in the same subordinate relationship vis-à-vis the director. There is sometimes a tendency to the formation within a primary group of smaller combinations, and this can lead to the formation of groups which I will call quasi-social (even groups of two or three people). But that is not a general rule. Moreover, if the primary group has not exceeded the critical size, this tendency does not lead to the formation of social groups in the proper sense of the word.

Derivative or complex social groups are formed from units which are themselves groups. Here we see the formation of a complete hierarchy of derivative groups of various ranks. To define groups by rank: 1) The primarly group has no rank; 2) If group A has rank n and is moreover a unit directly included in group B, then group B has a rank (n + 1). I should point out that group A is directly included in group B if group B does not include another group to which group A belongs. For example, a platoon in the army is included directly in a company, but is not included directly in a battalion, a regiment, a corps and so on.

Social groups can also be divided into *ad hoc* and official groups. Examples of the former could be a gang of robbers, a group of revolutionaries, a group of scientists founded on self-interest but independent of official or scientific organisations. Examples of the second could be a platoon or a company in the army, a section or a department in a scientific research institution, or a university faculty. Official groups are social groups which are recognised and approved in a given society. The relationship between the types of groups I have mentioned are of many kinds. A group can begin as a spontaneous group and then develop into an official group, and vice versa. A group can be simultaneously a spontaneous group and an official group (for instance an official organisation taken over by a band of crooks, particularly in the field of commerce). Spontaneous and official groups can overlap, intersect, coincide for a time and then diverge, and so on. For example, the official power-structure in a country may only partly coincide with the actual power-structure of a spontaneous group. Moreover they may have one and the same leader, and in this case the official leader can become leader of the spontaneous group only because he is the official leader. There are essential differences between these groups. For example, in spontaneous groups very often the most authoritative members of the group (authoritative from the point of view of the form of activity which underlies the formation of the group) will push themselves forward into the role of the director or leader, while in official groups the leader is appointed or 'elected' (more generally selected) according to different parameters. In their turn official groups have a tendency to degenerate into spontaneous groups. For example, in the management of a firm such personal—almost family—links can be established that the management is transformed into a clique or a gangster-type organisation whose members are united in the interests of collective self-preservation. Inasmuch as the group preserves its official structure which does not coincide with its structure as a spontaneous group, various consequences incomprehensible to an outsider (cynicism, vulgarity, venality and general boorishness, etc.) must result.

We must further distinguish social and productive groups. It is difficult to make a very rigorous distinction, since social groups are formed for some kind of activity, and productive groups overlay social groups (contain and swallow them). But for this very reason it is all the more necessary to make this distinction. Productive groups are formed not only (and sometimes even not so much) according to the laws which govern the formation of social groups, but also according to the laws of one kind of activity or another, on the basis of some historical data or other—as for example, the outcome of a prolonged war and so on. In seeking examples of productive groups, we have to use the same examples of social groups (a military unit, a factory, an institute and so on) but to consider them from a different point of view. Groups consisting of a large number of people were needed for the construction of the pyramids, complex irrigation systems, canals, military highways, and so on. That is the productive aspect. But within these large groups, social groups were formed, and the large groups taken as a whole could function in a rather complicated way as social groups. To put it briefly, the unadulterated social group does not exist. It can only be isolated as an abstraction, but that abstraction is completely legitimate and even essential within the framework of society. Productive groups becoming official conglomerates have a huge influence on the social structure of society. It is thanks to them that social groups become more stable units in complex social groups, and so on.

Productive groups likewise can also be divided into simple (minimal) and complex groups. I shall not consider this subject here (this is the field of political economy, social policy, law and so on) and shall limit myself to a brief observation. In a modern developed society a minimal productive group has the following characteristics: it has its own dominant or directing group, which is not subservient to other members of the group, but they are subservient to it; it has its own accounting system and funds, i.e. within the framework of such a group people are paid for their labour; it has its own methods for the exploitation of individuals, i.e. within the framework of such a group people have an opportunity to work; it has the opportunity (and even the right) of bringing people into the group and of expelling them (in particular by way of hiring and firing). There are other characteristics as well, (for example, in our country, the group will have its own party committee, the right to allocate apartments, to award holidays and business trips, the right to nominate people for awards or to distribute bonuses, and so on). Complex productive groups depend less on the conditions of one or another kind of activity, but they are on the other hand more circumscribed by considerations of economics, politics, ideology and so on. So the complexity of the productive structure of society obscures its social structure in other directions as well.

Social classes must be distinguished from social and productive groups. One single social class can include people of the most varied professions, nationalities, duties and so on—it can include for example, writers and artists, ministers, scientists and even sportsmen. A given class is made up of people of a specific level and style of life, of taste, of culture and so on. Personal relationships are established between them. Within the class there are frequent marriages, there is continuity in a profession and so on. Members of the class derive mutual benefit from it (by connections, by bribery, by acquaintanceship and so on). The class forms its own specific public opinion, its local ethic, jargon, fashion, and its own reaction to events. Classes partly coincide with professional castes. They have a tendency to operate as closed societies. The existence of social classes deforms still further the social mechanism of society. But the type of personality which is formed according to the social laws exercises an essential (sometimes even decisive) influence on the relationships between people of a given class.

Social groups of all ranks have critical minimum and maximum sizes (which incidentally are quite movable, changeable and relative). Social groups have a tendency to increase their size (as a consequence of the principle of self-preservation and consolidation) and a tendency towards differentiation. If the size of the group significantly surpasses the critical level, the group differentiates itself. The prime group divides into two sub-groups which have a tendency to become prime groups themselves. It should be said that if a prime group has six members as its norm it is not wholly necessary for it to increase to twelve members for division to take place. Any increase in the size of the group, even to nine members, can lead to a division and to a subsequent augmentation of the new group to bring them up to the norm. Within complex groups, prime groups are formed in one way or another. The reasons for the differentiation of prime groups are the mutual repulsion of individuals, clashes of interest and so on, manifestations whose bases I shall discuss later. Official status protects the prime groups from dissolution even in cases where the group is of a normal size. A reduction in the size of a group leads either to its liquidation or to a restructuring (in particular to a change in its rank).

Prime groups can be divided into those which are prime in a primitive sense and to those which are prime in a ranking sense. The distinction between these two varieties derives from the following circumstance. The directing organ of a group can consist of one person (for example the commander of a military unit, the head of a minor section in a scientific institute) or of several people (for example the regimental staff, or the board of management of an institute). In this way the number of people comprising the directing organ can increase in such a way that the directing group becomes a social group in its own right. It has all the characteristics of a prime group and, moreover, the members of such a group hold a higher social position than rank-and-file members of primitive groups. They carry on their own shoulders part of the authority of a director and are partial directors. There are intermediary forms between rank groups and primitive groups (for example a company commander, his deputy and his platoon commanders form a directing group in their own right, but this is not yet a fully official social group). Directing groups can in their turn be complex. Into this category fall the staffs of large military units, for example, ministries, the governing bodies of scientific academies and so on.

In a complex society (like a large modern state) so many and varied relationships are established between social groups and the individuals they include that it is in practice unthinkable to describe these relationships, still less to keep control over them (incidentally herein lies one of the sources of mutation), but in practice there is no need to do so. I shall mention just one curious manifestation. Relationships of official subordination lose all practical meaning after a given point, and social individuals and groups which are officially in a master/servant relationship turn out to possess equal rights or at least equal prestige; and sometimes indeed the actual relationship becomes the reverse of the official relationship. It would of course be interesting to examine the principles on which a real power system is formed as distinct from a nominal power system, but I doubt whether anyone would be able to do this in practice. And theoretical considerations of this subject fall outside the scope of my thesis.

A social group acting in the capacity of a social unit executes the will of its directing organ (the director or the directing group). Of course, this is at best a tendency and its fulfilment *in toto* is only an ideal. But as far as certain actions are concerned, at least, this does actually happen. The social actions of a group are the aggregate results of the actions of its members. The interests of the group are the interests of certain members of the group, and primarily of its leaders. To talk of the general or the common interests of the group is a myth, a deception or an empty abstraction. At best this comes about only as a rare exception. The leadership of a group obliges the group to accept as their common interest something imposed on it and external to the interests of the members. Of course, some consideration is paid to the members of the group but only to a minimal degree. This is a source of conflict and of uncontrollable consequences. Official education seeks to persuade individuals to accept external interests as their own, (along the lines 'this is being done for *you*', 'this is *your* firm', '*you*'re the boss here', and so on).

The values of the characteristics of a group as an individual are established by measuring the corresponding characteristics of the individuals who form the group and by reworking the results of such measurement by a certain standard method. For example, intellectual level (or potential) of a group can be established by measuring the intellectual potential of its members and by subsequently calculating on the accepted formula (calculating, that is to say, the arithmetical mean of the intellectual potentials of the members of the group). Certain variants are possible, but there are general principles into which these variants must be fitted. For example, the group can be neither more intelligent collectively than its most intelligent individual member, nor more stupid than its most stupid member, (in the way that the speed of movement of a regiment cannot exceed the speed of its fastest soldier nor be less than the speed of its slowest). In general, the value of a characteristic of a group is a standard function of the value of this characteristic of its leadership and of the remaining members of the group. The most common case occurs where the group characteristics are equivalent to the corresponding characteristics of its leadership.

The sources of realism

A couple of weeks after the events I have just described, read Instructor, Intellectual detected in Writer an undoubted literary gift and advised him to write something for the treasury of world literature. He remarked that many great writers had begun in the same way. Milton. Defoe. Beaumarchais. Ibanov. Soon, Writer wrote a short story called *We Stand on Watch*. Intellectual corrected the spelling and grammatical mistakes while preserving the author's creative individuality, and said that Writer was sure to become a laureate. The only trouble was that with his 'Corporal' he was overdoing it, and might land himself in trouble. Writer said that he didn't write for money or fame, and as far as 'Corporal' was concerned, he was just a literary device, a hyperbole. Writer was sent to the cooler as a self-styled corporal after it had got round all the garrison who it was who was concealed behind this pseudonym. Although Writer's story has become famous and is in every anthology, it must be reproduced here in its entirety. Here it is.

In the nth platoon of the nth company the following events took place. We were marching to the firing range. On the way Comrade Cadet Ibanov lagged behind. The platoon commander Comrade Lieutenant Ibanov repeatedly ordered Comrade Cadet Ibanov: 'Cadet Ibanov, catch up!' But Cadet Ibanov continued to lag behind. As a result when we got to the range, he had only fired at three targets and all the rest had fired at four or five. So, Comrade Lieutenant Ibanov announced before the whole company that Cadet Ibanov would have to attend two extra work-details. But then up came the regimental political officer Comrade Senior Lieutenant Ibanov. He asked Cadet Ibanov, 'Why, Cadet Ibanov, were you lagging behind your platoon?' Cadet Ibanov replied, 'Because my boots are three sizes too big.' Comrade Senior Lieutenant Ibanov then asked, 'But why did you choose oversized boots?' Cadet Ibanov replied, 'I knew what's what. It'll be winter soon. I'll be able to wrap my feet in newspaper to keep the cold out.' Comrade Senior Lieutenant Ibanov said, 'Good for you, Cadet Ibanov.' And he thanked

Cadet Ibanov in front of the whole platoon. In this way our comrade officers afford us a complete and meticulous education, to make new men of us, fully developed. Signed, Corporal.

Many years later Fellow-worker met the famous Writer Ibanov (Ibanov is a pen-name—his real name is Ibanov). They recalled ISMA. He had forgotten about his stint in the cooler, but he remembered his first story word for word. As they parted he said, 'I've done quite a number of brilliant pieces which have not gone unnoticed. But I admit that I was never able again to recapture such literary heights. Ah, youth! In youth we are always more talented.' Fellow-worker said that Writer was a comparatively harmless creature. He never went beyond stealing gaiters, going absent, boozing and gossip. Far more dangerous are the thought-informers. It is not so much that they betray the deeds or the words of other people, but their very thoughts and intentions. For example, a certain Ibanov says that they have not been given so much as a radish for their day-labour on the farm. The thought-informer turns him in as a slanderer of our agricultural organisation. A certain Ibanov says that the Enemy has penetrated as far as Ibanograd. The thought-informer reports that Ibanov does not believe in our ultimate victory. The thought-informer is better educated and better camouflaged. He is hard to detect. He can share a bed with you, and write reports on you in such a way that you never dream of suspecting him. There is only one consolation: the principal object of the thought-informer's attention becomes the most pure-minded citizen, vitally interested in the improvement of existing conditions and relatively competent in his affairs. The thought-informer has not only to report what is obvious to the Bosses, but he has to disclose the secret heart of the matter. His reports should be to a certain degree sensational, for the thought-informer is, by nature, vain. Which leads to certain apparent paradoxes. In the courtyard of our apartment block, there was a drunk who kept bawling hostile slogans at everyone in the street. No one touched him. But our neighbour, who'd been a party member since before the revolution, once warned him to take more care. He was hauled off in an instant. After he'd been rehabilitated it transpired that a

French translator (a woman) had denounced him. Intellectual, who had patiently listened to Fellow-worker's impassioned tirade, pronounced a sentence whose meaning he has not to this day understood: 'Just what he deserved. Next time he'll know better.'

The foundations of social anthropology

True science, read Instructor, is born from a generalisation of experimental data. Slanderer and Gelding were wily enough to creep into the canteen at the very moment when cauldrons-full of boiling soup were being distributed to the tables. Under the very eyes of the dumbfounded orderly and the kitchen staff they grabbed a cauldron each, gobbled the contents in a flash and hooked off so fast that the orderly had no time even to identify them. Back in the cooler they flopped down contented, their bellies swollen as far as they would stretch, and steam coming out of every orifice. The prisoners took turns to feel their bellies, some envying their success, others praising their courage, yet others drawing theoretical conclusions. 'The main thing,' Panicker said, 'is choosing your moment. If they'd been five minutes earlier there would have been no cauldrons, and five minutes later there would have been no soup.' 'There's another aspect to this,' said Deviationist, following Panicker's thought, 'and it's an aspect which has never been studied in modern science. Slanderer and Gelding swallowed eight helpings each of scalding hot, revolting soup in thirty seconds, whereas it would have taken Patriot and Writer twenty-four hours to get through it. Now why? Habit? Education? Physical fitness? Rubbish! It lies in the very essence of personality. I shall prove that the speed with which a man eats food does not depend on its temperature, consistency, or degree of inedibility. From the very beginning people are sharply divided into quick eaters and slow eaters. And there are no transitional stages! Nor are there any biological reasons! These are purely social characteristics which have no basis of their own, but are themselves fundamental elements in personality. Moreover these characteristics have a fateful influence on a man's life. A quick eater, for instance, will never carve out a serious career for himself. The best he can hope for is to be a company commander, an assistant professor, a scientific secretary, an assistant, a seminar leader, or such like. Have you ever seen a quick-eating Director, General, Academician, Minister?' Gelding said that he'd never once seen any director, general, academician or minister eating at all. But he agreed with Deviationist. Moreover in his view people could be divided just as clearly into quick shitters and slow shitters, and diarrhoea and constipation had no effects on these social characteristics. They just have different meanings for different categories. For a quick shitter, diarrhoea is to a degree comparable with the speed of light, and a slow shitter's constipation doesn't bear comparison with anything. 'Have you ever seen a quick-shitting director, general, academician or minister?' Deviationist said that this was a contradiction of the theory and was therefore impossible. Intellectual suggested that this humanology, whose bases had just been laid by Deviationist and Gelding, could be completed by a special section which would study lavatory, barrack and other kinds of shorthand. Panicker said that this had long been in existence, and went by the name of reactionary Freudianism. Man is a compound of social relationships. All else is nonsense. If you want to know what a man consists of, you must discover the kind of society in which he lives. 'And how do you study a society without knowing the man?' asked Gelding. 'That's very simple,' said Panicker, 'you just have to read the papers.' Intellectual said that the qualities of a man as a social individual were truly defined by the combination of social relationships which he was able to endure. But they are defined not in the sense of determining either his genetic or functional condition, but in the sense of the possibilities of defining the terminology and the methods of measurement. Deviationist said that such fine distinctions were pregnant with consequences and were therefore comprehensible to no-one. Along came Sergeant and ceremoniously announced that life had become better, life had become gayer. After lunch he released the prisoners from shithouse duty and sent them to peel potatoes in the kitchen. This sparked off an incredible rumpus, from which Sergeant finally realised that the prisoners were not prepared to leave the shithouse voluntarily, though he couldn't understand why. Patriot made the biggest fuss of all. He yelled that he was in the cooler not for something unmentionable, but for something for which other people are given medals and promotion. Sergeant said 'You're nuts, every one of you,' spat into the white-hot stove and left. This remark of Sergeant's enabled historians to discern in the prisoners' revolt the first spark of mass schizophrenia which later was to become a normal manifestation. After Sergeant had left, Deviationist said that what had happened was no surprise to him at all. On the contrary it would have been strange if it had gone differently. The most attractive aspect of prison life was the quite disgusting nature of the work. The product of the coefficient of disgust and the coefficient of productivity of labour was equal to unity plus-or-minus alpha, where alpha is a certain characteristic constant of formation lying between zero and unity. Take for example work in the shithouse. Give me a couple of men, promise double rations, and we'll have it razed flat in two hours. Otherwise we'll be at it two weeks, time enough for it to collapse on its own. Patriot said that those were bourgeois ideas. 'You may work for double rations, but what about us? We only get to load waggons or peel potatoes, is that it? No, you won't get away with that.' Intellectual said that historians would either accuse Deviationist of slander, which would not be a total evil, or would pass over his thoughts in silence. Panicker suggested a third possibility: they would accuse him of slander *and* pass over his thoughts in silence. Deviationist said 'Amen,' and the prisoners set off to work in the shithouse. This time the shithouse seemed to them to be particularly cosy. They talked about their homes, their mothers, and milk. And they all called each other 'pal'.

Group and individual activity
The group forms a whole for a given kind of activity, wrote Schizophrenic. A particular instance of this activity is command. Between the individual and a group activity there is a variety of relationships. I shall indicate the basic ones. Every activity consists primarily of people who receive on account of their work the means of existence, a social position, a career and so on. People were not invented in order to carry out an activity; rather is the activity carried out only insofar as a certain group of people foster it by virtue of their own social existence. The basic social tendency here is to accomplish any activity by engaging a minimum of effort over the widest possible front. So

there is a specific social coefficient n which is greater than zero. If it is calculated that for a given activity m people are needed, then in practice this activity will be undertaken by a number of people not less than the product of n and m. From my observations the value of n is often as high as ten and sometimes even as twenty.

A normal individual does not live in the interests of his activity but engages in the activity because of his interests. As an exception an individual might live for the interests of his activity, preferring his participation in the activity to any strengthening of his social position or career, but even this case presupposes a certain minimum satisfactory to him. I know from experience that usually this minimum exceeds the average level of the individuals who occupy similar positions.

An individual's social position does not depend on the state of his business, nor does the latter depend on the former. The individual strives to make the progress and results of his work maximally dependent on his own part in it. A group strives to make the progress and results of its work maximally independent of the part played by any given individual, (since if an individual is necessary, then he is better protected, and if he is superfluous, he is without protection; if the progress of the work does not depend on the particular qualities of a given individual, he can be replaced by any other individual.)

Member's joke

'When I was a student,' Chatterer said, 'I earned a bit on the side as a lab assistant in a brickworks. The factory was more like a medieval museum than a modern enterprise. Because there was a growing demand for building materials they decided on a radical modernisation of the method for making old-style bricks. A special laboratory was set up. They hired five doctors of science, fifteen research students, and fifty would-be research students and two hundred laboratory assistants. A corresponding member of the Academy was placed in charge. The lab assistants' job was to stick a whole lot of ultra-modern instruments into every possible nook and cranny in the medieval furnaces and record the data thus extracted in thick ledgers. The scientists perused these ledgers in search of a formula. It was a lousy job I must say, checking every instrument ten times a day and writing up the results. Not a minute's peace. I'd almost made my mind up to pack it in when I suddenly had an idea. Why bother to do all this running about? The furnace was always the same, so's the clay, and so are the instruments. The method had stood the test of centuries and there wasn't the least possibility of squeezing anything new out of it. Had it been possible, our ancestors would have worked it out for themselves. So, I decided, the measurements we get from the instruments will always be more or less the same. I combed through the ledgers over a two-day period and worked out the average data and acceptable deviations. After that I used to come on duty, spend half an hour filling in the ledgers for the next day and then take a nap or do some work for my exams. In a day or two my method became known, and all the lab assistants adopted it. We worked like that for nearly a year. The ledgers, duly completed, were taken off to the laboratory in special vans, where they were very carefully studied; finally they came up with a formula, on the basis of which they developed an experimental furnace lining. Instead of the eight hours' firing they used under the old method, they decided to fire for four hours but with the temperature increased 1.375 times and the humidity decreased 1.578 times. Actually the figures were even more precise but I can't remember them any more. After four hours they opened the furnaces and hauled out the brick-containers. There are no words to describe what happened then. You had to see it to believe it. All the bricks cracked, but each of them in its own way. There weren't two the same shape. And, my God, there were some strange shapes! You'd never see the like in any museum of modern art. I just fell about and howled with laughter. They had to pour a bucket of water over me. The corresponding member of the Academy took brick after brick, sniffed at them and slung them all into a pile for crushing. I begged them to keep the bricks for the sake of history, but this they steadfastly refused. Next day they sacked the lot of us, and a week later, they hired three hundred new lab assistants, brought in five more doctors of science, fifteen research students and fifty more potential research students and began to fill out new ledgers. The corresponding member became a full member of the Academy.'

'I know that kind of thing very well,' said Careerist. 'For five years we produced complicated calculations and handed the results we got to one unqualified mathematician who, by methods known only to himself, could work out the most complex and insoluble problems. He did his job and everything went on smoothly. Then one day this mathematician signed some petition or other and was fired. To replace him, they had to create a special group of one doctor of science and three assistants. But even then they couldn't cope, and the group had to be turned into a section, another doctor put in charge of it, with three further researchers and five qualified computer operators. While the section applied itself to the solution of theoretical problems without which, they claimed, calculations at this stage would be impossible, we had to get ourselves out of our difficulties by incredibly difficult and expensive methods. After another six months the section grew into a research department. They published a heap of papers and held a symposium. Then they all went off to another symposium. They published a collection of articles and began to talk about a specialist review. Once, for the want of something better to do, I decided to glance through the work books of the mathematician who'd been fired. My eyes almost literally popped out. It turned out that he'd discovered the banal truth that calculations at this stage of the operation were totally unnecessary and had no influence on the subsequent stages. He just used to write whatever came into his head. I told the Scientific Committee about it and they nearly tore me to pieces. They dismissed me as a reactionary, an obscurantist and a fool.'

Member said that this subject had been bothering him for a long time. He had written an important document full of statistics and substantiations, and he'd asked for a meeting with Deputy. He was going to see him today, so today he wasn't going to drink a drop. Chatterer asked Careerist how his trip abroad was coming along. Careerist said that it had been cancelled. Chatterer said that he always thought it would be. If they'd allowed the trip to go ahead he would have been very surprised. 'Young man,' said Member, 'it's no use surrendering to pessimism. Just mark my words: it won't be much longer before everything that all you young chaps dream about will be permitted. Everything in its own good time. They're not fools up there you know. They know what's possible and when.' 'Maybe the time will come when they allow these things,' said Chatterer, 'but I wonder whether by that time, there'll be anybody around willing and able to profit by that permission. The problem is not what they forbid, but the fact that there are so very few people who apply for a permission.' For the first time in his life, Member ventured on a joke. As he left, he said that if he didn't come back, they should regard him as being no longer a member of the Party. But that joke was his last.

A meeting with Deputy

At his own request Deputy had a meeting with Dauber. They talked for a whole hour. When Artist heard about it he turned green with envy. But he consoled himself with the thought that it would never occur to this newly-discovered 'genius' to exploit this chance for his own ends. He was more likely to do the opposite. Afterwards Dauber told Slanderer that the conversation had been almost totally trivial. Deputy had lavished upon him ecstatic praise, promises, hints and of course demands. But Dauber had been struck by one thing. 'Just imagine,' he said, 'Deputy suddenly began to moan to me about how difficult life was for them, and he told me this story. He had a young colleague, an able lad, fluent in three languages and with a spotless background. Peasant origins. He had distinction, tact, application, modesty. Deputy lent him a hand, and promoted him, skipping a grade. He even nominated him for an award. Then Deputy had to be away from his office for a long time, and when he came back there was no sign of the lad. "Where could he have gone?" I asked. "He's been devoured," they said. "How d'you mean, devoured?" I asked. "By the rats," they told me. And do you know what he said to me when we parted? He said, "I value your work, and I could authorise your mounting an exhibition." "Go ahead," I said, "it won't cost you anything!" "There's no point," he said. "No matter what I do, nothing will come out of it. You know our system." "I do," I said. "Art has always needed the protection of the powerful. On its own, real art is defenceless. Without your protection, they'll make a meal of me." "Even with my protection," he said, "they'll gobble you up just the same." Now what did he mean?' 'The cogs of our history are coming to be exposed,' said Slanderer. 'We are living in an amazing age from the point of view of opportunities to grasp reality. Everything is being laid bare. Mark my words, in the next few years we'll be stripped of all our fashionable rags and be exposed stark naked.' 'Who will do that?' asked Dauber. 'It's already being done,' said Slanderer. 'There'll be plenty of willing helpers. And the material is thoroughly intriguing.' 'It's amazing,' said Dauber. 'Taken individually, our lives are dreary, grey, monotonous to the point of loathing. Yet taken altogether, we're giving birth to a phenomenon which is creeping towards the centre of attention of mankind's spiritual life. What's the reason? Is it just the unhealthy interest of people with full bellies?' 'I don't think so,' said Slanderer. 'At all events not only that, and not to any great extent. More likely, people are beginning to think about themselves. They sense danger. In the last analysis their future is being decided here in our country. And at this very moment. Already yesterday.'

Social relations

From certain clear indications Schizophrenic realised that he wouldn't be given much longer to write, and so he began to hurry, writing in fragments without working out the details. He wanted, at least in his first draft, to carry his ideas through to their logical conclusions and clarify in his own mind that the manifestations he saw around him, which were officially regarded as alien, accidental, one-off deviations from an essentially noble, benevolent basis, were in fact essential, natural, regular, and universal consequences flowing from the very essence of the social existence of people in conditions in the highest degree suitable for such manifestations. Every time he locked himself into his little room, he beseeched fate to spare him another day, and feverishly wrote down everything that flowed through his head in a constant stream. Recently Dauber had disappeared God knows where. His studio was always locked and there was nowhere to stack the growing pile of pages. The previous day Sociologist had sought him out, chattered on endlessly and incomprehensibly about the state of affairs and promised his support. 'Let me read your thesis,' he asked Schizophrenic.

Social relationships comprise the relationships of an individual to his own group, of a group to a member-individual, of individual to individual within a group, of individual to individual outside a group but applying the same standards of relationships which exist within the group, of an individual to society as to a social whole, and of society towards the individual, wrote Schizophrenic. The relationship between an individual and his group are defined by two values: (1) by the degree of dependence of an individual on the group; and (2) by the degree of dependence of the group on the individual. The degree of dependence by the individual on the group has a tendency to increase towards a maximum, and the degree of dependence of the group on the individual tends to decrease towards a minimum. The former is realised in the tendency to create for the individual a situation in which everything that he receives from society he receives as a dependent of the group; in which everything that he can or wishes to give to society he gives as a dependent of the group; in which rewards and punishments are controlled by the group; in which all the productive and extra-productive conduct of the individual is controlled by the group and so on. When critics of society, and fighters for truth of all kinds allege that the principle 'from each according to his abilities, to each according to his labour' is not being observed, that is evidence of a childishly naïve incomprehension. 'From each according to his abilities' is far from implying a general disclosure of ability, as the demagogue propagandists would claim (if for no other reason than that people *en masse* merely average out, and abilities are by definition deviations from the mean); it is in fact a principle according to which what is demanded of an individual is what he should do in his given situation. 'To each according to his labour' does not mean an absolutely just share of the product in return for labour which has in fact been provided, but a share of the product which is considered just for a man in a given situation. It is the value of an individual's social position. If labour were genuinely measured on the basis of the expenditure of physical and mental effort, society would have a system of distribution very different from the one which exists. The value of what is usually called labour is a social value. And the labour of a man who occupies a higher social position is *a priori* valued more highly than the labour of a more humbly placed individual. A boss receives more not because he expends greater physical and mental effort than do his subordinates, nor because he is stronger or wiser than they, but because according to the social laws, his social position is more highly regarded than the social position of his subordinates. For this reason, it is considered that the boss works harder and better than those he directs. I would point out, incidentally, that for this very reason every attempt to develop scientific methods to measure people's social qualities is either doomed to failure, or practicable only in professional circles under control of those in authority. I have digressed a little from my theme. Returning to the idea from which I began, I should observe that the situation whereby career, wages, an apartment, travel warrants, the provision of a creche and so on depend wholly and completely on the group is not something accidental or transient. The official tendency to assign a man to a group fully coincides with social laws. Nor is it accidental that this becomes normal practice even in the use of expressions to describe the situation. Everything a man acquires and possesses is depicted not as something he has earned, but as a gift from society ('the state's given him all this, and yet he . . .').

It is important to note that when I speak of the dependence of the individual on the group, I am expressing myself figuratively. The fact is that the individual is dependent on other individuals, which merely gives an appearance that he is dependent on the group as a whole. This is the violence which people inflict upon each other—basically a mutual violence. As far as the inverse dependence of the group on the individual is concerned, this is subject to the principle that no-one is indispensable.

A social individual who has been able to achieve a sufficiently high degree of independence of the social groups within his society is a social person. The degree of personal freedom in a society is defined by the percentage of such persons in the population and by the degree of their influence on the life of the society. That is just in passing.

Social relationships within the group can be divided into relationships of co-operation, and relationships of subordination. Relationships of co-operation are based on this principle: the greatest danger for a social individual is that represented by another social individual of superior abilities, (taking certain key indicators of social existence—intellect, artistic talents, resourcefulness, eloquence, cupidity and so on). From this springs the desire to weaken the social position of another individual; if it cannot be weakened, to prevent its being enhanced; and if there is no way of preventing its being enhanced, to keep that enhancement to a minimum. Thus such frequently experienced characteristics as hypocrisy, tale-bearing, slander, intrigue, treachery and so on are not deviations from the norm but the norm itself, while the reverse of these characteristics are the genuine exceptions. When everywhere one hears catch phrases about people's unreliability ('you can't believe a word anyone says', or 'there's no one you can rely on' and so on), it is not the fact of this universal unreliability which should be surprising, but the fact that it is not accepted as something entirely natural. All it means is that favourable conditions have been established in which the social laws can flourish. Yet the inertia of old-style education, world culture and so on is such that unreliability is regarded as something accidental, inadmissible and remediable. But we can assume that this attitude will soon pass away. People are led to protest most violently when their actual colleagues, fellow-workers or peers achieve in a certain area successes which are significantly superior to the mean level (particularly among scientists, writers and artists, athletes and so on). In these cases people will exert extraordinary efforts to prevent their colleague's success, or to reduce it to the minimum, or at the very least to slip some tar into the honeypot. People's joy at the failures of the strong is expressed in the guise of sympathy. On the other hand, too great a weakening of the position of other individuals is also undesirable, since that can lead to trouble and worry. So it is no accident that as a rule an individual experiences satisfaction at the sight of cripples, or on hearing news of others' misfortune—a satisfaction which disguises itself as an expression of sympathy. An inevitable consequence of these principles of co-operation is a tendency to reduce individuals to uniformity. 'Be like everyone else' is the fundamental basis of a society in which the social laws play first fiddle.

Other principles, too, play a part in determining the relationships of co-operation (which of these principles are basic and which derivative I shall not go into here). For example, every individual strives to achieve maximum independence from all other individuals, and maximum dominance over at least one or two. Every individual tries to discharge on to others unpleasant work which he might otherwise do himself. If an individual can depart from normal standards of morality towards other people with impunity, and if he needs to do so, he will do so. If he can with impunity cause another person harm, and if he needs to do so, he will cause him harm. If an individual can with impunity appropriate to himself the fruits of another person's labour, and if he needs to do so, he will do so (there are countless examples of this—the award of prizes, patent rights, appointments to delegations, or plagiarism, to name only a few.) Every individual seeks to shuffle off his responsibility on to other people's shoulders; and so on. The list could be much extended. In general, these principles are familiar to everyone from his own personal experience, although of course each person sees them only as a failure in others. I shall mention just one more strange rule which frequently causes surprise but which is also completely natural. This is the law of substitution and compensation. If an individual needs to inflict harm on another individual but is unable to do so, he will compensate for this by choosing another more or less suitable individual as a sacrificial victim, selecting someone whom he can harm at the least risk to himself. We might here suggest the existence of some social-energy constant in every individual which obliges him to exercise within his own social sphere a defined degree of his inherent malice.

I shall go in more detail into the relationship of subordination later in my chapter on leaders. At this point I shall restrict myself to one general observation. A leader occupies a higher social position than a subordinate. The rank of a leader is defined by the rank of the social group he leads. The higher the rank of a leader the higher his social position. A leader also has productive functions, but in general application this loses significance and the position of the leader appears a purely social position. If a society needs a million bosses, there is no point in discussing their capabilities and exercising a choice on the basis of productivity. There will probably be ten million people wanting to become bosses and able to fulfil this role no worse than any others.

Social relationships of individuals outside their groups are based on the principle of submitting them to the rules which govern relationships of co-operation and of subordination. There are two reasons for this. Firstly, specific behavioural skills are developed. Secondly, every individual with whom a given individual has to have contact outside the confines of the group, is regarded as a potential colleague, boss, or subordinate. Apart from that, there are many occasions when in the course of his work, an individual has dealings regularly with other individuals (shop assistants, policemen, clerks, teachers and so on), which put him into a position, relating to them, indistinguishable from his relationships within groups. In this case, casual quasi-social groups are formed which act according to the principles of social groups. Moreover, in such cases the social laws operate more openly since here the restraining factors are less effective. The boorishness and arbitrariness of civil servants at all levels, the rudeness of shop assistants, the arbitrary behaviour of the police, the covert bribery to get work done, the unending stream of red tape and so on, these are not minor shortcomings, but at the heart of the matter. It's not surprising that all this exists, what is surprising is that in a situation of this kind anything ever manages to get done. It is true that what is accomplished is at the cost of a senseless waste of time and energy, of bad temper and an awareness of a total lack of vision.

This is not a personal attack on man. I do not say that man is evil. I love man. I merely want to say that if he appears to be evil, the reason lies in those cells of the social mechanism in which he is obliged to fit himself by force of circumstance. Man is good only when for a greater or lesser period he succeeds in escaping from these cells.

Some reflections about art

Instructor read on: Using a stub of pencil Dauber produced very odd drawings on the wall of the cooler. Deviationist was staggered. He couldn't take his eyes off them and told Dauber that he was a genius. Patriot said that Dauber was a painter with the stress on 'pain', and told him to draw a naked woman—and make sure she's got a good fat arse. He, Patriot, likes to have something to get his hands on. Intellectual said that Patriot's artistic education appeared to have stopped with the Impressionists. Patriot said that he didn't know who the Impressionists were, but he did know who the Peredvizhniki were—the 19th century realist school, men who could paint what was before their eyes. The guard commander came in and said that Dauber was a painter with the stress on 'pain' and that he'd do better to draw a naked woman with a good fat arse, because, he, the guard commander, liked to get . . . Then the Sergeant came in, bawled out Dauber for defacing the walls, and said that he was a painter with the stress on 'pain' and that he'd do better to draw a naked woman with a good fat . . . Then Colleague came in and said that Dauber was a painter with the stress on 'pain' and that . . . Intellectual said that he was amazed by this unanimity of aesthetic views, and asked Dauber to draw a naked woman for these fools. Dauber drew a naked woman with such pronounced sexual organs that even the prisoners were a little embarrassed. Patriot asked Deviationist to explain the meaning of Dauber's drawings. Deviationist said that a variety of interpretations were possible depending on the individual experience of life of the observer and on the orientation of his consciousness; and told the old story of a man who went to an abstract exhibition, where each picture put him in mind of women because he never thought of anything else. Patriot said that abstract artists weren't artists at all. Intellectual said that Dauber wasn't an abstract artist but an extreme realist. The only thing was that he didn't paint people and things, but thoughts. And since none of these fools had a thought in their heads, only clapped out notions, they could never understand what Dauber's paintings were about. Gelding said that he'd once read a book by Ibanov and Ibanova *Formalists in the Service of*. There it said in black and white just who Picasso, Neizvestniy and Dauber really were. Patriot asked him to tell all, but Gelding told him to fuck off. At this point Writer discovered that the bread rolls his girlfriend had brought him had disappeared. In response to this Intellectual said that Writer now found himself in a cleft stick: he could not avoid writing a denunciation about the theft, but at the same time he could not write it, since informers, according to the definition of the term denunciation, did not denounce themselves.

Leaders

As he was about to begin writing his section on leaders, Schizophrenic was sitting on the lavatory reading in the latest number of the Newspaper some verses by Writer on this very subject:

> How pointlessly you guide us through the years
> With science and her weapons ever armed.
> 'Tis better, far, to drive us on like cattle
> According as you think it's best we go.

'Well,' said Schizophrenic, 'I'll make no judgements about the literary quality, but he's certainly got to the heart of the matter.' And he used the verses for his own purposes.

The question of leaders, wrote Schizophrenic, is something of vital importance to sociology, for it poses the question of the composition of the social groups in any given society. In principle, a leader is appropriate to his group in the social sense ('Show me the priest, I'll show you the parish'). There are exceptions but they never last. The social type of a society is in large degree (if not fundamentally) defined by its type of leader. I shall not consider the distinctions to be drawn between official and unofficial leaderships, between fictitious and genuine leadership. Facts of this kind are widely known. Independently of these variants, the relationship between master and servant is one in which the subordinates act as an unthinking body totally lacking in will, while the leaders are the consciousness and the will of the body. The position of the leader is a more advantageous social position than that of the led, which must be clear to all normal people. So leadership is not a function carried out for the good of the people by noble martyrs. It is a position which is always the object of a bitter struggle. The higher the rank of the leader, the more elevated his position; the greater his advantage, the better protected is his position, and therefore the more bitter the struggle to attain to this position. That is a truism. The problem is not how to state that truth but how to formulate the social rules by which people become leaders, and according to which leaders act.

The basic principle of a leader's social actions is to represent his own personal interests as those of the group he leads, and to exploit the said group in his own interests. If a leader also undertakes certain actions in the interests of the group, that is merely one way to achieve his own personal aims, and especially one of the means by which he can advance his career (a good organiser has in some cases, but only in some, better chances to advance his career). But more often a career becomes more successful because of apparent, not real, perfections and improvements—one of the fruits of eyewash, disinformation and deliberate deception. Any hopes that the leadership will take steps, show concern, strive for improvements, and so on, are childishly naïve illusions. I repeat that leaders prefer making speeches about improvements to actually making improvements, (which anyway is normally beyond their capability), and if they do make any improvements it is out of a fear that otherwise their position will be weakened, or from a desire to consolidate their hold, or as a result of internal intrigue and so on. As far as the operation of the social laws is concerned, leaders not only make no effort to limit their operation, but try to develop that operation as much as possible, since leaders are themselves the most concentrated product of these laws. The inter-relationship of the group's interests to those of the leader can be seen as analogous. It can only arise from external causes, not from social causes if the leader of a group achieves his personal aims by securing the interests of his group. As a norm of society, the progress of a group's business tends towards independence from its leader not only from the point of view of his social position, but also from the point of view of the organisation of the business itself. As regards the social position of the leader, that has a tendency towards independence as a special case in the law which is common to all members of the group. The leader's concern is not concern for the group's business, but for his own advancement, his security of tenure, the use of his office to his own ends, especially towards the furtherance of his career.

The rules by which people move into the leadership class and make themselves an official career have an historical origin and become habitual. There is no point in hoping here for the action of spontaneous forces which might improve things. There are no such forces. There exists nothing but what is known and evokes only gloom and despondency.

The most important thing in an official career is the role played by the relationship between the real and the nominal evaluations of a person's qualities. As I have already said, these evaluations do not coincide. And although there is a tendency towards a correspondence, in the case of people aspiring to a leading role, or to a higher rank in the leadership, there is also a law according to which preference goes to people exhibiting the most favourable relationship between their nominal and their actual evaluation. This is not self-deception or a deception of the consumer. The fact is that in real social relationships it is only the nominal evaluation of a person which appears to be real, while the real evaluation appears to be only an unattainable possibility. If we all know that A is a careerist, prepared to sacrifice thousands of people in the furtherance of his career, but the leadership considers that A is a capable, forceful organiser, then from the point of view of the given society only the second assessment has any meaning. The first assessment can acquire a meaning only in the event of a struggle against this society. How the aforementioned favourable relationship is established depends on the type of situation we're in. There are two types. There is the routine type, in which preference is given to people with an average degree of survival capacity (this latter being directly proportional to the apparent and inversely proportional to a real evaluation of the individual), and the revolutionary type, when preference is given to people with a high capacity for survival. It is only in rare spontaneous groups that the leader can have a low degree of survival capacity. Inasmuch as the routine type of situation is standard, the leadership of a society is formed by people known to be merely average but who are endowed with specious significance, i.e. by people considered the least dangerous as social individuals. Since leaders of the higher ranks are chosen from among those of the lower ranks, we see here again the operation of that same law of selection; and with an increase in the rank of leaders there is a reduction in the real worth of the individual (including a reduction of his intellectual potential, his level of culture, and his level of professionalism). I should point out that as he rises through the ranks of the leadership, any positive qualities in the individual are reduced according to a formula: the initial value is divided by the number of grades which the individual has had to climb in his career, and multiplied by a coefficient of rank which lies between one and zero. Negative qualities are increased according to a different formula: their initial value is multiplied by the number of grades climbed and divided by the coefficient of rank. But the indices of positive and negative qualities of a post of a given rank are measured in such a way as to take into account the total number of possible steps (in a normal career a man should not miss any of the rungs in the ladder), so it is possible that in some cases the individual will not fully coincide with the post he holds. It sometimes, therefore, happens that a high post is held by a person who is too intelligent and too honest for such a post. But I repeat that this is an exception which does not derive from the social laws.

There are however factors which compensate for this tendency. The first is the existence of huge staffs of aides, deputies, research assistants and so on, and also the back-up of various kinds of institution. Moreover, the higher the rank of the leader, the bigger the group which implements his leadership. For instance, speeches delivered by the most important leaders are written by hundreds of qualified people. The leaders themselves, as they deliver their speeches, are not merely incapable of having written them, but in most cases are unable to understand them. However, all the people I've referred to are themselves social individuals. And they reach the leader's entourage according to normal career-making social laws. The only difference here is that a low intellectual level, slovenly work, carelessness and so on can be more cleverly camouflaged by a knowledge of foreign languages, an ability to turn up quotations and so on. The intelligence and talent of a group cannot exceed the intelligence and talent of its component members. And they must be inferior to that of the strongest members of the group. So the compensation under consideration is fictitious. It merely creates an illusion of intelligence, ability, diligence and so on. But after all, illusion is all that anyone expects. The second factor is more serious. This is the effect of the real inability to control an unwieldy social system. From a certain point on, any decisions taken by the leadership about a particular problem have one and the same result. For example, a decision to reduce staff leads just as successfully to an increase in staff as a decision to increase it. The third factor is that the functions of control become increasingly primitive, the higher the rank of the leader. The fact is that whatever position an individual occupies, because of his physical limitations he is able to come into contact with only a limited number of people and to reach only a certain number of judgements—and the more judgements he reaches, the less considered they are. And any average individual (average ability and average education) is able to master within an average time-span the functions of control at any level, provided he has climbed the rungs of the appropriate ladder. The difficulty here lies not in the activity of control as an intellectual activity, but in career-making itself as a particular kind of professional activity. The profession of a leader consists mainly in being able to hold his ground, to break through, to manoeuvre, to remove obstacles and so on. Only to an insignificant degree is it connected with the external business of leadership. For this reason, the people who have pretensions to become leaders are those least concerned about morality and those least talented from a professional view point. Any individual who embarks on a career in leadership will quickly come to realise that he has chosen a field which is by far the easiest from the point of view of intelligence and ability, and the most rewarding in material terms. The number of people who have set out on this career only to abandon it out of choice is so small as to be virtually non-existent. So there is nothing abnormal in the fact that old men in their dotage hold leading posts and will not voluntarily give them up. Moreover, in such cases the leader above a certain level merely becomes a symbol for a large group of people in power.

Finally, it should be noted that social mastery, in conditions where there is no other force on which it could depend in any real sense, leads to a system in which there are masters but no bosses who carry a personal responsibility, or who commit their own individuality to their business—it emerges as a shiftless, irresponsible, faceless system. The masters merely strive to take all they can get and to edge into the best position for doing this, regardless of any remoter consequences. It is, of course, quite absurd to think at all about consequences, since this is one of the most forbidden subjects in a society which, for the most part, lives according to the social laws.

For the reasons which have been stated, the system of leadership engenders a gangster's mode of consciousness and conduct, an awareness of the moral illegitimacy and instability of their own position, and a need for constant self-justification, confirmation, eradication and so on—in other words all that is widely recognised in common experience.   .

The tendency which is common to every social individual to claim credit for the positive results of others' activity, and to shift on to others the responsibility for the negative results, takes the following form in the case of leading individuals (including leading organisations). All successes achieved in any way by the given society (or social group) are regarded as successes achieved by virtue of the wisdom of the leadership. The actual degree and nature of the part played by the leadership in the achievement of these results does not of course play any part. Even if the successes have been achieved against the will of the leadership they will, nevertheless, according to this law, be regarded as successes of the leadership. Successes achieved under any given leadership must be successes achieved by that leadership. This law is of such cogency that even previously persecuted and subsequently rehabilitated cultural manifestations are depicted as the product of the great wisdom of the leadership. Even manifestations which have absolutely no dependence on the leadership (for example, fine weather, ancient monuments, natural resources and so on) are inclined to be regarded by leaders as a personal gift from them to the people. Furthermore, responsibility for all the negative consequences of the actions of the leadership is born not by the leadership but by those persons, social strata, or organisations, which the leadership considers suitable to bear the guilt for these consequences. The leaders are able to do this and they do it. The leadership never makes mistakes. Finding guilty parties is usually no problem. But there are occasions when it is difficult to find suitable guilty parties, and then they have to be invented. Since it is difficult, and even perhaps impossible, to distinguish between phenomena which are the consequence of bad leadership and those which would have happened under any leadership, people have to be found to take the responsibility for any evils which happen and which might be laid at the door of inept leadership. In such cases the leadership acts in a totally blind and formal way. The well-known cases when leaders have tried to represent their own criminal actions as being the will of the people, or as being approved by the people, are just one example of the operation of the laws we are considering. Hence the striving of leaders to represent their activity as activity for the good of the people, by the will of the people and enacted by the people. That is convenient. The successes of the people can always be represented as successes of the leadership, and failures can at least be represented as the result of the action of the people or of actions expressing the will and interests of the people. The tendency of criminal or amoral leaders to make as many people as possible accomplices to their criminal or amoral actions, does not reflect the evil intent of individuals, but results from the action of social laws which people are often very glad to obey. And if we are to combat the evil which infests our world, we must fight it not only in its individual and leading exponents, but in all people. We must fight always and everywhere.

Insofar as authority, according to the social laws, appropriates the mind and the will of society, it naturally tries to bring the actual state of affairs as close as possible to this ideal, and regards the wilfulness of persons who, without its authority, start thinking about society, about its laws, its system of government, its economy, law, press, art and so on as an unwarrantable invasion of a prohibited area. And if these persons begin to sort out the problems of society more successfully than the representatives of authority (which is not difficult, since the official level of comprehension tends towards a minimum of truth and a maximum of deception), they appear to the authorities as criminals, although there is no law forbidding anyone to try understanding what goes on around him. The absence of any legal prohibition is easily by-passed by the leaders' demonstrating that the comprehension of society by individual people is a notable slander which undermines the existing structure, since such a comprehension is at variance with official dogma.

On fate

In the morning, read Instructor, Defeatist was taken away. This shook the prisoners because Defeatist was the most harmless and insignificant creature among them. Gelding gave him his spare foot-wrappings as a parting gift. Deviationist said that the chastisers and the chastised had different criteria in

(157)

assessing degrees of guilt. Panicker muttered something about the vicissitudes of fate, and a discussion started up. They expressed every point of view which has been and is still held on this subject in a variety of religious and philosophical conceptions. Finally Intellectual won their attention. The word 'fate', he said, when they had all adjourned to the shithouse, has almost disappeared from daily usage, and if it is used, it's used in a different sense which has no connection at all with human fate. And no wonder! In its old traditional sense, the word 'fate' suggests predestination, the incomprehensible, the unthinkable, and so on. All that, of course, is alien to us. Our life is clear and transparent. Do what your father and mother tell you. Obey your teachers. Do as you're told by the bosses. Chance is a manifestation of inevitability, and what is inevitable is the law. There's a reason for everything, everything can be scientifically explained. So the concept of 'fate' is alien to us. But is it as straightforward as that? What is the predetermination of events? Let's say that a certain event took place at a certain time. This event can be considered to be predestined if, and only if, during the entire period preceding it, the assertion that this event would happen at the stated time was actually correct. Just try and prove that there had been no such events. Or try and prove that there are events to which this definition does not apply. Science is irrelevant here. To accept or not to accept the concept of predetermination is not a matter for science, but lies in man's relationship to the flow of his own life. It is one of the cogs of the most fundamental mechanisms of his behaviour. It is, you might say, an element in the stategy of his life. The cause of all that exists can be explained on this basis. I shall take it on myself to prove that in this matter nothing can be proven and nothing can be refuted. And science has nothing to say either for or against. But it seems that we have left fate out of account. Intuitively, when we speak of fate, we see in the life of man something which cannot be defined by natural or social laws, by a causal chain and so on, something, that is, for which we can find no reassuring explanation from the viewpoint of the means of explanation accepted in the given society. Fate is the name we instinctively give to something which essentially cannot be embraced by the concepts and principles of our philosophers. Note that one and the same event can at one time be an element of fate for a man, at another time not. One and the same event may be an element of fate for one man and not for another, can be an element at one time and not at another. So it is to all intents and purposes impossible to produce any explanatory examples. In this case, clarity must proceed not from individual examples but from the observation of a complex interweaving of the circumstances of many people's lives and of your own. Every epoch in which thoughts about fate have played an important role has had its own concept of the nature of fate. The problem we have to face is what is the significance of fate for a man in our society? I can offer you only a very crude and approximate answer to this question. An event which happens to a man is an element of fate if it satisfies at least the following conditions. It must not depend on the will of the given man. It may correspond with his wishes or it may contradict them. But that is of no importance. Fate is not something that is chosen. It just happens. An event which is embraced by a man's fate plays an important part in his life. It affects his status in life, his life and his death, his whole life-style. For a modern man, the events in his fate which are ascribed to his destiny are those which are unconnected with natural laws (an earthquake, for instance, may influence the life of a man but does not determine his fate), or with natural social conflicts and upheavals (a war, for example, may lead to a man's death, but death in war is not an element of fate in the modern sense). Nor can we include events which are considered 'a pure accident'. An accident is an accident, and nothing more. Fate includes only events in the life of a man whose occurrence or non-occurrence is entirely dependent on the free will of other people. It is people themselves who determine each other's fates. Thus, the fate of a man includes events which affect him, whose occurrence depends completely on the free will of others. Inasmuch as a man lives surrounded by a great many other people, and as it is practically impossible to establish precisely which actions of which people, as they affect him, were the product of free will, he perceives his fate as being the general pattern of his life which is in no sense determined, but which is not a succession of accidents either. Otherwise there can be no practical rapport with fate. So even in our society, in which people's heads are stuffed with scientific learning, the problem of a man's fate turns out in the end to be the problem of man's moral relationship to any and every other man, regardless of the exact nature of these men as individuals. Patriot said that this is metaphysics, and that man needs a concrete historical approach. Deviationist said that that was quite a different story. A demand for individually tailored moral canons is an end of morality as a socially significant phenomenon. Patriot demanded just one example of such a class-free non-historical morality. Intellectual said: 'Stop spying!' Patriot shouted 'What are you hinting at?', and gave Intellectual a shove. Intellectual thudded against the wall and the shithouse fell down. When the prisoners had crawled out from under the planks, along came Sergeant who was in charge of the building work, and said that they had done a fine job. Since the work was so far ahead of schedule, they could knock off for the day. Leadswinger said that he'd broken a rib. He was taken off to the sick bay from where he did not return. Informer said, but Patriot merely thought, about this: 'They have all the luck, the bastards!'

Puss's article

Oh, God, said Thinker, as he read through an article by Puss. What rubbish! Who would have dreamt that this fine upstanding gentleman was such a swine! Of course, there are a few tiny signs of thought in the article. Compared with Secretary's articles it doesn't look at all bad. His language is more or less correct. If I worked on it for a couple of evenings it might turn out quite well. So Thinker buckled to and found the work inspiring.

As Wife later said, Thinker made a real little jewel out of Puss's article. Benevolent readers said that he had managed to save Slanderer. After a brief exposition (but accurate beyond mistaking) of the main heads of Slanderer's opinions, Puss-Thinker's article launched into a restrained but forcefully aggressive critique of the reactionary ideas of apologists in office which were so fashionable Over There. Although these ideas had no connection with Slanderer's, they deserved nonetheless to be shot down. True science, as the article so justly put it, is not under the control of that inferior type of logic known as formal logic, but of that much superior dialectical logic which, in its breadth, its depth, its degree, its universality, its accuracy, its completeness and its accurate grasp of reality, surpasses formal logic as much as the hydrogen bomb surpasses decaffeinated coffee for psychological motivation. Dialectical logic teaches that all concepts and things are restless, changeable, shifting, that they never stay put but constantly switch identities mutually and with anything else; instead of the cookbook's principle of 'either/or', dialectical logic is dominated by the principle of 'both/and, and if you prefer, neither/nor.' Slanderer for his part wilfully ignores all these newest and greatest discoveries of the West which, immediately after their rehabilitation, began to confirm the correctness of our own views, and invents instead trivial homegrown theories, all old-hat, which events at once refute. The article ended with an appeal which for a long time afterwards became almost a slogan of Ibanskian democracy: everything obsolete and outmoded must be strangled in embryo.

The last meeting

As he walked past the garrison bath house, Chatterer noticed a new memorial stone incised in letters of marble with the information that here on this very spot the Leader himself was soon to deliver his latest speech. How excellent, thought Chatterer, that in this way my labour will merge with the common effort of my republic. Dauber was there already, and soon Slanderer came along. 'There are rumours that you're pulling out,' he said to Dauber. 'All lies,' said Dauber. 'My position is stronger now than it's ever been. I've had some orders and I've been promised an exhibition.' Slanderer said that he was glad to hear that. He was reminded, he said, of a story. 'Once, after a boozy weekend, we were flying badly. The commanding officer came along. He said, "If you don't want to serve we won't keep you. Is there anybody here who doesn't want to serve?" I raised my hand. And what do you think? Soon everybody was demobilised, and for the next six months they kept trying to persuade me to stay on. They even offered me promotion. In the end I got fed up and agreed to stay on. Then on the very next day I was demobilised—and with an appalling testimonial. Fortunately, the thaw began about that time, and I was sent to jail on quite another matter.'
Then they began to talk about the exhibition in which

Dauber had kindly been invited to take part. Slanderer said that he would never have agreed to participate in such an exhibition. There would be a lot of humiliation and little benefit. Dauber said that he was a painter and he couldn't go on without showing his work. Careerist said that this was not an exhibition but, as they said on the radio, a demonstration of outstanding successes and the flowering of talents, and since Dauber was not a mere talent, but a genius, it wasn't the right place for him to be. Dauber said he had a feeling that this exhibition would be of some importance, that he needed money, and for that he needed commissions, and to get commissions he needed official recognition; now, in their system, the fact that he was taking part in the exhibition was a tacit permission from the leadership to do deals with him, and if he refused, this would be interpreted against him as if he were getting above himself (that would be the interpretation of the higher authorities) or that he had not been allowed to show despite all his efforts (the interpretation of the rank-and-file authorities and of his colleagues), so that even if they let him show only a few insignificant trifles, that would still give him the possibility . . . and so on. 'In a word,' Dauber concluded, 'let's get on to something more substantial.' 'At home,' said Careerist, 'I've got a bottle of excellent French brandy. It was a gift from the chairman of a firm Over There. Let's go and sample it—and they can all go to hell.'

Conflict

Instructor leafed through the final pages of Schizophrenic's manuscript. Soon he'd reach the end, with no sort of conclusion in sight. After the old shithouse had been demolished, read the Instructor, they began to clean out, deepen and widen the cesspit. 'It may seem a paradox,' Panicker said of this, 'but it remains a fact: the cesspit is the foundation for the new glorious shithouse, and the bigger the pit the more magnificent the building to be erected on this foundation.' Patriot said that Panicker was a joker. Dauber inquired as to the meaning of the word 'sortir'—the Ibanskian word for shithouse. Gelding said that it came from the French word 'sortez' ('to satisfy one's natural needs') which, transplanted to Ibanskian soil, had acquired its familiar vulgar meaning. In the sixteenth century the great Utopian had put forward the idea of building a special building in which everyone would freely execute their natural functions. Patriot said that Gelding was a joker too. Gelding gave Patriot a thump in the mouth. When they'd been separated Patriot promised Gelding another five days for assault and battery. Deviationist said that there hadn't been any assault and battery at all. Patriot said that he was only joking. But a division of opinion had begun. About that time the population of the cooler divided into Left and Right. The Left slept on the right of the stove, and the Right on the left. Writer, who slept in the middle, had affiliations with both sides. Finally, Signatory came into the cooler, and as a sign of protest against shithouse politics, at night used to piss into Sergeant's bunk. He chose Sergeant's bunk for two reasons: first, Sergeant was a heavy sleeper, and secondly, his bunk was out of sight of the orderly. Sergeant had a very bad time of it, and even took a secret course of hypnotic treatment against incontinence. But on one occasion he nipped out without permission, leaving his greatcoat in his bed instead of himself, and Signatory was unmasked. In the cooler Signatory initially installed himself among the Left. After he had pissed in Intellectual's boots he was expelled to the Right and he began to piss conscientiously into Patriot's boots. Patriot detected in this the machinations of Deviationist and Gelding. And the split took on a form which was classical in the New History. Intellectual said the situation was clearly ripe for great changes whose consequences were well known.

The exhibition

When Dauber was invited to take part in the jubilee quarter-final exhibition for untalented artists of the first early middle age division, he was beside himself with delight. At last! 'There you are,' he said to Slanderer, 'even here something can be done! I am an optimist!' 'Ah, well, we'll see,' said Slanderer. Dauber sent more than a hundred magnificent engravings to the selection committee. They were all rejected and he was asked to submit something simpler. Finally, they accepted one tiny etching which Dauber had considered a failure and which he was going to tear up. A friend of Dauber's, who was organising the exhibition, put the etching in the darkest corner beyond a great many works by Artist. 'What have you done?' cried Dauber, angrily. 'It's the first time I've ever had an exhibition, and you shove me somewhere almost out of sight.' Friend got angry in his turn. 'How conceited can you get?' he said. 'You are exhibited all over the world and you want to spread yourself here as well!' Dauber couldn't think of anything to say and went off to the Bar. There, Slanderer and Chatterer were waiting for him. 'You were right, of course,' he said to Slanderer, 'and that kills me.' 'What kills you?' asked Chatterer. 'What Slanderer told you, or the fact that it was Slanderer who foresaw it?' 'Both,' said Dauber. 'Our life is so ordered that we can't avoid seeing the future down to the last detail. It's appalling.'

The Leader, himself, visited the exhibition. Beyond Artist's powerful canvases showing the Leader in the front line, the Leader posing beside a steam-hammer, the Leader visiting a modern rat-breeding station, the Leader saving a neighbouring nation from the danger of back-sliding, as well as other aspects of our busy and colourful life, he did not immediately notice Dauber's pathetic etching. It was hard to tell if it was a representation of a finger, a phallus or a chromosome in the grip of sudden madness. The Leader disliked the etching. 'Our people feel no need of this kind of thing,' he said, 'because our people need something quite different.'

That evening a special commission was set up to organise the struggle with Dauber and those like him. The commission included Artist, Writer, Friend, Thinker and Colleague. Thinker delivered a speech on false orientations. Colleague told the latest funny stories about the Leader. And Artist formulated a resolution: that Dauber's works were of no value and should be destroyed to avoid harmful consequences, and that Dauber himself should be regarded as having no existence, since there could in principle be no such monstrous deviation among our people. The resolution was adopted unanimously. Afterwards, Colleague and Thinker went to see Dauber, drank a bottle of his vodka, borrowed a hundred roubles to the end of the month, ridiculed the other members of the commission, and spent a long time trying to persuade Dauber to fix them up with some girls.

Artist salvaged a few of Dauber's engravings from destruction and took them back to his own studio. He decided to copy some which were more or less tolerable. But whatever he tried to draw (a finger, a penis, a nose, a woman's arse, a crank shaft, kidneys and so on), it always turned into a portrait either of the Leader, or of Deputy, or (in the best cases) of a high-yield milch-cow praised in a newspaper article. Writer said on this account that Artist had a very healthy inner core, and however hard he tried, he could never turn himself into some kind of imprexprabsturrealist. Slanderer said that they weren't even able to steal properly, these people, because they didn't know the right thing to steal. Some of Dauber's sculptures were melted down and turned into saucepans and smoothing irons, and the rest were slung out on to the rubbish tip. Afterwards young and progressive artists, who were pleased not to be aware of the existence of Dauber who had never existed and never could exist in the culture of Ibansk because of its general state of health, chiselled off lumps of stone from Dauber's sculptures and carved from them little unknown monsters. These monsters reminded the members of the commission of something they had once seen long in the past, but they were nevertheless allowed to exhibit them.

Conversations about the secrets of history

It is bitterly cold outside, read Instructor, but in the cooler it is warm; people are burning the planks destined for the new shithouse. In the camp of the Right, they're talking about food, women, decorations and socks. In the camp of the Left they're discussing the problems of world history. 'All this writing,' said Deviationist, 'is nothing more than consolation for the feeble-minded. What it all boils down to is simply that some people do dirt behind other people's backs, and when you add up all the little bits of dirt, you get a big heap of dirt. To justify it people invent what are known as objective laws. They think them up in such a way as to facilitate new dirty tricks; that's what's known as scientific planning.' Intellectual dismissed this concept as too pessimistic. 'There are still plenty of points of reference which are stable and solid.' 'There are points of reference,' agreed Deviationist, 'but they are extremely fragile. And, moreover, they bring benefit to Mankind, but suffering to man.' 'If you're talking about morality,' said Intellectual, 'you must recognise that morality itself is relative and changeable.' 'No,' said Deviationist, 'what you call moral is not morality. It is propaganda, proselytising, sermonising. In short it's something completely official. True morality is always unofficial. It is always unique. Either it exists or it does not. It has no basis except the decisions of separate individuals to behave in a moral way. It is trivial in content but incredibly difficult in execution. Don't betray people, keep your word, help the weak, fight for justice, don't be the first to grab the bread, don't force others to do what you could do yourself, live as if every move you made was always visible to everyone, and so on. What could be simpler? But have you met many people who live like that? It's possible to conceive a situation in which a whole society adheres to a certain level merely because that society includes one single truly moral man. If that man disappears it's a matter of chance whether another such man will turn up. There's no knowing.' 'There's not much comfort in what you say,' said Intellectual. 'It leaves no room for hope.' 'We are men,' said Deviationist, 'and hope is no concern of ours. And anyway if you need so desperately to hope, that's fully compatible with an awareness of being in a situation without issue, or indeed with having been condemned. A friend of mine said that humanity ought to be grateful to him for all the evil which he might have done it but had not. That is, of course, a point of view, but a passive point of view.' 'An active point of view,' Deviationist said, 'isn't any better. The vilest crimes of history have been committed in the name of good.' 'Where's the way out then?' asked Intellectual. 'In the shithouse,' said Deviationist. 'There is no way out since there's no need for one. It's an invented problem. Who would leave? Where to go? What to do? We need to look at everything from quite a different point of view—but from what point of view I haven't the faintest idea. When I was a boy I read in some book or other: "Men create for themselves an absurd and pointless journey, which has no meaning or aim, and which leads them unthinkingly towards the void. And only the powerlessness of each one of us in the face of the blind and pitiless strength of all gives this journey any appearance of greatness and nobility. The efforts of individuals to tear themselves away and seize their freedom can only succeed via self-destruction and are therefore in vain." I've always remembered that passage, but it's only now that I begin to understand it. It's a pity that it's too late. It's too late. It's time to sleep.'

'How strangely society is constructed,' said Gelding. 'On the one hand it's always ahead of its time, and on the other it's always hopelessly behind. And on neither hand does it live normally, i.e. at its own time. On the one hand there are rocket motors and chain reactions which don't find any sensible use until many years after the war. On the other hand there's the cavalry which was already an anachronism by the end of the first war. The legend of the First Cavalry Division was so strong that I, a man with higher technical education, even if it was unfinished, was called up into the cavalry. There was, admittedly, a tank regiment in the Division, but even that was divided into squadrons like the cavalry, although they didn't include a single man with secondary education. After a few months they decided to show us what a cavalry charge was like. For a whole month, we studied the route to the place where the demonstration was to be held. Despite that we were an hour late, and one regiment blundered over a cliff and never turned up at all. In the end there was some sort of bugle call, and our war horses, who had known the calls by heart ever since the civil war, charged forward. Within a moment we had all fallen off into the snow, and the horses carried on with the sabre charge on their own and then went back to their stables. We crawled about in the snow trying to recover what we'd lost. I'd lost my rifle sling and my neighbour couldn't find his bayonet. And as for our deputy platoon commander, he was brandishing his sabre so vigorously that the blade flew off the hilt and disappeared God knows where. There he was down on his hands and knees sifting through the snow and cursing the cavalry with every name he could think of. The court martial handed out four-week sentences. The next two months were devoted to analysing the exercise. When the war broke out I was again in the Cavalry. It's true that I was in a trench and my Penelope, who was as shaggy as Hemingway, was grazing peacefully somewhere in the rear. But all the same, as the Ballad says,

> This time luck was on my side,
> For the brass-hats made a rule:
> Anybody who could read
> Should be sent to flying school.'

In his sleep Gelding snorted and neighed gently. He was dreaming of a mass charge, a whole avalanche of cavalry. In front of all the others, mounted on a tear-stained deputy platoon commander, galloped his shaggy Mongol mare. She was waving a ramrod and shouting, 'I'll report you for this!'

Nightmares

'Schizophrenic is seriously ill,' said Wife. 'We must visit him and try to help.' So they all went to see him at the same time, and talked at him all at once. And he answered them all at the same time. And he didn't understand what they were saying, nor what they wanted, nor what he was saying himself. 'When You write about a social structure in which social laws (in Your understanding, of course) operate without any serious limitation, You must of course have our society in mind,' said Sociologist. 'I have no concrete society in mind,' said Schizophrenic. 'I am just carrying out an ordinary abstraction. I formulate a few rules of human conduct. At least people sometimes behave according to these rules. You must agree that that is true. I call these social laws. If You don't like my use of this word, there is no need to use it. It's not a matter of principle. Let's call them alpha-rules. No objections? Then I pose the question: what would a society look like in which people behaved exclusively according to the alpha-rules without any limitation being put on them by such established social institutions as morality, law, public opinion, an opposition and so on?' 'Such a society is an empty abstraction,' said Thinker. 'That's absolutely true,' said Schizophrenic. 'It is indeed an abstraction. But it is certainly no worse an abstraction than that Ism which you have been criticising for two hundred years as if it were a reality.' 'This Ism is stable, and it exists in reality,' said Dauber. 'But Your Ism could not exist in reality for a single day.' 'Quite the contrary,' said Schizophrenic, 'it is so stable that it becomes frightening. The vast majority of the population prefers it. In my Ism, as You put it, great masses of the people receive comparatively little. But at the same time, they work still less (again relatively speaking). So their coefficient of reward is quite high. Try asking our workers to choose: hard work and higher pay, or easier work and lower pay which is enough to satisfy fundamental needs. I am sure that the majority would prefer the latter. Then again here a large number of citizens can lead an idle way of life. Here the army of bosses has risen to such incredible numbers that it fully satisfies the vanity and ambition of humanity. Here men who are remarkable for their intelligence and their abilities are destroyed or reduced to such a level that they can no longer offer anything, while nonentities flourish and rise to the summits of society. And there are a great many more nonentities. Thanks to the officially established system of education and to the ease with which social habits can be acquired, a type of man is created who is adapted precisely to life in just such a society and incapable of living in any other. So the fears of the leadership of a possible mass emigration have no basis in fact. It is precisely this type of person who will go on to exert a feedback influence on technology, on the organisation of labour, the arts and other spheres of social life, supporting the tendency to develop the coarser branches of industry, the most primitive forms of labour organisation, the most depersonalised forms of art, deprived of any social content, which again is most acceptable to the majority. And the vicious circle is completed.' 'That's far too pessimistic a picture,' said Sociologist. 'From what point of view?' asked Schizophrenic. 'We stand at the very sources of what we desire. We must start everything all over again. And if we do begin again we shall have to live through again all the standard situations and models. Of course my position is pessimistic from the point of view of one life. History disregards the fact that life is short. But from the point of view of eternity there is no pessimism here. There are conflicts between people, there are uncontrollable consequences, there is a variety of regions and countries. Incidentally, if mankind is to perish it will not be because of differences and struggles, but because of unification and standardisation. Finally, the emergence of highly moral people is not impossible. Although morality is the most unstable aspect of a social individual, and a moral life is a life of martyrdom, the probability that such people will emerge is nonetheless better than zero. And we greatly underestimate the influence that such people would have on the course of history.' 'In many ways I agree with you,' said Thinker. 'And indeed You and I are pursuing the same activity but in different ways. And, as you see, with different results. The people at the top are not all villains and imbeciles. They do understand quite a lot. But in practice they cannot act. If you were to try to carry out just one tiny social reform on a statewide scale, then you might understand what that means in practice. It's easy enough for anyone to criticise and to devise utopias. We should all get together to make common cause.' 'I criticise no-one and I propose nothing,' said Schizophrenic. 'I do nothing in Your sense of the word. I just think. And what You call "We" in fact is the emptiest abstraction of all. And if what you say is sincere you cannot even guess how far apart our positions are. The condemned man and the executioner also work in harness. Executioners have always sought the co-operation of the condemned. And unfortunately as a rule they have achieved it.' 'But you, it seems, are a moralist,' said Colleague. 'No,' said Schizophrenic. 'Moralism is a formula of demagogy, deception and oppression. I am moral. But that in many ways is the opposite of moralism. A moral man is Little Red Riding Hood, but a moralist is the big Grey Wolf dressed up as Little Red Riding Hood.' 'Elsewhere in your first thesis,' said Colleague, 'You said that morality has no basis except the decisions taken by individuals to behave morally. In other words in your view morality is a product of free will. But that is a primitive mistake unforgiveable in a man like you.' 'I did not say that and do not say it,' said Schizophrenic. 'What do you mean?' asked Colleague, 'it's written down in black and white.' 'It is written down,' said Schizophrenic, 'but it is not I who am saying it but Deviationist. I have not yet finally made up my mind about it.' 'That is sophistry,' said Colleague, 'it was you who wrote it down just the same.' 'It doesn't follow from the fact that I write something down that I take it as truth,' said Schizophrenic. 'You yourself have just repeated a sentence which is written in my thesis. But you don't regard it as your conviction.' 'Of course not,' said Colleague. 'But there was some point you wanted to make in your thesis. What exactly?' 'I did want to,' said Schizophrenic, 'but this isn't a juridical question.' 'Well, answer it for us simply as a human question,' said Sociologist. 'I will not,' said Schizophrenic. 'You are not people whom I recognise as equal. I do not want to talk with you on any level other than on a juridical level.' 'But you know perfectly well that level doesn't exist either,' said Colleague. 'All there is is illusory legal phraseology. And what's more, no matter how impeccable your paradoxes may be from the logical point of view, for the ordinary man they look like inhuman deviations from the norm.' 'All the finest achievements of civilisation first appeared as deviations from the norm and were usually regarded as inimical to men,' said Schizophrenic. 'In every way civilisation is a deviation, a protest, a defence against the norm.' 'What's civilisation to you?' asked Claimant '—after all, we only live once.' 'We have stopped living,' said Schizophrenic. 'We no longer exist. So it would be better to think of those who will come afterwards. Who knows—it may be that my descendants will be interrogating yours.' 'That's of no significance,' said Colleague. 'After two or three generations biological parentage loses its significance for men.' 'But the weight of the past doesn't lose its significance,' said Schizophrenic. 'You just don't like our Ism,' said Thinker; 'that explains everything.' 'Even if I don't like it,' said Schizophrenic, 'is that a crime?' 'Of course it's not a crime,' said Colleague. 'It's something more serious—it's the possibility and the threat of a crime.' 'But I don't feel either love or hatred for our Ism,' said Schizophrenic. 'I approach it rather differently: I understand it.' 'You're naïve apart from everything else,' said Claimant. 'You surely don't believe that an understanding of the essence of our life has the slightest bearing? In the end everything is decided by man. And they always have false views on life, or invent them specially. Otherwise they wouldn't be able to operate. In order to attack some particular aspect of the Ism you must look like someone who's defending it.' 'Naïvety is also ideology,' said Schizophrenic. 'And a knowledge of truth is the first purely human duty. You know that as well as I do.' 'We know,' said Sociologist, 'and so we do not envy you.' 'I have done nothing criminal,' said Schizophrenic. 'Apart from legal crime,' said Wife, 'there is social crime. You've written constantly about that yourself.' 'I didn't use such an expression because it has two meanings,' said Schizophrenic. 'It can mean the carrying out of actions dangerous for or harmful to society, or the carrying out of actions which are intended to limit or oppose the social laws but which are neither dangerous or harmful to society as a whole—but rather the opposite. Which of the two did you mean?' 'Stop splitting hairs,' said Wife, and giggled. 'You are just as much a turd as we are.' And they all disappeared simultaneously.

On the other side of the partition the drunken landlord was

bawling out his equally aggressive wife. A baby was crying. The neighbours' television was turned up full. And outside the window the big world clattered on, constructed according to a theory which provided for just such a world and on the basis of the great achievements of the rehabilitated relativist cyber-nomats.

The balance sheet
Colleague put Schizophrenic's thesis and the conclusions of the experts, Sociologist and Thinker, into a file, and sealed it. Then he ordered measures to be taken to prevent the distribution of the thesis or to stop its distribution if any had started. But anyway, he thought, it'll die a natural death like the last time. No-one's going to read this rubbish. It's boring.

The report
The Leader's report was completed ahead of schedule and the plan was overfulfilled by 105 per cent. The Leader liked his report very much; and delivered it twice and ordered it to be published in three editions. The theme of the report was the accurate notion that in our country everything is just, apart from one or two peccadillos to which maximum attention must be paid, and that in our country everyone behaves correctly, apart from one or two isolated madmen and still more isolated enemies whom we unanimously condemn and towards whom we are taking the correct steps. The decision was taken that in the period until the next report, the main task of all his colleagues would be to broadcast the present one and to prepare the next. A hundred articles were published in the Journal, and two hundred more commissioned embodying explanations of the profundities of the Leader's report, commentaries by the Deputies on the Leader's report, and explanations by the Assistants of the Deputies' commentaries on the Leader's report.

The idea of a plot
After the Leader's report, Claimant observed in the broad circle of those he did not know that the Leader was far from being a fool. In the narrow circle of his acquaintances, Thinker said

that the Leader was not such a cretin as we had always thought. But this could damage him, as there were others in ruling circles who were still worse. And so he must be supported. And thus the idea of a plot began to float in the air. The aim of the plot was to reinforce the status quo. Three opposing tendencies took shape. The radical left wing insisted that no improvements should be allowed beyond those proposed and realised by the leadership itself. The moderate right wing sought to avoid any aggravation beyond that which was proposed and realised by the leadership itself. And the centrist bog aimed at nothing, but merely dreamt of leaving everything as it was, or if worse were in store, making sure that it would affect them as little as possible. And immediately disagreements appeared.

The end

Everyone expected the end to come and had exactly predicted it, read Instructor, when he reached the last page of Schizophrenic's manuscript. That is why the arrival of the end was unexpected. They were awoken in the middle of the night and told that an infantry regiment was leaving for the front, that their grievous sins had all been pardoned, and that they had all, with the exceptions of Patriot, Writer and Leadswinger, been assigned to the regiment. Patriot and Writer were returned to their respective units. In his sick-bay bed, Leadswinger rolled over on to his other side. The rest got their things together and joined the crowd gathering in the yard. The infantry sergeant bellowed: 'In columns of two, fall in!' And then: 'Sing to keep time . . . forward . . . march!' Panicker, who at the beginning of the war had been to regimental evening classes to become a company soloist, roared so loud that all the dogs in Ibansk joined in:

> Do not weep, my darling dear,
> Do not weep, dear hearts.
> If we really have to die
> It's written in our stars.

'Heads up, swing those arms, keep together!' The sergeant's roar shattered the silence of the night, and as the Ballad says:

> They march off with step so light
> Gone forever in the night.

(173)

When they'd left, the cooler was transferred to the cellar. Its normal history began. That is well known and they played no part in it.

Perspectives

When he had finished reading Schizophrenic's manuscript, Instructor spat on it out of disappointment and ordered it to be destroyed in view of the absence of appropriate evidence. Then he settled down to wait for further directives from below.

Boredom

Slanderer became insupportably bored. No friends. No family. No colleagues. No disciples. No-one to talk to. No pay. Not even any enemies. No-one. Nothing. It seemed things were much more serious than he had thought. Man had disappeared. 'Individuals like me are completely useless here. They are all alien.' Slanderer went to the Bar. There, as always, there was a crowd of drunks, and the sound of lively music. He couldn't understand where it came from. There was the Ibansk Frail Voice Choir singing popular verses based on Writer's words.

> Come my love, oh, let us sing
> Songs of our perdition.
> Being was the very start;
> Later—full cognition.

These last two lines, Slanderer understood quite differently.

> Beating was the very start;
> Later—full confession.

The hole where they used to go was crammed with people he didn't know. When he approached, a very young girl with broad shoulders and her bony backside half-naked, a cigarette in her mouth, blew smoke in his face and told him to shove off if he didn't want a thick ear. I wonder to what category, he thought, Schizophrenic would have allotted this phenomenon? To the anti-social? Hardly. This is not a protest, but an accommodation.

> When I try a drink to pour,
> My wife begins to curse.
> Everything's much as before
> Except it's getting worse.

(174)

And Slanderer went off somewhere as no-one needed him. But the music and its joyous words went on ringing out over the waste ground where the Bar stood.

> My little sweetheart often talks
> About her arsehole's schism;
> Once again through Europe stalks
> The spectre of the Ism.

3

THE GRAVESTONE

Epitaph to a living man

When it's barely dawn, you jump out of bed. You fling a few clothes on to your sleepy child. And you rush off to take him to the creche. And you see another man just like you taking a child just like yours to the same creche.

You grab your shopping bag and hurry off to the store. And you stand in line. There's the same man again, standing next to you. He's getting angry. He's late for work. And the salesgirl's slow. She's in no hurry. She's at work already. And she doesn't care a damn about her work. It's all the same to her. And then there are other people jumping the queue. And then they haven't got what the man wants. He has to hurry off to another shop. And stand in another line.

You just manage to squeeze into the tube-train. And that other man squeezes on next to you. He stands on your foot. You dive for a seat that he was aiming at as well on the basis of first come first served.

You run panting into your office. You clock on and beside you the same little man clocks on as well, and sits down next to you at the same desk. Like you he shuffles through some papers that nobody has any use for.

He goes along with you to a meeting. And to another meeting. And to another. And along with you he's dying of boredom. Like you he waits impatiently for the meaningless conclusion. You vote 'yes' together. You approve together. You vote 'no' together. You condemn together. Together . . . together . . .

You know everything about him. You know what his wardrobe's like, you know what his table's like. His sofa. How his lavatory flush works. What his blood pressure is. What his children are studying.

You know nothing about him. You don't know that every

day, every hour, inside his little head, a tiny book is being dreamt up. It will never be written. No-one will ever read it. It contains no events—just tiny thoughts. Gloomy thoughts. Pointless thoughts.

The little man is thinking his own miserable life. And this life is his principal and only book. And his last.

This little man is Nobody. He is merely your insignificant colleague.

This little man is Everybody. He is the absolute master of your fate.

This little man is you.

From Secretary's article

We are often asked if God exists or not, wrote Secretary. We answer this question affirmatively: yes, God does not exist.

Some peculiarities of the history of Ibansk

The history of Ibansk is made up of events which almost failed to happen; which almost happened but at the last moment somehow didn't; were expected but never happened despite that; were not expected but did happen despite that; happened but in the wrong way, at the wrong time, in the wrong place; happened, but are acknowledged not to have happened; did not happen but were generally accepted as having happened. This classification was put forward by Slanderer in a narrow circle of his enemies in a bar on Teacher Square after his fourteenth glass. His colleague, Puss, who had shat himself on quite a different subject, included this classification in his report. Slanderer disappeared. But to the surprise of his colleagues, after many years he emerged posthumously on the smooth and virginal surface of the cultural life of Ibansk, punched Puss in the face in full view of everyone, and set out to look for work. This happened after the Ibanskians, hot tears running down their faces, had accompanied the Boss on his long-awaited and final (as some naïvely thought at that time) journey, and after they had covered as best they could their naked arses which were embellished with multi-coloured scars and bruises and in theory at least were ready for the next general thrashing which was expected. To the great grief of the Ibanskians, the thrashing did not take place. And in terror they allowed themselves some timid rejoicing. Claimant was accorded the honour of being elected for his courage. Thinker called everyone coward, which was well-deserved, and reduced the number of citations from the Boss by half. And again nothing happened. Thinker successfully defended his thesis. Sociologist, instead of using the customary title of the Boss: 'The super-genius, the most brilliant genius of all the brilliant geniuses', used the greatly weakened title of 'the greatest genius'. Still nothing happened. And Sociologist went abroad again. No-one was arrested. 'My God,' Puss sobbed from joy after this, 'what will happen now? We have only one hope left—the Chinese.' The Chinese rejoiced no less than Puss, but went their own way.

In the panic which followed the return of Slanderer from non-existence, he was appointed the head of some organisation or other. Taking advantage of this brief moment of confusion, he was wily enough to publish a small booklet on a subject which it was still too early to write about and which afterwards became too late. In this booklet, he gave a distorted picture of everything, and, for the rest, his method of presentation was incorrect. The highest authorities who, after the joyful and tragic event already referred to, became even higher and radically altered their point of view, publicly declared of Slanderer that even a tamed wolf is always a wolf, and distributed a confidential letter in which they argued that the grave was the only cure for a cripple. Slanderer was immediately relieved of the heavy burdens of his high office and there was a move to send him back to whence he came as a parasite. But times had changed. And Slanderer (up to every trick) found himself a job as the most junior employee in some dead-beat little institute, on the lowest pay-scale. Since Sociologist was unable to prevent this, he took the credit for it. Thinker said that there was no longer any chance of resurrecting the Boss, although no-one was particularly trying to do so. And already on the horizon of the History of Ibansk there could be seen the picturesque silhouette of Hog. One hand of the silhouette held a tiny ear of maize which had not yet reached the lactic-wax degree of ripeness, and the other was frozen in an obscene gesture. One of the silhouette's feet was naked. The silhouette hiccuped loudly and mumbled slogans: OUR PRESENT GENERATION, FUCK YOU ALL, WILL LIVE UNDER THE TOTAL

ISM. And glancing towards the abstract painters, the silhouette raised a warning finger.

Director's funeral

One day, much to his own surprise, Director died. The doctors started a rumour that it was cancer. But Chatterer affirmed that that was a lie. Director had died of self-satisfaction and a cerebral haemorrhage. There had been an attempt to promote him almost to the very top, and he had burst a cerebral intestine out of sheer delight. That promising colleague Puss listened discreetly to Chatterer's remark and said (as did all those present in the cemetery) that first of all that was not funny, and secondly that this was no time to be making witty remarks. Every schoolboy knows that the brain is made up of two hemispheres which (in most cases, although, true enough, not in all) have convolutions and not intestines. Neurasthenic, who was standing beside them and dying of boredom, said that Chatterer was right, since the topmost leadership did indeed have their heads full of intestines and what intestines usually contain. Remember what Secretary said when Director promised to write a nine-ton theory of our practice! He said that Director would never manage it because he simply didn't have the guts.

Director was buried in the Old Whores' Cemetery. Apart from those who were obliged by law to be present at the funeral, and also those who could not avoid being present in the absence of any law permitting them to be absent with impunity, everyone came who had any chance of becoming Director or perhaps something even higher. They had put enormous efforts into ensuring that Director was buried here since in doing so they were thinking of their own futures. Indeed the funeral of the Director in the Old Whores' Cemetery created a precedent without equal in the past and very enticing for the future. It was a concrete application of the new directive to enhance the leadership role of the leadership cadres and to activate an initiative from below. Besides, they all looked with unconcealed envy at the Director's coffin covered in its pall of fiery scarlet. Their faces made plain their thoughts: 'That lucky bugger hasn't done too badly for himself! Look what he's landed himself this time!' Neurasthenic noticed this and whispered to Chatterer that these degenerates envied the Director.

'Just think, they're already wondering what will be said in their obituaries, who will write them, where they'll be published, and in which cemetery they'll be buried. It makes me shudder! How can people like this exist?' 'They're not people at all,' said Chatterer. 'They're just social functions without any trace of human nature. They've gone through such a process of selection and training that they don't receive any human element in the first place, and anyway there's nothing left by the end. There's no psychology here—there's nothing but social calculation. Their obituaries and their cemeteries are their inalienable privileges and their final ambition. Promise them a burial-place in the Wall, and they'll go to any length to make sure they get it.' 'That terrifies me,' said Neurasthenic, 'because they're going to make everybody like themselves. And then what'll happen?' 'They've done it already,' said Chatterer. 'The best thing we can do is to slip off and have a drink to the memory of Schizophrenic.' And they slipped out of the cemetery at the crucial moment when the coffin containing the body of Director, who had died from an access of delight, slipped from the ropes which held it and fell sideways. Puss scornfully watched them go and walked over towards Colleague. 'It'll be interesting to see,' said Neurasthenic, 'who they appoint in his place.' 'In this situation,' Chatterer said, 'the best Director would be a downright deadbeat who's achieved all he's going to achieve and has no prospect of getting anything bigger. Someone like that won't stop you from doing nothing. And he'll do everything he can to make sure that the highest authorities believe that you're doing everything you should as well as you should.' 'But what if you want to work?' asked Neurasthentic. 'You can't please all of the people all of the time,' said Chatterer.

And at that time no-one knew nor could know that in only a short while they would see alongside the grave of the Director the grave of Hog himself, who, for even only one hundredth of the Ibanskians he had beaten round the head in the past, should have been buried in the Wall. But the well regulated history of Ibansk was already beginning to misfire and create exceptions. And even less could anyone at that time have imagined that around the grave of Hog there was to be played out one of the most inept episodes in the history of Ibansk—such episodes, because of their very ineptitude, became the most characteristic manifestations of the deepest significance of our history.

The turning point

The life of Ibansk came to a decisive turning point. It was officially recognised that this very life which, by an act of genius, had been planned out on high more than a hundred years ago, which had been prepared for by the whole development of matter throughout the latter half of eternity, and which had been brought into being in complete conformity with its own most fundamental laws and formulae under the eye of the secret police—that this very life was revealing occasional oversights by certain malefactors. The Newspapers published sharply critical reports. On the No. 5 tram (Driver, comrade A; Depot manager, comrade B; Transport chief, C) passengers X and Y, who were strap-hanging near an old woman, citizeness Z, did not give up their place to an old woman, citizeness D. And it was only under the pressure of public opinion that passenger E was obliged to give up his seat to baby K, a seat on which citizeness Z was forced to sit down despite her objections that she had already passed her stop. And at the greengrocer's (Manager, comrade B) citizen A shoved citizeness C who had tried to jump the queue, and did not apologise to the cashier D, who had overcharged citizen E and therefore was quite justified in calling him a lout. Measures were taken in favour of the victims.

The empire of fine art

It has been proved that the new-born child is endowed with every possible ability. Any child, if it is properly educated according to our theory, can become a physicist, a blonde, a caretaker, a man, a purveyor of fizzy lemonade, or a famous film star. And in any event, an artist. This truth requires no demonstration, for no-one feels the need for one. Any parent who wants to see his gifted child become an artist and who possesses the necessary qualities, knows from his or her own experience that that indeed is so and not otherwise. As for other parents, this is not their concern, since it has nothing to do with them.

Thus parents who have the afore-mentioned qualities send their children to innumerable clubs and to special schools. It is of course more difficult to get them into the special schools as at this stage of artistic training a more searching selection of the most highly qualified parents is carried out. The most able of the children of parents educated in this way provide an impeccable *curriculum vitae* and are selected to go to much less numerous schools and institutes. At this stage healthy competition becomes much keener and attracts the attention of relatives, acquaintances, and other people whom everybody knows about but does not discuss to avoid difficulties. It does sometimes happen however that people in this category are unmasked. But this happens very rarely. More often it is they who do the unmasking. At each new stage the role played by the abilities of the parents is somewhat reduced, and the role played by the lack of ability of the children greatly increases. From a certain moment on, children who are aware of their own talents put out their claws, bare their teeth and, without any outside help, begin to devote themselves selflessly to the service of beauty and truth. The most able of those who graduate from the schools and institutes, having acquired the skill to sculpt or to paint leaders, heroes, cows and birch trees, and the skills to exploit these skills, take part first of all in mixed exhibitions and, with time, graduate to one-man shows, and are awarded commissions, prizes, titles, apartments, seats on councils and in academies; they make busts, torsos, statues, portraits, landscapes. In other words they ruin their own lives and, in particular, the lives of other people according to all the undoubted laws of beauty established by higher authority.

To ensure that these laws of beauty should be religiously observed and that there should be no regrettable errors, hordes of wise mentors were invented (in part—others appeared spontaneously) in the ratio of five-to-one (five mentors to one graduate artist). These mentors were drawn from the ranks of the most worthy artists supported in equal number by administrative colleagues and retired colonels who could not possibly be used in the world of science on account of the fact that that particular field was already saturated. These mentors established a powerful, well-organised, wholly self-supporting and perfectly self-perpetuating system, whose main function became the production of staff for reproducing itself on a larger scale, while the production of artists became very much a matter of secondary importance of which they would willingly have relieved themselves were it not for a hint from higher authority that this was not yet quite the right moment. The principal ingredients of this system are the following institutions. The Academy of Arts with, subordinate to it, a number of special institutes. Members of the Academy are included in all the other institutions of the system. The Artists' Union. This incorporates Unions of a lower rank, which in turn incorporate Unions of still lower rank. And so it goes on. The Union also controls innumerable Funds, Studios, Combines, Commissions, Councils. The members of all these institutions are included in some way or another in all the other institutions. The Ministry of Culture, which has a special Department of Culture, which has a special sub-division of fine arts. The Supreme Committee, which has a Department of Culture, which has a special sub-division of fine arts. A Special Department in another no less important Institution in charge of cultural affairs, which has a specialist sub-division in charge of fine arts. Innumerable special Publishing Houses, Journals, Newspapers. Still more innumerable special departments in all the other Publishing Houses, Journals, Newspapers. Plus a super-vigilant army of volunteer Ibanskians who maintain an exhaustive watch on every microscopic fragment of space and time in the world of the arts, and who have a very considerable experience in this. Finally, the Regulations, which are permanently enforced, and *ad hoc* Instructions. In principle this system is so dense that it cannot be penetrated even by cosmic rays, which prefer to go round it, which has engendered among modern physicists the mad idea, which has tormented them for a long time, that space is bent and that time is reversible. As Slanderer said, if you want to discover the secret of how hundreds of gifted girls and boys become transformed into thousands of talentless men and women, whom by tradition we still call artists, just study the system. The possibility of any genuine artist penetrating the system is about as great as the possibility of a man, after dying of extreme old age, being roasted in a crematorium oven, passed through a mincer, pounded to dust and flushed down the lavatory, turning up on the Ibansk sewage farm in a state fit to report 'ready for duty and military service in the nation's defence'.

And yet despite it all, cracks appeared in the system. And through these cracks crawled miserable abstractionist bugs and frivolous but officially unrecognised formalist cockroaches. Their appearance made life impossible. Progressive theorists bellowed as loud as they could that they were not in favour. Not even that helped. But after all, it was only half a disaster. Out crawled Dauber who was like nothing at all, and he began to laugh with glee. He was labelled an abstractionist. No effect! Then a formalist. Again no effect! Then an expressionist. Still no effect! Then a modernist. The hell with it, still no effect! 'He's nothing but a gangster and a currency speculator,' said the reactionaries. 'It's true,' said the Liberals, 'he's just a drunk, a homosexual, a drug addict and a lecher.' And then Dauber became the leader of a new trend in Ibanskian art, a movement which consisted of himself alone and had no direction, neither to the left nor to the right, neither backward nor forward. But Chatterer found a way out of the situation. 'In general,' he said, 'there are two forms of art. There is centripetal art which comes from within and centrifugal art which comes from without. For a long time I have tried to find a reasonable explanation of the former, and I have failed. On the contrary I have discovered that this form is essentially inexplicable. It is a kind of hole in space through which order and light flow into our dark and chaotic world.' Scientist said that Chatterer's idea was completely in the spirit of modern physics.

After incorrect directions in art had achieved proportions which the leadership considered threatening, steps were taken which redoubled their harmful consequences. In particular a plan was put forward to limit admission to the Union of Artists of Ibansk only to people aged sixty and above. And even they could be taken on initially only as candidate members. They could be admitted as full members only after a twenty-year trial period. 'That's excellent,' Chatterer said. 'There's just one clause that needs to be added to this regulation: Every application for admission to the Union should be accompanied by a personal coffin.' 'And by a gravestone,' said Dauber. 'As a sculptor I have a professional interest.'

Hog

If anyone had told the Ibanskians a year ago that Hog was to become Leader, he would have been laughed out of court. And if anyone had told them after Hog had come to power that soon Hog would denounce the Boss, he would have immediately been despatched to the very place whence, after Hog's denunciation, tens of thousands of Ibanskians began to return. These hordes had by chance survived beating after beating, and were numbered among those very few Ibanskians whom the Boss, unbeknownst to his Deputies and Assistants and all other Ibanskians, had lightly criticised for minor offences. But the incredible actually happened. Hog delivered—more or less intelligibly—his denunciatory speech, whose author, intended audience and purpose were all equally unknown. The Ibanskians were completely thunderstruck, not so much by what the speech said, (the Ibanskians, of course, had never known anything of the kind and had never heard a word about it, since it had all been done in the deepest secrecy, and today they know about it even less) as by the mere fact of such things being mentioned at all. And there was no-one they could denounce about it, since he who was speaking could himself denounce everybody and beat the living daylights out of them. And no-one was arrested for listening to the speech and winking at each other about it conspiratorially. There were victims even on this battlefield. Member, who until this time had held quite an important post, suddenly began to fight for truth, and was retired on a pension. Someone got drunk and shot himself through the head. The rest got off with only a few prickings of a conscience which hitherto they had never noticed.

'What do you think?' Dauber asked Chatterer; 'will justice be done?' 'That's a laughable question,' said Chatterer. 'First, if justice is done the number of victims will double at least. And secondly who is going to do justice? Whoever acquires control of the judicial function will simply continue what his predecessors started. In our situation justice is out of the question as an historical action. It can exist only as a moral phenomenon.'

What is to be sculpted?

To become a sculptor Dauber drank (at that time everyone got drunk, just like now), chased after women and studied the humane sciences which, in his innocence, he considered possible in Ibansk, and philosophy which, even more naïvely, he believed to be a science. 'That,' said Slanderer on this subject, 'is of no importance. It may even be preferable that there should be no smack of science in philosophy. Instead there are ideas. And a true sculptor should carve not people, heroes and animals, but ideas and thoughts. Let nine thousand nine hundred and ninety-nine of our sculptors carve cows and heroes. A useful activity, of course. But let just one deal in trivia and start carving ideas.' Schizophrenic said that there were some signs that ideas were immaterial and that they might therefore be a little difficult to sculpt. Slanderer said that it was worth trying because, you never know, it might work. If you're going to be original you might as well be original on a grand scale. So you need to sculpt problems. Posing problems is anyway more important than solving them. Problems that have been solved disappear into the past. Problems which have been posed give birth to the future—especially those which are in principle insoluble: they are eternal. Man begins where the effort to achieve the impossible begins.

Chatterer's analysis

There was a party in the bar on Teacher Square to celebrate Slanderer's unexpected return. The bar was still open at that time and was used as a rendezvous by the emerging Ibanskian intelligentsia. Naturally enough the conversation turned to Hog. 'You must give him his due,' said Careerist. 'Had it not been for him, Slanderer wouldn't be sitting here with us today.' Then all the others had their say. And they said everything that could be said in such a situation, with so many years of whispers and silence sitting on their shoulders. Although much of what was said was intelligent and even true, Chatterer said that it was nothing but raving nonsense. You're not stupid, he screamed at the whole bar, (everyone was shouting, incidentally, and so no-one was paying the slightest attention to what anyone else was saying) and yet you can't cope with the most trivial problem. This single event involves many inter-related problems. If you don't separate them and sort them out one by one, then this whole event will remain for you nothing more than a riddle, a miracle, a happy coincidence, a fateful mistake, a lunatic decision or a sensible act of wise politics. But here we have no riddle, no miracle, no accident, no error, no lunacy, no wisdom. And it would be wrong to say that it involves a little of each. Here we simply need a totally different point of view.

It is said that Hog denounced the regime of the Boss and dealt it such a blow that now his regime appears more or less to have disappeared. A lot of words have been spoken—but what a mass of ambiguity! What do we take the Boss's regime to be? A few individual historical particularities of the life of our society in this period, or the general basis underlying these particularities in given historical conditions? Hog has never dealt a blow to any regime. He tried to save this regime. And saving it he has undertaken certain actions which he himself has not invented. The uncontrolled consequences of what he has done are quite another thing. And who of those who sanctioned this action (and this action is the product not of an individual but of a corporate decision of those in power), who could have foreseen these consequences? We're so accustomed to swallow any filth without blenching and regarding it as a blessing from above, and taking any blessing as filth, that none of us could even consider the possibility of uncontrolled consequences. They were unthinkable, and so in principle they could not exist. If we want to be historically precise, a basic blow was truly delivered against the regime. But it was delivered from outside. The regime from the inside is invulnerable. The blow was dealt at the beginning of the War. It was at that moment that the regime swayed and tottered and collapsed in its illusory trappings and its stupid excesses. And then these excesses did nothing but agonise for many years. But in effect they had already been swept away. They were condemned from every point of view—economic, military, human. They became unacceptable to all—both to the leaders and the led who, during the War had the time to build up their 'noes' and their capacity for resistance. What Hog said came as a surprise only to the hypocrites and to the executioners. And perhaps to countless cretins. For millions of people, it was an ordinary normal way of life. Hog, as it often suits authority in our conditions to do, merely exercised skill in annexing other people's achievements and what had come about on its own. He doesn't deserve admiration. All he deserves is scorn and sarcasm.

(187)

Hog's action was partly an action of the ruling group, an act of self-defence. They feared for their own skins. If the earlier situation had been maintained, they would all have been liquidated one after another by those who were striving to preserve the status quo—that is to say by themselves, but in order, one after another. This action was in part advantageous for Hog in his struggle to attain and preserve personal power. Here we cannot even say that he pursued his own personal ends—such people do not have ends. He just blindly obeyed the mechanism of the seizing and holding of power. As a result he achieved something. But it is no act of humanity, but an act which for a little time has embellished their power and which has, incidentally, eased the life of many people. But that was their last concern.

And in this extremely advantageous situation for himself, he has behaved with extreme stupidity. He just opened the valve a fraction, leaked off excess pressure and then closed it again. Closed it too early. He didn't have the sense to understand that if you are going to strike people, you must strike them with all your might. Half-measures in such situations always end in defeat. You say that he wouldn't have been allowed to? That he would have been toppled? They would have had no chance! Before they could have got themselves together, he could have done so much that it would have been far too late to have taken any steps against him. The further he had gone, the stronger his position. It is true that he could not deal a really heavy blow. But not because he understood the objective impossibility of a heavy blow, but because he subjectively did not understand the possibilities before him. And because he had no wish to strike harder than he needed in order to carve out his own little niche. And because of his fear of unknown consequences. In our conditions any blow against the Boss, no matter how it is formulated, is a blow against the entire system, since the Boss is the most exemplary product of the system, and he in his turn is rooted in all the spheres of our life and in the souls of all our peoples. So even a feeble blow must have a loud resonance, literally a chain reaction which will destroy our illusions. It will not destroy the system, I say again, but our illusions. If Hog had been in the slightest degree intelligent, he should have been able to understand that and carry right through. But he began trying to obliterate the consequences of his action. And in so doing, he gave birth to a new false situation for which we all (and particularly He Himself) will have to pay. It is striking that They cannot understand what is clearly apparent: the system itself is unusually strong and stable. The War has shown that even the most stupid leadership is unable to shake it. Without all these idiotic illusions and myths about heaven on earth, in other words, if the system were open, it would be even stronger. The mistake lay not in denouncing the regime of the Boss, but in failing to pursue the matter to the end. Mark my words, this mistake will have fateful consequences in the future. I am not talking about the establishment of historical truth (soon all that will no longer interest the broad masses of the people) but of the creation of more or less normal conditions of existence in the present social system. Anyway, there is no further possibility of anything taking its place. We have to accept this as a given fact.

As for the removal of Hog, he will of course be removed. And quite soon. But for quite a different reason. The most likely is the destruction of the existing balance between the personal and the nominal system of power. In his time the Boss also created a system of personal power out of line with the nominal system, but then he brought the latter into line with the former. Hog is also trying to go the same way—an example of his complete lack of comprehension of the situation and of his inability to be original. But he's doing it like a caricature. He is original only in the stupidities he commits. What a grandiose idea to sow the wilderness with maize! And what grandiose forecasts—our generation will live under the total Ism!

Neurasthenic's objection
'All that may be so,' said Neurasthenic. 'But all the same he is trying to do something. He travels round the country. He makes speeches.' 'He does travel,' said Chatterer, 'and he does make speeches. In one place he even said that people are living badly, that they're starving. But just you try to say the same thing now! You'll be done for slander. Once he's talked about a shortcoming, that means that that particular shortcoming no longer exists. It's been put right.' 'Neurasthenic is right,' said Careerist. 'You can't simply cross everything out like that.' Dauber said that Hog was now taking an interest in the position

of the arts. 'The Boss took an interest, too,' Chatterer said. 'Hog's doing nothing original. They're obliged by their office to take an interest in everything they haven't the slightest interest in and which means nothing at all to them. But I'm ready to bet that you've got more slaps in the face to come from him.'

Slanderer's objection

Slanderer said that on the whole he shared Chatterer's view. But he thought that the individual psychological qualities of historic leaders could not be totally ignored. He was certain that a major part in Hog's action had been played by his natural strong constitution, his intuition, and his energy. Surely Chatterer would not deny that the personal psychological qualities of the Boss had created a suitable climate for the tragedy which occurred and had enhanced it. At this Chatterer swore like a trooper, swallowed a glass of vodka over-hastily and chased it with an over-hasty glass of beer. 'You're staying completely within the framework of the official interpretation of events,' he said. 'In his struggle for personal power, the Boss allowed himself, had recourse to, and all the rest. But surely you don't think that's the heart of the matter! Just think how many regions, areas, districts, unions, trusts, combines, factories, roads, housing committees, ministries, universities, managements, companies, regiments and so on, and so on, there are in the country. Just think how many people are needed to fill the millions of posts which all these forms of authority demand. And then drop the facts you've got into the historic conditions of our country. There was a revolution! And a counter revolution! And a civil war. And to all that, add the possibility which opened for everyone to have some job or another. And you begin to get the first pale idea as to who were the real authors and performers of the tragedy. And as far as individual psychological qualities are concerned, they have played absolutely no role at all. Anyway they never existed. They're just a fiction. It isn't a matter of their having played no role. I say again, they don't exist at all. What is the psyche from the social point of view? It is a badly organised awareness of its own sickly physiology and nothing more. The presence of a psyche from the social point of view is nothing but a deviation from the norm. And the Boss, Hog, and millions of their people are socially normal. They have no need of a psyche. And so it did not, and does not exist. And psychology as a science (or more precisely as a self-styled science) on the basis of which we judge some mythical psyche has in fact no relation at all to the psyche. It is a jumble of more or less literary chatter on physiology and of archaic drivel about the old logic of thought. Conversations about the psyche of such individuals as the Boss and Hog are conversations without a subject. The only interest they have is as gossip among intriguers. The hell with them all! Who are they anyway, that we should be bothering our heads with their miserable personas! We'd do far better to have another round.'

The explosion

Dauber finished his series of sculptures 'War' at the most unsuitable moment. An exhibition was being planned for those who not only had never been allowed to exhibit before, but who had significantly augmented the number of people who'd received a thrashing. And Hog himself was supposed to be attending the exhibition. It's still difficult to judge whether the organisation of this exhibition was a consequence of the wind of change, or of the perfidious intentions of conservatives, who wanted to show the leadership how far present-day youth had degenerated under the putrefying influence of the West. Slanderer alleged that in intermediate periods winds of change usually harmonised very nicely with conservative schemes and gave birth to intermediate forms which were characteristic of such periods, and he suggested that these forms should be regarded as independent without wishing to force them into more sharply defined classic categories.

The 'War' cycle is interpreted as a protest against war. 'Well,' said Schizophrenic, 'maybe it is but maybe it isn't. For example, take the sculpture "Man Removing his Gas Mask". Let's assume that the artist wanted to show how a man tears off his gas mask. The gas mask has saved the man from the poisoned air. The danger is now passed. He can take the mask off. Moral: what a vile thing is war! Is that funny? Of course it is. But take another look at the face of this happy fellow who's just been saved from death. What does it show? Joy? No, something quite different. The man's been tricked, told that the air is poisoned. They've made him wear a mask so as not to breathe the poisoned air. And here we see the man snatching the mask off because he can't stand it any more. And what does he find? He's amazed. It turns out that the air is pure. Everything is false! And "The Explosion" is merely inspired by the explosion of an atom bomb. In fact it's about something quite different. It's about the explosion which is happening now in the consciousness of the people of Ibansk. I think the cycle would have been better called "Enough!"' 'It sounds fine,' said Chatterer, 'but it's a bit high flown. I would have preferred something rather different: the fellow-worker's revolt.'

Fellow-worker's revolt

Citizen X, wrote Fellow-worker, often has guests. Judging by their clothes and their accents, some of them are foreigners. They have anti-Ibanskian conversations. For instance, yesterday, they were talking about Truth-teller's book which isn't published here and they spoke well of . . . Fellow-worker sealed the envelope and took it to the nearest post box, sighing to himself as he did so: see what this vile system drives decent people to do! When he got home, Fellow-worker began to work on some verses for his office wall newspaper. A marvellous subject, he thought. Something really to get your teeth into. Epitaphs on villains who are still alive! That'll give them something to think about. Fellow-worker had written verses since he was a child. He read them to his close friends. They praised them but advised him to keep them to himself. Although times were better than they were, people were still being taken away for far less dangerous things. It would be better of course to throw them away. But the best thing of all might be to hang on to them just in case. Who could tell what would happen in the future? There might suddenly be a zig-zag in a totally opposite direction. They might even be published and make him famous. And then, who knows . . . But what if someone denounces me suddenly! Our people are such swines! There's no-one you can trust. And Fellow-worker's brow was covered in cold sweat, his nose began to tremble, and he fouled his pants. But what am I afraid of? That's enough! I'm fed up with it! The verses he wrote turned out to be very malicious. That'll raise a laugh, said Fellow-worker. Of course, I can't possibly sign them. Secretary will be an opponent, that's for sure! But it might be worth

(192)

starting a rumour as to who's the author. I can always deny it later. No, that's still a bit too sharp. I'll just round the corners off a little . . .

The collision

When Hog saw Dauber's sculptures, he had an instinct of what they were about. Maybe he had been warned about Dauber and set against him in advance. But that was unlikely. There was no need to set Hog against Dauber. Everything was clear enough without that. There was a famous confrontation between Dauber and Hog. Hog almost lost a button. Dauber lost more and might have lost still more. But as Thinker justly observed, times had changed. The conversation between Dauber and Hog followed the classic Ibanskian form; 'You're a fool', 'Fool yourself', 'Look who's calling me a fool.' Finally Dauber said that as far as art was concerned, he was his own prime minister, and could sort things out a lot better than Hog and all his friends. Initially this outburst made Dauber far more famous than had the quality of the works which gave rise to the confrontation. The fact is of itself significant: any independent major artist in Ibansk is condemned to take social actions by his very appearance. Then the form was made responsible for everything. But the form was only a method worked out by officials to give them an excuse for refusing to show an artist's works. Later some sculptors appeared who were, in the form of their work, far more abstract and formalist than Dauber, while Dauber himself did perfectly respectable work. But the situation didn't change in principle since the purely social factors— the independence and the scale of the artist's personality—were still there and became more apparent.

Consequences

After the clash, Dauber was expelled from the Artists' Union. The left-wing members of the Union voted for his expulsion. They cold-shouldered him. This expulsion meant the end of any Government commissions, the withdrawal of his studio facilities, and a total ban on his exhibiting. There were other minor unpleasantnesses. Since they seem almost incredible, it's not worth mentioning them. On the other hand, he was not sent to jail, and he carried on working on his sculptures. When he left the exhibition, that self-same day, he began to work on 'Orpheus' and 'The Prophet'—self-portraits of his situation and his state of mind at that moment and throughout all the period that followed.

The rats

In order to have something to read on the bus, Chatterer picked up in a bar a book called *Everything About Rats*. It was of course a translation. The preface said that for several decades the authors had been carrying out an experiment with a rat colony. The colony was housed in a fairly isolated environment with the aim of observing the laws of rodent life in their pure form. But the environment was quite large and varied, and the diet conformed with normal and natural requirements. At all events, when they decided on the dimensions and internal structure of the living space, as well as on the food supply, the experimenters took into account corresponding characteristics in natural conditions. The book presented the results of their observations and their conclusions. In a number of cases, the conclusions were presented as mathematical formulae.

The aim of the experiment, Chatterer read, was to clarify the rules which govern the way in which rats behave towards one another. Their basis was the tendency, developed over a long evolutionary period, of individuals and groups towards self-preservation and towards an improvement of their living conditions in a social situation. By social situation here is understood a more or less stable agglomeration of individuals who come together to lead a life in common and to reproduce that way of life in a series of successive generations. Accordingly we refer to the rules of behaviour of the rats towards one another as social rules, without giving the expression any other significance, and without supposing any analogy with human society which operates according to entirely different laws. Human society also has institutions, developed through history and controlling people's behaviour, as for example legal standards and institutions, morality, religion, public opinion, art and so on. The rat society has of course nothing comparable. And although, at first sight, observation of that society seems to reveal many resemblances with human society, and consequently gives rise to gloomy thoughts, this phenomenon is of an entirely different nature. The reader may convince himself of this from the following account of the results of the experiment.

Rats have to learn the social laws, and do not inherit them. A rat brought up in comparative isolation is seen to be without ambition, unable to compete with the others for leadership, unable to steal other rats' food, to denounce them and so on. They learn from their own experience, by observing others, and from the training they are given by other rats and so on. The rules develop of their own accord. The rats are sufficiently intelligent to discover them for themselves, and the rat society offers them huge possibilities of applying the rules. In most cases the rats . . .

Chatterer was so absorbed by his reading that he rode right past his stop.

Claimant

As the historians of Ibansk explain, the roads that lead to the quagmire of power are covered in blood and tears. The foremost personalities of Ibansk have made their own substantial contribution here. And the most humanist of them recently invented a completely new path, drenched in urine, smeared with shit and snot and flecked with spittle. It is this very road that was chosen by the late Director who would almost certainly have achieved his goal had he not rejoiced too soon. Claimant and Director had their eye on the same position. And so they were intimate friends. Initially Claimant sought to overtake the late Director by winning the support of Theoretician and getting himself immediately elected a full member of the Academy. But Director tripped him up deftly by hinting to Theoretician what Claimant's intentions clearly were, and the attempt miscarried. Claimant lost heart and was taken to hospital with a second bout of appendicitis. When the news of Director's long-awaited death came, he was lying on the operating table. Thrusting his doctors aside and stuffing his stinking guts back into his gaping belly any old how, Claimant tore off to the cemetery and just managed to get there in time to deliver an emotional speech. 'Sleep, dear comrade, and do not dream of waking up again,' he intoned, brushing away a tear. 'We have picked up your great work and we shall carry it forward to its logical conclusion. The loss which science has suffered in losing you is irreparable. But we shall do our very best to multiply that loss.'

As he sobbed out this funeral oration, Claimant gazed around him, trying to choose a place for his own future solemn interment. I'll get Dauber to do the monument, thought the right hemisphere of his brain which, as modern science has established, has not yet been studied at all by modern science. I shall just have to warn him not to fool about. After all, it won't be the tomb of just any old third-rate professor but of someone . . . And if . . . But it's still too early to think about that. The left hemisphere of his brain which, as modern science has definitely established, controls verbal diarrhoea, had all this time been churning out without any pause Claimant's computerised funeral oration. He did, of course, know how to talk. There's no denying that. He made fewer mistakes than others, no more than three in long foreign words and no more than one in Ibanskian mono-syllables. Because of this he wasn't greatly loved by his colleagues, who thought of him as a white raven. What's he doing poking his nose in everywhere, they said to each other, it would be better if he got on with his own scientific work. 'Sleep, dear friend,' Claimant wailed for about the tenth time. 'We shall pick up our common work which has fallen from your hands and we shall carry it forward . . .'

Claimant understood that he now had a great opportunity. And he decided to become Director cost what it might. 'You have a real chance,' said Thinker. 'You should become Director. You just need to work it all out properly. You must find the essential link which will allow us to pull out the entire chain.' Claimant was greatly moved by this, and promised Thinker an editorial job, and a part-time post in the Special School with its special canteen arrangements for the privileged. After this Claimant went off on a trip abroad. Claimant's wife telephoned Thinker. 'Just a moment,' said Thinker as he leafed through his desk calendar. 'Come on Friday from three o'clock to half past four.'

The inevitability of error
'So,' said Thinker, condemning Claimant and therefore himself to failure from the very start, 'let's draw up a list of all the possible competitors, of all the people on whom the decision

depends, and work out the most advantageous line for the Journal to pursue.' As careerists who were just starting and who had achieved some success entirely by accident (i.e. not according to the laws which govern career-building in this kind of society), Claimant and Thinker had no idea of the most vital and fundamental social principle in career-building. Careers are not made, careers make themselves. If a career is in the making, it must not be interfered with. Any help offered to a career creates disturbances. If, on the other hand, a career is not in the making you simply have to wait until it takes off on its own. If this doesn't happen, then the career is meaningless anyhow. All that is required of an individual who is eager to make himself a career is to reveal himself to society as a potential careerist, and then await the consequences. As a rule the desired consequences follow. All you need is to have the patience to wait for them and recognise them when they arrive. Claimant, who had skipped at least five rungs of the legally permissible career ladder, and Thinker, who had skipped at least three, were equally ignorant of the other fundamental social principle of career-building. A careerist who has skipped even only one rung of the normal career ladder must convince everyone that he is now satisfied with what he has achieved and has no intention of leaping further upwards. Claimant and Thinker did quite the opposite. They let everyone know their intention of aiming still higher. And although all their subsequent actions were in full conformity with the rules of career-building, the outcome had already been decided. Finally, Claimant and Thinker did not know the third fundamental principle of career-building in Ibanskian conditions: no matter how progressive and forward-looking new or old tendencies may be, the careerist must convince all interested parties that he is less progressive and less forward-looking than the tendency currently in vogue. Claimant and Thinker put such effort into launching and spreading rumours about themselves as extraordinarily progressive and forward-looking fellows, that, despite their actual accomplishments, which were totally divorced from any sort of progress, many people in responsible positions began to believe that they were in fact progressive. And this put them on their guard. And in our terms, being put on your guard is almost the same as imposing a ban. And the well-known rule whereby people who want to make a change never change anything, while changes are only effected by people who had no intention of doing so—this has no significant role in this. And the man who does change things changes them unintentionally and with no thought of the consequences. Chatterer revealed all these considerations to Schizophrenic in that very same bar, which, at that time, was living through its last days. It was the eve of a strong campaign against alcoholism, which was a consequence of the almost total collapse of the brewing industry, and all the bars selling beer were getting ready to go over to milk. It's true that this raised the new problem, that of finding milk when there weren't any cows. But the problem now no longer presented any difficulty, since the waste ground on the far bank of the River Ibanyuchka had already been sown with maize. And from there, you see, it is only a few short steps to the achievement of the total Ism. 'But who might be appointed?' asked Schizophrenic. 'The Director will be Someone-or-other, and the Editor will be No-one-at-all,' said Chatterer.

The social functions of the studio

Dauber was given a studio. Twelve square yards of useable space, a miniature toilet of pre-revolutionary construction into which it was possible to urinate only via the nostril of the Prophet or through a tear in Orpheus's chest, and a mezzanine which just had room for a spring mattress and a couple of stools. At lightning speed Dauber flooded the studio with sculptures and drawings in such quantity that Chatterer had to draw up for him special instructions on how to reach his mezzanine with a minimum of damage—and the mezzanine, after the closure of the bars, became one of the centres of the cultural life of Ibansk. 'Now you've got yourself a salon on the real international circuit,' said Chatterer. 'Everyone comes to parade themselves here! Ministers, generals, streetwalkers, Italians, artists, informers, Catholics, the rehabilitated, signatories . . . Make no mistake—they're all on to you with their ears, eyes, noses and what-have-you all the time. See that little drunk over there, he must be a high-ranking agent.' 'I don't give a damn,' said Dauber. 'From a certain point of view informers aren't very different from our liberal friends. And at least they don't pretend to be suffering from world weariness. And anyway I want to play my cards on the table. I have no secrets other than those which everyone knows.'

The rats

Almost immediately, literally a few days after the beginning of the experiment, we began to think that our rat colony was condemned to an early end. A number of phenomena which were both extremely striking and completely inexplicable in the light of existing theories took place in succession. First of all there was the spontaneous formation, which subsequently received official confirmation, of exceptional groups of rats who began to give chase to individuals with the highest intellectual potential and tear them to shreds. Then the most remote areas of the colony cage were cleared of food and shelter and specially selected rats were herded into them and destroyed by every available means. We were unable to establish on what principles this selection was carried out. Several hypotheses were proposed but none of them was confirmed by the subsequent development of the experiment. These exterminations happened in waves. A theory which explained one wave turned out to be unacceptable for the next. Things were complicated still further by the fact that the exterminators were themselves exterminated in their turn. Simultaneously other processes took place in the rat colony, for which it has hitherto been impossible to find a satisfactory explanation. For instance, some areas which the experimenters had provided liberally with food were surrounded by detachments of rats and the food was destroyed. Other sectors, where there was no food, were converted into special feeding points. They were provided with the most miserable left-overs, and the rat population was given an opportunity of getting food in a savage battle with one another. But perhaps the most striking phenomenon was this: all the observation windows were progressively covered in rat dung, and the possibilities of observation were greatly reduced. Zones deep in the centre of the colony were specially created to be inaccessible to any observation. What happened in these areas we could judge only on circumstantial evidence: the huge number of corpses thrown out over the partitions, streams of blood which flowed out from below the partitions, constant and inordinate demands for food, and so on.

But our forecasts of the inevitable end of the colony turned out to be ill-founded. The fact that the experiment lasted several decades is eloquent testimony to that. As early as three years into the experiment, quite accurate calculations showed that the population of the colony had almost doubled (rather than being reduced by half as we expected) although the number of violently exterminated individuals persistently rose. And when suddenly this extermination fell sharply (again for hitherto unknown reasons—at times it almost stopped altogether—but then it began again, so there is no foundation for speaking of it as a temporary phenomenon) the growth of the population of the colony immediately declined. Another strange fact was that the level of food consumption per head rose noticeably, while the population grew and the supply of food to the colony remained static or was even reduced.

What is truth?

'Of course,' Careerist said, 'there have been some distortions. But they are not the most important thing. There have been successes too. And there were very many more of those. And these successes were achieved thanks to the Boss; you have to be brave enough to admit that.' 'These successes may have been achieved under Him,' said Slanderer, 'but in spite of, not because of, Him.' 'It's not true that they were due to Him, nor is it true that they were despite Him,' said Chatterer. 'It's not even true to say that He was involved in any way. Only one thing is true: they happened under Him, in His time. Just think about these expressions: "due to", "despite", and "participation". What do they mean? The first means the following: "If He had not existed, things would have been worse." The second: "If He had not existed, things would have been better." The third: "If He had not existed, things would have been different." The general logical construction of these expressions is: "If X had not existed, Y would have occurred." But these expressions in their turn are only the reduction or the substitution of the following expressions: (1) In reality X existed; (2) There are two expressions A and B such that the facts indicated in the expressions X and Y are respectively elements of the compounds A and B (or are respectively particular cases of A and B); (3) The assertion "If not A, then B" is true. Without this assertion, it is impossible to verify your assertions. Can such an assertion be obtained? In order to do this, you will need to repeat the past at least once more with certain variations. Wouldn't you wish to re-live what you have already lived through, for the love of truth, of course, but this time without Him? No? You're right, it's not worth it. In His place there would be another Him. And much the same thing would happen. If there were no Him at all, there would be no repetition of the situation. There would be no rule any more.' 'I can't argue with you,' said Slanderer. 'These are just logical tricks. And we are talking about life.' 'But we are talking,' said Chatterer. 'So we can't get by without logical tricks if we're trying to find the truth.' 'Everything must be told as it was,' said Slanderer. 'Nothing must be hidden.' 'But what are your criteria to distinguish between what must be said and what must not be said?' asked Chatterer. 'It's not possible to say absolutely everything. Say that you were allowed two volumes to tell everything that really happened. What would you write about? Deviations? Successes? In what proportion? Slanderer would insist on one proportion, Schizophrenic on another, Colleague and Sociologist on a third, and so on. Which of these is the true one?' 'Everyone must have their say,' said Slanderer, 'including the victims.' 'By definition the victims aren't able to have their say,' said Chatterer. 'Well, let others say it for them,' said Slanderer. 'Who?' asked Chatterer. 'And who will invite them to do it? Our kind leaders? Chance? Trickery? Favourable circumstances?' 'We're back where we started again,' said Slanderer. 'It looks as if any conversation on this subject is pointless.' 'No,' said Chatterer. 'Forgive me, but I have to end this conversation with a most banal lesson. Conversations about the past, in situations like this, have real meaning only when a lesson for the future is drawn from the past. The portion of truth in situations like this which are insoluble from a logical point of view is determined by the kind of lesson that you want to draw from the past. If we do not exclude the possibility of a return to the past, if we're afraid of the responsibility or if we fear the slightest accusation, we say: "Thanks to Him", "He played a positive part", "It can't be denied that He . . ." and so on. If we do not want there to be a return to the past, then we say: "In spite of Him", "Do not forget that . . ."and so on. And of course there are possible variants. In cases like this impartiality is only a means of disguising evil intentions or fear.'

A conversation with Theoretician

Soon after the confrontation with Hog, almost the highest theoretician in the land invited Dauber to go and see him. Dauber walked into the huge office and spotted a little man spinning round and round in his executive chair. The little man threw a bundle of letters on to the desk. 'So, you pervert young boys and girls,' he shouted in place of a greeting. 'How do you know that?' asked Dauber. 'Read for yourself,' said Theoretician. 'Anonymous letters?' asked Dauber. 'Anonymous letters,' said Theoretician. 'I never read anonymous letters,' said Dauber. They had a long conversation which was mutually incomprehensible. Theoretician, as the rules laid down, had the last word. 'Now,' he said, 'I think you clearly understand that you must immediately disarm yourself and cut yourself off from your friends.'

The main mistake

According to Chatterer, the principal mistake that Claimant and Thinker made was to have a studied, infallible programme of action, since in the matter to which this programme applied, any programme of any kind was in principle counter-indicated. The C/T programme comprised two parts—one part, which was secret and inchoate, and was absolutely clear to them as to everyone else, and the other part, which was open and constantly trumpeted abroad, and which neither they nor anybody else could understand at all. This is what the secret part consisted of. Firstly, wherever possible but never in writing, Secretary, or his colleagues and his lackeys, had to be discredited as a monstrous product of the Boss's regime, as a threat to the winds of change which were beginning to blow, as reactionaries, boors and idlers. Secondly, Slanderer and all other people of that kind had to be ignored, silenced and suppressed, but two or three articles unmasking their gross theoretical error should be published. Thirdly, an appropriate political error was to be found and unmasked in such a way that everyone would know about it, but that nothing should be published. With this in mind, attention was to be paid to the Wall Newspaper, since these hooligans from Slanderer's group were getting ready for something. They were not to be stopped. Just let them overreach themselves. Secretary and his henchmen of course would not take the risk of getting involved. Their reputation was tarnished, and they did not understand what it was all about. It would be no bad thing if these hooligans had a go at Secretary himself. That would get Secretary into trouble, nothing easier for them. And at the same time it would bring them back on course.

The open part of the C/T programme comprised these elements. A close and correct (not incorrect, as previously) contact with the natural sciences was to be established. To this end, the Journal was regularly to publish articles by outstanding scientists (i.e. scientists long senile) on the general problems of modern science (i.e. dreary waffle about problems a hundred years old). Secondly, close contact was to be established with construction practice. This would involve the regular publication of articles by top industrialists (i.e. the articles would have to be written for them, but their signatures would have to be authentic and original). Thirdly, the theoretical and professional standard of articles would have to be raised (i.e. maximum use of incomprehensible expressions, foreign names, obscure sentences and meaningless rhetoric). The concealed aim of this open part of the programme was childishly transparent: it sought to win the support of various bodies, to obtain complete independence from their colleagues, and to become indispensable to the highest authorities. But all this played no part, for it did not exist as an official fact.

Thinker met Puss and they reached agreement on an article on the relationship between science and ideology. He advised him to take a look at Slanderer's latest book. Of course there was to be no question of tearing it to shreds, but there was no harm in writing a perfectly straightforward review—particularly as Slanderer had said many silly things. The Wall Newspaper came out and was very successful. Claimant immediately found in it what he wanted and telephoned Assistant. The Newspaper was removed. A special commission was set up including Claimant. The names of the candidates for the post of

Director were published. Claimant was third on the list. This did not disturb him for he knew that the two ahead of him were to be excluded. The first one wanted the job but would not be allowed to go; the second did not want the job but he would not be allowed to arrive. As for the others, they would need a little working over. Incidentally Puss's article (which ought to come out soon) would have to point out that one of the competitors had passed Slanderer's book for publication, another was the editor responsible for it, and the third had even quoted from it.

The rats

From the beginning, read Chatterer, we discovered a quite remarkable phenomenon, namely a duality of behaviour in individual rats. We called one of these aspects the social aspect, the other, the official aspect. The relationship between these aspects is defined by the following principles. The official principle is the generally recognised form of the social principle. The official principle is . . .

Chatterer felt that he'd read something like this somewhere before, but couldn't remember where. For example, he read further on, the leader of a rat group cannot in social terms have an intellectual potential higher than the potential of the group, and in official terms, he may not be more stupid than the group. Because of a tendency for the social and the official to correspond, there is also a tendency towards the lowering of the group's intellectual potential. Many cases were recorded where, literally in the space of a few months, the intellectual potential plunged very steeply, dropping even below the threshold norm, which led in the end to catastrophic results.

Robots

The series 'Robots' shows transformations of the human body and combinations of parts of human bodies, parts of animals, and technical constructions. The theme of the series is the struggle within man of the spiritual and the animal, the natural and the urban. Schizophrenic said that this was rather vague. Your monsters are no accident. And they do not come from the mind, but from somewhere in the stomach and even the intestines. What exactly was the era of the Boss? continued Schizophrenic. Was it mass terror? General jubilation? The collapse of agriculture? An industrial boom? The collapse of culture? Out-standing successes? Despair? Joy? What exactly happened? Mistakes? Crimes? Plans of genius? What? Whatever you like. But that's not the main thing. The main thing is that this period brought to life a new type of social individual and a system of social relationships in accordance with the nature of that indi-vidual. The individual who appeared was a head taller than a man, but he had a tiny little head (or none at all) and a heart which was empty (or made of stone). Your 'Robots' are an exact portrait of this individual. He is not Michelangelo's 'David', nor is he Rodin's 'Thinker', as he is officially represented, but exactly your 'Robots'. And if we talk about the subject of 'Robots', then to be accurate we must say that it is the struggle within man of the anti-human against the human, and moreover a struggle in which the human suffers crushing defeats and is condemned to suffer. 'That sounds fine,' said Chatterer. 'And it is true. But I would have preferred some-thing simpler. For example—"Sketches from Nature".'

Personality

'Man is an animal who may combine any number of qualities,' said Chatterer. 'In order to become a social being (a citizen), a man should look into himself and not oppose himself. In order to become a personality, a man should have an external model which strikes his imagination, an unconscious desire to grow to be like that model, to overcome fear and to accomplish an action which professes his assimilation to the model. Despite more or less regular thrashings, the life of the intellectuals of Ibansk flowed by fairly peacefully and sometimes even happily until along came Truth-teller and began to ask everyone "Who are you?". Those who heard that question went off by different paths. The majority of them turned into citizens, and very few into personalities. At least potentially.' 'But surely isn't it pos-sible to be a citizen and a personality simultaneously?' asked Scientist. He was supported by Careerist, Neurasthenic and Dauber. 'It is obvious that Chatterer is just indulging in verbal pirouettes. The question's not even worth debating. But we're going to have to debate it, since we aren't talking about just words. What precisely do we mean by a citizen?' asked Dauber. 'And what is a personality?' 'A citizen,' said Careerist, 'lives from the interests of the common task. He is concerned about the interests and prestige of the state. He is a patriot.' 'Excellent!' said Chatterer when the argument had reached maximum confusion. 'Let us apply your ideas in practice. Is the Leader a citizen? A personality? And what about Truth-teller? Or Dauber? Let's leave words in peace. I've often remarked on the fact that our language, which was formed under the influence of Ibanskian literature of the last century, and of Western culture also mainly from past ages, needs a fundamental overhaul to allow us to discuss our contemporary problems in more or less rigorously defined terms and to have a chance of understanding each other a little. And this isn't trivial. The state of the language is some indication of the state of a society's spiritual culture.

'The problem is,' Chatterer continued after the argument had again risen to a peak and then died away because of a purely linguistic barrier, 'the problem is that we need to be able to distinguish between the state, the law, morality and so on as manifestations of and a defence of the anti-social, and the same institutions as manifestations and a defence of the social. Certainly, there is always a mixture in reality. But all the same we can see more or less distinct forms. It is only in the former case that we can talk about a so-called society of citizens in which the concepts of citizen and personality coincide. In the second case we see a divergence. Sometimes this divergence can reach the point where any significant personality is anti-citizen. So it is not by chance that we argue so much about whether such and such of our leaders was an outstanding personality or not. The arguments never lead to any result because the concepts we use are so ambiguous and the problems are on many different planes. Fame, popularity, a high position, participation in important historical events (wars, treaties, discoveries and so on) and other factors exclude the possibility of employing general expressions and values which were current in the past.'

Scientist said that the problems they were discussing could hardly be resolved scientifically, since the parameters were not sufficiently stable or measurable. 'Say for example we were talking about the measurement of personality. How can its parameters be measured?' Chatterer said that there were various means of research, and appropriate methods had to be found or invented. You were talking about the measurement of personality? Well, there are significant indicators. And they can be used one way or another in factual evaluations. For example, a strong personality tries as far as possible to refrain from regulating the destinies of others if there is no necessity. An insignificant personality tries to constrain other people's wills so as to appear strong himself. A strong personality strives towards simplicity and truth. The insignificant personality strives to deceive and confuse so as to appear a wise and complex man. If you work over these truths scientifically, you will arrive at a theory for the measurement of personality.' 'What use would that be?' asked Careerist. 'If it did nothing else,' said Chatterer, 'it would convince you that the Boss was a personality of total insignificance, wholly fitted to the society which threw him up.'

The rats

We will introduce the concept of the social individual, read Chatterer, without which no theoretical generalisation is possible. We will use the term social individual to mean a separate rat, a group of rats, a combination of groups and even an entire rat colony which is relatively speaking enclosed. This enclosure is also found in natural conditions provided that each rat colony is segregated by strictly defined boundaries. The movement of rats from one colony to another is severely punished by special groups of rats from both sides and is allowed only in the most strictly defined cases. Individuals are divided into simple and complex. A simple individual is one rat on its own, the complex individual is the group. But they have characteristics in common. Every normal individual has an organ with which . . .

Why is all this so familiar? thought Chatterer. Where have I read it all? And suddenly he remembered Schizophrenic.

Extracts from Slanderer's book

If we want to define sufficiently accurately and completely the particularities of modern ideological formations, wrote Slanderer, we must first examine, albeit on a very broad canvas, the social situation in modern science and the situation in scientific methodology, which forms a bridge between science and ideology, and certain purely phraseological peculiarities of scientific methodology, without which it is absolutely impossible to understand the textual aspect of ideological phenomena.

From this point of view, we must first of all bear in mind the fact that scientific activity is no longer exceptional; it has turned into a very run-of-the-mill mass phenomenon. In former times, scientists were isolated individuals; now there are hundreds of thousands of them, maybe even millions. In the past the word 'scientist' indicated certain personality traits. Now it sounds a little humorous and is being progressively overtaken by the expression 'research worker' which indicates a widespread profession. In the past the word 'scientist' conjured up associations of an educated and talented man. Now words like 'illiterate' and 'untalented' are used no less often of scientists than they are of artists or writers. Formerly a scientist was often a man valued for his ideas and discoveries. Today the worth of a scientist is often measured by the number of works he has published, by his degrees and titles, and basically by the jobs he holds. Because of the division of labour, the simple and sometimes even primitive intellectual standard needed for the great majority of people engaged in scientific work is ever more clearly seen. The work of the scientist has diminished in prestige compared with its level in even the most recent past. Yet to become a great scientist it is now necessary to have a higher level of intellectual development and to have contributed significantly to science, or, on the other hand to be a successful career builder. So to rise to the ranks of the major scientists purely on the basis of scientific discoveries is now more difficult than it was in the past. The social structure of scientific research means that people who are engaged on administrative work or who have managerial posts often use the talents and intellectual work of scientific researchers. All this establishes a very particular moral and psychological climate in science which is far removed from those idyllic pictures one finds in even the most critical and damning novels and memoirs of the science of the past.

Modern science is not a sphere of human activity whose participants are engaged only in the search for truth. Science contains not only the scientific principle—indeed, it may not contain much at all of the scientific principle as such, which is not at all similar to science in the generally accepted sense—but also an anti-scientific principle which is deeply hostile to the scientific principle, but which appears to be a great deal more scientific than the scientific principle itself. Alas, that is the way the world is made. Here everything has two aspects and is turned inside out. The scientific and anti-scientific principles are diametrically opposed. The scientific principle produces abstractions, the anti-scientific principle destroys them on the grounds that such and such has not been considered. The scientific principle establishes strict concepts, the anti-scientific principle makes them ambiguous on the pretext of thus revealing their true variety. The scientific principle avoids the use of materials which can be done without. The anti-scientific principle strives to bring in everything which can be brought in on any pretext. The scientific principle strives to derive simplicity and clarity out of the complex and confused. The anti-scientific principle seeks to confuse the simple and to make what is obvious incomprehensible. The scientific principle seeks to establish the normality of everything that appears abnormal. The anti-scientific principle seeks for sensation; it seeks to invest normal phenomena with an aura of mystery and enigma. Indeed, initially the scientific and anti-scientific principles, by other names of course, are regarded as equal facets of a unified science but later the anti-scientific principle gains the upper hand in much the same way as weeds smother the cultivated plants if the ground is not constantly hoed. Within the framework of science as a whole, the scientific principle is assigned a miserable second-class role. It is only tolerated as far as it supports the anti-scientific principle. There is a tendency to drive it completely away from science because it provokes a nagging of the conscience. All this is a typical case of the struggle between the social and the anti-social. The scientific principle represents an element and a means of the anti-social, while the anti-scientific principle is a brilliant expression of the social. So when we base our hopes on the civilising role of science, we commit a grave error. Science is a mass phenomenon, which itself is wholly and completely controlled by the social laws and only in insignificant degree contains the scientific principle (i.e. only in an insignificant degree contributes to the anti-social), while in conditions of the purely social, the element of the scientific principle in science tends towards zero.

The rats

The qualities of social individuals can be divided into negative and positive. An example of the former is intelligence. An example of the latter is stupidity. We want to draw your attention to the fact that . . .

Claimant's birthday

Claimant's birthday celebration was conceived as a unification of all the forces of the Ibanskian liberal thinking intelligentsia. The dinner followed its normal course. They ate. They drank. They proposed toasts. Claimant held forth incessantly. Sociologist tried to shout louder than him, and Wife louder than Sociologist. Then Claimant got drunk and went off in a corner with Thinker and Dauber. The company split up into little groups. In one of these, a restless little fellow who tried to look younger than he actually was, and who was the closest friend of all the leading Ibanskian personalities, started on a flow of interesting tales about the Chinese. He even told the well-known story of the grammatical error which had led to tens of thousands of Chinese having their heads cut off instead of their pigtails. Everyone knew it, but he told it so well that everyone laughed delightedly. On the same subject, Careerist said that in England once he had been at a reception given by a famous mathematician (and he mentioned a name celebrated round the world). There were all kinds of celebrities there, including an Ibanskologist known to all of you. He was talking about certain events in the past of Ibansk which are all now erased and forgotten. One lady exclaimed, 'My God! If they go on like that they'll all kill each other off very soon!' The mathematician asked the Ibanskologist for some empirical data, and plunged into some complex calculations. Half an hour later, by which time everyone had forgotten about this conversation, the mathematician announced that according to his calculations, it would take the people of Ibansk a hundred years to kill each other off. At first everyone was amazed, and then they all burst out laughing. After Careerist had finished his story there was a brief uneasy silence, which was quickly followed by laughter. 'But it's true,' Thinker said, 'that they look at us in the same way that we look at the Chinese.' 'There's one difference,' said Careerist, 'and that's what I said to those English people. The story about those Chinese from antiquity is not a fact which affects our life here today. But what that Ibanskologist told those English people is a fact of their own life. And it's such a serious fact, that there's a great deal about their life that can't be understood if that fact is ignored. And these cretins are unable to understand that.'

Another group was discussing Slanderer and Schizophrenic. Neurasthenic said that Schizophrenic was writing a completely lunatic thesis in the currently fashionable style of sensational revelations. Of course, there was nothing very specific in it. But it could cause trouble just the same. And it wouldn't be as easy for Sociologist to save Schizophrenic this time as it was last. 'That's right,' said Wife. 'If it hadn't been for Sociologist, Schizophrenic would have been kaput. And it seems that Slanderer's completely played out, gone to pieces. There was a time when he didn't write at all badly, and gave interesting lectures. But now it seems that he's got nothing left to say. Well, time passes and criteria change. Young people nowadays are very talented and better educated than they used to be. By the way, one of Thinker's articles has been translated Over There. And one of my pamphlets, too. Some people have said that it's too much of a popularisation, but all the same, I've managed. . . .' Puss said that he had begun to work on a very complex and important subject. It was the kind of thing that needs years of thought. But the publishers insisted that it should be ready for the press in a month. That's just not a serious approach! It's not quite the same thing as digging a hole! Over There they just dash off any old thing, and they haven't the faintest idea of . . . That article of mine that was translated. . . . Yes, into English. . . . It was a good article. . . . Actually, it's not every day that you'll read a thing like that . . . I spent two years on it. . . . That's why it's such first-class work.

At this moment, the word went round that Assistant was coming. Claimant sobered up in a second. Puss came out in red blotches and went to the lavatory just in case. They all rose to their feet and spent the next two hours standing rigidly to attention, little finger along the trouser seam, holding their breath and awaiting the arrival of the distinguished visitor. When he turned up, he was only just looking in, but he stayed until the small hours. He refused a proper meal, and just ate a goose stuffed with apples, a Pekin duck, a jar of black caviar, a jar of red caviar, a slice of roast veal, a shashlik and a great deal else besides. He drank a glass of vodka, a glass of brandy, three bottles of beer, another glass of brandy and another of vodka. Simultaneously he lobbed into the ever-open mouths of those who hovered religiously around him such a collection of banalities that Wife's phrase 'Among that lot Claimant stands out like a white raven', which she had once uttered in an access of civil courage, after downing a third glass, lost all its feeling of comedy and assumed a tragic aspect. Finally, Assistant (a great politician, whatever else you say about him, Puss later remarked) announced good news for all. Claimant had been accorded a high honour for bringing out twelve jubilee editions of the Journal containing one hundred and twenty jubilee articles. Thinker had been awarded an honour as well, not as high as Claimant's, but still high. After that everyone began to wink knowingly at each other. Not bad that! Thinker does all the work himself, while all Claimant does is hang about in anterooms and sit on platforms. Ah well, that's life, said Thinker gloomily. Claimant and Thinker (and everyone else, invited and uninvited) had been aware that these awards were on the way (indeed, between ourselves, that's why this party had been arranged) but they were still both surprised and encouraged by the news. It was now completely clear to everyone that the question of who was to succeed Director had already been resolved. And so a relative peace could reign. But Wife warned that they must still be vigilant. 'We have won, that's beyond any doubt,' she said. 'But these bastards won't give up without a battle. We must be ready for anything from them.' 'If we'd described what we'd have to go through before . . .' said Claimant, 'we'd simply not have been believed.' 'No great cause is ever won without a struggle,' said Wife, shedding a tear. 'Hey, that's a good one' she thought to herself. 'I'd better write it down before someone pinches it.'

The rats
We can use the term social actions to describe those actions of individual rats or groups of rats which concern other individuals or groups, and which affect their interests in some way or another. These actions are premeditated (the rat individuals or

rat groups somehow weigh up the effect of their actions on other individuals), free (individual rats can perform them or not perform them), and egotistic (individual rats perform these actions in their own interests). At this point we must reject any identification of the awareness, freedom and self-interest of rats with analogous social actions in man. The awareness of social actions in man indicates that those actions have been thought out and evaluated from the point of view of historically acquired legal and moral (and perhaps other) criteria. The freedom of human actions indicates that mankind's existing social institutions and customary way of life guarantee the possibility of carrying out actions of various kinds (e.g. freedom of speech, freedom of conscience, freedom of movement). The value placed upon man's own interests implies that man will take account of the interests of others, and implies the discovery of the optimal variants of behaviour (agreements, mutual concessions, contracts, word of honour, and so on). There is nothing of this kind in the actions of rats, since they exclude evaluative criteria and institutions which have been built up historically and passed on from generation to generation, which are protected by society, and which alone have permitted human society to distinguish itself from animal societies and to undergo non-biological progress.

Chatterer's opinion

Neurasthenic said that he had foreseen this outcome. By and large, they had won. Now they would just share out the jobs. In general the question was decided. Chatterer said that that was nonsense, self-deception, illusion. Claimant and his gang were proclaiming their wishes for reality, and spreading rumours which were favourable to them. Rewards were of no importance. Nowadays everyone got awards. But all the same Claimant would not become Director. Chatterer's words were relayed to the competitors, to the envious and to the malcontents. Everyone knew that Chatterer was no fool, that he never spoke lightly. But no-one understood why he was so certain of what he was saying. His forecasts always came true, and his statement caused alarm. Thinker tried to pump first Neurasthenic and then Dauber as to where Chatterer got his information from. Dauber said that Chatterer never received any information, which was why he always spoke the truth. Neurasthenic said that for the moment *no-one* had any information. All that anyone had was suppositions. Yet the basis of Chatterer's certainty was very simple. And he did not conceal it.

'Claimant will not be promoted,' said Chatterer, and offered to take bets on it. 'Why? It's very simple. You believe that Claimant is a talented careerist, although totally insignificant as a scientist or as an author in general. I agree. But the fact of the matter is that a talented careerist in the circle of careerists is as rare a thing as a talented writer among the vast number of successful Ibanskian writers. But the most successful method of making a career in Ibanskian conditions, and this is certainly the method that has been chosen by that undoubtedly talented careerist Claimant, gives enormous advantages to the *un*-talented careerist. Even the Boss himself seized power and established his own system of power not because he was a genius at his own filthy business, but exclusively because even in that very business he was a total nonentity. He was completely fitted to that business as a person. The leader of rats cannot be a lion. The leader of rats can only be a rat.' All the colleagues heard what Chatterer had to say with interest. Some of them later told Thinker and Claimant what they had heard, others told Secretary and his mob, and yet others told Colleague and Instructor. Claimant suggested to Thinker that it might be worth publishing one of Chatterer's worthless little articles and so seal his lips. Thinker answered that he had already tried to talk to him, but that he wouldn't listen.

Extracts from Slanderer's book

Science does not have a direct influence on the ideology of a society. Its acts via scientific methodology, which sums up all the elements of science which are significant from the ideological point of view. But methodology itself is a product of society.

The last decades have seen the emergence of a great many bodies devoted to scientific methodology: groups, sectors, departments, divisions, seminars, conferences, symposiums, colloquiums, journals, reviews, associations, congresses and so on. A vast quantity of material has been written and published in accounts, reports, notes, articles and books. And an even greater quantity remains unwritten and unpublished in the feverishly thinking minds of men. Throughout all recorded history there has not been so much thinking and talking about methodology, nor so many pages written about it, as in the past few decades. In a word, methodology, like physical training, has become a mass phenomenon. This is regarded as a sign of the times: science has become so complex and difficult that without methodology it can develop no further, and scientists can now take no step ahead without first studying the methodology of that step. There is, of course, an element of truth in this. But more often people turn to the methodology of science for other reasons: they do not have at their disposal the factual data they would need for an ordinary experiment; they do not wish to take up science; they are bored with science; they have no talent for science and so on. All the rejects of science pour themselves into methodology from all those branches of science which have over the years become more or less mixed up with it. In a word it is possible to discern the reason for the astonishing spread of methodology not so much in epistemological difficulties, as in the social possibilities of turning the discussion of these problems into a source of income.

The literature of the methodology of science is growing at an alarming rate. But this is doing nothing to calm the brain-fever. This mass of publications, far from clarifying matters, has still further complicated not merely the solution of the problems, but also their formulation and their basic comprehension. And there is no attempt to dispose of this kind of difficulty. It is indeed cultivated. Specialists in problem-solving are yielding place to specialists in the relevant literature which does not go any way towards solving them. The attempt to understand someone else's opinion is yielding place to an active incomprehension, so that it is now impossible to give voice to a thought which will not be distorted by colleagues or rejected on some pretext or other.

It is difficult to name a single methodological term which has not been rendered meaningless by the efforts of specialists who have swamped it in ambiguity. If you try to discover what a 'cause' is (and you might think that there's no more widely used or commonplace term) you will be given dozens of incompatible answers.

The ambiguity of terminology is closely connected with a

new type of discussion of disputed problems. In theory, a scientific discussion should consist of some scientists putting forward certain clearly stated propositions, and other scientists contesting them. Precision of terminology, and hence a precise grasp of the sense of the propositions put forward, are essential conditions without which no such scientific discussion can take place. But in discussions of the new type the non-observance of these conditions is the very basis of the discussion. So there is the same degree of probability that these arguments should result in truth as there is that the coupling of a fox-terrier and a motorcycle should result in an elephant. Truth is lost in the argument.

From a science which in essence gave simple yet positive advice, methodology has become in essence a collection of critical works which give complex and purely negative refutations to any positive solution to a problem. And if the methodologists *do* produce any positive counsels, it is genuinely impossible to escape the comparison of their advice with that of the alchemists. Just as the alchemists cheerfully sold their formulae for the fabrication of gold, formulae which they themselves could never realise, so the methodologists cheerfully tell everyone how to make scientific discoveries, although they themselves have managed never to make any discoveries even in their own special fields. And what curious advice they give! There is a story that goes: 'How do you determine the sex of a hare? A biologist catches a hare and examines it. A methodologist releases the hare and watches it run off. "If it's a he—it's a male; if it's a she—it's a female."'

Naturally enough scientific methodology strives to keep up with the development of the concrete sciences and to be modern and forward-looking. But it does not do this by developing its own system of concepts and its own system of methodological principles of perception, but by assuming spontaneously the ideas, concepts and propositions of the concrete sciences and translating them into methodological phraseology. This in particular applies to new approaches to old problems, approaches which have become very fashionable recently. This is the approach based on systems, models, structures, functions, information. To get some idea of these generalising theories, the reader might try, for example, to construct a methodological theory of functions which would embody mathematical functions, a functional approach and the function of the trade unions in the textile industry. In the final analysis, the kaleidoscopic use of words like 'system', 'systematic', 'information', 'structure', 'functional', 'model', and so on, in the powerfully running tide of methodological literature, more often than not merely reflects the feel of the age, and not the results of serious research. Put briefly, in the field of scientific methodology the true motivation is no longer a disinterested search for truth, but a desire to occupy a cosier position among that enormous army of people who live off a small number of commonplace problems. This inflated interest in methodology, and the high-flown style of expression which methodology involves, coincides amazingly closely with the processes which one observes in science, and of which I have already spoken. One of the indicators of the psychological situation which has established itself in science is a longing for something out of the ordinary, something sublime. There is a longing for the work done by any average research worker to resemble the work of a Newton, a Galileo, an Einstein. There is a longing to clothe the prosaic labours of a rank-and-file scientific worker in the romantic garb of something extraordinarily difficult, and to preserve the idea of the exceptional nature of the scientist's work even if this means that its real worth has to be cloaked in mystery. It is as if the methodology of science has been specially invented to free scientists from this nostalgia for a position they have lost and to give them the consolation they so much long for. It reflects completely the inferiority complex of the average research student or doctor of science who has merely produced a few dozen original publications.

The rats

Individual rats form groups. Not all their groups can be considered social. For example, a gathering of rats round a crust of bread is not a social group. Similarly, rats who are fighting for the leadership, and the crowd of curious observers of this fascinating spectacle, do not constitute a social group. A social group consists of rats who have been forced into it by more or less constant conditions of their existence. It contains a stable division of functions, and primarily a division into a leading part and a led part. The leading part, unlike a simple individual, consists in this case of one rat or (in more complex formations) of a group of rats . . .

The prognostication is shown to be true

Newspapers, magazines, radio, television, books, articles, speeches, pictures, placards, films proclaimed the wisdom of Hog and the successes achieved under his wise leadership. 'It really would be a good moment to remove him,' said Chatterer. And that very night a new Leader was appointed, and Hog was removed. When, shortly after this, a certain foreign scientist learned that Chatterer knew Dauber personally, he asked him how that famous confrontation between Dauber and Hog had ended. 'Surely you must know,' said Chatterer, 'Hog's removal immediately followed.' Those present laughed heartily. As usual, Ibanskian tragedies had degenerated into grotesque farce.

The reference

'The man on whose initiative I went mad,' said Schizophrenic, 'is a typical paranoiac. He first latched on to me when we were students. He attacked me at every seminar, at every meeting. He wrote denunciation after denunciation. Everyone knows that. But no-one laid a finger on him. He is a useful man. He's a member of many committees.' 'It's always the same everywhere,' said Dauber. 'Just listen. I needed a character reference to go on a trip to Italy. The reference had to be passed by the Bureau. The Bureaucrat said that I was immoral, alcoholic and debauched. So, of course, I didn't get my reference and the trip fell through. It would have. Even if I had been given the reference, as has often happened since. But that's not the point. Literally six months before all this, the Bureaucrat had got involved in a dirty business. When he was drunk he picked up a prostitute down by the station, took her back to his studio and then refused to pay her. The girl managed to get his party card out of his pocket, took it off to the police and made a scene. The Bureaucrat should have received a severe dressing down, but he was let off with a fatherly warning.'

Inferno

By and large the critics held the same view about the engravings Dauber had done as illustrations to Dante's *Inferno*: they saw them as a representation of the life of man in modern society. 'But it's not clear to me,' said Chatterer, 'what kind of man they have in mind. Surely they can't see their happy existence as an inferno? I think that your *Inferno* is not about them, but about us. Or at least about us in the first place. As far as they're concerned, it's about them only insofar as they will come to it themselves sooner or later. Your *Inferno* is about the position of the creative person in our society. Or it might be more generally about the position of man in social conditions. And I would not call it a pessimistic hell. It is not a hell of repressed and terror-ised people. It is the hell of a strong and combative personality, a personality who is victorious despite his defeat. Or, of course, it could be that it's precisely the opposite. Your *Inferno* needs a text. But not Dante's text, another. But for the time being I do not clearly see precisely what text. I can merely discern its general shape.'

From Slanderer's book

A significant part of the methodological boom of our time is taken up by discussions about logic and discussions about everything imaginable using the language of logic. But the use of the language and principles of logic does not so much play the part of an effective method of problem-solving as one of pres-tige and camouflage. And, strangely enough, an ideological part. It is enough to utter the word 'implication' in a lecture theatre full of doctors of all kinds of science for a deathly hush to fall, and for everyone to freeze in the expectation of a miracle.

The diary of an artist's model

'Here,' said Dauber to Chatterer, 'read this. I can let you see it because you're a moral man.' Chatterer leafed through the school exercise book. It was a diary left behind by one of Dauber's models. 'It's a terrifying document,' said Dauber. 'I swear that it's all true.' The diary was made up of entries like this. 'Went to X's studio. Still young. Nice guy. On the table: vodka, sausage, oranges. He says: "Get undressed." I get undressed. He says "I fancy you." Had a drink. Had a fuck. Had another drink. Had another fuck.' After a few pages she's through with X. 'X is a bastard. He twisted me out of money. And he made me do some disgusting things. Went to Y. Still not old, although he's bald. On the table: brandy, sausage, tangerines. He says "Get undressed." I get undressed. He says I've got quite a nice shape. Had a drink. Had a fuck. . . .' 'That's all taken as normal in the artists' world,' said Dauber. 'And the models themselves accept it as the norm. They combine business with pleasure.' 'You say it's a terrifying document,' said Chatterer. 'Do you think it's any better outside the world of the artist? My present boss is a complete nonentity. Every year he changes his lab girls and secretaries. Then he finds them a job somewhere else, fires them, or helps them get another post. Not all of them, but nearly all. And they're all girls straight out of school. And nearly all of them got their jobs because he knows their families. Their parents must know what's going on. After all, there's nothing anyone can do about it. It's a stage that they're all going to have to go through. And they do get a certain benefit from it. It's got to the point where I'm afraid to go to work. It distresses me when I see these kids, and disgusts me at the same time. The girls think that they're building their lives as they want them to go, in the spirit of the times. But in fact they're playthings in someone else's dirty game. And there's nothing that anyone can do about it because officially it doesn't exist, it's all sewn up. Say a word about it publicly, and you'll be called a slanderer.'

Grandeur

Hog's denunciatory speech was something unprecedented in the history of Ibansk not because of its content (after all, in our country everything has been said), but by the formal mechanism by which he acted. Everything was correct. The mechanism worked correctly. But the result was not correct. Schizophrenic said that there was no paradox in that. It was simply that there was no cause and effect relationship between Hog's speech and the confusion of minds that followed. It was just a matter of coincidence and succession in time. The two phenomena were effects of the same cause. But the authorities had need of guilty people. Even a fool could see clearly who was guilty. Chatterer said that fools always saw everything clearly, but no one understood him.

But this analysis of the situation turned out to be premature. After Hog's removal from power he did not disappear into oblivion and disgrace as his predecessors had done, but on the contrary, became a figure more important than he had been even at the apogee of his power. He grew wiser and took on the appearance of a citizen. He publicly regretted that he had not pushed his denunciation to its conclusion, that he had not allowed all Truth-teller's books to be published. He also said in public that he had been mistaken in his judgment of Dauber's work and that he was interested in his life. As time went by his greater and lesser stupidities began to be forgotten. The name of Hog came to be associated with the two greatest developments in the history of Ibansk. One was the unmasking of the Boss and the rehabilitation of millions of victims. The other was an unprecedented broadening of cultural and economic links with the West. Then Hog died, and there occurred a third remarkable event: he was not buried in the Wall, as he merited from every point of view, but in the Old Whores' Cemetery beside the grave of some Director or other. When they decided on his burial place, the authorities had intended to deal a blow to Hog's prestige, but instead it was of great benefit to him. It put Hog in an exceptional position. If Hog had been buried in the Wall, the authorities would have recognised him as one of their own, but this recognition would have been a punishment in itself, for Hog would have been lost among the dozens of former leaders rendered insignificant by their very number. His burial in the Old Whores' Cemetery they regarded as a punishment and an exclusion from their ranks. But this punishment singled out Hog and raised him to eminence far better than all his own actions and any number of paeans of praise which our grandiose system uses to glorify those in power. Hog's tomb became a symbol and a place of homage. Thus was created a second holy place in Ibansk, a small and unofficial holy place compared with the grandiose and official one, but because of that, more human.

Extract from Slanderer's book

The multifarious media (radio, cinema, magazines, popular scientific literature, science fiction and so on) ensure that the mind of modern man of average education is stuffed full of scientific information. There is no doubt that this leads to a raising of the general level of knowledge. But at the same time this is accompanied by a faith in the omnipotence of Science, and Science itself acquires features very remote from its normal academic pattern. Scientific information which penetrates the minds of people does not fall on virgin soil, nor does it retain its primitive form. History has committed to modern man the ability to rethink on ideological grounds the information he receives, and he has a need to do so. Now society presents him with scientific information in such a form that the ideological effect becomes inevitable. Science merely provides the phraseology, the ideas and the themes. But the way in which this material is treated in men's minds does not depend on Science alone. It should suffice to say that Science is highly specialised, and that its results have meaning and are susceptible to proof only in a very specialised language. For mass consumption these results are translated into common language, with simplifications and explanations which create an illusion of clarity but which, as a rule, have nothing in common with the initial material. The achievements of Science are presented to the public by a particular kind of intermediaries, 'theoreticians' of a given science, popularisers, philosophers and even journalists. All these people comprise a huge social group with its own social functions, habits and traditions. Thus the achievements of Science arrive in the heads of ordinary people in such a professionally predigested form that only a certain verbal similarity with the basic material recalls where those achievements originated. They are seen in a manner quite different from the way in which they were regarded in the world of Science. And their role, too, becomes quite different. What we are seeing, properly speaking, is the creation of a kind of *doppelgänger*, parallel with the concept and the proposition of Science. A certain number of these *doppelgänger* become an element of ideology for a certain time, a time which may be long or short. Unlike the concepts and propositions of Science, which tend to be precise and verifiable, their ideological *doppelgänger* are imprecise, ambiguous, unprovable and irrefutable. From a scientific viewpoint they are meaningless. For instance, the assertions of the physical sciences about the wave properties and corpuscular properties of elementary particles, when taken out of physics and submitted to an ideological re-working, are turned into assertions embodying imprecise and ambiguous words like 'wave', 'corpuscle', 'simultaneously' and so on. These days we can prove that physical bodies cannot, as it were, be simultaneously waves and corpuscles, but on the other hand they can be so, in a way somewhere deep inside the material. That is a fairy story. But it is a fairy story intended not for children, but for educated adults who have a thirst for mysteries and enigmas. To be able to tell fairy stories of this kind requires an ability to manipulate language in delicate and complex ways; it requires a specialised training in physics and a certain facility in the methodology of Science.

Society puts people under pressure to express their respect for Science's ideological *doppelgänger*. It is for this reason that many propositions of the theory of relativity, at one time persecuted for heresy in their ideological incarnation, are today all but canonised. Any attempt to express anything which appears to disagree with them will be greeted by a rebuff from influential social forces (for example, by accusations of obscurantism, of reaction and so on).

Not all scientific truths are accorded the honour of having ideological *doppelgänger*; only those which are the most convenient. Thus one well-known theorem about the incompleteness of certain formal systems, and one which has sense in logic, is converted into a truism about the impossibility of completely formalising Science and becomes 'a self-evident truth', while another truth—about the existence of certain problems which are in essence insoluble—has been spared this fate, although a much greater number of similar sentiments could be derived from it. Here too there are disgraces and congratulations, rehabilitations and promotions, apparently all taking place within the framework of Science. But in the present case ideology longs to gain the appearance of a science.

The rats

Social relationships within a rat colony are respectively the relationship of individual rats to their group, of the group to the individual rat, of individual rat to individual rat within the group, of individual rat to individual rat outside the group compared with the relationships within the group, of the group to the colony as a whole, and of the colony as a whole to the individual rat. The relationship of the individual rat to the group can be defined thus . . .

The wall newspaper

When the people of Ibansk discovered (with, of course, the permission of the authorities) that the Chinese covered their walls and fences with placards carrying all kinds of criticisms or eulogies, called Da-Tsi-Bao, they went into hoots of laughter. Just like Barbarians! What else could you expect from the Chinese! The strange thing is that the Ibanskians somehow or other forgot that they themselves had these very same Da-Tsi-Bao plastered on the walls of every institution. The only difference was that in Ibanskian they were called wall newspapers. The reason for this lapse of memory is plain. People had got so used to wall newspapers that they had long since ceased to pay any attention to them, and so for the average Ibanskian they virtually no longer existed. And yet wall newspapers are an essential element in the life of Ibansk. If they fail to appear, someone has to answer for it. They come out regularly for every festival, every important jubilee and for re-election meetings. In the same way that all Ibanskian newspapers are alike and can be distinguished only by their title, all Ibanskian wall newspapers are alike and can be distinguished only by the walls on which they're plastered. They can be distinguished from proper newspapers only by their method of production (they are either typed or hand-written), by their print number (one single copy), and by their frequency of appearance.

Such a wall newspaper came out even in the Institute. And there, like everywhere else, no-one paid the slightest attention to it from one re-election meeting to another, at which point the old editorial board, which usually included half the workers, (the painters to do the headlines and slogans, draw portraits and paste in pictures cut from magazines; representatives of every subdivision to put the articles together; representatives of every organisation to check them; appropriate people to edit the wall newspaper's sections on 'production', 'culture', 'youth', 'sport' and the like; suitable people, selected in high places, to occupy the post of editor, of five assistant editors and twelve observers to supervise the work of the various sections; appropriate people, who knew how to write verse and compose long slanderous diatribes, to work as poets, feature writers and columnists and thus ensure the necessary sharpness of criticism and self criticism which, as is well known, are the driving force of Ibanskian society), this old editorial board would be re-appointed for a new term because they had fulfilled their responsibilities so well. The Institute would have gone on with the familiar wall newspaper *Ibanskian Thinker* were it not for a wind of change which had blown as high as the fifth floor where the Institute was housed. But the wind of change blew as high as it did despite the fact that from time immemorial the lift had been out of service for repairs, condemning those workers whom age and idleness had rendered obese and stupid to a whole new set of fashionable Western diseases—heart failure, cancer, cerebral thrombosis, dyspepsia, paranoia, and so on. It was then that all the liberals, the demagogues, the bawlers and the young hooligans of the Institute checked and rechecked everything at every level of management, convinced themselves of the rightness of their general line, and brought out the famous and fateful number of the *Ibanskian Thinker*.

A crowd of workers immediately gathered around the paper. 'Well, well,' some said, 'it's straight from the shoulder this time!' 'What a scandal!' said others, 'that's really going too far!' 'Ha, ha!' said yet others, 'they've scored a bull's-eye this time!' Yet others smiled enigmatically and began to ponder the denunciations that they planned to send off immediately to various authorities. Others again, convinced that this had nothing to do with them, sighed with relief and nonchalantly returned to their places of work (or more accurately, places of non-work). And yet another group, observing that they had been attacked in the paper, rushed off to the office to complain that their image had been distorted and their dignity deeply insulted. In other words something indescribable had happened to the paper. Claimant forced his way through the crowd, skimmed through the editorial, glanced at the silhouette of Teacher, shown sniffing a spray of lilac against the background of a television mast and an elevated railway bridge, at the articles from the 'Production section' and various socio-cultural sections, and finally lit upon his own face, distorted almost

(225)

beyond recognition in the section of satire and humour. He was prepared for anything, but not for that. Claimant was depicted at a meeting of the editorial board in the persona of Louis XIV, with the other members (even Thinker!) shown as pawns. Thinker was shown as a rather larger pawn. Beneath the caricature was a caption written in Ibanskian but transcribed into Latin characters.

Here's the truth, it's plain to see,
The Journal, well, the Journal's me.

The cartoon was completely accurate, for Claimant, as everyone knew, made a point of never paying any attention to the opinion of his subordinates. That, of course, was nothing of any consequence, and his subordinates fully merited this treatment. But at a time when everyone everywhere was talking openly about the re-establishment of legality and democracy, it was a blow below the belt. 'T-r-r-raitors!' hissed Claimant, 'Now just you wait!' Within fifteen minutes the paper had been torn from the wall. Within half an hour an extraordinary commission had been set up under the chairmanship of Assistant. Claimant was not a member of the commission, but played first fiddle in the wings. That evening, all the leaders of the liberal tendency met in Sociologist's apartment. After the guests had sat down at the table covered as usual with rare dishes from the specially reserved shop, and Colleague, who had been held up at a private meeting, eventually appeared, Claimant stood up, raised his glass of Ibanskian vodka imported from abroad and said: 'A group of irresponsible hooligans from the clique headed by Slanderer, Chatterer and Schizophrenic have committed a vile betrayal of our common interest in our common Task.' Treason, treason, treason . . . echoed round the table from the masticating jaws . . . treason, treason, treason . . .

The rats

The problem of leader-rats is central in ratology since it is the problem of the nature of the social group of any given rat society. In principle the leader corresponds to his group from a social point of view ('Show me the priest, I'll show you the parish'). There are exceptions but . . .

For the cause

After the replacement of Hog by the new Leader, and naturally of the old Theoretician by the new one, this latter expressed a wish to meet Dauber. The meeting took place and the conversation gave Dauber some new hope. True, not for long. In the waiting-room he met Claimant, who had just been appointed to a new post, and who immediately told Dauber all the thoughts which he intended to propound higher up. 'Now it's all going to warm up,' he said, with genuine enthusiasm. 'We're going to publish Schizophrenic, Slanderer, Chatterer, Thinker, Wife, Neurasthenic and all the serious characters who aren't stupid. We've wasted enough time! We really must get down to it!' Dauber told Thinker about this encounter. Thinker pulled a long face and said: 'How can you talk to that skunk. He's nothing but a turd. A sly, hypocritical turncoat. There's no believing a word he says. I know the likes of him.' 'But he seemed sincere enough to me,' said Dauber. 'What do you expect?' said Thinker angrily. 'He always is sincere in what he does because he always gets himself into a position to be sincere. All he was doing was rehearsing for you the speech he prepared for Theoretician.' 'But what do you mean?' said Dauber with surprise, 'you're a friend of his!' 'That's beside the point,' said Thinker, 'I have to do that for the good of the Cause.'

'It's a strange friendship all the same,' Dauber said later to Chatterer. 'What does he get out of it? He leads a pretty miserable existence!' That depends on the point of view you take,' said Chatterer. 'He didn't have an Ibansk residence permit. Claimant helped him get one, and an apartment. He left this apartment to his ex-wife. And in return for his merits (what merits?) he was then given a good single room in a decent flat. Just think what that means in our conditions. For nearly twenty years Slanderer has been paying ridiculous prices for every sort of garret and maid's room. Now Thinker's upset because other people have got flats. And why doesn't he chip in for a co-operative apartment? No way, he wants one free! Mark my words, he'll soon get one. On top of that he takes the chair at nearly half the meetings of the editorial board. He sits at the head of the table and leads the discussion. He makes intelligent remarks. He has the last word. For a vain man that's not doing too badly. And then he's able to print his own rubbish regularly! And all those references to his own lousy books which would never appear in other circumstances! And those business trips abroad! And there are a lot of people who would give half their lives to appear on television as he did recently. No, my dear Dauber, he gets a lot from his friendship with Claimant. A great deal. And he has a panic fear of losing all that. He's bright enough to see that he's not going to be allowed any higher, and that's why he's trying to get as much as he can without being noticed, and to preserve the appearance of respectability. And Claimant gets something from him too, or rather thinks that he does. Claimant is a cretin, and he's got so used to thinking of everyone else as cretins that he's got into a state where he imagines that Thinker is irreplaceable as camouflage, while in reality people like him are legion. As soon as Claimant realises that, he'll throw him out. And the more so since Thinker is already beginning to compromise him in the eyes of the authorities. Theoretician said somewhere in passing that Claimant was a good enough kind of fellow, but that the people around him, and Thinker in particular, were very dubious indeed.'

Extract from Slanderer's book

One of the most curious features of the vulgarisation of the achievements of science and of scientific methodology is the attempt to pass off concrete scientific discoveries not only as a revolution in the understanding of some particular field of scientific activity, but also as a sensational revolution in the logical bases of science as a whole. Sometimes this is done directly, with the statement about the unsuitability of the 'old' rules of logic in some new field of science. For instance, it's become almost a prejudice in some circles to consider that microcosms need logic of a totally different kind to macrocosms. Sometimes it is done indirectly, by criticising as false and outmoded the commonsense of ordinary people who are not party to the great secrets of modern science. But essentially all this is speculation on the fact that the language in which scientific discoveries are discussed is ill-fitted to this purpose from the point of view of logic. This is truest of all as regards modern physics. This has produced an enormous literature whose direction is quite clearly defined. While in its time fulfilling its noble role of defending and disseminating new ideas in physics, this literature has at the same time pursued its own egoistical aims, which have had an adverse effect on its intellectual level, particularly after the point where these ideas of physics no longer needed to be defended and had indeed acquired a truly Chaplinesque fame. The desire to impress the reader at whatever cost, to force him to believe that the objects of the microcosm, of space and time, and so on have properties inconceivable for ordinary commonsense, has become a condition of its existence and a *leitmotif* of this literature. For instance, space is said to have acquired the ability to compress and to extend itself, to deform itself and to re-form. To time is ascribed the capacity to move (to move more slowly or more quickly, backwards and forwards). But the literature passes over in silence the fact that all these properties are normal from the point of view of commonsense. And if commonsense protests when it hears them ascribed to space and time, this is not because commonsense is uneducated and conservative, but because, even at the most primitive level of commonsense, it is clear that space and time have within them something which prevents them being regarded as empirical objects which can be felt, compressed, stretched out, broken and so on, and that this something is a series of tacit agreements about the meaning of the linguistic expressions employed, and the rules of logic, which linguistic practice has to a certain extent assimilated. They are all tricks played with the concepts of space and time which have been used for many years to excite the imagination of readers, and which are based on the imprecision and ambiguity of accepted expressions and also on the change of meaning which they have been made tacitly to undergo. These are merely tricks of the language which is used in talking about space and time. A science whose language corresponds with logical standards cannot come into conflict with ordinary commonsense if this latter is regarded as a combination of genuine affirmations of empirical experience plus certain rules of logic which people have assimilated in one way or another. Verbal manipulations on 'the latest achievements of science' and a complete disdain for the logical foundations of terminology, built up as an ever deeper penetration into the essence of the microcosm, of space or time, and so on, that is the other aspect of the realisation of the good intentions of the literature we are considering. This kind of methodological literature proliferates equally in other specialised scientific fields. And that is ideology.

All these speculations on the logical imperfections of the language and linguistic tricks are not made by chance. Nowadays there is no further capacity for astonishment at discoveries made in the physical sciences. People have got used to them. But no-one can ever get used to scientific 'revolutions', which are in conflict with logic. A fact which is logically impossible, but of which the authoritative magicians of science assert that it is happening according to the latest scientific discoveries, is seen as a miracle by the highly developed culture of the twentieth century. It is difficult, of course, to believe that several thousand people could be fed with five loaves. But to believe that the impossible can be accomplished, that the unrepeatable can be repeated, the irreversible can be reversed and so on, that takes long and patient study. Moreover scientific discoveries themselves seem surprising only to specialists properly so-called, who in most cases do not understand the true meaning of their discoveries. Taken as it is, the world is grey and simple. The complexity of the world is nothing but an accumulation and confusion of simple things. The world does not contain any mystic secrets. These have to be brought in from outside.

The gravestone

In his will Hog asked that Dauber should make his gravestone. Everyone thought that Dauber would refuse. Everyone reckoned that Dauber should refuse. Slanderer, who went to the funeral, and put some flowers on the grave (actually not on the grave itself because it was impossible to get to it because of all the secret policemen present, but symbolically, not far away), told Dauber that he must make the gravestone. Dauber said that he had already made his mind up firmly on the matter. 'I might do myself harm by agreeing, and so I can't refuse. And secondly, it will be the revenge of art against politics.'

'Hog's wish that Dauber should make his gravestone,' said Chatterer, 'is an historic event. Centuries will pass. People will forget about space flights and hydro-electric stations. But in the history of our times this fact will figure alongside wars and revolutions. But they won't let you erect the gravestone.' 'Why not?' asked Dauber. 'Because, first of all, a Hog plus a Dauber equals a Double-Hog, and a Dauber plus a Hog is a Double-Dauber. A great political phenomenon plus a great artistic phenomenon would together produce the most important and durable sight in Ibansk.'

Neurasthenic suggested to Dauber his idea for the form the stone might take. A granite base carved with an ear of maize and the words 'Our generation, fuck you all, will live in the total Ism', and above, a hand making an obscene gesture, the ring finger replaced by a penis. Dauber said that it seemed a good idea. But there were some possible variations. For instance, the pedestal could support a huge pink arse with ears and topped with a forage cap. But his approach would be rather different. An artist could not be more malicious than a politician.

The exhibition by the Prodigy

The Prodigy's exhibition was held in the central exhibition halls. It was advertised in all the newspapers and magazines, on radio and television and on posters. A special film was made, and there was no charge for admission to the exhibition. The Prodigy was still under thirty but he looked like an adult. He had begun to draw when he was five months old and since then he had turned out about a thousand works. They were all on show. As the commentators pointed out, his drawing was still very weak, and his colouring like a child's, but he had everything still ahead of him. He would of course have to study. In the main, the Prodigy painted horses and scenes from the two World Wars. In an interview the Prodigy said that ever since his childhood he had been attracted by philosophical problems of the meaning of life. 'I've a brilliant idea,' Neurasthenic told Dauber. 'Let your beard grow, and we'll call you a prodigy and organise a superb exhibition.' 'It won't work,' said Dauber. 'I can at least draw, and that's something I can't hide even from our academicians.'

The wall newspaper

As became clear later, the wall newspaper contained nothing of any special merit, and Slanderer, Chatterer, and more particularly Schizophrenic, had nothing to do with it at all. Slanderer

(231)

was looking for a job, Chatterer sat trembling in expectation of being fired from his, and Schizophrenic was still doing time in the sanatorium for his last thesis. But this didn't have the least importance, since it was clear to everyone from where the wind was blowing—and where to. Everything considered, all the fuss could have been avoided, the more so since Claimant stated publicly that he wasn't in the least offended by the caricature, that indeed that was not the question. But since the fuss had started, it was impossible to avoid it: someone would have brought it up all the same, and then it would have been quite impossible to avoid. And so the Commission launched into a detailed study of the wall newspaper, co-opting for this purpose (on the advice of Claimant, who was the commission's Grey Eminence) Thinker, Sociologist, Wife, Neurasthenic, and everyone else who could be brought in and put to any use.

At first sight, the paper looked like this. On the front page there was a picture of Teacher against the background of a television mast with a spray of lilac between his teeth. 'There's nothing original there,' said Wife. 'It's all old hat.' 'No,' said Neurasthenic, who had been brought in, as it later transpired, to play devil's advocate. 'We've not seen this before. On the one you're thinking of there was a steel furnace, and not a television mast, and it was a spray of mimosa he had between his teeth.' 'No, it was a dove,' Puss corrected Neurasthenic. 'There's no need to distort the facts, young man. You do have, I understand, some connection, however remote, with science. In my article, which has, by the way, been translated and published in English, it's all set out in black and white. . . .' Claimant said that he agreed with this, and Thinker began haltingly to read out the leading article. They found nothing prejudicial in it. Indeed, it would have been surprising if they had, for it had been written (or rather re-written from last year's edition) by the editor himself, checked by the secretary in person, re-read and edited by the acting director himself, and approved by the regional instructor. The result was that there was nothing left in it, to the point where the only thing left in it was nothing. 'This would be an interesting subject for dialectical logic,' said Neurasthenic, and he looked at Puss. 'Affirmation and negation in this instance mean the same thing.' 'Instances of this kind,' said Puss, 'crop up at every touch and turn in our dialectical reality. One merely needs a highly developed intelligence to be able to understand them.' 'Of course,' said Neurasthenic. 'When I was a child, in the days of Boss, I happened to visit a little town on the border between two areas with two different languages. I saw two notice boards. One hung on one side of the station, the other on the other. One said "Comrade Boss lives here" and the other said "Comrade Boss lives not here". I asked a policeman how anyone could be here and not here simultaneously. He arrested me, but I was soon released on account of my tender years, and they arrested some others instead. They, of course, didn't understand dialectical logic.' Claimant told them both to stop playing the fool.

The leading article was followed by the section on 'Production'. There too, on the whole everything was in order. It is true there was one critical article, but this was not brought up until later, and for a different reason. This article said that the sector of theorisation of practice, illuminated and directed by theory, had planned for the next forty years a collective monograph by 180 authors in nine and a half volumes. But this time-scale and work-force were clearly too limited for the team, who were working successfully under the direction of Secretary and Academician. It turned out to be necessary to increase the size of the monograph five-fold, as so far no author had submitted his material for discussion, and by all appearances none would do so in the next few years since the subject was both new and difficult, demanding an enlargement of the team to make room for new young and dynamic talents, as an underestimation of the discoveries and practice of modern science could have a negative result, and for these reasons it was rational to push the publication date back by ten years. 'This all seems quite in order,' said Claimant, and gave instructions for the noting and verification of the facts referred to, (since Competitor was running the sector, not to mention Secretary).

After 'Production' came 'Socio-Cultural Life'. Here everything was in order for the same reasons as was the leading article. True, there were two articles which attracted the commission's attention. One was critical of colleague A who was always late with his dues, and ended by calling on colleague A to pay his dues on time. The other said that colleague A always paid his dues in advance, and called on all other colleagues to

(233)

follow his example. Puss said that this was logically impossible. 'It all depends what kind of logic you're talking about,' said Neurasthenic. It then became clear that these were different colleagues, and that moreover one of them had been a student under Slanderer. Unfortunately, this one turned out to be the one who paid in advance. Nevertheless, Thinker wrote his name in his notebook. One article attracted the particular attention of Claimant, but he didn't let on, just winked at Thinker. This article dealt with the work of the department headed by the other Competitor. Its tone was eulogistic. Only at the end of the article did the author remark that, after having overcome the consequences of the cult of personality, work had progressed excellently, but that it was still too soon to rest on their laurels and assume that from now on everything would look after itself. Thinker looked through this passage, and formed the same idea as Claimant.

The rats
From the very first day of the ratorium experiment we have observed the formation of rat groups, the emergence of leaders, the ferocious leadership battle, the appearance of a leadership hierarchy and so on. We even thought for a moment that in this lay the basis of the bases of existence of the rat colony, which would explain all the peculiarities we observed. But we soon came to the conclusion that this opinion was erroneous. For example, on numerous occasions we noticed that terror increased in areas where a system of leadership was well established, and decreased in areas where there was a ferocious battle to attain and consolidate leadership. Similar cases were observed for the colony as a whole at various periods. Similarly, all possible combinations of situations in the leadership system and in the food supply system were observed. Statistical data produced no argument in favour of one hypothesis over another, and it was therefore impossible to establish any stable correlations.

When he had read this section of the book, Chatterer called its authors cretins. They were confusing the most elementary things: empirical laws, established on the basis of a generalisation of observed data, and abstract laws, whose formulation required theoretical and practical experience of quite a different kind. The best they could achieve by their experiment would be to clarify certain consequences of the comparative isolation of the colony. But this could have been foreseen in advance, without any need for decades of observations which *a priori* excluded the possibility of discovering empirical laws. Of course, if thousands of facts are observed, it is possible to produce some sort of generalisation. But to this end, it is necessary to have a very special orientation of mind, which they lack. One day when I have time, I shall have to analyse their figures. If only I could get hold of all their experimental data!

And yet, Chatterer read, the observation of the leadership struggle has enabled us to make an amazing discovery. This is perhaps the most significant discovery made in the whole course of the experiment. We have discovered a system of self government unique to the colony, and have been able to determine its structure. But the strangest thing about this discovery is that the system of self government has always been clearly in evidence, and it is impossible to explain in rational terms why we went so long before noticing it.

It's inexplicable, thought Chatterer, because it is perfectly clear without any need for explanation. They didn't expect to find anything of this kind, and didn't want to find it. The fact kept thrusting itself under their noses, and they kept averting their gaze. And when it was no longer possible to avoid it, they suddenly discovered it! A striking discovery indeed! And Chatterer was reminded of something that had happened to him. A very prominent Western scientist, S., a colleague, had had a long stay in Ibansk. They often met. S. was able to study the life and work of the Ibansk scientists in some detail. And yet when he returned home, S. behaved as if he had come straight out of the leading article of an Ibansk newspaper. He invited Chatterer to come and stay with him in a specially rented seaside villa. Chatterer received the invitation a month late. His friends found this very amusing, and called S. a degenerate. But Chatterer replied, thanking S. for his invitation, and explaining when he had received it and the date he had sent his reply. S. however, showed utter incomprehension and was offended. They don't understand, Chatterer thought, even when they see for themselves. When they observe things, they accept the observed fact, but reject the basis which seems to them without sense and therefore without existence. And so they accuse us personally, and feel a sense of superiority.

Crime and punishment

The academic edition of Dostoevsky's *Crime and Punishment* with illustrations by Dauber became the focus of a battle involving the leading personalities of the cultural life of Ibansk, many of them people in very high positions. The book was published despite fierce resistance. It came out at the time which later turned out to be the apogee of the liberal epoch which started after the death of the Boss and ended some years after the removal of Hog. In Chatterer's opinion, this period would have been better called the epoch of confusion. At any other time, before or after, a book with illustrations like those of Dauber would have been unthinkable. Like Dante's *Inferno*, *Crime and Punishment* merely served as Dauber's excuse to comment on our society in terms more or less related to the subject of the book. Schizophrenic interpreted Dauber's drawings as follows.

One theme, and one alone, which in one case is the presentiment of something yet to happen, and in the other a reflection on something already past, is formulated, and resolved, in a somewhat contradictory fashion. In the case of Dostoevsky it is the theme of the individual's responsibility for mass crimes—for Dauber, it is the mass's lack of responsibility for individual crimes. For Dostoevsky crime is a deliberate deviation from a natural norm, and punishment is the norm. For Dauber, crime is the natural norm, and punishment is a deviation from some criminal norm. 'I by no means wish to say that that is what was in Dauber's mind when he created his drawings; it's far more likely that he was thinking something completely different. It is simply that I cannot find any other sense in them. It is indeed a case of inventing punishment, creating it as an antidote to the criminality of the mass. This is not a juridical problem but a profoundly social one. At the present time it has become extraordinarily simple from the point of view of general formulae, and extraordinarily difficult (almost insoluble) from the point of view of a concrete programme of action. In his series Dauber has no such programme. No-one has. It still has to be invented.'

Extract from Slanderer's book

I shall call the dominant ideology of a given society 'fundamental' and ideological formations of the type considered here 'local'. The fundamental ideology is influenced only superficially by local ideologies, and even so only to a point where this influence is useful to the fundamental ideology or offers no threat to its existence or its prestige, and only in those cases where the fundamental ideology either wishes to be influenced or cannot, for reasons beyond its control, avoid being so influenced. According to circumstances, local ideologies try to make themselves indispensable to the fundamental ideology, to influence it, to weaken, destroy, reform, improve it, and so on, in short to do everything they can to consolidate their position and to eliminate or remove competitors, etc. Their relationships are very similar to those which exist between a great power and its small neighbour states. Sometimes their interests coincide to the degree that they can be seen as a single entity. The special nature of these relationships lies in the fact that the more the fundamental ideology finds a local ideology to its liking, the closer that local ideology is to its total extinction.

Dauber and modern West European art

For theoreticians, said Chatterer, Dauber isn't so much an enigma as an embarrassment. It's obvious that he isn't a manifestation of our artistic world. All his ideas come from Over There. If not, where else could they come from? All our ideas are known well in advance. And between ourselves, we theoreticians, know what ideas like ours are worth. It's said that there are some ideas which used to be our own, which went Over There and which are now beginning to come back to us. But for a start, those are fables or myth-makers. And secondly, even if they were our ideas in the first place, they've been Over There. And if they've been Over There, they're not ours any more. So purely theoretically, Dauber cannot be a manifestation of our artistic world. But is he a manifestation of Western art? According to the decision of the Academy of Arts, the Union of Artists, the Ministry of Culture, and of even higher institutions, of all the specialists in the theory of art, and of all connoisseurs, modern Western art includes those Western artists of a century ago who cannot yet be thought of as being old, but who are in some respects similar to our own, and who do not provoke feelings of revulsion in the members of these institutions, and in addition all those artists who sympathise with us in some way or another, irrespective of their age, school, or geographical provenance, and whom it is permissible to regard as artists. So according to the definition of the concept itself, Dauber cannot be classed as a Western artist. In these circumstances, the artistic phenomenon which we call Dauber simply does not exist.

The exhibition of bones

The main event of the Ibansk cultural season was the opening of an exhibition of old bones brought from a friendly, but not neighbouring state, and put on show in the Museum of Fine Arts. Because of the exhibition of bones, the museum was closed. Two months before the exhibition, people began to sign up for the vouchers which would give them the right to join the queue for the exhibition when it came. The opening of the exhibition was performed at a very high level. Dauber didn't manage to get in at all. Neurasthenic, who did manage to get in thanks to his connections, said that the exhibition was interesting enough, but not so interesting as to be worth queuing for hours to see. Chatterer said that people were desperate to see something real and unusual. They were ready to look at anything at all, provided that it came from abroad. Dauber asked whether there would be a queue for his exhibition, if he ever managed to have one. Neurasthenic said that if Dauber was billed as a Western artist, the place would be mobbed. And if he was advertised as one of ours, there would still be queues, although rather shorter. But as time passed the queues would disappear altogether. Chatterer said that he thought an exhibition by Dauber would have a devastating effect. Even his friends hardly knew what he'd been doing for the last few years, or thought it must be worthless because he always left everything lying around in his studio. But all this discussion was a waste of time anyway, because Dauber would never be allowed an exhibition. 'You can't mean "never",' said Dauber. 'Never,' said Chatterer. 'Whatever official success you might have, you'll never have an exhibition. The only thing you might get is quite the opposite.' 'What do you mean?' asked Dauber. 'You know perfectly well,' said Chatterer. 'Yes,' said Dauber, 'but I don't even want to think about it.'

Extract from Slanderer's book

Ideology and science are mutually exclusive phenomena. By that I do not mean that they are enemies. Enemies can live in peace, and sometimes in good friendship. I mean merely that science and ideology are qualitatively heterogeneous phenomena. Science presupposes (at least in its tendencies) a meaningful, precise and unequivocal terminology. Ideology presupposes forms of language which are meaningless, diffuse and imprecise. The terminology of science stands in no need of explanation and interpretation. The phraseology of ideology demands exegesis, associations of ideas and so on. Scientific statements assume the possibility that they can be proved or disproved, or at least that it can be established that they are essentially insoluble. Ideological propositions can be neither proved nor disproved, for they have no meaning. From this point of view, the widely held idea that ideology is made up of signs is false. Science consists of signs, but ideology consists of pseudo-signs. Ideology is anti-significant. It is a linguistic formation only in the sense that it uses the raw material of language. So many manifestations in modern science turn out to be situated in the realm of ideology. Finally, if the term 'scientific' is used to denote science as a whole, including those aspects which are anti-scientific, one can think of scientific ideology as pertaining to the anti-scientific. In this connection, the term 'scientific ideology' indicates an ideology of the kind that sucks the marrow from science properly so-called, and camouflages itself under this mask. But ideology as a science properly so-called is a non-sense. It comes from quite other sources, and has quite other targets than the knowledge of reality. It is rather the opposite. It is only when compared to a different form of ideology that such and such an ideology can pass as a product of knowledge or enlightenment. But this stage is ephemeral. Essentially, ideologies cannot be distinguished one from another by their degree of scientific understanding of nature and society.

The fact that ideology is anti-scientific should not cause it too much concern. In our days it its none too honourable to be a science. It is far more honourable to be an ideology, for ideology dominates and science submits. Science's efforts to dominate are laughable. If it dominates, it does so only in its role as an ideological organisation, and not as a science in the true meaning of the word. The efforts of ideology to put on a scientific face are an historically transient phenomenon.

A scientific ideology is just as much an absurdity as is, for example, a scientific art. As far as art is concerned, one can distinguish between art itself as a particular form of activity, and the science of art, that is to say its theory. It is known that works of art are created by artists, not by scientists who have studied art, and artists do not formulate the theory of art. It can happen that one person can both create works of art and contribute to the theory of art, but that does not change anything. In the case of ideology, we must make the distinction between the creation of ideological objects—texts, or cult objects—which is not a science, and the science which studies this ideological activity and its artefacts. But in practice this is never done. It is tacitly accepted that people who create, preserve and protect ideological artefacts are indeed scientists. And as ideological texts are considered to be products of science, then a scientific study of them seems to coincide with their preparation. But this is not true. The more difficult the distinction is to make, the more persistently and carefully it should be made. There is no more in common between ideology as a particular activity creating ideological texts and the science that studies this activity and its texts, than there is between art and the theory of art. Ideological texts are constructed according to rules which differ in principle from those of scientific texts. The weakness of modern official ideology lies mainly in the attempts that are made to give its texts the appearance of scientific texts. And this indeed is done. No science comes out of it, and no account is taken of the structural rules of ideology, which are clearly not used. The result is a science and an ideology both equally lamentable from the point of view of professional realisation.

It might seem that in view of the exceptionally important role played by ideology in society, it should be developed as well and as professionally as possible. Yet it is in this very aspect that it offers such a pitiful spectacle. Can this be by chance?

Puss's article

When he had leafed through Slanderer's book, Puss said what a scoundrel he was, and began to re-phrase Slanderer's thoughts to the demands of the Journal, attributing suitable absurdities to Slanderer and brilliantly refuting them with arguments taken from Slanderer's own books. Claimant took charge of Puss's article himself, having first asked Neurasthenic, as a friend, to edit it. Neurasthenic said the article was balderdash, but agreed to edit it. He had submitted an article of his own to the Journal, which he desperately needed to have published (elections were drawing near, and he had published hardly anything yet!) A refusal would automatically have resulted in his own article being dropped. Puss's article turned out quite well, and Puss was very pleased with it.

His ambition given wings by this success, Puss conceived the idea of a monograph on the battle of ideas in our epoch. Thinker took up the idea with him. For greater confidence, and unknown to Claimant, they invited Secretary to join them as co-author. 'First,' said Thinker, 'that way the book is certain to be published. Secondly, after that no-one will attack us. Thirdly, we're certain to get our fees. Fourthly, Secretary is an ass; he won't make head nor tail of it, and we'll be able to push through our own ideas.' The monograph found its place in the publishing plan. In anticipation of the fees, Thinker borrowed a large sum from Sociologist, used it to buy an ikon for one of his girl friends of indeterminate nationality, and presented it to another girl friend from one of the embassies, having first spread the ikon with red caviar from a delicatessen reserved for him alone. There was only one thing they had overlooked: At no time in his life had Secretary ever written a line of his own. Others had always written for him. Thinker's productivity was even lower than Puss's, and Puss, at best, could squeeze out one small article a year. But it was Secretary who found the way out of this problem. He suggested that they should base themselves on one of his old books, written in the time of the Boss, and re-write it taking the new directives into account. 'I've got myself mixed up in some dirty business,' said Thinker at one of

Sociologist's parties. 'Puss and I were called into the Section and obliged to work with Secretary on a book about the "Battle of Ideas".' 'You could do a good book on that subject,' said Wife. 'Secretary's only there for the sake of appearances; you can ignore him.' 'Incidentally,' Puss said to Thinker, 'I've still got some notes for the second part of Slanderer's book. It's sheer rubbish, of course, but it wouldn't hurt to look through them . . .'

An historical judgment

The life of a thinking Ibansk intellectual is first and foremost conversation. And conversation is first and foremost a disorderly and sterile debate. Historical phenomena must be judged by their consequences, yells Scientist. So they can be, yells Chatterer. But why *must* be? Do you really think that's the only method? And what do you mean by 'historical phenomena'? Is this conversation we're having an historical phenomenon? Or Deputy's visit to our Bar? Or a speech by the Leader? Or a declaration by Truth-teller? And how do you establish cause-and-effect relationships? Why do you consider the very fact of a revolution to be a cause of terror? Why do you believe collectivisation to be a cause of hunger? What do you mean by talking about causes in this context? You've got to understand that all these words you are using have lost all meaning. If our conversations are even going to start having some glimmering of significance, they have got to meet these conditions at the very least. They have to describe the standard means used to establish (and even to measure) the nature and the strength (the degree) of influence that an event has on people. They have got to distinguish between the influence an event has at the time, and the influence it exerts on posterity. To do this, we must first carefully determine temporal boundaries defining what is regarded as 'contemporary' with a given event. We must equally determine the time frame work of what is to be regarded as the period of historical posterity. This period does not cover the full interval that elapses after the event. If we use a certain number of methods to determine the influence of events on the life of mankind, then, after a certain lapse of time it becomes impossible to use these methods to verify one's statements. Finally, we must bear in mind that contemporary evaluations of an event do not coincide with those of posterity. An event which may be of great importance for those who are contemporary to it may have insignificant historical consequences. But there is a dependence between the two periods. If all the concepts are accurately defined, and the methods of measuring the degree of influence an event has on the life of mankind are clearly established, then it is possible, by pure deduction, to reach certain general consequences from this basis. For example, if an event is of no social significance to its contemporaries, it can be of no social significance to history. Cases where it appears that an event from the past suddenly acquires significance in later history arise purely as the result of a confusion between concepts and facts. In reality, something different is happening here. What happens in reality is that contemporary events which are socially significant are associated with events from the past for a variety of reasons, and their significance is attributed to the events of the past. But these past events really only provide raw material for the work of the imagination, of phraseology and so on. The significance of the event in history cannot exceed its contemporary significance, not because of any objective laws, but because of the linguistic rules which are accepted for the discussion of these events. For an event to become historically significant, it must first of all be significant to its contemporaries. These purely linguistic relationships are still further obscured by the fact that a great many events of contemporary significance are not publicly discussed, not written about in newspapers and so on. For instance, what have you read about Truth-teller's speech? And have you today seen any newspaper without a photograph of the Leader and a description of his visit to our Bar? And yet what event produced the greater impression on the people of Ibansk? The visit? But that produced no impression at all. It's not a case of people forgetting it happened—no-one saw it, not even those who were watching.

After Chatterer's harangue, tumult broke out again. Everyone yelled with one voice that he was wrong. 'If even you don't understand that the concept of error is applicable to what I've been saying, what can I sensibly talk about to other people?' 'Only someone who makes statements can make mistakes.' 'But I've been talking merely about agreements without which it is impossible to make statements—I haven't stated anything yet.'

Fall in!

'I've always lived with the feeling,' said Chatterer, 'that at any moment I'm going to hear the order "Fall in!", and I shall run out, join the ranks, and march off wherever I'm ordered to.' 'I can understand that,' said Slanderer. 'I've lived all my life with the feeling that someone's going to bang on my door, say "Get your things together," and I'll go off where I'm taken.' 'We must cleanse ourselves of the past through repentance,' said the Visitor. 'It's only sinners who should repent,' said Chatterer. 'And how can you cleanse yourself of the future?' asked Slanderer. 'It's not the past which weighs so heavy, but the expectation of the inevitable.' 'You must resign yourselves,' said the Visitor. 'There's not much more to wait for. Just be patient a little, and it'll all be over, and there'll be nothing left. And Nothing can't suffer. And it can't have any problems.' 'As for me,' said Dauber, 'I live with the feeling that for ages now people have been saying to me time after time, "Fuck off".'

The rats

Chatterer decided to carry out an experiment on his own account. He decided to develop an abstract theory derived from certain propositions in the book, and later to see what the book said about these subjects. So, Chatterer said to himself, let's start. The ratorium constitutes an enclosed group of rats forced together for whatever reason and condemned to a prolonged co-habitation. Either this group remains a chaotic group, in which case it will perish because of self destruction—it is even easy to calculate the exact moment—or, somehow or other it will put itself in order. Since it exists at all, and multiplies, and from a certain point of view prospers (it should be noted that the average weight of the rats has increased, as has the length of their tails; their claws and their teeth have grown, and their coats are more glossy), that argues that order has been achieved. But at what cost? The ratorium is autonomous. There is no pressure from outside. Physical environment and food remain the same. The only factors which engender order are the rats themselves. They cannot, all of them, take charge of organising a system of order, since, if they did so, chaos would result. Consequently there is a division of function—between those who impose order, and those who submit to it. That is merely the beginning of a system. Those who seek to impose order are many. It is possible to calculate the minimal number using the tally of members of the primary groups. They in their turn form an hierarchic system of groups and leaders.

Having developed his hypothesis in this way, Chatterer read the appropriate chapter of the book and discovered that he was indeed right. And he was greatly astonished, not by what the authors of the book had written, but by the accuracy with which he had predicted the results of their empirical observations. In all probability, he thought, people usually predict the general outlines of social phenomena fairly accurately, but never believe in their forecasts, and so it may seem that they are unable to penetrate the complexities of their existence. People need their faith in their own intelligence restored—that is one of the essential conditions for the progress of society. It is odd to see how far modern science destroys this faith, whatever is said on the other side. A faith in reason is not a scientific phenomenon. It is faith—in other words the fundamental basis of ideology. By striving to appear scientific, official ideology destroys the foundation of the foundations of everything that is most human in humankind—belief in one's own reason.

Successes

The affair of the gravestone passed off more successfully than could have been hoped. Dauber drew up his sketches. The Commission of the Artists' Union examined them and approved. The only change they proposed was the use of red granite in place of black and white marble. It would look better, they said, and not so eye-catching. But Dauber stuck to his guns. Then there was a special commission, which also approved Dauber's drawings, but suggested that instead of the combination of black and white marble he should use grey and red, or at the very least light grey and dark grey. Otherwise people might interpret the stone incorrectly. Then there was the very highest Commission. The Commission approved the drawings, but laid down that the gravestone should be made of single-coloured marble. A year later everything cooled down, and the highest authorities approved Dauber's drawings. 'Phooey!', said Chatterer. 'Minor successes never lead to a real victory. A major victory can only come from a series of defeats.' 'There'll be defeats all right,' said Dauber cheerfully. And he began to work on the maquette of the gravestone. The model was small and did not produce the desired effect. Rather the reverse, for it produced a rather comical effect because of the Hog's minute head. 'It's a good thing the scale model doesn't give a proper idea,' said Dauber gaily. 'That means that all the councils and commissions will pass it. But when you see it full size it'll take your breath away.' The Union Commission passed the model—but once again they raised the question of the materials. 'The material you're using,' they said, 'is like a red rag to a bull.' They didn't even consider the form of the stone. The model was approved by higher commissions, then higher, from one side and the other, and in the end by the very highest. Dejected by this unaccustomed success, Dauber prepared to sculpt the full-size stone. But here came the long awaited defeat.

The wall newspaper

It was supposed that the real reason the paper had been removed from the wall was the 'satire and humour' section. Here there really was something to get heated about. The cartoon of 'The Old Whores' Cemetery a hundred years hence' showed the gravestones of theoreticians who were at the moment in perfectly good health. And the gravestones bore shocking epitaphs. For instance, the stone on Troglodyte's grave bore this verse:

> For a century he reckoned
> The world came first and reason second;
> He shunned idealism's trap—
> And science too—a yawning gap.

The pedestal was decorated with the well known boots wearing a cap and moustaches, with little Troglodytes peeping out of each boot. Puss was shown in an incredibly indecent and scandalous fashion, but so as to be instantly recognisable. On the pedestal there was this inscription:

Adam was fashioned out of clay,
Eve from his rib, says Holy Writ.
The idiot who lies here today,
Was made by Thinker out of sh*t.

'It's a distortion of my personality!' yelled Puss. But Neurasthenic said it was foolish to take the caricature personally. But it was Secretary's tomb that was the worst of all. On the pedestal there was a greeny-brown pile of something crawling with worms. From the heap there arose a fetid miasma bearing the titles of Secretary's books. And on the worms were written words like 'Denunciation', 'Slander', 'Plagiarism' and so on, some of them still more insulting. And there was an epitaph in letters of gold:

A titan's lifetime now is past,
And what a heart has throbbed its last!
How can we tell, we here forlorn,
If such-like filth can be reborn?

In the middle of the cemetery there was a tall obelisk which bore this inscription:

Pause here awhile, friend, and contemplate,
For here within this plot beyond recall,
The mentors of your fathers lie in state,
Panders and mental eunuchs one and all.

When they had examined the 'satire and humour' section, the Commission retired to deliberate. The entire Institute held its breath waiting for the decision. Two very senior faculty members had heart attacks. Five juniors had to be sent away to be dried out. Another was caught red-handed, and the reputation of the Institute was marred.

The decision

'What's going to happen?' members of the Institute staff whispered to one another. 'What's going to happen? Nothing special,' said Chatterer. 'The situation is serious of course, and so it mustn't be taken seriously. No-one can know what they're going to write. And so it isn't too difficult to predict. The fact is that all major decisions are reached according to the following principles. Some people provoke the decision. Documents provided by others are studied. In reaching the final formulae, ideas are used which have not the slightest logical connection

(247)

with them. The object of the decision becomes people who have absolutely nothing to do with the matter in hand. There is no cause and effect link between any of these aspects. They are not even co-ordinated. The act of decision itself which brings some appearance of co-ordination in from outside. You want to know what's going to happen? It's extremely simple. Who started the whole thing off? It wasn't Secretary and his mob, but Claimant and *his* mob. Why? So as to deal a blow to their competitors and to give a good impression of themselves higher up. Who are their competitors? The Acting Director, the Head of the Theoretical Section, and the Head of Department. The first can be sunk for a serious mistake, the other two for anything you like—that's of no importance. The Acting Director has not made any mistake, but you can always pin a serious mistake on him from outside by exploiting the situation and saying that he let that mistake in the paper through. The mistake is clear enough—all the conseqences of the deviations of the cult of personality have long since been put right, as everyone knows, but some criminal elements go against the general line and claim that they still exist. And in the end the blow will be directed against Slanderer, Chatterer and Co.'

The following day a confidential letter was read at the Institute. During the past year, it said, the Journal has improved the quality of its work. There have been interesting articles critical of Secretary and the Head of the Theoretical Section. They must take account of this just criticism and step into line. But the Journal has committed a crass mistake in publishing a series of articles which go against the official line. These articles claimed that not all our deviations had yet been overcome. This primarily concerns a certain department (headed by comrade X), and certain unworthy and repulsive insinuations in the form of vicious caricatures inspired by an irresponsible group (Slanderer, Chatterer and others). With the intention of correcting this situation, the Acting Director will be relieved of his responsibilities and a new Acting Director appointed, the Heads of the Section and the Department will be severely reprimanded, and the problem of Slanderer and Chatterer will be put down for consideration. The letter also noted the true vigilance which had been shown by Claimant.

'What did I tell you?' said Chatterer. 'Yet all the same, this fool will never become Director. When there are too many victories, the whole affair ends in defeat.' The next day it was discovered that the list of candidates had changed its composition, but that it had grown longer. Claimant had now dropped back to fifth place. When he had started his little game, in which he believed that he held the strings, Claimant had not imagined that in doing so he would himself become a pawn in someone else's little game. He did not know that in this game his fate had been decided long since, and he had been allowed to go on playing for a little himself simply because he had not finished doing everything expected of him. But in high places it had already been decided that Claimant was not suited for the job of Director, as he was far too far to the left and too progressive. Claimant was not too bad in himself, but he was too subject to the influence of those around him. It was Thinker and Sociologist who were primarily regarded with suspicion. They were so stuck up! They thought themselves very superior just because they had read a few Western books! It had been decided to move Claimant to a no less elevated post (seeing he's a scientist, let him do some science!) which completely excluded any possibility that Claimant could ever pursue the career he had mapped out for himself. The fate of Thinker was not considered, for he was just an insignificant detail. Chatterer predicted that Claimant would be promoted out of the game, but in such a way that he could not rise again. Thinker tried all he knew to discover how Chatterer had come by his information. 'My God, what idiots,' said Chatterer angrily. 'How can they possibly fail to understand that between the Secretary's mob and Claimant's mob, there is a still more powerful mob, which according to the general law of social change must take over from the Secretary's group. It was only pure chance that Claimant's group took the initiative, taking advantage of a coincidence of favourable historical circumstances. But these circumstances have had their day, or nearly.'

The defeat
The secretary of a boss who wasn't very highly placed, but who on the other hand was by no means lowly placed, took up a seal, blew on it, and raised her arm in a gesture that had about it an air of finality. All the papers had been stapled and signed. They

bore all the seals that were needed, except for this one, and the secretary of the boss who was neither too high nor too low, was about to place it on the very last page, which her boss had already signed. Finally, thought Dauber, thank God, that's the end of all this paper work. Now I can get to work. But . . . But the secretary did not apply the seal—she did not complete her final gesture. She slowly lowered her arm, carefully put the seal away in her drawer and locked it. 'One moment please,' she said, 'I must make a telephone call to . . .' and she mentioned a wholly unfamiliar name. 'I have got Dauber with me,' she said into the phone, 'and he . . .' For half an hour the secretary sat with her ear glued to the phone, while Dauber sat with his hand stretched out, waiting for that last document which almost had the final seal of permission on it. 'Telephone me in a few days,' the secretary said, as she replaced her receiver after a final 'Very good', and put the paper into her drawer.

'I would like to know what's been going on,' said Dauber. 'Was that a directive from above? No, they've given their agreement. The Union of Artists? No, they've given in already. And on top of that they think that I just produce rubbish and that this will damage me. The secret police? They couldn't give a damn about it. A personal initiative by the secretary or her boss? But what am I to them?' 'Don't try to find the answer,' said Schizophrenic. 'There isn't one. Not because it's difficult to establish the truth, but because you're trying to find answers to the questions "Who?" and "Why?" There are no "whos" and "whys" here. There is an impersonal machine which takes on no responsibility. So many things could have happened. Are there people who don't want you to make this gravestone? Yes, there are. Are they doing things to try to stop you? Yes, they are. In cases like this, even a word is action. Even a smile. Even a silence. Even a refusal to make a telephone call. Even making a telephone call. All it needs is to feed material into the machine by one of its access points—and there are millions of those—and it can produce an entirely disproportionate result. Just think, the fate of one of Slanderer's books was decided by an almost imperceptible pause in a lecture given by one of Slanderer's high-placed supporters. Someone interrupted his eulogy with a trivial question. He was confused for a moment and mutterered something incomprehensible. This

(250)

was interpreted as a directive to action, and all the rest was dismissed as camouflage. I have analysed a whole series of defeats that Chatterer has suffered. I've taken ten cases, all different, all involving different people. But the effect was always the same. In your case, it's a serious business. Exceptionally so. In practice, it was officially turned down right from the start. The positive official decision wasn't hypocritical. That was real too. It may be the case that they genuinely wish you well. But they're just cogs in the machine as well. They may even be unaware of the fact (although this I doubt) that in taking a positive official decision, they do so in such a way that it becomes in fact a negative decision.'

The bases of natural science

In Ibansk, a science which enjoyed a great flowering was that of meatology. To be fair, it should be said that initially things didn't go too well. At the start, the meatologists reared the Fly and the foreign Chromosome, and on this basis developed theories which were foreign to us. Naturally they were greatly praised for this in the West. But they made life quite impossible for the Ibanskians. Things had to be put right. So in their place the Great Veterinarian was appointed. He was quite incredibly stupid and tongue-tied. The Ibanskians said he couldn't tell Gogol from Hegel, Hegel from Babel, Babel from Cable, Cable from Beigel, Beigel from Table, but he came from the right social background, and had views which fitted in at the time in question. So he quickly made up for lost time. Relying on the work done by the founders of this branch of science, he began, on the wide open spaces of the Ibanskian wasteland, to carry out his famous experiments on crossing watermelons with maize. And he achieved remarkable results. In the outskirts of the city of Ibansk cows were exterminated. Milk began to come from powder, and meat from abroad. After Hog had been removed, it was alleged that the Great Veterinarian had gone too far. Chromosome was rehabilitated. Claimant hurriedly dashed off a bold book in which he unmasked Veterinarian and wrote approvingly of Chromosome. The correct relationship between Theory and Natural Sciences had been achieved. The Journal began to print regular articles by a rehabilitated Fly and Chromosome specialist. 'I've made sure of the support of the

natural scientists,' Claimant thought to himself. 'Now we'll
clamp down on Them,' he said aloud. People knew whom he
was talking about, but thought that he would smash Secretary,
Troglodyte, Veterinarian and other supporters of the Boss.

Bewilderment
'Look,' said Chatterer, showing Dauber the latest number of
the Journal. 'The avant-garde intelligentsia of Ibansk is going
in for strip tease.' Dauber looked through the articles by Puss
and Thinker, and swore violently. 'What's come over them?'
'Our friends have disclosed their true faces,' said Chatterer.
'The period of confusion is over. Now they are going to have to
get rid of everyone who is more significant than they are, or who
even knows what they're really worth. That way they will
enhance their own values. Just let me draw your attention to the
way it is done. There is sharp criticism of mediocre out-of-date
work by senile old men and charlatans. The better-looking
work will be allowed through—indeed, sometimes there may
even be battles to get it through. In fact, those works are every
bit as bad as the rest, if not worse. But this produces an illusion
of progress. And if in the course of all this one or two or three
really good pieces of work fail to appear, that's a mere trifle.
(There's little enough good work any way). It's not worth
bothering about. In our job we can let through a thousand
pieces of work and hold up one—that's enough to get you
condemned as a scoundrel, if that one work was the only one
which showed progress and all the others were run of the mill.
Thinker's always been like that. But before, he's always had
faith in the fact that there would never be any real men here.
And at that time he still didn't have power. There's no mystery
about it, no psycho-drama. There is only fear, greed, parasitism
and mediocrity.'

All mixed up together
'It really isn't a case of Claimant's mob on one side and Secretary's mob on the other,' said Neurasthenic. 'The real situation
is quite different. Secretary is everybody's boss, and in one
sense Claimant is subordinate to him. But there is another area
in which Claimant does not obey Secretary. Secretary, Puss and
Thinker are writing a book together. The acting director works

part-time with Sociologist. Wife has just defended her thesis under the direction of Claimant's nearest enemy; her official opponent was one of Secretary's closest henchmen. Shall I go on? We form one single close family. Its division into enemy groups is nothing more than healthy criticism and self-criticism, the interests of the cause, concern for the future of Ibanskian science and the purity of the Ism. The groups of Claimant and Secretary are not even concentrations in some dense medium. There is a certain tendency among many people to act in such a way that some of them seem to want to help Claimant become Director, while others want to stop him. And this senseless fermentation of a quagmire—or rather dung-heap—is subjectively experienced as a battle for some kind of principles. Here the disparity between passions and judgments on the one hand, and reality on the other, grows to such monstrous proportions that sometimes I feel we're all living in a loony bin.'

Schizophrenic's vision

'Where am I?' asked Schizophrenic of a dashing, handsome lad in a terribly well-known uniform which Schizophrenic simply couldn't identify. 'You, dear comrade, are in the capital of our fatherland, the forced-labour-caravanserai Genghis-Khan,' replied the lad, and whistled to summon up a number of colleagues in plain clothes. In the middle of the camp, Schizophrenic saw, there was a tall synchrophasotron. Truth-teller was squatting on his haunches on top of it, strumming a balalaika. Dauber was busily engaged making from horse-manure a statue of a Mongol activist who had overfilled his quota for cutting up Slavs by three hundred per cent. Close by, Chatterer, neatly impaled on a stake, was delivering a lecture on Ibanskian art. Thinker stood near him with a machine-gun, taking great care to see that Chatterer kept sitting symmetrically. Around them, sitting cross-legged, was a multitude of rats. 'Art,' said Chatterer, adjusting his position, 'can be divided into official and unofficial art. Official art allows the subject to be studied *en masse*. In principle, any rat-mongol with sufficiently gifted parents should be able to become an artist emeritus, a prize-winner, an academician, a deputy. The images of official art are familiar and widely accessible. Even Genghis-Khan himself or

(253)

a Batu or a Mamai, could understand them. It does not reject exaggeration provided that it remains truthful. So if the artist shows a Mongol's legs as being more bandy than they actually are, or his horse as being even more shaggy than it actually is, then that is revolutionary romanticism, urging us ahead. But a straight-legged Mongol mounted on an English mare would be pure abstractionism.' 'That's true,' screeched the rat-mongols, waking up for that very purpose, and loosing a shower of arrows at the synchrophasotron. 'Official art,' continued Chatterer, feeling rather flattered, 'calls us to live. But it can also accuse, unmask.' 'Forbidden!' screeched the rat-mongols. 'Of course, I mean within limits and under controlled conditions,' Chatterer qualified. 'Moreover, it is subject to the following conditions. It must be as untalented as optimistic art. The faults which it attacks should be shown as isolated and temporary, and it should illustrate the fact that we are combatting these faults with great success. Non-official art comprises one part which is permitted, one to which everyone is indifferent, and a part which is banned. The part to which people are indifferent won't remain so for long if it becomes in any way prominent. So there are only two aspects to consider. Any unofficial art can be permitted if it meets the following conditions: It should not be more talented than official art. It should not be widely discussed in society. It should not place the artists in a privileged or exceptional situation compared with artists who are officially recognised. It should lack content, or at least in this respect stay within permitted limits. So we are left with forbidden unofficial art. Society struggles against this by all possible means. And of course, society always wins. Artists like that one over there,' said Chatterer, pointing at Dauber, 'shouldn't exist at all, if it weren't for two absolutely exceptional circumstances: the period of confusion which followed the battle of Kulikovo, and the flirtation with the West. The former circumstance allowed the Dauber to save his skin, the latter, to become famous.'

Chatterer finished his lecture, adjusted his stake, and asked if there were any questions. The model pupil Batu raised his finger. 'Tell me, professor,' he said, 'could Dauber have appeared there in the West?' As he spoke, he showed off his French accent and his American jeans. 'Dauber arrived at the right time and in the right place,' said Chatterer. 'He couldn't have turned up Over There. If he could have done he would have done, for everyone who has a chance of turning up Over There does so. People don't watch too closely Over There. Over here, if he'd turned up before our time, he would have been strangled.' 'That's true,' screeched the rat-mongols, 'he'd have been strangled.' 'Or even later it would also be impossible,' said Chatterer, 'they'd strangle him then, too.' 'That's right,' screeched the rat-mongols. 'Let's strangle him.' And they flung themselves on Chatterer and dragged at his feet until his stake came out through his throat. The audience burst into stormy applause. Thinker shrugged his shoulders scornfully. 'What could I do?' he said to Dauber. Batu thanked the lecturer for his interesting address, and ordered the rat-mongols to march on Ibansk. 'As for you,' he said to Dauber, 'you can get the hell out of here. We won't detain you. Company, keeping step by singing, forward march,' shouted the Sergeant.

> Ine, tsvy, unt dry unt fear,
> Bitter froyline ine glasbieer,

bellowed Thinker. And the rats, carrying their scaly tails at the high port, began to advance on Ibansk.

Thoughts about death

'I am constantly pursued by the thought of death,' said Neurasthenic. 'I think about it as well,' said Careerist. 'But I'm afraid. I only need to think that any moment there might be nothing else—I'm terrified.' 'I think about the past,' said Scientist. 'Where has it gone? Yet these people had an existence. They wrote poems. Proved theorems. Suffered in the camps. Where's it all gone? Is there anything of it left in our memories? And what is memory? That's not the question.' 'That's not the question,' said Visitor. 'What is a normal human life? Your well-being? No. A normal human life is the continuation of the life and work of others, when they regard your life and your affairs as theirs, and when someone continues your life and your affairs. And taken all together you form a whole. When this happens, you get a state of participation in eternity, and the fear of death disappears. If people in this situation think of death, it's not a painful or frightening thought as it is with you, but just a matter of fact one. And how do you live? You don't give a damn for your predecessors—indeed, you haven't any. And if you did, you'd try to forget about them and to put yourselves forward as the initiators of everything. There will be no-one coming along to continue your work, and you know it. You will be spat upon as you have spat upon your predecessors. Parents? Children? Here it's even worse. Yet even from a strictly biological point of view we have lost a great deal. People say that life expectation has increased by twenty years. No, it's been shortened by forty. A normal man is a unity of at least three generations. Add it up. And we—we are just truncated people, people without a past or a future. We're just a passing manifestation. That's why we're so afraid of death. The fear of death is just a recognition of this breaking of the thread of time.' 'Where's the way out?' asked Neurasthenic. 'Religion,' said Visitor. 'In the state of modern knowledge, religion's an empty word,' said Scientist. 'Religion isn't only knowledge,' said Visitor. 'Apart from that it's a human community.' 'A community of old women,' said Neurasthenic. 'Be quiet,' said Chatterer. 'He's right. We need to have an anti-social community of people, and that needs its own unofficial religion. If you don't like the word religion, try ideology instead.' 'Very curious,' said Neurasthenic. 'Perhaps you've handed out our roles already as well?' 'Perhaps,' said Chatterer. 'Who's got what?' said Scientist. 'Well, something like this,' said Chatterer: 'Truth-teller, the prophet. Dauber, the ikonographer.' 'What about the Messiah?' asked Neurasthenic. 'Slanderer? Schizophrenic?' 'No,' said Chatterer. 'They are apostles. The Messiah will come.' 'Where?' asked Neurasthenic. 'In you, in him, in him, in me, in all of us.' 'And where does he come from, your Messiah?' asked Scientist '—from science? From art? From prison? From politics? From the salons? From reason? From the heart? From the liver?' 'From everywhere,' said Chatterer. 'Who knows, perhaps he's here already. And we are blind and so have not yet recognised him.' 'But why do we need him?' asked Careerist. 'To restore the broken thread of time, and cleanse your soul of the fear of death,' said Visitor. 'Well,' said Neurasthenic, 'that's all very nice. Are we to take you seriously?'

Reaction gathers strength
The jubilee year came to an end. For the next three years the Journal went on publishing the remainder of the material it had

produced. People began to prepare for the next jubilee, due in ten years time, and to publish preparatory material. But because for some reason (probably the machinations of reaction!) there was a delay in the directive establishing the period between the two jubilees, there was a gap which no one knew how to fill. At a meeting Secretary declared that the editorial board was overwhelmed, and put in for reinforcements. A commission was set up, including shock workers from various enterprises, pensioners and leading representatives. The commission began the interrogation of the victims. Claimant hastily returned home from his special extra paid holiday. 'I only need to take a week off,' he yelled at Thinker and all the other editorial staff, 'and look what a bloody mess you get into! Totally helpless! I've got to do every damn thing myself! If you don't want to work, why not say so straight out! I won't detain you!'

Thinker proposed an ingenious scheme—to bring out a series of joint numbers: Ibansko-Polish, Bio-Armenian, genetico-Germano-Chuvash, and also a number devoted to the union between the natural sciences, science and physics. It was decided to begin with an interview with Academician, who had just completed the one hundredth volume of his monumental work *One Moment of One Discovery*. As Academician suffered from incurable verbal diarrhoea, which made it necessary to supply anyone who interviewed him with a special gag fitted with a silencer to clamp his mouth closed, the interview was handed over to Thinker himself. Then Claimant ran into Puss, who at the time was writing an article for the principal reaction leader, Troglodyte. The article was a vicious attack on Claimant. 'I've had a marvellous idea,' said Claimant, and the rest of the conversation was held in whispers. 'Not a word to anyone,' said Claimant. 'And not a word to Neurasthenic, either,' said Puss. 'He can't be trusted. Not by you, nor by us.'

Notes by Slanderer
Only an official ideology can become a truly valuable or even a great ideology. Unofficial ideological formations, are, as a general rule, dependent, deformed and unstable. In the future I shall be dealing exclusively with official ideology. I do not intend in doing so to attempt to construct a global theory of

ideology. I merely want to draw attention to certain aspects of the matter which are important from the point of view of the perspective of social change.

An official ideology is an ideological doctrine and an ideological organisation of people. The tasks of this latter are as follows: to support the doctrine and keep a watch on its purity (protect it from revisions and heresies), its unity (protect it from sects and splits), spread it abroad among the people, ensure that it is treated with respect, root out those who show themselves mistrustful of it, and so on. The ideological organisation is not just one among the various organisations of a society (it is not for instance analogous with a ministry of some branch of industry, or the army). It is an organisation of society as a whole from this point of view. It penetrates all spheres of social activity. Apart from many institutions at various levels (Departments, Institutes, Schools, Groups and so on) ideological work is the task of a multi-million strong army of agitators, propagandists, correspondents, journalists, writers, artists, scientists, from the most lowly to the highest placed. Newspapers, journals, radio, television, books, films, concerts, theatres. Almost every boss at times is an ideological worker. And there is a huge army of volunteers—particularly pensioners, particularly retired colonels. Almost every citizen who has reached a certain age and who has had a half-way decent education is potentially an ideological worker. And he is fitted to be so, indeed, because of the special way in which ideological functions are directed in our society, and by the grandiose structure of ideological education (if I may use such a phrase). It is only thanks to this system that the ideological doctrine becomes such a powerful factor in social life. Without this system it would be unthinkable as a social phenomenon. Without this system it is nothing but an accumulation of texts which can be considered from the most varied points of view—from the historical, the physical, the logical, the critical, and the aesthetic viewpoints. However, if we wish to consider them as ideological texts, we should not forget, not even for a moment, about the activities of this powerful organisation of people. And anyone who intends to attack ideological doctrine without bearing this circumstance in mind will look like a naïve infant or a lunatic. But that is still not all. This is only the beginning.

The period of past confusion was instructive from many points of view. It was instructive, too, from the point of view which concerns us here. Before the beginning of this period it seemed that it would be enough to break the ideological shackles, which had transformed able writers, artists, scientists and so on into untalented liars and cretins, for a new dawn to break. This period offered people enormous possibilities. But was much done? A little. The problem is not whether people had time enough, or freedom enough. There wasn't any alternative any way. The absence of any pressure from this 'alternative' was one of the reasons why the possibilities were not exploited. Everything that people could do, they did. They did all they could. The fact is that the great mass of the people could do nothing else because they did not need to. As became manifestly clear, the great mass of the people who were in one way or another involved in ideology (incidentally, analogous phenomena occurred in other spheres of social life) turned out to be in favour of that form of the official ideology which belonged to them and which they themselves consumed. It suited almost everybody. I am not saying anything about its economic or political consequences. I am not saying that it was good. I am not saying that it was bad. I am merely saying that it suited people. And it would be wrong to think that it was maintained only by violence. It was also voluntarily accepted. I shall not attempt to calculate the percentages of voluntary acceptance, indifference, and forced acceptance. I am no apologist for this ideology. But I think it my duty to state the following fact. Even if for some reason or another the apparatus of ideological constraint ceased operation (for example if it were physically destroyed) certain elements of the official ideological doctrine would retain their importance as elements of some official or unofficial ideology. We are after all dealing with a great ideology. If it were not so, it would not be a problem. And incidentally the general scorn for the official ideology in no way diminished its greatness.

Another success

At his own risk Dauber made a full size clay model of the gravestone. When Chatterer saw it, his jaw dropped. 'I never thought it would come off so well,' he said. 'It's the effect of the scale,' said Dauber. 'And then, even though it's only a little tiny part of me, I've done it without any compromise. That's me, all right. And in marble it won't look at all bad.' 'If you ever get the marble,' said Chatterer. 'And yet it's a Dauber of twenty years ago, and only part of him at that. And all supposing they ever let you put the stone up.' The commissions, the examinations, the decisions were resumed. And this time the outcome was successful. Finally, the chief architect of Ibansk said he would like to see the stone. Twice he set out to see it, but never arrived. On each occasion he was called for an urgent conference on a high level. But now he promised to come for sure provided nothing unexpected cropped up.

The rats

We have established that specialist expert-rats carry out a selection from among the young rats using criteria which only they understand. The experts observe the young for a certain time, then they choose one, surround him and sniff him. Then an assembly of the rats which have already been selected is brought together. The newly selected rat runs into the middle and squeaks something (the squeaks of rats have been recorded and classified: more of this in the next chapter). Then two or three other rats come to the centre of the assembly and also squeak. Then the rats raise their tails. Usually, almost all the tails are lifted. Some abstain. Throughout the entire period of observation, there were only two occasions when a minority of rats raised their tails. On these occasions the chosen rat was immediately torn to pieces and eaten. In all probability this is a ritual act, since all present had usually eaten their fill already. After the tail raising procedure the chosen rat merges into the mass of others, and from then on it is impossible to distinguish him from the mass. From the rats which have been selected in this way, they then elect leaders of all ranks. The election system is so well organised that we observed hardly any errors. We shall describe the elected rats as 'designated'.

Yes, said Chatterer. There can be no mistakes here. But not because the system is rational but because it is completely irrational. An error is always an error of thought. Where there is no thought there can be no mistakes.

We also established, Chatterer read on, that in the complex

leadership system of the colony, there is a regular changeover between the rat-leaders, accompanied by certain measures which at first sight seemed to us inept, but which gradually convinced us of their rationality. These measures are applied in the following order: 1) the stage where the designated rats are promoted into the circle of leadership candidates; 2) the stage of penetration (the result is mutual habituation within a limited group of rats); 3) the push through to leader rank (winning the post); 4) the replacement of the old leader's supporters by his own (a process which usually involves a massive extermination of the old guard); 5) mass terror, with the aim of making every rat docile and timid; 6) some improvements in the ratorium, aimed at winning popularity and justifying what has happened. The rationality of the massive exterminations which systematically accompany these various stages lies beyond any doubt. On one occasion we tried to prevent these exterminations, but the result was pitiful. The old rats who were in the system of control carried out such a fearful pogrom that it was several years before the ratorium regained its normal appearance.

This was the only point at which Chatterer let an inaccuracy slip by. The figures he had predicted were only half of those which the experiment had produced. But he ascribed this discrepancy to the external intervention which had interrupted the normal course of things, and which, from the scientific point of view, was an irregularity in this type of experiment.

Notes by Slanderer

Ideological doctrine deals with the world at large, man and human society. I stress doctrine and not science, if we by science understand the scientific approach as we have defined it earlier. If we were to define the essence of ideological doctrine briefly and in general terms, it would come to the following. The world, man (i.e. you) and society (i.e. the system of a large number of 'yous' with all their weapons, their means of existence and so on) are organised in such a way (or exist according to such laws or obey such laws, NB obey!) that the society in which you live is the best society of all possible societies. Your leadership has a profound (more profound than anyone else) understanding of the laws of the world, of man and of society and builds your life in full conformity with those laws. It does the best possible for you. It lives and works very hard in your interests. And your life is beautiful. It is beautiful thanks only to your wise leaders whose efforts are directed by the most correct theory, and so on. Briefly, here we can see all the attributes of divine wisdom, goodness, farsightedness and so on and so on. But there is one peculiarity here which we should consider. This is the twentieth century, which is rather different, as far as man's living conditions are concerned, from those ages which gave birth to ideologies as important as Christianity, Buddhism or Islam.

Doctrine of the world? There are powerful natural sciences. There is physics, which has clearly expressed its claims to certain areas which hitherto have been regarded as integral parts of philosophy (and philosophy has become part of ideology—'has become', to avoid saying 'is'). Doctrine of man? There is anthropology, physiology, medicine, psychology, pedagogy, genetics, logic, linguistics and so on. Doctrine of society? There is history, sociology, political economy, social literature, social journalism and so on. Moreover man regularly receives limitless supplies of information of all kinds on these subjects. Consequently ideology has to face a problem: it must take up a specific position vis-à-vis all this (and this position is familiar—a position of control, supervision, tutelage, censorship) and win its own territory from science, literature, and the other cultural fields, territory where ideology will not merely be an overseer, but the master, the executive, the creator, the preserver. This territory will become an integral part of the ideological corpus. And ideology holds such territory. It is a certain general doctrine of the world as a whole (*Weltanschauung*), a certain doctrine of cognition and thought and the whole domain of the social sciences. The recent and unhappy attempt by sociology to win if not autonomy, at least the right to bear its own name, is an eloquent demonstration of the vigilance with which ideology defends the sphere of the social sciences. I repeat, by winning control over the social sciences, ideology does not itself become a science. In what concerns the world as a whole and cognition (thought), ideology has a competitor which it is not so easy to overcome; logic. And logic is not so much a competitor as a permanent threat of being caught red-handed.

Supreme authority

'In our country,' said Careerist, 'the supreme authority is also the lowest authority. You must know R. by name of course. Well, he's finally been fired from the chair he's held for years. He'd created an entire school! It was a very high-class chair. By the way, he was my supervisor for a time. You remember the business of those letters? Some went to him as well. He's an honest decent man and he couldn't refuse, even though he doesn't have the slightest interest in politics. It was suggested that he should make a public statement saying he's been tricked. He refused, of course. The very next day he was relieved of his functions. To keep the chair alive, a certain Nil was appointed director. He's an absolute nonentity. He's an obligatory member of every delegation that goes abroad. He doesn't have to go through all the complicated formalities that the rest of us have to put up with—he just goes *ex-officio*. When Nil was appointed they said that it was just a matter of form, and that R. would still in practice be running the department. And for some time that was what actually seemed to happen. But that was only the surface appearance. In fact, it was the beginning of something quite different. The life of a university department consists of a multitude of tiny matters of detail, and it's only when they're all totted up that the results of the way the chair is run can be seen. There are all sorts of elements—checking the students' course and diploma work, selecting post-graduate students, giving the go-ahead for publications, considering reports, introducing new special courses and closing down old ones, deciding who supervises which students' work, marking exam papers, distributing work, deciding who's ready to defend their theses . . . and almost every decision involves a choice. None of these choices taken by themselves is a matter of any great difficulty, because you can always argue the case so that you can't subsequently be attacked. But little by little, if we consider all the choices taken together, a clear tendency begins to emerge. Say, for example, there are two research projects, A and B. At first sight it seems there's no essential difference between them. Indeed, project B at first sight looks the bolder, more progressive. But R. knows that project A has more possibilities. It's true that it's more difficult, and needs firmer direction and a more determined and able scientist. Nil knows that R. knows this, and he does the very opposite. He is the director. It's not a desperately important matter—not a matter of principle, so R. doesn't argue about it, out of tact. He's simply lost when he comes up against people like Nil. So project B is selected for the post-graduate work. Let's say there are two students A and B. Almost identical performance. Perhaps B is slightly more promising. But R. prefers A, and therefore Nil prefers B. Nil is supported by the social organisations in the university, the party and so on. So B is selected for the post-graduate course. This goes on quite openly. Everyone can see it, everyone can understand it. But no-one can resist it. The dean? But all his life he has envied R. Every night he's dreamt of ways of squashing him. And anyway, why make a fuss about nothing? The whole faculty gradually becomes demoralised. When the case of one of R.'s students or post-graduates is discussed, it's all nagging, cavils, fault-finding. And all this is done, of course, completely correctly and for the best of reasons. When Nil's students and post-graduates are being discussed, everything's fine. A few minor defects, but faults that can easily be put right. Go ahead, with a good recommendation. It looks as if both have passed in the normal way. But men are men. And gradually they begin to show a preference for Nil. Anything for a quiet life. The more interesting students keep on going to R. for a time. But there aren't very many of them—and sometimes none at all. And R. is a fussy, choosy man, who won't accept just anyone who comes to him. A post in the department falls vacant. There are two contenders, A and B. One is attracted by R., or at all events not attracted by Nil. The other is quite happy to do what anybody wants. Their formal qualifications are pretty much the same. B is selected. The department begins to fill up with people who are only a little more able than Nil, then of about the same calibre, and finally less well equipped even than he. And all this has gone on quite lawfully, openly, with the approval of the highest university authorities. Nil's people are more skilled at sorting out their personal affairs, R.'s people are scientists, who don't know how to resist this sort of thing. R.'s favourite student is obliged to leave the department. And there's a reason for this: he spoke out of turn at a meeting. Another one gave him away. A third quietly slipped off into the sidelines. L. went off to a better paid and more peaceful job. Yes, L., you heard. In the end R. found himself completely isolated. And almost without any work to do. Of course he couldn't stay in the department.'

'But surely,' Dauber said angrily, 'didn't the results of the department's work show who was worth more?' 'How? The students are studying normally, meeting their other obligations, passing their exams, getting jobs, doing post-graduate work, writing theses. The courses are going on. Examinations are being set. The academic board meets regularly. Life goes on normally. Even rather better than in some departments. The educational programme has been improved. Some effective new measures have been introduced. The staff of the department are happy with their lot. Those who aren't either look stupid or leave. Moreover, it's put about everywhere that R. and his group are working in the department, which is greatly honoured all round. Of course the results do show the effect of all this. But in such a way that the sources are concealed and those responsible can't be identified. The effects are shown on a national scale, in the state of some branches of science or the economy. For example, say a setback in some field is discovered. Something didn't fly properly, or didn't explode. Guilty men will be found all right, but not the right guilty men, and not in the right place. People like Nil are invulnerable. By the way, he's been proposed as a Corresponding Member of the Academy. He won't be elected, of course. But even to be proposed is a recognition of his merits. There again, he might just possibly be elected.' 'I've read all this in general terms in Schizophrenic's book,' said Dauber. 'But I must confess that I didn't really believe that all this happened like this in your scientific world. And what's the way out?' 'What way out are you talking about?' said Careerist. 'Nil's people do certain things no worse than R.'s people, and R.'s people are a social nuisance: they are proud, dignified, even honourable. Nil's people are obedient, and ready to do anything they're asked. R.'s people gain in strength when they feel that society needs them. For example, it's necessary to catch up with, to overtake an able adversary—in short to enter into competition with him. The way out is to suppress the adversary. Then there'll be no need for R.'s people. No more problems. It's true that then some other processes will start up. Nil's people are maintained at a certain level thanks to R.'s people, who are tolerated because of the general situation. If R.'s people disappear, then along will come an Infranil who will devour Nil and replace Nil's people with his own, or force them to reduce the standard still lower.' 'It's appalling,' said Dauber. 'Nothing out of the ordinary,' said Careerist. 'It's normal. It suits most people, perhaps even nearly all. There are only a few individuals who suffer. In the long term everyone suffers, of course, but Nil's people suffer least. And they couldn't care less. Deep in their hearts even decent people are quite glad at R.'s fall. It lets them feel righteous anger and at the same time feel that they themselves are slightly more important.' 'How do you yourself react to this story?' asked Dauber. 'Like everyone else,' said Careerist. 'As you see, I'm complaining about it to you. Incidentally, we've had to assess Nil's work—it was a positive assessment, of course. I voted "for". I am neither you nor R. I'm an ordinary mortal. I like my comfort. I've got a family. I'd like to go abroad for a couple of months. There's a possibility that I might be able to. If I'd voted against, that'd be the end of that. And again, my son is just about to enter this faculty. Now there Nil really is somebody.' 'While I've been listening to you,' said Dauber, 'I've been having a growing feeling that I was observing through a microscope a cancerous tumour developing in the body of a man I am fond of, and that I couldn't do a thing to stop it. The awful thing is not that all this is happening. That's probably always happened everywhere, and always will happen. What *is* appalling is that it all goes on without any disguise, without any psychology, without any moral drama.' 'We mustn't paint too black a picture,' said Careerist. 'After all, we're alive, we work, we even laugh. And we have rich, intelligent conversations. What more do you want? The present moment is life itself, not a preparation for life.'

Fear

Despite all the measures designed to prevent it, the Ibansk intelligentsia had a fairly full idea of the dissident literature that had been produced over the last few years. At all events, people talked about it as if it had become a compulsory subject in political education classes. 'Truth-teller's last book,' said Scientist, 'is overwhelming. It made me feel afraid.' They began to

(266)

talk about fear. Chatterer said, 'I distinguish between the animal fear we find in man, and the human fear we find in the animal. The animal fears murders and violence in general, evils that it can see or foresee. Man fears the impossibility of doing the good he is capable of. It is dreadful, of course, that there are many people who have the capacity and the occasion to do evil, but it is still worse that there are few people who have the capacity and the occasion to do good. What is truly appalling is not that there are exceptions to the rule, but that there is a rule from which there must be exceptions. It is, of course, extremely important to ascertain the fact of murders, violence, terror and the rest, and discover the guilty. But it is something else which interests me—the horror of a situation in which no-one is killed, but in which something much more dreadful happens, where people who are capable of becoming Men are not allowed to do so.' 'I understand what you mean,' said Dauber. 'But this position condemns you to inaction.' 'It all depends on what you mean by action,' said Chatterer. 'For instance, we are talking—that's action. It's not as sensational as Truth-teller's book, but it's action all the same. In the last analysis a book is written to make people talk. Sometimes inaction is a preparation for action.' 'All the same, it seems to me that you are underestimating the active side of man,' said Dauber. 'Truth-teller's book has a lot of examples of cases where the action of even a small number of people produced an effect.' 'What effect?' asked Chatterer. 'Material for a book, certainly, but no more. And anyway these are phenomena which stay outside the threshold of history. Historically they do not exist and have never existed. In other words, if you're a mouse and don't like your situation, how are you going to advise mice to turn into elephants?'

Notes by Slanderer

I recall a conversation with Scientist. I said that the so-called world doctrine (*Weltanschauung*) was a purely ideological phenomenon, which had nothing in common with science except its verbal form. Scientist, who has always held philosophy in contempt, on this occasion, to my surprise, came to its defence. Subsequently I was able to establish that despite their apparent disdain for philosophy, the representatives of the concrete sciences support it to a considerable extent. Their very disdain is a form of recognition, a purely subjective and generally accepted way of expressing the fact that in their heart of hearts there is nothing more positive. It is true to say that our *Weltanschauung* is closely bound up with science. It is easy to scorn what others have done. Try to propose something better!

'There is a certain amount of truth in all that,' said Scientist. 'Take for example the proposition that everything in the world is in a state of change. That is really so! It's a commonplace, of course, but it's true.' 'Are you sure of that?' I asked. 'What about invariable objects? And how does a circular square change, for instance?' 'That's sophistry,' Scientist protested. 'You understand perfectly well what I mean! What's the point of this verbal cavilling?' 'Yes,' I said. 'I know what we're talking about. And for that reason I don't regard this as verbal cavilling. We're talking about precise linguistic expressions. And I am right to regard them as facts of language. These "cavils" are essential if, of course, you are striving for clarity. For example, you argue that everything in the world is interlinked. What do you mean by that? That any phenomenon is connected with any other phenomenon? And what do you mean when you use words like "interlinked" or "connected"? Why are you so sure of this? Think about it and you'll soon convince yourself that your statement is an empty, meaningless phrase. But you don't even begin to suspect what traps there are lurking in statements like that. Very well, let's suppose that we have made this sentence more precise, and we've reached a statement that says that all phenomena are brought about by a causal link, or by some other link. Here you use the word "all". In other words, this includes phenomena which are *not* brought about by a causal link. So this means that phenomena which are not brought about by a causal link are brought about by a causal link.' Scientist protested. 'We are talking about existing phenomena,' he said. 'When do they exist? Now? Yesterday? And where do they exist? But all this does not resolve the paradox. Let us say that all existing empirical phenomena (let's add that further reservation "empirical") are brought about by a causal link. According to the very rules which control linguistic expressions, every existing phenomenon brought about by a causal link is an existing empirical phenomenon, and it is therefore equally concerned in the general statement. So we still have our insoluble paradox—a phenomenon which is not brought about by a causal link is brought about by a causal link. Exactly the same thing goes for the statement "Everything changes". If we take this even in the limited form "Every existing empirical phenomenon changes", we still have to cope with the next problem—what about empirical phenomena which do not change? Do we accept that such phenomena do not exist? Fine! But from the point of view of the construction of scientific expressions, this is the same as accepting the following: we shall describe as empirical those phenomena which have such characteristics, including the property of mutability. But this doesn't suit ideology. For ideology, the statement that everything changes should be the conclusion of mankind's long and arduous searches to understand the world. It should be a great discovery, not a commonplace agreement about the meaning of words. So begin to dig right down to the essence of the matter, set out your results publicly, and you'll know what it feels like. Ideology is also fixed in linguistic expressions. But linguistic ideological phenomena are formed, function and have an effect on people according to rules quite different from those of linguistic scientific expressions.'

'Very well,' said Scientist. 'Let's accept that you are to some degree right about the doctrine of the world as a whole. Although there is still a great deal that is not clear to me. But what about the doctrine of society? That's not philosophy! That is science!' 'What is the difference?' I asked. 'Let us take, for example, the idea of a classless society.'

Absence of clarity

The arguments ended either in nothing, or at best, in insults. But they always began again. And their subjects were nearly always the same. Was the Boss a genius or not? Was Hog a great statesman or not? What would have happened if there hadn't been a revolution? What would have happened if the Boss hadn't existed? What would have happened if Truth-teller had been published? And so on in the same sort of spirit. Even decent people come in lots of varieties, said Chatterer. Some determine their position immediately and go straight into action: they write, they make speeches, they protest and so on. Others lack intellectual clarity, particularly those for whom the search for clarity is a calling and sometimes even a profession. People cannot all act in the same way. If my vocation and my action are the search for truth, then why should I dash out into the streets shouting 'Down with . . .!'. Take T. for instance. He grew up in a village. There were a lot of children in his family. They worked on a collective farm. The work was fiendishly hard, and all they got back were a few crumbs. And sometimes they had to work at night to earn even that. Naturally they stole, or they would have starved to death. And yet they had entered the collective farm willingly. Do you think they were tricked? No. Most people knew perfectly well what life on a collective farm would cost them. And if later they had been offered a farm of their own again, most people would have refused. They often talked about it at home. And they had no reason to lie to each other. So what was the explanation? There are a number of aspects to consider. In particular, in T.'s family, all the children had got on in life. One had become a factory director, another a colonel, a third a doctor of science. The sisters had gone off to the city where they'd become housewives or simply workers—one was a driver. But the main thing was that they had all got themselves settled, they'd all got their little attic rooms (and that was a great thing in those days). And even collective farm work wasn't made up entirely of drawbacks. For one thing, the people had all their worries taken off their shoulders. Machines had begun to appear. I don't want to tell you things which everyone knows. It's simply a matter of taking account of the real situation. And that situation was that the revolution and all the measures which followed it were a huge benefit to the people. Otherwise there is no way that you can understand everything which has happened and which is still happening. You have to be a complete idiot to regard the revolution and everything that the government has done since as sheer crimes and stupidity. There are no wise revolutions. There are no revolutions that are not criminal. And it is not true to say that there was a good part and a bad part, and that one of them was the stronger. There is another factor: history. And another: historical problems. Not yesterday's, but today's and tomorrow's. Take, for instance, Truthteller. Why does he produce such an effect? Because of the awful facts of the past? Rubbish. That is only raw material for thought about the present. They are the literary and ideological form taken by the reflections of a contemporary about our contemporary problems. It is a manifestation of modern life based on the facts of past history. And he is interpreted differently depending on whether it's seen from here or Over There. Let's talk frankly. Does he deal with problems with which most people here are directly concerned? To a small degree and in passing. Waste and apathy and so on. That's not a social problem for the population at large. What about the interests of the bureaucrats? Are they really threatened by massive repression? No. As for the rest, that is trivia, for they are the power. The intelligentsia? And who are they? Those who belong to the world of science or culture are for the most part just as much bureaucrats and penpushers. And so they are in a similar position. Have they any reason to be discontented? Yes. But what degree of discontent? People are always discontented. And their discontent is not such that it could become social discontent. So what remains? A very heterogeneous opposition, in which, no matter how mad this may sound, there are just as many representatives of people in power and close to it, as there are people who are persecuted and oppressed.

A new defeat

'That's marvellous,' said Chatterer, 'just one more blow, and I'll begin to believe that you'll finally get permission to go ahead with the gravestone. But what exactly has happened?' 'I don't understand it myself,' said Dauber. 'The chief architect came along, and he was very enthusiastic. He showered so much praise on the model that I was quite embarrassed. And then all the time he seemed to be trying to find out what people higher up thought about it. I said, it's all fine. It's all been agreed. All the papers are signed. All I need now are your permission, and an order to the management of the cemetery. And that's it. And he kept on fidgeting around the model. I think I've tumbled to his game: he hadn't been given any orders from above. They'd left the decision to him. If there was a row, he'd be guilty; if it all turned out well, they'd take the credit. But he's crafty. He's not going to take any responsibility. Now the whole affair depends on him alone, and he won't do a thing without guarantees. He doesn't need an approval of the gravestone as an example of sculpture, but a directive from above to put the stone up at all. It doesn't make any difference precisely what stone it is. But there hasn't been such a directive.' 'What happens now?' asked Chatterer. 'Back to Square One,' said Dauber.

It's men who take all the decisions

'From what you say,' said Dauber, 'nothing depends on the will of men. Why not?' 'Because everything depends on it,' said Chatterer. 'That's just a play on words,' said Dauber. 'Very well,' said Chatterer. 'Let's say then that there are some things which depend on the will of men and others that don't. Is that the kind of thing that you wanted to hear me say?' 'No,' said Dauber. 'That's of no importance. But aren't there things that happen of their own accord?' 'Yes,' said Chatterer. 'But we only discover their consequences after thousands of years—again through the will of men. Can you feel the movements of continents? Within the geological eras of a society social life is autonomous. Take any sphere of life and you will see that everywhere people are faced by the problem of free choice. I am obliged to speak in paradoxes again. It is freedom itself which engenders dependence. I defy you to find me a single instance in our social life where the decision a man takes does not depend on his will. Everything depends on how many people say "no", and where, when and how they do. That is the basis of everything. It is senseless to expect anything else. There is simply nothing else in the nature of society and of man.' 'So you mean,' said Dauber, 'that these people who immolate themselves by self-arson in public places, who go on hunger strike, who kill themselves, who write their stupid little books. . . .' 'Yes,' said Chatterer, 'even they make up our history.' 'But, you know, I know a lot of these people,' said Dauber. 'They are ill-educated, many of them are mentally sick, abnormal, incompetent, unstable . . .' 'But you would engage in such a terrible battle and at the same time preserve your mental balance, your good wages, your creative ability, your family's and your own health?' asked Chatterer. 'Then why do they keep up the battle?' asked Dauber. 'Because they can't do anything else,' said Chatterer.

Types of tragedy

For a creative person, said Neurasthenic to himself, the greatest tragedy is not to be able to do what he believes himself capable of. That is well known. My contribution to this problem will be to prepare a typology of tragedy. I can distinguish here three types of tragedy. The first type is the tragedy of Truth-teller. He needs nothing from society except a chance for his voice to be heard. The second type of tragedy is that of Dauber. What he demands from society, apart from that, is a large amount of materials (for example bronze, stone, a studio, space and so on). The third type of tragedy is that of Slanderer. What he wants from society is people, for he has a prime need to make men. Truth-teller and Dauber also need people and to influence people. But their direct creative product is words, books, paintings, sculpture. Slanderer is an educator. For him books are secondary, a support, an accessory. The main thing for him is to be able to mould men's concrete consciousness. All the representatives of these three types can be deprived of the possibility of following their vocation. But by different methods and with different consequences. Truth-teller has been expelled from Ibansk by force. Dauber will flee of his own accord. But what about Slanderer? Slanderer would not leave on his own account, and even if he wanted to they wouldn't let him. Slanderer should simply have disappeared, dissolved, vanished into thin air. I don't know what is worse and what is better. But what is even worse still is that we do not even feel the tragedy of what is going on. We do everything in our power (and in this we are all-powerful!), to lose the tragedy in the jumble of day to day trivia. We could have lived surrounded by flowers. But flowers horrify us. So we trample them in our own mud and filth. There is no need to, but we do. Then Neurasthenic, greatly moved by the beauty of his own thoughts, began to reflect on how he was going to defend his thesis.

The publication of a book

It is not true, said Neurasthenic, to maintain that it is difficult here to get oneself published. On the contrary we are obliged to go into print. There are even norms we have to fulfil. For instance every year I am obliged to bring out eight or nine thousand words—a book every two years. That's quite something. And every year the Institute is obliged to publish an entire library of scientific discoveries. And bear in mind that our brief is to publish only creative, original work at the highest level which is a contribution to future developments in science. And the level of our work should be higher year by year. An entire grandiose system has been developed to guarantee this irresistible progress.

It goes without saying that there is a general directive defining the development of all science for the given historical period. And everything that happens happens within the framework and in the light of this directive. The directive passes downwards from step to step in the form of every kind of executive document until it gets to the workers at the bottom of the pyramid. These people plunge their heads in their hands and begin to wonder what they're going to plan for the next ten years, then for the next five years, and finally for the year that is staring them in the face. The precise content of the plan is of no particular importance because, whatever happens, everyone will go on doing the same thing. The main thing is to invent a new title which will please the authorities, or at least won't irritate them. The invention of titles is a difficult job. Then the titles are stuck together to form the broad plan of the group, the section, the department, the institute. The draft plans now move back upwards, enriched with concrete content. When they have been completed and confirmed at a high level, they come back down again, this time as directives. Now the worker who has included his research project in the plan is obliged to produce his work within the specified timescale for discussion by his research group. When he's come successfully through all these stages and taken account of critical remarks, the worker acquires the right to include his book in the plan prepared by the editorial board. After this the manuscript is corrected and again goes through all the stages, gathering at each stage documents with seals, signatures and comments. After discussion at the Scientific Council and at the Board of Management, the manuscript is sent to the publishing house, where it is read by a junior editor, the senior editor, the literary editor and the editor-in-chief. It is then included in the publishing schedule. After many meetings between the author and the editors, the manuscript ends up at the press where the text is set up. The first proof is execrable. The second is bad. The third is still bad, but a little better. The fourth, finally, is still bad but bearable. After a further series of seals and signatures, the edition is printed, and after a visit to Glavlit (a pseudonym for the censorship), it is published.

If you are idle and don't keep to your schedule (for this read: if the subject is difficult and demands a more serious approach!), or if you've written something extremely mediocre (for this read: if you have revealed a high degree of competence, a good knowledge of the subject, an ability to find creative ways of solving the problem!), this whole system is not even observed. It is as if it had never existed. You are either pressed or given more time, you're praised, or given a welter of advice. All your friends offer to give you the helpful comments you need. You might even manage to get a fee, and you will certainly get a bonus. But God help you if you produce something out of the ordinary or, horror of horrors, outstanding! If you do, every cog in the system will immediately come into play, and every cog will show its own irresistible power. You will discover that anybody, no matter who, can sink your book, or at least freeze it on any pretext for an indefinite time, even under the pretext that it contains a new, unapproved point of view, that it wouldn't do to hurry, that more discussion is needed. In these circumstances it makes absolutely no difference if you have a whole string of publications behind you, if you are well known and have a good reputation. Any work out of the ordinary is treated as if you were a beginner, trying to launch your first garbled concoction. Everyone who has any hand in evaluating an outstanding work suddenly turns out to be a specialist in the field, even if this very field has first been discovered in your book. And everyone turns out to be better qualified than the author, even though they have never published anything on the subject. If anyone who has anything to do with the preparation of the work for publication finds himself unable to understand any part of the work, this means that the author has made some error. Everything in the work must be correct, nothing must be incorrect. Everyone feels responsible for it. They all have only one concern—the interests of world science (or national, depending on the circumstances).

Not to publish? Certainly anyone can write without being

published for some time. Writing for your desk drawer, or maybe for the waste-paper basket. But a man cannot carry his own road with him for long. He must either leave it behind him, or do nothing. Or behave as everyone else does.

Happiness

'What a joy it is,' said Schizophrenic, 'that we are all fictitious characters. We can talk about suffering without experiencing hunger, cold or pain. We can talk about the discomfort of life without having to repair a tap, hunt for bed-bugs or complain about noisy neighbours.' 'Yes,' said Chatterer, 'we're very lucky that we have no real existence. And besides we can make discoveries without having to worry about publishing our books or getting our fees. We can produce masterpieces without suffering sordid arguments about getting them exhibited. This does have a certain charm and beauty of its own.'

Plagiarism

Claimant's plan was brilliantly simple: Plagiarise! Puss, who was writing an article for Troglodyte, was to insert in it a fair-sized chunk taken from some publication which was sunk in oblivion. He was to insert it without any alteration at all, otherwise it would not be plagiarism. In conditions where everybody copies everybody else without indicating their sources, you need something more than a mere borrowing, usually involving a few insignificant changes, to commit a plagiarism. You need a very considerable passage of at least several pages to make the situation legally incontestable. The idea of a plagiarism imposed itself naturally. Troglodyte had already been accused of plagiarism by the relatives of his former colleagues (posthumously rehabilitated) on whom in the past he had written open or secret denunciations. But all that had come to nothing. First, Troglodyte had lifted articles and entire chapters (some indeed insinuated that he had stolen entire works, but this remained unproven, for the victims of repression were even more degenerate than Troglodyte himself); now, it is always more difficult to prove a large-scale theft. It is indeed almost impossible. Secondly, at that time everything was explained by the tragedy of the situation, the more so since Troglodyte's theft had been so ludicrous that the commission of inquiry, made up mainly of young and progressive people, simply wept with laughter. But now everything was different. Now there was no falling back on historical necessity. A blow against Troglodyte would be a blow at the very heart of reaction. 'But take care,' Claimant said to Puss, 'to insert the plagiarised passage in the article after Neurasthenic has finished correcting it. Otherwise it's absolutely certain that that idiot will correct the plagiarism as well.'

When Neurasthenic, who was an inveterate idler by nature, was rewriting the article that Puss had written for publication under Troglodyte's name, he inserted a good dozen shorter or longer paragraphs from a leading article on the same subject which had appeared in the Journal of the previous year. The article was published in the Directive Journal with amazing speed. The very next day all the responsible institutions were inundated with dozens of letters accusing Troglodyte of literary theft. A commission was set up at the highest level. At this point circumstances came to light which had to be hastily concealed, and it was ruled that the incident had never taken place. What had happened was that Puss had inserted in Troglodyte's article a passage from an article by Deputy, which had been taken by the author of Deputy's article from an old article by Troglodyte which he had stolen from his rehabilitated predecessor. And the passages inserted by Neurasthenic in his turn proved to have been lifted from an editorial in the Journal at the time when Secretary was the editor. No attempt was made to discover where Secretary had lifted it from as, all things considered, the chain might have led right back to the Founding Fathers, and perhaps even further. Although the affair of the plagiarism seemed to come to nothing, all the interested parties derived some satisfaction from it, and interpreted it in their favour.

The opposition

In our country, said Chatterer, the opposition is a fact. And it plays a social role. But it is not homogeneous, and that is the first thing that must be born in mind. It has no common interests which could unite it. This is its general structure. First of all there are the liberals, who strive for power and imagine that they could organise life better than the conservatives. But their liberalism degenerates into demagogy or stupidity.

Secondly we have the pragmatists, who are unhappy about the poor progress that is being made purely in the field of production. They are not even liberals. They come wholly and completely within the framework of the system. Thirdly there are the people who are discontented by the fact that within this system they have no room to manoeuvre and to achieve their ends. This group even includes some criminals. They have no concern for moral and social considerations. They want, and are not given. Fourthly, there is the creative intelligentsia, who have no chance of realising their potential because of directives from above and the efforts of their colleagues who implement those directives. Fifth, there are people who are acquainted with the Western way of life and are discontented that they cannot live in the same way here. Sixth, there are people who have become the depositories of a general discontent with the excesses of the regime, and principally with its terror and oppression. Foremost among them is the Truth-teller. The seventh group includes people who have suffered in various ways from the conditions of our life. Hog was one example. Eighth, there are people who have thought deeply about the essence of our life independently of oppression, the West, business interests and so on, and who naturally arouse general hostility. Such were Slanderer and Schizophrenic. All the opposition groups, with the exception of the sixth and the last, parade themselves in virtuous garments. The last group strips them of this disguise. That is why the position of this group is the hardest of all. The members of the sixth group have at least the secret sympathy of almost all the opposition. But if we now consider concrete individuals, then quite often they cannot be clearly classed in one group or another. They belong partly to one and partly to another. And if we take the opposition mentality, its diversity may appear to make it even less definable. So to look for any unity of action after all that! It does not and cannot exist.

Of course the opposition cannot fail to leave traces behind it. And it exerts its influence on the course of Ibanskian history. How! You already know of cases of individual and even collective actions. They cannot be ignored. They have their effect. But that is not the main line of opposition activity, which passes through the work of the whole apparatus which directs society. There are indeed cases where an action of the apparatus directed against certain elements of the opposition finally results in the accomplishment of some of the wishes of the opposition. Unfortunately history works in such a way that the ideas are put forward by one group, realised by a second, and their fruits are enjoyed by a third. And man has only one life.

It is the mediocre who survive

'Mediocrity has a better chance of succeeding in our art world,' said Dauber. 'I know from experience. Neurasthenic says that the same thing is true in science. But surely it can't be in industry? There at least there are certain rules which impose a specific level and style of work.' 'At all events,' said Neurasthenic, 'every discipline has its own rules, its own level and its own style of work. That goes for yours as well, and for science. What's the difference? And then I'm talking about mediocrity as the general average, and not about success in the specific area of work, but about social success. These are very different things. It's quite clear that in art mediocrity cannot achieve great success in the creative sense, but it can achieve success in the sense of titles, honour, money, exhibitions. A mediocrity can become famous and be respected by all as an outstanding talent. That is social success. You know all that perfectly well. And to be a mediocrity is not so bad. I never use value categories because they're too vague. That is also true of a whole range of institutions once they're considered as social individuals.' 'Going by my observations,' said Careerist, 'Neurasthenic is right. You see, if an institution begins to work noticeably better than others, it draws attention to itself. If it is officially recognised in this role, it soon turns into a fake or a showplace, which also in time degenerates into a run-of-the-mill fake. If this does not happen, other institutions, which are piqued by its success, will take appropriate steps. The possibilities here are unlimited. For example, for any good work to be produced, even for any normal work, laws, instructions, rules and so on have to be broken. There are so many of them and they are so formulated, that there is no way to avoid breaking them. So there is always something for enemies to snipe at. Then there are divisions and dissentions within the management. For instance someone's envy and desire to oust the director. There may be denunciations and so on. In a word, as time goes by, somehow

(279)

or other success will turn out to be either unlawful, or over-inflated, ephemeral or abnormal and so on. The most satisfactory variant is the golden mean with, just for appearance's sake, a slight improvement but not enough to annoy others. In brief, it is best to be like everybody else. This as a whole tends to a reduction of the level of activity below actual technological potential. Certainly the laws of production do impose a certain level and style of work. But here too variations are possible. There are establishments which are ruled by this technical principle: if the work is done it should be well done; if the work is done badly then it is not done at all. For example you can't fly to Venus in a badly made spaceship. But there are other establishments where the technical principle in force is quite different: even work badly done is still work done. There is no need to look far for examples. From this point of view it is in practice impossible to determine the attitude of our industry. So it is difficult to say how general social tendencies actually influence the functioning of industry in the country as a whole. It is a very interesting and complex problem. But as far as I know, no-one is working on it. For it is the official view that in our country production is stimulated by competition for the best results and by mutual aid.'

Abstract from Chatterer's manuscripts
First I could never understand why people who create an illusion (an imitation) of work achieve greater successes than people who actually do real work, why the imitation of work is more viable than work itself. I cannot claim to have worked through to the end of this problem. But I can claim to have begun to understand something about it.

At first sight the problem is amazingly paradoxical. In many cases work needs very few people (sometimes literally two or three or at the most five). The imitation of work involves the participation of enormous masses of people, who can be counted in dozens or even hundreds. At first I thought there must be some law by which work needed some kind of human envelope, similar to the way in which bones and muscles are wrapped in a layer of fat. Later I became convinced that in most cases the imitation of work arises without any actual work, independently of the actual work, or destroys the actual work,

(280)

while itself flourishing still more. The actual work can often be done in a few days or months. The imitation of work can last for years or decades. I have tried to find some general mechanism which could explain these phenomena, but in vain. It was not that I was unable to find any, but that I became convinced that every case depends on different circumstances. An analysis of these could produce only certain general judgements which, while having no power of proof, left no room for doubt. Here are some of them. The performance of real work demands a limited number of people. The number of people who are drawn into the imitation of work is in principle unlimited. An acquaintance of mine, an outstanding imitator of science (both as to texts and as to the organisation of research) brought off the remarkable coup of founding a research establishment of several hundred people and spending more than a million for work on a problem that wasn't worth a spent match and which could be solved in a few moments—and negatively at that. Attempts to unmask him failed, since some high placed organisations had an interest in the business, and as far as his enemies were concerned, they were swindlers as well. Real work needs a final result which should be mercilessly checked and evaluated by outside authorities according to principles independent of those who have done the work. The imitation of work needs only an apparent result—or rather the mere possibility of justifying the time that has been spent: checking and evaluation of results carried out by people who've taken part in the imitation, who are connected with it and who have an interest in perpetuating it. The progress of real work is imperceptible routine, even boring and laborious. Imitation is all bustle and go. It can be regarded as a grandiose theatrical production, made up of meetings, symposiums, reports, travel, inter-group battles, changes of leadership, commissions of inquiry and so on. Real work demands a stringent selection of personnel based on professional criteria. Real work rejects those who are not chosen, without worrying about their fate. It is easy to take part in an imitation. There is a kind of selection process which establishes a certain professional gradation. But it does not exclude those who are rejected, who continue to take part in the imitation. To put it briefly, the imitation of work is, as Schizophrenic would say, a purely social phenomenon protected by all

(281)

the means of social defence. For the imitation, the work itself is only a pretext, a means, a form. Real work, though, is an anti-social phenomenon. Of itself it is defenceless and needs protection. It is only tolerated to the degree where its disappearance or its poor state of health might threaten the existence of the imitation. Work demands intelligence, ability, determination, conscientiousness, self-criticism and other rare human qualities. Thus it needs individuals the least well adapted to society. The imitation of work is satisfied with an average social individual with a socially average professional training.

Usually no distinction is made between the imitation of work and real work, and the former is taken for the latter. Often the imitation of work contains real work and allows it more or less to survive. It feeds a large number of people, and some of them, thanks to this, manage to do some useful work. However sometimes the imitation of work becomes the cause, or one of the causes, of certain serious consequences. This is true in particular when the object of the work is large masses of people. For example, during the war, the real work of the command of operations was overlaid by a powerful imitation of the system of command. The consequences of this are well known. And it is hard to deny that the imitation of the work of ensuring state security made a major contribution to the extermination of huge masses of people who were no threat to the security of the state.

Deception

Once again they hired a truck and some labourers, and once again they drove to the stoneyard. They waited outside the director's office for an hour although he had nobody with him, and it was his official time for seeing clients. At last a bell rang and the secretary disappeared through a door covered in fly-blown leatherette with a lot of notices pinned to it. Twenty minutes later she emerged and asked Dauber to come in. Dauber had met the director before, and the director must have recognised him. But the director didn't reply to Dauber's greeting and didn't invite him to sit down. 'What do you want?' he asked with unconcealed scorn and assurance of his own superiority. Dauber saw 'no' written all over his face no matter what his wants or needs were. 'Not at the moment,' said the

director. 'Come again next Thursday. There'll be some then.'
'Are you sure there will?' asked Dauber. 'Give me a firm date so
I don't waste my time. We've hired a lorry today'. 'I told you
it'll be here, so it will be here,' said the director. And without so
much as a goodbye he called for the next customer.

When they were driving home, they laughed about it. 'Just
imagine,' said Dauber, 'Michelangelo spends an hour in a
waiting room (if you can call that hut a waiting room) to see that
filthy lout. He goes in. "What do you want?" "Well," he says,
"I'd like a bit of marble. I want to carve a Pietà." "No," says the
lout. "Come back next week." They're such bastards, people
like that. They stop decent people working.' Next Thursday
they went back. The director wouldn't see them, he was too
busy with some highly-placed people. 'It's enough to drive you
mad,' said Dauber. 'What's the answer? Have we got to start
again from the beginning?' 'I don't think so,' said Careerist. 'It
seems to me that in this case we can see the general principles of
our organisation at work. In this case it doesn't make a blind bit
of difference whether you're Michelangelo, Neizvestniy or
Dauber.' 'But it's bloody senseless,' spluttered Dauber. 'A
senseless waste of time and money. We'd come to an agreement! Why couldn't he simply have said next Thursday rather
than this!' 'It may be senseless from your point of view,' said
Chatterer. 'But in fact there's a very deep meaning here. For
example you take your shoes to be repaired. It's only a five-
minute job. But you spend at least half an hour in the queue.
You hand over the shoes. You get a ticket which says they'll
take a week. Oh, you want them back sooner do you? Very well,
put "urgent". And they tell you it'll take one day, or two or
three. It makes no difference. The main thing is that they've
given you a precise date. If you're inexperienced at this sort of
thing, you go back on the appointed day, you stand in the queue
and they tell you they're not ready, come back tomorrow. You
don't go back tomorrow but the day after. You queue up again
and they tell you there's a delay at the factory, come back
tomorrow. If you are experienced, you don't come back on the
appointed day but several days later. You queue up, and they
tell you they're not ready, come back tomorrow. You think:
What the devil is all this mystery? It really is a mystery. In such
situations one can't avoid the standard procedures of deception,

queuing, insults and exasperation. You must always be in a state of confusion, anger, and ready for all sorts of unpleasantness. There is a sense in all this. You must regard everything that you get without difficulty as a gift of fate, a triumph, a blessing, and you should think yourself happy if you eventually manage to achieve what you had reckoned to achieve without effort. From this comes your attempts to reduce to a minimum your number of contacts with people on whom you depend for anything, i.e. it leads in the final analysis to a self-imposed restriction of demand. From here too comes the habit of grabbing everything that comes to hand, i.e. a lack of control of consumption which depends on external circumstances. On the other hand people are forced to waste time to no purpose, time which they could otherwise turn to good account, for such purposes as thinking about their life, about art, or generally about themselves and their self-improvement. Bear in mind that when people spend their time in queues getting upset about the details of day-to-day life, their personalities are degraded. It isn't while standing in queues that great discoveries are made. It isn't while standing in queues that a sense of honour and human dignity grows stonger.'

'It's another aspect of all this that disturbs me,' said Careerist. 'Lies and deception add up not simply to disorder, bad workmanship and total indifference to people—there's more to it than that. When we were still students we tried to find a formula of deception which would enable us to work out the real situation every time. For example, you were given an appointment for Thursday this week. You work out the formula and you find out that you should come back on Wednesday fortnight. Then you can apply similar formulae to any similar appointment. If you're told that the plan has been fulfilled by 125 per cent, you do your sum, and it works out at 92 per cent at the most. But there is no such formula and in principle there cannot be. The trouble is that in our society deception is irregular both in quantity and form. Its presence is fundamental. It is regular in qualitative terms. You know that in reality it was, is and will be different. But you never know in what concrete form and to what extent you will be deceived.' Chatterer said that that was in perfect agreement with his theory. You can adapt yourself to regular deception and regard it as a literary form of the naked truth. Deception which is susceptible to calculation and prediction is the official form of truth.

'But there must be means of fighting against that,' said Dauber. 'The state must have an interest . . .' 'Rubbish,' said Careerist. 'People do fight against it. But who, how and to what purpose? That filthy lout, as you called him, he's fighting too. And incidentally you can't take it out on him. Perhaps the reason he didn't see us was that at that very moment he was coping with a commission of inquiry who'd turned up to see if he was keeping up his norm. My dear man, if the director was part of a cosmic plot against Dauber, I would shout to the heavens: "Life is beautiful!" But alas he's concerned even less with higher considerations than he is with your goodself. In a certain sense he is even your fellow sufferer. Or at all events he's on your side. I bet he's got everything you need, and more than he knows what to do with, but he doesn't give it to you not because he doesn't want to, but because he can't owing to the incredibly complex organisation of his incredibly trivial business. You could rub his nose on the piece of marble you need, and he'd still be convinced that he hasn't got anything like it in the yard.' 'So what do we do now?' asked Dauber. 'We go back next Thursday,' said Careerist.

Notes by Slanderer

'From a purely logical point of view the allegedly scientific idea of a classless society is grotesquely illiterate. That is why it is irrefutable. It is simply absurd. The only meaning it can contain is the one prescribed by the appropriate authority. It is an example of pure ideology. What I have just written is quite enough on its own to get me removed from my job and perhaps even worse. And try after that to get work in your speciality! And no chance of a labourer's job if you're too highly educated: each man to his proper station. And no-one will listen to you, and far less try to understand your arguments. This idea is an ikon, one of the idols of our religion. The very fact of casting doubt is a heresy.' 'All that is true,' said Scientist. 'But all the same this idea did contain some good sense! The people who invented it were very far from idiots! They had in mind certain distinctions between people in a given society and the specific

(285)

relationships between them. Let us say that there is indeed something rational in the idea that with time the exploitation of man by man will disappear.' 'I am not speaking of the origins of this linguistic phenomenon but about its present role,' I replied 'The idea of a dualism of the wave and the particle has clearly come from physics, but within the framework of ideology it has acquired all the attributes of an ikon or an idol—of a secondary and transitory idol, but an idol all the same. And then let us examine the linguistic expressions which figure here. The word "exploitation". What does it mean? Use? Instead of the expression "the exploitation of man by man" use the expression "the use of man by man", and you will immediately see the crass stupidity of all the fuss about this subject. Can a man live without using another man for certain aims including personal aims? For instance Careerist is driven about by a chauffeur in his official car. Is not that a use of the chauffeur in his own personal interest? And the same goes for his own work. And for you too. Isn't that so? And what interests can you think of which are not personal? Non-personal interests are an absurdity! Even when one speaks of the interests of society, it is thought desirable that everyone should make them their personal interests. Only a corpse or someone who is mentally ill does not have personal interests.' 'Very well,' said Scientist. 'But the division of people into classes is a fact which has to be admitted. How do we cope with that?' 'I don't deny it,' I said. 'But what is a social class? Either you include a rigorous enumeration of groups of people considered to be classes in your definition of "social classes", or you do not. In the former case we get the folllowing: Social classes are certain groups of people and nothing but these groups (slaves, slave-owners, serfs, feudal lords, the proletariat, capitalists and so on). And then the idea of the construction of a classless society will have to be this: we will build a society in which these groups do not exist. But will there be something in their place? If we take the latter case we will have social classes as groups of people who have similar social characteristics. If we specify those characteristics we shall come back to the former case without admitting it, and if we do not specify them, we shall get the following. It is always possible to produce a classification of a greater number of individuals than two if at least two of those individuals are different. For example, in any society we can divide men into those who are excluded from the active social sphere (those who are satisfied and do not kick over the traces; those who are isolated), and those who are included. These latter are divided into those who are "for" and those "against". The "for" group consists of opportunists, scroungers and careerists. Careerists are divided into active and passive and so on. And at all events the division between the bosses and the rank-and-file is a fact. In a society in which the overwhelming majority of the population receives the means of existence formally as wages for labour, and in fact as wages for a social position, in which the army of bosses rises to astronomical proportions and in which the basic cell becomes a group in which the major social relationships are those of command and subordination, in such a society these divisions have just as much importance as the division of men into capitalists, land-owners, workers and peasants and so on in traditional class societies.'

The concert

Scientist had promised to take Chatterer to one of Singer's concerts. Chatterer liked Singer's songs, but not to the point of losing his head about them. But he was curious to see what the author of these famous songs and his entourage looked like. So he willingly accepted Scientist's invitation. The concert kept on being postponed. Then there was a rumour that Singer was going to emigrate; then that he was being expelled. And then it became clear that he did not particularly want to leave, and nobody was very keen on letting him go. In general everything remained much as before, only far worse. The concert was to be held in a private flat in the suburbs and people made their way to it almost as if to a meeting of conspirators. The flat was crammed from floor to ceiling with a very mixed crowd. The greater part of them were young men with beards and sweaters, and women not of the standard pattern. There was so much smoke in the room that Chatterer could hardly make out Singer himself in the far corner. He was sitting at a small table with bottles, smoked sausage and a microphone. The assembled company looked like plotters or members of some obscure religious sect. The whole thing produced an impression of misery, as if the participants were taking part in some shameful secret. Singer sang his old songs which Chatterer had heard many times before, yet the whole impression was very dramatic. Chatterer did not sleep that night. He lay in the grip of some incomprehensible fear. The first Christians must have felt like this at their meeting in the catacombs. What was it? A cult? Great art? A mass? At first it seemed to him that Singer was strikingly out of place in these squalid surroundings. But he immediately realised that this was a mistake. When he looked more closely at the people who were there, he saw intelligent, wise faces. To say nothing of Scientist! At the age of twenty-five he was a Doctor of Science and had already made his name. And I myself must seem to them some kind of holy fool! And then it seemed to him that Singer was out of place among these Olympians. This time too he was mistaken, and realised before he had even formulated the thought. And his disquiet gave way to anguish and gloom.

An argument about ideology
'Truth-teller's proposal to renounce official ideology is childishly naïve,' said Careerist. 'It's a long time now since the leadership took account of it in its actions. So he's only saying it for appearance's sake.' 'So why not renounce it officially?' asked Scientist, 'if it only makes for trouble.' 'There is no way of renouncing it completely,' said Neurasthenic. 'And it wouldn't make any sense because no-one believes in it anyway. And its real role in society is insignificant compared with the one ascribed to it by Truth-teller.' The argument that began stopped only because everyone got tired of talking. 'What do you say about it?' Dauber asked Chatterer. 'Clearly, from the scientific point of view,' said Chatterer, 'Truth-teller's position is absurd. But therein lies its strength. Serious conversations on this subject will have no effect at all. Everything serious is regarded as grey, boring, passive, banal. The suggestion that something is serious makes a large-scale success impossible. And absurdity is in the spirit of the time. Absurdity creates an illusion of breadth and audacity. The more absurd the claim, the stronger the protest expressed. Absurdity is sensational. It is an excellent literary device for producing a mass effect.' 'But what do you think about the essence of the matter?' asked Dauber.

(288)

'From one point of view,' said Chatterer, 'ideology plays an enormous role in the life of society. From another point of view it plays none at all. It has an influence on everything, but it can never be pinned down. Because of this we get these contradictory judgements which vary between zero and infinity. This is the origin of the naïve illusion that the leaders of the country can change the official ideology at will, with a noticeable effect on their conduct. The leadership is powerless to change the official ideology of any society at will, even if they wanted to, even if they didn't believe in the ideology. A lack of faith in the truth of an ideology plays no role here, if for no other reason than that it is totally meaningless to talk about the truth of an ideology. But even if the leaders were able to change the ideology, this would have no effect on the social essence of their power and the nature of their activity. What is important for social mechanisms is the very existence of some ideology, its formal functioning, and not its content. The content of an ideology is determined by the concrete historical conditions of the spiritual life of a society. As for the formal mechanism, it is determined by its social nature and structure. If we consider ideology as a science and as a guide for conduct, then it does not need great intelligence to observe its "falsity" and its "sterility". But if it is an ideology, it is for the very reason that it is neither a science nor a guide to conduct, but a very particular form which serves as a framework for phenomena which are very different from, even at times directly opposed to, its declarations. To say that it is the source of all evil is senseless. It is equally senseless to say that it is a source of good. There are no false ideologies. Nor are there any true ones. Its role in society must be described according to a quite different system of concepts. A society like ours would be unthinkable without some form of ideology. It is an ideological society at its very base. Any other official ideology would have brought down exactly the same imprecations on it from Truth-teller. For him an attack on ideology is merely a convenient form of attack on something different. And if you dislike the textual aspect of ideology, think of something better. Try to do some work yourself in the field of ideology, and you will find that no matter how opposed your views may be, you will end up singing the same tune. All ideological arguments of our time somehow or other seem to revolve round the same subjects. Is this by chance? Of course not. They are an inevitable product of our time, and there are no other subjects—others are either insignificant or not broad enough.

'People often talk of the incomplete or even inadequate nature of our ideology. That is a factual error. Our ideology is a complete and even impenetrable whole. Not in the sense that from a certain point of view it is incapable of improvement or expansion, but in the sense that as a special kind of social construction it excludes the possibility of improvement or expansion. It has no such need. Within its framework individual works can be created which will produce a powerful effect. These could include ideological texts which differ from the official ideology and which from some point of view are more interesting. But they will be either ideologoid works, or ideological élitist literature, and not ideology in the full sense of the word. They will be as it were a spiritual dessert, to follow the bread and butter of ideology.

'The birth of ideology is not within the control of human beings. It is a secret which is in principle impossible to elucidate, even when the whole process unrolls itself before your eyes. When men are still in a state to interfere in the creation of ideology, they do not yet know what ideology is. And when they do begin to perceive it, by then it is too late. That is why ideology comes into the world complete, in possession of all its attributes. The texts have a history. But ideology of itself has no history, for its birth in this sense is an act of realisation of its social function, not of its form and content. Ideology is accepted as a fact; it is taken into account or not as is a natural need, and not as a product of human reason or folly.

'We must also bear in mind that the leaders of the country do not form a homogeneous and monolithic group. They are not even a social group at all. They are a large number of persons dispersed in various groups, a large number of social groups, associations of persons and groups which establish links between the members of the ruling system. The most important element in the process of selection of persons for the leadership, in their career and the stability of their position, is their relationship to the official ideology. A man who gets into his head the idea of reforming the ideology in some way (or even worse of renouncing it altogether) is not going to be given access at any level to the path which leads to power. And if he gives voice to a similar idea once he has come to power, he will seriously weaken his position, perhaps even to the point of losing power altogether.'

'That is obvious,' said Careerist. 'That is obvious,' said Scientist. 'That is obvious,' said Dauber. 'That is obvious,' said Neurasthenic. 'But we aren't talking about that.' And the argument broke out again. And everyone said exactly the same as before.

'But all the same, what exactly is Truth-teller?' asked Dauber. 'Don't try to find analogies,' said Chatterer. 'There are none. Truth-teller is a great child-man, who has suffered unjustly, cruelly and senselessly. He is problem number one of our time. He is something much bigger than ideology, politics, morality. He is the focal point where all the problems are concentrated. If only men can contrive to preserve all this long enough! . . .'

When

'. . . But when will all this end?' asked Chatterer. 'Not before people stop queuing at the tomb of the Teacher,' said Visitor . . .

The error is discovered

By sending a hundred anonymous letters each to various bodies, inspiring the writing of another fifty each by their friends, and despatching a letter of their own to Director, Secretary and Troglodyte finally managed to get a special commission set up to look into the activities of the Journal. In their letter, Secretary and Troglodyte drew particular attention to the fact that Claimant had no experience of life, since he had been born on a school bench, and had surrounded himself with internal émigrés who were always travelling abroad and concealing their true nature when they got there. They used fashionable little foreign expressions, and avoided using words of our own which state our position openly and unambiguously. Secretary and Troglodyte had repeatedly drawn attention to this, but their voice had been one crying in the wilderness. As for Thinker, Claimant's closest aide, he may have been a talented self-taught degenerate, but he was, nevertheless, alien to us from top to toe. Taking the broad view, they insisted . . .

But the forces of progress were not slumbering either. Claimant and Thinker, on their side, exerted considerable efforts, and included in the Commission people whom they could trust. Secretary and Troglodyte also had reason for satisfaction, for they found these same persons equally trustworthy. The Commission was given the brief of discovering the error. So the Commission began to look for the error. The Commission included Wife, Neurasthenic and Friend. Greatly flattered by being chosen, they did not press home the charges levelled against Secretary and Troglodyte, but neither did they oppose the allegations brought against Claimant and Thinker. As a mark of recognition for her efforts, Wife was given a trip abroad. Neurasthenic was allowed to defend his thesis, and Friend was promoted. 'What the hell do they think they're playing at?' raged Claimant. 'They've fouled up the whole business.' 'What else could they do?' said Thinker. 'If it hadn't been them, it'd have been still worse.' Finally, the error was discovered. Puss's article had omitted a quotation from the basic texts, and thus could be interpreted in a wholly different sense. When he heard about this, Puss shat his pants again, and immediately repented, laying the guilt on Slanderer. Furthermore, he found an error in an article by a new, unestablished author, and drew the attention of the Commission to it. The error was regarded as a gross distortion, and was referred to in the final report. Although this new author was a fool who would stoop to any chicanery, he was fired. For many years afterwards his name was to be found in resolutions and reports, until eventually another mistake more appropriate to the times was discovered in another, more appropriate, author; both error and author were included in a new resolution, and began to be referred to in new reports, until. . . .

Double-think

'What a sickening condition to be in,' said Neurasthenic. 'How much time I've wasted through being on that idiotic Commission. And the worst thing was having to pretend to take it seriously.' 'You could have refused,' said Dauber. 'Why are you a member of the Union?' asked Neurasthenic. 'And why do you agree to be a member of the committee for the defence of so-and-so against what's-his-name?' 'I can't do anything else,' said Dauber. 'Well, do you think I can?' said Neurasthenic, 'Yes, I understand,' said Dauber. 'Whatever you do, there's no way of avoiding the double-think.' 'That's true,' said Neurasthenic. 'What double-think are you rambling on about?' asked Chatterer. 'There's no double-think. That is something completely different. Double-think is a literary idea of the last century, when people were still taken seriously. This is something else. There are standard social mechanisms. Some people believe that they accept these standards voluntarily, others feel that they are imposed on them. You surely wouldn't argue that everyone does their military service voluntarily? So why don't we talk about that as double-think? Some people accept service as a duty, for others it is a spiritual drama. Neurasthenic's reaction to his Commission falls into this latter category. For some reason or other he forgot about his dissertation. And how is he linked with Claimant? At the moment, not in any way. His article's already been published in the Journal, and he's not thinking at the moment of doing a new one. Was this Commission really vital for him? No. He was neither for nor against. As far as his personal career is concerned, it has just been a momentary irritation. Let's not exaggerate! Let's not promote our trivial little daily hang-ups to the elevated rank of a double-think! Double-think sounds far too theatrical. We're dealing here with something altogether humbler. We're in a fairground booth. And then we must bear in mind that whenever a normal man is faced with making a decision, he has at least two possibilities to choose between, and only one of them can be put into practice. The other possibilities remain mere possibilities, although they sometimes have an illusory appearance of having been implemented. For example, whispered conversations in bed with your wife. Any officially expressed set of thoughts naturally presupposes in the same person the possibility of a different set of thoughts which is opposed to the official line, at least in part. So the business of Hog is not an example of an outstanding mind, but a trivial example of a more or less common banality. After all, you've all been in the army, and you know how people behave when they gain a certain amount of power, or, conversely, when they lose it. Do you know, by the way, what distinguishes a writer of a genius from the run of the mill? Do you think it's the depth and the breadth of his understanding of humanity? Nonsense! It is exclusively his capacity to invent something of his own from within himself and to attribute it to anybody you like. And later, literary critics really observe this in people, since people potentially contain everything you could wish for (inasmuch as they contain a total vacuum).' Neurasthenic said that he categorically disagreed with this, since such a concept impoverished mankind. Dauber supported him, and said that such a concept justified an absence of principle. Chatterer said that principle was a moral quality, introduced into man from outside as a limitation of his social potentialities. And it was irrelevant to the subject under discussion. And as far as impoverishment is concerned—that could only arise if there was something to impoverish! 'You get angry about falsehood in others, yet you're afraid to recognise it within yourselves. If you really want to know, the most fundamental basis for all these abominations is not the immorality of the average and inferior members of the human race, but the deficient morality of its best representatives.'

Cybernetics and society

Neurasthenic described the latest action of the Ibanskian leadership as sheer stupidity. 'Even a babe in arms could have seen where it would end,' he said. Scientist did not agree. 'It may seem now that the result of the action was clear in advance,' he said. 'But if you take the data which were available before the action was taken, just try to work out the best course on that basis!' And Scientist began to talk about the arduous problems of managing a society and taking the best decisions. In conclusion he described the radiant perspectives which were opened up by the development and application of cybernetics. 'Believe me,' he said, in winding up his highly competent and expert discourse, 'believe me, cybernetics will have a great role to play in social life.' But he was laughed to scorn.

'That is complete rubbish,' said Chatterer. 'Let's say, for example, that Group A has to work out its line of conduct towards Group B. In an abstract sense, A seeks to establish the line of conduct most beneficial for itself. But let's say that Group A is internally divided, and itself consists of a number of heterogeneous persons and groups. The question arises as to who will work out this line of action, and how? This is not a scientific meeting. Although it must be said that these days scientific meetings can be models of incoherence, and so my comparison no longer makes sense. Inside A there are people, groups and organisations which exist simply because there are problems of inter-relations with B. And the problem under consideration is approached not as a scientific attempt to discover the best line of approach; it is approached as an element in the problems which these people, groups and organisations are tackling on their own account. This is not a question of intelligence or stupidity, but of the actual relationships between the groups which has nothing to do with intellect. One can use computers to determine the best variant, as Scientist proposed. But this does not change the situation. The computers are operated by men. It is men who programme the computers. Now we see that the arena in which our little problem is being fought out has moved somewhat. The same thing will happen in the choice and evaluation of material fed into the computers, and also in the evaluation of the results and in the decisions based on them. Nothing will have changed. For instance, take this crowd of people who have to take the decision as to whether Claimant will become the director. This crowd includes A, who thinks that Claimant is the best candidate, B, who has tipped Theoretician the wink that Claimant has been cheating, and C, who has been writing letters to every conceivable body to denounce Claimant, and so on. Is this crowd intelligent, stupid, far-sighted or blind? These concepts can only be applied to a social group considered as a whole, as an individual. But here we do not have a social group. Even in a case where a group exists, there are occasions when a group of geniuses can take decisions worthy of idiots. So what can you expect of a large number of heterogeneous people, brought together by chance for the resolution of a problem which they despise, which they do not understand, and whose existence they do not even suspect. The main problem is not that these people are incapable of solving the problem in a way which we would regard as intelligent, but that a system of social relationships is being formed which obliges them to make decisions which seem stupid even to those who make them.'

The infection of evil

'We get angry with the Western intelligentsia,' said Dauber, 'because they don't come to our defence, or don't do everything they could in that direction. But what right have we to complain? They have got their own affairs and interests. In general they don't care much about us.' 'That is so,' said Visitor. 'But you don't have to be very bright to realise the simple truth that if somewhere in the world people are suffering and you are indifferent to that suffering, that will serve as justification or as a model for sufferings which you may have to face in the future. Evil is infectious.' 'Evil can be localised,' said Dauber. 'You can close frontiers and isolate the country. Just you try to find out, for example, what's happening in China.' 'Maybe,' said Visitor. 'But the isolation of certain parts of the world leads to decadence and isolationist tendencies in others. And that reduces the inner capacity of every area to oppose evil.' 'How do you know that?' asked Dauber. 'From the experience of history, my personal observations, and theory,' said Visitor, 'You could construct a theory of social systems in which my statements could be proven as theorems. But they're quite evident, even without that. The problem is not that people do not recognise them, or understand them. The problem is that some people want to do evil, while others want something else which lies outside the problem of Evil and Good.'

Cunning

This time they decided to resort to subterfuge. Dauber went to the stoneyard. Chatterer and Careerist stayed in the studio and waited for his phone call. If the call came they were to go out, grab the first truck that passed and drive to the yard. 'I am a private individual,' said Chatterer to Careerist. 'My ideas are the result of observing what everyone can see. But you are a public person. You have a position. Connections. Acquaintances. You have an entrée into the most elevated spheres. Tell me what you see from your bell-tower?' 'It's even worse.' replied Claimant. 'But is there a solution?' asked Chatterer; 'can you propose anything positive?' 'Of course I can,' said Careerist. 'There's no shortage of proposals. For instance, this isn't a bad idea: things could be so arranged that they were difficult to destroy and at the same time easy to control.' 'That's no solution,' said Chatterer. 'As time goes by, people will get used to it and what was strong will become fragile. What was easy to control will become difficult.' 'Yes,' said Careerist, 'that isn't a solution. I am a technician. Thinking is more in your line. What do you propose?' 'I've considered thousands of variants,' said Chatterer. 'There is no solution in principle. The problem isn't to think of something very intelligent. You can't think of anything intelligent, as the essence of the problem is simple to the point of triviality. And there lies the basic difficulty. What is needed is simply a policy of reform from the leadership, and pressure in this direction on the leadership from below. We need freedom of speech, freedom of movement, social rights, an opposition, a right from the leadership to take a chance, and other similar minor rights.' 'But if you see everything so clearly, where's the problem?' 'Clarity in one thing,' said Chatterer, 'produces confusion in another.'

Then Dauber telephoned. Chatterer and Careerist stopped a passing lorry and made a quick deal. When they reached the stoneyard they discovered that it was closed for stocktaking. The director had confused Dauber with somebody else. 'Fuck me,' said Dauber, and proposed a return to the studio to drink to this joyous event.

At the wholesale vegetable market

Everyone who could not find some suitable excuse for evasion was dispatched to the wholesale vegetable market. This is one of the forms of forced or partly forced labour, similar to the sending of groups of students during their holidays to every corner of the land to bring in the harvest or to help in building work. 'I wouldn't take it on myself to judge how stable this kind of work is, nor what contribution it makes to the national economy,' said Neurasthenic. 'But what I've seen with my own eyes has made a nightmare impression on me. I have seen flocks of overfed, drunken or half-drunk bosses and bizarre individuals wandering about without any apparent aim in filthy warehouses. Rotting vegetables. Crowds of people, more often than not with higher education and even with university degrees, torn away, occasionally from important work and more often from some form of idleness. There isn't the slightest possibility of using them properly. Day after day passes in complete idleness. Men slope off and organise little drinking parties. They tell each other funny stories. This entire idiotic system of deliberate waste of time is trampled in the mud.' Chatterer preserved an enigmatic silence, and this irritated Neurasthenic. 'What are you thinking about?' he asked. 'I was wondering what Schizophrenic's answer would have been,' Chatterer replied. 'I think it would have been something like this. If some fact of our life appears to you to have no connection with good sense, try and find in it some legitimate social basis. In the end, scandals like we see here might not take place. But something else would come instead. And in general terms what we have here is an acute shortage of labour where it is vitally needed, and a gross excess where we could do without it. Speaking even more generally, it's a lack of everything useful and important and an excess of everything useless and trivial.' 'But why do you think that this is normal?' asked Neurasthenic. 'Just read Schizophrenic. He's got all the explanations,' said Chatterer. 'But I've read all that,' yelled Neurasthenic; 'why do you keep on at me about Schizophrenic. He's nothing but a child.' 'Maybe he is a child,' said Chatterer, 'but God speaks through his mouth. Just think, it's only after hearing him talk that I realised why we find it easier to build a nuclear reactor than a decent potato store, why we find it easier to produce ten thousand doctors of science specialising in the theory of potatoes, than ten warehousemen who know how to look after actual potatoes.'

Problems of control, theory and so on
'It's Schizophrenic's theory, it's interesting when he deals with problems of control,' said Careerist. 'But there's a strong feeling that he himself has never worked in the system of control and isn't familiar with its details. It may, of course, be that that is all to the good.' 'Why?' asked Neurasthenic. 'A knowledge of the material never hurts when you're constructing a theory.' 'That's not necessarily so,' observed Chatterer; 'there must be a certain limit even there.' 'That wasn't what I had in mind,' said Careerist. 'If Schizophrenic had been more closely acquainted with the practice of control he would have been indescribably horrified and could not have written any more. It seems to me that our reality cannot be described in any theory. For instance

try to resolve a paradox of this kind. In our country everything is planned and controlled down to the last most insignificant detail. Yet officially we give people freedom of action. In the end even small systems which should be the easiest to control become uncontrollable in practice. They can only be controlled as far as official reports are concerned.' 'There's nothing mysterious about that,' said Chatterer. 'Schizophrenic's theory explains it easily enough. The tendency to a minute and detailed watch over everything is the consequence of certain social laws, and the tendency towards anarchy, the consequence of others. Irresponsibility, the absence of any personal interest, lack of information, deception, deliberate idleness and so on—all this produces the inevitable consequence that quite large groups of people are beyond the control of the leadership. And as to the abundance of facts and the horror they can produce, this is no obstacle for a true scientist. Science does not coincide with the everyday way of looking at facts. It may be that there is a multitude of facts which could stupefy the imagination, but in its approach to these facts science restricts itself to a small number of unimportant formulae. And on the other hand, there may be isolated facts of which people in general are virtually unaware, but which are enormously important from the scientific point of view. For example, it may be a matter of total indifference from the scientific point of view whether a thousand people have been punished or a million. But a phenomenon as unique as the persecution of Dauber or the exile of Truth-teller, can become an object of concentrated attention since that phenomenon alone may be the meeting point of far deeper and far more important social problems.'

Careerist said that he wasn't a specialist in these problems and would not defend his opinions to the last. From his observations there were two decisive moments in the organisation of a system of control (a problem which greatly interested him). First, there was the choice of a small number of points of control (parameters, to use the fashionable word) which were effectively controlled. If these points were mastered this allowed more important aspects of social life to be brought under control as a consequence. The second was the selection of a small number of instances where the intervention of the controlling organ was essential. 'Do you know, for instance, what distinguishes an experienced pilot from a beginner? A beginner thinks that the aircraft must be watched over every second or it will begin to misbehave, and he never leaves the controls alone for a moment. But the experienced pilot knows that if the aircraft is flying more or less normally it is best to let it fly itself without interference. He should only interfere when the flight pattern varies excessively.' 'But society is not an aircraft,' said Chatterer. 'Who determines these points of control and the moment when it's necessary to intervene? That does not depend on some more or less purely cybernetic consideration, attempts at improvement, attempts to find optimum variants and so on. It depends on the nature, the interests and the aims of those in control, on their relationships with their subordinates and on other social factors. Society isn't merely a machine for the production of lengths of printed cottons, tons of potatoes or steel, thousands of doctors, scientists and other mass-production items.'

At this point Scientist joined in and began to explain the importance of the construction of theories to forecast and explain social phenomena. 'As far as explanation goes, that is evidently nonsense,' said Neurasthenic. 'The same goes for forecasts,' said Chatterer. 'How can a theory be made to produce the best forecasts? Theoreticans start from the premise that the object itself does not depend on them, and construct amazingly complex mathematical systems of no practical value. This is not because the theoreticians are fools, but because the object itself is idiotic, i.e. "incorrect", and excludes any possibility of "correct" theory. What is the solution? It seems natural to adapt the object to the theory: to simplify it and standardise it.' 'That's an excellent idea,' said Careerist. 'That is exactly what happens in reality. Not immediately, of course but progressively. It takes much time and effort. Wittingly or unwittingly the state tries to perfect society in such a way that it becomes easier to govern scientifically.' 'If I didn't know that you were speaking ironically,' said Chatterer, 'I would have a very poor opinion of you. Despite its apparent naïvety, Schizophrenic's theory is astonishingly precise and effective. According to his theory, all attempts by the state to improve social life, if such attempts are undertaken, are put into practice by people and organisations who are immersed in the field of action of social laws with all the consequences that flow from them. You surely can't be unaware of the attempts that have been made over the last decade to improve and simplify the apparatus of control? How have they ended? Things are now more confused and tangled than they were before. It is true that over a long period of time the totality of the actions of millions of people and organisations will indeed produce a certain stability. But this is only the resultant of all the various forces at work, and can only be achieved if it is in complete accord with their social nature. It is far from being the realisation of some ideal cybernetic system of control.' 'Where then is the solution?' asked Scientist. 'Why seek a solution?' said Careerist, 'there is no need for one. All we need is a certain measure of stability.'

Horses for courses

Theoretician summoned Claimant and gave him to understand that people were looking to him to undertake great responsibilities. And so he should give evidence of taking things seriously. He was surrounded by people who were not serious. He should set himself apart from them. After this conversation, Claimant spent a good fifteen minutes persuading himself that this must be done for the good of the Cause. When he met the members of the Commission, he told them sincerely about everything. And despite his feelings of sympathy for Thinker, Sociologist, and Friend, he was obliged to admit error: yes, they had indeed been guilty of error. The Commission drew its conclusions and produced its proposals. These were taken into account. Thinker, Sociologist and Friend were removed from the editiorial board. They were replaced by Secretary, Neurasthenic (a talented young scientist who would soon present his doctoral thesis!) and Colleague, of whom no-one had heard so far. Claimant was thanked and released from his post. He was delighted. After all, he knew what this meant. The new post which he so much longed for was within his grasp! After this Thinker went to a new full-time job in a Secret Establishment, and to a spare-time job in the analogous Open Establishment. Sociologist went for a prolonged stay abroad. Wife declared a general and optimistic period of mourning. 'Just wait a while,' she said, 'until Claimant has settled into the job of director, and we can form a powerful cell there.' When he heard about this, Claimant said to his spiteful wife, who was starving herself in the cause of beauty, 'what clowns I have to deal with! I wouldn't let them near the institute, even if they had me at gunpoint! Now I really know what they're worth!' And Claimant began to reflect on how he would reorganise the institute, whom he would bring in, whom he would fire, whom he would promote and demote; and how thanks to all this the level would suddenly shoot up; and then! . . . And he began to snore, poisoning the atmosphere of Ibansk with gases emanating from ill-digested exotic foods bought from the shop for the privileged.

Writer's trick

According to the official press, Truth-teller had been justly punished. The intellectual élite of Ibansk showed commendable restraint. The bravest of its representatives expressed their approval, the remainder held their breath and waited for someone suddenly to force them to do the same. Only Writer produced another new trick. He wrote a letter to the Leader in protest, and gave an interview on the subject. Dauber said that he found Writer's gesture completely incomprehensible. What was it? A sincere reaction? A wish to curry favour with the public and restore his reputation? Had he been ordered to do it? 'A little of all that,' said Neurasthenic. 'He's an obliging man.' 'But he'll get into trouble for it,' said Dauber. 'He could even be expelled from the Union.' 'Not at all,' said Neurasthenic. 'He'll just be shouted at a bit and let off. It's all for show. In fact, everything to do with Writer is all for show. If it was in my power and if I wanted at the moment to inflict the most terrible punishment on him, I wouldn't punish him at all.' 'Still, it is an act of civic courage,' said Dauber. 'A protest that's inspired by the authorities, or tolerated by them, isn't a protest at all,' said Chatterer. 'I'm certain that Writer will quietly recant. Just wait until tomorrow.' But they didn't need to wait until tomorrow; as it turned out Writer had already recanted today.

Sincerity

'An historic drama has been played out before our very eyes,' said Dauber. 'And we have remained silent. Could it be that we have been cowardly?' 'That depends,' said Chatterer. 'If it was only a question of cowardice. Cowardice is a temporary phenomenon. A hundred cowards produce at least one brave man. That's not the question. Most of our intelligentsia quite sincerely give the authorities their full support. Their position is not one of cowardice but of complicity. For example, you're in sympathy with Truth-teller. But you've got your own personal problems. You can't be involved in the sufferings of others. The only important thing for you is your own personal suffering. And anyway you're irritated by Truth-teller's success. And anyway it's not your affair at all.' 'That's broadly speaking true,' said Dauber, 'But what about you?' 'I sympathise with Truth-teller as well,' said Chatterer. 'But what about you?' 'I sympathise with Truth-teller as well,' said Chatterer. 'But if conditions were different, I would be more likely to cross swords with him. In a certain sense his position is the opposite of mine. He is preoccupied with the past, and the past in the future. I am preoccupied with the future and the future in the past. So I am condemned to keep silent and sympathise. If I were to argue against him, I would appear to be a traitor. And I don't want to be. Nor do I want to join the crowd of his supporters. That's not my game either. I don't want to take any part in it. I'm not afraid, but I simply don't want to. I live on quite a different plane, which *a priori* condemns me to solitude. My books, like those of Slanderer, and Schizophrenic, are equally unacceptable both here and Over There. They are not topical. Slanderer and Schizophrenic perished because they were alien everywhere. Their fate was natural. Truth-teller has survived only because of his support from Over There. He survived thanks to a social principle and entirely within that framework, but in a framework far wider than that of Ibansk. Were it not for that the situation would have been different. He would have been stifled by his dear literary brothers. And if he had been published he would have been brought low by the terrifying indifference of his self-satisfied compatriots. In a situation where all normal forms of reaction and conduct are turned on their heads, a normal man can sometimes seem a coward, sometimes a traitor, sometimes two-faced. I am a scientist although in our terms that sounds comical. I wish to have no part in any politics. My politics is my work. I wish to belong to none of their parties or groups. I recognise only one party—the party of which I am the only member. Surely that's not a crime? I have worked for many years, but I have found nothing which has given me any true bearings. I can develop any argument for or against any opinion. But I have no opinion of my own. Discontent and exasperation do not make up an opinion. Nor, even more so, do indifference and despair. To take an active part in public affairs demands a fairly considerable degree of lack of understanding. And that I do not have. I am sure of only one thing. We stand now at the very beginning of a long and difficult epoch in the battle of the Ibanskian creative intelligentsia for a way of life which it would find more or less satisfactory. But in the conditions of Ibansk the normal way of life for the creative intelligentsia is a struggle for improvement and transformation. And the nearer the Ibanskian intelligentsia approaches to its ideal, the more chances there will be of history repeating itself. But I want to have no part in this history. I am tired. I am a researcher, not an activist. As a researcher I know that every isolated process finds within itself the sources and causes of all the phenomena of which it is composed. No matter how wild it may seem, even the régime of the Boss was a defence against itself, that is to say a protest against the debauch of social principle, a reaction born from the laws of that self-same principle. As a researcher I know that sooner or later this society will develop a form of culture appropriate to itself. This process is a tragedy for people like you and me. But for others it is a blessing. And here there are no objective criteria which can tell us who is right. As a researcher I have come to the conclusion that our society is not sick. It is healthy. But it has its own ideas about health and sickness. Just look at the young people! They are handsome and happy. They don't find life boring. If they were to listen to us they would think us out of our minds. So where then is your problem? Your problem is the problem of your "I". It's the problem of an "I" which is strong, talented, enterprising, combative. If the state had taken you to its bosom at the right time, you would have been theirs. You would have served it with faith and truth. At this moment the state is cultivating you. Going by your commissions, you are the leading sculptor in Ibansk. You're world-famous. You have enough money and a decent studio, as you must admit. What more do you want? The titles of Honoured Artist? Peoples' Artist? Academician? An even bigger studio? People to write monographs about you? And by what right? Besides, even that wouldn't satisfy you now. It's too late. My problem is a problem of my "I" as well. But my "I" is weak, defenceless, standing outside the battle. If the State had come to my defence at the right time I would have been a well-established professor, more or less famous; I would have delivered lectures, had a chair and students. I might even have founded a school. And all this would have been to the benefit of the State and not at its expense. But the State did not want either to take you to its heart, nor to protect me, and it does not want to do so now. Therein lies the essence of our personal drama. Even if the State did not want to do this for you and me, it will do it for other Daubers and Chatterers who will be better than us. And there lies the essence of the general drama of people like us. Only people like you can, from time to time, win through. People like me never can. You do not think of a life for yourself in the framework of this human community. But I cannot imagine a life for myself outside it. So it seems that it is mere chance which has brought us two together. What kind of unity of action, then, can one sensibly speak of, when we consider the reactions of our intelligentsia as a whole?'

Law and interpretation

The discussion was set in motion by a statement from Careerist, who argued that Truth-teller's essay was genuinely anti-Ibanskian. This led to an incoherent argument which was only ended by Chatterer's comment that all conversations on this subject were meaningless.

'The first thing one has to do,' said Chatterer, 'is to distinguish between the text and its interpretation (or exegesis). Any text allows a limitless number of interpretations, none of which is to be found in the text itself. For example, take the text: "A is a good man". This could be interpreted as putting forward the proposition "B is a swine", or "B is a hypocrite". Neither of these interpretations is contained in the text being interpreted. The author of the text bears no legal responsibility for the interpretation of his text, whatever that interpretation might be

and no matter who has suggested it.' 'Agreed,' said Neurasthenic. 'But all the same, there are various systems of law.'
'There are various systems of lawlessness,' said Chatterer. 'If
the author of a text is responsible for its interpretation, that
automatically implies the abandonment of a juridical point of
view. What kind of text is to be considered anti-Ibanskian?
Note well that here we're talking about the evaluation of a
text—and a juridical evaluation. In other words there must be
criteria for judgement. So here we must distinguish between
legal usage and legal rules. The expression "legal usage" is
imprecise. It would be more accurate to speak about "rules of
punishment". But let's keep on using the former for the sake of
monotony. What does "legal usage" consist of? In police practice this is what actually happens. If a certain group of people
(generally either people in power, or those closely connected
with power) believes that a given text can be interpreted as
anti-Ibanskian, and does so interpret it, then juridically speaking the text becomes anti-Ibanskian. But this practice cannot be
formulated as a juridical rule, since this would be to destroy the
fundamental principle of any system of justice, namely the
principle of the independence of the law from the executive.
There is only one solution: on each occasion the legislature
must make a law which would declare the given text anti-
Ibanskian. But even our legislature is not prepared to go to such
extremes of legal illegality. So the solution lies elsewhere—in
expertise. A special group is appointed to consider whether the
text is Ibanskian or anti-Ibanskian, and by so doing to commit
an unlawful act. For expertise only has the power to state facts,
and not to give evaluations. Only the judiciary should make this
evaluation, basing themselves exclusively on the only criteria
which exist for this purpose, namely laws which have been
specially passed. If no such laws exist, the text cannot be subject
to judgement. By its very nature a judicial judgement by an
expert is an illegal act. Moreover if the accused himself is
obliged to make such a judgement, that too is illegal. The
accused is entitled to insist that the judicial evaluation of his text
should be made on the basis of the words and phrases which
make up the text, and on the basis also of existing rules.

'What matters above all is not whether a law is bad or good.
What matters is whether or not the law exists. A bad law is

nevertheless a law. Good illegality is nevertheless illegal. I shall take it upon myself to prove the mathematical theorem that any society with a rule of law, no matter how bad that law may be, allows the existence of an opposition. The very existence of an opposition is a sign that the society lives by the law. And the absence of an opposition is an indication that the society is lawless. But let us look more closely at the question. Let us take a certain text A. Let there be a legal system B, according to which this text is assessed to be hostile to the given society (as an "anti" text). Consequently the author of A is prosecuted. And if, for example, I say "N asserts that A", I am not asserting A, I am asserting that N asserts that A. When then, from the point of view of society B, is the nature of a text of the type "N asserts that A"? Is that an "anti" text? Fine, but how will the prosecutor look, when in court he accuses me of asserting the text "N asserts that A"? Will he be seen as a man pronouncing an "anti" text? No? But why? Where is the formal criterion which lets us make this distinction? Admittedly I have used the word "asserts" once, and the prosecutor has used it twice. But if such a law is adopted, all I have to do is to pronounce in advance the following text: "M asserts that N asserts that A". I have only cited one logical progression. But there are many more. Construct for me a code B of laws which permit texts to be assessed as "anti", and I will undertake, for any text which is so assessed, to construct a text which cannot be so assessed according to code B, but which all the same will be understood as an opposition text. Every rigorous law is *a priori* a possibility of opposition. But people are afraid of a rigorous law. Existing law contains a norm and a whole system of provisos which allow the law to be circumvented, in other words a disguised form of illegality. It remains a law as long as it in no way threatens the established authority. But as soon as any hint of such a threat appears, this law becomes a form of illegality. So Truth-teller's essay can be interpreted as an opposition work, but in no way as an anti-Ibanskian work if the term "anti-Ibanskian" is a juridical term. We have no juridical norms which could allow it to be classed as anti-Ibanskian. In the given case your way of thinking is typical of the way of thinking of a society which ignores the law. What can you expect of others in these circumstances?'

Self-defence

'The case of Dauber,' said Careerist, 'is unprecedented.' 'It depends on your point of view,' said Visitor. 'From a purely social point of view, that's not the case. This last epoch has produced many people like him. You could name dozens of writers, artists, scientists and so on of the same social type. Very few of them have become world famous. Many of them integrated themselves into official society. Many perished. Dauber is one of a type, merely rather more striking than most.' 'All the same you wouldn't deny that he has immense talent, a great capacity for work, that he's very brave and that he isn't concerned about material advantage,' said Claimant. 'No,' said Visitor, 'but Slanderer and Schizophrenic were no less talented, no less industrious, no more demanding and just as brave. And where are they now?' 'Dauber's works have a wide public response,' said Careerist, 'unlike those of Slanderer and Schizophrenic.' 'Yes,' said Visitor, 'But don't jump to conclusions. First of all, despite everything, Dauber's works are very far from politics and even from ideology, while Slanderer and Schizophrenic talk about the very essence and basis of both. You can look at Dauber's works and experience their effect. The books of Slanderer and Schizophrenic are hard to find (for all practical purposes they have been withdrawn from circulation) and even harder to understand. By their very nature they were not intended for a mass audience. And secondly it is not the case that the secret of success lies in the works themselves. In fact people choose a man whom they find suitable and convenient, and look to his works to express their own state of mind. Incidentally, I. and E. enjoy no less success than Dauber, and you know perfectly well yourself what they are worth.'

'Visitor is right,' said Chatterer. 'Dauber is suitable raw material for sociological observation. Take, for example, the problem of self-defence. There are official and unofficial forms of self-defence. The former are well known. The latter have never been fully studied. They include, first of all, anti-official human groupings. Some of these themselves form social groups which are enmeshed with official groups, which feel their influence, which consist of the same social individuals and which as communities themselves obey, at least in part, social laws. It is only thanks to their anti-official position that the individuals which make up these groups and the groups themselves take on certain features which allow them to be regarded as anti-social phenomena. At the slightest opportunity they try to lose these features. Their victory consists of the liquidation of their anti-social nature and the affirmation of the social principle to the status of a rule in an even clearer form than previously. This form of self-defence is appropriate for weak individuals who, as a rule, lack social possibilities. If strong personalities happen by chance to find themselves in a community of this kind it is only in the capacity of leaders or organisers, and in such cases they are in practice using the community in their own egotistical interests. Other communities of the anti-official variety are not social groups since the members of the group have no stable regular and necessary links between one another, and there is no division of functions within the group. Such communities form around major artists, writers, poets, actors, scientists and so on. People are drawn into these communities merely as a result of their own individual links with the central personality. If this personality is removed from such a community, the community dissolves. This particular personality cannot be replaced. These communities are purely personal communities. They offer support to a creative person, which can sometimes be very powerful support if the devotees have weight in society. The same can be said of some professional communities, but the protection they give falls within very narrow limits. And moreover this is only true when the person protected is of the same rank as his defenders, that he does not wound their professional self-esteem, and that he has a real need to be defended in some capacity other than that of the given profession. A second form of social self-defence is self-sacrifice. Here the most significant role is that of enforced heroism, when the force of circumstance thrusts a man into the role of a protester. Generally speaking people do not voluntarily become enemies. They resist this. Society itself makes its own enemies. Sometimes they are convenient enemies against whom it is easy to wage a showy struggle. Sometimes they are vitally necessary enemies who defend society and bring it benefits, in other words future heroes. Here it is a kind of self-preservation instinct which comes into play. A third form of self-defence is to become a significant personality by use of one's own abilities and the products of one's own personal labour, and by these means to achieve a certain degree of independence. This is personalism. But in our case powerful personalities are the exception. It is impossible to become a powerful personality without the knowledge of the authorities. And the authorities permit the existence only of an imitation of a powerful personality, or a personality they can control. The final form of self-defence is to use the lack of homogeneity of associations of people and the divergence of their interests when one finally leaves the framework of such an association. As an example, international relations come immediately to mind. But similar phenomena are possible even within the country. Just recall the affair of "Prometheus" and relations between the ministers of culture and electronics. The case of Dauber is a combination of all these forms which was able to arise in the conditions of the period of confusion and disarray which we have just lived through. If you add to that an ability to make the most of a situation and a good organising talent . . .' 'All this is so,' said Neurasthenic. 'But it is desperately boring. The romantic effect of an unexpected result disappears altogether.' 'You find it boring,' said Visitor, 'because you don't take this business seriously enough and because you don't want to learn a lesson from it.' 'A lesson?' said Neurasthenic scornfully, 'a lesson for whom?' 'For other people,' said Visitor. 'It's a waste of time,' said Neurasthenic. 'There are no lessons to be learnt.' 'That's not true,' said Visitor, 'People do everything from examples.'

The end of Slanderer's notes

When he reached the point in Slanderer's notes where he began to set out the official ideology in what he regarded as a more refined form, Thinker said that from here on Slanderer had lost his grip, and threw the notes into the dustbin. But that was a mistake. At the end of the manuscript there was an analysis of the reasons why any work directed towards the real improvement of the official ideology in the name of that ideology and to its benefit (in actual fact and not merely in appearance) was one of the most dangerous forms of activity in the society of Ibansk. It could have been slightly rephrased and published in the

Journal, given a different emphasis and presented as Thinker's own thoughts. On the last page of Slanderer's notes, Thinker noticed these words: 'If you want to be a friend, you will become an enemy. Such is the sad fate of every decent man who dares to do good.' But Thinker did not grasp what these words meant.

The manuscripts disappear

You've got no right to complain about your lot, said Chatterer to himself as he set about the task of examining and destroying his archives. Schizophrenic didn't have a table of any kind. Slanderer didn't have a desk. You've got a desk of your very own! And what a desk! The dream of any graphomaniac! Schizophrenic lost everything. Slanderer managed to get a few things published, but the bulk of his work vanished. What about you? You published far more than Slanderer. Your archives aren't very large. And on top of that you're alive and well. So progress is clear. It's fashionable to say these days that manuscripts don't burn. What idiocy! One or two escape, and then people draw the most far-fetched conclusions. It may be indeed that they don't burn to the extent that people don't set fire to them. But they aren't being written. And if they are written, they vanish. How that happens, no-one seems to know. It's like my article. It was sunk by those reactionaries Secretary and Troglodyte almost twenty years ago. At that time it would have had a real effect. Even today I wouldn't have been ashamed of it. But what can I do with it now? I can't publish it. I don't want to keep it at the bottom of a drawer. It isn't mine any more. So—into the dustbin with it. And what about this other article? That was sabotaged by Claimant and Thinker. Liberals! Friends of my youth! Like-minded thinkers! At that time this piece could have been published without the slightest risk to them. Now, there isn't the slightest chance of it seeing the light of day. In two or three years' time I wouldn't agree myself to publish it. So that one goes the same way as the first. Almost my entire life into the dustbin. Perhaps even my entire life. Can such things be? Intellectually I understand why, but my heart can't get used to the idea. Who's the madman in all this story? I'm not taking, I'm giving! I'm not saying give me, give me! I'm begging that someone should take what I'm offering!

A phenomenon

'F.'s been buried,' said Scientist. 'Who's he?' asked Careerist. 'Surely you must have heard of him,' said Scientist in surprise. 'He's the true founder of this school of thought that's so fashionable at the moment. . . . More than twenty years ago he wrote a book which provoked a whole flood of articles (with no reference to the source of course) but which was never published. Dozens of little hangers-on grabbed hold of his coattails. Then there was a wind from the West. Everything was tarted up with new words and foreign terminology. And it took off! It became a new field of scientific research. Journals, symposiums, congresses. A new institute, tons of books and articles. And all emptiness. Only F. worked like a real scientist. He was shoved on one side, of course. At first there were some references to him, but soon it seemed that he had never existed.' 'That's the usual story,' said Dauber. 'Most of the great cultural innovators die unrecognised.' 'This is something quite different,' said Scientist. 'He was recognised. Everyone knew who he was. He didn't get official recognition in terms of awards and titles. His colleagues were more concerned about that kind of thing. But they knew who F. was all right. If they hadn't valued him at his true worth everything would have turned out differently. They regarded him as a threat to their own position. At the cemetery there were great paeans of praise, great eulogies. There was talk of publishing his work. Maybe it really will be published. Although it's unlikely. They'd rather steal his ideas—of course without any reference to his name. But of course with references to the West. And over there they'll take part of his ideas and rediscover his results. F.'s ideas won't disappear, that's clear to everyone, but they won't survive as F.'s ideas, but as someone else's, someone else whom it's convenient to refer to. Perhaps some day a conscientious scientific historian will turn up. He'll dig up F., study our times. He may be surprised that there could have been such a phenomenon. But he won't be surprised that F. left no traces; there will be traces of one kind or another.' 'If this F. had had power,' said Careerist, 'it would all have been different. If he'd been an academician, a prizewinner, a Hero. References to his work would have cropped up everywhere. He'd have had his own School. To keep students, you've got to have power, the ability

(312)

to find them jobs and keep them employed. These days ideas alone aren't enough to hold anyone.' 'What if F.'s fate was only an imitation of the fate of a real scientist?' said Chatterer. 'Where are your criteria? Just imagine that F. works for years on his own, and people say that he's doing real work. And just next door there's a gang of swindlers who are producing a grandiose puffed up imitation of work. But then in these conditions F.'s life can be considered from the point of view of its own authenticity. Almost thirty years of life and work in solitude! What intelligence and what will are capable of distinguishing here between work and the imitation of work? And what if F. himself was engaged in an imitation of work which, compared with an officially inflated imitation of work, would only resemble real work from the point of view of his individual destiny!' 'It's possible,' said Scientist. 'It's hard to say. There were some Americans who came here a short time ago, and they said that F. was a truly great figure—at least, the most significant figure in this field over here. And so who knows . . .?' 'What did he die of?' asked Dauber. 'Of loneliness and despair,' said Scientist.

The formula of silence

'Who still knows that Slanderer used to be a brilliant lecturer?' said Neurasthenic. 'Who listened to him? Did he have a great deal to say? Who knows that Schizophrenic was a painter of original talent and did thousands of drawings? Where are they now? Perhaps a few examples still exist in private collections. But if they do, it's only because they have some personal connection with the collectors. Who knows that Chatterer was a magnificent writer on problems of culture? At one time he was officially commissioned to write a book on non-conformist ideas in culture. I have read it. If it had ever been published, it would have been nothing short of a masterpiece. Where is it now? For people of this kind, our formula is clear: don't make a sound! If you do, we'll destroy you! If you keep quiet, you won't get hurt. We'll give you a little room, and a wage. Don't expect too much, but you'll be alive, and you'll have enough to eat! And for people like you, even that's too much! I don't agree with Singer that silence is golden. Silence isn't well paid here.' 'That depends on what kind of silence,' said Visitor. 'Enforced silence doesn't pay. Voluntary silence—that's another matter.'

On consumption

'We've discussed everything,' said Neurasthenic. 'The only thing we haven't argued about is consumption.' 'And what is there to argue about in that?' asked Careerist; 'everything's perfectly clear,' 'Absolutely,' said Scientist. 'Obviously,' said Dauber. 'It's not as obvious as all that,' said Neurasthenic. 'Look at me, I'm a research worker, and I earn less than a bus driver. Chatterer is a doctor of science. So is Sociologist. As a scientist Chatterer is worth a thousand of Sociologist. But in money terms he gets only half as much. And I'm not even counting Sociologist's official car, his rent-free flat, his country house, his paid trips abroad, his access to the stores reserved for the privileged, his extra fees.' 'Sociologist came to see me not long ago,' said Dauber. 'He wanted to buy an etching. I told him my lowest price. You should have seen his face! He started straight off to complain about how hard life was. He said that a Western scientist in his position would have a cottage, at least two cars, trips round the world, five-star hotels, a yacht.' 'I very much doubt,' said Neurasthenic, 'whether a Western scientist lives any better than Sociologist. I've been there and I've seen them.' 'And what price were you asking for the etching?' asked Chatterer. 'You know perfectly well,' said Dauber. 'Do you think that was dear? I'll tell you. . . .' 'No need,' said Chatterer. 'I know it already. My wife earned a hundred roubles a month. Then she did a course at an evening institute, and got a job that paid ninety. Calm down, I'm not comparing your creative capacities. I don't see any injustice in that. I'm merely stating a fact: you asked more for that etching than she earns in a month.' That led to a row, as usual. Names were tossed around. Everyone was brought in: anonymous bosses with their unoffical increases and their rake-offs. Fashionable tailors and hairdressers. Photographers. After an hour the initial question had been totally confused, and all the slanders and sensational news exhausted. Everyone had poured out his just fury about the injustice of wages and salaries. 'So,' said Chatterer, 'now to the question of consumption. I don't want to attack your possessions. I am prepared to concede that you have unjustly little and that in justice you should have more. Nor do I want to compare us with the West. I want to draw your attention to the fact that we always pass in silence over the most fundamental question of our way of life. It's as if it did not exist, as if it was of no importance. We aren't allowed to travel abroad? A scandal! We aren't allowed to speak, and we get arrested if we do? Another scandal! Your book isn't published? Yet another! And yet, respected thinkers, there is such a thing as a salary. There is an official basic salary. And there are occasions when the disparity is enormous. It can happen that A gets twenty times as much as B. There is an official supplementary salary (in the form of increments, bonuses, fees). There is a concealed supplementary salary (motor cars, apartments, villas, special shops, trips abroad, and so on). There are the legal and illegal products of personal initiative (sales of market produce, bribes and backhanders). But why go on about that? In both our official and our clandestine trade people are constantly buying and selling goods at prices which pre-suppose the existence of a very wealthy stratum of population. There was a queue for lounge suites costing four and a half thousand roubles—forty months' salary for my wife. Just look in jewellers' shop windows, in furriers. Look at the money people pay for co-operative apartments. And then there are the crowds of people who can pay surprisingly easily for any tourist trip abroad! What are they using? Money saved from their earnings? Very well. Let us leave this side of the business to Truth-teller. Let us just accept the clear fact that society is divided into groups of people who somehow or other have got very different levels of consumption. It is important to assess the place of this phenomenon in our way of life. And among the multitude of questions which arise in this connection, it would do no harm to clarify the following: what are the attitudes to this of our liberal intelligentsia and our conservative leadership? And here we have a most interesting situation. Our leaders of all ranks and varieties have no doubt about the justice of their privileges, and do all they can to strengthen and increase them. The people as a whole grumble a little, but in principle they do not consider this unjust; they've got a right to it, they're the leaders after all! Taken as a whole the intelligentsia feel frustrated and unhappy with their situation. But not so much as to revolt. They try to find some lawful or unlawful (but God forbid, not social) means of compensation. Part of the intelligentsia (who are not too badly off by our criteria) have a rather sharper feeling of being hard done by.

The leadership tries to put pressure on this section. The leaders do not want to see this section living better than they, the leaders, do. And in thinking thus they are acting according to their concepts of justice: they are the masters, and so they should live better. Moreover, they're constantly telling the people how overfed the intellectuals are, thus giving an impression that they're fighting for justice and at the same time distracting attention from themselves and finding scapegoats. The situation gets more complicated because the liberal intelligentsia is preoccupied with its own personal interests and falls into the trap. From the point of view of wages, the intelligentsia thirsts for justice. But this desire is not just from the social point of view, since in theory the distribution of resources should correspond to the social structure of society. In the present case, the intelligentsia is acting as an anti-social force. Its struggle for justice takes on the form of a struggle for inequality. This puts a powerful trump card in the hands of the leadership, and completely cuts the intelligentsia off from what is known as the people. Add to this the desire to create one's own culture and the chance of creating one's own life-style. And you get a complete isolation of a section of the intelligentsia from the rest of the population, although in geographical terms we are completely mixed together. And besides that, since the great mass of the intelligentsia prefers to sort out its affairs on the quiet, and in culture and life-style it is not markedly different from the rest of the population, and since its most crafty representatives live very advantageously (while complaining all the louder), then the cream of the intelligentsia are in complete isolation even within their own sphere. Sociologist and Schizophrenic both belong to the intelligentsia. The former is a twister, the latter is a true scientist. One flourishes, travels round the world representing the Ibanskian intelligentsia, constantly complains about his hard lot, and criticises our way of life. And, you will note, with complete impunity. He even gets rewarded for it. And Schizophrenic? Have you ever heard him complain or criticise? But where is he now? Who even knows him by name?'

The imitation of civilisation

'There's an international symposium going on here just at the moment,' said Neurasthenic. 'Is it interesting?' Dauber asked.

'That depends who for,' replied Neurasthenic. 'It's really a tremendous con-trick. It looks genuine from outside, but it's really total eyewash. I'm coming more and more to the opinion that many areas of our culture are basically deceitful.' 'Not only culture,' said Careerist. 'It would be better to say that they're imitative forms,' said Chatterer. 'The same thing goes for the arts,' said Dauber. 'These forms of imitation activity are so convenient and effective in our society,' said Chatterer, 'that our entire life takes on the character of an imitation of civilisation.' 'But maybe in time these imitative forms will take on some real content,' said Careerist. 'I've come across examples of that sort of thing.' 'In our case, even the examples are just imitations of examples,' said Neurasthenic. 'Imitation may take on some form of reality, but to about the same extent as a provincial actor playing the part of Napoleon actually becomes Napoleon,' said Chatterer.

Truth-teller's letter to Chatterer

This same ill-starred wall newspaper contained what purported, jokingly, to be an open letter from Truth-teller to Chatterer. At first these lines were forgotten—there was too much else to think about. But in the light of Truth-teller's latest actions, the staff were asked to react. So they wrote a condemnatory letter. That was said to be too little! So they signed an approving letter. More still was wanted. So they launched a slander campaign. Still not enough. So a meeting was called to consider what could be done. 'We have to take radical steps,' said Claimant, and resurrected the wall newspaper. Immediately everyone remembered the Letter. The letter was inoffensive, but included two allusions: one referred to Chatterer's claims that his works were significant, and dismissed those claims as ridiculous; and the other said that it was high time that Chatterer's works were examined from this viewpoint.

'Hmm, yes,' said the Acting Director, when he had re-read the letter. 'We had overlooked this. It was an alarm signal. And we did not react. We must take steps.' Steps were taken, and noted in the resolution. Chatterer began to look for work. But not very energetically, more for conscience's sake, because in his present situation he would have been foolish to expect to find work in his speciality. It was simply a case of waiting for something to turn up, without hoping for anything. When Chatterer read the offending verses to Dauber, Dauber commented that a poet of genius had died in the person of Fellow-worker. But genius and crime were nevertheless incompatible. 'Quite the opposite,' said Chatterer. 'In our society genius without crime is unthinkable.'

The spiritual leaders of the opposition
When they left the studio, Journalist and Neurasthenic began to talk about the spiritual leaders of the Ibanskian opposition. Journalist said that Dauber was at least one of them. 'That's not quite the case,' said Neurasthenic. 'Through Dauber you receive something of what has been thought by others, and partly by Dauber himself. Dauber is a little hole which can be seen from outside, and through which the spiritual pressure of our society can burst into the world outside.' 'So who then are your real leaders?' asked Journalist. 'They have no right to fame,' said Neurasthenic. 'Not even a right to exist.' 'Perhaps they are kept secret,' inquired Journalist. 'Not at all,' laughed Neurasthenic. 'Something quite different. I'll try to explain. If you stay here longer, perhaps you'll sort it out for yourself.' 'Well, what about Truth-teller?' asked Journalist. 'Truth-teller's coming closer to the truth,' said Neurasthenic. 'But even he is a fire-cracker, an explosion towards the outside world. The spiritual leaders of our opposition stay inside. They explode silently. And internally. If you want to learn to understand our life, you've first got to learn how to walk about upside down.'

The visitor
'They've been looking for something that doesn't exist,' said Visitor. 'A doctrine of the world? That doesn't exist, since the general laws of the world are merely conventions about the meaning of words. A doctrine of society? Nor does that, since the laws of society are merely rules of conduct invented by men. A doctrine of man? Nor does that exist, since man is everything you like—i.e. nothing. Man is just an accidental visitor to this world. When he exists, he has already ceased to exist. He has no bearings, everything is true. But at the same time everything is false. Everything has a deep meaning—but everything is mean-

ingless. They are all intelligent people but they are given no choice. Choice is excluded—and science even more so.' 'That's strange,' said Dauber. 'Everyone says the opposite is true.' 'That's because they're looking for a formula of existence,' said Visitor. 'What they need is a formula for life.' 'Does such a formula exist?' asked Dauber. 'Possibly,' said Visitor. 'Give me an example,' said Dauber. 'For example, good and evil,' said Visitor. 'I don't know what that means,' said Dauber. 'They are like the formal symbols used by logicians,' said Visitor. 'They are variables, which you can replace by your own concepts of good and evil. The abstention from evil is good. The abstention from good is evil. Good is alienable. Evil is alienable. If you do evil, you receive evil. If you do good, you receive good in return. Then there are sufferings, contentment and peace. Here as in logic there are rigorous laws. No-one can forbid you to break the laws of logic. Indeed, they are very rarely observed. But if you want the truth, you have to keep those laws. In the same way, no-one can forbid you to break the laws of life. They are observed even more rarely than the laws of logic. But if you want to preserve something of humanity in you, those laws must be obeyed.' 'They clearly have to be studied,' said Dauber. 'Alas,' said Visitor, 'they still have to be invented.' 'What about religion?' asked Dauber. 'The old religion does contain a doctrine of life,' said Visitor. 'But it cannot satisfy the demands of practical life which modern man makes of it, in the same way that Aristotelian logic is inadequate to the demands of modern linguistic practice.' 'We do have some strange conversations,' said Dauber. 'What is strange,' said Visitor, 'is that people haven't talked about this in the past, and talk about it so rarely now. Mankind is facing a choice—for the first time in history, bear in mind. People have got to reflect on our experiment. They have got to think about it in all sincerity and without pity. And that is why they must talk. At this moment conversations like this are mankind's main duty.'

Unexplored possibilities

'Here comes the dénouement,' said Neurasthenic. 'The editorial committee has been dissolved. Claimant has sold out Thinker, Sociologist and Wife. They've been expelled from the editorial board. Claimant has survived for the time being. But all the same he will never become director.' 'Serves them right,' said Chatterer. 'But all the same, they're better than the others,' said Dauber. 'They are no worse and no better,' said Neurasthenic. Nor yet the same. They are simply out of a different story. Once, when all this was just beginning, I told them: "we have some possibilities, but not for long. These possibilities must be used to the full." Slanderer's prestige should have been enhanced, Schizophrenic's works should have been published. In the end they could have published Chatterer and his group. But what did they do? They helped to suppress Slanderer, Schizophrenic, Chatterer and all who were with them. They stirred up the mud, that's all they did. They proposed nothing that was new in principle, and just got on with their own little private affairs. They quite deliberately and consciously let opportunities slip away, that's what they did. If you set out those missed opportunities on a national scale, you see the total situation. The very first act of this past epoch contained everything that has happened since, analogously, in every socially significant group. The first assault wasn't even taken seriously. Opportunities were allowed to slip consciously and willingly, because those who had come to power did not want to use that power in such a way as to let others get on with their work. There was a schism. At first we all marched together. We bore within ourselves a potential for creation and action, and a thirst for power and well-being. At first it seemed that all this was within everyone. But when the chance appeared of bringing both aspects to fruition, it turned out that the two things were incompatible. They were divided between different people. And we ended up by destroying with our own hands our capacities both for creation and action, by latching ourselves on, with a few minor losses, to the traditional system of power and well-being. That's all.'

The end of the Rats' Paradise
And yet the the Rats' Paradise (as we called the experimental ratorium) ceased to exist at a moment when we least expected it, read Chatterer. Somehow or other lice got into the ratorium, multiplied at amazing speed, and created their own society on the model of the rats. And then . . .

A parable about oneself

I will tell you a parable, said Chatterer. I joined the army before the war. We were sent up to join our regiment, and they took us into the mess hall. There were eight men to a table. A big chunk of bread was handed out to each table. An intellectual looking lad said he'd share ours out. He did it like this. One piece was bigger than all the others. The next was a bit smaller. The rest were any old size. He stuck his knife into the biggest bit, and yelled 'Grab for them!', and shoved the second biggest piece over to a tough character sitting next to him, who had taken him under his wing. That was one of the most important moments in my life. Either I should bow to the general laws of social existence and grab the biggest piece I could, or go against these laws—i.e. take no part in the struggle. I had only a fraction of a second to draw on my entire experience of life. I took the piece which had been left lying on the table—the smallest. That split second determined the course of all my later life. I had forced myself to stay outside the struggle.

A party at Sociologist's

Sociologist came back from a trip abroad. He was bubbling over with pleasure. He had brought back a whole heap of gifts. There were quaint little peasant dolls, a pot of caviar, a bottle of vodka. And a mink coat for Wife. 'We spend all our time torturing our own minds and the minds of others,' he said to Colleague and Thinker, who came to meet him at the airport, 'yet Over There they've resolved all these problems in the best possible way.' That evening he gave a party. The guests were Claimant, Colleague, Instructor, Thinker, Someone, Careerist, Scientist, Puss, Neurasthenic, Fellow-worker, and a much criticised young author who turned out to be one of Wife's students. After everyone had eaten and drunk their fill, talked and leafed through the art books he had brought, Sociologist delivered a speech. 'I am overwhelmed by what I have seen,' he said, his voice quivering with sincerity. 'Over There they live as in a fairy story. Their wise leadership conducts the only just and far-sighted policy, both at home and abroad. The arts and sciences flourish. All the people are beautifully dressed. There is an abundance of food of all kinds. There are no housing problems. All those envious rumours are pure slander. There are, of course, some shortcomings. But only a few, and they are immediately corrected. And there are people who are not satisfied. But where are there not such people? Particularly among the intelligentsia. People like that are always discontented, even though they don't know why themselves. But there are remarkably few malcontents there. You can count them on the fingers of one hand. And they are very quickly corrected or cured.' Everyone listened to Sociologist's speech open mouthed in astonishment and admiration. 'There's an example for us,' said Claimant, and Thinker proposed that they drink to Ibansk's following this example. And everyone cheerfully raised their glasses with him.

A dream

Once again all the papers were signed. Once again all the seals had been stamped. And they were overcome by a certain sadness. Surely they hadn't won through to the end? Surely Chatterer hadn't been wrong? They hired a lorry and some workmen and drove to the stoneyard. But at the yard they could only get a piece of black marble which was to be used to depict the black side of Hog's activities. The director of the yard refused to give them the piece of white marble which was essential to show the beneficial side of Hog, saying that there was no such thing in the yard, although the very piece they needed was lying in the middle of the road and they had had to drive round it. Dauber shoved a fistful of documents signed and sealed by the very highest authorities under the director's nose. The director yelled that he didn't give a bugger for that, no matter what they'd got written on them. They'd nothing better to do than sit there signing papers, while down here we're all breaking our backs with the work. If they had to work here, they wouldn't make such a song and dance. And the complications began all over again. No doubt the whole story would have ended here if it hadn't been for Careerist. 'Forget it,' he said. 'Let's go.' And they went to another stoneyard which had nothing to do with art. For half a litre of vodka the storeman let them choose their own piece of white marble. The yard was full to overflowing with it; there was no demand for it since no-one could find a use for it. This joyful event was celebrated with a prodigious drinking party. 'Just don't get too cheerful about it,' said Chatterer.

'Creating a masterpiece is easy enough. You've still got to get it set up in the intended place.' 'We'll do it', said Dauber, flushed with success and wine. 'That would be sad,' said Chatterer. 'For a fact of this kind to be truly historic, it is necessary that it shouldn't happen.' Careerist said that in that case it would simply be another fact. And he went off to an important meeting in high places. 'All the same,' said Chatterer, 'there is something demeaning and false about all this. It's more the capitulation of art before politics than the other way round. No matter what alliance is formed between art and politics, it always turns out in the end to be a misalliance.' But Dauber had already drunk himself into a stupor and fallen asleep, his head resting on the piece of black marble, his feet propped on the white piece. Chatterer looked at the bronze bust of Hog. Dauber's cap, which was perched atop it, gave Hog the look of a cheeky, sly costermonger from the vegetable market. Chatterer put out the light and slammed the studio door behind him. A mixture of rain and damp snow was falling. Traffic crawled along the busy street throwing up showers of viscous mud. Faceless shadows passed to and fro. A night without hope was beginning . . .

And Dauber had a dream. He dreamt he was in a beautiful city flooded with sunlight. All about stood Dauber's sculptures, in the very form in which he had always dreamt of making them. Here was Truth-teller Street. At one end stood a 'Prophet' a hundred metres high—and at the other, an 'Orpheus' two hundred metres high. And what's this? Hog Square! And in the very centre an enormous pedestal, supporting a hairy hand raised in an obscene gesture and bearing the inscription: 'Our present generation, fuck you all, will live under the total Ism'. Dauber's engravings were on show in shop windows. 'They've understood,' Dauber thought with some satisfaction. 'They have realised my worth!' In front of one window he saw a group of boys and girls. He was always fond of young people, and he could not resist approaching, and listening discreetly to what they were saying. 'We've had this degenerate thrust down our throats so far I'm sick to death of him,' said one lad with a finely drawn spiritual face. 'And this last load of crap!' said a girl with a finely drawn spiritual face. 'I've been lent an album of engravings by Artist and poems by

Writer.' 'Hurray!' cried the boys and girls with their finely drawn spiritual faces. They turned out their pockets to buy a bottle of wine and hurried off to examine this album of engravings by Artist and poems by Writer. Dauber felt sick. He tried to wake up. But he could not.

The end of Claimant

Claimant was appointed to a high post. It was higher than that of Director, but was as far away from Ibansk as the post which had once been held by Slanderer. Moreover, this post effectively prevented any further promotion. Any further move would be a demotion, and a complete exclusion from the game. The job of Director was given to Someone. 'The bastards,' said Claimant, 'I'm not through yet!' And he rushed to the lavatory in search of consolation. And there he saw before his very nose blazoned in letters of fire on the lavatory wall:

Look back, shitter, before you sit!

Claimant looked over his shoulder involuntarily, and on the wall behind him read:

All that was, will be! All that will be, is!

Claimant tried to understand, but failed to do so, as he fell into the cess pit. In the pit he found waiting for him the Boss himself, Director, Secretary, Troglodyte, Hog, the new Leader, and even the Leader who would come in time to replace the new one. 'I salute you, rising generation, still unknown,' said the Boss to Claimant (in the words of Pushkin). And embracing him firmly he began to absorb him in a passionate kiss. 'Help!' cried Claimant in horror. But it was too late.

4
THE LEGEND OF DAUBER

The manuscripts from the rubbish tip

The newspapers had already several times failed to inform their readers about the fragments of manuscript that had been disco-vered accidentally (i.e. without the permission of the authorities) on the recently opened and almost immediately abandoned rubbish tip. These manuscripts told of imaginary events from the time of the Boss, the legendary founder of Ibansk. According to the legend, the Boss first led the ancestors of the Ibanskians out of a dark cave and along a radiant road, and built a joyful future for them. When he had done this, and had overcome all his enemies and friends, he grew proud, and began to punish those who were left. From this came enormous progress. In his old age his vision suddenly cleared, and he pardoned all those who had survived. In honour of this gloomy event he was renamed Hog, and it was decided to set up a monument to him. But fortunately people changed their minds just in time. Around the monument grew up Ibansk—an imaginary settlement of the urban type, which in practice could not have existed because of the falseness of its original premise, and which, even if it had been possible, would not have been possible in Ibansk. The fragments were discovered by surviv-ing schismatics (from the old Ibanskian word 'schemers'), who sold them for assorted currency to the survivors of the foreig-ners (the name given in olden days to the ancestors of the neo-Ibanskians, who now inhabited the most backward parts of the country). The foreigners tried to turn this to profit (from the old Ibanskian word 'profiteer'), but to no avail. Soon after the fragments of manuscript had been found and immediately destroyed, another discovery was made. As milk pipes and meat cables were being laid in the region of Claimants' Square, a piece of plaster was incautiously uncovered which bore a resemblance to a human figure distorted by suffering.

However, as investigations revealed, this was just a late forgery of the work of an unknown master of the Epoch of Confusion, a period when there was no suffering (since there was no confirmation of any of the rumours that there had been sufferings during that period). The learned arguments resumed even more fiercely when some so-called writers and ex-scientists who, in the cause of self re-education, were working on the foundations of a new monument to the art of antiquity, discovered, thanks to the negligence of a secret policeman who had nodded off for a moment, some fragments of a new manuscript which confirmed once and for all that the legend of Boss-Hog was purely fictitious, and that all further discussion of the subject was inadmissible. Below we reproduce these fragments in abbreviated form, but in their original order. Ibansk, 5974.

Problems

'Our life is made up of attempts to solve insoluble problems,' said Chatterer. 'They say that the Boss never existed. But what about his boots? They are preserved as a sacred relic. The boots surely couldn't have ruled the country without the Boss?' 'Why not?' asked Dauber. 'You'd be better employed helping me to solve a more important problem. How can I procure the plaster that's lying in my studio? I got hold of it legally. But now I have to go through the administrative procedures to make it look legal. If I don't, then I could be charged with breaking the law. But the legalisation of a legal operation is illegal.' 'Drop it,' said Chatterer. 'That's what I've done,' said Dauber. 'That's what everyone does. But the possibility of finding myself in court remains. And they could haul me up any time they feel like it.' 'Just keep your head down, and they'll leave you alone,' said Chatterer. 'If you stick your neck out, that's when they might take their opportunity. But don't think they've thought this up specially for your benefit. It's a typical way of keeping social individuals in a state of submission. And don't think that it's been invented deliberately. It happened all on its own, and it's more prophylactic than punitive: it's an attempt to create in man's subconscious a psychological background that tells him that his very existence is unauthorised and even illegal. As long as you spend your time sculpting cows or cosmonauts, you won't be aware of that psychological background. But as soon

(326)

as you begin to produce the kind of monsters you usually make,
it'll come up out of its cellar shouting "Stop!"'

A hole towards Europe

Back in those romantic days when Hog was learning to count on
his fingers at the Academy for the Liquidation of Illiteracy, he
once heard from the tip of his ear (in those days you didn't
listen, you eavesdropped) that somewhere, far, far away, there
was a mysterious land. This land was so backward that it was
even behind the Poles. But then a Great Tsar appeared. He saw
the backwardness all around him, and he decided it had to stop.
So he rolled up his sleeves, got down to work, and opened up a
window on Europe. After this, progress began. When Hog for a
time put an end to general persecution, he got it into his head
that he would do something similar. Not a window, of course.
But at least a hole—a very small hole. He summoned a Council
including the most influential people in the land—his Wife, his
Son-in-law, his Nephew, his Brother-in-law, his Godfather,
Colleague, and many others, who knew where Abroad was,
what people ate there, what kind of clothes people wore. 'I
want,' he said, 'to make a hole through to Europe.' 'Hurray!'
cried his advisers, 'that's what we've needed all along,' and they
all rushed off abroad. The hole was made according to the
theoretical rules. It had a valve, which opened one way and
closed in the other. But which direction was 'one way' and
which direction was 'the other' was kept so secret that now they
do not know themselves which way is which. And so, just in
case, they decided not to let anyone pass either way. But it was
too late. Progress had already started. The first people to go
were the Ensemble of Sinners and Dangers, who are still touring endlessly there. From time to time members of the Ensemble come back to Ibansk to hand over foreign currency and the
information they've collected, sell their foreign finery and
receive new instructions. But they are immediately despatched
on their return journey. After the Ensemble it was the turn of
the Academy of Sciences, which immediately took part in a
conference and established contacts, while sticking to their
principle of not establishing any contacts at all. 'Our task,' said
Academician, 'is to denounce. . . . I beg your pardon, to
enounce our gospel to them.' And he denounced Sociologist for

flabbiness, and Sociologist took his revenge by denouncing Thinker for improper conduct (Thinker had visited a brothel without taking Sociologist along). Afterwards Thinker complained to Sociologist that for some reason he had been stopped from going abroad, something he'd got accustomed to, and without which life was now unthinkable. Sociologist promised to try to find out what the problem was and to help in any way.

Idleness is the source of creativity

'You're being idle again,' said Dauber. 'I've always been idle,' said Chatterer; 'the difference is that I'm not getting paid for it any more.' 'So how are you living?' asked Dauber. 'I get by,' said Chatterer. 'Translations. Confidential reports. "Co-authorship" for half the fee and no mention of my name. I "checked" some fool's doctoral thesis.' 'You know a lot about my work,' said Dauber. 'If you've nothing better to do, write something about that.' 'To write about art you need to know at least something of the language of aesthetics and art criticism,' said Chatterer. 'And I despise it completely.' 'Fine,' said Dauber. 'These days the dilettantes write more interestingly about art than the professionals.' 'The other thing,' said Chatterer, 'is that you have to have a talent for that kind of thing, and in principle I am anti-literary.' 'I don't give a damn for the beauties of style,' said Dauber. 'Write whatever comes into your head. Not necessarily about me.' 'Very well,' said Chatterer, 'I'll try.'

Pseudonym

Following the rules of modern science, wrote Chatterer, I shall refer to Dauber for the sake of anonymity by the symbol E.N. The more readily to distinguish those passages of my work which deal with E.N. from the remaining passages, I shall mark them with an asterisk. They may be left unread. Indeed, they might have been better left unwritten. But I promised E.N. that I would write them, and as a man who in the opinion of the authorities is untrustworthy, I have grown accustomed to keeping my word. As our forbears used to say, if you call yourself a mushroom, get into the trug. It's true that not even the Ministry of the Gifts of Nature knows these days what a mushroom is. A great linguist of my acquaintance said that in all probability the word means 'criminal', since the word 'trug' is clearly a variant of the word 'jug'. Terrified by this association of ideas, I rushed home and deleted this sentence about the wisdom of our forbears just in case, even more so since any references to our ancestors are never as inoffensive as they may seem at first sight. For there are ancestors and ancestors.

I

There is a monograph about a great scientist which begins with a long and boring introduction in which the author recounts when and where he was born, when he got mumps, how he was miraculously cured of diarrhoea, who his maternal grandmother was, where his father served in the army and under what circumstances he married his supposed mother. It isn't until about page forty that the author writes that he eventually came across the works of the great scientist, and that they produced a profound impression on him since the thoughts of the great scientist coincided in every respect with the author's views at that time. So if I begin my study of the work of E.N. with a description of my 'I', I shall not in that respect be original. Moreover, since I am to a certain extent a typical consumer of E.N.'s output, my considerations about myself can be regarded as a primitive means of generalisation. And my idea of E.N.'s art can be regarded as that of a consumer.

So, following the classical tradition of works about great men, I shall begin with a description of my 'I'. I am a man in whose courtyard a hole was dug a year ago, a hole which has remained unfilled ever since. They promised to fill it in before the big holiday. The big holiday came and went. So they promised to do it in time for the next. That too, came and went, and we're still waiting for the next. But we've got used to the hole. If in the end it does get filled up, we'll miss it. A bulldozer calls in every so often, snorts around for about ten minutes, and then either breaks down or falls into the hole. A couple of hours later a bigger bulldozer comes with about ten men. They settle down near the hole and have a smoke. Then they go away. Towards evening they come back with a few pints inside them. The big bulldozer heaves the little bulldozer out of the hole, and they all go off somewhere, leaving the hole in an even worse state than before.

My wife's just come back from the shops. She says she's been overcharged again, and they've been rude to her as well. 'It's not just the money. What I really can't stand is the way that everyone seems to take you for a fool,' she says. I tell her to ignore it all. It's time she got used to it and treated it as normal. Just allow for it. If the price ticket says that a kilo of so-and-so costs three roubles, just reckon that 900 grammes will cost three and a half. In that way you'll even get some change. 'It doesn't bother you at all,' says my wife. 'You were brought up in the good old days. But I'm a living person.'

The hole into Europe

Through the hole into Europe there began a seepage of pictures, manuscripts, sculptures, ikons, people. One man even managed to take his mother-in-law through with him—an event without precedent in world history. Nothing of that kind had ever been seen before, not even in the days of the Great Tsar, when anyone could go abroad with their bullock carts, their entire household staff, their cattle, their pigs, their sheep and their chickens. The foreign press wrote that as usual the Ibanskians might stay quiet for a while, but then they would suddenly do something to startle the world.

All this began with a completely harmless incident. A half demented student, who had written a garbled and delirious thesis which he was afraid to submit because of its bold, progressive ideas, in an access of *folie de grandeur* lobbed the manuscript into the grounds of a foreign embassy. The ex-student was immediately arrested. A foreigner came out of the embassy building, disdainfully picked up the manuscript of the student turned genius between his finger and thumb, and threw it back again. The ex-student was freed and, despite his strenuous resistance, was forced to take his manuscript and have it immediately published in the West. Rumours about the event began to spread at once throughout the creative intelligentsia, who drew significant conclusions from it. The ex-student's example was followed by Candidate. He had written a completely orthodox book, but had dared to say in it one or two things in his own name rather than in the name of the founding fathers, who had not said anything on the subject—who indeed had had no time to do so. The manuscript was accepted for publication by the appropriate Ibanskian publishing house. But Candidate was still afraid that it might be stopped by the censor (this habit of mind was a hangover from the days of the Boss) and took a copy of the manuscript abroad (the wind of change of the Hog era!). After this, Candidate took fright, repented, and wrote a well documented denunciation of all his friends who had not restrained him from the slippery slope.

The most decisive action in this direction was that of Slanderer. He had spent many years in jail for no particular reason that he could understand, and he had made a thorough study of the law. He declared that we have the right to publish what we like and where we like, provided that it is neither a state secret nor anti-Ibanskian. The main difficulty is getting over the frontier. If it's picked up by the customs, they won't let it through, and that's all. If it *does* get through, that's your good fortune. But Slanderer was soon made aware of his childish naïvety and the wisdom of his old grandfather, who used to say 'The law is a tiller: you turn it the way you want to go'. Progress, however, had begun—and enormous efforts were needed to stop it and liquidate its undesirable consequences.

The fact that the penetrability of the hole had grown to quite horrifying dimensions is amply illustrated by examples like these. One underground Modernist painter took through a painting ten times bigger than the Sistine Madonna. An underground Expressionist sculptor took out a cast iron sculpture weighing ten tons. While the sculptor was being X-rayed and having his anus probed by the customs officer's finger, the sculpture just stood their blocking everyone's way. Eventually the senior officer bumped his head on it, and ordered it to be moved immediately towards the West. Within half an hour the masterpiece was in Europe.

My artist

E.N. told me that I'd only need to start and it'd all be flowing out of me. . . . Well, all things considered, I've made a start. And maybe the time has come to recall why this beginning was made. E.N. is my artist, in the sense that everything he does is about me. About my life. Not about my life in society—I have never had such a life, or, at all events it has been so negligible that it hardly exists. My social life is so trivial that it could not

(331)

engage the attention of a major artist. I am talking about the life which has gone on inside my head and which has left no visible trace on the outside world. In this imaginary life I have done a great deal. I have solved the most complex problems of existence, and in the best possible way. I have delivered courses of lectures to a large understanding audience. I have founded an interesting journal. I have improved the level of agriculture. I have unmasked entire armies of parasites and corrupt bureaucrats. I have arranged an exhibition of E.N.'s works. I have even filled up that hole in my courtyard. When E.N. draws or sculpts, it seems to me that he is watching what is going on inside my head. To understand the essence of E.N.'s art, it is necessary first to describe the social type of people who could describe E.N. as 'their artist'. The rest will flow from that. But this social type does not yet exist as a mass phenomenon. There are not many people yet who are potentially capable of recognising E.N. as 'their artist'. There are even fewer who have already done so with deep sincerity and faith. I have observed hundreds of people admiring E.N.'s work. But only a few have truly recognised themselves in them, identified with them. I understand that one must distinguish between the purely aesthetic approach to works of art and the active relationship in which the work becomes something lived and experienced, in much the same way as one must distinguish between an admiration of the picturesque rags of a beggar and a real compassion for their wearer. Much has been said about the aesthetic beauty of E.N.'s works. That beauty is by now almost self evident. But I have never heard anyone speak of their living force. Even his friends remain silent on this point. I do not claim that E.N.'s works depict the spiritual life of people of a particular social type. That would be sheer stupidity. I merely say that in our times only people of this particular social type are developing the potential ability to derive from E.N.'s works an intellectual (and not merely an.aesthetic) satisfaction similar to that which a sincerely believing and sensitive person derives from a beautiful religious service.

Interview

If an experienced customs officer is in principle able to detect a manuscript, a picture, a sculpture, an ikon, a mother-in-law and such like material objects concealed in the false bottom of a suitcase, it has not yet become possible to stop the flow of words cascading out of Ibansk on to the world arena in the form of interviews. The Ibanskians are so used to the idea of the interview that people have even begun to communicate with their friends through the medium of foreign journalists. Let us say, for instance, that the home of Ibanskian A has been searched by the authorities—and quite justifiably, of course: it could all have been quite easily avoided by not keeping forbidden books at home or passing them on to friends. Instead of going round to his acquaintances and telling them what's happened (after all, one can't keep quiet about a thing like that!) A calls in some foreign journalists, and the next day the whole world (including A's friends) knows all about this remarkable event. Or, for instance, Ibanskian B wanted to go abroad (no! really?) and wasn't allowed to leave. And wasn't told why. There again, B calls in the foreign journalists, and the next day the news that B has been refused permission to go abroad is on everybody's lips. Indeed, the way people talk about it, you'd imagine that abroad can't survive another moment without B's presence. The word 'interview' has become a commonplace. A pensioner who was looking for a public lavatory kept on going up to passers-by to ask for an interview on the subject. The passers-by began to dodge him, and the pensioner was arrested by the police who had been hurriedly summoned. Although the pensioner swore that he wasn't an intellectual, and offered as proof a fly-blown diploma from the Senior Academy for the Liquidation of Total Illiteracy, no-one believed him.

Daily life

'Why've you been so long?' asked my wife. 'I've been queuing,' I said. 'They've palmed you off with two broken eggs again,' she said. 'You shouldn't be allowed near a shop. You're asking to be cheated. It's written all over your face.' 'The world's within a hair's breadth of war,' I said, 'and there you go carrying on about broken eggs!' 'I don't care twopence about the war,' she said. 'If they only had to do the shopping and stand in the queues, they'd soon. . . .' An image forms in my mind. The United Nations. Kissinger, Sadat, Pompidou and the rest queuing for butter and eggs. Golda Meir is cheating them. Churchill jumps the queue, claiming that he's going to be late for work and that he's got a crying baby at home. 'By the way,' my wife says, 'you were going to talk to G. about our son. Don't forget that this year the children of intellectuals are finding that admission to colleges and institutes is virtually closed to them. And if he doesn't get into an institute, then he'll be called up into the army.' 'That's nothing to worry about,' I said. 'Let him serve his time.' 'I've nothing against the army,' said my wife. 'But why don't Their children have any problem about getting places in institutes? It's not our son's fault that you aren't a worker or a peasant.' N.K. rang. 'You haven't heard about the awful thing that happened to me last night,' he said. 'I went out to the lavatory. And there was this old woman who began to scream and yell at me. You should have heard her language! There she was, bawling her head off—something or other about modern youth, about the way they grow beards, even something about the pernicious influence of the West. . . . Me, modern youth! I told her, "youth is a social concept, not a definition of age. Until you're in charge of something or someone, you're young. And your insignificance is written all over your face." Just think,' he said, 'she called the police, whistled for them!' 'Perhaps she's right,' I said. 'Maybe you were pissing erroneously?' 'Maybe I was' he said. 'You know how filthy it is there. I placed myself at the closest safe distance.' 'But you haven't been charged?' I asked. 'No, thank God', he said. 'So don't worry,' I said. 'You won't be reported to your employers.' 'I realise perfectly well,' he said, 'that all this is trivial nonsense. But all the same, I can't work. By the way, N.M. has finally decided to leave.'

A little history

I rang N.M. 'I'm very sad that you're leaving,' I said. 'What else can I do?' he said. 'You know perfectly well why.' 'I wish you luck,' I said. 'I'll never forget you,' he said. 'The main thing is that I don't feel that I'm making a mistake. I hope we'll meet again some time.' N.M.'s departure was a real loss for me, even though we saw each other very rarely. We had first met about twenty years earlier. At that time N.M. had just come out of the camps. He'd served ten years for some poems he'd written. We were introduced by my good friend K.K., a very sympathetic character. Now he's a well known specialist in aesthetics. At this meeting, N.M. read the poems he'd written in the camps. This was at the time when philosophers were beginning not to quote the Boss. I'd just come from a meeting of the Scientific Committee, where we'd been discussing a doctoral thesis which criticised the Boss. I had got up and said that it was all a bit too easy, that even a donkey could kick a dead lion, and that during the Boss's lifetime the author of the thesis had crawled behind him in the dust and licked the very marks of his boots. One of my old acquaintances said à propos of this that I was an impenitent cult-follower. This acquaintance knew perfectly well that I had spoken out aginst the Boss while I was still a young man. During the war he had served in a provost detachment, and as a student he had fulminated against cosmopolitans, Mendelites—indeed everyone against whom it was thought proper to fulminate. Now he had become so progressive and leftist that there was nothing for me, an almost innate anti-cultist, left to say to him. There were many like him. N.M.'s poems were beginning to lose any sense at all. At that time E.N. had already made firm and irreversible steps towards the status of the major artist he is today. I had been friendly with him for some years, and I was absolutely convinced that he would come through. In the situation at that time in all socially significant spheres of our life, two camps could be clearly distinguished. One of them consisted of obscurantists and reactionaries. No-one considered themselves to be members of this group. The other camp was made up of all those who were against the obscurantists and reactionaries, and who strove towards democracy, liberalism and progress. All the others saw themselves as members of this camp. They were divided into the young and the old. The young maintained among themselves that the old were obscurantists, and among themselves the old maintained that the young were trouble-makers subservient to Western influences. When either group spoke openly, they tried to use rather different terms. This was the beginning of the usual battle for important posts, bonuses, high salaries, degrees, titles, trips abroad and other such benefits. And there were, too, some isolated beings who had realised from the very beginning that they must stand aside from all this, do what they had to do, with all the effort, time and talent that demanded, and, by pursuing their own personal affairs, place themselves in quite another sector of existence. E.N. was one of these people. I don't know whether he chose deliberately to act in this way, or whether it was the intuition of a remarkable man. I am inclined to the latter explanation, for it was only later that people came to understand the social situation clearly. But the fact remains that, when a panic starts, it is better to stand aside and seek one's own best way out of it so as to avoid ending up in a cul-de-sac. That is what E.N. did, Here there was no calculation. Everything happened of its own accord. In fact he was forced by circumstances to be original. What was the decisive factor here? Perhaps it was his awareness of his own immense vitality and an almost unhealthy appetite for work. The famous artist G., whom at that time I knew well, said repeatedly that E.N. had schemed, fiddled, grabbed for what he could get. I am prepared to accept this. E.N. schemed and fiddled in much the same way as Chaliapin schemed to become a bass, or as Beethoven schemed to write music extraordinary for his times. K.K. followed the crowd, among the young, but perhaps closer to the old. And so through all these past twenty years he has felt very uncertain. For some reason or other N.M. never came to very much. I telephoned K.K. to tell him that N.M. was leaving, and that it was time to say goodbye. 'I'm ill,' he said. 'There's no point in going to see him,' I said, 'he's got his hands full without having to put up with us. Just ring him.' K.K. did not telephone. I feel very sorry for him, and sad for all of us. There's hardly any trace left of our youth.

Youth

Wet snow was falling. It was the beginning of November. The trench of the punishment battalion was knee deep in mud. And there was no escape from the cutting edge of the wet ice-laden wind. Impossible to lie down; impossible even to sit. No-one even felt like eating. It was a kind of petrification, waiting for the inevitable. And nothing more. No thought. No memories. No desire.

> Ah, love me, lass, while I am free.
> While I am free, I'm yours,

Panicker intoned mournfully.

> For soon you'll see no more of me,
> And heed another's calls.

'Shut your gob!' yelled the Lieutenant. 'Can't you find anything more cheerful to sing?'

> I found you barefoot, bald and without teeth,
> And I spent hours in putting you to rights,

Panicker struck up unwillingly. The platoon woke up, and more from habit than from any real enthusiasm, took up the chorus:

> But you did deceive me,
> Decided to leave me,
> Oh why did you twist my balls so?
> Hoi!

'Stop this fucking row!' bellowed the Sergeant. 'Get fell in!' 'Oh, it's hard, very hard, in the trenches. But up there it's even worse. At least there are walls down here. There are none up there.' 'At the double' shouted the Sergeant. 'Why are the cunts dragging us out here?' said Panicker. 'Can't you see?' said Deviationist, pointing to Academician. 'They're going to give us a lecture.' 'They can stuff their lectures,' said Pimp. 'Shut your mouths!' yelled the Sergeant. 'Fall in!'

The absurd*

Wet snow was falling. Drunken youths demanded lights for their cigarettes and prevented me from walking a straight and uninterrupted course. I was trying to invent something for E.N. Inventing truth is a difficult thing to do. And apparent life is not well suited to phrase-making. Everything is so lacking in form that nothing can be seen. Everything is so rectilinear and geometric that it makes you feel sick. As soon as you reach out for something that seems to be important and durable, you realise soon enough that it's nothing of any significance, or something which doesn't even have a name of its own. And an infinite morass of words which in reality can designate nothing. E.N.'s drawings are understood on the same level as a commonplace pamphlet. A shabby intellectual with a fashionable beard and a beggarly salary, being read a lecture by a lavatory attendant—a lavatory attendant with the intellect of a statesman . . . and the titanic figures in E.N.'s work . . . what possible connection can there be between them? Absurd. Yes, absurd. But

(337)

it is a real not an imaginary absurdity. The fact is that N.M. was attracted by E.N., and not by anyone else. When my acquaintances ask me to explain E.N.'s drawings, I become confused and come out with all kinds of rubbish. I talk about music that one needs to learn to listen to, about beer which one has to get used to. The reference to music passes by unnoticed. The reference to beer produces an effect. When E.N. himself begins to explain his work to visitors to his studio, I leave so as not to see the expressions on their faces.

Our friends*

'Look,' said E.N., 'here are two monographs. Published by official houses. In theory they shouldn't touch me with a bargepole. Yet both monographs refer to my work. K.K. and N.M. are our friends. In theory they ought to go to any lengths to help me. But what actually happens? K.K. takes care to see that his magazine never says a word about me. Our building is officially regarded as the finest from the point of view of the combination between architecture and sculpture. It's even been proposed for an award—true enough without any mention of my name. But K.K. fills half his magazine with articles about a mediocre building of the same kind in T. For six months N.M. was always on at me to write an article for his paper. In the end I broke off my own work and wrote it. And what happens? Two years go by. Everyone forgets about the article. The manuscript can't be found. What's going on?' B.P., who had dropped in to borrow fifty roubles from E.N., made a few vague remarks about directives from above. 'That's nonsense,' I said. 'Directives are a result, not a cause. Even directives from the Boss were merely a formulation and culmination of the aspirations of the masses, not schemes dreamt up by a villain. What's going on, you ask? Nothing out of the ordinary. Life is terribly normal, and our friends are acting like ordinary normal people as well. They are protecting themselves against the consequences of your existence, that's all. Such a clearly defined and expressed social process is going on in your connection that it simply appears unlikely.' We've grown accustomed to these social laws cutting a path through a whole multitude of chance circumstances like more or less apparent tendencies. But here there are no chance circumstances, no tendencies. It's brutally to the point. That is what makes it seem confusing. It's far from being the first time we've talked about this. And I am not talking with the aim of educating E.N., but to clarify my own mind by speaking out loud. Of course, K.K. could have published articles about E.N. and N.M. could have published his own article. They should have done so if only because they were personal friends, to say nothing of the fact that they all belonged to a certain spiritual confraternity, along with E.N., and that they are therefore his brothers in spirit. They could have done this, and as people who hold important posts, they could have done so without any professional risk to themselves. But they did not do so. They failed to do so voluntarily, not because they were under constraints. They did not wish to do so, although for self justification they had to hint at certain reactionary intrigues, and at bans imposed from above. I repeat that such bans do exist. But in such cases all the higher authorities usually do is to give permission to colleagues and friends to hinder a man from becoming too important for their social peace of mind. For colleagues and friends are the highest court of appeal for a creative person. They are the only true censors and the only true effective power. Why did our friends not want to do anything for E.N. which might lead to a strengthening of his social position? Because in fact the situation is not one in which they and E.N. stand shoulder to shoulder like the forces of light opposing some dark forces, but one in which they stand opposed to him, as the very representatives of those dark forces. E.N. has served as an involuntary indicator of their actual social status. They had enough intelligence to be aware of this. But they did not have enough courage to recognise the true situation. And on top of that, the staggering scale of E.N.'s personality overwhelmed their own miserable standing as socially significant individuals. I am talking of K.K. and N.M. as typical representatives of an entire social category. So E.N. became as it were the personal enemy of a whole group of people working in different areas of cultural activity. If it had been possible, they would have erased him from their past. But they were not able to do that. They had missed the moment when this could have been done. And impotence engenders hate. E.N. is no particular problem for reactionaries (the dark forces). Their relationship to him is on quite another plane, which has nothing to do with art as such. In case of need they could even defend him against the forces of light. They won't let him go very far, they'll keep him on the edge between semi-recognition and semi-repression. And they will use his friends and colleagues as intermediaries. Our friends are typical representatives of that category of our society in which E.N. is obliged to live and work. This category has no stable title, which is entirely appropriate in view of its actual instability and amorphousness. It can include almost by chance scientists and artists who are in a privileged or exceptional position in their professional field: because they are better educated, better known, more success-ful, freer to express controversial opinions on controversial subjects, because they are familiar with Western life and cul-ture, because they have contacts with cultural organisations and can use them, or because they have access to higher authority. In a certain sense they are our intellectual elite. In many para-meters the position of this social group is twofold. In the narrowly professional sphere they are a remarkable manifesta-tion. When they compare themselves with others, they come to the view that they are truly outstanding people (megalomania, let us say). But in society as a whole they are, on another plane, a mass phenomenon. Their exceptional nature is merely the result of a division of labour. It is purely illusory. Seen against the mass of people like them, they turn out to be wholly unremarkable people. From this comes their inferiority com-plex and their efforts to find a more stable social base. People from this category strive to acquire every reward conceivable in our society—domestic comforts, degrees, titles, ranks, decora-tions, prizes, trips abroad, high salaries and fees and so on. And alongside this, they wish to appear persecuted, forgotten, neg-lected. They feel this way because they have constantly before their eyes a stream of less well equipped, less able colleagues, who have risen to higher positions and achieved a more privileged situation. One acquaintance of mine who had recently come back from the U.S.A., and who for some reason had been refused permission to go to England, launched such an attack on our way of life that I began to feel like a backwoods conservative. All the same, he did go to England some time later. They try to make themselves seem wholly trustworthy in the eyes of authority. They are capable of doing all in their power to achieve that, and even to do it better than their reactionary predecessors. But at the same time they wish to look like persecuted opponents of the regime. They even offer their ability to play dirty tricks better than their reactionary forbears as evidence of their progressiveness and civic courage. This duality does not relate to any sense of there being two opposing forces within them, but to the sense that what they pretend to be does not correspond with their social essence. In essence they are ordinary careerists, informants, executants; but on the surface they are unjustly persecuted seekers after truth, justice and beauty. They present no enigma to the authorities; they are an enigma only for themselves. For people like this, the appearance of truly remarkable persons like E.N. is wholly unwelcome, for these latter strip from them all their 'creative' attributes and leave them nothing but their social function.

Social life

'I spend virtually all my life in the studio,' said Dauber. 'There's nothing to read. Television bores me to tears —nothing but ice-hockey or speeches. We went to the cinema one day, and for the next two we were gagging on our food. There's nothing to talk about with colleagues. If you leave aside purely business conversations and visitors (that's work) I haven't spoken to more than two or three people regularly for many years. Almost my whole spiritual life consists of conversations with them. There's hardly any other social life.' 'You're lucky,' said Neurasthenic. 'People come and see you.'

Children

Children, comrades?—streams of snot,
Burps and screaming's all you've got.
Sleepless nights and troubled days—
Life's pure hell, that's what I says.
(from The Ballad)

From a piece of filth which bore some vague resemblance to a wallet, Pimp extracted a photograph of a small girl and showed it to Intellectual. 'Look,' he said, 'isn't she pretty?' The photograph passed from hand to hand. 'There were eleven children in our family,' said Defeatist. 'We were always hungry. Lived in filth. Wore rags. You should have seen what I looked like when I went into the army! But all the same it was a good life. Happy and gay.' 'I was an only child,' said Deviationist. 'Of course, it was a lot worse for me than for Defeatist. Nice clean room. Regular meals. You should have tasted my mother's rissoles! But it wasn't too bad, all the same.' 'I haven't got any children,' said Intellectual. 'And I won't have any now. I don't regret anything. I'm even just a little proud that I once pissed in that bastard Sergeant's boot. At least I've achieved one social act in life! There aren't many people who can say that. The only thing that I regret is that I haven't got a son. Or better, a daughter! Or better still, a son and a daughter! There's something positive about having children. My father used to say that in these days children were the only thing worth bothering about. Children are the only thing which unconditionally relates us to the human race. Children are an eternal and absolute basis of morality. If you deal with everyone as with a child, that's the whole secret of life. Everything else is just an illusion. I didn't understand my father then. And I still don't understand him. But I wish I could understand him and think as he did.' 'As for me,' said Panicker, 'I see this business differently. You remember when we were sent out to unload those wagons? Well, while you were all rushing about using up your strength, I had time to find a girl, marry her and give her a baby. So if I get sent down, at least I won't have any alimony to pay. Which is always something.'

Sociological analysis*

I was told this story by an eyewitness. Once upon a time, in the liberal era, there was a gathering of artists and writers. The majority were young and talented. They were discussing a variety of subjects, including the relationship between academicians and the young. E.N. was persuaded to speak. He drew a huge backside on the blackboard, and said the following: 'The academicians have all joined hands and placed themselves around this arse to lick it. In return it gives them money, titles, cars, medals, villas. Behind the academicians is an enormous crowd of young people who are pushing forward. The academicians cry that the young ones are trying to come to bite the arse, and kick them out of the way. Poor, poor backside! It does not know that the young ones don't want to bite it. They're pushing forward to lick it, but to lick it with better qualifications and for a larger reward.' In due course, the dear colleagues forgot this brilliant sociological analysis, although they were very angry with E.N. at the time. But they will never forget and forgive him for what he does in his studio. One artist who looked through E.N.'s last album said as much. So what do you want? To do such extraordinary things and at the same time count on their benevolence? No, they'll never forgive you that! Who are 'They'? The huge army of artists and people who are connected with the arts in general. All that this painter had done was to apply a general social law to the particular case of E.N.

The no-exit people

'My wife and I had received a private invitation to visit one of the brotherly countries,' said Neurasthenic. 'But they wouldn't even let us go there. So I got up at dawn and went to this department which our common friend Colleague has nick-named the Department of No-Exit Visas and Travel Bans and applied for an appointment with the director to ask why we'd been turned down. I spent all morning hanging about there only to be told that I couldn't be told the reason for the refusal. And on top of that they won't let us go anywhere for a full year. Of course, they won't let us go anywhere after that, in all probability—but this year it's for certain. I was sure they wouldn't let us leave. I got used to that idea a long time ago. My wife's even stuck up a map of the world with little black crosses to mark the places I've been invited to and not been allowed to visit: She calls it her map of international non-communication.' Dauber said, 'I've had an invitation to go to G. It's taking a long time to get the papers together. Perhaps it's not worth doing. They probably won't let me go.' 'Of course they won't let you go,' said Neurasthenic, 'but get the documents together all the same. That is an action. And a refusal is an action. At least don't let them get away with it scot free.' 'It's strange,' said Dauber, 'all our friends go abroad quite regularly, and that doesn't seem to provoke any particular emotions. But the last time I was turned down and got angry about it, what was the reaction then? "Oh, listen to him, didn't get what he wanted! So he thinks he needs to go abroad, does he?" But I actually do need to go. It's my profession!' 'I met an old acquaintance recently,' said Neurasthenic. 'You should have heard him laugh when I told him how we'd been refused permission to go to a brotherly country. "You don't know your luck," he said (not bad, is it?). He said, "for the past three years I haven't even been allowed to crawl out of one hole to get into another, and there you go talking about London and Paris and Rome." But you know, if we had been going to that brotherly country, he'd have accepted that as our due. Why?' 'It's very simple,' said Chatterer. 'If you had been going, that would have meant that you had that amount of social privilege. That's the rule. So that would have put you in a higher social rank than him. But since you weren't allowed to go, you must be in the same social rank as he is. And since you want to go abroad, that means that you're trying to climb out of that rank—i.e. do something dishonest from his point of view.'

Secrets

'Today we are having a very important meeting,' said Neurasthenic. 'A decision's got to be taken. Assistant is coming in person.' 'Oho!' said Journalist, 'I'd like to be in on that.' 'Well, come along with me then,' said Neurasthenic. 'But I'd need a permit,' said Journalist. 'No, you don't,' said Neurasthenic. 'No-one will pay the slightest attention to you. And if Assistant knows there's a foreigner in the hall, he'll say things he's got no right to say. Here we're very fond of foreigners and we don't like keeping secrets secret. Our secrets are designed for wide dissemination. The more secret a secret is, the faster and further it spreads. An old friend of mine once came here on holiday. We went to a restaurant. After the first glass he began to tell me and everyone else in the place about the location of secret rocket launch pads and new types of rockets. Just next to us was sitting a foreign spy who was in the process of encoding his report about rocket bases. He'd got all his information for prodigious sums of money from speculators. Well, you can imagine what kind of information that was. In the end he called for the manager and asked him if he could persuade my friend not to speak so loudly because it was disturbing his concentration.'

'You see,' said E.N. 'I'm drawing. Whether or not someone has been stopped from going abroad makes no difference to that. I work spontaneously, independent of the flow of current events.' 'So be it,' I said. 'Let's allow that you just dropped in here from outer space, and that nothing that you do has any connection with our life here on earth. What then? I'm thinking about the future. Is there going to be any sort of connection then? With whom? And will it last? What will your art mean to those who may choose to make you the spokesman for their personalities? And whether you like it or not, it is these "WE" who will give your works a strictly defined meaning. We will grow in number with the years, and in the end we will canonise you. That is the fate of all great artists whose work has a social resonance. So the meaning of your works lies not within the works themselves, but in those stable and continuing social phenomena which give birth to a particular kind of people or to specific traits of human character.' In their relationship to social laws people are divided into two unequal groups. One of these includes the overwhelming majority of the human race. The representatives of this group behave usually in complete correspondence with social laws, i.e. with the historically developed rules of social behaviour. The other group consists of that tiny minority who perform vitally important actions in defiance of the social laws. Very few of them can do this systematically. And literally only one or two individuals can find the strength within themselves to sustain the titanic battle with society. It is only thanks to this strength that they are sometimes able to accomplish some great work for the good of that very society which has been trying to destroy them or to bring them down to the level of the normal social type. This group of people we call anti-social. A man's adherence to this group does not depend on his behaviour for or against any given political system, or on whether he shares any particular ideology. E.N. is an example of people of this kind. He had been driven to become an anti-social element not only by the circumstances of his individual destiny, but also by the special conditions which surround the life of an artist in our society, which transform the struggle of an artist to affirm his individuality into a daily battle. So the conversation which E.N. had with one well-known Western writer seemed to me to be pure comedy. For several hours at a stretch this writer tried, by dint of references to the history of culture, to contemporary philosophical concepts and scientific data, to persuade E.N. to fight for his creative individuality. You should have seen the expression on E.N.'s face! This is how he spoke about it later. A man has spent ten years in a labour camp. He has lost the habit of consorting with women, and satisfies his needs with men. One day a representative of the international association of homosexuals turns up at the camp and tries to persuade him that from the view point of the most recent achievements of culture, science and philosophy, sexual relations with other men is the finest form of masculine sexual activity. You know, for a whole hour I couldn't understand what he was getting at. And when the penny finally dropped. . . . I can just imagine what a Charlie I must have looked!

Decision

The hall was full to bursting. The members of the conference were sitting two or three to a chair, standing on the window sills, hanging from the chandeliers with their imitation crystal lustres, clinging on to the frames of the portraits of handsome Leaders and Deputies, hardly distinguishable one from another, all with astonishingly wise and honest faces of men who were ready for anything. There was no air left to breathe. People were saved from suffocation only by the ability, gained after decades of countless meetings, to breathe a mixture of sulphuretted hydrogen and demagogy. Journalist immediately fell into a state of coma. 'He's not up to it!' said Troglodyte, jerking his thumb towards Journalist. 'Not up to it at all,' said Claimant. And they shook hands. Assistant had to climb over people's heads to reach the platform. As he clambered over one bald pate (that of Thinker, according to some, Claimant's arse according to others) he slipped and ricked his neck so badly that he had to read his speech while facing simultaneously towards and away from the audience. The assembled company took this as a directive and all tried to do the same. Because of this Claimant's chances dwindled once more. After the report and the debates, in which previously selected, checked and double-checked conference delegates delivered previously checked and double-checked enthusiastic speeches, the resolution was put to the meeting. In the executive part of the resolution, the paragraph on concrete propositions included the following point: with the aim of pursuing the elevation of the general level, the conference resolves to occupy strongpoint N. Troglodyte voiced the objection that our forces were insufficient. But he was immediately unmasked and declared guilty by Claimant. 'What's the punishment battalion for?' he declared triumphantly, and left on a business trip to Italy. Claimant's chances immediately improved. The proposal to take N. by storm was unanimously adopted, and was immediately included in the General Plan. Both junior and senior colleagues included this subject in their individual plans. The Management planned a report on the progress of the fulfilment of the plan to capture N., which would, it was hoped, attract the participation of authors from outside the Institute. Thus it became quite impossible that N. should not be taken. 'But why,' Journalist asked, 'did they decide to take specifically N., and not D?' 'What difference does it make?'' asked Neurasthenic. 'Do you think D.'s better? Let them storm whatever they like, as long as they leave us in peace.'

Refusal
'They've turned me down,' said Dauber. 'And they haven't explained why. What do you think that can mean?' 'Don't worry your head about it,' said Chatterer. 'You can think of as many reasons as you like, but they'd all be wrong. Don't regard your case as an exception, but as part of the general rule. That way you'll be making no mistakes. For us, a trip abroad isn't a normal means of human communication in the twentieth century. It's a privilege which is accorded only to people of a certain category. That's common knowledge. You don't belong to this category. They don't explain the reasons for their refusal because they have no legal or moral arguments to justify them. That, too, is common knowledge. The only thing that makes your case unusual is that it will produce an international echo.'

Interview
Soon everyone knew that Dauber had been refused permission for his trip. The studio filled with foreign journalists. An

interview had to be given. Dauber talked mostly about his artistic projects. As far as the refusal was concerned, he said that he had not been told the reasons. Why? Because clearly they had no rational justification. And at the same time because in refusing him permission, they could kill two birds with one stone. Once a man has been refused permission to go abroad without being told why, he becomes alarmed and worried. He has to try to think up reasons by himself, and take upon himself some imaginary guilt. The body which has turned down his application without having to give a reason acquires the attributes of being privy to great secrets, and in so doing takes on the role of Providence. And man can only tremble. This idea produced a powerful impression on the journalists. Neurasthenic, who heard Dauber's interview the following day on a foreign radio station, said that THEY would never forgive him. 'But what can THEY do?' asked Visitor. 'If they were to judge Dauber, they would stand themselves before the tribunal of history.'

Food

As soon as breakfast's down our throats,
Lunch is the the thing that gets our votes.
And when lunch has left the table,
We'll bolt our supper when we're able.
All the rest we shrug away—
How else to get through the day?

(from The Ballad)

Thus the worthless round is seen . . .
Best place to be is the canteen.

(from The Ballad)

The meal was soon over. The men of the punishment battalion huddled together shivering from cold. They could neither sleep nor stay fully awake. 'It's easy enough to talk about stuffing yourself,' said Deviationist. 'Which of us hasn't gone through that? Which one of us wouldn't stuff ourselves with any old scraps provided they had a few calories?' 'Here's what happened to me once,' said Gelding. 'I was on guard in the stables—last watch. It was time for me to hand over, but some bastard had stolen a bridle. My relief wouldn't take over. I had to wait and sneak off to nick another bridle from the next squadron. Everyone did that. There were dozens of bridles missing in the regiment, but on paper they were all present and correct. You spent your time stealing bridles from one another. Anyway, in the end I got myself relieved. I was late for supper, of course. I got to the canteen, and what d'you think! There were about thirty bowls of porridge left. Every bowl big enough for four men. My head swam at the very thought of it. Another late arrival turned up from guard duty, and we got down to work. Believe it or not, I got through eight bowls with no trouble. And I'd probably have carried on, but I just happened to look at this other bloke. He'd eaten fifteen bowls. I could see that his eyes were beginning to turn up and porridge was coming out of his ears. And then he began to slide out of his seat in a very strange way. I was horrified. I tried to stand up, and I couldn't. The porridge was suffocating me. I undid all my buttons, struggled outside and got back to the barracks half dead. I recovered in the end, but the other lad died.' 'That's nothing,' said Panicker. 'When we were in training three of us ate a lunch intended for a whole platoon. The redcap arrived and swore he'd easily find out who'd done it. The thieves would be so full they wouldn't be able to eat dinner that evening. So we had to eat our dinner as if nothing had happened. The redcap was shaken, and begged us to own up, and promised not to punish us. All he wanted was to see what such astonishing eaters looked like. But what were we? We were just ordinary rank and file starvelings. Of course we didn't confess.' 'In our squadron,' said Panicker, 'there was a navigator who decided to rear a goat. It was a very friendly beast. Followed us everywhere. Once we were sneaking out of camp without a pass, and the goat tagged along. No matter how much we shooed it away, it wouldn't leave us. So we got this idea. It's the first—and I would guess the only time in my life—that I've ever stuffed myself full to bursting with fresh roast meat.' 'We had a vineyard belonging to a wine co-operative alongside our second airfield,' said Deviationist. 'Of course, we all used to sneak off for a quiet browse. The vineyard bosses were stupid enough to ask our command for help in protecting the grapes. Our commanders got a bit on the side from the vineyard bosses, so they agreed, and we were sent off to patrol the vineyard. You should have seen the result. Within a week everything had gone, right down to the bark off the vines. The vineyard bosses begged for the patrols to be withdrawn. But that wasn't quite so easy. While the argument was going to and fro, the season ended, and we stopped going to the vineyard even though we'd been ordered to guard pretty well to the end of the year. So we had our share of vitamins all right! You might say we'd had enough to last us the rest of our days.' An orderly arrived. 'Sergeant, Intellectual, Gelding, Murderer,' he said. 'To the battalion commander.' 'Go and get me a prisoner who'll talk,' said the Commander. 'Don't come back without one!'

Worldly hypocrisy

'Once,' said Dauber, 'I won a competition in U. against some famous Western painters. It was unprecedented. And what happened? I came home with a bouquet of eulogies which I showed to the Artists' Union. I wanted to give an account of my trip. But no-one wanted to listen. Yet it was laid down that I had to give an account. And I accepted. Anyone from here who goes anywhere gives a dozen lectures at least. Of course there wasn't a line about me in the papers. But if anyone else had won this competition, we'd never have heard the last of it in Ibansk. All right, have it their own way. Let's say that's normal. But my friends and acquaintances! Imagine, not one of them so much as congratulated me. It's not that they didn't know. They all knew perfectly well. And kept their mouths shut. As if nothing had happened. Or at best, they sniggered a bit. Really, in U., what a joke! At about the same time B.A. went to P. He didn't win any competition. Just took part, without winning a thing. Submitted rubbish. But after that, no-one talked about anything except that piece of nonsense that B.A. had shown.' 'Apart from anything else,' said Neurasthenic, 'this is a sign of complete and utter provincialism, and a total lack of education or decent manners. I become more and more convinced that the critical literature of the recent past has done a great deal of harm by attacking worldly hypocrisy. It's been based on a very banal principle, that a man who behaves decently towards others (smiles, says he's pleased to see you, sympathises when things go wrong, and so on) thinks something else privately—(that he looks down on you, envies you, is pleased with your failures, upset by your successes, and so on). This was seen as hypocrisy. It was considered that people who were of little worth were passing themselves off as decent and good. But that isn't only (or always) hypocrisy. It can also be the result of good education, which is one of the social means of self defence that people use against their own selves. It's the ability to control oneself, without which no normal relationships are possible. Without this good education life becomes a nightmare. Without it, it's virtually impossible even to meet anyone. We cannot talk of man as if he possessed something secret and genuine which developed a mask to suit any given situation. A man's character includes what he is at home, and what he is at work, and what he is among his friends and acquaintances, and what he thinks and what he says.' 'Yes, but there's more than a lack of worldly education here,' said Chatterer. 'You'd have to talk more about anti-worldly education. To ignore and trample underfoot everything that is outstanding and to hold up mediocrity for praise is a particular kind of education, not a void. Hypocrisy that takes the form of a negation of hypocrisy is hypocrisy squared.'

Language*

The idea of considering E.N.'s work as a new language comes as no surprise in our time which has gone mad for models, formalisation, systems, structures and so on. And it is an idea wholly lacking in content until we establish precisely what is meant by considering a manifestation of some kind as a language. When I developed this idea to Neurasthenic, he said that he had thought it up himself long ago. But, as he admitted later, for him even the twittering of sparrows or the caterwauling of amorous cats or the whining of dogs constituted a language. If we consider a form as a language, we have to use concepts like 'sign', 'meaning', 'sense', 'alphabet' and so on. The photograph of an object is not the sign of that object. The same thing is true of a realistic drawing. The sign does not represent, it signifies. The lack of similarity between the sign and the original or, at least, their deliberate dissimilarity is a necessary condition for an object to become a sign. From the appearance of a word, for instance, it is impossible to judge the appearance of the object it represents. The significance of a sign is known if one knows exactly what it signifies. The transformation of an object into a sign presupposes a voluntary act. The meaning of a sign is taken as known if one knows the significance of all the simple signs of which it is composed, and all the rules which govern the composition of simple signs in the complex whole. These rules of composition are not signs themselves; they have their basis in the active creative nature of man. The significance of complex signs is established by first establishing their meaning: i.e. it presupposes the use of certain linguistic components which are not themselves signs. When we speak of the alphabet of a language, we must distinguish linguistic means which are not themselves signs, but which make up signs, and simple linguistic units to which concepts of significance and meaning can be applied—meaningful units of language. This distinction can be clearly seen in the distinction between the alphabet and root words of normal languages. From what has been said it should be clear that the concept of meaning cannot be applied to every work of art. For example it is absurd to speak of the meaning of a portrait of a cow or of a statesman, even if it is painted by an artist as eminent as Artist. It is absurd to speak of the meaning of the countless sculptures (both equestrian and standing figures) which adorn the squares of Ibansk. The concept of meaning is only applicable when the work of art acquires certain properties of significance. The dissimilarity between what the artist carves or paints and the actual objects (including their transformations) is an essential condition which must be fulfilled before one can talk about the meaning of a work of art. One way of creating a work of art which possesses attributes of meaningfulness is the deformation and transformation of real objects, for example of parts of the human body. This also produces manifestations which are, at best, signs only in part. On the one hand they may show a certain similarity with actual objects. But on the other hand they are tranformed in such a way that the 'resemblance', in the naturalistic sense, is destroyed. The combination of signs of this kind allows the sign-constructions which no longer have any analogy with reality. In these combinations we see the complete disappearance of representation, which still survived in their individual elements. It is strange that completely naturalistic elements can be included in such combinations to such effect that they seem

(352)

even further from reality than the most improbable transformations of actual objects. E.N. did not invent any particular alphabet in the visual arts. He invented something else. He developed a whole system of semantic units and rules governing their composition into complex formations—into semantic phrases and texts of a particular kind. One can compile definitive lists of the semantic units and rules of composition. It is a difficult task. But as time goes by art critics will complete it exhaustively. E.N.'s semantic units have a visible appearance and an invisible meaning. As visible phenomena they are fragments of drawings, engravings and sculptures. They can even exist as independent, self-sufficient works. As phenomena which have meaning they are symbols of ordinary human passions, desires, experiences—indignation, disappointment, anger, hope, enthusiasm, insight, torpor and so on. But these meanings are not allocated once and for all. They are subject to variation and change. They depend on the various combinations in which they are placed, on the subjective states and peculiarities of those who see them, and on many other parameters.

A prisoner who talks

'There's a whole art in capturing a prisoner who'll talk,' said Murderer. 'For example, the prisoner you take should be the best informed man in the entire enemy army. So ideally he should be the chief of their general staff. And then again, his disappearance should pass unnoticed. So in that respect ideally he should be some jerk from the sanitary platoon. How can we best reconcile these two requirements? It's very simple. We grab the first man we find.' 'That's the principle we used at K.,' said Sergeant. 'We crossed the front line. The night was as black as your hat. We stumbled over someone. Grabbed him. Gagged him. Shoved a sack over his head and brought him home. Lost one of our own. Got back to the unit. Undid the sack. And then what? He turned out to be one of ours. From the division next up the line. He was out on a recce as well. And they'd got the one we'd lost. You can imagine the kind of interrogation they went through.' 'What do they want to take a prisoner for?' said Gelding. 'Everything's perfectly clear anyway. You only have to look. If they'd only ask me I could draw them a complete map in five minutes—what's what and where it is.' 'Who do you think you are?' said Murderer. 'Who'd trust you?' 'So why are they sending me on this mission?' asked Gelding. 'That's another matter,' said Murderer. 'Your job is to bring back a prisoner. It's him they're going to have to trust, not you.' 'Why?' asked Gelding. 'Because he's an enemy,' said Murderer. 'They've got to have a prisoner,' said Sergeant. 'It's laid down. They're got to put it in their report.' 'The Sergeant knows the score,' said Intellectual. 'They play everything by the book.' 'They play everything by our necks,' said Gelding. 'Of course it's never their own necks,' said Intellectual. 'Anyway, lads,' said Sergeant, 'we haven't any choice. So we're going to have to go out and catch this bloody prisoner. With a bit of luck one or the other of us will survive.'

The basis of optimism
'You look at life far too gloomily,' said Journalist. 'Governments always and everywhere have used carrot and stick policies. You've had your share of the stick. Now you're waiting for a bit of carrot to come your way.' 'You're right,' said Neurasthenic. 'But you're not taking one particular circumstance into account. You're supposing that the stick and the carrot are administered in equal proportions to one and the same people. But we are imaginary characters in an imaginary country. In our country some people get the stick, and others get the carrot. And incidentally, when they hand out the carrots, the first lot get another beating. You're thinking of us Ibanskites as if we were all in the same situation, and as if we didn't have any inter-Ibanskian relations. And yet almost all the people you meet and who complain to you about their terrible lot belong to that very set of people who own the carrots and wield the stick.'

Genuine art
'And where are the criteria which let us draw a distinction between real and unreal art?' asked Scientist. 'Personally, I don't find any problem here at all,' said Neurasthenic. 'For instance, I visited Artist's studio. I looked, and I thought that in

principle I could learn to do what he was doing. In other words, it was a load of rubbish. Then I went to Dauber's studio. I looked, and I thought that even if I studied for a hundred years, I could never do anything like that. The same thing's true of poetry. For instance take Writer's verse in today's paper. I could churn out that kind of stuff by the mile. So it must be nonsense. I could have invented the whole of Writer's work in six months. But O.'s poems—never.' 'You've got too high an opinion of your own ability,' said Scientist. 'Quite the reverse,' said Neurasthenic. 'I'm completely untalented.' 'Right,' said Scientist. 'Let's see you improvise.' 'Very well,' said Neurasthenic. 'If I pause for a moment, I shall have failed.'

A success

'Well,' said Gelding, 'we crawled right up to them. Suddenly a mine blew up close by. Murderer and I dived into a hole. Then two of theirs came crawling out. Damned if I know what for. We grabbed one and set off home. We were almost back to our trenches when the bastards shot Murderer in the arse. So I had to lug two of them home.' 'Perhaps they'll give you an amnesty now,' said Defeatist. 'Send you back to school! Some people have all the luck!' 'I can't bring myself to believe that Intellectual isn't here any more,' said Deviationist. 'It's unjust. Why? I can't explain. Sergeant, Murderer—that's just. That's war. But Intellectual—that's unjust.' 'Listen to what I've just written,' said Panicker:

> The chief he called us in at evening-tide,
> And in a fearsome voice his orders cried:
> I want a prisoner who can tell me all:
> So bring me one or don't come back at all.
>> Well, no use grumbling. War, they say, is war.
>> It's not his fault—a fact we can't ignore.
>> Since that's the order, better get it done,
>> Find him a captive ere the rise of sun.
> So out we crawl into the blackest night
> Cursing that prisoner with all our might.
> Where are you fucking bastards tucked away?
> We've got to find one by the break of day.
>> For every man comes time to meet his fate.

(355)

A mine explodes and massacres my mate.
And I survive, I seem to be all right.
I need a captive ere the morning light.
As I crawl up, a soldier goes to crap.
Oh, you're the one I need, my bonny chap.
I slap his naked arsehole with my hand.
And say 'You're coming to the promised land'.
   And so I got them both back, rather late,
   The prisoner and some pieces of my mate.
   The prisoner seemed a pleasant sort of chap,
   But information!—all he knew was crap.

'That's not bad at all,' said Gelding. 'If you left out "fucking bastards" you might even get it printed in the paper.' 'It'd be better the other way round,' said Deviationist. 'Print "fucking bastards" and leave the rest out.'

The strangeness of ordinary things

'I have got into a very strange situation since the interview,' said Dauber. 'From one point of view things have improved, but from another everything's come to a standstill. For one and the same order, I'm being chivvied by some people who've no reason to give a damn about it, while other people, who have the most interest in getting the job finished, are dragging their feet. I keep seeing old informers who I'd almost forgotten about, and all the latest crop, who were never out of my studio, seem to have disappeared altogether.' 'There's nothing special or strange about that,' said Neurasthenic. 'According to the rules of the system, everyone who has anything to do with you or your work should react. For the moment no-one knows how to react. They're merely showing that they're prepared to react when they're told how. They're trying to sniff out their instructions. There aren't any instructions yet, because even upstairs they've reached no decision. Everything's in a state of ferment which will produce something sooner or later. What exactly it'll be is hard to predict. It might turn out to be something that even they would never have expected. At all events, there are inevitable rules which will finally come into play. First everyone who can do you any harm in this situation without getting punished, or at least only lightly punished, will do so. Secondly, anyone who can do you any good in this situation without getting punished, or at least only lightly punished, will not do so. Thirdly, your interview is in principle something which merits punishment, and so the the greater the benefit it brings you in the short term, the greater the damage it will do you in the long term. The punishment will surely come. It will only be a question of time, form, and steps to be taken. There's always the possibility that they will punish you with kindness. For example, they may let you go abroad, or authorise one of your official commissions. They might even give you some kind of honorary title.' 'I've nothing against that,' said Dauber. 'I'm not a politician or an ideologue. I'm an artist.' 'Of course,' said Neurasthenic. 'It all depends what kind of artist.'

Women

Women! Huh! Just look around,
They're just trouble, I'll be bound.
If you've an urge you can't resist,
Quietly do it in your fist.
Guard your purity, says I,
And much harm will pass you by.
Your greatcoat won't get soiled and dirty,
And the M.P.s won't get so shirty.
Further, you'll not catch V.D.,
That's a bonus, you can see.
You won't give scope for idle chatter,
And save your boots—no trivial matter.
That's the way, believe you me,
To live long and happily.

(From The Ballad)

After they'd eaten, they began to talk about women. The meal had been meagre, and the conversation was theoretical rather than practical. 'If you were to tell me that the Venus de Milo was outside in the bushes and I could do what I liked with her,' said Panicker, 'I wouldn't move a muscle. But if you were to offer me a bit of bread I'd go out and bring back what's left of Sergeant and Intellectual.' 'Grub like that,' said Gelding. 'It's hardly worth the trouble of undoing your pants. Let alone doing them up again.' 'Speak for yourself,' said Pimp. 'I wouldn't mind a couple of goes right now, one after the other.' Everyone knew that this was no idle talk. When the battalion had been in the rear at D. (those were the good days), Pimp spent every night touring villages forty miles around and had himself a good two dozen women who happened to come to hand. And in the morning he'd be on parade as if nothing had happened. 'The only snag is,' he used to say, 'I'd never see their faces and I don't know their names. If I get killed, whose features will I see before my eyes, whose name will my dying lips whisper?' 'In our training school,' said Defeatist, 'there was a cadet called Dickie. He was tiny. Someone once joked that Dickie's dick was bigger than he was. The rumour spread through the garrison, and Dickie made a killing with the officers' wives. Although they soon scotched the rumour, he'd had time to accumulate a massive experience, and he became the terror of the garrison command. He'd bribe (and he made a lot of money out of his exploits) all the orderlies, sentinels and watchmen, and he slipped out of camp every night. He even managed to cut himself in for a share of what Colleague received from his harridan wife. In the morning he drew marks on the wall over his bed. Thick marks indicated the number of women he'd had, and thin marks, the number of times he'd had each of them. If you believe his accountancy, he was remarkably talented.' 'How did his career end?' asked Deviationist. 'The usual way,' said Defeatist 'Jealousy. Someone reported him and he was sent to a punishment battalion for sneaking out of camp.'

Secondary problems

'In your studio I have seen all manner of people and all manner of human passions,' said Visitor. 'There've been some very odd cases. For example, take the problem of Schizophrenic-Neurasthenic. The former is one of those creative people who can be described as doing whatever they want to and are capable of doing, whatever happens. Neurasthenic is an able and intelligent man; from a certain point of view he could be said to be more intelligent than Schizophrenic. But he is one of those people who never quite make up their minds to embark on a piece of work which is beyond them but which they believe themselves to be more capable of doing than people like Schizophrenic. Neurasthenic is an imitation and a reflection of Schizophrenic. If the former did not exist, then neither could

(358)

the latter. The former engenders the latter, but by their own existence condemn their creation to infertility. No-one has as great an interest in the destruction of Schizophrenic as Neurasthenic does. But if the former were destroyed, then the latter (his reflection), would disappear as well. The latter does not understand this. He claims he has an independent existence.' 'It's the problem of Salieri,' said Dauber. 'You know, the lesser man's envious hatred of his betters, Pushkin said it all.' 'No,' said Visitor. 'This is something different. It is perhaps the problem of self-destruction of creativity. A creative personality consists not of one individual, but of many, at least two (probably more often than not two) individuals. A creative individual is a group of individuals each with their own functions. Mozart and Salieri are two parts of one whole on one particular plane, Schizophrenic and Neurasthenic on another, Dauber and Chatterer on a third. From this point of view you are unthinkable without Chatterer. In one way Chatterer could be said to be the co-author of your works. And even I, if you've no objection. An outstanding creative personality is merely the official representative of a creative group.' 'From what you say,' said Dauber, 'it would appear that the director of an institute where some great scientific discovery is made is the author of that discovery.' 'Well, why not?' said Visitor. 'But there is a certain difference between that director and me,' said Dauber. 'There is indeed,' said Visitor. 'You are different types of representative of a similar group of creators.' 'What a nightmare!' said Dauber. 'Why a nightmare?' asked Visitor. 'Why then don't you regard the law of gravity as a nightmare?' 'Because it doesn't suit me to do so,' said Dauber. 'Well, there you are!' said Visitor. 'When people wanted to shrug off the law of gravity, they invented the aeroplane.'

The methods of decent people

Dauber had a phone call from the architect S., who had some time previously persuaded Dauber to do a bas-relief for the façade of a building which S. was working on. 'Hello, old man,' he said. 'I'm afraid I'm going to have to disappoint you. The bas-relief's been axed. What? No, it's nothing to do with you and your little difficulties. They didn't even know that it was you who were going to be doing the bas-relief. It was dropped from the plan, whoever was doing it. How are things, otherwise? I heard that you were having another exhibition Over There. . . .' 'What's all that about?' Dauber asked Chatterer. 'The most likely thing is that it's the beginning,' said Chatterer. 'Probably he provoked the banning of the bas-relief himself. Probably he was the first to agree to it. Probably he defended it without any great conviction. At all events, working with you would have damaged his professional position. If you come out of it all right he won't have lost very much, the more so since his conscience is clear. He wanted to bring you in but he wasn't allowed to. He keeps his reputation for being a decent man—and he's guiltless in the eyes of the management as well.' 'But he and I have been friends for twenty years,' said Dauber.

Instruction

For two hours they had formal instruction. They perfected the forms of addressing a superior and how to salute officers. Then they spent some time grumbling about the absurdity and inhuman character of these exercises. The Lieutenant said that they had a purely pedagogic function. 'Pedagogy is a very serious thing,' said Pimp. 'We had one lad at flying school who had very slow reflexes. The instructor—a great pedagogue— worked out a cunning idea. He started giving all his orders in advance. And the cadet began to fly solo, passed out and went to the front.' 'What became of him?' asked Deviationist. 'He dropped his bombs after the squadron had got back over their base,' said Pimp. 'That's nothing,' said a voice in the darkness. 'In preliminary training we had one lad who was afraid of landing without an instructor even though he could fly perfectly well. His instructor decided to be cunning as well and unscrew his joy-stick in midair and throw it over the side. The student got wind of it, so he took a spare and hid it in his cockpit. So they took off. The instructor unscrewed his joy-stick, showed it to his pupil, and threw it over the side. "Right", he said. "Now it's up to you to fly this aircraft on your own—and land it yourself." Then the cadet showed the instructor his spare joy-stick and threw it over the side too.' 'How did it all end?' asked Pimp. 'The instructor went mad,' said the voice, 'the trainee landed the plane, went to the front and won a stack of medals and then ten years inside.' 'What for?' asked

Deviationist. 'For telling little stories,' said Humorist. 'Nowa-days the word is the most serious act one can perpetrate. Words are punished more severely than acts.' 'Yes,' said Deviationist. 'In our world the word is followed by the final act.'

Unfounded hopes

When he tried to pronounce the word 'intercontinental', the Leader dislocated his jaw. This gave rise to rumours which began to circulate among the intellectual avant-garde. 'This'll probably do for him at last,' everyone said immediately, with a knowing smile, (well, it's high time he went!) and began to nurture unfounded hopes. The hopes turned out to rest on a very unsure foundation since the broken jaw was artificial and was replaced by a new one of better quality (it was rumoured that these jaws had been specially made for the cosmonauts), as a result of which no-one thought any longer about the removal of the Leader from power. It was too soon! 'It doesn't matter,' said Scientist. 'Soon the Leader will be making a speech about the problems of science. He's bound to mention the achievements of genetics. And since the boys are going to slip in the phrase "deoxyribonucleic acid", he'll have a heart attack for sure.' 'And then what?' asked Careerist. 'Do you think the next one will be any better?' 'He might even be worse,' said Neurasthenic. 'But all the same, we'll get a certain pleasure from it all.'

Social structure

'In your country,' said Journalist 'the Ism hasn't yet been fully realised, all the same. You've got state capitalism.' 'Fiddle-sticks!' said Neurasthenic. 'That's the rubbish produced by your Ists who've never come here to see for themselves. What we've got is state feudalism.' 'I disagree,' said Dauber. 'What we've got is more like state slavery.' 'You're wrong as well,' said Chatterer. 'You're all forgetting one decisive factor. Our country was invented on the basis of unrealisable premises. We are the fruits of a sickly schizophrenic imagination. So all the concepts you have used here are inapplicable. Slavery, feudal-ism, capitalism—these all fall within the framework of civilisa-tion. And we are an anti-civilisation. If we *had* fully realised ourselves, we would have had to pass through all the stages through which civilisation has passed, but with a minus sign in front of each.'

Semantic composition*

I have now come to what is without any doubt the most difficult point in this exposition of my understanding of E.N.'s art. And so I shall here go to rather greater length, and I shall refer to things which may bring a smile to the faces even of representatives of official aesthetics and official art history. But I see no other course open to me. The secrets of our existence do not lie in some hitherto unknown depths of the world, but simply in a different approach to certain well known phenomena on its surface. There are works of art in studying which it is appropriate to draw a distinction between what the author wants to say and the way in which he says it. Certain of these contain within themselves the raw material for the answer to the question 'What?' For example, many classic works of literature fall into this category. But among them there are also (true, in smaller number) works which within themselves do not contain any raw material for the answer to the question 'What?' Such, for example, are many ikons and frescoes in our churches. The works of E.N. are precisely of this latter kind. But if as far as ikons and church frescoes are concerned, the answer to the question 'What?' is supplied by a religious ideology dating back over the centuries, in the case of E.N.'s works things are very different. In order to answer the question 'What?' as it relates to the art of E.N., we must undertake some preliminary work. We have to develop a system of general statements about the modern world, and the place of man and his fate in this world, i.e. construct a certain ideological conception. This conception has already been born and exists, although in a rather amorphous form, only fragmentarily and in the context of spiritual life in general. E.N. has lived, and still does, in the field of this conception. In fact in his drawings, etchings and sculptures he works towards its incarnation, he works on the creation of cult objects of this conception. But the conception does not yet exist in the form of precise texts which are reasonably widely recognised. What Schizophrenic has done was a step in this direction.

But at the same time it was a step in the other direction, the direction opposed to ideology. And while there is no precisely defined conception, the products of creation remain at another level. They are no longer works of art in the normal meaning of the term, although people go on approaching them as such. They are something greater, and something different. Since E.N. has created a whole world of objects which can potentially become manifestations of the cult, that simplifies the task of those who will in the future develop this conception. Here we see mutual influences. But I shall leave the question of what form this ideological conception associated with E.N.'s art should take, and pass on to a more technical aspect of the matter. I have said that semantic units in E.N.'s work are linked by special rules of composition into semantic phrases and texts. The main thing here is that these rules of composition have a nature which is not immanent to art as such (i.e. they are not determined by the means of representation), but which is immanent to the ideological conception which is under consideration. Without this latter, they are an incomprehensible accumulation of incomprehensible shapes. Without these ideological connections, there are neither sentences nor texts in E.N.'s works. So we must first raise ourselves above the level of E.N.'s works to a certain supposed ideological conception, and then come down again; i.e. we should as it were bring to E.N.'s works a meaning which they contained in the first place, but which we now bring from outside, as something completely extraneous. Here, as we see, what is at work is a general principle of the functioning of the material incarnation of ideological phenomena. It is interesting that in E.N.'s work the semantic phrases are not necessarily made up of semantic units set out side by side (e.g. in one room, or on one sheet of paper), and that juxtaposed units may be units from different phrases—the basis and the concealed rhythm of his polyphony. One needs to have a good memory and considerable knowledge of a large number of E.N.'s works before they can be read as sentences and collections of sentences. Of course, they could be set in order, which would make it easier for non-initiates to study them. But to do this, one would have first to construct general rules for the ideological grammar of the language.

Of great things and small

'The Monument to the Fallen is going ahead very fast, unlike everything else,' said Dauber. 'Why should that be?' asked Neurasthenic. 'The opening ceremony's soon,' said Dauber. 'They won't make it in time without me.' 'That's clear enough,' said Neurasthenic. 'But then they'll remove your name from the list of artists and designers under some pretext or other.' 'That's perfectly possible,' said Dauber. 'They've already ordered a trivial alteration to part of my design and are trumpeting about it as if it were some radical revision. Anyway, I'm not that keen on being the designer of that thing.' 'It's not a question of what you want,' said Neurasthenic. 'It's a question of what they're going to do. There are situations where all human acts have one and the same meaning. Why? Because in this situation they all represent a preordained reaction.' 'Oh, the hell with them,' said Dauber. 'What unimportant trivia!' 'That's all very well,' said Neurasthenic. 'A thousand little successes never add up to one big one. But a thousand dirty little tricks always add up to one huge abomination.'

Extra rations

From somewhere or other Pimp and Gelding procured two loaves of anthracite—an incomparably hard variety of black bread. 'Where the hell did you find that?' asked the Lieutenant. 'Down there,' said Gelding with an airy wave of his arm. 'We swapped it for a watch.' 'Oh, if we had a dram or two to wash it down with,' sighed Panicker. 'This might do the trick,' said the Lieutenant, producing from his bag a pair of almost new chrome leather boots. 'Do you think you can raise anything with them?' 'Nothing easier,' said Defeatist, who grabbed the boots and returned to the dug-out half an hour later with a saucepan full of raw alcohol. 'In our dear and distant school,' said Deviationist in a voice full of nostalgia, 'one day when we'd had a few we worked out a whole theory of scrounging. But unfortunately, any genuinely scientific theory has a limited area of application. For example, just try to put into practice this fundamental principle: If the cook has a daughter, marry her. If not, marry the cook! As for our great national Ism, all it will procure is ten out of ten for political education. And a fat lot of good that is to us here! There was a time when I knew this theory by heart. It was very elegant! Electrodynamics is crude by comparison! And electrodynamics, I'd have you know, is one of the most beautiful theories in science. But compared with scroungiology, electrodynamics is no better than Pimp here compared to Don Juan. But now I can only remember odd fragments here and there. For instance, the basic assumption of scroungiology is this : nothing is impossible. Do you remember old Leadswinger? He was a real swine, but he knew his theory. You can't deny him that. Well, one day, by dint of applying this principle, he managed to fish out through an air vent barely wide enough to get his arm through, but which came out directly over the stove, a whole pot full of melted butter without spilling a drop. He swallowed the butter, and the saucepan as well, and got away undetected. A bit later on he coughed up the saucepan thoroughly cleaned out. On the other hand, Fellowworker, who was a complete novice at the theory, spent a whole month squatting by this hole trying to pinch a pencil off the stove through it. Of course, he didn't get anywhere. The methods for scrounging have to be worked out bearing concrete conditions in mind. It's really high class dialectics! When you set off on a scrounging expedition you have to evaluate the general situation, the time available, the special peculiarities of the kitchen staff and the orderlies of the day. For example, if your section is having a bit of a flap, don't waste your time thinking about it, just make a bee-line for the kitchens or for the serving hatch, take the first thing that comes to hand, (a loaf of bread, a pan of soup, a chunk of bacon or even a bar of soap) looking very busy all the while, and leave quietly. If you've got a lot of time to spare, you can, for example, go into the dining hall under the pretence of reading a book because it's so much quieter than the barrack huts, and then pick your moment to nick something. There's always the chance, besides, that the kitchen staff may give you something. Depending on what kind of people they are, you can either use the traditional psychological method or the parapsychological method, (it's very fashionable at the moment!) Here's an example of the traditional psychological procedure. You go to the hatch and you look at the cook with an innocent expression on your face. You get kicked out by the supervisor. You come back and start looking at her again. You get thrown out by the orderly officer. You come back and start again. Just look at her, without doing anything else. Sooner or later the cook'll get sick of it, and shove a bowl of porridge in your face out of desperation—Here, cop hold of that and get the hell out from under my feet! Para-psychology needs a very superior intellectual level. You go to the hatch and stare fixedly not at the cook but at the saucepan. The main thing is to concentrate all your attention on it and not let yourself be distracted. After ten or fifteen minutes the saucepan will begin to rise off the stove all by itself. And after half an hour it'll fall piping hot into your hands.' 'That's just a load of bullshit,' said Pimp. 'Anti-scientific, idealistic bullshit.' 'Oh yes?' laughed Deviationist. 'What if they're facts?' 'Did you see that with your own eyes?' asked Pimp. 'Not me, no,' laughed Deviationist, 'but people have seen it. And you have to believe eye-witnesses. Just remember what you dreamed when Sergeant and Intellectual got themselves blown up by that mine!' A sinister silence fell on the dug-out. 'How bloody gloomy!' said the Lieutenant. 'Let's get on to something more cheerful!'

When I was just a beardless youth,
To be a flyer I trained,

sang, or rather sobbed, Panicker.

My only girl friend, that's the truth,
Was my swift aeroplane,

the rest of the platoon joined in drunkenly. People from the neighbouring dug-outs gathered to listen to the 'flyers'. It became a little warmer.

The years have passed and disappeared,
Lost in the toils of war.
Where are you now, my handsome bird,
Who had no chance to soar?

A typical exception

'I entirely agree with those who say that we constitute a tiny part of the population,' said Chatterer. 'But does that mean that our problems do not exist for this society? For instance, Dauber is probably the only artist in our society of his stature and style. And it's true to say that the reaction he provokes reveals what our society is from one point of view. That explains why there are no such artists—or almost none—in our country. Or why they do not flourish. Our problems are not typical in the sense that they are neither common nor widespread. But they are more fundamental, since they are characteristic. They serve as indicators or as characteristic problems of our society.' 'It is not quite clear to me,' said Dauber, 'how they are characteristic.' Chatterer replied: 'Say there is a physical medium you want to study. You can approach the problem in a variety of ways, and in particular the following. You introduce into the medium an experimental body whose properties are already known. Then you observe the reactions of the medium. Finally you define the medium by this reaction. What is peculiar in our situation is that characteristic bodies of this kind grow up of their own accord in the given medium, and are not introduced from outside, they are indeed its legitimate product. Yet at the same time they suffer the effects of this their native medium as if they were elements alien to it. And since these bodies have a soul, since they dream, love, hate, suffer, create and so on, they have to face very specific problems. Society does all it can to get rid of these problems and to make it appear that these are not its problems. But alas they *are* its own problems to an infinitely greater extent than those problems which it claims as being organically characteristic of it.' 'Naturally,' said Dauber, 'society tries to conceal its shortcomings.' 'No,' said Chatterer. 'These aren't shortcomings. It's the other way round. Society is trying to conceal and liquidate its most healthy elements.'

Ambiguity*

Almost all the critics who have studied E.N.'s work have remarked on the ambiguity of his position. On the one hand he is never allowed to exhibit, he is denounced on every suitable and unsuitable occasion, his name is deleted from the lists of every artistic organisation, he is not allowed to go abroad, he has no titles of any kind. From this point of view he holds the lowest position in our artistic system. On the other hand he is commissioned to carry out work of a kind which in our country is only confided to a handful of sculptor-generals. Why? Can it be coincidence? The existence of a struggle between two opposing forces within the country? It seems to me that it is a great deal more serious than that. In theory E.N. should have been a recognised official sculptor. He could have produced works of genius to incarnate the ideology of our society in sculpture. Those people who commission him to produce grandiose bas-reliefs and monumental sculpture are aware of this. But our society has grown up in specific historical conditions and lives now in a specific international context. It has well defined historical traditions. Just take one example. The mania for columns which dominated our architecture before and just after the war. Where did that come from? From the past, clearly enough. Now we have passed through this stage. We have assimilated modernistic architectural forms. And we have to all intents and purposes abandoned the traditions of the nineteenth century realists. But for the time being these are isolated instances. On the whole our art is still dominated by representational traditions (particularly among artists themselves) and from this point of view E.N. appears as an enemy to official art. His colleagues cultivate this idea of him with great energy—hence the humiliation of his position. Thus we come to the further paradox—E.N. is an enemy of the present state of art as it exists here for the reason that he could have become a brilliant exponent of it.

Where is justice?
'One day,' said Humorist, 'they sent a chap to our regiment who came from the very top echelons. You see, he had to be given a decoration, and for that he had to take part in some fighting. They gave him to me as a gunner. It wasn't much of an operation. There was just a bit of flak and a couple of fighters who were on the prowl, And he threw up all over the aircraft. When we got back, I told him to clean up the mess. He looked at me and said "Do you know who you're talking to?" I took out my pistol. "If you don't clean it up " I said, "I'll shoot you." He cleaned it up.' 'What if he'd refused?' asked Panicker. 'I'd have shot him,' said Humorist. 'For a little thing like that,' said Gelding. 'Sometimes a little thing can be a symbol of something important,' said Humorist. 'How did it all end?' asked Deviationist. 'We both got what we deserved,' said Humorist.

Genuine art
'You're right,' said Neurasthenic. 'One does detect a certain ambiguity in our old writers. Why is that? They became writers

by virtue of the old criteria—in other words they were talented people. But according to the modern canon, they had already begun to tell lies. The writers of today have been relieved of this contradiction. They are selected as writers in the light of the tasks which they will have to perform. For this purpose mediocrity is amply sufficient. As the several tens of thousands of writers are also several tens of thousands of mediocrities, complete harmony reigns in the world of literature.' 'In other words, if I understand you rightly,' said Journalist, 'your literature is not art in the full sense of the word.' 'No,' said Neurasthenic. 'It is indeed art in the full sense of the word. Exactly like yours is. It is merely that in your country the level of the average writer is a little higher, and the type of person who becomes a writer is slightly different. Maybe as well some individual talents manage to survive. On the whole the difference is the same as in any mass-production industry. We prefer to read your writers for the same reason that we prefer to wear imported trousers or eat imported chickens.' 'Nothing unusual there,' said Journalist. 'So why all the fuss?' 'What fuss?' asked Neurasthenic. 'You ask, we answer. Speaking the truth doesn't yet amount to making a fuss. It's you yourselves who do all the fussing as you observe. We're just going on living.'

Man and scientific-technological progress
'In the end everything will be decided by the progress of science and technology,' said Scientist. 'Housing, day-to-day comforts, transport, clothing, even food—are they not all the products of modern science and technology? And in principle their possibilities are unlimited.' 'That may well be,' said Neurasthenic. 'But I don't seem to have seen any scientific technological meat in the shops yet.' 'We really are amazing people,' said Chatterer. 'We see a problem. We formulate it in such a way that we immediately pass on to another. And then we go on to discuss a third which has no connection with the other two. We began with the question, does the development of science and technology have an influence on the structure of society? We formulated this in such a way that another question appeared: does the development of science and technology have an influence on the subjective state of people? And what we're actually talking

about is how this development influences man's living conditions. And when you come down to it, what's the real problem here? It's a fact: some people take two hours to fly to Paris, and others fight each other to get on to buses and tube trains in the rush hour. So there is something in the structure of society which does not depend on scientific or technical progress. What does this 'something' consist of? The formula of human happiness is not made up of absolute quantities of well-being and misery, but of the relationships between them. A man, for instance, will not become happier if his situation is improved by ten per cent, while that of others is improved by fifty per cent. The level of happiness as a subjective state is directly proportional to the social value of the man, and inversely proportional to his own idea of his subjective value. The former has a tendency to fall, the latter tends to rise, independently of scientific and technical progress. And what is man? What qualities do you have in mind? Blood pressure? The kind of furniture he's got? Among other things man is honour, conscience, an aspiration to freedom of will and choice, freedom of movement, creative freedom and so on. And man, too, is a citizen. What part does the development of science and technology play in that? None at all. The man-citizen has still to be carved out of the man-beast. And quite other sources must be used. According to special rules and using special methods. And every time one has to start again from the beginning, and to fight. And this is another story. A man is not made into a citizen by science and technology, but by art, morality, religion, ideology, a long experience of resistance. Not just any art, any morality, any ideology. And not just any battle for one's "I". The problem here is to know precisely what art, what morality, what ideology and so on are capable of turning a man-beast into a man-citizen. It is also a matter of knowing who should be given the job to do it. Should it be Writer or Truth-teller? Dauber or Artist? Slanderer or Troglodyte? If we remove this concrete and personal aspect of the matter, we come to an official, empty plan: man must be educated. Dauber knows from his work as a sculptor how imperceptibly the true sometimes becomes the false. Not to mention the fact that the experience of resistance can give birth to an anti-citizen.'

A correct position in life
If you want to live in ease
Learn the art of catching fleas.

(From The Ballad)

'The worst thing in life is fleas,' said Pimp. 'When there are a lot of them. One flea is just a flea. A dozen fleas is bearable. But hundreds of fleas attacking you from every side is a nightmare. You can't see them. You don't know where, how or why they're biting you. There's no escape. It's better to take on a pride of lions barehanded. Or even wolves. Or even jackals, at a pinch. But it's senseless to try to defend yourself against hordes of fleas.' 'Fleas aren't the worst,' said Gelding. 'I served in the cavalry. There the fleas died of exhaustion. I must say that the cavalry isn't a school of life. It's an academy of life. The most important thing to lead a happy life is to learn how to live normally when you're arse forward and upside down. We'd barely managed to teach ourselves how to mount our companions-at-arms of pre-revolutionary antiquity, before they began to teach us. . . . Guess what? Trick riding! We get to the riding school. In the middle of the manege there's a sergeant with a whip. Volt to the left! Dismount with sabres drawn! Scissors jump! Well, in the end you get yourself turned round so you're facing the beast's tail, and then comes the big event of the season. Army horses don't only learn the words of command, they learn soldiers' jokes as well. As soon as your witty old Osoka, Akula or Lorelei notices out of the corner of her left eye that you've taken the risk of raising your legs, she gallops out of the manege at full belt and dashes over to the head-quarters block. The whole of the HQ staff rushes out to see, and from the colonel downwards they all nearly kill themselves laughing. Then its off to the HQ of the next regiment in the line, and the same scene's repeated all over again. Then it's the sick bay, then the veterinary quarters, then the club, then the adjutant's office. And all the time you're clinging on to the brute's mane and tail with all your strength. Right under your nose you can see those bloody great hooves pounding up and down. Just one blow could splinter the skull of a mammoth. And your poor little empty head would be crushed into bloody pulp. Everyone thinks it's very funny—except you. And when you've been carted round all your own divisional offices, it's off

(371)

on a twelve mile gallop to the HQ of the next division. And here your Penelope really shows what she can do! She does everything but stand on her tail! You've never seen the like of it in the circus! And when the divisional commander's pissed himself laughing, you gallop off back to your own squadron's manege and get back into line as if nothing had happened. Volt to the left! Dismount with sabres drawn! If ever I get out of this mess in one piece and survive to have any children, the first thing I'll teach them is how to live arse forward and upside down. Let my children be happy, at least.'

The flow*

E.N. is not the artist of a particular moment, nor even of a series of particular moments, but of a whole flood. This is very clear in his graphic work, and less so in his sculpture. In sculpture he is best known as the creator of monumental works, in the ordinary meaning of the term (even if his work is original), and on the official level he does a lot of work of this kind. But I am very familiar with all the work which does not leave his studio, and the vast amount of pieces which are still at the project stage. Over the many years of our friendship I have learnt to get a visual idea of these projects as they would look when they were completed. There too, the dominant trend is towards the flow form, which he discovered and brought to perfection in his graphic work. If these projects are ever come to be completed on the gigantic scale which is intended for them, mankind will be blessed with one of the most overwhelming masterpieces in the entire history of art. I in no way exaggerate, for even on a small scale and in disjointed fragments the sculptural flow which E.N. has created is a unique phenomenon in the plastic arts. E.N. did not come immediately to the flow form. Here is a rough sketch of its evolution. E.N. is a sculptor. One can see in his early work a tendency towards problems of transformation. He does some drawings—but only for the purposes of sculpture. At the time I called them sculptural graphics. The drawings are beautiful of themselves. They acquired their own value in the eyes of his admirers. This exerted a certain influence on E.N. In addition to this there was the impossibility of realising certain of his ideas in a sculptural form compared with the ease of realising them on paper. As a result E.N.-graphics began.

(372)

During his graphic period, which is still going on, E.N. has kept on working as a sculptor. But his aesthetic evolution has taken place mainly in his graphic work. Here two lines have led directly to the flow form: virtuoso etchings of complex composition, and series of large numbers of etchings all deriving from a single moment of emotion. His illustrations of Dante and Dostoevsky were a watershed. They were not yet a flow, but they contained something which prevents them being considered simply a series. During this time E.N. makes hundreds of etchings on different subjects, or, more precisely, without any specific content in the usual meaning of the term. Or their content is abstract: birth, reversal, destruction, ripening, and so on. During this graphic period, E.N. acquired vast experience of the treatment of abstract themes, and in the material he produced his work is clearly organising itself into spontaneous cycles, connected by many kinds of links. A kind of distinct and definite order was established for separate collections of prints. More than once I drew E.N.'s attention to the fact that many of his prints could be brought together into orderly and internally connected cycles. I think that other people probably noticed this as well. I think that E.N. noticed it himself. The important thing is that the phenomenon I am describing came about informally at first. Then it was understood as a fact and served to determine future prospects. Finally it was brought to fruition in cycles of drawings conceived in advance and physically united in a single whole. I refer to E.N.'s unprecedented albums. Thus a new form of graphic art was born, that form to which I have given the conventional name 'flow'. Later, the flow form, found through graphic work, exercised an influence on sculpture in its turn. But what is 'flow'? It is a synthetic form. To describe it would need extensive research and historical comparisons. I will limit myself to a few comments on the subject. Flow must be distinguished from the individual composition of the print as an ordered whole. The state and the flow of states must, if seems to me, be distinguished from the static and the dynamic. A state can be dynamic, a flow may be static. The flow forms of E.N.'s works contain both the static and the dynamic. Figures which are in the highest degree static can often be discerned within them. Then one gets the impression here that the artist has made enormous efforts to halt an irresistible movement. I believe that E.N.'s works would not appear anything like so dynamic (and every reviewer remarks on his dynamism, which commands attention because of its effect) if they did not include a very clear, if less obvious, static element. For me, the distinction between the steady state and the flow is not so much a distinction between the static and the dynamic, but something on quite a different plane. Further, the flow, as an ordered, uninterrupted succession of a rather large number of drawings, etchings and sculptures must be distinguished from the series: in a series, each element has an independent meaning, if, of course, the concept of meaning is applicable; in the flow, however, each element presupposes some other element and extends its significance, while at the same time retaining its significance as an independently meaningful phrase. Even outside the scope of the albums, where this is quite plain and assumed in advance, E.N.'s etchings frequently move the spectator to seek out others from which they derive or towards which they are progressing. Not all the etchings fit into this role. Sometimes, assortments of etchings are arranged in complete cycles, which have a beginning and an end and an internal coherence which responds to the feelings of the spectator. Finally, to the extent that it is semantic unity and homogeneity which form the basis of a flow of drawings, etchings and sculptures, the flow of a work of art may be considered and experienced in the same way as a ballet or a symphony. Of course, E.N.'s works give aesthetic pleasure both as elements of a series, and as self-sufficient units independent of others. But this pleasure is of quite a different order if one can learn to consider the works as a flow in the sense in which I have tried, very roughly, to define it.

Social orientation

'All that is just passing trivia,' said Journalist. 'One triviality just gives place to another,' said Visitor. 'But the system of trivia remains. Let's go in here and I'll show you something. See this queue? Three people. Just watch, they just stand there and wait. Do you see how many people there are behind the counter?' 'Yes,' said Journalist, 'but don't they sell anything?' 'It's impossible to answer your question,' said Visitor. 'There are no reasons. Indeed, to talk of reasons in this case is meaningless. Look, the queue has grown to twelve people. They're beginning to get annoyed. Look, those people there are going to try to jump the queue. Do you think they're in a desperate hurry? Not a bit. That lad over there has just got served out of turn and now he's hanging about with nothing to do. In a moment someone in the queue will say something to the ones who've gone out of turn. There you are, see? And there's bound to be someone in the queue who'll come to the defence of the queue-jumpers and accuse the other of talking out of turn. What will he get out of it? Nothing. So why does he do it? No reason. Now someone's beginning to sound off at the sales staff. Someone else is starting to tell him off. Now just consider the people in the queue. They're just ordinary people. If you see them in the street it'd never cross your mind that they could become an element in a social problem that I've just demonstrated to you. So how much time has been wasted? How much annoyance and bad blood has been generated? You may think that's all trivia, but for us it's a way of life. I could take you on a tour of all the vitally important points where people come up against other people, and show you that our life is crammed full of these trivia. We come up against them every single minute. In large things and in small. At work and at home. Everywhere. We can't get away from them. I've heard you say that every Ibanskian you've ever met is a neurasthenic. I don't want to use medical terms, but there's some truth in what you say. Human nerves can stand quite a heavy load, but on one condition—that the load must be rational, i.e. that we must know its reasons and its aims. But here everything is irrational. You asked why people behave in this way, to what purpose. There are no reasons, no aims. There is no evil intent. In this system you will not find the usual bases of human behaviour—"why?", "for what reason?". In other words, what is lacking here are the criteria of social orientation. In scientific terms, here the individual cannot determine his position in social space, for he has no system of reference. Hence we find all these peculiarities in the behaviour of everyone in every situation where he is in any way dependent on another person. But this behaviour is regarded as perfectly normal. Everyone considers his own behaviour as normal, because he is responding to circumstances, but that the behaviour of other people is abnormal,

(375)

because it is irrational and in defiance of common sense. Hence we get the customary formulae—"People have gone out of their minds!", "Everyone's gone mad!", "What's got into everyone?" Have you ever heard anyone shout "I've gone out of my mind!" "I've gone mad!" "What's got into me?" So what's the solution? To climb as high as possible into the ranks of the leadership. That's what many people do. But not everyone can manage it. And anyway, if they choose that course many people fall into a quagmire of another kind, similar from many points of view to the one they're trying to get out of. You can try to re-educate yourself, to deliberately impose limits on yourself. But many people aren't capable of that. Or perhaps the solution lies in social reforms. I am no liberal. I don't even count myself among the progressive forces. So I can allow myself to say things which others would be ashamed to say. Who will carry out these reforms, what kind of reforms, and how? People like Claimant? Heaven preserve us! They haven't even taken power yet, and they're twisting your arm already! Or could it be along Truth-teller's programme? From a practical point of view that's absurd and unachievable. I've studied this problem for many years. Our progress is wholly in the hands of our top leadership. And even if our leaders wanted to, they cannot anticipate by much what actually lies within their means.' 'What about your own personal programme?' asked Journalist. 'That only concerns myself,' said Visitor. 'I don't hide it, and I'm quite willing to hand on my experience to anyone who wants it. But this is really only for strange loners like me. The principle is to create within one's inner self a system of reference according to which all the surrounding irrational reality is a normally organised society where one feels completely at ease.' 'In other words,' said Journalist, 'you've got to adapt.' 'You could put it that way,' said Visitor. 'But in the end, what is the important thing for people? The sum of happiness.' 'But surely that's what your official ideology is constantly preoccupied with,' said Journalist. 'It appeals to science, to the law, to truth, to cause and effect, to plans, and so on,' said Visitor. 'That is why it places itself, without needing to, on a level of lies and hypocrisy, although it is senseless to accuse it of mendacity or hypocrisy. So try to work out what it contributes to the sum of human happiness!'

The decision

'There is a Decision,' said the Important Commander to Commander Lessimportant. 'It poses you a difficult, but rewarding, task. For the Festival, you are to take Point N.' 'It shall be done,' said Commander Lessimportant. And he sent for Commander Evenlessimportant. 'For the Festival,' he said, 'you will take Point N.,' 'Point N?' said Commander Evenlessimportant in surprise. 'There doesn't seem to be any point in that, and there don't seem to be any forces to do it with.' 'It's a Decision,' said Commander Lessimportant. 'The people have got to have something to be festive about on the Festival. Take N., or else. . . .' 'I'll take it,' said Commander Evenlessimportant. 'But there aren't many troops.' 'I'll let you have the punishment battalion,' said Commander Lessimportant. 'Thank you for your confidence,' said Commander Evenlessimportant. I shall take N. at exactly twenty zero zero hours.' And he set off to take N. 'I order you to take N. at twenty zero zero hours,' he said to the Subaltern. 'Very good, sir,' said the Subaltern. 'But we haven't got many troops.' 'You'll have a punishment battalion,' said Commander Evenlessimportant. 'We'll take it,' said the Subaltern. 'But forty miles through that mud—they'll be fagged out. They won't be easy to whip into the attack. And then the only weapons they've got are rifles.' 'Get a provost squad in the rear,' said the Commander '—and arm *them* with machine-guns. The main thing is not to forget that they're people as well. In our society it's man who's in the number one spot. The thing is to know how to handle people.' 'Very well,' said the Subaltern. And he set off for the punishment battalion, to try out his approach to people, who are the most precious asset in our society. The men of the punishment battalion were semi-conscious after their forty mile forced march, wading up to their knees in mud, so tired that they'd even forgotten about the breakfast, lunch and dinner that they'd missed. 'Look,' said Deviationist. 'See? It's the end.' Three hundred yards behind the punishment battalion they could see well fed, warmly clad lads falling in, armed with machine-guns. 'Yes, I see,' said Panicker. 'Ah, well. Never mind. I've always come through so far. I'm a survivor.'

Power

'Just dig below the surface of any of our bosses,' said Neurasthenic, 'and you'll discover lurking behind his titles a mediocre engineer, a second-rate researcher, a poor student, a rote-learning schoolboy, a layabout, a sneak, a coward, a deceiver, and so on. Get them all together and give them a simple fourth form dictation exercise. They'll make at least two mistakes in every sentence. To say nothing of what they'd make of the problem of the swimming pool with an inlet pipe and an outlet pipe.' 'But things still get done,' said Journalist. 'They can't all be like that.' 'They are all like that,' said Neurasthenic. 'Things get done because they exploit to their own benefit the intelligence, the patience and the courage of others. The vital fluids of society flow through veins and arteries which do not depend on them. All they do is to suck them out.' 'Then you should change your methods of selecting people to go into the power system,' said Journalist. 'That's not possible,' said Neurasthenic. 'Society is made up of millions of points where men are pushed towards power and prepared for it. You can't keep an eye on all of them. And anyway, who would? The people who do monitor them in practice (tens of millions of people who form part of the system of power) do precisely what is needed—which leads to the result we started with.' 'But surely this situation can't go on for ever,' said Journalist. 'Our history has a traditional solution to this problem,' said Neurasthenic. 'Supreme power gradually builds up around itself an "enlightened" layer. This is made up basically of their own children, children-in-law and so on. This layer begins to exercise a certain influence on the supreme power, which in turn begins to put a return pressure on the layer. The final result is a movement of one millimetre in a hundred years. Come back again in a hundred years, and see for yourself.'

Heads I win, Tails you lose

'The only person who wins is the man who is able to arrange games where he can't lose,' said Neurasthenic. 'Take your gravestone, for instance. If it's put up, fine. If it's not, that's fine, too. I don't even know which would be better. Or take the business of T. If he's allowed to go to the congress, that's excellent. He knows the language and he's a good orator. And he's got something to say. It'll have quite an effect. But if he isn't allowed to go—that's good, too. There'll be a lot of fuss about it. And it's hard to say which will produce the greater effect—his presence or his absence.' 'You're right,' said Chatterer. 'But to get this result you need to conduct the game in such a way that your opponent aims his blows at a point where you no longer are—i.e. at your past. And for that you need an enormous reserve of past-ness. So that even death can work to your advantage.' 'So we've got work to do,' said Dauber. 'Work! Look at this idea I've had. . . .'

What type are our problems?

'Here we are walking along a street,' said Journalist. 'Of course the houses aren't very beautiful. But they're quite decent. Your leaders really have some concern for the living standards of the workers.' 'And you attribute this,' said Chatterer, 'to their remarkable spiritual qualities and their paternal concern for their children, the people. You think that all this is a gift from nice kind people who could have chosen not to do it? Think what would happen if they tried to stop building! Apart from anything else, the construction industry is a sphere of social life which keeps millions of people in work. Just analyse the whole system—the work of the planners and administrators, of the construction firms. The process of building and letting.' 'Yes, I know,' said Journalist. 'But that's not what I was talking about. Look, this street isn't at all bad. Plenty of plants and trees. First-class buses.' 'Yes,' said Chatterer. 'But look, over there this beautiful street has been dug up. They're always making holes somewhere. Look, they're cutting down the trees—and it would have been perfectly possible not to—would it have been so difficult to make a three-yard detour?' 'I'm not talking about that either,' said Journalist. 'I know all that. But look at this office block. It's a fine building. The people going in are well dressed. They look healthy and civilised. They get a guaranteed salary. Holidays with pay. Bonuses. There are kindergartens for their children.' 'Yes,' said Chatterer. 'And is that a result of the touching solicitude of the leadership? You've seen these offices. But here are others—and some more over there. Just count up how many there are in this building, in this street, in this town. Look at them more closely, go in and see what the people in them are doing. What their relationships are like. What dramas blow up over who gets the bonuses. How long they have to wait for a kindergarten place, or a salary rise.' 'I understand all that,' said Journalist. 'But where do your problems stem from? I can't make it out.' 'You can't because you don't want to. You're looking in from the outside, and so you're expressing our official point of view. I keep on trying to draw your attention to the sources of our problems, and you simply refuse to look at them. Let's say that everything you've said is true. Let us even accept your use of the word "solicitude", even though "solicitude" here makes no sense. It simply boils down to presenting the natural course of things as being due to the merit of certain people and organisations. But take a closer look and you'll uncover the laws which give rise to these very problems. The action of these laws, and the examples from which to illustrate them, stretching way back, are summed up in events which you might never have suspected of underlying these laws. Indeed, the action of these laws may seem purely haphazard events. Take Dauber's case, for example. Or that of T. Surely they are unusual cases?—exceptional, if we take the proportion of such people to the overall total of people in their profession. The social laws apply to everyone. And the result of this (to take Dauber's case) is that almost all artists are turning into artists of Artist's type, and if anyone manages to become an artist of Dauber's kind, he'll be dealt with in one way or another. Or take this road which has been dug up immediately after it's been asphalted. The next road hasn't been dug up, nor that one there. Is that by chance? An oversight? Look at this new building where the lift has been repaired ten times already at a cost greater than that of a new lift. Is that a triviality, mere chance? And here, in this office over here, a dullard has been appointed to a senior post and a capable man has been passed over. Trivial, you say? Doesn't it always happen like this? Such things happen in your country? Well, so what? If this sort of thing happens elsewhere, does that make things any easier for us? Have we ever claimed that our problems are not your problems? The heart of the matter isn't altered by the fact that we share some of the same problems. The main thing is that by their very nature these problems need a different kind of approach from the one which is constantly imposed on us. I am prepared to admit that they'll build a huge number of houses, give everyone their own apartment, grow trees in every street, shorten the working hours and increase the pay, and what have you. But despite all that, the basic facts from which our problems derive will remain the same. The social laws will still make themselves felt on our style and standard of living, in crises and catastrophes, because they lack the limiting factors which civilisation has invented and which are the very essence of civilisation—law, morality, public opinion and so on. The great majority of people may find these crises unexpected and incomprehensible, although they will be predictable and explicable to thinking people. The kind of thing that might happen could be a stupefying torpor overtaking our young people, with all the consequences that would entail, a total decline in some areas of science, the collapse of some part of the economy. Just now experiments are going on aimed at prolonging life to the age of a hundred or even two hundred years. Just imagine what would happen if the elixir were discovered! Who would be allowed to live two hundred years? Who would carry out the treatment? How could it be set out in ideological, moral or legal terms? You can imagine what lengths people would go to to win the prize of two hundred years of life. People are condemned to a constant struggle. The idea of a world-wide kiss and be friends is a myth. Or it's a form of oppression.' 'Well, what do you suggest?' asked Journalist. 'Nothing,' said Chatterer, 'apart from some kind of reflexion.' 'You really are strange people,' said Journalist. 'There's nothing strange about us at all,' said Chatterer. 'We are you, with only a very slight difference. We start off by going to the same school as you, but then we part company and go and live in different villages.'

Help to the strong
'The weak have learnt to look after themselves,' said Visitor. 'The strong have turned out to be defenceless.' 'The strong need help,' said Dauber. 'That's something history hasn't seen before. Help the poor little strong man! What does that sound like?' 'Very touching,' said Chatterer, 'but there's no future in it. If the strong need help, there's no helping them.'

The bosses are wiser than the subordinates

'You keep on going on about these laws,' said Neurasthenic angrily. 'Any fool could discover laws like that. Everyone knows them. The main thing is to explain exactly why things happen the way they do and not in some other way.' 'These laws aren't all that well known,' said Chatterer. 'After you'd read Schizophrenic's thesis you began to feel as if you'd known them for a long time. But you should have tried to discover them before. Maybe the explanations you are after are just as trivial. But you try to discover them for yourself!' Neurasthenic took umbrage and went off to do something else. 'We have grown so used to treating other people's work disdainfully,' said Chatterer, 'to appropriating their thoughts and putting too much value on our own ideas, that we don't even notice what a monstrous habit it is. We only see it in other people, and then only when we suffer from it ourselves.' 'Well, what is your point of view?' asked Dauber. 'It'll come as a disappointment to you,' said Chatterer. 'There is no need to explain the laws, since they are invented only for this particular purpose, and they include no generating mechanism, since they themselves constitute the ultimate mechanisms. Let us take as an example the law which states that the bosses are wiser than their subordinates. Neurasthenic demands an explanation as to why this is so, since he had a thirst for complex formulae and deep mechanisms. The bosses, too, would like an explanation, since they are convinced that the boss class includes the wisest individuals. Yet the question "Why?" has no sense here. The fact is that the very position of the subordinates makes it disadvantageous for them to be wiser than their bosses, since this would weaken their social position and might even lead to conflicts in which the wise subordinates would always come off worst. Hence the subordinates always try wittingly to be more stupid than their bosses—and succeed voluntarily in becoming so. A process of mental self-abasement goes on, as a result of which the intellectual level of the bosses becomes on the average higher than that of the subordinates. And that is the very law which Schizophrenic crystallised in the form of an aphorism: the bosses are wiser than the subordinates. If you are a boss and I am a subordinate, it follows that you are wiser than I.' 'I agree with that, too,' said Dauber. 'In fact I've always thought so myself.'

Without soul

'Take any ordinary day-to-day situation which involves a lot of people,' said Chatterer. 'If you can find the slightest element in it which you can describe with a straight face as a spiritual drama, I'll stand you a bottle of cognac. These days people get by without ever using the mechanism we call spiritual life. First, it is too delicate and fragile a construction for us. It snaps on the first contact with others. And then we have too little time for this spiritual mechanism to operate. It demands a certain distance between people, and an unhurried life style. And secondly, there is no place where it could work. Spiritual life in the proper sense of the word presupposes quite a high degree of independence from society, and a highly developed sense of moral responsibility in the individual. It grows up like a special mechanism linking the individual to society under these conditions. It is not needed if there is nothing for it to bind together. Psychologism is a type of social relationship, and not an innate human characteristic. Intellectualism is the banner of our age. We often say that our life seems to offer marvellous subjects for psychological literature. You don't even need to rack your brains to think of them. Just write everything down as it really is, and you'll produce works of genius. But just you try! In our conditions art which claims to be psychologism is false by virtue of that very claim, since psychologism is totally alien from our life. What about facts? Try to describe them, and you will see how sinister and impoverished they are. Your art is anti-psychological and anti-factual. And that is why it is true. It is intellectual and ideological. But that is quite a different matter.'

The genius of instinct

'The government has various ways of attracting the creative intelligentsia on to its side,' said Chatterer. 'But in conditions where the creative intelligentsia is numbered in tens of thousands, and where truly creative people are counted on the fingers of one hand, the most effective method it has is to eliminate the most outstanding and original. If our writers were asked to vote for either a lowering of their fees or the banishment of Truth-teller, most of them would prefer the latter.' 'In other words, the government's actions against Truth-teller are reasonable,' said Dauber. 'No,' said Chatterer. 'The

(383)

government merely thought about how they could get rid of Truth-teller, and not about the fact that they needed to get rid of him. This latter is a fact of a social kind, and not a product of reflection.

The weather
. . . An interminable autumn merging into an interminable winter . . .

The real and the unreal
'When I was young I used to go to see a girl who worked on a pig-farm,' said Visitor. 'Twenty miles through the mud. And in the intervals between my rare visits, she filled my place with a malingerer who passed himself off as a wounded war veteran. I kept on going to see her and I prayed to fate to send me a true love and a true springtime. But now, as I approach the end of my life, I see that this trollop with her pigs and the mud were my true love and my true spring. I had a comrade once. We slept together under the same greatcoat, shared every crust of bread. And he reported all our conversations to the proper quarters. I knew it and I prayed to fate to send me a real comrade. My life has gone by. And it turns out that my comrade who denounced me was my truest friend. Then I decided to leave the army. I broke off a successful career. There was endless trouble after that. My family were fed to the teeth with me. In the end my wife couldn't bear it any longer and took our child and left me. Now I only prayed to fate for one thing: I'll endure all the difficulties you can send, but give me the chance to accomplish just one real worthwhile thing in my life. My life is almost over. There's no sense in expecting anything now. Add it all up: it seems as though that idiotic step I took was the only real action of my life. So what is real, what is unreal?' 'The real is only an abstraction from what actually happens,' said Chatterer. 'It realises itself as unreality, and is unreal itself. When it is over, it is cleansed in the memory of flesh and blood, and elicits a certain feeling of tenderness. Only the past has any real value. Only the expectation of the past creates an illusion of the beautiful.' 'You're right,' said Visitor. 'The annoying thing, though, is to live alone. It's not the fact that life is difficult that makes you feel afraid, but the fact that no-one

wants to know how you're getting on, because in principle
everyone knows what your life is like. Our life has no secrets
and provokes no curiosity in anyone. Once, when I was a boy, I
skied down a hill that no-one had ever dared ski down before. I
was very upset because no-one had seen me do it. I was on my
own. Afterwards I did it several times before witnesses, but the
effect was the same as if I had been alone. I achieved nothing
from it. Later in life I sort of got used to that, but it's a pity all
the same. Not for me. I'm sorry for the witnesses—it's even
worse for them.'

We are all colleagues
'Tell me frankly,' asked Neurasthenic. 'is Sociologist one of
your people?' 'Yes,' said Colleague. 'And Thinker?' asked
Neurasthenic. 'Ours as well,' said Colleague. 'And Wife?'
asked Neurasthenic. 'Ours,' said Colleague. 'What a nightmare,' said Neurasthenic. 'Why a nightmare?' said Colleague.
'All our colleagues are our people.' 'But I for one, am not,'
said Neurasthenic. 'You are—potentially,' said Colleague.
'We've got our eye on you.' 'Of course, that's not to say I've
any objection in principle,' said Neurasthenic. 'If I'm paid
well, of course. I could do you reports every bit as good as
Sociologist's. And incidentally Sociologist is a hack, a dilet-
tante and a liar.' 'Yes,' said Colleague, 'recently he's begun
to lie a lot, and turn in hack work. And his prestige abroad has
slumped, too. We'll have to replace him soon. We'll talk about
it later.' 'And what about Truth-teller?' asked Neurasthenic.
'Truth-teller was a potential colleague of ours as well,' said
Colleague. 'If Hog hadn't gone mad. Truth-teller would
be in charge of the writers by now.' 'Hog!' said Neurasthenic in
surprise. 'But it was Hog who let Truth-teller speak out.' 'Yes,'
said Colleague. 'But he got frightened and ordered him to
be suppressed.' 'It is a nightmare, all the same,' said
Neurasthenic. 'I'm surprised to hear that from you,' said
Colleague. 'You can't be a member of our society without
being conscious of its influence on you. The first thing that
happens when a person is born here is that he becomes our
colleague. Then he learns to walk, talk, write. And once he's
learnt all that, he begins to write denunciations. The fact of

(385)

the matter is that our colleagues are divided into two groups—actual and potential. The actual colleagues are sub-divided into a further three groups—regular, sporadic, and the shamed-faced. The regular colleagues are either on the staff or systematically carry out our instructions. The sporadic ones only carry out our instructions once in a while—sometimes even only on a single occasion. The shamed-faced either do not suspect that they are collaborating with us (but in practice that doesn't really happen—I personally don't know of a single such case) or pretend not to suspect. There are very many of that kind—an incredible number. We're flooded by them. Potential colleagues are the rest of the population. They remain "potentials" either because they do not find it acceptable, for one reason or another, to collaborate with us, or because we have no opportunity to use them, or because their time has not yet come.' 'But what about the opposition, then?' asked Neurasthenic. 'We make the opposition ourselves,' said Colleague. 'Either by mistake or because we need them. If you scrape off the surface of our most determined opponents, you will find a Sociologist, a Thinker, a Wife or a Claimant manqués. Opponents are nothing, not worth serious attention.' 'What does merit attention?' asked Neurasthenic. 'Those who stand outside or above,' said Colleague. 'Independent people. Those are the alien bodies in our society. There are very few of them. But they are dangerous because they are in control of themselves. One such independent person could cause us infinitely more trouble than an opposition party a million strong. Personally, I'd allow such parties to exist. In our society they'd degenerate into a farce any way. Without any effort on our part. Just for internal reasons. And in general I'm opposed to compulsion. You can get the same results without violence. And even better. You just need to have patience and know how to wait. When you use force against people they get the impression that they're able to do a lot. If you give them freedom it rapidly becomes clear to them that they aren't capable of anything. The ability to do anything is a mutation.' 'That sounds very scientific,' said Neurasthenic. 'Where did you get these ideas from?' 'I've read Schizophrenic and Slanderer in my time,' said Colleague.

Perspectives

'Say that I were expelled or died,' said Dauber, 'what would my future here be?' 'People would soon forget you,' said Chatterer. 'After a few months life would be going on as if you had never existed.' 'Surely, I must be of some use here,' said Dauber. 'You are indeed,' said Chatterer. 'But in our society everyone has to prove his usefulness and impose it on others. In our society Competition doesn't count for anything. Competition is a struggle between the strong. It makes you remember. But here it's a struggle of the weak against the strong. And in this struggle, the weapon of the weak is the forgetfulness of the strong. The strong man must fight for his necessity to society, even when he is unique. In the latter case in particular. The more exceptional the person is whom society needs, the more ferocious the battle he has to wage with society to confirm this need. Moreover, the strong are very eager to sink their former culture in oblivion. The more refined and delicate that culture is, the greater the conscious effort needed to keep it alive. If a man is to be remembered, we need constant reminders of him. Historical memory is also the fruit of labour. If you threw Shakespeare out of the school textbooks and closed down the institutions which keep his memory alive, he'd be forgotten in a couple of generations. Anyway, you're needed here not in a personal capacity, but because you fill a vague need. Someone else could take your place, or it could remain empty. Needs are not necessarily met. And needs of this particular kind are only recognised as needs when there is something available to satisfy them, or even when circumstances make such satisfaction obligatory.'

The pseudo-lie

'We live surrounded by falsehood,' said Neurasthenic. 'Of course it goes without saying that the newspapers, the radio, magazines, cinemas and so on lie. That's laid down as part of their function. They're doing their job. What I'm talking about is our ordinary life. For example, today I was talking to our head of section. He was trying to get me to take on a thoroughly lousy research subject, and he lied about its great theoretical and practical importance. In return I lied to him, accepting the importance of the subject and arguing that it ought to be given to R. who is much more experienced and educated than I am. In fact R. is a drivelling idiot. I managed to get myself another subject, no less revolting, but which sounded more European. Then we discussed a book by that other cretin S. Everyone's praised it, even though everyone knows that it's sheer rubbish. I praised it as well.' 'That's not lying,' said Chatterer. 'That is a form of pseudo-mendacity which is completely natural to our society. And maybe to others. That is a deceptive falsehood. Imagine this kind of situation. A certain N delivers a lecture to a group X with the aim of persuading them of something or other. N himself considers his speech to be mendacious. Clearly he has his own criteria in reaching this view. Then let B, for instance, say that N's speech is a lie. Are you certain that his criteria are the same as N's? So it is possible that B. has different criteria from those used by N. He also believes that N is lying. But for him this has a different meaning. It is clear that N will defend himself by producing arguments. But what arguments? Those giving an appearance of truth in accordance with certain criteria which are officially recognised within the group X. If he succeeds in this, he is not lying from the point of view of group X's criteria. Where then is the truth, and where the lie? Your personal criteria are your personal business. You can regard yourself as a liar. You can regard everyone else as liars. But the only criteria to have any validity are the official criteria—the ones embodied in plans, decisions, reports, reactions. Here there can be errors, but not lies. It is merely that our official criteria, from whose standpoint people's words and deeds are judged, are such that from the standpoint of our own subjective criteria our behaviour looks deceitful.' 'All that is so,' said Neurasthenic. 'But it was I myself who convinced the director of our section of the importance of his research subject. I invented it myself, even though I knew that it was nonsense. Now it'll be included in the plan. And it will be officially considered to be important. In other words I have assisted in the introduction of what I consider to be a false criterion.' 'That's true,' said Chatterer. 'But when you invented the subject and sold it to your director, you were arguing in the light of the official situation—i.e. in the light of the official criteria. Your subject was only accepted because it fitted in with them. So it wasn't you who invented them.' 'But I took part,' said

Neurasthenic. 'At the very least I took a hand in upholding them.' 'Yes,' said Chatterer. 'But your action cannot be assessed in terms of truth or falsehood. It belongs to a different picture.' 'To tell what is true, Needs a bottle or two,' said Scientist. 'You'll have heard, of course, that at Institute Z. they've invented artificial caviar. That was all a confidence trick from the start. They needed money for experiments which for the moment didn't have any practical application. Five years of grants handed out for caviar research frittered away on some compounds that no-one wanted! (It turned out in the end that some of the compounds they produced were more important than their ludicrous caviar). The time came round to account for their spending. Somewhere or other they got hold of a bucketful of real caviar, set it out in little dishes, and invited a panel of experts to tell the real stuff from the artificial. Of course, they couldn't. And so to the delight of the institute they got another enormous grant to pursue their research to the stage of mass production. And on that money the institute produced its famous discovery. They forgot about caviar. Of course, it should be said that they did manage to produce artificial caviar—very similar to natural, and at a very similar price. The only trouble is that it turned out to be wholly indigestible. But in itself that's an advantage over the natural kind. You eat it, you defecate it, wash it out, sprinkle it with eau de cologne and back to the table with it.' 'To serve to foreigners,' said Neurasthenic.

Without a past

'In my youth even I tried to write something,' said Slanderer. 'Of course, I threw it all out. It wasn't worth keeping. The only thing that's left is this scrap of paper. Listen:

> Let Bugler sound reveille once again,
> Let Sergeant swear and kick us from our cots.
> Let's get fell in and sing a loyal refrain,
> And let the foe blast off his shells and shots.
> As kids we left our mothers' love and care,
> And ate the army's shit they called our food.
> Those endless night-time talks when we laid bare
> Our inmost secrets to the informers' brood.
> Our virgin love we gave to whores and tarts.

It's not all this that's caused our broken hearts.
What's so much worse is that it's still the same,
As if we'd never lived nor made our vow:
"Just wait! Perhaps They are the masters now,
But give us time, we're going to fling Them out,
Show Them what's what, tell Them a thing or two,
And all their crimes and lies we'll make them rue!'
  If Bugler blew reveille once again,
  And if the sergeant dragged us from our sleep,
  Then would we . . . simply sing the same refrain,
  And add Our own sins to Their festering heap.
Just to think that more than twenty years of my life have
vanished nowhere,' said Slanderer, and tore the paper into
shreds. No-one stopped him. And no-one picked up the scraps.

Work and 'work'

'Two years ago,' said Scientist, 'a new head was appointed to
our scientific section. An imposing man, full of his own importance. If you saw him in the street you'd take him for nothing
less than a minister from a neighbouring state, so democratic
you'd hardly believe it! As far as science is concerned, of course,
he was an absolute nobody.' 'Well, perhaps he was a good
administrator,' said Dauber. 'In America good administrators
are rated higher than scientists.' 'That's what I want to talk
about,' said Scientist. 'Along came this outstanding
administrator, and it all started! We've had it for nearly three
years now! Every month every one of us has to turn in little
memoranda saying that we have done everything laid down for
us to do that month (although we do something completely
different, or nothing at all!) These memoranda go first to our
direct superior. On the basis of these memoranda (as if they
were the only contact we had with him), our boss gets his
secretary to fill out more forms, and then there are more papers
for the technical staff, grade one research workers, grade two
research workers, and so on. Briefly, forms are filled in for
every possible administrative subdivision. All this paper con-
verges on the secretariat and the accounts department. There
are people specially appointed to examine them. The whole
purpose of this exercise is to show, according to the forms, who
has either not done what he should have done, done less than he

should have done, or done what he should have done, but inadequately. Any guilty party is revealed on pay-day, for instead of receiving his salary he is summoned to the head of the scientific section, who spends a couple of hours talking to the victim, establishes that there's been a misunderstanding, and gives him a form entitling him to receive his pay. Over the whole two years I cannot recall one instance where wages haven't been paid at all (which anyway would be against the law), or where anyone has been punished in any other way (it's a matter of principle that in our establishment everyone fulfils his quota!) Once I raised the question at a productivity meeting. I suggested that forms should only be filled in where individuals had *not* fulfilled their plan. That would mean five or six forms a month at the most. You've never heard a row like it! Everyone without exception must have a form filled in! Why? The reason's very simple. Let us call the scientific work of the establishment A. Let us call B the activity which consists of preparing and circulating forms about A. In theory A is our principal activity, and B is secondary. But only in theory. From the social point of view it is a matter of complete indifference whether A gave rise to B or vice versa. All that matters is which of them is socially more significant. From the point of view of social life, it is B which is real and A which is illusory. It's of no importance whether A progresses well or badly. But that's not the question. To come back to B. What would be an intelligent way to organise B? The way I proposed. Incidentally, I did rather well at school. But the way our great Administrator has organised B, a slow second-rate plodder would do the job admirably. In its present form the fulfilment of B demands not a shred of intelligence, not a trace of talent of any kind. The qualities it demands are a complete lack of soul, petty pedantry, impenetrable stupidity, and an appalling greyness. Plus the ability for its participants to stoop to any shoddy practice such as denunciation, slander . . . even forgery. In the view of the so-called service department B, scientific activity A needs no kind of talented organisation. And so activity B becomes central and essential. In a word, one could say that B is The Activity, and the scientific work we do is only a context for B. And such an Activity by its nature precludes ability and intellect. It is by nature anti-intellectual. It would be even less prepared to tolerate an able administrator than A would be prepared to tolerate an able scientist.'

Religion

'Do you pray?' asked Visitor. 'Yes,' said Chatterer, 'sometimes.' 'Who do you pray to?' asked Visitor. 'To God, of course,' said Chatterer. 'Not to my colleagues, for sure, nor to the director!' 'And what do you say to him?' asked Visitor. 'That depends,' said Chatterer. 'Sometimes I call him every name under the sun, but not often. Sometimes I thank him for what exists. When things are going badly, I pray that they shouldn't get worse. When things aren't too bad, I pray that they should stay that way.' 'And does it help?' asked Visitor. 'Yes,' said Chatterer. 'Prayer changes the way you see things and has a certain calming effect.' 'So you're a believer,' said Visitor. 'I'm afraid I have to disappoint you on that score,' said Chatterer. 'If I may, I'll give you a brief lecture. There are three forms by which a man can address himself to another man, a group of men, or an organisation—a request, gratitude, or blame. That is an address of a personal level. Now remove this personal element. Imagine that man addresses himself—but to no-one. But as a linguistic form address cannot be so incomplete. This void must be filled by something. So this abstract personification is God, by a purely linguistic process.' 'Those are just semantic devices,' said Visitor. 'Well, what can you do about it?' said Chatterer. 'We live in a civilisation. We can't tear ourselves out of it, and here everything is in language and passes through language. And even religion takes on here the form of a purely linguistic activity.'

The fear of truth

'The panic fear of hearing the truth about oneself is a sign of the times,' said Visitor. 'It's not the fear of being unmasked, but simply the fear of the truth about oneself. People are desperate to be deceived. The art of self deception has reached such heights that now's the time to hold congresses about it, set up institutions to study it, publish textbooks about it.' 'But that's obviously a general rule,' said Dauber. 'People in the mass have never had an accurate idea of themselves and their age.' 'Yes, but that was for different reasons,' said Visitor. 'In the past it was out of ignorance. But now? Now it's because literate people can and do understand their essence and their situation in society. That humiliates them and pains them. In our days the fear of truth is not a fear of the unknown, but a fear of something that is well known. People are afraid of themselves because they know who they are.'

Who has betrayed whom?
'Have you heard?' said Dauber, 'T. hasn't come back from abroad.' 'Yes,' said Neurasthenic. 'I've read the letter from his colleagues. They call him a traitor.' 'A traitor?' said Visitor. 'But they know him very well. They know that he's not a traitor. T. and I have been friends from our youth. He got first-class marks at school, and he was a brilliant student at the institute. Then he was arrested on the basis of a denunciation from his closest friends. Did his school speak up for him? Did his institute? His neighbours? His friends? Even his family didn't let out a squeak! And he was their only son! So who betrayed whom? Then the years went by. He became an outstanding scientist. His whole life was lived in full view of the world. Then a campaign of some kind was started up against him and he was in trouble again. Was there a word in his defence from his colleagues? His students? His friends? I ask again, who betrayed whom?!! More years passed. We entered our "liberal" phase. T. became very well known—abroad as well. He was invited to conferences abroad, but others went in his place. People were elected to the Academy who were nowhere near his equal. A group of scientists in which he was the leading light were nominated for a state prize—he was discarded. And all that happens in the full view of everyone. Everyone knows T.'s qualities, and the qualities of those who get sent to the conferences, get elected to the Academy, get awarded the prizes. So, who betrayed whom? . . . Finally he managed to establish a faculty which began to be discussed abroad. His colleagues did everything in their power to destroy it. And in the end they succeeded. People talked about it in corridors, in corners of restaurants. But no-one raised a finger to stop this criminal act. And what about his students? Where are they? What have they done to defend their leader and teacher? So in this story, who the hell is the traitor?!!!'

Who are we?

'In your country,' said Journalist, 'I have met a great variety of people from all sections of society. And you all talk about the same thing, with a few slight variations of style. You talk of apathy, of irresponsibility, of the shortage of vital commodities. You complain of the way you are tied to the place you live, and the place you work. No freedom of initiative. Nothing to read, nothing to see. Your leaders are fools and money grabbers. This is stupid, that is stupid, and so on. You hear the same thing from a worker, a writer, a minister, an actor. Everyone talks and talks. But no-one does anything to get things changed.' 'I have often met people from the West,' said Chatterer. 'Writers, artists, scientists, students, businessmen. And you all say one and the same thing to us: that we all say one and the same thing, talk and do nothing. Every time I've asked them one question, and I'll ask you the same one: Have I spoken to you of these things? No, I haven't. Nor shall I. I've spoken to you of quite different matters. But you, like all those who have come before you, just close your ears. For you I do not exist. For you, people like me do not exist. And it's not that there are so few of us here. The problem is not to see things as they are. You don't have to be very bright to do that. The problem is how to live once you've seen things as they are. We know perfectly well who we are. And we complain partly because we're rather ashamed of what we are, and partly because we want to show off about how deeply we think. Incidentally, people who are close to the highest authority and who are best provided for complain far more than those who have no such privileges. They can see things more clearly, and they have sharper appetites. And what's more, they can look thoughtful and courageous without any fear of the consequences. Of course, we all want things to be better. And what's more, since we've been able to observe your life we have lost our innocence. But to want is one thing . . . to be able to do anything about it is another. We can realise our ambitions only through our life here. And that means that we may complain in one voice, but we act in different ways and we want different things. You're not right about our inaction. We all act. Have you met Academician? Did he complain? Of course he complained. Do you suppose he does nothing about it? He certainly is doing something! He's doing everything in

(394)

his power to get rid of Troglodyte and Secretary. He's already got his hands on half the posts they used to occupy. He's getting his own lackeys in everywhere. Do you think things will get any better because of that? No. He thinks it's better because he's got hold of those posts rather than anyone else. But it's he who's done more than anyone else to suppress Slanderer. Have you met Claimant? Did he complain? Of course he complained. Is he doing nothing? Certainly not. He's sorting out his complaints and his ambitions as best he can in his position and given his character. He genuinely believes deep in his entrails that he is engaged in reshaping the country on a Western pattern. You've talked to Sociologist and Thinker dozens of times. Do you think that they are doing nothing? They hate the sight of queues in the shops, mud in the streets, disorder in general. But do you think they're deeply upset by what they see? They'd even be upset if it all vanished. There'd be nothing to talk about then. There wouldn't be anything to make them feel superior to everyone else. How could they feel that they were victims? And what do they want? To publish their life's work? But it doesn't exist! To open the way to genuine talents? But exactly how many talents have they opened the way to? They've acquired their power only because in present conditions Troglodyte and Secretary are unable to distinguish between talent and mediocrity and have begun to let the occasional talented work slip through. Thinker and Sociologist won't let such work through, not those two. They're doing very well in that respect. And we've got people who are trying to transform our life, as well. You know about them. And you know that they are actually doing something. And you know how they are treated. They are regarded as enemies, as slanderers, as traitors and so on. Who are they? They include people you've talked to and who've complained to you about their lot and our appalling living conditions. They include some of the people whom you listed in your last article as the spiritual leaders of our intelligentsia. I believe you're writing a book about us? Do you want a bet? I bet there isn't a word in it about me or about this conversation. Or if you do write about it, you'll turn it back to front. I don't hold it against you. Your behaviour isn't determined by what you hear and say here, but by your social position back home. You're a man after all. What do you expect of us? We're just people, we're not simply actors in a play which you have chosen to watch.'

Art and scientific-technical progress

'It is often said that art has an immense influence on science,' said Chatterer. 'Innumerable examples are produced in support of that statement. And the greater the standing of the scientist and the artist who is exerting the influence on him, the more convincing the example is. Thus, Einstein acknowledged the influence of Dostoevsky. And if Einstein himself admits the influence of Dostoevsky, what more proof can you need! But try to trace just one directly observed case where art has influenced science, apart from in the recollections of some great cultural figure. The situation is wholly imaginary. I assure you that the most you'll discover is the existence of a variety of psychic layers superimposed in time. Subjectively this superimposition is experienced as a cause and effect relationship. In fact it is meaningless to seek here any causal law, for scientific and artistic creation have their respective places in different conceptual systems, which exclude by definition any application of a causal link between the phenomena they describe. It is true that a certain similarity can be found between these two processes. But a similarity is not a connection. Moreover, similarities can be discovered in any two processes chosen at random. In brief then, everything which has been said about the influence of art on science is nothing but pure fiction which commits us to nothing.' 'I agree with you,' said Dauber. 'But what about influence the other way?' 'Of course, such an influence exists,' said Chatterer. 'And there are as many examples as you like. Space flight and nuclear physics are the most characteristic examples of scientific and technical progress. Have they had an influence on art? Of course they have. But is that influence much greater (relatively speaking, of course) than the discovery of the bicycle? Great art is born not in the depths of space or of the atom, but from the human soul and human life, lying on the surface and open to the sight of all—from what is known and accessible to everyone. Great art is merely one of the forms of organisation of our familiar life on earth. Scientific and technical progress provides images and subjects. But it does not provide the basic problems and prin-

(396)

ciples. If it does touch the essence of the matter, it does so only inasmuch as it gives rise to a new spiritual situation, or sharpens an old one which already exists in certain strata of society or in society as a whole. That is where art comes on the scene. I am not talking about art in general, but about whichever art it is which is specially orientated towards spiritual situations of this kind. Not an art which depicts scientific technical progress and its consequences, but an art which responds to the spiritual states of people who come under the influence of these consequences. That is what you do. You offer people the consolation they seek.'

How to handle people
'My sons,' roared the Commander in his powerful voice. 'Your country does not demand . . . Your country asks. . . . Your country beseeches . . . in the name of . . . I declare a general amnesty . . .' bellowed the Commander. 'Hurrah,' shouted the amnestied men of the punishment battalion. 'For the Fatherland, for the Boss, forward to N!' yelled the Commander. 'Hurrah,' came the cry from the amnestied men. 'Have you any requests?' asked the Commander. 'Yes, I've a request,' said Deviationist. 'Could we do it just for the Fatherland?' The Commander looked at Deputy, Deputy looked at Colleague, Colleague looked at the Commander. 'Very well,' roared the Commander. 'Hurrah,' yelled the condemned soldiers. And staggering from exhaustion, they set off to capture N.

Stupidity is always stupidity
'The thing that upsets me most,' said Neurasthenic, 'isn't that they're careerists, but that even as careerists they're untalented.' 'Like everywhere else,' said Dauber, 'talent is always a rarity. But you won't deny that the Boss, for instance, was a talented careerist.' 'I shall indeed,' said Neurasthenic. 'He only got to the top because he was phenomenally mediocre in every respect.' 'How do you mean?' asked Dauber. 'There are volumes of reminiscences which show very clearly that he was a man well out of the common rut.' 'Name me the man who, in your view, is the ideal of mediocrity,' said Neurasthenic. 'Good. Now place him at the head of our Union. Leave him

(397)

there for ten years. And he'll begin to turn out such amazing material that you'd be able to publish a collection of the best aphorisms of this cretin. If a complete mediocrity feels that his hands are untied, he'll begin to behave as if he were a genius. And through the efforts of enormous numbers of people, an illusion of genius will be created. Take this lousy business of Claimant! Thinker and I have talked about it dozens of times. But who am I in his eyes? A no-good Neurasthenic who can't even get himself a flat or organise a decent defence of his thesis. And here we're talking about matters of great importance to the state. And yet the problem itself could not have been more trivial. I said to him: you're a chap well above the average—at least the leadership and their entourage think so. Yet you behave like an outstanding mediocrity. That's not normal. You ought to do one of two things. Either go some place where your talent will look like mediocrity, for example, to Sociologist's. They're all like that there. Or try to convince people that you're a shit like everyone else, and stay where you are. So he patted me condescendingly on the shoulder, and told me I didn't understand the first thing about politics. And you know yourself how it all ended. So you see, according to these very rules which determine career formation, the most able careerist is the one with the least talent as a careerist. The best asset is a complete absence of any qualities which are in any way remarkable. The decisive factor is your readiness to carry out a certain type of social action. But we're using the word quality in quite an inverted sense, in the sense that a man is capable of actions like denunciation, lying, slandering, issuing orders to kill, or being the killer himself. A readiness to do such things is not a sign of talent in the sense that we talk about talented singers, artists, athletes, scientists or politicians. A talent is inborn, but social behaviour is not. The concept of talent is not applicable to the Boss, Hog, Claimant and Troglodyte: they owe their success not to any inborn qualities, but precisely to a lack of them. Their readiness to stoop to anything compensates for their lack of innate qualities and for their total insignificance.'

We and them, again*
My book has been discussed. I have never been under any illusions about the intelligence or the morals of my colleagues. I

have known them personally for many years. In addition to that, I know that there is a special social law which applies to moderately normal creative beings like my colleagues: either they play mean tricks out of stupidity, or commit stupidities because they are mean people. And yet until very recently I had idealised them. This was partly because of my natural desire for a decent environment. But it was mainly because during the 'liberal' period we have just lived through, many people of no worth were able to pass themselves off as courageous and important because they wanted to, and because they had the skill to do so. What's more they were able to achieve this without any personal effort or sacrifice, and indeed to their own benefit. They were widely distributed, perhaps even dominant, in our circles. They formed something of a border between people who were vague and indeterminate. The years passed. To maintain themselves in their chosen role they behaved just about well enough to preserve their reputations. That gave rise to certain illusions, mainly in their own view of themselves, and also to high ambitions. But the era came to an end. The role no longer had a *raison d'être*. But they did retain their claim to be the judges of all things. I have felt the consequences of that on my own skin. One could of course say that my individual case was a mere concatenation of circumstances. But in social life a general trend does not show itself merely through individual instances, it is also made up of the sum of these individual instances. During the years that had passed, my colleagues had amassed a lot of hate for me. I had always felt it but had been able to ignore it. But now it burst out fully and quite openly. It was a long time since I had seen from so close the amount of filth secreted by human minds. The impression is of being up against an extraordinarily insignificant force which, by virtue of this very fact, is invincible. I had had the same feeling during the war when our dug-outs had been raided at night by armies of fleas. The combination of this sense of a hostile strength and one's total impotence made me want literally to scream. E.N. says that the same thing happens among artists as among scientists. The methods of battle are the same as well. I don't have anything against fights. But that is when you fight man to man, using your fists. Even clubs and knives, if you like. Or teeth. But when people begin to fight me with snot, I just drop my guard. I say that people have accumulated too much evil and hatred within themselves. I am afraid that these localised explosions may spread and become general explosions and grow to an alarming size—if, of course, they are skilfully directed. E.N. says he shares my impression that things are moving towards something very serious. I tell him there are many of us who think this way. Indeed, people will even be disappointed if THAT doesn't happen. They don't have a presentiment of THAT, they're longing for it! And they do everything they can to see that THAT should happen. My little individual case provides an excuse for us to talk about everything that is happening in the world and causing alarm. I watch E.N. working, and my little affair begins to look insignificant and not worth bothering about. I have said that E.N. is my artist. That was putting it too weakly. E.N.'s art is an inalienable part of my existence. I cannot think what would become of me without it. I enter E.N.'s studio like a temple, and cleanse myself of the filth of the world. And what, E.N. says, what if THEY are right, and everything I am doing is rubbish? Where are the criteria which tell us what is great and what is worthless? What is the point of breaking all this up, melting it down, burning it?!! There must be a criterion, I say, for if there were not, there would be no E.N. You have such a criterion. It is your own reason. That is the supreme judge of what you are doing. And as far as melting down and burning are concerned, that's not the problem. Something else is much more terrifying. The death of a man is that man's tragedy. The death of millions is a huge tragedy, but it is a human tragedy. But there is a further kind of tragedy—the tragedy of the whole of mankind. But people are mankind, says E.N. Not quite so, I say. People are scattered through space. Mankind is stretched through time. That is another aspect of existence. Mankind lives so that from time to time new shoots will appear, producing branches of the extra-ordinary which grow far beyond the level of the common mass. If you cut these branches off, it may seem that nothing results. It may be that cutting them would pass unnoticed. But who can tell what consequences will follow this at first sight harmless pruning? And who can tell what the human race has already deprived itself of by this kind of action. You are one of these branches. Your tragedy is a tragedy of mankind. The tragedy of opportunities destroyed. And what about you? asked E.N. My situation is even worse, I said. I don't even have a tragedy. I never even managed to germinate.

Doctrine of existence

'Many of the traditional phenomena of Ibanskian life are being reborn here,' said Neurasthenic. 'Take Visitor, for example. He's in the process of inventing a whole home-grown theory of existence. Do you know how many other people have tried this before in Ibansk? You say that he is disinterested? So were they. You say he's not trying to make propaganda? No, but he doesn't hide his ideas, either. And if a man doesn't seek to hide his ideas, he's taken as a propagandist in Ibansk.' 'And what is his doctrine of existence?' asked Journalist. 'I've heard it more than once, but I can only remember fragments,' said Neurasthenic. 'It's sheer primitive nonsense, and I didn't try to remember it. His teaching involves a system of rules for the preservation of physical and mental health, rules of behaviour towards acquaintances (including friends and relatives), towards colleagues, bosses, to people you meet by chance, or with whom you are obliged to come into contact, to subordinates, to people you depend on, to people who depend on you, and also rules of behaviour relative to material goods, to honours, to your career, to success, to failure and so on—in brief, a system of rules of conduct for every event in life.' 'Does he follow them himself?' asked Journalist. 'All things considered, yes,' said Neurasthenic. 'He's spent his entire life in self-education, and it's only now that he's an old man that all this has come together into an overall conception. His doctrine has a positive aspect and a negative. The positive side speaks of what a man should do to preserve his physical and spiritual health, and the negative deals with what he should not do. The former are precepts, the latter prohibitions. What I'm telling you is my own summary of Visitor's ideas. His is neither so tidy nor so frank. I told you that he is self-taught. The rules of life apply to acts which concern oneself or someone else. Any that fall outside that definition are of no relevance. But Visitor is deeply convinced that if his teaching were rigorously followed no such acts could exist. The essential principles which guide our existence do not vary according to the situation. If an act is obligatory (or forbidden) then it is obligatory in every situation (given of course the conditions set out in the rule). For example, if you have promised someone you will do something, you must do it irrespective of what kind of man he is or how your relations with him may have changed and so on. Your relationship with a person does not depend on your relationship with other people, nor on his relationship with others. And so on in the same spirit. It's incredibly boring. On this basis he develops his own system of psychogymnastics and abstentions. Don't drink. Don't smoke. Don't take on important jobs. Own as little as possible. Spend as little as possible. Eat as little as possible. Sleep as little as possible. Have as few contacts with people as you can if these contacts involve any degree of social dependence. Do not seek honours or fame. Stay silent when others talk. Learn to listen if you want to be listened to. Never complain. In a word, be something like a yogi, but in our style and bearing in mind the specific nature of our life here.' 'That's very strange,' said Journalist. 'The strangest thing is his psychogymnastics,' said Neurasthenic. 'This is really the pinnacle of his achievement. Do you know how old he is? Well past sixty. He's held some very important positions. At all events, he ended the war as a colonel. You've seen how he dresses? Well, he lives on thirty roubles a month, and economists say that the minimum you can get by on is sixty.' 'How will it all end?' asked Journalist. 'As usual,' said Neurasthenic. 'It'll degenerate into an anecdote. Either he'll die a solitary death from a common cold, or he'll get sent to jail for poking into something that's none of his business. I know one man who spent twenty years developing his biceps with dumb-bells in the cause of self-defence. He used the result of his titanic efforts just once. He thumped a drunk who'd asked him for a cigarette, and, when he refused (for of course my acquaintance was a non-smoker), insulted him in filthy language according to the old Ibanskian custom.'

Mass art or élite art*

Is the art of E.N. mass art or élite art? That is a question of words, not of the essence of the matter. What do we mean by mass art or élite art? First, art which is accessible to the masses, and art which is accessible to many are not one and the same thing. When we here talk of the masses, we have in mind the least cultivated and worst educated strata of the population, and those strata which, although they have been given both education and culture, have lost both because they had no need of them, and who live as though they had never heard of either. In this group we can include for example the huge army of technicians, teachers, doctors, officers and so on. The art of Picasso, for instance, is incomprehensible to the masses in this sense. But we cannot say that it is comprehensible only to a few people. The number of people who can understand it is huge. Is it élitist or not? E.N.'s work can be sold in mass editions. If his albums were printed, there would be huge queues to buy them. They'd be sold out in a few days. E.N.'s sculptures should be produced by industrial methods. Even if we admit that his success would be restricted to the sphere of the scientific intelligentsia, this sphere alone is a typical mass phenomenon. But circumstances force E.N. into the role of an élitist artist in the sense that almost all his works remain in his studio, where they can be seen only by him and by the very small circle of his friends and acquaintances. If in the concept of mass art we include that of mass production of art, and its distribution to a fairly wide circle, mass effect, mass experience, mass standard reaction and so on, then E.N. is potentially the most typical artist of this genre. That is what he is meant for. Great art of our time is unthinkable unless it is mass art in that sense. That is why he is not given the chance of getting into this class. He is obliged to be élitist.

> An impetuous attack
> Of attacking we'd be charier
> But for a kick in the posterior.
> Then through the mud our way we make,
> Carrots and cabbage in our wake.
> If these 'mines' we then defuse,
> They give us vitamins to use.
>
> (From The Ballad)

'There's another kilometre to N.,' said Panicker. 'We crawled a lot further than that when we were in training.' 'There was an incentive then,' said Deviationist. 'We'd get through five cabbages and fifty carrots each on a crawling exercise there.' 'Those were the days,' said Panicker. 'Fags out,' said the

Lieutenant. 'Remember lads. In our situation the one who throws himself on the guns has the best chance of surviving. Forward!' Heaving their mud-caked boots with difficulty out of the clinging slime, the lads set off to the assault on N. After a hundred yards the Lieutenant fell. The amnestied and condemned men of the punishment battalion flattened themselves in the mud. Behind them the machine-guns stuttered. The Lieutenant got up, took one pace forward, and fell again for good. Deviationist got to his feet. So did Panicker. They were followed by all the others who were still alive. And they advanced further. The Lieutenant stayed lying in the mud. He was lucky. He had been killed, which was why he had a life ahead of him. But a fictitious life, it's true.

Consequences

'It follows from Schizophrenic's postulates,' said Neurasthenic, 'that the progress of a society which bases itself on such premises is possible only if the leaders of that society so wish it. Personalism both as a way of life and as an ideology is to be ruled out. Liberalism degenerates into trash. And the opposition in principle cannot formulate any serious positive programme of change. It rises up and fades away again like some sickly phenomenon and wins no support from the population at large.' 'These conclusions are very demoralising,' said Journalist. 'They're not all that terrible,' said Chatterer. 'After all, this is an abstract country, not a real one.'

In reality everything is different. In reality, the progress of society is impossible even if the leaders want it, personalism is out, liberalism is born like trash, and the opposition isn't born at all. So there is no reason for pessimism. 'And who is this chap Schizophrenic?' asked Journalist. 'Nobody,' said Neurasthenic. 'Just a man who one day suddenly noticed that, despite everything, he was still a member of a particular society, and was so amazed by that fact that he lost his head.' 'But he didn't lose his head because he was amazed or because he didn't understand,' said Chatterer, 'but because he had foreseen everything and understood everything.' 'And because he'd left no room in his soul for hopes and illusions,' said Visitor.

'Hello,' said Fellow-worker, when it became clear that he wasn't going to be able to pretend that he hadn't seen Chatterer. 'Hello,' said Chatterer. 'How are things?' asked Fellow-worker, and without waiting for an answer, said that he was doing very well, thank you. That his institute had got an excellent new director. That he and Secretary, Thinker and Puss had just finished an epoch-making piece of work, and that they were even getting a special bonus bearing in mind the special importance of their volume in the struggle against trends from Over There. That Troglodyte would probably be retired on a pension because he had been in hospital for almost two weeks after a massive stroke, and that that was a great victory for US. That he'd stopped writing verse a long time ago. That he and Wife had just got back from abroad, where everything on the whole was rubbish. Nothing interesting at all. That OUR BOOK would be a whole head higher and wouldn't leave stone on stone. 'Excuse me,' he said, finally, 'I'm in rather a hurry. A meeting. Yes, just think, we're going to have a new journal. First-class editorial board. Sociologist. Me, of course. Best wishes to Dauber. How's he getting on? There've been rumours. . . . It was a mistake for him to get involved in that. . . .' When he'd gone on for another hour or so, established what seemed to him to be the best explanation for Dauber's behaviour (his ambition, his envy of Truth-teller, his egocentrism, his lack of self-confidence, his isolation from the finest achievements of world art, his dubious entourage and so on) Fellow-worker left without saying goodbye.

Who are we?

'We may seem an enigma to you but we're not in fact much more complex than an amoeba,' said Neurasthenic. 'Indeed, as far as ease of comprehension goes we're a good deal simpler. It's because you approach us through this whole system of your own prejudices, our official camouflage, and our general desire to conceal from foreigners what we really are.' 'But perhaps people hide because of their own ignorance,' said Journalist. 'That never happens,' said Neurasthenic. 'You can't hide what you don't know. If we hide something, that means we know it. And we know that it's not worth showing.' 'So why do you talk about it?' asked Journalist. 'Because I want us to become better,' said Neurasthenic. 'And to do that we shall have to conform to certain models, and make a great effort of self-control. And if people are going to do this on a large scale, not just individually, they will have to be prepared to strip down to what they really are. People should be ashamed to let others see their filth, and they've got to take steps to get rid of it. But for the time being we try to hide it.'

On the problem of survival*
E.N.'s problem is primarily one of survival, for a creative artist, in modern conditions. From the purely creative point of view Slanderer and Schizophrenic were no less important than E.N. But they are no longer here, and E.N. is. Wherein does the strength of this man lie? In his personal qualities? In a coincidence of circumstances? In his links with or support from the intelligentsia? In support from certain governing circles? All that of course has had a part to play. But that's not the main thing. At first no-one here allowed E.N.'s art any serious significance. It seemed that he was standing somewhat aside from the main-stream of the spiritual life of society, did not hinder its triumphal official progress, and was privately engaged on some absurd trivialities. During that period he was able to develop. By the time people realised this, it was too late. He had become immense, and had attracted the centre of the spiritual life of our society closer to himself. In this period he had been able to identify his own creative interests with the personal interests of a substantial number of people who had a certain influence on developments.

Fathers and sons
'Young people,' said Neurasthenic, 'don't give a fuck for us. They don't even know we exist. And if they do know anything about us at all, then it's always twisted and deformed in some way or other. We simply have no contacts with youth at all.' 'Why not?' asked Chatterer. 'I've taught for many years, and I've had contacts.' 'So what?' said Dauber. 'I'll tell you,' said Chatterer; 'no contacts. We're isolated not only in space but in time as well.' 'But there was surely someone before us,' said Dauber. 'Indeed there was,' said Chatterer. 'But we only disco-

vered after we had become what we are now.' 'But there will surely be someone after us,' said Dauber. 'Of course, but they will only find out about us (if they *do* find out) when they become somebody in their own right. Who that somebody will be is impossible to foretell.' 'I was invited round to Fellowworker's yesterday,' said Neurasthenic. 'We talked about the war, the Boss, Hog, Claimant and Truth-teller. The usual sort of small-talk. But when there was a moment's silence, Fellowworker's little daughter remarked that one girl in her kindergarten hadn't eaten her porridge and so the teacher had had to punish her by not taking her for her walk. Young people have their porridge and their punishments as well. And they don't give tuppence for us.' 'But all the same there is a certain continuity of ideas,' said Dauber. 'It's merely that the same old problems keep cropping up endlessly,' said Chatterer. 'Then along comes some genius or other to discover some kind of evolution.' 'But is it conceivable that nothing leaves any trace?' said Dauber. 'Why talk about there being no traces?' said Chatterer. 'Traces remain, but they sink into the depths and disappear without trace.'

Morality is absolute
'It is by his own will and his own desire,' said Visitor, 'that man becomes what he is in the moral sense. An average man has before him a sufficient number of examples to teach him to tell good from bad. The average man knows from experience what good and evil are. One cannot become an evildoer by force of circumstance or by ignorance. One cannot be paid to become a decent man. If a man is a rogue it is because he wanted to become one and has striven towards that end. Man himself bears the full responsibility for his morality. Anyone who takes this responsibility away from man is immoral. The assessment of acts as good or bad is absolute. It does not depend on who performs the act, on whom the act is performed, on the relationship of either party to third parties, or on the relationship of third parties to either party. Evil and good are evil and good at all times and in all places. Anyone who insists on the relativity of good and evil, i.e. on some relationship between the morality of actions and the circumstances in which they are performed, is *a priori* negating morality. In this case morality is replaced by

the appearance of morality, or antimorality. Not in the sense of amorality—amorality falls within the limits of moral judgments—but in the sense of morality with a minus sign.'

Labour is not lost, but it is in vain

'There you are, I have done what you asked,' said Chatterer, handing Dauber *The Legend of Dauber*. 'Do what you like with it. I hope you'll forgive me all the faults in this essay. It was written off the cuff after all. But don't think there would have been fewer errors if I'd taken a longer time to write it.' Dauber read the piece, and said that that was what he'd always thought. Chatterer shrugged his shoulders. Then the essay got lost somewhere.

The business of talking

'Our conversations are pure chatter,' said Neurasthenic. 'We must put a stop to it. We're beginning to repeat ourselves and chew the same thing over time and time again.' 'You're right,' said Chatterer. 'But now we've finished talking. So what next? Talking is my vocation. The product of all my activity is ideas transformed into words. It's of no interest to me whether or not they lead to anything. I'm not vain. And it's not such an idle occupation as all that. In our era mankind has found itself faced with the problem of making a conscious choice of which way to go. And so on a universal scale mankind has been reflecting on its past experience, its present situation and its future prospects. And so naturally enough people talk a great deal about these subjects. If you really want to know, the business of talking may well be more important today than space flights and physical experiments. And since society is thinking and talking on this universal scale, professional thinkers and talkers are bound to appear—if it were not us, it'd be someone else. Sooner or later they'll turn up something—at which point it'll no longer be mere idle chatter.' 'It's easy enough to put a stop to that,' said Neurasthenic. 'No, you can't stop it,' said Chatterer. 'You could create a system of bans which would make the business of thinking and talking the preserve of ideological sects with all their warped narrow-mindedness, dishonesty, hysteria, intolerance and so on. It'd be a nightmare.' 'Wouldn't be the first time,' said Dauber. 'There was a time when truth was revealed to the Ibanskians by the simple-minded, hysterics, epileptics and clowns.' 'And artists,' said Neurasthenic. 'There's another hazard here,' said Chatterer. 'The business of talking has become a mass phenomenon. And for some reason it's dominated not by a search for clarity, precision and candour, but by an ambition to drown all contemporary social problems in a turbulent stream of meaningless words. It's not by any evil intent, but by some people's wish to assert themselves, and also because people have lost the habit of making a logical approach to language. From the logical point of view, man's linguistic practice is a subject worthy of the brush of a surrealist. The speeches of politicians, prosecutors, lawyers, journalists, propagandists, scientists and so on, who claim more than anyone else to be logical, in fact produce outstanding examples of illogicality and ineptitude. I have no illusions as to the outcome of any attempt to instil greater logic into our language. The voice of a man calling for logic is that of a man crying in the wilderness. He has no more chance of being heeded than the voice of a man who cries "Do not kill!" And yet if there is the slightest chance, no matter how slender and remote, of exercising any influence at all, by applying logic to language, on the way men think about their lives and the fate of mankind, then that chance must be seized. When people repeat themselves and chew over the same things time and again, they are also, incidentally, engaged in the logical processing of their ideas. That is, of course, a substitute. But who can suggest any other means accessible to many people without special training? It should be noted that professional logic, whose successes have won so much acclaim, has itself turned into a typical mass phenomenon, and as a result it has quite lost touch with the problems of improving language logically.'

Personalism

'In your circle,' said Journalist, 'I have never heard you discuss the fate of the Ibanskian people, of Ibanskian science, of Ibanskian art. Surely you must be disturbed about these things?' 'The Ibanskian people,' said Chatterer, 'don't need us to worry about them. They are entirely happy with the care shown by their leaders. It's a very long time now since the Ibanskian people were a downtrodden and ignorant mass whom heroic, enlightened intellectuals had to set on the true path. The Iban-skian people are quite well enough educated, well enough read, and they know perfectly well how matters stand. They know what they want to know. And on the whole they have what they want as well. The activity of the leadership corresponds with the interests of the people. At all events, there is no question with us of any conflict, even potential conflict, between the people and their leaders. I would stress that this is not because the leadership represses the people. The leadership does not repress the people. It is because the leadership is of the people, and the people are of the leadership. The people bear full responsibility for the activity of the leadership. The people are the co-partners of their leadership in all its actions, good and bad. There is someone to take care of our people. Let's not take the bread from their mouths. But who will worry about us if we, we ourselves, are not capable of doing so?' 'As far as Ibanskian art goes,' said Dauber, 'that needs my concern even less. It would be a crude mistake to think that our art situation is bad here. Art flourishes. It is fully in tune with the spirit of the people. And with the spirit of the leadership, of whom there are enough to form the entire population of quite a large state. I want personally to do what is within my strength, and nothing more.' 'But in seeking self-expression, you are obliged to do things which look as if you were fighting for the freedoms of art, of speech, of movement and so on,' said Journalist. 'And isn't that a form of concern for the fate of your people and your art? Surely the people of Ibansk must be grateful to you if you manage to soften emigration controls, to get writers like Truth-teller published, and painters like Dauber exhibited?' 'The people don't need this,' said Chatterer, 'and the leadership even less.' 'But someone must be interested in achieving this,' said Journalist. 'Yes,' said Neurasthenic. 'A minute group—by comparison to the total mass of the population—a group of dissident intelligentsia who have no social force in the land, who are not even competent to defend themselves.' 'But in the future the country would benefit from the development of this group,' said Journalist. 'The people and the leaders of the people never think about that kind of future,' said Chatterer. 'And catastrophes, crises, and other such negative phenomena can always be put down to external circumstances—and to

(410)

dissident intellectuals. Of course, if a country does produce an influential group of critical intelligentsia who are capable of defending themselves, then such a country will in the long run profit from their presence. But this "if" is a matter for the course of history, not for a single day. Moreover, as experience shows, society is able to exist (how—is another question) without such a group, by transferring its functions (in a form obviously caricatured and neutralised) to a completely obedient section of the liberal intelligentsia and petty officialdom made up of people like Writer, Artist, Thinker, Sociologist, Careerist, Fellow-worker, Claimant and so on, who can always be called rapidly back to order should the need arise. All this tragi-comedy over Claimant, which you've witnessed, is a case in point.'

Who are we?
'We are your lawful child,' said Neurasthenic. 'Of course you took contraceptive precautions, but they turned out to be ineffective. But we were conceived by you. As one of our great theoreticians put it, we were born on the great highway of world civilisation. And if we do not behave as you might wish, that's not unusual. We're not the only people like that. You may deny us, you may try to make it appear that we and you are complete strangers. But that's just a waste of time. We exist in this form only thanks to the fact that you did and still do exist, and we are your lawful heirs. And we exist in your home whether you like it or not. And we will dispose of your heritage as best pleases us.' 'You draw a gloomy picture,' said Journalist. 'Why gloomy?' asked Neurasthenic. 'It's not up to you or to us to judge what's better and what's worse. It will simply be different, and there will be no further scope for an unwelcome comparison. And mankind has no problem of choice before it—that's all a myth. So we'd better think how best to organise life on this basis.'

The judgment of one's peers
'The Union's been asked from up above to give its opinion about my interview,' said Dauber. 'They've recommended expelling me from the Union, and even from Ibansk.' 'It's good that they've said such extreme things about you,' said Chatterer. 'Up on top they've got a panic fear of taking extreme

(411)

measures. And so they'll have to protect you against them.'
'And what good will that do me?' asked Dauber. 'None at all,'
said Chatterer. 'Except that the method they use to smother you
will look like a demonstration of humanity and toleration.
That's progress just the same!'

In the camp of the defeated

'Let's take stock,' said Neurasthenic. 'Here's a man whom you
made friends with almost twenty years ago who's been betray-
ing you for quite some time and now he's done you dirt quite
openly. On top of that, he's made it look as if it were you that
had wronged him. And he has no pangs of conscience. A man
who has been repeating for ten years that he is in no way a
scientist (unlike you), that all he wanted was to get his degree and
a share of the cake, suddenly begins to lecture you as if you were
a first-year student, tears your work apart, despite the fact that
you've spent half your life on it and he doesn't know the first
thing about it, and ends up by spreading slander about you.
People whom you've always tried to help and with whom you've
been on good terms suddenly start to put false interpretations
on everything you do, to put words into your mouth which you
never said nor thought, or to turn on you in hatred over something of no moment. The fact is, that's all in the day's work. But
for some reason we're feeling especially sensitive just now. Why
is that?' 'Because,' Chatterer replied, 'we are now living in the
camp of the vanquished.' 'But who is the victor?' asked
Dauber. 'No-one,' said Chatterer. 'We have all been defeated
by ourselves. We have not been able to cope with all the garbage
that has heaped itself up inside us.' 'You're right,' said Neurasthenic. 'We are perishing in a bloody battle for a few miserable
benefits, for privileges and honours. Friend has devoured
friend out of petty jealousy. That's the way we're going.'
'And by way of compensation,' said Chatterer, 'we are now
choosing our last victims and rounding off the affair.' 'What
victims?' asked Dauber. 'Those who are left, the strongest and
the most independent. Like you, for example. We have first of
all, whatever the cost, to make it seem that they are made of the
same crap as we are. Then make them believe it. Then drive
them out of our circle as foreign bodies. If we are able, destroy
them.' 'Surely you don't count yourself among these people,'

said Dauber. 'No,' said Chatterer. 'But then we don't really exist. We are THEY.' 'And what will happen now?' asked Dauber. 'A free fall to the very bottom,' said Chatterer. 'But perhaps that's an exaggeration,' said Dauber. 'Seek the answer within yourself,' said Chatterer. 'If you can find anything at all to cling on to, you are right. If not, can you hope to find anything in other people? Seek, and you will understand yet another paradox of our existence: in a situation like this the force which looks the most liberal in the country is the leadership and even the apparatus of law and order.' 'You're right,' said Dauber, and gladly began producing examples. 'These are not exceptions, but the general rule,' said Chatterer. 'Within the limits of Schizophrenic's postulates, even the functions of the opposition must be taken over by those against whom the opposition is directed and who repress it.'

Problems come at night

When night came, Fellow-worker told himself finally that he'd had enough, that he'd taken as much as he could, and began to reflect on his life. After a moment, his attention switched to that epoch-making volume he was producing under Secretary's direction, which was to be a stock-taking, an examination of future prospects, a sledge-hammer of a book. That, of course, is the main thing, said Fellow-worker to himself, and he began to read the grubby scraps of paper which he had managed to snatch from that parasite Thinker. What a load of tripe, thought Fellow-worker. Oh, God, the man's an idiot! Everything'll have to be done again from scratch! If, after all that, those stinkers don't pay me my royalties! After all the work I've put in! And yet Secretary doesn't seem in all that hurry to nominate me. I'll have to give him a prod. And Fellow-worker reverted to thinking about life, which implacably recedes, leaving behind it mountains of epoch-making papier mâché. The lads from the newly reformed Provost Detachment had asked him to write some verses for their wall newspaper. Witty, but serious. Fellow-worker chuckled maliciously and began to write a humorous anthem for the Provost Detachment.

> We stuff ourselves with porridge every day,
> That's why we live the best in every way.
> And with our lusty voices proudly say:

                    Left!
                        Left!
                            Left!
                                Right!
You are alone! We come in might!
                    And if you want to eat your fill,
                    You'll have to be like us as well.
                    If not, it's best you make your will!
We're certain of our past, oh yes, we are.
We don't need criticism from afar.
The critics—they're the guilty ones for sure.
                    Left!
                        Left!
                            Left!
                                Right!
You are alone! We come in might!
                    Stay quiet, or else we'll beat you black and
                        blue.
                    Join the enemy, and that's the end for you.
                    You'd do as well to march the way we do.
The Boss, our Father, taught us in his prime,
We're right to beat or kill at any time.
Because we sing of progress in our rhyme.
                    You are alone! We come in might!
                    Our own good sense will teach us right,
                    To tell the black sheep from the white.
                    You are alone! We come in might!
                    Left!
                        Left!
                            Left!
                                Right!

                    Paradoxes
'But all the same we can't get by without any hopes and illusions
at all,' said Dauber. 'We can't get by any more with hopes and
illusions,' said Chatterer. 'Anyway, to all intents and purposes
there aren't any left. And people are no worse off for that.' 'You
deliberately put everything into the form of a paradox,' said
Dauber. 'On the contrary,' said Chatterer. 'From the monstrous paradoxes of existence I try to extract more or less straight-

forward statements. Look! Our population knows perfectly well what our system of existence is. They know that this system is far from ideal, as it's claimed to be by our newspapers, radio, television, films, books and so on. And yet this system is fairly comfortable for the vast majority. They curse the system at every point and at every level. But they wouldn't change it of their own free will for any other system. Our leadership shouldn't be priding themselves on running the best system imaginable. That's not their merit now. In theory they should be preening themselves on the fact that despite our system, for which they bear no responsibility, they have been able to achieve something which lies outside the framework of this system. And what happens?' 'There's no point in going on,' said Dauber. 'I keep going round in circles all the time myself, and I thought I might have got lost. But it seems I'm on the right road.'

News from the future

'Sooner or later secrets become widely known,' said Dauber. 'Our meticulous descendants will get down to the truth in time.' 'That's an optimistic black comedy,' said Chatterer. 'Do you want to know what our descendants will really discover? Here's a news bulletin from, let's say, 8974. "In their excavations of a piece of waste ground on the outskirts of Ibansk, geologists have discovered more than ten million cubic yards of human bones. By modern standards this is an insignificant figure. But since the population of Ibansk in those days was many times smaller, such a mass burial naturally provoked no interest in the ranks of the specialists. Thanks to the efforts of a large number of researchers and of appropriate organisations, no explanation has been found for the large number of skulls pierced by a round hole in the back of the neck, and with the cranial cavity filled with the bran of optimism and illusions. Some attempts were made to revive the reactionary theory of the actual existence of Boss-Hog. But these attempts were swiftly quashed. The martyred-atoms method was used to establish that if such a mass burial had indeed taken place, then it would relate to a much later, post-Hog period. Scientists have used the prime sources to prove that such a burial ground could never have existed on Ibanskian soil. Later excavations of the

(415)

waste land using the most modern methods, have once more confirmed the accuracy of this theory." Do you see what I mean?' said Chatterer. 'It's futile to rely on our descendants. Truth about the past is only possible when it does not provoke any emotion. If the past is still a matter of emotions, it is impenetrable. Go on living in the present.'

The last hope

'The processes of society are accelerating all the time,' said Scientist. 'That's just a trite phrase,' said Chatterer. 'If an expression is constantly repeated everywhere, it's a sure sign that it is just a piece of ideological nonsense, even if it's come to light in the best scientific way, by leaping out of a nuclear reactor or crawling out of a chromosome. We can only show its psychological basis. In the past, people went to some lengths to calculate when events would happen, and on the whole they weren't disappointed—they came when they were supposed to. But now people often find themselves expecting an event to happen at a certain time, and it actually happens earlier. Careerist, for instance, married his young secretary. Well, he's a man of the world. He knew that his wife would take a lover. But basing himself on the old historical rules, he expected this to happen in eight years' time. Well, she made a cuckold of him after eight days. It is these repeated errors in forecasting that have come to be known as the acceleration of the processes of society. To speak of this has come to be accepted as a sign of high education and a progressive spirit. But do expected events always happen earlier than expected? How many of them happen later, or don't happen at all? Has anyone calculated the relationships? But let's accept that the pace of history is accelerating. Where does that leave us? You expect that according to your calculations you're going to get your real drubbing in two years, and in fact it starts happening earlier, say in a year's time.' 'But positive phenomena are speeding up as well,' said Dauber. 'Of course,' said Chatterer. 'You look forward to a certain freedom to go abroad, for example, in two hundred years, and it actually comes a great deal earlier—say in a hundred years. A mere hundred years, and then if you haven't done anything really stupid during that time, you'll be allowed to go and have a look at Paris under the eye of Colleague or Sociologist.'

There is no other way

Of the several thousand soldiers who formed the punishment battalion, a few dozen survived as by a miracle and dragged themselves to N, which the enemy had abandoned. The rest had remained lying in the mud. Deviationist, Humorist and Panicker wandered around the deserted fortifications looking for food. 'Why the devil did we take this dump N?' grumbled Deviationist. 'It's ridiculous. Just mark my words, by the evening we'll be withdrawn to our starting point.' 'If of course,' said Humorist, 'we aren't massacred by this lot. Just in case. To avoid talk. An amnesty before a battle is a trick to con the dead, not the living.' 'How do you know what's senseless and what's not?' asked Panicker. 'Maybe they have no option.' 'What do you mean by that?' asked Humorist. 'Do you mean that they acted the best way they could in conditions over which they had no control? Or that they acted as they did because that was in their nature? That's very far from being the same thing. The former example presupposes intelligence and a rational approach. The latter, not.' 'But someone somewhere must have taken a decision to take this N,' said Panicker. 'Someone gave it some thought.' 'Who thought of it and where is something we'll never know,' said Deviationist. 'But since we've captured N, that means that whoever it was must have thought it all through. Someone will get medals, titles, promotion for that. If we abandon N, then it'll be because we have to for either tactical or strategic reasons. Maybe it'll be so that His Majesty King Break-Barn-Brick-Corner may be confirmed in power and bring his long forgotten people directly to the full Ism without passing through the intermediate stages. Or maybe it might have to be done as part of Operation Eyewash. And in that case too there'll be medals, titles and promotions. Or perhaps they won't need to. In which case those who took the decision will receive medals, titles and promotions.' Silence fell. Despair gave way to hope. And therefore to alarm and fear. From the direction where, an eternity ago, they had gone into the attack, the wind brought them snatches of singing.

We stuff ourselves with porridge every day. . . .

(417)

'In our country even songs are reported,' said Humorist. 'It's of no matter who started the idea of capturing N,' said Deviationist. 'Once started, it became a factor in a totally different game wholly divorced from any kind of rationality. Those who said "yes" preserved or improved their position. Those who said "no", and I doubt whether there were any, worsened theirs. It's all very simple.' 'The awful thing is that it *is* all so clear and obvious,' said Humorist. 'There'll be no more mysteries for centuries.' 'The Lieutenant's been killed,' said Panicker. 'Gelding, too. Pimp as well. We've been lucky. We're still alive, lads!'

We're certain of our past, oh yes, we are. . . .

The singing was now louder and closer. The sound of marching feet could be heard, and the squeak and rumble of caterpillar tracks.

The Boss, our Father, taught us in his prime . . .

'Look,' said Humorist. 'They're coming.' Fountain-pens at the ready, the well fed, warmly clad boys of the Provost Detachment were making towards them—Troglodyte, Thinker, Secretary, Sociologist, Claimant, Puss, Colleague, Director, Wife, Careerist, Academician, Instructor, Fellow-worker, Scientist, Artist, Writer. They were followed by a great horde of Zeros who drove them in the right direction.

Our own good sense will teach us right,
To tell the black sheep from the white.
You are alone! We come in might!
Left!
Left!
Left!
Right!

Not much time left

'What do you feel at the moment?' asked Visitor. 'Utter confusion,' said Chatterer. 'What do you want?' asked Visitor. 'Peace,' said Chatterer. 'So you must have faith,' said Visitor. 'Faith does not breed confidence,' said Chatterer. 'Resign yourself,' said Visitor. 'They won't let me,' said Chatterer. 'We are obliged to feel anguish and fury.' 'Then fight,' said Visitor. 'I cannot,' said Chatterer. 'There's no point.' 'Very well, then,' said Visitor, 'be patient. There's not much time left.'

(418)

No pretensions

'All my commissions have been cancelled,' said Dauber. 'My fate is decided.' 'It is decided,' said Chatterer. 'Why?' asked Dauber. 'Because you wanted to be independent,' said Chatterer. 'Tell me frankly, if your sins were to be pardoned at this moment and you were restored to your former situation, would that satisfy you?' 'No,' said Dauber. 'If you were elected to the Academy?' asked Chatterer. 'No,' said Dauber. 'If you were given the prize?' asked Chatterer. 'No,' said Dauber. 'If they let you go abroad?' asked Chatterer. 'No,' said Dauber. 'If they gave you an exhibition?' asked Chatterer. 'No,' said Dauber. 'And if you were expelled from the Union, would you be distressed?' asked Chatterer. 'No,' said Dauber. 'If they took away your studio?' asked Chatterer. 'No,' said Dauber. 'If you were expelled from Ibansk?' asked Chatterer. 'No,' said Dauber. 'If your works were destroyed?' asked Chatterer. 'No,' said Dauber. 'In other words, all your trials and tribulations are irrelevant?' asked Chatterer. 'No they're not,' said Dauber. 'But for them, I couldn't have answered "No".' 'So what is it you want?' asked Chatterer. 'To work,' said Dauber. 'And you, what do you want?' 'Nothing,' said Chatterer. 'I don't even lay any claim to being punished.'

II

THE

DECISION

An essay on the logic of
one period of the history of Ibansk

The aim of this essay is to determine the principal result of this period.

The author had no help from anyone in preparing this essay. No-one has read this essay. No-one has proposed any helpful criticisms. Far less have there been any friendly comments. The author wishes to express his gratitude to all concerned.

Of course many people have guessed that the author was in the process of writing something. The main people to have guessed this were members of the Omnipresent and Omniscient Organs. It is their job to know about everything before it happens. For an entire year they carried out a systematic observation of refuse disposal in the courtyard of our building. But they allowed themselves an error unforgivable for such a powerful and experienced organisation: they examined the wrong dustbin! Our block is served by the dustbin on the left, and they rooted about in the dustbin on the right. In all probability the error occurred because the author, on an occasion when he was explaining the disposition of the dustbins to an old friend, was standing with his back to the building while his friend was facing it. A few close friends also had the feeling that something was afoot. They were very much afraid that the author might suddenly write something serious and did all they could to discover what it might be. But look, said the author, I'm not Truth-teller or Singer. I'm just a rank and file member. Pacified, his friends clapped the author on the shoulder and advised him to go on writing. But they could see from his eyes that there was something not quite kosher about what he was doing and, just in case, prudently put about rumours that the author had some 'anti' book in mind. However, the author is obliged to disappoint them. He has indeed written a book. But it is in no way 'anti', more of an apologia. An underground book in defence of the Ibanskian way of life—has there ever been anything like it before? Certainly not in western history. But in the history of Ibansk, that is apparently becoming the done thing.

Ibansk, any year you like.

(423)

The choice is yours

Your accomplices have acknowledged their guilt and have repented, said Colleague. You are the only one to remain obstinate. And you are wasting your time. Whatever happens, we won't let you get into court. So put that idea aside. We'll send you for a medical examination. In the present state of medical science, give them a day or two and there won't be a psychiatrist in the world who won't pass you as mentally deranged and undertake to cure you. But you'll retain your capacity to understand your own situation. And that can be like torture. You will suffer constantly. For ten years. For twenty. Until the end of your life. And no-one will make a fuss about what's happening to you. Your accomplices will avoid mentioning your name. As a scientist you are not so distinguished that your disappearance will be noticed and linked with politics. If you acknowledge your guilt and recant, you'll get only a short sentence. The story of Truth-teller will have no place in the indictment. That's agreed already. You'll be allowed to live and work normally in your special field. I'll give you twenty-four hours to reflect. No longer. The choice is yours.

That's progress, thought Bawler. Now they're giving us the right to choose our own punishment. In exchange for our co-operation, of course. What changes we're seeing! In the past the innocent rushed to confess and repent. But now even the guilty have the face to make bargains. No, my pets! All that's not been in vain. Not in vain. Ten years? Twenty? A trifle! It's nothing more than a moment. And then there's nothing.

An objective view from outside

Journalist had spent a whole month in Ibansk living in the Intourist hotel near the Shithouse, observing Ibanskian society from the inside. He had written a big book about how this society looked objectively, i.e. from the outside. The book was a great success in Ibansk. A review in the Newspaper observed that even bourgeois representatives of the West were obliged to acknowledge . . . and then there was a long extract critical of Ibanskian reality. In return for this Journalist was allowed to export from Ibansk two jars of red caviar and an ikon. So Journalist's book is patently reliable. And later we will have occasion to quote it more than once in the context of our description of the period of Ibanskian history which concerns us.

In the period under consideration, wrote Journalist in his book, Ibansk saw a powerful upsurge in its spiritual life. Proof of this came in the publication of the sharply critical verses of the outstanding poet Snottyhanky, hero of the nation's youth, the army and the Secret Police, and also in the renaissance of the Ibanskian National Theatre, which reinterpreted a number of old plays and staged a topical new one by the extremely talented publicist Brother, which he had written in collaboration with Shakespeare and Dostoevsky, and which dealt with the situation of Hamlet in the Institute of Physics of the Academy of Sciences (known for short as SOHITIOPOTAOS). The play opened with the deathless monologue of Hamlet, a graduate student in physico-mathematical studies, who had been refused a tourist visa for foreign travel by a bunch of reactionaries headed by the local Party Secretary, who feared, not without reason, that he would defect. So the play opened with Hamlet's monologue:

> To be or not to be—a silly question
> Considered in the context of Ibansk,

and continued to the tumultuous applause of the intellectually inclined audience until such time as Hamlet was finally permitted to visit Mongolia. One should really have seen the audience at that moment! They felt that victory was theirs. If They had tried to ban this play, the audience told each other in whispers, we'd have shown Them. . . .

Among other important phenomena of the cultural life of Ibansk, Journalist referred to the forthcoming unveiling of the memorial to Hog, the work of the modernist sculptor Dauber, who, it was rumoured had been a close friend of Hog's; to the publication of a series of articles by Wife about the New Left in the West, and a series of articles by Thinker about the Old Right in the West; to shamizdat publications—a typewritten magazine critical of the extremes of the regime; to the political ballads of Singer; and to the unpublished novels of Truthteller, which were not so much cultural as political phenomena.

'Well,' said Dauber, 'that's a pretty full and objective picture. Apart from that, nothing very important happened here.'

'He's a right bastard, your Journalist,' Teacher said to

Neurasthenic, who had drunk two monthly salaries with Journalist. 'Well, what do you expect of them?' said Neurasthenic. 'They're like well brought up young ladies who think that if you open a villain's eyes to the evil of his ways, he'll immediately feel ashamed and become a good little boy.'

A page of heroic history

As is well known, the Boss, apart from having the most powerful intellect ever known to history before or since, also had the most powerful prick. According to legend, he used his prick to destroy his most committed enemies. He did it this way. He would summon his enemy late at night, urge him to recant in the interests of the Brotherhood and to name his accomplices, and would then produce his mighty member and deal a light blow with it on his enemy's empty skull. During the process he let out a yell of 'A-a-a-a-h!'. The enemy's skull would shatter into fragments. 'And now,' the Boss said kindly, 'pick up tha' shit and booger off. And joost treigh t' be a bit brighter i' t' fewcher, tha' grit cretin!' The enemy swept up the last remaining pieces of his now useless skull, which until a moment ago had been crammed with the useless bran of Ibanism, and humbly departed to compile a report on his closest friend and colleague, with whom he had spent fifty years of his youth, sharing a one-man solitary confinement cell.

Songs were written in honour of the Boss's prick, towns were named after it, processions were held to glorify it. At the corner where Boss Street (now Leader Street) met Boss Avenue (now Leader Avenue), a public urinal was erected in honour of the Boss's prick. On its walls Artist, winner of all the prizes and bearer of all titles, drew a large image of the Boss's prick in full working order, with all the leading statesmen of Europe and America sitting astride it. Below the picture, a marble slab bore in letters of gold these verses, penned by Writer, the winner of nearly all prizes:

> If in our affairs your dirty nose you stick,
> Beware, for all you'll get is . . . prick!

As the Boss was much engaged by his duties as head of state, viz. sorting out questions of linguistics, Artist used a stallion as a model. This stallion belonged to the legendary Military Leader, who was subsequently elected to the Praesidium and appointed Chief Director of Culture.

The birth of Ibansk

Ibansk, with all its problems, decisions, and what have you, was invented by Schizophrenic, during a session in the Dive with Colleague, Chatterer, Bawler, Thinker, Wife, Dauber and all the rest. He did his inventing after he had tossed back a half litre of vodka and washed it down with five glasses of beer on an empty stomach. The reason he didn't eat was not any petty snobbishness but because the only people who could afford to eat in Ibansk at the time were speculators, bosses and their lackeys. Schizophrenic was in great form. The assembled company hung on his every word, particularly the informers, to whom the Ibanskians had begun to pay less and less attention, making them the butt of some very sharp jokes, thus demonstrating their native boldness. Deprived of their former power, the informers for a time felt rather melancholy. But they began to put even more zeal into the composition of their denunciations, which also gained in style, since the number of people with higher education had increased tenfold since 1913. Moreover, two million colonels had been demobilised, being fit for nothing else. It's true that they were very fit for a re-working of the theory of Ibanism. But were there enough vacancies? A hundred thousand, or two hundred if you really tried. But what was to be done with the rest?

So Schizophrenic drank his vodka and his beer and held forth. The rest drank their vodka and beer and hung on his words. The barmaid, Toad, who served them, brushed up against their faces with her scrawny posterior and her mighty bosom. The informers held their breath. There was a scent in the air of a secret organisation, of an attempt to overthrow the regime. 'I am categorically opposed,' yelled Teacher. 'You can't have Toad as the head of state. If you do, her future favourite, Puss, will seize power. And he'll establish a tyrannical regime even more savage than Boss's.' The ambitious Puss swelled visibly from his own importance, and promised to preserve the democratic freedoms. But only after all informers and executioners had been put behind bars. 'That'll never happen,' said Colleague. 'If it did, no-one would be left free.'

(427)

What times they were! It's hard now to believe that they ever existed at all. But those witnesses who have survived say that there is some truth in these reports.

But only two people accompanied Schizophrenic to his last home: Chatterer and Dauber. Even Neurasthenic didn't show up. His excuse was his official appointment as contestant against a thesis being defended by some fool or other. In fact he didn't turn up out of cowardice. 'I would have made a monument for him,' said Dauber. 'It wouldn't have cost me anything. But those bastards would only nick it. It's not only that they'd nick it, they'd destroy it and sling it on the rubbish tip.' 'Well, let them steal it,' said Chatterer. 'All the same, we ought to put something up.' 'I haven't time, just now, old man,' said Dauber. 'And frankly speaking, I've got other worries as well.' 'That's true,' said Chatterer. 'It's not really your business. Your business is the memorial to Hog. Whatever they say, that's a noble task. And the main thing is, it'll have an effect.' 'Please don't get angry,' said Dauber. 'Well, cheerio—I must dash.' Chatterer went to the office to order a metal plaque costing fifty roubles, which would bear the name and the dates of the brief and unrecognised life of a remarkable citizen of Ibansk. How times have changed!

The monstrous hymn

After Schizophrenic had invented Ibansk, this latter demanded its own special anthem. A closed competition was organised, with special invitations and entrance permits. And while they were waiting for the outcome, a poem by that winner of all prizes, Writer, a poem which has passed into the golden treasury of Ibanskian poetry, was appointed acting temporary anthem.

> Forging
>   together
>   a radiant
>   day after tomorrow,
> Seeing
>   the future
>   in time
>   through a prism

We do not recognise
                        nor desire
                                no . . . nothing,
Nothing but
            the Ism!
America
        And Europe—
                    up your arse
                            with them!
We
    weren't born
                yesterday
                        ourselves!
We'll overtake
            them
                    and show them
                            a fine pair
                                    Of buttocks!
Just envy us,
            parasites!
And if anyone
            has in mind
                    to scare us,
Watch out!
            You'll get an
                    enema
                            up your bum!
We shall
        inevitably,
                you mother fuckers, you,
Live
    in the glory
            of the total
                    Ism!
The Leader was much pleased with this anthem, for which he
was decorated with the Order of the Gigantic Prick for his feats
of arms, and was henceforth regarded as the author of the
anthem. Those who had taken part in the competition were
mobilised, for the Leader had decided on an unscheduled
re-edition of his more than complete works. This was to be

published, at the request of the workers, in verse, and to this end the most talented poets of the age were to be recruited. For his part, the young poet Snottyhanky, favourite of the nation's youth and the Secret Police, came in for a sound dressing down, and then a villa.

There is no music to the anthem. It is performed silently, all standing with their thumbs firmly pressed to their trouser seams, until the order is given to arrest everybody.

The first hour

All day the Mother had ploughed the infertile soil. As evening fell she unharnessed her mare, lay down on the stove and gave birth to a new baby boy. When she had recovered a little she gave her son a scrap of black bread wrapped in a rag, and went off to see to the beasts. But the baby began to cry. No-one could understand why, for all was going well. 'Oh, what a bawler he is,' said the Father. 'What're you crying for, you little silly? At all events it won't get you anywhere.' And the baby fell silent, as if he had understood it all from the very beginning. That is how Bawler appeared on the earth.

When Bawler finished primary school, his parents began to consider his future. 'Let him be a cobbler,' said the Father. 'He's got golden hands.' 'Let him learn the tailor's trade,' said the Mother. 'He is so intelligent.' 'He should stay on at school,' urged the teacher. 'I've been teaching kids for fifty years and I've never seen one like this. Children like this are born once in a hundred years. He could become the pride of the nation.' The Father and the Mother did not know what 'nation' meant, although the Boss's definition of 'Nation' had already been circulated throughout Ibansk, and they did not contradict the teacher. 'Let him stay on at school,' said the Father. 'We'll manage somehow.' 'Yes,' said the Mother bursting into tears, 'we'll manage. We won't let him starve to death here.' They found a few rags from somewhere. They sold his grandfather's Sunday boots, his Father's rifle, which hadn't been fired for years, and his Mother's wedding ring, which had been pre- served by some miracle. They put a brass cross round Bawler's neck and sent him off to his Uncle in the city. The Uncle, who lived in a communal apartment in a damp cellar, was in the kitchen filling a box of potatoes intended to last all winter. When Bawler arrived, his Uncle flung a dirty rag over the box, and cursed violently. 'You can live here if you like,' he said, and went out to drink the money his nephew had brought.

The neighbours swore for a long time. But people are kind when they own nothing, and in the evening someone fed the boy. Someone else said, 'Well, you might as well live here, since you're here.' 'Fine,' said Bawler. He rolled himself into a ball under a blanket which gave no warmth, and the following verses came into his head:

My belly is endlessly empty,
A-perished with cold now am I;
And I would go home to my mother—
Aye, if God gave me wings I would fly.
I'd ask her for bread and for blankets,
She'd give me her dear hand to hold,
And I'd stay here with her for ever,
And never go out in the cold.
But mother will say, oh my darling,
There's no warmth here, no food, and no rest.
No chance of success, no horizons,
So while there's time—go, that's the best.
My mother will say, oh my darling,
Just look at the void all around,
We'll die if we stay, but you slip away
While you can—without making a sound.

He thought that this was poetry. But it was really prose of unrelieved gloom. Ibanskian life was not yet ripe for poetry. Poetry could only be a lie.

How the time flew by! It's a long time now since the Father died for no reason at all. A long time too, since the Mother died, exhausted by her life of slave labour. A long time since his brothers and sisters had scattered out into the world and into an alien life. Long ago his wife had betrayed him and left him for a better life. His daughter had rejected him. His friends had disappeared. His accomplices had betrayed him. Nothing remained of the phantoms of his existence. 'What is all this?' Bawler asked himself. 'After all, I was kind, brave, hard working, generous, honest. So what happened?' 'That's life,' he answered his own question. 'Normal, ordinary life. This whole

(431)

story has passed through my mind without my paying any attention to it.'

New times

'But times have certainly changed for the better,' said Wife at Colleague's housewarming party, as she sat displaying her plump forty-year-old thighs adorned with purple veins and some foreign objects for which as yet there is no decent term in the Ibanskian language. 'We've achieved a great deal. I'm just back from England, for example. I was lecturing on the future development of shithouses in Ibanskian society. It was a huge success. I almost didn't need an interpreter, so it was me they sent rather than Troglodyte. Not Secretary, not even Academician.' 'I'm off to Italy tomorrow,' said Thinker, crossing one velvet-clad leg over the other, and stroking his bald patch with a hairy paw with its dirty finger nails. 'I'm going as leader of a group of unmarried mothers, for a symposium on the problems of artificial insemination without preservatives.' 'I entirely agree with you,' said Colleague. 'You can't turn the clock back. We won't allow it. Those times are past.' Fellow-worker laughed discreetly and respectfully, helped Colleague to the lavatory, all imitation marble, and unbuttoned his flies for him. An old member, pre-war vintage, emerged and tapped Fellow-worker on the shoulder in a friendly way. 'That's a good lad,' it said, and then spat full in his face. And they decided to write a book together on the conflict of ideas in our era.

A page of heroic history

When the Boss died, as unnaturally as he had lived (rumour has it that he choked on one of his own quotations), his prick was embalmed and placed in the Pantheon of Ibansk's greatest sons. But the honeymoon period lasted only a very short time. The prick had hardly had time to push its neighbours out of the way and take up the central position which it merited when the Hog came to the rostrum, and stumbling over every vowel, consonant and sibilant, delivered his famous denunciatory speech. The prick had to be taken out of the Pantheon and temporarily buried outside like any run-of-the-mill head of state. The tomb was sealed with a block of cement, as the prick had a tendency to draw attention to itself. The cement block bore the words: A leader of some movement or other at the beginning of the century. The Dive was renamed the Pavilion. Artist painted on the wall a new picture more in tune with the spirit of the times. It showed three Junoesque half-naked women with tanned faces and heels and one well-built half-naked Mechanic. The Mechanic (the name generally adopted to denote tractor drivers, stable lads and accountants) was clutching an unripe apple and wondering which of the women to give it to. The women were giggling with delight. The Mechanic's expression was reminiscent of the one observed on Hog's face in America when he had not been handed the next page of his speech, and was then handed the wrong one. If this apple had been a bottle of vodka, thought the Mechanic, I could have divided it equally between these three tarts. But this is a real problem, I tell you. I'll never manage it without cybernetics. Beneath the picture there was a marble plaque with some lines by Writer carved on it:

> Do not fart so loud, my girl.
> Not a word and hold your tongue.
> We shall overtake the Yanks
> In milk and meat before too long.

Underneath in small print there was a footnote: the word 'tongue' must be pronounced to rhyme with 'long'. The rising generation of Ibanskian intellectuals took to using the Pavilion for their drinking bouts and their long daring discussions. They called it The Three Graces to show that they were educated and had a refined critical attitude.

The birth of Ibansk

'Give me my postulates you like.' Schizophrenic said, 'and I will deduce from them any social system you like, just like that, to order. If you give me liberty and equality, from them I can deduce a system of paternalistic terror and privilege. If the premise you offer me is violence, I can deduce a system of fierce democracy. The content of the postulates is of no importance. To construct any society it is quite adequate to have a certain number of individuals and leave them to themselves. You give them a certain aim, and let them get on with creating whatever seems best for them. The definition of the aim is also of no importance. Let us, for instance, take your Ism, that invention

(433)

of a super-genius. The aim is merely a way of giving shape to history. If you perform a large enough number of experiments under identical conditions you will eventually produce all the logically possible variants. None of these has any historical necessity. From a strictly scientific point of view we can speak only of the degree of probability of the possible variants, which does not give any practical guidance if we are attempting to forecast specific events. Historical necessity is merely an ideological distortion of the past which seeks to justify the present and to provide some guarantees for the future.'

The Boy, who was sitting opposite Schizophrenic, and who had recently agreed to become a secret police informer, no longer understood a word of this drunken babble, so he shrugged his shoulders and decided to report simply that Schizophrenic was rejecting the fundamental principles of the Ism. 'An idea,' said Wife, 'becomes a material force only when it takes over the masses. That is an elementary truth.'

'It's elementary rubbish,' said Schizophrenic. 'In fact individuals don't give a fuck about ideas. All that is asked of them is that they shouldn't complain when ideas are attributed to them.'

After this Schizophrenic drained his vodka and invented Ibansk. Just like that. Simply for a joke. 'It's funny,' he said, finally. 'You only need to invent any old rubbish for it to be accepted as an historical law.' 'That's only half the trouble,' said Teacher. 'Take care. As a rule people become the victims of their own inventions. One day, just after the war, a friend and I decided . . .'

The second hour

One day there was a school inspection. It was discovered that Bawler was wearing a brass cross round his neck and that his shirt was verminous. The cross was thrown away and the shirt was sent to be laundered by a member of the parents' committee. It fell to pieces while it was being washed. There was a meeting of the staff council where it was decided to give Bawler a voucher to get a new shirt. Now see here, they told him, just you remember the way the state looks after you, and study hard. There was no point in trying to persuade Bawler to study. He studied so hard that the parents even of model pupils began to get worried. When the Special Commission on Professional Career Prospects decided that Bawler would become a tailor (since he was the quickest at threading a needle), the parents were somewhat pacified. But the Commission was disbanded.

Bawler was a good friend. He was liked even by the best students because he didn't stop them coming top of the class and had no ambitions in that direction himself. In any case the adults took good care to see that that never happened. But one day the maths teacher rebelled and said that minds like Bawler's appeared only once in a hundred years—he was one in a million. But the teacher was under suspicion, which this of course confirmed. And as a punishment, Bawler's marks were reduced.

He had no-one to protect him, and he learnt to be a fighter. There was no-one to look after him, and so he tried all the clubs. He had no home and so he spent most of his time in other people's houses. And he saw everything. Once he was invited home by the boy who sat next to him, a handsome well-brought-up child, who was treated with deference even by the headmaster, and who was personally taken home each day by his teacher to protect him from attacks by hooligans. Bawler was quite overcome by the number of rooms in Neighbour's apartment, and by the abundance of beautiful and incomprehensible objects. Back home in the village, he said, we just had a one-room izba. And such a crowd of us! Six children for a start. The others had left home. And that's not counting the grown-ups. We had a lot of fun! That was when there was enough bread, of course. Neighbour's beautiful mother gave Bawler a piece of cake. 'What's that?' Bawler asked. 'It's cake,' said the mother. 'Have you never had cake before? Just try it!' Bawler tried it, and choked on a crumb. 'Don't you like it?' asked the mother. 'No,' said Bawler. 'My mother works from dawn until late at night like an ox and we don't even get enough bread to fill us up!' 'That is a provocation,' said Neighbour's papa. 'I would like to be your friend,' said Neighbour. 'But papa has forbidden it.' 'But what about equality?' asked Bawler. 'We're for equality,' said Neighbour, 'but against egalitarianism,' and he moved to another desk. The seat next to Bawler stayed empty. After school the headmaster sent for him. A sheath knife lay on the headmaster's desk. 'Here he is, the bandit,' said the teacher.

'This knife was found in his overcoat pocket. He is a member of a gang.' Bawler wanted to say that it wasn't his knife, that he didn't own an overcoat, but he decided to stay silent. He realised that it would be useless to speak. He was expelled from the school, and there were demands that he should be sent to a juvenile detention centre. But soon Neighbour's papa was arrested, along with the teacher. The students were told that they were enemies of the people and that they had conspired to get Bawler expelled. But Bawler didn't believe anyone. Many years later he met Neighbour who now held a very important position. 'In our society, as you know,' said Neighbour, before the question had even been asked, 'children do not have to answer for the sins of their parents.' 'Agreed,' said Bawler. 'But parents should feel responsible for their children if they ever want to be in a position to be avenged.'

A page of heroic history

By his nature the Boss was the most mediocre of mediocre men. There was absolutely nothing to distinguish him from his contemporaries except perhaps a quite immoderate tendency to be an informer. And he spoke like any ordinary major statesman of average illiteracy. But when the possibility of becoming the leader opened before him he noticed one very important law which governed careers in leadership. People adore it when a leader is remarkable not for his intellect or his beauty but for some visible defect, for example that he is lame, hunchbacked, a stammerer, bald, and so on. People do not like brilliant handsome men. People like someone they can pity. When a pitiable leader suddenly announces that two times two is four, the nation is ecstatic. Look, look, they cry. That's our fool for you. He may look like an idiot but he's got the mind of an academician. He's not as daft as he looks! So the Boss decided to acquire a defect worthy of a leader—a leader for all times and for all nations. What should it be? The answer was not far to seek—an accent. Scientists gathered at a special secret conference and began to consider what accent the Boss should acquire to make him totally different from everybody else. The decision was taken: the accent of a baboon. This time at least the Boss showed outstanding talent. Within a few years he learnt to speak with such a brilliant baboon accent that any Ibanskian, even half asleep, could tell the Boss's voice from any other sound on earth. As a final check of the power his accent gave him over the masses, the Boss visited a baboon breeding station. The male baboons took the Boss to be a female and violated him en masse. After this the Boss acquired a slight stammer and walked all bow-legged. His left arm was agitated by a nervous tic. All this greatly enhanced the effect. The time has come, he decided. And he called a meeting. 'Sithee, Ah've geet a propozishun,' he said to his bewildered colleagues. 'As fra' neaw, Ah'm not joost t'leader, Ah'm t'che-e-ef!' His competitors began to stammer, but they couldn't begin to resist him. 'Na'then, get shut o' them boogers,' said the chief. And they were all got rid of. The scientists as well. So that the secret should never be revealed.

The geography of Ibansk

Where is Ibansk? If this question is to be answered on a proper scientific basis, we must have recourse to the most lunatic ideas dreamt up by the most progressive and after them the most stupid physicists of our super-scientific age. But lunatic ideas do not exist, although according to secret police files there are very many lunatic people who have ideas. If lunatic ideas did exist they would almost certainly have been discovered by the physicists themselves, of whom there are almost as many in Ibansk as there are members of the secret police. And in Teacher's opinion, the problem itself is improperly formulated. It should have been posed thus: how do you get into Ibansk? It would then immediately become clear that the problem is very simple. To get into Ibansk one must write an application, provide a character reference, fill in a questionnaire and furnish a *curriculum vitae*. The *curriculum vitae* must include the names of all deceased relatives, both one's own and everybody else's. They must be prepared to sign a guarantee that they will stay where they are and that they won't tell anybody. One must pay one's dues, appear before a commission of pensioners in senile decay, turn out one's pockets, and agree to everything. After one has done all this one no longer needs to know where Ibansk is to be found because one is there already. A much more difficult problem is to know where to find what cannot be found in Ibansk. But to do this one needs a denunciation.

Ibansk occupies almost the entire land surface and has frontiers with every country in the world. These frontiers are a source of great irritation to the Ibanskians. Not because they are not allowed to cross them. They have grown used to this in as much as they have never acquired the habit of being allowed out. What irritates them is that there are in this world fortunate people who through no merit of their own live abroad. Here we are, grafting away for a pittance, suffering, never seeing a thing, while Over There they . . . !!!

Left-wing intellectuals began to rack their brains to discover the whereabouts of this centre of population populated by no-one, which has common frontiers with all the world and which pokes its nose into everybody's business. But at this moment that avant-garde poet Snottyhanky, who it is recalled, received a slight censure and much consolation, stepped forward and said:

> Gloomy reflections press upon
> My immature and virgin mind.
> Where is Ibansk? Not here. Not there.
> It's right up your behind.

'Hark at him!' said the left-wing intellectuals, exchanging knowing glances. They had not yet realised that their time was long past.

The weather

'Wi cain't expect as eawd Moother Naycher'll gi'us enny prezents,' said the Boss. So he made an order that the best possible weather should be established in Ibansk, bearing in mind the season of the year, local conditions and the needs of agriculture. The people went to work with a will. They gave up their Saturdays to voluntary work. A plan was prepared. On the initiative of textile workers fierce frosts were introduced six months before the onset of winter, interrupted only by blizzards and even fiercer frosts. 'Loife's gerrin' better all't'toime. Loife's gerrin' gradely 'appier, an' awl,' said the Boss. The economists calculated that the Ibanskians had already overtaken Europe and were close behind America in terms of the number of degrees of temperature per head of population. The philosophers declared unanimously that the pole of heat had been transferred to Ibansk as the classics had forecast. (It seems that there was some confusion over the type of degrees in question.) And there was no significance, the philosophers said, in the fact that we were still behind America. In fact we weren't behind America. Although it was true that we had fewer degrees per head of population than they had, our degrees worked better because they were not being put to the service of the exploiting classes, but to that of working people.

After the Boss's death these meteorological excesses were corrected. 'Och, mon, we cannae expect ony bluidy favours frae tha' . . . wha' the fuck d'ye ca' yon hoor . . . aye, Mither fucking Nature,' said Hog. 'It's time the noo tae tak'on yon bluidy Yanks. Maize likes fine a bi' o' sun.' And so a fierce heat was introduced, occasionally giving place to hot dry winds and even fiercer heat. The Ibanskians sold all their furs to foreigners, gave up meat and began to eat bananas.

After Hog had been deposed the usual wet and muddy weather returned of its own accord, succeeded by torrential downpours which turned first to snow and then to frost.

Periodization

The history of Ibansk falls into three unequal halves. The first half is known as the Lost Period. That is the biggest half. During this period part of the Ibanskian people were in the camps, another part was set to guard them, and a third were preparing the cadres for the other two. And altogether they were successfully engaged in the building of the Ism. This period is described in detail in the works of Truth-teller. No-one in Ibansk read these books because they contained nothing but lies. For instance, Truth-teller alleges that during this period fifty million Ibanskians were suffering their just desserts, while according to the files of the secret police themselves there were only 49,999,999.

The second half was the Perplexed Period, referred to in Western historical writing as the Accidental Disarraynaissance. This is the smallest half. This period is described in part in the works of Double-dealer, which have also not been read by anyone in Ibansk.

The third half is the Prosperous Period. It is difficult to assess its duration since it has only just begun. But it seems that it could well exceed the other two in every respect. There is no-one left to describe this period, as Truth-teller has been expelled, Double-dealer has fled the country and the Shamizdat writers have all been jailed. And although Double-dealer prophesied that a holy place never stays empty, this prophecy has only come true in the case of places much closer to home.

The difficulty of dividing the history of Ibansk into periods lies in the fact that the third period has begun on the one hand, but on the other it has not begun. Or, to put it more accurately, it has begun below but has not yet begun above. The people of Ibansk, with the exception of the most elevated leadership, have already moved in to this third period. They are ready for anything and are surprised that they haven't had their starting orders from above. But the highest leadership issues no orders. It is living on the illusions of the second period and is trying to behave decently. But is it possible to deal decently with our people? So it is no use for the authorities to be patient; there will come a time when they will grow angry because they see that no one is obeying them.

In brief, said Chatterer, what is actually happening is of no importance. What is important is the state of consciousness with which the Ibanskian intellectual regards his life. And he thinks in this way. Liberalism is over. The old leadership will soon be removed. The new leaders will accuse the old of having had too liberal an attitude towards opposition and of flirting with the West. In other words, *sauve-qui-peut*. The Ibanskian intellectuals do not believe in a brighter future and so there will not be a brighter future. It will not come, no matter what the leadership intends. It will not come because of what has already happened. And regardless of the possibilities, they cannot prevent the consequences of the past. For the future cannot amend the past. The most it is capable of is to become itself a decent past. But that only concerns future generations who at this moment are only just learning to walk.

The third hour

For the summer holidays Bawler went back to the village. It was just the time when the peasants were beginning to be driven into the corrective farms. They were of course being driven as volunteers. The man from the ministry delivered a speech in which he described in glowing terms the earthly paradise which was on the point of coming to the countryside. Everyone who had not managed to escape in time signed on the dotted line. 'Well, men,' said the half-tipsy ministry man, 'not too many regrets at seeing the back of the old regime? Say what you feel—there's nothing to be afraid of.' There were almost no men left in the village but the ministry man addressed the women as men as a mark of respect. 'I am not sorry on my own account,' said the Father. 'I am going to die anyway. It's the cattle I feel sorry for. They're going to die for no reason at all.' The Father was seized. He was dragged away from the meeting immediately for anti-Ibanskian agitation. No-one did anything to help him. And Bawler came to understand one of the elementary truths of existence. If the leadership thinks that they are doing you good, then they are indeed doing you good. The leadership can do no evil. And if they kindly allow you to be even fractionally against, it's at that very moment that they want you most of all to be for. The most hated enemy of the leadership is anyone bold enough to take advantage of the freedom conferred on him by that same leadership. If the leadership allows something it does not wish to allow, that is the most stringent form of ban. After this Bawler never again believed in official permission. And Bawler understood, too, that if a man decides to become a man he will always be alone. No-one will come to his defence. From that time onwards he can depend only on himself and on no-one else.

For five versts, Bawler, weeping bitterly, followed the cart in which the drunken bosses were taking away his sober, quiet, kind, wise Father, who had never done any harm to anyone and who had felt such pity for the innocent cattle. When he was returning home he passed through a neighbouring village where he was surrounded by a gang of kids who had decided to beat him up because he was a weakling, according to the old ancestral tradition. Bawler flew into a terrible rage. He beat up all ten of the kids so severely that their parents complained to the authorities in the town and demanded that he should be sent to jail. The apple never falls far from the tree, they said.

The methodology of research

When Double-dealer began to write his book about the Period of Perplexity, he found himself confronted with the problem of the methods of research and exposition. And he discovered the following.

The life of the Ibanskians is very lacking in events and almost totally lacking in spiritual experiences. Of course even here there are sometimes extraordinary happenings—for example earthquakes, air crashes, epidemics of diarrhoea, droughts, foot and mouth disease, palace revolutions and just punishments which overtake people who think. Sometimes one even comes across dissident thinkers who have been made so by the pernicious influence of the West, and they are destroyed in the egg. Sometimes . . . But no-one ever tells the Ibanskians about anything like that. Why should their radiant and joyful working days be clouded over by trivia of that kind! The only emotions which the Ibanskians are allowed to experience are joy at their successes, gratitude for the care the government exercises towards them, and pride in the wisdom of the leadership. So the means of ordinary literature are not suited to describe Ibanskian life. The very fact of the existence of great literature is an indication that something actually exists which is a worthy object of its attention. If a country has no great literature, that does not necessarily mean that the country has no talented writers, or that the government suppresses them and gives them no opportunity to develop a true literature. It rather means that there is simply nothing in the country the description of which would produce genuine literature even if there were any talent, no matter how weak or how severely repressed it might be. What is frightening is not so much that writers are not allowed to write, but that there is nothing for them to write about. What should writers consider? Should they write about trades union or party meetings? About standing in queues? About the difficulty of finding an apartment or of getting a rise? About the business of finding acquaintances who could help to get your son into university?

From a scientific point of view Ibanskian society is a huge and complex system in its dimensions and in the diversity of its elements, while remaining a primitive organisation which seeks total uniformity, and which is stabilised at a minimum level of positive parameters and a maximum level of negative parameters. And as the distinction between parameters as positive or negative is relative, and depends on instructions from above, on the same basis Ibanskian society can be seen as a social system with an optimally high level of organisation, extremely diverse, and stabilised on a maximum of positive and the minimum of negative parameters. It was not by chance that Journalist said in his book that in Ibansk everything was exactly the same as in the West, but just a little bit the opposite. So, if scientific methods can be appropriate for a study of the Ibanskian way of life, this is only the case if they make an abstraction from the distinction between Ibansk and the West. Why, in such a case, should one risk one's life by writing a study of Ibansk if one could win approval by doing exactly the same thing about the West? So Wife, Sociologist, Thinker, Neurasthenic and others do not just happen to spend their time writing about the West. They know very well what they are doing. But is what they are doing understood, either in Ibansk or in the West?

'So then what method should I adopt?' asked Double-dealer. 'None at all,' said Chatterer. 'This crap isn't worth studying. Just write what passes through your mind. The secret police will work out for themselves the methods you've used.' 'That's all very well,' said Double-dealer. 'But I don't want to go the same way as Truth-teller.' 'Don't then,' said Chatterer. 'Don't think about it. At all events, there is no other way.'

Singers

During the Period of Perplexity there appeared in Ibansk a great number of singers who wrote their own words and music and performed their songs themselves. They usually gave their performances in private apartments in return for a drink and a bite of food. That was largely because food and drink were a necessary element both for the performer and his audience. Among the singers the one who stood out most sharply was Singer, because of his clearly defined social and political orientation. He had become a singer quite by chance. He once went to a party of this kind, picked up a guitar and suddenly began to sing:

Hear this, you insects, henceforth this is law!
From at this moment, now and ever more.
The powers that be will rule how you behave
From birth to death, from cradle to the grave.
The food you eat, the drink you drink—*they*'ll choose

(443)

Your style of pants, of shirts, of socks, of shoes.
They will decide the kind of books you'll read;
And what you write—that too will be decreed.
Yoghurt will keep your bodies fit and strong.
As for your minds—you won't go too far wrong
With radio news of harvesting of grain,
Or that the plan's overfulfilled again.
When at the polls, you'll vote the way you're told,
To show commitment—otherwise we'll scold.
To let you see what's going on abroad
TV will show how World Cup goals were scored.
But joys like this demand a certain price,
Just you remember—that is my advice.
What price? you ask! What's that to you, I pray—
It's our affair. All *you* need do is pay.

The authorities were not over fond of songs like that. But the times were such that they looked at them through half closed lids. The children of the authorities relayed the songs in their homes and their country villas with all the power of their tape recorders. The authorities themselves listened to them when they were alone, saying to themselves: he isn't half going it, the bastard! All the same, there's some truth in what he says! But what can it achieve? Nothing can be done about it anyway.

My position and my station
Mean that I must know the law;
Wave your arms in desperation—
And you're in the quicksand's maw.

And the authority ordered his wife to bring another bottle of brandy. And he drank it on his own, locked in his study.

Chronology

What Western historians have called the Period of Perplexity is a period in the history of Ibansk which falls into the period between the period when the Boss was the leader and the period when the Leader became the boss. But Western historians suffer from an incorrect metaphysical method and an erroneous idealistic theory. So they have failed to understand the main thing, and have got the rest confused. Ibanskian historians unanimously reject the existence of the Period of

(444)

Perplexity for the indisputable reason that in the history of Ibansk there has been, is, and always will be, only one period—the Period of Prosperity. In Ibansk there is a distinction between two degrees—the lower and the higher. But these are degrees and not periods. Degrees are described by the concepts 'lower' and 'higher', and periods by the concepts 'earlier' and 'later'. Since the higher degree has not yet arrived and is constantly being postponed for very weighty reasons, for the time being the lower degree is acting as the higher. So it is, by order, higher than everything which ever was or is now Over There in the West. And there is no demand for any division into periods. Western historians, of course, know nothing about this and deliberately keep quiet for the benefit of capital. In a word, there is no principal difference between the periods of the Boss and the Leader and they both follow the same general line.

One Western theoretician, who had studied in secret in the Ibansk Institute of Progressive Professorship because he wanted to ridicule his Western colleagues without giving himself away, posed the following question: Was there in fact any period during that period which Western historians call the Period of Perplexity but which in the view of Ibanskian historians never existed? The Ibanskian historians sought guidance from the highest authorities. It's none of your bloody business, was the answer from above, and they published a memorandum which said that the Western historians were grossly interfering in the internal affairs of our past and we could not tolerate this. We do not interfere in your internal affairs. Do what you like, but bear in mind that the entire written history of mankind is nothing more than the pre-history of Ibanskian history and a survival of the past in human consciousness. The imprudent historian was accused of anti-Ibanism and his name was stricken from the rolls. After that he had to be recalled from abroad and retired on a pension.

'If the Period of Perplexity existed,' said Teacher, 'it must have begun significantly earlier and have ended earlier still—before it started. In other words it ended before it began, and began after it had ended.' And Teacher produced an incontrovertible formula which proved this with brilliant clarity. Chatterer said that Teacher had found an accurate mathematical expression of Schizophrenic's ideas. 'Immortality awaits you,' he said. 'I've been called to see the investigator tomorrow,' said Teacher. 'What for?' asked Chatterer. 'It's about Bawler,' said Teacher. 'That's the end of the Period of Perplexity,' said Chatterer. As for the beginning, there was none.

But Chatterer was mistaken.

There was a beginning.

The fourth hour

When he reached the top class, Bawler took part in the mathematical olympiad. He solved all the problems quicker than anyone else and suggested several original variants of the answers. But no-one had any personal interest in his success. And he was not suitable for a variety of other reasons. He wasn't even included among the honourable mentions. And he realised that it was not possible to be talented without the approval of the collective and of the leadership, and that in Ibansk people of talent were appointed from the most deserving candidates. In Ibansk true talents are not revealed through results or recognition, but by the way people behave and through their personal destiny.

At this time Bawler fell in love and began to write strange poems.

> To advance the rising generation,
> Giving them a good clear way ahead,
> We will carry out extermination,
> And construct our socism instead.

The girl grew alarmed and asked him to write something more lyrical. So he wrote:

> Oh, what joy there is about us
> As the snows begin to thaw,
> And the birds beneath my window
> Sing their waking song at dawn,
> And the tinkling, chattering streamlets
> Babble down the mountainside.
> Then the fear comes in to greet me:
> I will soon be put inside.

She was even more frightened, and left him for another. On the way she dropped his poems in at secret police headquarters. And so Bawler's file acquired its first document. There's something fishy here, the secret police decided. And they instructed

(446)

Bawler's friends to keep an eye on him—an order which they gladly obeyed.

The essence of a period

The essence of an historical period is revealed by its results and its consequences, i.e. after the period is over. But if the result of a period is the absence of results, and its consequences are the liquidation of possible consequences, then the essence of the historical period can be established only before it has started, on the principle: what might have been if it had happened. The essence of such a period can be determined potentially but not actually. The Period of Perplexity is just such a one.

So what is the essence of this period?

Thinker's opinion

The progressive forces of society lost their head when they came face to face with the unexpected possibilities of progress, did not know what they should do for the sake of progress, and did not make the progress which they could have made had they not lost their heads. The reactionary forces took advantage of the confusion of the progressive forces, gathered their strength and foreclosed the possibility of progress. When the progressives came to their senses and worked out what should be done, it was too late.

Troglodyte's conclusion

The theoretical leader of the reactionary forces, Troglodyte, on the basis of the experience of this period reached a conclusion which was valuable in practice, but useless in theory because of the inability of the reactionary forces to follow it: if you want to sow panic in the ranks of the progressives, you must suddenly present them with a clear opportunity to achieve progress. This must be done suddenly not only for the benefit of the progressives but also for the benefit of us reactionaries. And after a little time, when they imagine that they have beaten us, seize them with your bare hands and make them into even more reactionary reactionaries than we ourselves are.

Neurasthenic's opinion

The progressive forces have lost the chances which were offered them because of wasting their time on trivia—family quarrels, and the hunt for academic degrees, positions, prizes, trips abroad, apartments and so on.

Secretary's comment
Another leading theoretician of the reactionary forces observed that the progressives should be given everything they dream of in secret but never mention openly. If, for example, a progressive declares that such and such a proposition of the Ism is out of date, this must be understood as a desire to become a Doctor of Science.

Academician's opinion
The leadership lost its head, coming face to face with the unexpected possibility of making progress, and showed itself incapable of directing this initiative along the right lines. Somebody should have been sacked, and I should have been appointed. I would have shown them. . . .

Theoretician's opinion
We have allowed excessive softness to be shown towards the dissidents, who, under the influence of ideological sabotage from the West, have begun to spread smears and slanders.

The Bitch's opinion
They should all have been put up against a wall.

Dauber's opinion
FUCK YOU ALL!

Teacher's opinion
This is all fiction. Here, look at this formula for the organisation of social systems of the Ibansk variety. Seen from one angle we have a perfect organisation and a perfect order. From another angle we have a total disorganisation and a complete disorder. See, they coincide. It's true that they could be given plus or minus signs. But what difference would that make? In all the subsequent calculations they are squared. And anyway, all values of order are merely a mirror image of the values for disorder, and vice versa. So it is a matter of complete indiffer-

ence whether we consider the period as the introduction of disorder or the restoration of order. This period showed a real growth in the index of organisation. But that is on quite a different level and for quite different reasons. From this point of view your social factors are expressed in such negligible quantities that it is quite impossible to take them into account in the calculations. Your problems, my dear intellectuals, do not even exist from a scientific point of view as a real factor in social life.

Neurasthenic's objection
In periods like this very small causes can produce very large effects. Your formulae should be corrected to take into account the increase in social values.

Teacher's objection
As far as your small causes of big effects are concerned, that is a typical prejudice of the old philosophy. Mathematically speaking, if the causes and effects are commensurate, then the effects cannot be larger than their causes. As for the corrections you ask me to make, I have tried to do so. Even if their indices reach the value of infinity, the social parameters produce a result which is significantly large, but fictitious. It is an illusion.

Slanderer's comment
I do not understand the reasoning. But the conclusion is correct.

Bawler's comment
Here's how you could rewrite your formula. Now you'll no longer be able to get these paradoxical results.

'Bravo,' said Teacher. 'You're a genius. That's a real discovery!' 'I'll make you a present of it,' said Bawler. 'But this discovery has one weak point. To demolish this system would need an amount of force close to infinity. Where is it to be found?' 'Or close to zero,' said Teacher, 'if you combine our formulae. Then it would destroy itself without any effort whatsoever.' 'Yes,' said Bawler. 'But how long would it take?'

Chatterer's opinion

You have talked about reactionary forces, progressive forces, the leadership, the intelligentsia, the intellectuals, the opposition, dissidents and so forth. As if they are some kind of homogeneous entities, whose members are in more or less stable contact with each other and who behave as some kind of whole towards the outside world. But they are no such thing. These are just words convenient for purposes of classification. In reality there are no such groups, combinations or conglomerates. For instance, Truth-teller never once met Double-dealer, and didn't know of his existence until very recently. He was even hostile to him initially. The same thing is true of Double-dealer and Dauber. In reality there are hundreds of millions of individuals and hundreds of millions of groups of individuals linked by thousands of millions of threads into some kind of whole. The people you have been talking about are dispersed in the cells of this whole in the most diverse places—in groups, in organisations. The men you have mentioned occupy cells in this whole. Even if they communicate, as we do for example, they do not form social groups. Even if we accept the possibility of some combination of effort by the intellectuals, for instance in the form of some particular journal, you still won't change the system in principle. An intellectual who works on this hypothetical journal is still a member of some other group, organisation or institution. He must be listed as a worker there, must actually work there, must draw his salary, experience the pressure of that particular collective, and so on. If he allows himself to overstep the mark in his hypothetical group, he will immediately find that action is taken against him in his real social group. And the same goes for all the categories of people you have referred to. Even to the leadership. They make a grave mistake in the West when they regard these groups of people here as being analogous with their own. Even the expression 'Ibanskian scientists' has a different meaning here and there. Here the expression can be a general term to indicate individuals so dispersed through Ibanskian society that it becomes impossible to define the meaning of the term. In this case, the only terms that can have any meaning are those such as 'an Ibanskian scientist', 'an Ibanskian intellectual', 'an Ibanskian artist', and so on. Alternatively expressions like 'Ibanskian scientists', 'Ibanskian artists', 'Ibanskian writers' and so on could indicate the Academy of Sciences—an official organisation embracing thousands of bodies, in which the number of people who could be described as 'real scientists' is incredibly small, or the Artists' Union, made up of thousands of people of quite different kinds and styles, or the Writers' Union, and so on. It is curious that all these things are widely known but that this knowledge appears to exert no influence on the way people think. And this suits the official point of view down to the ground. Ibanskian writers have held Truth-teller up to ridicule. In the West—astonishment: how could they do such a thing! Yet they couldn't have done anything else, since they are social organisations which live by their own social laws, and not according to the principles of honour, dignity, independent opinions and so on of some mythical writers' organisation. Ibanskian scientists have attacked Double-dealer. In the West people are shocked: how could they do such a thing! They're scientists after all!

Neurasthenic's opinion
It is true that if at this moment say fifty more or less important intellectuals got together and made a joint political statement, the effect would be shattering. But try to get these intellectuals together for just one single action! It's not just by chance, incidentally, that there was such a violent attack on the signatories. That smelt far too dangerously like an opposition grouping.

Chatterer's opinion
So I am inclined to take the view that there was no perplexity. There was rather a stripping bare of the social mechanisms of our life. Our social system operated in the full view of everyone, calmly, unhurriedly, like some autonomous, pitiless machine which spontaneously established a state of things which suited it better. It merely transformed itself slightly, and adapted itself to changing circumstances. And from an historical point of view it did so with amazing rapidity.

Bawler's thought

Soon all this mess will be over. And what'll be left of all their chatter? Everything will drop back into its rut. And no-one will have a thought to spare for all those who have worked in silence through this period of intrigues. They've already been partly eliminated. Soon they'll get round to the rest. And more little boys and girls will have to be born who are capable of sacrificing everything—or at least a great deal. But will they ever be born?

Live like everyone else

I asked without pause
How to live by the laws,
And still be completely contented;
But I have to admit
That the answers I get
Tend to drive me quite simply demented.
Your foes and your friends
All lie without end;
They yell, 'It's a most complex question.
Tobacco and booze is
Out. So are floozies.
You must follow the bosses' direction.'
And the years they fly by
And people still try
To dissuade you from giving up trying.
The purer your life,
The harder your strife,
None will help you when they hear you sighing.
From boredom supreme
You sometimes will scream
The howl of a stricken hyena,
You'll stay silent from pain
Or you'll shriek yet again,
But none will condone your demeanour.
But it surely should be
Worth seeking the key
To living your life standing tall;
Though all are combined
To agree with one mind
That 'you'd better live our way, that's all'.

'But really, there's nothing to whine about,' said Sociologist, reaching the conclusion of his expert report on Singer's song. 'Life in Ibansk has greatly improved. Look at the facts. It's only smoked sausage that has disappeared—there's still plenty of boiled sausage about. The price of meat hasn't risen by 500 per cent, as was expected, but only by 350 per cent. Thirty dissidents haven't been sent to jail, as was planned—only 29.3. And even there they didn't get ten years as they should have done, only seven, with four extra in special regime labour camps.' 'They think they can do what they like,' said Colleague. 'That's true,' said Wife. 'They're constantly getting in the way and stopping us from getting on with our work.'

The truthful lie

This is the way things happen here, said Neurasthenic to Journalist. If it's publicly avowed that some trend in scientific research has been undervalued, that means that it's been completely obliterated. If it's admitted that in some cases doctor's degrees have been awarded not according to merit, it means that doctor's degrees have become a way of building a career, getting rich, winning prestige, of blinding people as to your shortcomings. It isn't a matter of the deceptive form that these official declarations are made in. People have got used to that, and anyone who wants to can make allowances for the system. The fact is that the processes giving rise to such situations, which are criticised even at an official level, take place in the full view of everyone. Their consequences are clear from the very beginning. But there are no forces who can resist them. For example, take this business of the doctor's degrees. In my area alone several hundred people a year have their doctoral theses accepted. Do you think these people are scientists? Even by our debased criteria they're almost a hundred per cent ignorant charlatans. But these are front-rank men, their closest henchmen (who are in fact the authors of their masters' lousy books), careerists on the make, members of highly placed organisations and so on. They are passed by section meetings, departmental meetings, meetings of the academic council, editorial committees, commissions. Everyone knows what's going on. But everyone pretends to be discussing new ideas, valuable results, deep thoughts. It's just one farce after another.

(453)

Year after year. But make a squeak of protest and you'll be torn to pieces. And in a situation like that, if by some miracle a genuinely talented productive scientist does emerge, they'll manage somehow or other to crush him. Or to bring him to heel—as an advertisement. Or rather as a cover. But there you are, you can begin to see the outcome of these farces, which are an embarrassment even to those who take part in them. Steps have to be taken—and they are being taken. How? By another series of farces played by the same actors. They're prepared to carry out any orders, to put any measures into execution. But in their own way, taking good care that they don't suffer themselves in any way. For example, stricter rules of selection for candidates for the doctor's degree have just been introduced. And who were the first victims of the new order? Those who should normally have been the first to become doctors. You talk to me about higher authorities? They're farces as well. Different, but still farces. You may think it's their job to make sure that our doctors should be real scientists? But for them a real scientist, like a real artist or a real writer or what have you is their bitterest enemy. If it's authentic—they're against it. What they want is plaster imitations, disguise, a touch of rouge. Their real business is giving orders, discussing, taking decisions. And making sure that the authorities at a lower level react in the right way in their own farcical productions.

The fifth hour

It was a friend's birthday. Everyone had a drink or two, and got talking. The conversation turned to the problem of power and individual freedom. Who gave them the right to use me as a pawn? said Bawler. There's no such right. It's not a right. It's a gross intrusion. To talk of right presupposes freedom. But here we have a deliberate perversion of elementary principles. Legalised interference is one thing, but if you want to use the word 'right', you have to speak in terms of an arbitrary right or, if you don't like this term and would prefer to appear human, you could call it 'right number one'. The legalisation of resistance to arbitrary measures is something else again. Here we must speak of a right-freedom. Of course, this could provoke unwanted associations. As everyone knows, we here are living in the paradise of liberty. Very well, then, let's refer to it as 'right

(454)

number two'. And, say what you will, 'right number one' is the reverse of 'right number two'. Constraint is the opposite of freedom, even though they both concern the same phenomena, and each is defined linguistically in terms of the other. You talk to me of revolutions, of wars, of building sites, of space flight, of dams, of exhibitions, and other indications of the correctness of the doctrines under which we live. But what's all this got to do with me? That's their business, not mine. I never chose to be born into this world. I certainly never asked to be. I didn't sign a declaration the day I was born promising to approve of everything they do. I found the world as it had become quite independently of me. I owe nothing to anyone. I should repay the cost of my education? And how much did it cost—not a lot. And who am I supposed to pay? And what about all those years my mother worked for nothing? Is that state philanthropy as well? I worked on the corrective farm myself, and what did I get for it? Damn all. Very well, I'll work. And they'll get back ten times what they've given me. But that's another story. No point in going on. My moral right is to accept some of the things in this world I've been presented with, and to reject others. For me the world is a primordial basis.

His friends did not understand Bawler's harangue. They understood only that Bawler knew and understood something forbidden, something which was inaccessible to them. And they wrote a joint denunciation to the secret police asking them to save their comrade who had fallen under some evil influence. That there was external influence could be in no doubt at all. For surely Bawler, who had been to the same school as they had, read the same books, was worse dressed than they, ate less than they did, went to the cinema less, never went to the theatre at all and had no wise grown-up friends, couldn't have thought all that out for himself. And the words he used were not our kind of words.

In the evening an unknown young man came down to the cellar and asked Bawler to come for a walk. Bawler instantly understood what it was all about, and began to gather his meagre possessions together. Inside he didn't find things too bad. For the first time in his life he had a bed to himself and three meals a day. Important bosses had long talks with him. He left them bewildered with his questions and opinions. They wanted to know who had taught him to talk this way. But no-one had taught him. The things he said they found new and astonishing. And they couldn't relate them to anyone they knew about. They decided to let him out for a spell to watch his contacts. And he went straight back to the village without going home or saying a word to anyone. From this moment on he took all the major decisions in his life on the spur of the moment. It seemed to be the only effective way of staying at liberty.

Six months went by. One day late in the autumn a neighbour told Bawler's mother that someone had been asking about her son in the nearby town. Grabbing a crust of bread and a handful of small change, Mother rushed to the field where Bawler was working. Run, flee, she said. She didn't shed so much as a single tear. But when he had gone and she realised she would never see him again, she fell on the grey, wet, cold ground and bit it in anguish. Help him, Lord, she whispered. That's all I ask. Just help him. He's my whole life. All my suffering. And yours, too, Lord. What are you without him?

At the railway station there were some drunken peasants who'd been enlisted for the Far North. They sat, grey and pitiful, moaning in a plaintive monotone:

Soon we'll hear that mournful whistle,
Soon the train will round the bend,
Come to take our loved one from us,
Come to take away our friend.

Bawler jumped on board a goods train as it slowed down to pass through the station, and hid in the middle of a load of logs. An icy wind blew through the cracks. Never mind, he told himself. You'd better get used to it. This is only the beginning. His tears fell on to the crust of bread, making it soft and tasty.

If only someone had invented an instrument which would make visible a young pure soul after it had been through a pitiless pogrom! How innocent the battlefields of our great wars would look in comparison!

No-one would ever be able to forget that sight!

When they picked up his traces in the town, he managed to get away and join the army as a volunteer, and they lost sight of him. They only caught up with him many years later.

You will find no hiding place,
You'll find no escaping us;

For you're a no-one, vile and base,
But we're the mighty working class.

The sun is forever

After many years of cold and damp, the Sun came out. On the radio it was announced that even the weather was joining in the celebration of our successes. At the same time there was news of the spread of the class war, of poverty, of price increases and wage cuts Over There. The Leader broadcast on television that this had been achieved under the wise leadership of the leaders he led. The freely trusting Ibanskians went wild with delight and elected an Honorary Presidium. Accepting a Telegram of Congratulations on the record-breaking speed with which the plan had been overfulfilled, thanks to the spirit and initiative of the masses, the Universal Lathe Operator declared: We assure our beloved and wise leadership and our beloved and brilliant Leader personally that we believe even in what we actually don't believe, and shall accomplish that which in fact we shall not accomplish. The Leader was deeply touched, and saw this as evidence of an exceptionally high level of awareness. With people like that, he said, it's not just the Ism we'll build, but something even better. Just give us time to get over our temporary difficulties, and we'll tell these Americans and all that lot where to get off.

The famous philosopher Foot-rag, a thorough degenerate and complete boor, author of the extremely stupid book *Dialecticodialectic Higher Logic* happened to meet Neurasthenic in the street. 'The Sun,' he said, a deeply meaningful expression on his face, 'the Sun, my son, is here to stay. It's high time to throw our umbrellas into the dustbins of history, where your Marcuses, your Carnaps, your Russells, your Picassos, Parsons and all that crap are.' 'Well, we'll see,' said Neurasthenic, opening his umbrella. At that moment rain, snow and hail began to descend from the sky in sheets, and the Sun disappeared as completely as if it had never existed. Foot-rag was soaked to the skin and frozen to the marrow. When he had dashed home, he succumbed to a mood of glum optimism and began to write a denunciation of Neurasthenic, who had gone out carrying an umbrella in broad sunshine, thus expressing his lack of faith.

Chatterer was going from no-one knows whence to no-one

knows whither, heedless of the weather. 'How are things?' Neurasthenic asked him. 'As usual,' said Chatterer. 'Out of work?' asked Neurasthenic. 'No, I'm working,' said Chatterer. 'Can't manage without work. They'd chuck me out of my room as a parasite.' 'If they want, they can sling you out even if you've got work,' said Neurasthenic. 'Could be,' said Chatterer.

On television, the Leader said that not even the bad weather was disturbing our festive mood.

A sentimental story

'There are some beautiful villa sites round here,' said Bawler. 'Indeed there are,' said Teacher. 'But they don't half fleece you for them, the swine.' 'Who do they belong to?' asked Bawler. 'Third- or fourth-class civil servants,' said Teacher. 'For instance my boss was in charge of an important region of Ibansk. This villa over here belongs to a retired secret police colonel. That one to a retired university rector. The pension my bosses get is bigger than my salary.' 'So why do they let their houses out?' asked Bawler. 'They'd remain empty otherwise,' said Teacher. 'So why not let them, particularly if they can charge that kind of rent. They're not averse to money, these people. A lot of these houses are rented. In ten years or so they'll have completely covered the purchase price. It's not at all bad here, as you can see. But it's nothing compared to the villas for writers or academicians. And then a few miles from here there are the villas belonging to the Council of Ministers. They're even better. And I won't even mention what the higher-ups get. In town one way and another you don't pay any attention to all this. We don't rub shoulders with them in day-to-day affairs, and so we don't see anything of their life-style. But here it's all on the outside. They can't hide anything. When you look at all this it's easy to believe that they have a true love for their way of life, for their Ism. It's something well worth loving. They live well. And they won't voluntarily give up anything. And there are a great many of them. They are the basis of everything. If you dig down as far as you can into our so called liberalism, you will find its essence here. Even liberals want to have their slice of the cake. Nothing surprising about that, you say? I wouldn't dispute it. No, alas, there's nothing surprising about anything. Basically everything's pretty banal.'

(458)

'Anyway, the hell with the lot of them,' said Teacher. 'Shall I tell you a sentimental story? You see this sort of palace over there! It's a secret police building. Everywhere you go you'll find these secretive, vacant-looking private houses. Sometimes one of their staff comes here for a break or for a special assignment. The houses are always fully equipped of course. Now in this particular house Double-dealer rented a room with a balcony. When he was refused permission to go to first one congress, then another, when he was flung out of the university and no-one would publish his books, he suddenly found he'd got a lot of free time on his hands. So he got the idea of writing a book. Actually, *the* book, the famous one. And he decided to get as far away from informers as he could. And he took this little room right under the roof of the secret police. Now whether he'd talked too much himself, or whether the landlord suspected something (that tenant spends all day typing, and the landlord is one of those who don't need much persuasion to do a bit of spying on the side), at all events it came to the ears of the secret police that Double-dealer was writing something. They knew perfectly well who Double-dealer was. And they were afraid of a repetition of the Truth-teller episode. So they took the business seriously. This splendid palace was immediately taken over by an operational group. It sounds like a subject for a thriller. Here we have a solitary, exhausted, humiliated man in the process of writing an immortal book. He snatches a bit of sleep when he can. Eats what he can find. And on the other hand we have a dozen fit young men, well paid, well looked after, using all the weight of the most up-to-date equipment and criminological methods to try to discover what this solitary little man is doing, and thinking of ways to stop him.'

'Well how did they manage to miss him?' asked Bawler. 'Just imagine, he led them right up the garden path,' said Teacher. 'He wrote two books simultaneously, one an academic work, and the other the famous one. He hid the academic manuscript very carefully, but in such a way that the landlord noticed it. And he carefully threw the drafts in the wastepaper basket. But he left the important book on his desk along with his typing paper. He went on like that for three months. In the space of those three months he finished both books. Finally the academic work was confiscated. They had to have some trophy at the end of this immaculately organised operation. When the important book came out in the West the landlord found himself in deep trouble. He was a long-standing party member and a distinguished informer, and he almost hanged himself in despair. They say he's hardly recovered yet.' 'How did he send the book to the West?' asked Bawler. 'That I don't know,' said Teacher. 'But he's a resourceful character with a good head on his shoulders. He probably thought up something ingeniously simple. Anyway, why are you interested? You haven't written something of the same kind?' 'No,' said Bawler. 'There's a friend of mine I want to help.' 'Well,' said Teacher, 'let's think round the problem. After all, we are scientists, and some people say quite good ones. Let's show that we haven't wasted all those years of problem-solving.'

They were interrupted by Teacher's daughter, sent by her mother to summon them to dinner.

Love of foreigners
As the popular song says:
>   True Ibanskians, if you please,
>   Respect our friends from overseas.

But that isn't wholly accurate. Ibanskians adore foreigners and are prepared to give them their last shirt. If the foreigner doesn't take the shirt, he's called a swine. And quite rightly. Take what you're given, without waiting to get yourself thumped. So take it, damn you, if you don't want a thick ear. There's no need to play hard-to-get. They're being good-hearted, showing good feelings. So go on, make the most of it, they're not like this every day, and if you don't . . . But if the foreigner accepts the shirt and goes on behaving as he feels like doing, he'll still be called a swine. And that's only right. He could've refused it. But if he accepts, he ought to abide by the rules. We've acted with the best intentions, with open generosity. But as for him . . . It's no use looking for gratitude. They're swine, and that's all there is to it. But if the foreigner takes the shirt and then behaves like a proper Ibanskian, then he's an even bigger swine, because then he's clearly one of our own people, and with our own people there's no need to stand on ceremony. Ah, the Ibanskians say in such circumstances, he's one of ours, the swine!

And the Ibanskians love everything foreign. First of all because foreign goods are dearer and harder to find. They have to come from under the counter at three times the price. Secondly, if you're wearing foreign clothes you feel just a little bit foreign, just a little bit as if you were abroad. And the dearest dream of an Ibanskian is to be taken for a foreigner. And then perhaps you might perhaps be let through to the front of the queue, might not be arrested, might get a hotel room without an order from the top authority or the intervention of the chambermaid. But the most important reason why an Ibanskian wants to look like a foreigner is that other Ibanskians might look at him and say: Look, there goes another foreigner, the swine!

The sixth hour

But there was a beginning. No-one noticed it, though, because it took place inside each of them, and not outside, and everyone kept it hidden. Otherwise it could not have happened. And there would have been no beginning. A beginning is always a secret.

It happened when Bawler lay shivering on the bare boards of the freight wagon which was taking him off to the far outposts of Ibansk to serve in the army. They can never be forgiven, he said to himself. From now and always your main task is not to forgive. You are alone. That's something at least. A unit is the beginning of a series. But that's still not much. What weapons can be used to oppose them? Intelligence? Science? Of course it would be possible to construct a precise science taking account of this society. After all, it isn't really very complicated. Or rather, it is primitive. And a science of this society would hardly bring its creator the glory of an outstanding scientist. Moreover, the conclusions of science apply to phenomena which repeat themselves and not to exceptions or to individual cases. They are obtuse and indifferent—and because of Their obtuseness and indifference They are cruel. What They call education is merely trophies to hang on the wall. So you can't bring Them down with science. With what then? Madness? Capriciousness? The courage of despair? Recklessness? No, it's too early still. They wouldn't notice it. That's for later. What must be tried first is self-effacement and obscurity. You must

(461)

put an end to vanity once and for all. You are alone. Glory is of no use to you. From now on you and only you will know what your business is. Even those who are to be the object of your actions will not know who you are.

He recalled all the forms he had had to fill in when applying to join the army. That made him laugh. They lie to you at every turn, but from you They demand unconditional truth. They're certain that no-one will dare deceive them. And strangely enough They almost never are deceived. Yet They deceive all the time. Later he was to observe cases where They were deceived and was struck by the way in which They were incapable of detecting even the most contrived deception. His documents had been filled in from his own words. He had not said where his Father was, that he had been expelled from his institute without being allowed to state his case, that he had thrown his membership card of the Union of Youth into the dustbin when he left the headquarters of the secret police. And of course he said nothing about his dealings with the secret police.

He was calm.

He knew what he had to do. A mighty work.

In the end it is men themselves who decide.

He thought. As our beloved leader once said, the cadres decide everything. I must act upon people. My actions must be individual, stubborn, unhurried. There must be no external display. External display is the means of mass action, and now is not the time for that. First, individuals, dozens, hundreds, thousands of people like me must work within society. It is only after that we shall be able to organise mass demonstrations. And as a joke he thought up these lines:

It's useless to seek a verse-form to extol us,
And neither is prose quite a suitable way;
Better far to get hold of a gallon of petrol
And make for the square in the heat of the day.
Go out on the square with a match or a lighter,
Pour the juice over you—just calm and slow—
Light the flame carefully, calmly apply it:
It's worth having lived, choosing that way to go.

This was more than twenty years before the first boy, who had not then even been born, set fire to himself in the square. In one word, he said to himself, someone has to begin to stir up this heap of rubbish. And that's what I shall do.

He could not have known then that this task he had chosen for himself would be appropriated by Them, and that They would proclaim it all over the world as their own work, that They would speak of it as a benefaction from them to all people. He could not know that it would be one of the closest associates of the chief executioner who would announce this. A sly, semi-literate intriguer with the intellect of a bath-house supervisor would heave himself up onto the pedestal of the Liberator, and thus into history, insolently pushing out of his way all those who had any right to be there. No-one would point to the blood dripping from him. And no-one would ever make the slightest reference to people like Bawler. Even people who knew about Bawler's true work and who were in his debt would stay silent. They would shove him on one side, preferring to consider what he had done for them as rather the product of their own efforts.

Oh God, good God, why aren't you here?

Where are you—Devil take you!

For God's sake, God, rise up and come!

It's very hard without you.

The idea of inequality

You force me to talk all the time and then you accuse me of babbling on, said Chatterer. Well, never mind. I don't charge you anything. The most progressive idea under our conditions, if you want my opinion, would be the idea of inequality. In the conditions of the Ibanskian society the idea of equality is the exact opposite of what it would be in the West. Here it has much the same sound as the title of revolutionary applied to a secret policeman or a party hack. Here the idea of equality is a principle of power directed only against subordinates. Its essence is to ensure that no man, whatever his personal ability or the quality of his work, should acquire privileges which are reserved for people of a particular social rank to which he does not belong. Subjectively this is unjust. For example, subjectively there is no way of justifying situations in which two officials indistinguishable in effort or ability receive different incomes and privileges because they occupy different posts, or where a talented and productive scientist receives as much as his unproductive and untalented colleague because they occupy similar posts. Any attempts the authorities may make to introduce some justice degenerate into empty demagogy since they do not directly affect the hierarchy which determines the distribution of money and jobs. There is only one answer: to establish a just inequality by creating conditions which would allow for the social promotion of individuals in accordance with their personal abilities. But this would contradict the very idea of the hierarchy which *a priori* excludes any distinction between the personal qualities of individuals. As a result of this situation, which remains insoluble at the level of reason, the creative potential of society has tended to diminish and social stagnation has tended to spread. This stems from the fact that quantity, here, cannot substitute for quality. Two imbeciles can never add up to one intelligent man. The level of social awareness in a society can never exceed that of its most cultivated citizens. Similarly, the creative level of society can never be higher than that of its most talented representatives. And in reality this level is indeed generally inferior. As you see, there is no way out.

A page of heroic history

During the era of the Boss a pan-Ibanskian standard was laid down for trousers. There was to be one type of trouser for all ages and sizes, for all professions and all circumferences. They were wide at the waist, at the knees and below. The crotch hung down to the knees. They had well delineated flies and pockets down to the heels. They were ideologically consistent trousers. Ibanskians were unfailingly recognised by their trousers throughout the world. Even today on the streets of Ibansk one can still sometimes see examples of these living memorials to the glorious epoch of the Boss. They are flaunted brazenly by the Boss's former collaborators now retired on pensions. But are they old trousers which are being worn out? Doubt is permissible. Once Journalist asked the owner of such a pair of trousers how he had managed to preserve them so long. The pensioner demanded to see Journalist's identity documents, and then said that he had had the trousers made quite recently. As Journalist left, he heard the pensioner hiss with rage: They're getting out of hand, the villains, they should have been put up against a wall long ago. Of course that's just a slightly comic curiosity. They could have put people up against the wall just as easily if they'd been wearing tight trousers. Or even with no trousers at all. It might even have been more convenient.

The pan-Ibanskian trouser was developed in the context of the bitter struggle against deviationists and class enemies. Leftist deviationists wanted to make the trousers even wider waisted and bring the crotch down to the ankles. They were counting on realising the total Ism in the next six months and stuffing the starving workers with food. Fortunately the Boss intervened and corrected their error. 'T'leftists,' he said, "'av made wun ov them theer typickle errors. They've coot'emselves off from t'masses and gon' agate rushin' ahead o'theer selves.' The leftist deviationists were liquidated by the rightist deviationists. These wanted rather to widen the trousers at the knees and eliminate the flies. They had no faith in the creative potential of the masses and put all their hopes in the bourgeoisie. Once again the Boss intervened in time to put them right. 'T'reight deviationists 'av made a typickle error. They've coot'emselves off from t'masses and gon' agate rushin back'ards.' The rightist deviationists were liquidated by the left.

When the Boss died and the Ibanskians had got over their drunken rejoicing, rather narrow trousers began to appear. They were followed by really tight drainpipe trousers. A merciless battle was launched against the drainpipers. Their trousers were hacked to pieces in public, they were expelled from universities, fired from their jobs, fined, and denounced in the press. But on the other hand they were no longer shot. This repression was not the work of the secret police but of the broad masses of the people on their own initiative. It wasn't the narrowness of the trousers themselves which caused such terror. Indeed the fashion was advantageous, for it led to an immediate doubling in the country's textile output. But narrow trousers were a sign and a symbol of a growing intolerance of authority, of self-assertion and cynicism. In the end, however, narrow trousers, like cybernetics, were purged of all ideological deviations and recognised officially as corresponding with the ideas of the Ism. By which time, they had already passed out of fashion.

As the Boss himself said: 'A new-born bairn meight skroike a

bit at fust, but it awl turns out reet in th' end: an' it'll tak ower
from th' old uns.'

A hymn to trousers

When narrow trousers won their right to exist, this hymn to
trousers became widely sung in Ibansk:

> There was a time, a famous time,
> In our great and famous land,
> When every pair of pants we wore
> Was cut by the Party's hand.
> The very old, the very young,
> The fathers and their sons
> Were always dressed identically
> In those marvellous pantaloons.
> The postman knocking at your door,
> The worker on the factory floor,
> And discharged soldiers proudly wore
> The selfsame pair of pants.
> The ones who never said a word,
> The ones whose voice was always heard,
> The bosses, too, as you've inferred,
> Wore the selfsame pants.
> Crooks and people who went straight,
> Jokers, pillars of the state
> Wore, both daily and *en fête*,
> The selfsame pair of pants.
> They never thought as they flapped by
> That such beauty could ever die;
> They never cast an envious eye
> On narrow foreign pants.
> It's not because our land was poor—
> An inference that we deplore—
> That every manjack of us wore
> The selfsame pair of pants.
> In those splendid years of old
> (Our motives, high and pure and bold,)
> Our age-old dreams had to unfold
> In the selfsame pair of pants.
> But now those years have whistled by,

We've drained their cup, yes, drunk it dry.
And now their old ideas we try
        In modern drainpipe pants.

No-one ever discovered the author of the hymn. Some thought it was Singer. Others ascribed it to Snottyhanky—and a few even thought it might be by Bawler.

The gravestone

The day the Sun came out for the first and last time, its first rays fell on Hog's gravestone. One might have thought that it had come out for that very reason. On top of Hog's bronze head was a layer of dirty snow, like a child's hat that needed washing. A moulting raven perched on the snow and noisily croaked throughout the Old Whores' Cemetery: Cro-o-k! Cro-o-k! And the expression on Hog's face looked as if he had just shat in the black and white marble trousers which were intended by the artist to express Hog's complex and contradictory nature. Opposite Hog, standing calmly at attention, was the statue of Director which had originally been a statue of the Great Commander, which had recently been replaced by the equestrian statue of a condottiere. 'It's turned out pretty well all the same,' said Dauber. 'At all events it's uncompromising.' 'That's true,' said Chatterer, 'if the lack of any demand for compromise can be regarded as uncompromising.' 'How do you mean?' asked Dauber. 'After all, there was a struggle! They were fighting against themselves and not against you,' said Chatterer. 'By the way, it seems that they've decided to move Hog into the Pantheon and to send the gravestone to be broken up because it won't be needed any more. In a word,

   * I have made him a monument, become now invisible,
      In the Old Whores', and not by the Wall.
     It may well be said that the man was quite risible;
      But flies leave their mark—elephants, not at all.

'Who wrote that?' asked Dauber. Chatterer shrugged his shoulders. At that moment the Sun disappeared behind the clouds, and it began to rain and then to snow.

* The first line of this verse is an echo of a line of Pushkin, from the poem *Exegi Monumentum*.

Tragedy and farce

Among the many irrefutable truths that the Ibanskian intellectuals had to digest was the one that states that history repeats itself, but the first time as tragedy, the next time as farce. The tragedy has already taken place, and the farce isn't anything like as terrible. But this consoling truth has not stopped Ibanskian intellectuals from shitting themselves at every possible moment. On this theme Singer wrote a song:

It was called tragedy in the old time:
A word out of turn—a political crime.
A shot in the neck before you could utter—
And just to make sure, your name in the gutter.
But now it's a farce, I tell you with candour—
Just an idea and they'll do you for slander.
Into the nuthouse without more ado;
If you can grasp that, well—it's more than I do.

'That's a work of genius,' said Brother. He copied the poem in his notebook. That evening he read it to a company which included Play Producer, Colleague, Sociologist, Actor and Thinker. Although the Period of Perplexity had already begun, Singer was sent to prison. It's true it wasn't for his verses, as it was rumoured, but for homosexuality. 'We must save Singer,' Brother cried, and began to collect signatures. 'A farce which constantly repeats itself is in fact a tragedy,' said Chatterer. Brother wrote this phrase down in his notebook and used it later in a progressivist article.

Unity

In the beginning there was nothing, and for that reason there was complete unity. There were of course disagreements but not on essential matters. For example, Colleague invited everyone round to his home where a great pile of undrunk drink and uneaten food remained from the birthday party of his highly placed papa. Teacher refused to eat left-overs even if they'd come from a king's table and not from that of some decaying minister, and invited everyone to the Three Graces instead. Puss said that children weren't answerable for their parents and urged everyone to go to Colleague's where he hoped to be introduced to the minister and tell him about his views. With this in mind he had learnt by heart a few Latin quotations

(468)

about the law. Snottyhanky insisted on a bar nearer his home. As always, Puss moaned that he didn't have any cash on him and bummed cigarettes from everyone in turn. Everyone knew that Puss had plenty of money because he was mean and was saving up to buy a villa. But that was a very venial sin. After all it doesn't cost much to stand a round! And Bawler, who had been paid ten roubles for unloading a wagon of potatoes, said that he would pick up the check.

The disagreements began later, and for quite another reason. It wasn't when Puss stopped drinking and smoking other people's cigarettes, or when Fellow-worker had defended his thesis, when Thinker had become an editor, when Colleague had got an apartment even more magnificent than his father's, who by this time had retired on a pension, when Wife had been abroad a few times, when Chatterer had been dismissed twice, or when Teacher. . . . It was even later, when a clear distinction appeared not only between their positions and standards of living, but in their concepts of the world. It was when Colleague ordered Bawler to be brought to him and asked his name, his age, his occupation. . . .

On this occasion the disagreements were quickly sorted out and they all repaired to the Three Graces. While they were waiting for their beer they passed the time in slandering the leadership and telling stories. 'One day,' said Colleague, 'an Ibanskian soldier rushed into a chemist's shop, grabbed a bottle marked "Water of the Tsars"—or aqua regia in Latin—and rushed off. "Stop!" yelled the chemist. "That's water of the Tsars!" "Okay," said the soldier, "I'd like to taste what the Tsars used to drink." The next day the soldier turned up in the chemist's again. The chemist was amazed. "You're alive!" he said. "But that was a mixture of nitric and hydrochloric acid!" "So that's what it was," said the soldier. "I wondered why I burned a hole in my boot when I was having a piss last night."' When they'd all had a good laugh, they began to praise the exceptional virtues of the Ibanskian soldier. 'It's quite remarkable,' said Teacher. 'What you're praising about our soldiers are all the worst things about our society: bad food, poor clothes, a totally senseless way of passing the time . . .' 'That's a law,' said Chatterer. 'The less difference there is between a country's way of life in time of peace and a soldier's

way of life in time of war, the better the soldier is prepared for
war.' 'That's never been proved,' said Teacher. 'I've seen a few
things myself, and I must say that rumours about soldiers are
greatly exaggerated.' Then the beer arrived and the absurd
discussion ended. 'Let's drink bad health to them all,' said
Brother.

On God

'It's generally accepted that there are no such things as miracles,' said Double-dealer. 'That's not true at all. They do
happen. Yesterday I was complaining to my wife that I couldn't
work any more, couldn't write. I brought it all out. If only some
insignificant little university in the West would invite me to
give some lectures. And at that very moment there's a ring at
the bell. A registered letter. An invitation! Now, of course, I'm
beginning to have doubts about the non-existence of God. And
if we're allowed to go, I'll be able to believe in him.' 'God
exists,' said Teacher. 'But not for everyone. He only exists if
you're a god yourself, or close to it. Apparently you are a god.'
'What about you?' asked Double-dealer. 'For the time being I
feel no need to believe,' said Teacher.

Special courses

One of the most striking features of the Period of Perplexity was
the abundance of special courses of lectures, delivered by the
most diverse people in the most diverse scientific and academic
institutions on the most diverse subjects. Lectures were even
delivered in people's homes. Slanderer began a course which
caused a sensation. It started off in an ideological institute, but
he was driven out of there and he transferred it to an academic
institution as far removed as possible from ideology, and completed it in a tiny room which he hired at a cost of half his hard
earned fees. Or, more precisely, it was never finished as the
Period of Perplexity itself came to an end.

I do not claim to have made any earth-shattering discoveries,
said Slanderer. These days discoveries are made in such numbers that we should long ago have reconsidered the very meaning of the word discovery. Take, for example, the queen of
sciences—mathematics. Mathematicians of the past considered

everything that could be solved without special difficulty or without great talent as mere schoolroom exercises. But these days mathematicians claim as scientific discoveries theorems that can be proved in a mere two or three steps. And if in mathematics things have gone as far as that, what must be going on in the other sciences? The hurricane of scientific discoveries in our time is very largely (maybe even fundamentally) a social wind and not a wind of knowledge. Of course real discoveries are made as well. Quite a lot of them. More than in the past. But in most cases they are concealed, unsensational, not like real discoveries. In a hundred years we shall know who in our time were real scientists and what was discovered of real value; I don't mean here simply the discovery of facts, but our understanding of facts. But I'm just saying that in passing.

But what he had said in passing provoked great interest among his audience. It was something unorthodox. There was no constraint about it. It was something that stayed in the memory.

I merely want, said Slanderer, to draw your attention to the most ordinary and well-known facts and to say that in the life of our society they have a far greater importance than our high-level official ideology and our no less high-level science ascribe to them. I am not repudiating science, quite the contrary. I consider that in present circumstances it can contribute something comparable with what classical mechanics contributed by its observation of the laws of motion or what quantum mechanics did for atomic physics. The difference between our present circumstances and micro-physics is that in our case there is no need to discover the facts themselves. They are there before our eyes. All the facts, I repeat, are clearly to be seen. We have no need of any confidential statistical data jealously guarded as important state secrets. The facts, I say again, are self-evident. They need only to be assembled so as to produce a theory affording a sufficiently sound and convincing basis on which to predict the pattern of future phenomena. Mark my words, very soon the most important state secrets will not be the disposition of missile sites or of the numbers of cattle in the country, but the most widely known and common manifestations of our daily life.

A place in history

'I could write something which would get me grabbed by the scruff of the neck,' said Snottyhanky. 'But where's the sense in that? At the moment I'm read by millions, and one way and another I have an influence on people's minds, particularly on young people. Bear in mind that in our days the very techniques of art have a revolutionary influence. It isn't important just what you write about but how you write about it. But if I do anything politically scandalous I'll simply be swept out of the history of Ibansk. Twenty years of work will go for nothing.' 'Of course,' said Teacher, 'the form of art has a role to play, particularly when there's nothing to say. But if there is something important to say there's no need to think about the form. That appears of its own accord, and in a way appropriate to the content. And how long do you intend to cling on to your place in Ibanskian history? For a century? A millennium? And which history? The official version? And is the official history of Ibansk worth hanging on to? You're not a baby. You know perfectly well that the work of a moment could be enough to leave nothing at all behind. Nothing of Ibansk, nor of the planet, nor of the galaxy. You want to live for the sake of a place in history? Do you really put such a low value on your life? If you want to show this sickening history in all its filth, if you want to destroy its false self-righteousness, that's another matter. At least it would be brave. But to count on a place in history comes down in the end to villas, petty vanity, mentions in the press, fine clothes and a seat in the presidium.' 'What are you insinuating?' Snottyhanky asked indignantly. 'Just wait,' said Teacher. 'You might learn something! Ibanskian history is capricious. At the moment it needs to have an appearance of authenticity. But as time goes by it'll toss you aside like a worn out glove and Truth-teller will be written back into its pages. So you'd better hurry, or you might be overtaken!' Snottyhanky turned pale and dashed off to write a satirical poem on Ibanskian reality. The poem turned out to be very sharp and it was gleefully printed in the Newspaper.

> When from the furnace out they poured,
> The workers in their sooty horde,
> Their faces grimy past belief,
> Lit only by their yellowed teeth,

They made my heart feel proud within
Although ashamed of my clean skin.
That grime did all their faces smother
But none of them looked like another.
I realised: outside the masses
There is no poet, no Parnassus.

'Sheer genius!' said Teacher. 'Now, even if you asked to get out of Ibanskian history they won't let you leave. Or only for a short interval.' 'That's brilliant,' said Brother, and printed a long article in the Journal about the place of the poet in the ranks of the advancing army. 'The swine,' said Snottyhanky. But he wasn't quite clear whom he meant.

The seventh hour

Tragedy began with a comedy. The enterprise was almost broken off at the very start. Bawler had become friendly with a lad who began to tell him such horrifying things that Bawler felt like a novice. Those few facts which he knew personally and which seemed so appalling, and the knowledge of which seemed to be a terrible secret, were mere innocent nothings compared with what his new friend was telling him. Soon they were joined by yet another. This one regarded the Boss purely and simply as his own personal enemy. 'I don't know what's going on,' he said. 'We didn't have a bad life. Everyone told me that the Boss was a genius, a great humanist, our father and our friend. But I hate him and all his gang. I don't believe a single word they say.' 'You should be more cautious in your dealings with him,' the first lad said to Bawler about the other. 'There's something about him I don't like.' A few days later Bawler was summoned to the Special Department. From the very first question he realised that one of the two had denounced him. Which one? He had to decide instantly. And he fixed on the first. It was only many years later that he worked out the logic of this decision. The problem did not lie in knowing certain revealing facts and in being able to make critical judgments, but in the whole moral state of a person. He saw many times later that the most fiercely anti-Ibanskian conversation took place among members of the secret police and informers, and in general among people who spent their lives under the protection of power. The secret police assembled so many facts about their own unlawful and arbitrary activity while they were preparing the speech that Hog delivered, that Bawler felt almost ashamed to produce his own information, which was quite trivial in comparison.

He had only a moment to find a way out. If he lost his head they would begin to dig deeper, and deeper. And that would be the end, and he'd have had it. 'Your informant,' he said, naming the first lad, 'is doing his job badly. I've wanted to tell you about this for a long time but I had no right to.' 'How do you know that he's our informant?' asked the Special Investigator. 'It's elementary,' said Bawler. 'I went through a special school. I am telling you about that because of the special circumstances we're in. I've got a special mission.' The Investigator came to attention on hearing this talk of a special mission. This was the beginning of Bawler's golden age, which gave him a breathing space. He wasn't even put on fatigues any more. He asked that this special treatment should stop because it might break his cover. If the highest authorities ever got to hear what the other ranks were saying among themselves, all the officers of the unit would have been shot on the spot without more ado. It was the first lad, the informer, who was the most impassioned. 'What could I do?' he said to Bawler. 'One day I was pulled in for saying a word or two out of turn, and they said either be an informer or we'll stick you inside. Of course I agreed. I'll pay them back in the end, God help me!'

Soon a recruiting drive began in the regiment for junior secret police officers, and Bawler's second friend was one of those chosen. The first swore like a trooper. They promised it to me, the bastards, and they go and choose that little plaster saint. It's obvious why. His father must be in the same system. At first Bawler was bewildered by all this. But when he'd thought it out he laughed till he wept. The hell with all this play-acting, he said, it's all a lot simpler than you thought. You can't live in filth without getting dirty.

When a recruiting drive began in the regiment to select candidates for flying school, Bawler told the Investigator that he had to be among those selected, as that was the particular purpose of the recruiting drive. The informer wept when they parted and asked him to write. They never met again.

Groups

Another characteristic of the Period of Perplexity was the variety of ideological groups. They arose on most diverse pretexts, in the most diverse places, and in most diverse forms. The most important and stable were those which, under cover of scientific research, were actually meeting places for ideological sects. The members of the groups, for the most part, didn't recognise themselves for what they were, but thought of themselves as genuine scientific research workers. And for some time they were regarded by others in the same light. Groups of this kind were even formed within the framework of the Ism, with the aim of developing a genuinely scientific Ism. These groups were the first to break up, not so much because their members were out and out ignorant charlatans, but because they began to win some official success and to compete with the ordinary representatives of the Ism.

The ideological nature of these groups was revealed rather later, when they were deserted by the occasional genuine scientists who had happened just by chance to start their careers in this milieu and, charlatanism no longer breeding success, the creative sterility of the groups became apparent to all. Certain of these groups turned into official organisations. Although these were just as sterile from the scientific point of view, they turned out to be extremely useful in other ways. They served particularly for the establishment of international relations of a certain kind, for the infiltration of various international organisations, and for generally throwing dust in people's eyes. Look here! they could say. You keep on talking about our stagnation and repression and persecution and similar horrors. It's all slander. We've got everything! Sociology? We can send you a delegation of a thousand! Cybernetics? Every other person you meet is a cyberneticist! Epistemology? We've got a special institute just for that! Systems research? Haven't you seen our journal? There you are then!

The groups came together as seminars, symposia, colloquia, lectures, reports and so on. And, of course, they talked about science. In fact, they talked about nothing else. But how they talked! They talked in such a way that no-one could fail to read between the lines. There was never a word about the Ism. All it got was winks and nudges and little sly grins. Some young genius from somewhere or other would stand up and start sounding off without pause for breath. 'Let us consider society as a homogeneous system comprising a number of hyper-personalized elements, represented by a homomorphic sub-group of corteges . . .' There was nothing for the authorities to refute. The diehards of the Ism went ashy pale in acknow-ledgement of their crass ignorance, tucked their tails between their legs and crawled off to find cover where they could. But everyone knew what it was all about. One or two more dis-coveries like that, and we've got them where we want them . . . Or, for instance, there'd be a symposium on the Ismatic crit-ique of Psychoanalysis, chief rapporteur Thinker, or Sociolo-gist, or Wife or even Fellow-worker. Or all at the same time. It made no difference. And the talking went on. The main thing was to say as much as possible, as vaguely as possible, using dozens of incomprehensible terms, and references to dozens of Western names. The best to choose were those who had just published one small article. This was the last word in science. Just two or three words to say that nothing in this was a contradiction of the Ism, just to keep the authorities happy. So everyone knew what was going on. That was essential.

And in the corridors, the apartments, the restaurants, the bars and the offices of respectable organisations, the discus-sions went on endlessly about the situation in the country at large, life in the West, about the Boss, Hog, about drainpipe trousers and mini-skirts, about neo-realism and surrealism, about camps and arrests. Everything here was denigrated. Everything from Over There provoked raptures. In other words, people were beginning to wake up after the forced hibernation of the Boss period, to open their eyes to reality, impatient to give full rein to their creative potential which had been repressed for so many decades.

The eighth hour
The day after Bawler, having completed flying-school, joined his regiment at the front, his immediate superior, a senior pilot, asked him a favour. He wanted him to go to the medical officer, say he'd caught a dose of clap, and ask for some sulphidine. The senior pilot had already flown thirty missions, won two decora-

tions and was nominated for a third, and he was afraid he might miss that third medal if they found out about his clap. He was a nice enough lad. But he was oblivious to the notion that for Bawler to begin his career with clap on his record card would block his way to decorations and promotion from the very start. Bawler couldn't refuse him. Although he later flew more than sixty missions, all he ever got was one iron clasp—and the lowest grade at that. As a rule he should have been entitled to at least five medals. And the next day the senior pilot was regaling everyone around him with the story how he'd got Bawler to take his place. Everyone in the regiment knew that Bawler was perfectly healthy. And they laughed at him. And the commanders always struck his name off the list of those recommended for decorations. Now he is grateful to them for that. They developed his scorn for titles and rewards. But it was hard for him at the time. He was still under twenty, and at that time he'd never even had a woman. And he wasn't sorry for himself so much as for the others: he couldn't understand how people who seemed quite decent could stoop to such mean tricks. Later he came to understand that it is ordinary decent people who stoop to the meanest acts.

The business of the clap was soon followed by another, and Bawler once again found himself an object of interest in the Special Department. But as luck would have it, he was wounded, and after he'd been discharged from hospital he was retrained on another type of aircraft and transferred to a different regiment. Here is what happened. He was sitting in the squadron dug-out playing chess with the regimental engineer. The squadron commander came in and asked him to taxi his plane, which was on the apron, to a far corner of the airfield. When he came back into the dug-out, he found everyone laughing their heads off. When he discovered what it was all about (one of his bombs had got stuck in the bay), for the first and last time in his life Bawler lost his temper. 'You bastard!' he cried. 'You coward! You might have told me what was wrong, then I could have taxied more gently.' And he slapped the squadron commander in the face. The business was hushed up because if there had been a court martial the full story would have come out. That would have damaged the reputation of the regiment, and the squadron commander wouldn't have received a decoration he'd just been recommended for after a number of attempts. But the incident wasn't forgotten.

The senior pilot for whom Bawler had collected the sulphidine died the next day from untreated gonorrhoea, and the squadron commander was blown up while trying out a motorcycle. So his sacrifices were in vain. Sacrifices are always in vain, Bawler said to himself. They leave an impression of torture, falsehood and sterility. Actions should be judged and experienced only by their aims and their results. And the main result of an action is what it does to yourself. The lack of any external result should not be a disappointment. We are not bargaining in a bazaar—we are standing face to face with our own conscience.

There were all sorts of legends about Bawler in the division. His friendship was sought by the most intelligent, best educated pilots. We ought to keep an eye on that lad, said the Second in Command of the regiment to the head of the Special Department. There's something funny about him. He speaks German fluently, and he's learning English. There's something slightly wrong there. But Bawler was lucky. He was shot down.

Unity

After his second glass Puss began to look wistfully at the picture of the Three Graces on the peeling wall of the bar. 'Not bad, are they, those birds,' remarked Colleague, intercepting Puss's gaze. 'Something to get hold of.' After his third glass, Puss pronounced significantly that Toad was better stacked than the graces. 'She's a bit on the elderly side,' said Teacher. 'But it seems that older women are in fashion these days. If she put her teeth in, she'd look quite attractive.' 'From what I can see,' said Colleague, 'she quite fancies Puss.' 'That's right,' said Fellow-worker. 'Some people have all the luck.' Puss took these remarks completely seriously, and when Toad brought him his fourth glass, he slapped her scrawny bottom. Meeting no opposition, he grew bolder and slipped his hand up her skirt. Toad, who was collecting the empty glasses, giggled with pleasure, but she wouldn't let Puss's wandering hand get any higher than her purple drawers, tightly fastened top and bottom by drawstrings as thick as a finger. All would have been well had not the next table been occupied by a group of General

Staff colonels, among whom was Toad's latest lover. For a long time he suffered Puss's impure advances stoically. Not for nothing had he been at the front. The Colonel, who had once worked out a draft order for the re-cooking of gnawed bones to extract additional value from them, had been quite close to the front line twice, which had earned him five decorations and promotion to colonel at thirty. It was this brilliant career which had finally overcome Toad's virtue, and decided her to share her charms between him and the cellarman. But everything has its limits. 'Hey, you, snotface!' the colonel barked, as Puss prepared to pursue Toad into the kitchen. 'Leave the girl alone!' And he hurled a hunk of bread at Puss, hitting him in the eye. Puss, overcome by the watered beer, almost shat himself and apologised. But Teacher saw things differently. He poured his remaining beer down the neck of the colonel sitting nearest, whose response was to thump Colleague in the face. A general brawl started. When the police arrived they couldn't tell who was guilty, and joined in on the side of the colonels. Reinforcements were summoned. In the affray Fellow-worker, who had kept out of things so far, grabbed a fur hat belonging to one of the colonels and shoved it in the dustbin. Puss, his trousers bursting, was thrown out as well. As he grew bolder he spat several times in the hat, and referred to it as a symbol of this autocratic power. The battle was carried on by Teacher, Colleague, Bawler, Chatterer and some volunteers from among the bystanders. When the colonel discovered that his hat had disappeared, there was an awful silence. 'Take them all to court,' yelled the colonel. 'Into the punishment battalion with them! Strip them of their rank!' Puss, who had grown pale with terror, for he was for the moment an untrained second-class reserve private, crept quietly over to the dustbin and with two fingers extracted the saliva-stained hat. 'Take your miserable hat,' he muttered through his teeth. The colonel was so astonished by this unexpected turn of events that he automatically dealt Puss a mighty blow over the head with his empty glass. It was the first time in all his brilliant military career that he had harmed a human being. Puss dropped like a corpse. Aghast, the colonel fainted. At this moment the police reinforcements arrived. As it was quite clear that the colonels were solely responsible, they were allowed to go in peace, and the students' names were taken just in case. Puss was taken to hospital with a fractured skull. Colleague who was suffering from a black eye, invited Teacher, Bawler and Chatterer to come home with him, and Fellow-worker tagged along without being asked. That was the first and last time in his life that he almost took part in a battle. While the warriors treated their wounds, Fellow-worker wrote the following verse:

It wasn't for nothing we bellowed our threat:
If you hurt us, we'll give as good as we get.
For a kick up the bracket—a punch on the jaw,
If you make us feel bruised—we shall make you feel sore.
Give as good as we get, and perhaps even more
To defend our ideals—or even a whore.

'Brilliant,' said Teacher. 'Now I know why you're such a coward. It seems you're a poet.'

Objectivity

'I want to form an objective picture of Ibanskian life,' said Journalist. 'That's out of the question,' said Neurasthenic. 'Why?' asked Journalist. 'Because you're in a privileged position,' said Neurasthenic. 'You don't have to worry about your apartment, you don't have to go to meetings, rush round the shops, stand in queues, try to get a rise, fit in with the censorship. And all that makes up the essence of our way of life.' 'But I'll be living like an ordinary Ibanskian,' said Journalist. 'In that case you won't have any time or energy left for observation, and irritation is no help towards objectivity.' 'So what's the answer?' asked Journalist. 'There's no need to go to Ibansk to understand Ibansk,' said Neurasthenic. 'All you need to come here for is a bit of training and practice in the language.' 'But there must be things that can't be seen from outside that are quite clearly visible from within,' said Journalist. 'No,' said Neurasthenic. 'All we've got are things that can't be seen from inside but are quite clearly visible from outside. Don't believe that we have got secret underground hideouts where terrible dramas are played out. Our most terrible dramas are played out in full view of everybody. They make up our daily life. Take any committee session, any open meeting, any speech, any newspaper. Just watch, and read and listen. That's what our real life is like, it's not a camouflage or a deception. There's no

(480)

deception. It's you who deceive yourself with the best of good intentions. You see what you want to see, because you want to give everything some sense. But there isn't any sense anywhere. For example, you hear that some region or other has been given a decoration. Region! Some Deputy or other has been there. Made a speech. Handed over a decoration. That's not something happening on a stage. That's real life. Life, not a mirage. It's a good deal more real than those empty gestures of defiance our intellectuals make when no one's looking. And if those cellars that intrigue you so much actually do exist, then everything that's going on down there is just as grey and routine as any ordinary meeting. It's the same tune all the time and everywhere. That's the way it is, that's the rule, and that's that. We've got nothing behind the scenes, because we haven't got any scenery. We ourselves are behind the scenes. As for the spectators, we try to liquidate them so that they shouldn't notice what we really are. The whole horror of our existence lies in the grandiose scale and inescapability of triviality.'

Groups

The composition of the groups was very varied, ranging from talented scientists who later made their name in science, (they could be counted on the fingers of one hand), to ungifted charlatans, hoping to make easy gains if the circumstances turned out right (they formed the majority of the members). The circumstances turned out as right as could be. Careers were made. Reputations for being decent and progressive were on the increase. There was even a new type of intellectual, a group whom Chatterer called the 'allegedly repressed'. Their ideal was to eat chicken tabaka or shashliks in elegant restaurants or in luxurious apartments, washing them down with good dry wines, and drinking French cognac or Scotch whisky, sleeping with every man or woman who happened to come along, while at the same time giving the impression of being unjustly oppressed and persecuted. The classic examples of this type were Thinker and Wife.

Scientific and academic establishments were at first delighted to give house room to this kind of group. And that's putting it mildly. Everyone wanted to keep up with progress and be in the avant-garde. New sections, chairs, departments and even institutes were established. Even entire new branches of science.

One such group was the one which formed around Teacher. In the opinion of specialists who tried their hardest to keep him out of official science, Teacher was an able scientist, who was contaminated by absurd social ideas and didn't know how to behave in decent society. The members of his group were basically quite decent people. But, like most normal people, they were not talented, and they tended to be immoral. They plagiarised their teacher's work, and published articles based on his ideas but without giving him any of the credit. And when the situation deteriorated, they quietly and gradually betrayed him and deserted him. Those who later became the most effective destroyers of Teacher's ideas were drawn from their ranks.

Almost nothing was preserved of Teacher's work. There are a few snippets from little known journals. And a small part of a manuscript of the theory of social systems, which Boy published under his own name when he established himself as an expert on Teacher's work, and made a brilliant career on his account in the world of science.

The state

All the traditional concepts of social science lose their sense when applied to Ibanskian society, said Slanderer. This refers in the first instance to concepts of the state, brotherhood, politics and law. The official point of view on these matters is well known. And I shall not trouble to set it out or enter into polemic with it, since it is a non-scientific phenomenon.

The state is the system of social power in a given society. In Ibanskian society it is a system made up of a vast number of people and organisations. At least a fifth of the adult population is engaged in some part or other of the system of power. If the society as a whole is regarded as a social individual, the state is its controlling organ, its will.

The overwhelming majority of the representatives of power are low-paid officials. That is a power of misery or a miserable power. This is very important. Hence comes the inevitable tendency to compensate for low earnings by exploiting one's position in the apparatus. So there is nothing surprising in the fact that many low-paid representatives of authority live considerably better than their highly-paid fellow citizens. So power is materially attractive, even at the lowest levels. The great majority of the representatives of authority have in theory a negligible share of power. Whence the tendency to compensate for this by exceeding official powers. Here there are almost unlimited possibilities. Nor is it surprising that the most insignificant officials of the apparatus have an enormous amount of power at their disposal.

It is for this reason among others that the lowest ranks of power bear such a hatred for the scientific-technical intelligentsia of higher rank, a hatred which by way of compensation is directed at the most defenceless and impecunious members of the creative intelligentsia. Hatred for the intelligentsia is a general feature in the ideology of the broad masses in the Ibanskian power structure, if only for the reason that at the lowest levels its members are drawn from the least educated and the least talented strata of society, while the higher echelons consist of people who, in terms of education and ability, have always had to yield place to those of their contemporaries who have become scientists, artists, writers and so on.

Ibanskian power is both omnipotent and impotent. It is omnipotent in the negative sense that it can do any evil it likes and remain unpunished. It is impotent in the positive sense that any good it may do remains unrewarded. It has a huge destructive force, and a wholly insignificant power of creation. Any economic success the country may have owes nothing to the authorities as such. These successes are, as a rule, seen by the authorities as a necessary evil. The same is even truer of successes in the field of culture. That is in no way a function of authority. The illusion that these things do result from the exercise of power springs from the Ibanskian practice of making decisions about everything, preparing plans for everything, handing out orders about everything, and writing reports on everything. In fact there is no connection between these activities and any success the country may achieve. They represent merely a formal superposition. The existence of a self-sufficient power here assumes the form of controlling everything—even the weather, even the biological nature of man.

In Ibansk the omnipotent power is impotent to carry out the most trifling reform on a nationwide scale if this reform is required for the better organisation of society, in other words if the reform is positive. It is capable of destroying in a trice entire branches of science and the arts, or of the economy, of putting an end to age-old traditional ways of life, of exterminating entire peoples. But it is quite incapable of defending the tiniest fragment of creative activity against its environment, if the environment wishes to reduce this fragment to dust.

Power of the Ibanskian type is in principle unreliable. It is incapable of fulfilling its promises in a systematic or durable way. This is not because it is made up of frauds and swindlers. Even with the best will in the world, the power is inhibited, by the very conditions of its functioning, from keeping its word. This applies of course primarily to positive intentions and only to a certain extent to negative ones. Why is this? The people who have promised to do something are easily replaced by people who regard that very promise as an error (for the purpose of discrediting the people they replace). As the norms regulating living-standards tend to instability, and as the authorities tend to favour reforms, the situation can so change that earlier promises become either meaningless or forgotten. For instance, Hog is replaced. Who will remember that he promised free public transport by a certain year, and a hundred per cent increase in the housing stock? As a general rule the authorities always have a false image of the state of things in the country, a necessary element of which is an overestimate of the good and an underestimate of the bad. In principle power excludes a scientific view of the society it governs, and consequently bases its intentions on false premises. For instance, Hog was convinced of the success of his maize-growing programme. Had anyone tried to convince him that this enterprise was doomed in advance because of the very social principles in operation, he would have wasted his breath!

The unreliability of the promises made by the authorities becomes an habitual form of government. Deep down, no-one trusts the authorities. And the authorities don't trust themselves. And when they make decisions they have this idea *a priori* in their minds, unaware of it though they are. And I repeat that this applies merely to their positive activity. As far as their negative activity is concerned, they only need a signal. It is easier to destroy than to construct.

To all this we must add an almost total irresponsibility so far as the conduct of government business is concerned. Power takes the credit for everything positive, whatever its nature, and so arranges its affairs as to bear no responsibility for setbacks and shortages. To this end there exists within the power structure a collective guarantee system. Here punishments are an exception and not very much to be feared. It is not much of a punishment if a vice-minister is demoted to be a deputy vice-minister. In the worst case scapegoats can be found to take the blame for everything.

The Ibanskian authorities are represented as having been freely elected by the population. This contains both a monumental lie and a profound truth. The falsehood is well-known and requires no comment. How can there be any talk of free elections if candidates for elected office are chosen by the authorities, if there is only one candidate, and if those who are elected have only one function—to applaud superior authority and to approve everything they are instructed to? Yet the Ibanskian system of power is the product of the goodwill of the people. It is absurd for the Ibanskian authorities to try to preserve sham elections, by which everyone is thoroughly bored and which provoke only ridicule. They should simply oblige the population to consider the free choice of power from another point of view.

On glory

Truth-teller's interview was broadcast by Western radio stations. 'I am not a vain man,' said Teacher. 'But at this moment I would like to be famous.' 'I understand what you mean,' said Bawler.

> O God, you can see that I'm weeping.
> You can see that I'm down on my knees.
> It's success, O my God, that I'm seeking.
> I need to be famous, God, please.
> You know that I am not ambitious.
> Self-seeking just isn't my creed.
> My fame truly is not the issue.
> I'm alive, and that's all that I need.
> I need fame to give strength to my story,
> It's all been hushed up for too long.

And now that my mind is in fury
I want it to come over strong.
Now fame would give strength to my passion—
As steam makes a steam-hammer go—
To give them a more severe thrashing,
To deal them a far sharper blow.

Payment and retribution

'All the blessings which the Ibanskian people rejoice in have to be paid for,' said Neurasthenic. 'For instance, the leadership does not want to look ridiculous, stupid, cruel or unjust. And the people must therefore think of the leadership as serious, wise, kind and just. And not only think of them in that way. The people must behave as if their leaders were indeed wise, kind, just, credible and so on. And by analogy all other aspects of life should be regarded in the same way. You will of course have noticed that individually every Ibanskian reviles our society and our leadership, but when they are together they praise everything we have and are prepared to tear any detractor to pieces. There is no contradiction in this. In the former case we are showing our awareness of the realities of our life, in the second we are paying for the advantages it gives us. Payment is made in public. Our awareness is experienced individually and is of no social value.'

'But in time this leads to catastrophic consequences,' said Journalist. 'That is of no importance,' said Neurasthenic. 'If the catastrophe is transitory it is regarded as a chance occurrence. If it lasts a long time it is not regarded as a catastrophe. Malcontents believe only prophets, who speak only nonsense. People who are satisfied believe no-one, not even the leaders in whom they have complete trust. Belief is a subjective state, and trust is a social contract. Now for the leaders any prediction which is out of line with the demagogy of the moment is a slander. The result is that those who pay do not know that they are paying for the sins of others. And so no one gives a fuck for anything.'

The ninth hour

The barrack room. A drink. A crust of bread.
The blue tobacco smoke above my head.

(486)

The oil lamp sways and flickers in the breeze,
The squeeze-box oompahs out its endless wheeze.
But I'm in luck. I'll be with you tonight.
The others have no chance of such delight.
The moment Lights Out sounds, I'm off my mark
To find a cosy corner in the dark.
My greatcoat under us, the stars above—
The first time ever I will swear my love.
And in the hut, the lads won't close their eyes
Imagining your breasts, your hips, your thighs.
But then she says, 'You fly at break of day—
So what's the point of rolling in the hay?
Canoodling here's a pointless thing to do.
Next time we meet, they might be burying you.
's no use, lieutenant. Sorry, but we're through.
I've got a Stores bloke when I want a screw.
And you're too good for me. So stay alive.
You'll find another girl if you survive.'
I go back to the hut as dawn breaks through
And hide my misery. What else could I do?
The lads all ears—'Well, that's another score.
And something else: she'd not been fucked before!'
But to myself I say, 'You poor fool, you.
There's only one thing left for you to do.
Don't plot your course home on today's flight plan,
There's no way you will ever live again.'

A declaration

You know why I like you, said Teacher. Because you keep quiet
and never moralise. These days that is astonishingly rare. These
days everyone tries to teach you something. Everyone tries to
open your eyes to what you must and must not do, just as if that
was a mystery accessible to only a few. The problem is not to
know what to do and not to do, but in deciding on one's own
relationship to the rules. From this point of view all those
scoffers who point out all the festering sores of the Ibanskian
way of life remain massively supporters of that way of life. That
is the swamp in which they find themselves. They want only the
privileges which they believe are theirs by right. They are more
intelligent than everyone else, better educated, they have been

abroad, they have read foreign books. That is all just words, words, words. You could go mad from so many words. I am a man of action. I have had enough of all this. I need action. No matter what action. Any kind of action, so long as it is action. Action has its own laws, very different from the laws of the word. A word does not mark the starting point of an action. The starting point of an action is action. From the point of view of words the starting point of an action is always absurd. For instance, self-immolation. How does the action differ from the word? By its consequences. The action is visible, forbidden and punishable. And the word, if it is visible, dangerous and punishable, is also an action. But to become an action the word must be spoken loudly enough. Is that only a theory, you ask. I am convinced that the progress of a society is invented and not just discovered like something which is hidden in the nature of the society. Progress is anti-natural and contrary to the laws of society. If there were no men of action equipped with an inventive fantasy, there would be no progress. The theory of the progress of society as an objective, natural and historic process which is accomplished according to certain objective laws, means in fact one thing and one thing only: keep your head down and sit quietly, everything will happen all of its own accord under the leadership of the authorities.

Unity

They hadn't managed to get remotely drunk enough before the lights were switched off and they were turned out of the restaurant. 'What the hell!' said Colleague. 'This is just the time when decent people begin their night out, but here they close any place where you can expect some fun.' 'Let's go to the station,' said Teacher. 'They stay open till 1 o'clock.' 'Balls,' said Fellow-worker. 'By the time we get there and place an order it will be throwing-out time again.' 'I've got the best plan,' said Schizophrenic. 'Let's buy a couple of bottles from the doorman and drink them in a doorway. It'll save buying food—besides it'll be more romantic.' 'No,' said Brother, 'come round to my place. My wife'll be pleased to see you, and there'll be no need to buy anything. Some friends brought us a bottle of home-brewed vodka from the country.' Teacher voted for Schizophrenic's idea because he had a gut mistrust of

Brother. But after a stormy argument they decided to go to Brother's.

When they got to Brother's apartment, everything turned out as Teacher had predicted. After a long discussion on the threshold Brother's wife finally, and very unwillingly, let them into the kitchen and went off to bed without so much as a hallo or goodbye. 'Bring out the hooch,' said Fellow-worker. 'What hooch?' asked Brother in surprise. 'Are you off your head?' 'Why you bastard,' roared Teacher, flinging himself on Brother. 'I shan't leave it like this,' Brother snuffled through his flattened nose. 'I'll take you to court. You'll all be witnesses.' The cheerful mood was destroyed and they went their separate ways home. 'You overdid it,' said Schizophrenic. 'There's no teaching people like that.' 'I didn't do it for him, I did it for myself,' said Teacher.

Business life

The business life of Ibansk follows a strictly defined course. It is decided at a high level to raise everything, to increase everything, to improve everything and to eliminate all shortcomings. These aims are fully realisable as there are usually very few shortcomings, and these usually just in individual cases. Decisions of this kind are usually taken at a time when the old leadership is being replaced by a new lot, and the new leadership attribute all shortcomings to the old leaders while keeping quiet about their achievements so as to be able later to claim them for themselves. But if they fail to overthrow the old leadership, the old leaders, under the pressure of present demands, change their old good intentions for even better new ones, or more precisely, present their old idiotic intentions as brilliant new ideas. Since it is impossible to improve and correct everything immediately, it has to be done in a very strict order of precedence: blast-furnaces, computers, cattle, potatoes, poetry, novels, chromosomes, alcoholism, absenteeism. Atoms, rockets and opponents are improved and eliminated systematically. They do not have to take their turn. No open resolutions are taken about them. Everything is done in great secrecy.

A strict order of precedence is also observed within each stage of the improvements. For instance a directive is issued to increase meat and milk production and to catch up and overtake America. Europe isn't even mentioned, it's such a trivial comparison! If we're going to do it, it must be on a grand scale! A number of concrete measures are then taken: (1) to increase the number of head of horned cattle producing powdered and condensed milk (in millions of horns); (2) to increase the yields from every milchcow (in millions of half-litre bottles); (3) increase the number of head of beef cattle (in millions of shashliks per head of population); (4) to increase the meat output per beast, and so on. Although in Ibansk cows have long since disappeared (they have been replaced by motorcycles and electric milking-machines), the decision to increase the number by fiftyfold quite staggers the Western press. And of course the Ibanskian press almost chokes with self-satisfaction. The Ibanskians themselves know perfectly well what all this is worth, don't read the papers and tell each other funny stories about it. Western specialists in Ibanskology, and in particular our most determined enemies, proclaim with a single voice that the Ibanskian leadership has at last decided to tackle the acute food shortage and has prepared practical measures for an upturn in agriculture. This is regarded by all as a clear swing towards the democratisation of Ibanskian society. The Ibanskian leadership confirms this publicly, while at the same time assuring the world that in principle we have nothing which needs to be democratised since we are already extremely democratic, and could in no way be more democratic. That friend of Ibansk, the American millionaire Shark, calls on businessmen to make deals with Ibansk on mutually disadvantageous terms. The Ibanskian newspapers begin to publish articles denouncing Western morals and testifying to the severe food shortages the West is suffering. Economists produce incontrovertible figures. For example in America, where there is an acute meat shortage, there is only one kilo of meat per head per week, while we have just decided to raise our production to fifty kilos per head per week. Under the cover of this hullaballoo the leaders take the opportunity to jail a few opponents.

At the same time all the forces of society are directed towards the finding of a solution to the problem in hand; all grab hold of the weakest link and begin to drag the entire chain behind them. Sector plans are proposed. As a result the time needed to complete the task is halved and the target figures are tripled. The shockworkers of the Ism take on vastly increased commitments and stand poised at the spearhead of the working people. The Universal Lathe-operator commits himself to milking single-handed all the billygoats in Ibansk, and Thrasher to shearing a hundred tufts of wool from every black sheep. The whole political education network begins to study the directive and to set examination questions on it. Bachelors of Art quickly and slickly defend their Master's dissertations, and the Masters their Doctorates. The philosophers theorise the practice of the building of the Ism, and raise it to a still higher level. The Journal publishes a series of articles and organises a round table which includes the champion of Charles Darwin who has managed to transform a monkey into an Ibanskian. A group of colleagues sets off on a foreign study trip. The newspapers and the walls of houses burgeon with appeals to workers with the udder, the pelt and the snout to increase their milk yields, skin more cattle and boost pig production. The latest achievements of science are applied to production. Cyberneticists suggest that classical music should be relayed to pigsties, which will produce piglets whose tails and ears grow amazingly long in a very short time. Cows are shown abstract and surrealist paintings with an accompanying commentary by leading Ibanskian art critics, with the result that the cows become even more stupid and yield their milk with no resistance at all. On its front page the Newspaper publishes a poem by the disgraced but pardoned Snottyhanky, the favourite of young people, the secret police and the Americans:

> The friendly cows both large and small
> We shall triple twice.
> Harvest up a hundredfold
> Milk yields that times thrice.
> And we shall
> > begin
> > > to see
> The envy
> > of the
> > > bourgeoisie.

The Journal prints yet another series of articles on the abolition of frontiers. There is a move to propose Claimant for election to the Academy. On the quiet a few more suspect elements are rounded up, and convicted of currency speculation, homosexuality and breaches of the passport regulations. A number of others are committed to lunatic asylums as a prophylactic measure.

The measures are published. The completion periods are fixed. And during these strictly established periods the workers with the udder, the pelt and the snout begin to produce reports that the plan has been overfulfilled ahead of time. The dates on which the plan has to be overfulfilled and the percentage of overfulfilment are agreed in advance. The same thing goes for the applications for the jobs of the leaders of the struggle for early overfulfilment. Finally, the decorations and the titles are handed out. Despite all this, meat, sausages, vegetables and so on are either in short supply or not available at all. But that is merely a slander by corrupt and parasitic elements who have succumbed to the pernicious influence of the West. The highest leaders go abroad to pursue the cause of world peace and take advantage of the opportunity to buy bread, meat, potatoes and toothpaste.

After a certain time this general trading cycle is complete and everything begins again on a higher level. As is well known, Ibansk is advancing towards the total Ism, advancing in the form of a spiral whose higher curves are below the lower, which permits this triumphant forward march.

After the measures concerning cattle, potatoes and maize had been taken, they were followed by others on literature, television, films, ice-hockey and 100-square chess. Finally they got round to science. And what they found plunged them into bewilderment: Ibansk, it turned out, was full to bursting with Doctors of Science. Oh, ho! So that's what the matter is! So that's why there are all these shortages, deficits, errors, deviations! We shall have to get to grips with the Doctors and liquidate them as a class.

The beginning

'Let's begin, my captain,' said Soilophagist. 'Very well, let's begin,' said Teacher. 'Our association is very odd. You are for, I am against. You believe, I do not.' 'Nonsense,' said Soilophagist. 'We met at the front so I know you well. People like you don't change. You are one of our people right down to your roots. If you really want to know, I trust you more than all our demagogues put together. You won't drop me in time of trouble. You won't betray me. So let's leave this silly squabble. We're long past being children.' 'Yes,' said Teacher, 'we're not children. But are you sure where this scheme's taking you? The people who are liked least of all here are sincere Ibanskians and reformers. If they sniff you out you'll simply be liquidated. And no-one will hear anything about it.' 'The same goes for you,' said Soilophagist. 'What have we got to fear? Just remember the conversation we had before the battle. It's a gift of fate that we're alive. The main thing is to get the job done. At least we've got to try. There's no other way.

'First of all let's establish the main lines of our work. Then we can get on to thinking about the actual material. There you've got all the cards in your hands. From my side I can give you material that no other Ibanskian scientist in any field or discipline has access to. Then we can get down to concrete propositions. And here you will have to listen to me. I'm a practical man. I know from experience that not everything that looks alright in theory works out in practice. Not everything that seems absurd theoretically turns out badly in practice. You will have to do all the basic calculations we need. We'll have no-one to help us. I've got no-one except you whom I could trust. We'll have to think where and how you're going to work. Bear in mind that a huge group has been set up to do something similar for the Leader. They'll have the support of the services of several dozen institutes and laboratories. You can see that the forces are very unequal. And that they'll be working officially. But if they find out about us we are both kaput.

'Just for your guidance, these are the principal directions for the selection and use of the documentation. Wanton and senseless squandering of state funds. Low productivity. The parasitic nature of large groups of the population. Parasitic organisations. Irresponsibility and depersonalisation. And so on, in that spirit. Do you follow me?' 'I follow you,' said Teacher. 'You think of some positive proposals without consulting me. And then we'll compare our conclusions. Our aim is to prepare a system of measures which would automatically guarantee economic progress and an elimination of waste. Something like

(493)

competition in a bourgeois society, but wholly and completely within the principles of the Ibanskian society. The problem isn't that I'm afraid of something. I am not afraid of anything. It's just that, for me, this is a base, a point of departure. I have thought about this subject a lot and I have come to a definite conclusion: what we have is a great historical outcome, while everything else is a step back.' 'Unfortunately,' said Teacher, 'I can't raise any objection to that, although I very much dislike this historical result. But the fact that one day we shall die is also something that we don't like. So what's to be done? In general you can rely on me. I am completely at your disposal. Let's make a start. At least we are doing something. Although to be honest I have no faith in any concrete success.' 'I'll take that on myself,' said Soilophagist. 'Cognac? Whisky?'

They did not know that their entire conversation had not only been overheard but recorded. Nor did they know that as a result a decision had been taken about it. Let them go on working. As soon as they had finished, then . . . There had, after all, been some progress in society. Mainly in the fields of bugging and recording what was bugged.

On social systems

The main difficulty in the understanding of social phenomena, wrote Teacher, does not lie in the detection of sensational facts, in compiling statistical data, or in gaining access to jealously guarded state secrets, but in finding a method of classifying what is evident, a method of understanding the commonplace. From this point of view it makes no difference whether ten people have been repressed or fifty million. Nor is it of any importance whether anyone was repressed at all. For instance if today it was accepted that there were no innocent victims in Ibansk, that would not change the essence of Ibanskian society. The authorities instinctively feel far more threatened by books about the laws of our glorious and radiant daily life than by books about concentration camps. Truth-teller's book was published. But Slanderer's book about social systems, which contained not a word about repression, was quietly killed. Schizophrenic's fine works on the same subject were confiscated and destroyed.

I do not know whether this is the conscious purpose or not.

But objectively when the authorities indulge in spectacular repression of sensational prison-camp writers, by that very fact they distract attention, particularly that of Western critics and politicians, from the essential, and are able without any fuss to stifle the slightest attempt to get down to the heart of the matter. The camps could have not existed. They could have not been restored. Although they are a characteristic phenomenon of Ibanskian society, they are not the only one and not the most important.

For the moment I am not in a position to present the method I referred to earlier in a finished form, for I simply do not have one. I merely want to sketch in its most general contours and certain specific details which I have managed to produce, albeit only in draft form. I conceive my task as being merely to stimulate research into social phenomena in one specific direction, towards the construction of a general theory of empirical systems and its application to systems of the Ibanskian type.

The signatories

From every point of view Ibanskian society is the best. That is common knowledge. Every citizen hears that repeated every moment of his life. He cannot fail to be aware of it. So if an Ibanskian is in a normal state of mental health he will not criticise Ibanskian society nor protest about its alleged sore points. Ibanskian society has no sore points and cannot have. That was established long ago by the classics. And there is nothing here to protest about. So, if anyone does criticise and protest, the conclusion follows with cast-iron logic: he must be mentally ill or a criminal. Naturally if a protester or a critic appears anywhere he is politely grabbed and put inside for reorientation or for cure. That reorientation or cure will last until he shouts 'Hurrah!' and sends a telegram of congratulations. And while experienced specialists are restoring him with tender care to the state of a normal Ibanskian citizen, his friends, relatives, colleagues and associates will be preparing a document addressed to the Leader, the Pope, the Patriarch, the Secretary-General of the United Nations or the Head of the Secret Police, demanding the release of the hospitalised or re-educated innocent critic. And they collect signatures. The people who sign a letter of this kind are known as signatories.

(495)

Initially signatories were carefully selected and arranged in hierarchical order: at the top of the list came the Laureates, then Academicians, then Professors; somewhere in the middle there were the Generals and Doctors, followed by the rest who were accorded this honour only by virtue of their relations and contacts. Later, when it became clear that this activity wasn't without its dangers, the organisers began to catch anyone who passed within reach and put under their noses a signature sheet bereft of the text of the petition. And many people signed, some on principle, some out of indifference, others because they didn't like to offend, and yet others because they feared they might be taken for cowards.

It was unexpectedly discovered that petitions of this kind had a real effect. The authorities were obliged to release two or three detainees from the lunatic asylumn, and in their panic they even released one *bona fide* madman. In his delight he found a piece of paper and wrote on it in block capitals: 'LONG LIVE THE IBANSKIAN CONSTITUTION!' He took it out onto the street before he'd even had time to shave. The mounted police had to turn out to disperse him. The signatories of this petition found themselves assaulted by a tempest of repression at their place of work, a repression which was unseen by foreigners but so effective for the signatories and their families that the epidemic of petition signing ended as abruptly as it had started. The Ibanskian liberal was prepared for a lot, but not for a reduction or the complete loss of his already miserable salary, not to mention other advantages like getting theses accepted, getting a better apartment, winning a bonus or getting permission for a trip abroad.

The majority of the signatories acknowledged their guilt and recanted. Some few remained obstinate. But initially no-one knew about them and later they were completely forgotten.

The tenth hour

The war was drawing to its end. And the high command decided to carry out one final major military operation according to all the rules of the art. One for the Manual of Strategy. Intelligence sources revealed the whereabouts of an important enemy airfield, defended by a few dozen fighters and six AA batteries. The high command worked out the following plan of attack. One squadron would destroy the runways. A further two squadrons would take out the anti-aircraft gun positions. And the remaining two regiments of the division would destroy the hangars and the bomb and fuel stores. Commonsense demanded a different, simpler plan. The enemy would be quite unable to replace his aircraft, his bombs, and his fuel supplies. So the obvious course would have been to make a single raid to destroy the bomb and fuel stores and the hangars and make a low-level retreat. In this case losses would be minimal. There would be no need to attack the AA positions or the runways, which would be of no further use to the enemy. And yet that was the most dangerous part of the operational plan. But this option would not have found its way into the Manual of Strategy.

The most dangerous role in the high command's plan fell to the first squadron. If they attacked at dawn they would almost certainly all be shot down. There would be fewer losses and better results if the attack were launched in darkness. But the aircraft were not equipped for night flying, and only one man in the regiment was capable of leading the squadron to its target. This man, however, was in the cooler, awaiting a court martial for his part in a brawl. The regimental commander himself paid the cooler a visit. 'Will you fly?' he asked. 'Certainly I'll fly,' said the Man, 'if you get me out of the cooler and cancel the court martial.' 'I can't do that,' said the commander, 'that would be against regulations. But the court martial will give you proper credit for the operation.' 'But do the regulations allow you to take me out of the cooler to lead a mission?' asked the Man. 'What if I get shot down?' 'Then your family won't hear anything about the court martial,' said the commander. 'It's ridiculous,' said the Man. 'What difference does it make to you to cancel the court martial? Because I'm bound to be shot down. You've nothing to lose.' 'Then why are you bargaining?' asked the commander. 'For the same reason as you, as a matter of principle,' said the Man. 'Perhaps you've gone yellow,' said the commander. 'You made a big mistake in using that word,' said the Man.

The squadron took off at dawn without him. When the crews arrived at the airfield he was sitting near the guardroom. 'So you're ducking out, are you?' they said to him. 'That's right,' said the Man. 'Just as if we didn't matter,' said the crewmen. 'As if anyone here mattered,' said the Man. The squadron took off. And they did not come back. There was something about this whole episode that was indefinable, but extremely unpleasant. Something cruel and unjust. A matter of principle, he said to himself. But what have principles got to do with any of this? Principles are alien to this society. They have never understood them and never will. Any men of principle are swiftly pushed into dead ends and condemned to all kinds of suffering. People here simply don't possess whatever organ it is that generates principles. In this present case I feel a bit guilty about the crews, but I don't owe anybody anything. Their obligation was to prevent me being put into this position. But they forgot about that. Situations where a man is forced to overlay their oppression by his own moral principles must be avoided.

> You see the flames enfold the sky,
> You hear the bombers dive;
> The boys are flying off to die
> While you alone survive.
> And then your life whirls past your eyes,
> You see your wasted days,
> From youth to age, to your demise,
> One thought with you always:
> There was that incandescent sky,
> There was that day you didn't fly;
> You watched your gallant comrades fry—
> And yet you lived—oh why? why? why?

But in fact nothing like that ever actually happened. It was just the delirium of a night before a combat mission. Just before the dawn an orderly came running into the cooler and beckoned to him with no further explanation. The Man tightened his belt, put on his flying helmet and went to the briefing room. On the way home he was shot down. A few days later he managed to make his way back to the regiment. 'Where are your orders?' asked the Military Policeman. 'Where are your papers? What happened to your gunner?' 'You go fuck yourself,' he replied. He didn't care any more. He knew he'd be put inside just the same. But times were hard and pilots were needed. He was let out and he flew again. He was shot down several times.

(498)

You watched your gallant comrades die,
And yet you lived—oh why? why? why?
You're losing your grip, he said to himself. That's enough of sentiment!

A polemic about fate

'If Bawler had had enough to eat when he was a child, and sheets to sleep in,' said Thinker, 'he wouldn't have got mixed up in all this nonsense. He'd have become a great scientist.' 'Bawler could never have become a scientist at all,' said Chatterer. 'He's far too intelligent and talented for that. He's done something more than just make scientific discoveries. He has committed an historic stupidity.' 'What stupidity?' asked Thinker. 'I don't know,' said Chatterer. 'And, all things considered, we shall probably never know.'

Unity

'You do not like our Ism,' said Puss, lasciviously peering up Toad's worn and grubby skirt, from which the hem of her nylon slip peeked provocatively. 'Yet the Ism is the incarnation of all our aspirations.' 'The aspirations of idiots,' said Colleague. 'Even if he doesn't like it,' said Thinker, 'it's hardly a crime.' 'Just shut this cretin's gob, with Toad's tit if you have to,' said Wife. The Boy was much dismayed, and decided to report the entire conversation without changing a word. Let them sort it out for themselves. Fellow-worker flung an arm round Claimant's neck and burst into song:

> When vicious minds come to conspire
> And combine mutu-ally,
> They produce a deaf-mute choir
> And a legless ballet.

'He's very good, the old bastard,' said Colleague. 'A real waste of talent.' But Fellow-worker, beating time on Claimant's pate, improvised without taking breath:

> Once informers reigned supreme,
> Now antillectuals are the cream;
> We won't have to wait too long
> Before they sing the selfsame song.

The Boy, who was rather tipsy by this time, plunged into a state of sincerity and tried to find someone to pour out his soul to.

No-one paid any attention to him. 'I was called in yesterday,' he said at last to Teacher. 'Called in There! What for?' asked Teacher. 'They proposed that I should become an informer,' said the Boy. 'My congratulations,' said Teacher. 'What did you say to them?' 'I promised to think about it,' said the Boy. Teacher knew that situations of this kind occur only after a person has already agreed, and that the Boy was asking advice merely to ease his conscience. But he was somewhat surprised by the sheer cynical simplicity of the problem. 'All the same, you won't get out of it,' he said. 'That's true,' said the Boy. 'And it's better for Them to have one of our own people rather than someone from outside.' 'What a crank he is,' thought Teacher. Anyone from outside always starts off by being one of our own people. But he said nothing. It's always better to know the people who are informing on you personally, he decided. And anyway he won't be reporting literally everything! He is one of ours, after all! But Teacher was mistaken. A clear month ago the Boy had already written a circumstantial report on the activity of Teacher's group, of which he was an active member.

Denunciation

Among the people I know there isn't a single person who hasn't at some time or another been taken as either a secret police agent or an informer, said Chatterer. When Truth-teller's first book was published it was said, even of him, that he'd written it on the orders of the secret police. To say nothing of Dauber. Ninety per cent of Ibanskian artists are convinced that he's at the very least a secret police colonel. If not, they could never understand why he's stayed at liberty so long. What are the causes of all this? There are many, beginning with the most harmless. For example, let's take the currently fashionable way of discrediting someone, to show oneself in a favourable light. And then there are more serious causes. I'll list the main ones. First there's the ideology which is stuffed into everyone's minds to the effect that every action of the opposition is committed with the knowledge and under the control of the secret police. The secret police knows about everything that is happening from the very start, and if something happens, that means that it must have been decided in advance. The action has taken place because it has been allowed to happen in the pursuit of a particular aim, and it has been stopped in time from going further than was intended. Otherwise things would be worse.

Secondly, there is the monstrously inflated number of secret police staff and their regular informers. They have representatives in every kind of enterprise. And at least one in ten of the adult population is an informer. And on top of that every citizen regularly carries out the functions of an informer, often without even suspecting it, and at all events without seeing anything wrong in it. For example, respectable citizen A is called in and asked whether he has noticed anything blameworthy about citizen B. Citizen A is indignant and rushes to the defence of B. And in the process he reveals everything he knows about him.

Yet the secret police apparatus and all its grandiose system of information is a typical—perhaps even a super-typical —Ibanskian institution. It selects for its purposes the most sociable individuals who turn in due course into run-of-the-mill scroungers, layabouts, liars and careerists. They function effectively only when the need arises to set a hundred such collaborators on to one defenceless man. In cases like that they perform miracles of idiotic ingenuity and perspicacity. The stupid, the idle and the deceitful are as a rule virtuoso inventors of absurdity. So all the grandiose apparatus of investigation, denunciation and surveillance is still not enough to explain the informomanic psychology of Ibanskian society.

The underlying basis of this phenomenon lies in a general system of mutual denunciation which is rooted in the very foundations of society and which becomes the norm, the customary form of its existence. We are conditioned to this daily phenomenon from our childhood and are not even aware of it. But just try and look at our life from outside. Look at our newspapers, our films, our magazines, our novels, our meetings, our symposia, our assemblies, our conversations, our reports and so on. What are they all? Nothing but denunciations, denunciations, denunciations. Denunciations of ourselves, our neighbours, our colleagues, our superiors, our subordinates. What is referred to as a system of control and accountability is in fact an official system of denunciation as the normal pattern of life in society. Information about the progress of work in hand, about results achieved, and so on, occupies a minute place in all this. Results can be seen without any need for progress reports, conversations, communications and so on. All this is done not as a matter of control, or of a genuine need to know, but as a purely social phenomenon. It is through all this that every citizen has, as it were, an invisible dossier—and in many cases a real, visible dossier—which can be brought into play at any time. Every individual is held up to the light from all directions in such a way that none of his inner secrets can be hidden. And indeed, the individual learns not to have any secrets and to avoid acquiring them. And a man without secrets is nothing but a cog in the social machine. A hollow, empty object. A naked form who can do nothing but perform a function.

So the apparatus of the secret police is not an anomaly in the life of our society. It is its legitimate creation and expression. If there were no secret police, society would somehow or other perform its functions, maybe in yet more terrible forms. For example, perhaps every apartment house, every institution of any kind, would contain its own secret cell. The secret police are even perhaps a little better than the body which has produced them, in the sense that they are to a certain degree professional. And even if there were no need to catch spies and enemies of the people, even if we were not ruled by the principle which, in his time, Writer expressed so well:

> The secret enemy of the masses—
> He's never far away
> As the war between the classes
> Sharpens day by day,

even then the secret police would have taken the form we know as a true expression of one of the real aspects of the Ibanskian way of life. And also, in passing, as an expression of the mysterious Ibanskian soul—mysterious, that is, for Westerners.

Brother

'The most enigmatic person in Ibansk is Brother,' said Fellow-worker. 'I don't want to hear a word about that scum,' shouted the infuriated Thinker, who was a friend of Brother. They had just been watching Brother on television, where he had developed a new interpretation of the theme of Mozart and Salieri, a subject on which Thinker was regarded as the leading specialist. 'How could they let him do it!' said Neurasthenic in bewilderment. 'Such an odious figure . . .' 'There's nothing special about that,' said Sociologist. 'After the pogrom of Truth-teller, Double-dealer, Shamizdat and the rest, there's now a need to create the illusion that intellectual life is flourishing. The Ibanka theatre, Brother, Snottyhanky and people like that are being pushed forward. Soon there'll even be public references to Dauber.' 'There's nothing enigmatic about Brother,' said Wife. 'He's just an ordinary informer.' 'I think he's on the staff of the secret police,' said the Boy. 'Nonsense!' said Colleague. 'They don't need blatherers like him down there. And if he is an informer he's a volunteer. But I think it's most likely that he's got different functions. What functions? Those that we've just seen him performing.' 'He's a provocateur', said Thinker. 'That may very well be,' said Wife. 'But he's a charming man and very far from stupid.'

Yet they were all mistaken. Brother was indeed an enigmatic performer on the stage of Ibanskian history of that period. He was the incarnation of the breadth, depth, complexity and rebellious nature of the Ibanskian soul. He was enigmatic because he was typical. Exaggeratedly typical. He didn't know himself who or what he was. When for example he swore to Truth-teller that the rumours that he belonged to the secret police were being circulated by the police themselves, with the aim of dividing and weakening the movement, he was speaking the truth, since no one had instructed him to go and spy on Truth-teller and report what he was up to. But he was also telling a lie since, when he left Truth-teller, he went straight to his friends in the secret police and told them about the new and stupendous book that Truth-teller was writing at the time. 'Lads,' he said passionately, 'we must do everything we can to see that this book is published. You must convince Theoretician that there's nothing anti-Ibanskian in it. I'll bring you some extracts to read, but only in the utmost secrecy. Truth-teller is our man deep down, as you'll see for yourselves. I can vouch for him. I give you my word as an Ist that he won't let you down.'

Progress in penology
'I've been offered a chair in the Academy of Penology,' said Thinker. 'Where's that?' asked Chatterer in surprise. 'Are you

sure it exists?' 'Of course it does,' said Thinker. 'You can't imagine that our society is making progress without that progress affecting the most important aspect of its existence! Indeed, progress is greater here than in your science. At the present time every warder has at least secondary education. A staircase officer must have been to university. The chief officer in charge of a block must have his doctorate. And prison governors must rate with professors.' 'What faculties are there in this Academy?' asked Dauber. 'Every kind,' said Thinker. 'You have to give them their due; they've put the most modern scientific discoveries to use in the most radical way. For example they've got faculties going full steam already: the Institute of Ideology, Building Science, Cybernetics, Physical Education, Medicine, Methods of Execution, Psychology. . . . We lead the world in this field. There are more than a thousand foreign students in the Academy.' 'That's wonderful,' said Chatterer. 'Educated jailers! Just think, if any of them were to try and get a job in France or America. What are your qualifications? Diploma of the Ibanskian Penological Academy. Excellent! We'll pay you double! We need fully-trained specialists!' 'Why all this irony?' asked Thinker. 'Education never hurt anyone. Actually they're doing valuable scientific work. You'll have seen in the papers that A and B have been elected academicians, and A, C and D have been awarded prizes? They're all members of the IPA. There are enormous possibilities. One thing they've established is that the rations for criminals were so low that they ought to be increased, and that political prisoners were getting such large rations that they ought to be reduced. They've just been awarded a prize for that research.' 'Well,' asked Dauber, 'have you accepted the job?' 'Why not?' said Thinker. 'The people are better than they are here. At least they aren't full of complexes. It's their job not to kick people when they're down. They'll give me an apartment for a year. I'll get paid for being head of department, for the title (and that's effective straightaway), and for services rendered. And then there are all kinds of additional benefits. They've got their own privileged shops and restaurants. And the level of teaching is higher than a university. For example, in the Faculty of Ideology they teach sociology, social psychology, psychoanalysis, and the history of religion, all at a very high level. Two foreign languages. Courses abroad. After all, the name of the institution doesn't matter. It's a first-class academic and scientific centre. In my view this is the path that any real progress in Ibansk will have to take.' 'That's only the way it'll begin,' said Chatterer. 'It won't take long for your IPA to turn into an ordinary Ibanskian institution, closed off, restricted, privileged, in other words a collection of scroungers, careerists, layabouts, liars and oppressors.' 'The whole thing scares me silly,' said Neurasthenic. 'What a prospect to see the running of prisons put on a modern scientific footing!' 'Why is it all needed?' asked Dauber. 'It won't have any real effect on criminals, and there aren't that many politicals. They're easily enough suppressed without the help of science.' 'It's easy enough to knock things,' said Thinker. 'Jailers are people as well. They've got just the same right as anyone else to a full life. They need to be able to perform at the highest levels of modern civilisation. And they need prisoners as the raw material for their activity—in the same way that a general needs soldiers, a teacher needs students, a miner needs coal, or a pilot needs a plane. If there aren't any prisoners to work on then this whole grandiose penological system, and beyond that the entire edifice of jurisprudence lose any sense.' 'It's a nightmare,' said Dauber. 'How can you say such things?' 'There's nothing shocking in what I'm saying,' said Thinker. 'Good and evil, love and hate have nothing to do with the problem. The jailer has no personal involvement with the prisoner. For the jailer the prisoner is not a personality, he is merely the area, the object and the product of his professional activity. Personal relationships are possible only between mutually independent individuals.' 'I've never known him talk so much,' said Dauber, when Thinker suddenly left their company. 'He's trying to justify himself,' said Chatterer. 'To persuade himself.' 'Do you think he'll take the job?' asked Dauber. 'Of course he will,' said Chatterer. 'Once the theory has been advanced that the Penological Academy is more progressive than the University (and he's probably right there if you consider freedom of teaching), then how can any progressive thinker fail to fall in with it, particularly as it has lots of other advantages.' 'But what about his reputation?' asked Dauber. 'I think his most ardent lady friends will get taken on by his Academy,' said Chatterer. 'Well there'd certainly be nothing unusual about that,' said Neuras-thenic. 'I never suggested that it was anything unusual,' said Chatterer. 'That is normality.'

Brother

When Brother persuaded Truth-teller to write to the Leader asking for help, he was sincere. But when he added that the Leader had quite a good opinion of Truth-teller, it was pure invention. It was invention, too, when he told Dauber that he had come to see him on behalf of the secret police. But when Dauber threw him out, accusing him of being an impostor, and he yelled in reply that they would expel Dauber and not let him take a single piece of work with him, he was sincere. But at the same time he was not sincere, as he immediately rushed off to his friends in the secret police and begged them to save Iban-skian culture because Dauber wanted to leave. Dauber, he said with conviction, is our man deep down. I'll vouch for him. I give you my word as an Ist that he won't let you down. And in a brief report to Theoretician he wrote that Dauber's fame in the West was largely political, because the West had more artists like him than they knew what to do with.

When the need arose to hide the originals of the collective letters, Brother took it upon himself. He concealed them in an old divan belonging to a schoolfriend. And when the school-friend began to be bothered day and night by suspicious charac-ters who wanted to photocopy the letters or take extracts from them, and he begged Brother to take them away, Brother was deeply and sincerely outraged by the ingratitude of the Iban-skian people. 'Oh, you people of Ibansk,' he said, his drunken tears coarsing down his unshaven cheeks. 'Just for once you've been given the chance of helping to set your people free, and you . . . Very well then, the hell with you! Sling all this shit away. No-one's needed it for ages.' 'What a creep you are,' said his Friend. But Brother did not take umbrage, and borrowed some money off him till next pay-day. 'You can spit in his face and he'll still say thank you,' Friend would say. 'What bastards our people are,' Brother said later to his Chief. 'I left him the papers just for one night and he took them all off to the secret police. By the way, who was that bugger who just left?' He was talking about Bawler who had bumped into him on the threshold. 'He looked like a typical informer to me.' 'That's what they say,' said the Chief. 'But it's funny all the same. To do a thing like that by way of the secret police themselves! Cognac? Whisky?' 'Why not?' said Brother. 'Then I've got to get off to the Ibanka. A meeting of the artistic council. But those shitheads can wait. They can't get anything done without me anyway.'

Brother was regarded as one of the spiritual leaders of the progressive Ibanskian Intelligentsia of the time and he had become famous in the West. And so he was involved with everything, could get in anywhere and received invitations from everybody.

'He's the worst kind of filth,' Chatterer said of him. 'A typical Ibanskian, but turned inside out.'

The tenth hour

'I don't understand what you want,' said Engineer. 'You're only twenty-three and you're a captain already. You've got a stack of decorations. You're a very able lad with a brilliant career ahead of you. What more do you want?' 'Let's analyse the situation calmly,' said Bawler. 'I'm a fighter pilot, yet who's been appointed squadron commander? He's never fought. And his qualifications are inferior to mine. But I'm just his deputy. His acting-deputy. Take the commander of our second squadron. He's a major. He's flown only half as many missions as I have. But he's got more decorations. He's even been nominated for the title of Hero. Now why? I was promoted captain and got a few medals because I was needed at the most difficult time. Now I'm not needed. I've no career ahead of me. As you know I wasn't sent to the Academy. I could have passed the exams standing on my head. He failed. But he was kept on for the preparatory class. No, my dear optimist, I've got no prospects and never will have. They only have to look at me and I only have to open my mouth for them to see straightaway that I don't belong. They've got a flair for it!' 'Do you think things would be any better Over There?' asked Engineer. 'Believe it or not,' said Bawler, 'but for me it's not a problem of better or worse. I've got a lot of things to think about and reflect on. So I need not only external independence but internal as well. And I need to be right in the centre. There at least there is some kind of life, tension, direction. And food for thought. Here all we have is drink, whores, cards and service duties. Later there might be a family, a comfortable life and a career.' 'A normal modest life,' said Engineer. 'That doesn't suit me,' said Bawler. 'Check. And mate, I think. Do you want another game?' 'No,' said Engineer. 'I'm bored playing with you. I have the impression that I'm a better player than you but for some reason I don't understand I always lose.'

The Brotherhood

You know just as well as I, said Slanderer, the role that the Brotherhood plays in the life of Ibanskian society. But nevertheless I shall dwell rather longer on this question than usual, since it is the key to the understanding of all the visible side of Ibanskian life.

It is superfluous and impossible to define what the Brotherhood is. All that we need here is merely a description of this phenomenon and the way it functions, similar to a description of the human nervous system. The Brotherhood is an empirical reality of Ibanskian society with its own structure and function. I merely wish to draw your attention to certain of its characteristics which are of major importance in any analysis of the epoch in which we live.

The Brotherhood in Ibanskian society is the essence, the nucleus of State power, the association of all forms of power into a unified system. It can either be regarded as a social power as such, or as power in its purely social function. And to understand the Ibanskian concept of State, one must understand the essence of the Brotherhood. Here we must discard our personal sympathies and antipathies and be wholly objective. Otherwise error is inevitable. A slight degree of apologia might even be preferable to tendentious denigration. I believe that the apologists of the role of the Brotherhood come closer to the truth than do its enemies. At all events in Ibansk, the Brotherhood is not only what the demagogues and propagandists make it out to be; it is the only force able to maintain order in society, to contain, up to a point, an unruly eruption of social forces, and to guarantee a certain progress. It is not the most powerful force, it is the only force. And it is impossible to ignore this factor. It would be an unserious approach. I would point out in passing that the mass repressions of the period of the Boss took place to some extent because certain forces in the land had succeeded in placing themselves above the Brotherhood and in submitting it to their power.

The Brotherhood consists of people. So if one wishes to understand it, the first question to consider is that of its membership. It must be accepted as an indisputable fact that membership of the Brotherhood is purely voluntary. It is clear to all why people join the Brotherhood: it is mainly from career and profit motives. But it is, I repeat, voluntary. Many people long to become members of the Brotherhood, but it is a blessing not accorded to all. More of this later. There are cases where people are obliged to join the Brotherhood for work reasons. For example, non-members find it almost impossible to get work in the fields of many humane sciences. But this does not gainsay the voluntary principle. People freely choose these spheres of activity themselves, usually knowing in advance that they will have to seek membership of the Brotherhood. The higher management of all kinds of institutions are usually members of the Brotherhood. They seek to move into management of their own free will, and for this purpose they join the Brotherhood. Anyone who says that he was forced to join the Brotherhood against his will is a hypocrite.

It is possible, and it happens, that once people have joined the Brotherhood they do not believe in its ideals or its moral purity, that they despise the Brotherhood discipline, its demagogy, its assemblies and so on. There are very many people like this. But this is of no importance since people behave formally as sincere members of the Brotherhood should behave. What matters is actual behaviour. There is nothing immoral in this since there is no way of detecting that a man is merely playing a part, that he is not a sincere supporter of the programme, the ideology, and the demagogy of the Brotherhood. If such cases are detected (and this happens very rarely), the person concerned is expelled and that is the end of that. The hypocrisy which can accompany the act of joining the Brotherhood does not contradict the voluntary principle, but on the contrary confirms it, for in cases like this, application for membership can only be based on the calculation and the decision of the individual.

The voluntary nature of Brotherhood membership is the basis of the whole of Ibanskian Statehood. It is a task for those who take pleasure in resolving paradoxes to explain how a power system of the most total and unbridled constraint can be built on a completely voluntary basis. The oppression which it exercises is the resultant of the free will of individuals, not any malevolent design of tyrants. The tyrants are just as much pawns in the hands of a power which has been allowed to develop voluntarily as are their victims. The alleged unlimited power of the tyrants is an illusion produced by a situation where the victims of the power are themselves all-powerful.

The second principle governing membership of the Brotherhood is the principle of selectivity. Membership of the Brotherhood is voluntary, but not all applicants are accepted. The selection takes place according to strictly defined principles. It is this selection process which determines the direction which will be the sum of the will of all the separate individuals who make up this collective power. Once it is established the system of election of people to membership of the Brotherhood is reproduced in a stable form day after day, year after year, with a few minor modifications which reflect the modifications of the general make-up of the population.

It must further be recognised as a fact that it is far from the worst citizens who are selected to be members of the Brotherhood. Take any average Ibanskian institution and consider the composition of its Brotherhood organisation. Of course in view of the enormous size of the Brotherhood many of its members are villains, libertines, drunkards, corrupt and so on. That is inevitable. But relatively speaking the proportion of criminal and amoral elements detected officially within the Brotherhood is lower than in the non-Brotherhood population. I do not mean by this that only good people are accepted into the Brotherhood. Judgments of this kind would be quite inappropriate. The Brotherhood selects individuals who by the official criteria of Ibanskian society are the best citizens. These individuals must be mentally healthy, have a modicum of political education (in other words they should read the newspapers and remember what they have read), they should observe everyday moral standards, accept normal standards of discipline at work, be socially active (be a militant) and so on. We use other terms to describe these qualities: careerism, a greed for profit, lack of principle and so on. But these terms are ambiguous. They have both a sociological and a moralistic meaning. Sociologically speaking, for example, careerism is a normal and healthy phenomenon. In the moral sense it is something rather different. It means making one's career by morally reprehensible means.

In other words the Brotherhood selects citizens who have clearly defined social characteristics. From a formal point of view they meet all the demands of morality, law and labour. They are not to be despised. As for their so-called real aspect, it has no official existence. So it cannot be unmasked. And no-one, apart from a few opponents and doughty fighters for truth, has any interest in unmasking it.

The problem of emigration

After several years of senseless red-tape, Double-dealer went abroad. For good. 'I can't imagine why you attach such importance to this,' said Soilophagist. 'It's only an isolated case. And whatever you say it's a betrayal of his own people. Abandoning his own people in their hour of misery . . .' 'It's not a question of numbers,' said Teacher. 'The problem of emigration is the litmus paper of our society. The question is how we react to it. And we react in a most abject way. Twentieth-century man has the right to choose for himself where he lives according to his own desires and his own capabilities. There is nothing at all criminal or immoral about that. It is criminal and immoral to hinder that freedom of movement. Take our own life within the country. Masses of people leave the outlying districts to come closer to the centre and into the centre itself. As far as the districts they are leaving are concerned, that too is emigration. But we have resigned ourselves to this as something entirely normal. And what is this misery you're talking about? It's strange to hear that from the lips of a statesman. And if it's the good of the people that you're so concerned about, that can never be achieved without the observation of elementary human rights including the right to choose where you live.' 'These are empty abstractions,' said Soilophagist. 'I'm well aware what slogans like this lead to in practice. They lead to a brain drain and the ebbing away of creative potential . . .'

'Nobody here had any use for Double-dealer's brains,' said Teacher. 'He was set apart from everything and kept in isolation quite independently of his hapless book, and even before it was written. Incidentally, there's nothing anti-Ibanskian in the book, rather the reverse.' 'We're never going to see eye-to-eye about this,' said Soilophagist. 'It's a matter of principle.'

It's very strange, thought Teacher. Here we are beginning to witness our most fundamental concepts laid bare. There was a time when they were thrust into the background and regarded as unimportant. Yet now—and this is an indisputable fact—we are dividing not over problems which quite recently seemed crucial and highly political, but over barely perceptible questions which never used to attract the slightest attention. The problem of emigration has become a problem of society only over the last two or three years. And it has been transformed into a problem which virtually determines whether or not we accept the very fundamentals of our way of life. No matter what the would-be emigrants say, what they are escaping from is the Ism. That is a fact. And our leaders are well aware of it. The divisions are not occurring over problems which affect the masses, but over problems which concern only a very few individuals. The fact that those individuals are affected so deeply is what makes the division so revealing.

'Very well,' said Teacher. 'The hell with the emigrants. After all, you and I aren't emigrants. We are not running off anywhere. Let's work for the good of the people. Let's not abandon them in their hour of need. The only thing I wonder is, how the people will read our good intentions? I'm afraid that it'll be worse for us than for Double-dealer.' 'So be it,' said Soilophagist. 'At all events it's too late to turn back. Just look . . .'

The sciences
    The sciences they nurture all our youth,
    And give hope to our old folk—that's the truth.
wrote one ancient Ibanskian poet. The situation has changed more than somewhat since then. The sciences have developed and become an independent productive force. Today it is not so much the young people who are nurtured by the sciences, as the old. For example, Academician and Troglodyte both eat more

on their own than the entire first-year class of the average university faculty. On the other hand, the youngsters have the hope of coming through and one day turning into old men. As Dishcloth said, 'Everything is transformed into its opposite by a spiral process of negation of negation in the form of leaps and bounds from quantitative changes to qualitative, all of which happens here under the direction of . . . and according to a predetermined plan, which . . .' 'Excuse me, old man,' said Neurasthenic. 'I haven't got the time. Just you carry on as you've started. I'll be back in an hour to hear the end of your remarkable thoughts. Don't forget, it's pay-day today.' As soon as pay-day was mentioned, Dishcloth broke off in mid-syllable and dashed off to the institute. As a major scientist he had the right to go straight to the head of the queue at the cashier's office.

Ibanskian sciences are divided into natural and artificial. The natural sciences are held in high regard, since they have become an independent productive force, as the predictions and the directives of the classics said they would, and contribute to the construction of the material and technological basis of the integral Ism. But generally speaking, the Ibanskians have learnt from their own personal experience that it would be perfectly possible to build the integral Ism without such a basis and that it might even be easier because there would be less red tape. All those meetings of heads of departments, decisions to be taken, exploratory work planned, and then you're ready to start. And if anyone takes it into his head to . . . But all the same, they felt a bit ill-at-ease in view of what the classics had said. The poor old dears had dreamt of putting everything on a sound material-technological basis, so that it should all be properly in accordance with cast-iron objective laws. So if anyone let out so much as a squeak of protest he would have his nose rubbed in the basis. There you are, you son of a bitch, that's what you're up against! Cast iron laws, that's what! Against historical necessity!!! And you'll get it in the neck. Or better, in the back of the head. It's more scientific.

On top of everything else, there's abroad. Oh, if only it didn't exist! Then we'd be through in two ticks. But Over There they keep on inventing things, and we're obliged to keep up with the competition, to prove our superiority. We hardly have time to steal one machine from them before we have to start thinking about the next. By the time we've introduced something, it's out of date already! And all this means that we can't get by without science. And there's the threat, of course. That's the main thing, the threat. We must resist. Defend everyone. Because without us, they'd all be lost, all these other bastards! So when you think about it, no-one minds spending money on science. So let it go on developing. We've nothing against that. Who said we had? Slander! We've always been for it. Science, ho, ho, ho, it's a very serious thing, science. Who knows, it might come up with something good! Yes, science'll come up with something, the old whore! And if it doesn't, we'll . . . It will invent something good, it will. It daren't fail to. After all, those are scientists sitting on their asses there, not just some . . . So what are we paying them for? And big money, too! If it's not enough, we'll fork out some more. And if they don't come up with anything, we'll just turn off the tap, and they can live like everybody else. They'll come up with something, all right! And then there'll be such a bang! That'll show them a thing or two Over There! That's enough from you, you mother fuckers! You've glutted yourselves on the blood of the world proletariat and the oppressed under developed nations! Now you'll have to answer to us for that! Now it's our turn! What have you done with our papooses, eh? Bang! What have you done with our bison? Bang! Who dared to raise their hand against . . . Bang! Oh, if only there wasn't abroad! Then of course we could fling all our resources into the peaceful use of the atom, of course! Into space flight! Don't think we're going to hang about here on earth for the rest of eternity!

Of course, not everything's quite up to the right level yet. There are some weak points. Things are making progress, but not quite as fast as we'd like. That's because they keep on interfering. We keep on trying, and they interfere. We're on their side, but . . . There's a bread shortage. No meat. It's all exaggerated, of course, but there's no smoke without . . . They say that science can help. They're lying in their teeth, the bastards! But what if it was true? Say they did come up with something really good! They did invent caviare after all! True it can't be eaten. Indigestible shit. But you can sell it. The Americans shovel it in till it comes out of their ears, and then come back for more. They must come up with something—they daren't not! And then we'll be able to run things the way they should be run. Just call them in at twenty hours, give them their orders and sit back and wait for the results. And if we have to wait too long, just tell them to get a move on, and they'll do anything they're told to. We're not paying them good money for nothing! And so they've got to come up with the results. They daren't fail. They must. And the plan's got to be over-fulfilled, what's more. And ahead of time. And if it's not—sack them and bring them to trial.

Putting it briefly, it was all a lot simpler when there wasn't any science. We got by all right without the theory of relativity, or chromosomes or negative feedback, without information at all. It wasn't a bad life. At least there weren't any Truth-tellers, or Singers, or Double-dealers, or Shamizdat. And we still don't know where all that'll end. You stamp on one and another crawls out of the woodwork and begins to bellow its head off to the whole world—help! We're oppressed! They won't let us out! They put us in jail! We're being forced into mental hospi-tals! These vermin have got to be crushed. Crushed in the egg. And if we really can't get by without science, everything's going to have to be checked, watched, verified. We've got to pick out people we can trust. You can't just have any old person invent-ing things!

On the other hand, they've promised to lengthen life expec-tancy to two hundred years. No more disease. Cosmic flights, too. They're purifying the air. And they show funny films. So if you're elected or selected when you're eighty, you'll still be able to get a good hard-on when you're over a hundred—so hard even the Boss'd envy you! So they think they'd make everyone happy. The scientists may think we'd need five hundred years to thank them. Just think of all the meetings and discussions there'd be in a hundred years! And how many anniversaries! All those prizes and decorations! So many it'd take ten men just to carry them! And all the speeches! At a volume a year, editions of a hundred volumes! But we'd have to have a good hard look at the printing works. They've been left a little behind this irresistible movement forward. The last complete edition had to be printed abroad. That'd be a bit embarrassing if it ever got out. But they won't get to hear about it, the bastards! Just let them try . . .

There are rumours that the Americans have developed methods for transplanting any organ you like. We'll have to send a delegation—of secret policemen, of course. And we might slip a couple of doctors in. But there's a risk they might defect. We'll have to pick them carefully. Reliable chaps. But it's a risk worth taking. If they can give you new organs for old . . . well, then . . .

The tragedy of the comic

Life in Ibansk is comical if it's seen from outside. But Heaven help you if you find yourself playing a part in this comedy. Once the Boss made a bet with his son that he could never get an examination mark as low as D or even C. There was quite a large sum at stake, and the Son decided to try to win it. He chose as his examiner an old villain with no scruples at all. He entered under a false name, and gave wrong answers. Since there was an instruction that no D's were to be given (because the institute had entered a competition to get a hundred per cent pass rate) the Professor gave him a C. Of course, the professor didn't know that he was His Son. When the Son gleefully produced the marked paper with his real name on it, the professor had a heart attack. The Son visited him in hospital several times to try to persuade him to give him a C. The professor was afraid he was the victim of a provocation, and insisted on giving him A. The Son wouldn't let him have the marked paper. Finally the professor resorted to cunning—he promised to give him a C, but marked the paper A instead. The Son was furious, and in revenge put about the rumour that the professor had accepted a bribe to give him an A. The bribe allegedly was that the Son had promised to get him a seat in the Academy. The professor was sent to the camps, where he soon expired, thus never realising that he was the victim of his own stupidity and not of the regime's senseless cruelty. And he died in vain, for the rumour the Son had started came to the ears of the President of the Academy, who issued instructions that the professor should be elected on the next occasion.

Doubts

The more Teacher dug into the mass of information which the Soilophagist had supplied to him, the more convinced he

(516)

became that it was complete nonsense from a scientific angle. From a scientific angle, all these data could have been predicted with a very close degree of approximation. He had already done so himself several times. Before analysing the material he could foresee the probable result. After a few weeks of hard labour he got pretty well the same answer. That, of course, was a splendid confirmation of his theory. But his theory had no need of this kind of confirmation. And it seemed a pity to waste his time for nothing. But Soilophagist recognised no theories. He demanded tables, graphs, percentages. Who the hell needs all this, thought Teacher. Who's going to be convinced by all these graphs and tables. Everyone knows that any figures they see in our country are pure fabrications, and there's no chance of anyone believing that they are accurate. And the conclusions that can be derived from this sea of figures are self-evident without any analysis. You can hear them in the bars, in kitchens, in corridors, in buses . . . Everywhere and from everybody. My God, what is this business I've let myself in for? I'll have to get out of it somehow or other. It's not my kind of game at all.

The rehabilitation of cybernetics

Cybernetics was rehabilitated, along with a whole series of other bourgeois pseudo-sciences, such as structural linguistics, formal genetics, concrete sociology and so on. The Newspaper published an editorial directive *Cybernetics in the Service of the Ism*. The Journal published a series of explanatory articles by the leading Ibanskian structuralists, geneticists, cyberneticists. The editorial made some minor allusions to certain errors in evaluation and to some deviations, but made the direct and straightforward statement that the true scientific comprehension of cybernetics was first arrived at by the classic authors of the Ism, who, even though they had never heard of cybernetics, had been able to leave some appropriate quotations for posterity—and for Ibanskian scientists. It was convincingly demonstrated by the articles of the specialists that cybernetics and all the other modern sciences had been first discovered in Ibansk. Soon on every street there blossomed Institutes and Laboratories of Cybernetics and the other new sciences which were now of inestimable value in the development of the Ism.

(517)

Every house had its own sociological laboratory. It was about this time that Sociologist worked out his famous interrogati . . . I beg your pardon, his famous questionnaire, in which for the first time in the history of world science he included such fundamental questions as: Do you love your Leader? Do you want to build the Ism? Do you trust the justice of the Secret Police? And many others. This questionnaire was later banned for humanitarian reasons. Just in case someone either through carelessness or stupidity should answer 'no'. If that had happened, he or she would have had to be jailed for slander—and that would have been premature.

Thanks to the rehabilitation of cybernetics and other Ibanskian sciences, the progressive forces were suddenly presented with a means of ideological and organisational unification sanctioned from above. They were offered premises for meetings, platforms for speakers, presses for propaganda. The authorities had swallowed the bait of history, and did not know what was happening. They remained unaware, for instance, that the appearance on the platform of some bespectacled weakling would be seen by his audience as an open protest against the regime. In the past he would simply have been jailed, and deservedly so. Now he was allowed to hunch his way on to the platform, mumble a few words about entropy and information (rather than matter and consciousness), and to write his x's and y's on the blackboard just as if so many glorious decades of Ibanskian history had gone by completely unnoticed. And when, to take another example, that stuttering schizophrenic wrote on the blackboard the function of psi from alpha to beta, the assembled intellectuals took it as a call to overthrow repression and win freedom. No-one understood the meaning of the function, either because it had none or because its meaning was exclusively a call to freedom.

By virtue of their highly developed Brotherhood instinct, the reactionary forces felt that in Ibansk any new ideas would acquire in their early stages a certain ring of ideology and would become hostile to the Ism. And they gave due warning that this would happen. 'I don't understand a great deal of this,' said Troglodyte, 'but I feel that all this does not belong here.' 'Just you wait,' said Secretary. 'We'll end up having to send the troops in.' The reactionary forces knew from experience that

(518)

new ideas only begin to bring new support to the Ism once they are hopelessly out of date and have begun to grow boring. But they were howled down by the leaders of the progressive wing of their own camp, and they themselves were obliged to set off full steam towards progress, and indeed to take a leading role in the venture. Troglodyte was appointed chairman of the cybernetics committee. Under his experienced leadership the progressive forces immediately proved that the new ideas upheld the truth of the Ism on its new stage of development, and were beginning to overtake the West on the cybernetic front. Ibansk had already overtaken the West in meat and milk, and the Ibanskians had long since forgotten about either. 'He's not such a bad old stick,' the progressive forces said of Troglodyte. 'The main thing is he doesn't interfere with the work.' 'It depends on whose you mean,' said Teacher.

'You must be in clover now,' said Neurasthenic to Teacher. 'Nonsense,' said Teacher. 'We're all cyberneticists now. The first thing our progressives did when they took over was to shove me out of the way and accuse me of being an ignorant amateur. It's almost laughable! The fellow who accused me of that had transcribed an article from a Western review of cybernetics, written by a Western mathematician as the last word on the subject. And all that this Westerner had done was to pirate my ideas which had been published five years ago. Indeed, he referred to me as his main source. It's only recently that we had no more than five or six cyberneticists, and they were all under secret police surveillance. They'd nearly all done time. Last week we had a symposium and more than a thousand specialists turned up. So there's not much clover about. Rather the opposite. At least until now I was something out of the ordinary, something negative but at least recognised. Now there isn't even that. Prospects? Oh, they're clear enough. We're moving into a boom. Things'll be blown up beyond all measure. All manner of rabble will gather round trying to get in on the act. People will write theses, collect titles, decorations, prizes. Some will go off on foreign visits—the highest reward possible for services to our society. And then the boom will begin to blow over. In the meanwhile any scientists worthy of the name will have been eliminated and crushed. Then there'll be a period of total disillusionment. Every idea of any unifying

(519)

ideological significance will have been exhausted. All that will remain will be the usual official mass phenomenon with all the official attributes of Ibanskian institutions. And since there can't be any new ideas on this scale, the progressive forces will disintegrate into social atoms—into isolated individuals with a weird way of behaving. There are no prospects here at all. The opposition must stop decking itself out in alien rags and tatters of science, art and economics. It must speak out in its own name without resorting to camouflage.'

Changes

On the roof of a new semi-skyscraper which was the editorial offices of the Newspaper and the Journal, green words flashed out in the night sky:

```
PAP     RING    HAT
URN     LLS U   HAT
```

'What does it mean?' asked Journalist. 'We'll find out in a moment,' said Neurasthenic. In a few flickerings of an eye the green words were replaced by flashing bright red words:

```
T EACH BAN   AN Y           OLD
  AD   HEM          THE   ARE S
```

'Translated into decent French,' said Neurasthenic, 'that means:

NEWSPAPERS BRING US WHAT IS NEW,
THE JOURNAL TELLS US WHAT TO DO.
LET EACH IBANSKIAN YOUNG AND OLD.
READ THEM BOTH WHEN THEY ARE SOLD.

As you see, our advertising techniques are every bit as good as yours.' 'But all the same,' said Journalist, staring rather stupidly at a glowing shop sign which said UPERMARK, 'there've been enormous changes here over the past few years. For instance, yesterday I met Snottyhanky who was reciting some marvellous verse. Really daring.' 'Look,' said Neurasthenic, 'this is by Snottyhanky as well.'

EVERY IBANSKIAN MUST KNOW
AT LEAST ONE SCIENCE,
                    WHICH ONE?
                              NO CODOLOGY!
THAT SCIENCE

                    THAT POINTS THE WAY
                                        THAT WE MUST GO
        OUR SACRED WEAPON—
                            OUR IDIOTOLOGY!
'That's very lightweight,' said Journalist. 'You're bound to
have that sort of thing. But what do you think about this?' asked
Neurasthenic, pointing up to another neon sign:
        WE MUST DO DEALS
                        TO STRENGTHEN OUR ECONOMY
        BUT EVEN IF CLASS TENSIONS
                            SEEM LESS TIGHT,
        DO ALL YOU CAN
                        TO BUILD OUR IDEOLOGY
        AND COMBAT THEIRS
                        WITH ALL YOUR
                                MIGHT!
'Yes,' said Journalist. 'That's no joke. Some arse-licker must be
making a tidy profit out of drivel like that!' 'That arse-licker,'
said Neurasthenic, 'is your beloved Snottyhanky. Let's go have
a drink.' 'It's not a bad idea,' said Journalist, nodding towards a
bar above whose door flashed the letters: COCK BAR. 'How
about there? Surely they can't be closed already? That's
strange. It's still quite early. How about here then? Oh,
damn, a queue! It'd take us an hour-and-a-half to get in. No,
that's not for me.' Journalist stood plunged in thought. He
didn't even react to the huge placard in the café window showing the Leader in a speech-making pose and below, the caption:
        TO UNDERSTAND THE POLITICAL SCENE
        STUDY LEADER'S SPEECHES AND KNOW WHAT THEY MEAN.
Neurasthenic was on the point of saying that that was another of
Snottyhanky's gems, that the portrait was the work of a triple
laureate . . . but he simply couldn't be bothered to open his
mouth for such nonsense. He waited. 'Let's go to the Intourist,'
said Journalist. 'They won't let me in there,' said Neurasthenic.
'To the National, then,' said Journalist. 'It's been full up since
opening time,' said Neurasthenic. 'Well, we could go to my
hotel and have a drink in my room,' said Journalist. 'Do you
really want to get me into big trouble?' asked Neurasthenic.
'What bastards!' said Journalist. 'Will things never change
here?' When Neurasthenic pointed to the sky sign again, which

                            (521)

by now was flashing up words from Snottyhanky's new poem, Journalist simply shrugged his shoulders. 'I know what it'll say without even looking at it,' he said.

TURNING MY FACE TO THE SKY
MY SLOGAN I CRY WITH DECISION
FORWARD!
       NO SNAGS ON THE WAY
TO THE DAWN
       OF THE INTEGRAL
          ISM.

Rewards for merit

'Look,' She said. 'Our friends and neighbours have elected Troglodyte and Theoretician to the Academy. There's a long article here about their distinguished scientific merits. God in heaven, what's going on! They're absolute nonentities in science!' 'That's precisely why they've been elected,' He said. 'That's why there's an article. Teacher, incidentally, has been elected to three Western academies. But we never see a line about that. Why? Because he's risen to be a major scientist without the permission of the authorities. Even against their will.' 'Can these Troglodytes and Theoreticians have a clear conscience?' She asked. 'Of course,' He replied. 'People get a great deal more pleasure out of unmerited rewards than they do out of ones they really deserve. If a reward is merited, that means that a man has done something and that people are aware of it. And the fact that he has accomplished something, and that it's well-known of itself strengthens his position in society. The reward merely confirms that and in a very minor way intensifies it. So it very often happens that people are not overexcited about rewards that they deserve. It's not a pose, they are quite sincere about it. And beyond that, people are much less upset if they're deprived of rewards they really merit than if they don't get rewards they don't deserve but which they thought they were going to get. Name me one genuine scientist who's been turned down by the Academy and had a stroke as a result. But when nonentities fail to make it they all, without exception, end up in hospital. An undeserved reward strengthens a man's social position all on its own. And in those cases that's all that people are after.' 'Surely we aren't all like that,' She said. 'No, not all of us,' He said. 'Most of us don't have a chance of getting anywhere near that kind of social level. We simply aren't allowed to. There are just a very few of us who fight a battle with ourselves and sometimes win a victory or two. Man, in the highest sense of the word, is a social individual who has overcome the normal social individual within himself. That is a cultivated product, something which has to be artificially nurtured. A natural man is a person like the Boss, Troglodyte, Theoretician, Claimant, Colleague, Sociologist and the other people whom we know, with a few exceptions.' 'You don't belong in that crowd,' She said. 'Of course not,' He said. 'Nor Teacher, nor Chatterer, and not even Neurasthenic up to a point.' 'But what will happen to you?' She asked. 'We will be systematically destroyed,' He said, 'until some form of defence and self-defence comes to light.' 'But will it ever come to light?' She asked. 'If it does,' He said, 'it will be contrary to the laws of this society. If it does happen, it will be by mere chance.'

The Brotherhood

The Brotherhood, said Slanderer, occupies a special position in Ibanskian society in the sense that it is neither a separate social group, nor a conglomeration of such groups. It is only the Brotherhood apparatus which forms social groups and which is subject to the general social laws of society. The members of the Brotherhood as social individuals are members of social cells outside the Brotherhood, and exist and operate within these cells. If a member of the Brotherhood is also part of its apparatus he does not participate in the corresponding social groups as a member of the Brotherhood, but as a member of this group with certain work and functions to perform. To be a member of the Brotherhood is not a profession. The member is a worker, an engineer, a teacher, a scientist, a writer and so on, who has been chosen to be a member according to well-defined rules, but who has a particular role to play in society. What then is this role?

Almost all people who exercise power in every cell in society (at least in the most important cells) are selected from Brotherhood members. At the very least they are regarded as potential members of the Brotherhood and usually end up by joining. So the members of the Brotherhood are those individuals from whom people are chosen to exercise power of all kinds. They constitute a reserve of power.

Moreover, rank and file members of the Brotherhood are at the base of the organisational hierarchy of the Brotherhood, reaching right up to the very top, i.e. the apparatus. Although they themselves do not form separate social groups the Brotherhood apparatus, which is constructed on this base and selected from its members, is itself a system of social groups of a particular kind. It constitutes the supreme power in the land at every level of the hierarchy of power. It possesses all the power. When people talk about the distinction between the power of the Brotherhood and economic power in Ibansk, or even about conflicts between the two, they display their total lack of comprehension of the essence of Ibanskian power. There is no economic power whatsoever. There are economic functions of power which are entrusted to specialised organisations. But there is only one power—the power of the Brotherhood—since economic power itself is made up of members of the Brotherhood. It is quite another thing to say that the apparatus of power is itself made up of people and organisations who live according to general social laws. Here conflicts can arise. They can arise even between different groups within the very apparatus of the Brotherhood. And even between individual members of one and the same group. But this does not affect the basic principle or the structure of power.

Within social groups members of the Brotherhood constitute a voluntary and secure power base, both from the point of view of the Brotherhood hierarchy and from the point of view of the hierarchy of power in its control and management function. Properly speaking, the duality which exists in the organisation of society (its social organisation on the one hand and its economic organisation on the other) creates the conditions which permit the existence of a form of power as unique as that exercised by the Brotherhood.

The classics, in their time, predicted that once the integral Ism was reached, the State and the Brotherhood would wither away. I have no wish to discuss this question. I will merely make one observation. Experience of Ibanskian history suggests that we're far more likely to see the withering away of such sham forms of power as the so-called elective assemblies, which

are a pure charade for propaganda purposes, than we are to see
the Brotherhood disappear. As regards the decay of the
Brotherhood as a political organisation, here I am in full agreement with the classics. With one minor correction: in Ibansk
the Brotherhood has not been a political organisation for a very
long time. I shall return to this question later.

> Hymn to the glory of the member
> Think what you like, say what you like,
> It's always been the same,
> The . . . Member is our staff of life
> And so it will remain.
> Think what you like, say what you like,
> You've got a form to sign;
> A . . . Member's there: 'You'll have to wait
> Or come another time.'
> Think what you like, say what you like,
> Lie down to take a rest,
> And someone shouts, 'Get up and vote!'
> A . . . Member? Yes, you've guessed.
> Think what you like, say what you like,
> You'd like to win a prize;
> A . . . Member reads your entry form:
> 'No—not in any wise.'
> Think what you like, say what you like,
> You've written your great book;
> The publisher, a . . . Member, states:
> 'Not worth a second look.'
> Think what you like, say what you like,
> You'd like to go to Rome.
> You've filled in all the documents,
> But the . . . Member says, 'Stay home!'
> Think what you like, say what you like,
> Speak to no matter whom,
> 'You're not a . . . Member, then?' he'll cry,
> 'Join now while there's still room.'

No-one knows the name of the author of this hymn. It has been
suggested that it was Singer. But in the opinion of Colleague,
who was in personal charge of the investigation into the case of
Bawler, almost all bawdy verses with political content came

from Bawler's pen. But Colleague was unable to prove this as Bawler himself refused to acknowledge the verses as his, and many officially recognised poets did not deny their authorship when their names figured in rumours.

'You're not a . . . Member yet?' they cry,
'Come off it—who're you kidding!'

The sciences

The artificial sciences occupy a special position in Ibansk. The ordinary Ibanskians neither know them nor understand them despite the fact that they study them throughout their lives and so call them, jokingly, social sciences. Nor do the specialists understand them, although they do recognise them. And since they have chosen to pursue them right to the tomb they seriously call them the social sciences. Moreover, they are the source of their daily bread. And when this bread takes on the outward and visible forms of a university post, high office, a good salary, huge royalties, a rent-free apartment, honourable idleness and even, heaven knows why, a certain degree of fame, the artificial sciences become for them supernatural sciences. There is no place here for humour. If one is tempted to resort to irony, then there is always the West as a target, the West where the social sciences are in a complete state of decay, for instead of serving the cause of the avant-garde proletariat, they are at the service of rotting imperialism. They cannot even really be described as sciences. The authorities of Ibansk also consider the artificial sciences to be social sciences. But in this case the word has a resonance of warning and threat. A threat aimed at those who are subject to the action of the laws of the social sciences. The Ibanskian authorities do everything in accordance with these laws. If they have done something which seems to have turned out not quite right, well, you must accept that it is in accordance with social science. Just wait, you slobs, you'll see for yourselves that all this has been done for your own good. And anyway, there is no other way of doing it. Science! We don't count for anything. The laws! Just dare to question them. There's another threat aimed at our own specialists. So what are you complaining about? We pay you money. And good money at that. And you just stay in the same place marking time. So get on with your theories, you parasites, you avant-garde practitioners! Get on with pushing our avant-garde theory even further into the avant-garde! How many times do we have to tell you you must be fertile, fertile, fertile . . .

The Ibanskian social sciences follow the line of the Brotherhood. In this respect they differ from the natural sciences in Ibansk; although they follow the Brotherhood line to a degree, they do so to a lesser degree than do the social sciences. It is still permissible to argue about the natural sciences. But there can be no argument about the social sciences. They toe the line in every sense of the word.

They follow the line in the sense first of all that the number of members of the Brotherhood which they include is no less than the number in the apparatus of the Brotherhood itself and in the secret police—which considers the social sciences as its civil arm. They follow the Brotherhood line in the sense also that they reflect class interests. Social sciences abroad reflect the interests of the exploiting classes and so are not sciences at all. Ibanskian social sciences reflect the interests of the proletariat, of the very poorest peasant class which is under the control of the proletariat, and of the working intelligentsia which has come to their support and which is controlled by both of them. And so they are authentic sciences. It is true that in Ibansk the proletariat no longer exists, still less the poor peasantry. As for the intelligentsia which joined them initially, they too have been exterminated and the new intelligentsia is not really an intelligentsia any more, but merely a collection of workers in the interests of . . . In Ibansk today everybody is a worker with the exception of Truth-teller, Singer, Dauber, Double-dealer and other isolated renegades. And the Ibanskian social sciences have exported their class basis. In these days they reflect the interests of the world proletariat and of the oppressed peoples whom the world proletariat leads. It is for the time being hard to say whose interests the social sciences will reflect when the integral Ism is established throughout the world. On one occasion Troglodyte was foolish enough to insist that the social sciences would perish. He was put right, but not very firmly. After all it may well be that they really will perish.

The summit, the basis and the most profound essence of Ibanskian social sciences is undoubtedly diabolectical Ibanism.

Some reflections

Why are we so intolerant of one another? wondered Soilophagist. After all, we're all striving towards a better life. We're all
representatives of one nation. And we all wish our people well.
Could it be that we all have different views of this better life and
of the means by which it could be achieved? Certainly we have.
But all the same we could discuss our differences and reach
agreement. Areas of agreement can always be found. Surely
Teacher cannot be right when he says it is impossible to find
such areas of consent. If that were so, for what and for whom
would I be making all these efforts? Why should I be risking my
neck? Strangely enough, I am risking more than all of the others
put together. Why should all this be? Is it possible that Teacher
is right and that if my programme were put into practice it
would not resolve a single problem in our society, or that it
might even make them worse? To hell with theory! To hell with
intellectual prognostications! The people cannot be worse off if
there are more apartments, more bread, more meat, more
textiles. They can't be worse off if transport were to be more
flexible and more comfortable, if it were easier to get higher
education, if there were a wider choice of newspapers,
magazines and films. That's beyond dispute! Surely results like
that are worth a sacrifice of one's time and maybe even of one's
life. Teacher thinks that nothing will come of all this. Why?
Something must come out of it. Maybe they will steal my ideas
and throw me on the rubbish heap. Maybe my ideas will be
distorted. But at least something must get into their thick heads
and then pass on to change the life of our people. It surely
cannot be that nothing would get through. Let them take my
thoughts and alter them as they think best. I don't insist that I
should be credited with them . . .

But nobody heard Soilophagist's thoughts, and no-one
recorded them. Not even Teacher knew about them. It was a
good thing that there was still no eavesdropping on thoughts.
Soilophagist had another thought in mind . . .

Brother

'That Brother's a strange chap,' said Dauber. 'He hides the
manuscripts of protest letters in his home. Nothing happens.
He distributes Shamizdat typescripts—yet when the authors

are tried, he's only there as a witness. He helps Truth-teller, and still nothing happens.' 'He's an informer,' said Neurasthenic. 'A provocateur.' 'No,' said Chatterer. 'This is something else. He helps in order to hinder. He hinders in order to help. He saves people, the better to ruin their reputation. He ruins people in order to save them. The aim of all his intriguing is very simple: he wants to bring everyone down to his own level. We are all wading through the same shit. We are all one and the same shit. Truth-teller gets out of it. Singer gets out of it. Dauber gets out of it. Fine! Long live Ibanskian culture! And yet it can't be allowed because they are part of the same shit as we are. Truth-teller escaped from it. And Singer went off in a different direction. Now Dauber is on the point of slipping away to somewhere in eternity. He needs help. After all, he is a genius. But the help has got to be such that he stays plunged in this self same shit. So that people can say to themselves or to each other with a sigh of relief: Well, he didn't quite make it as a genius and he stayed wallowing in the same shit that we all have to. Alas, people will say, that's our tragic fate. All we talented Ibanskian intellectuals are all condemned to sterility. Mark what I say, Brother works on no-one's behalf. He works only for himself.'

The State

It follows from what has been said already, wrote Slanderer, that no palace revolutions can have any influence on the general character of the Ibanskian state. And you must not believe that the State has been imposed by force on Ibanskian society against its will. It is a product of the free will of the citizens of Ibansk. Not that they had a meeting and decided once and for all that it should take on its present form. There has been a complicated, tangled and terrible process of establishment. But in its present form the Ibanskian State reproduces itself on the foundations I mentioned earlier. And if within the society there have been greater or lesser abominations of the kind about which Truth-teller wrote and Hog spoke, and of which many of our contemporaries have been witnesses, victims or participants, it would be a grave mistake to seek their origin in isolated persons or even in groups of people or in entire organisations. These abominations are the legitimate product of the daily activities of the best citizens of this society, just as are society's rightly acclaimed successes. They are the fruit of their labours.

Changes

'All the same,' She said, 'there have been colossal changes.' 'Yes,' He said. 'But can you tell which of them are the product of time and which the product of the new social system? There have been changes in the West as well, and pretty considerable changes. But the social structure hasn't essentially altered. If you want to establish what part the system has played in these changes, you have tò find relative values, and they may have to go as far as the second or third degree—not merely quantities per head of population, but place on the scale of values per head of population. The type of import and export.' 'I don't understand that,' She said. 'And no-one except you does understand it. People simply take facts as they are. Are we better fed? Fact. Are we better housed? Fact. Are we better dressed? Fact. Is the general living standard incomparably higher? Fact. Everything else is nothing but the conjectures of our critics.' 'Yes,' He said. 'They are conjectures.'

> When it was kings who ruled this state
> We toiled and strained and hardly ate.
> We had no freedom—no such thing
> Existed when we had a king.
> But now that kings are in the past
> How things have changed! There's food at last.
> No hard work now. And so instead
> We snore our lives away in bed.
> And freedom? Well, I have to tell
> We've had our fill of that as well.
> They've stuffed us with it—Holy Smoke!
> Another spoonful and we'll choke.

On the advantages of abstraction

Do not forget that we are beings from an imaginary, abstract country. We are disembodied. Abstract individuals can manage without eating, without clothes, without families and so on. And at the same time they can carry on conversations on elevated themes with an appearance of total detachment. The advantages of this situation are incontestable. Now, when we

(530)

abstract Ibanskians are sometimes tossed a smoked sausage or two, or given three square metres of living space per head of population, we fly into transports of delight and begin to snigger over the difficulties of life in the West where the number of varieties of sausage has dropped sharply from fifty to forty-nine, and where houses stand empty because of the class struggle. We, as is proper for abstract individuals in an abstract country, are engaged in something far more important. We are building the Ism. And the Ism can be built from slogans, directives, reports, accounts, appeals, resolutions, initiatives, and from other especially solid material. This story was going the rounds thirty or forty years ago. A meeting was called on a corrective farm. The agenda was (1) the building of a barn, and (2) the building of the Ism. In view of the absence of planks point (1) was deferred and the meeting passed immediately to point (2). In the past this story always raised a laugh. But wrongly. For it contains a truth. Ism-building materials we have in abundance. The Western world is at the moment suffering from a severe shortage of them. We could make some profit out of this. All we need to do is to lay an Ism-pipeline and begin to pour down it all our remarkable, well-tested building materials. All without any shade of self-interest. For we have enough of these primary materials. We would even be ready to pay someone to drain off a part of them. Otherwise we might suffocate under their sheer weight. But you must understand that even abstraction has its own laws. So, the abstract Ibanskian who does not eat or drink, or struggle to get an apartment, a villa or a car is logically possible. But the abstract Ibanskian who never makes a speech, never writes a report, never welcomes delegations, never applauds and so on is a logical contradiction. That is why his existence is impossible.

Utopia

'This society,' said Brother, 'is developing towards utopia. Society is putting forward radiant ideals towards which men aspire in one way or another.' 'Drivel,' said Chatterer. 'Why drivel?' asked Dauber. 'The facts support . . .' 'What is utopia?' asked Chatterer. 'It is an abstraction based on a given reality. Utopia is built in the following way. You take the positive and the negative aspects of this reality. The positive aspects are either implicitly admitted or deliberately exaggerated. The negative aspects are erased. There are two ways in which this can be done. First, by recognising that given aspects will not exist in reality. Secondly, by admitting the possibility of conflicting aspects. If you try to construct a utopia which offers us radiant ideals, you will arrive at Ibanskian society but without careerists, informers, parasites and so on. All the inventors of utopias make the same mistake. They ignore the fact that both the positive and negative aspects of reality which play their part in the formation of a utopia are both engendered by one and the same society. The former are unthinkable without the latter. They are rigorously interdependent. It is impossible to eliminate a bad aspect of reality without eliminating some good aspect connected with it. It is impossible to create a good aspect, without at the same time giving rise to some associated bad aspect. It is the same as in aerodynamics. It is impossible to increase the speed of an aircraft without increasing its frontal air resistance. The same kind of interdependence exists in social life as well. One cannot, for instance, eradicate gangsterism in America without at the same time eliminating, or at least very considerably restricting, free enterprise and democracy. If all these interdependences are established, if every possible logical combination is envisaged, you will not find a single known utopia, since utopias are logical contradictions owing to the very way they are constructed. And so they can never be realised in practice. And as far as radiant ideals are concerned, they have always been prosaic and unilateral. That is why they can sometimes be achieved. After all, we aren't in any hurry. Let's do an experiment. Invent a utopia. Explain it to us. And we will analyse it in public. It may seem mad to you, but in our days only one kind of utopia can produce radiant ideals. Do you know what that type is? It would be a degenerate form of utopia consisting of a multitude of the negative aspects of our reality. In effect, it would be a pitiless analysis of our day-to-day existence, with no glossing over and no exaggerations. No prettying-up, no blackening. It would be an objective, dispassionate, scientific description of what we are.' 'But that,' said Brother, 'that is truly utopia. Who would be capable of creating it? Who would allow it? That is truly pure fantasy.' 'But there's something in what he says,' said Dauber, when

Brother had rushed off to a meeting of the artistic council of the Ibanka Theatre. 'Do you really think it is possible to make a scientific description of society?' 'In our super-scientific age,' said Chatterer, 'it is fashionable to reject any real science of society. And that is exactly what the authorities want—and scoundrels like Brother. But I'm telling you the truth. If the authorities asked me in the interest of the State to construct a scientific theory of our society, even if it had to be kept secret, I know people with whom I could do it in two years.'

Take care, you are already in the future

'I've just been to the opening of the Palace of Children,' said Journalist. 'It's a beautiful building. We have to give you credit for that! Our government could never give our children a present like that!' 'You're very strange people,' said Neurasthenic. 'You're born, you're brought up and you live in an atmosphere of commonsense, but as soon as you come here not an atom of that commonsense remains. You must understand that here you are in a new kind of civilisation. Here there are a great many things that are beautiful to look at and seem to be real. But if you touch them you'll find that they're covered in poisoned thorns. Have you any idea what this magnificent building cost? How many people made themselves a tidy profit out of it? How many parasites benefited? Do you know what kind of clubs will operate inside it? There'll be a great many different art clubs. And you know what the situation in the arts is like here. That won't be put right by thousands of palaces like this one. But even that's not the most important thing. You say it's a gift for our children. You might think that that means for all children. But you'd be mistaken. It's not really intended for children at all, but for adults. There was a report in the papers today that new apartment blocks were ready for letting in the Green Region. Do you know what's in these buildings? Ten-roomed apartments, with swimming pools and two lavatories. And who are they for? Yet the newspaper reports talk about them as a splendid gift to the Ibanskian workers.' 'It's impossible to argue with you,' said Journalist. 'You leave no room for anything that's alive.' 'So don't bother to argue,' said Neurasthenic. 'Just remember from time to time that you are in the society of the future. And so take care.'

Principles of selection

'This action of your government seems strange, to say the least,' said Journalist. 'There's nothing strange about it,' said Neurasthenic. 'It's just common stupidity.' 'But surely there must be at least one intelligent man among them,' said Journalist. 'That's quite impossible,' said Neurasthenic. 'No intelligent man could ever get there.' 'But why?' asked Journalist. 'Because of the principles of selection,' said Neurasthenic. 'If the only people you select are dwarfs, freaks, sickly weaklings, and so on, would you find among their number even one giant, one Adonis, one genius? If we discover among them an individual of near-average ability, we see him as a giant or a genius only because our instinct tells us to expect nothing of the kind. If you take the ablest of them out of his social sphere and try to live close to him, you would be struck by his phenomenal greyness. These people only produce an impression because they have rubbed shoulders with the famous and been involved in important decisions and actions, in other words only as an abstraction from an inaccessible reality.' 'But the principles of selection could be changed,' said Journalist. 'Go ahead and try,' said Neurasthenic. 'It's your country. You try,' said Journalist. 'It's your idea, not mine,' said Neurasthenic. 'As an inhabitant of this country I know that these principles cannot be changed. It isn't in our power.' 'But there is a point of view which holds that any thousand people are worth any other thousand,' said Journalist. 'That's within a multitude of people of one category,' said Neurasthenic. 'If there is no artificial system of selection. It is true that any thousand heads of department of a given level are equal in value to any other thousand at the same level. But this principle is not applicable in this case. Here we are talking about an artificial selection and of the evolution of people under these conditions. Here we have got into the habit of thinking that all people are identical on an intellectual and psychological level, and that from this point of view the brain does not evolve. But who knows how people differ from one another from this viewpoint? Who knows what biological consequences for human evolution will follow from a systematic selection of imbeciles, mediocrities, toadies, informers, cowards and so on to occupy the most privileged strata of society? I personally am convinced that this cannot be done with impunity. Just as the human race has suddenly and brutally found itself face to face with problems of environmental pollution or of dwindling natural resources, one day they will find themselves just as deeply face to face with their own dwindling intellectual and psychological potential—and on a massive scale. And no amount of education will be enough to counterbalance this deficit. If mankind gets a grip on itself, which is most improbable, it will still take well over a century to recoup the wasted intellectual potential of even a small group of people by dint of an artificial isolation and protection. It will not be they, of course, who are protected, but all the rest will be protected from them.'

Dreams

'If we manage to get out,' said Double-dealer, 'I'll send my son to school in the most conservative institution I can find. So that there's no danger of any avant-garde ideas wafting over him. Why do I say that? I am after all descended from serfs.' 'It is simply that we have stuffed ourselves with revolutionary ideas,' said Teacher, 'and now they make us want to vomit. We have felt their effect on our own skins.'

The laws of poetry

'Whatever they say about us,' She said, 'we Ibanskians have some undeniable qualities. For instance . . .' 'I won't quarrel with you,' He said. 'We are a marvellous people.'

> We Ibanskians are the best
> By every kind of means.
> We're wise and brave—by any test:
> We've got it in our genes.
> From the goodness of our hearts
> We'll teach you how to live,
> On what to eat, or what to drink
> The best advice we'll give.
> We'll tell you what you ought to read,
> Or rather, what to ban.
> What moral guides your children need
> To grow as best they can.
> But we are mocked unmercifully,
> Hegemonous though we are,

Our own life being so beggarly,
The worst of all by far.

'You always look on the shadowy side of things,' She said. 'Not on the shadowy side,' He replied, 'but on the side that casts a shadow.' 'So be it,' She said. 'What's the difference?'

'There is a difference,' He said. 'Do you know what doesn't cast shadows?' 'What?' She asked. 'Spectres,' He replied.

'I always feel there's something terribly familiar about your improvisations,' She said. 'There's nothing surprising about that,' He said. 'Many people write and talk about the same subject as I do. And poetry has its own laws. Given the same subject, the same mood and the same type of person, everyone will write pretty much the same. And I'm not a poet. It simply comes off the top of my head. I don't try to make myself different from other people, and all I do is imagine the essence of things, i.e. what everybody else does. Just give me a subject. I don't know what I'll come up with, but it'll probably be something that will seem familiar to you. That's a sure sign that I'm not a poet. Or that I'm a very bad poet. Or that I'm a genius, which is much the same thing.' 'Very well,' She said. 'Here's a subject for you: a beggar's rags and the sublime in art.' 'It's a very banal subject,' He said, 'but all the same, let's have a go.'

Shall I seek beauty in rags that are vile?
Or claim that there's beauty right here in this mire?
Must I spend all my life in a task so futile?
No! I'll not! That's a fate that is loathsome and dire.
We still have the freedom, or so it may seem,
To hold differing views on this subject today.
Rags are vile, I shall cry, rags are frightful and mean.
What is mean must be ugly's the least I can say.

'Now let's see,' She said. 'Do you know where I've read that before?' 'No I don't,' He said. 'Just you try and find a single sentence which has never been enunciated before! That's beside the point! And anyway I could perfectly well refrain from writing these verses.'

The eleventh hour

The spin is regarded as one of the most highly skilled manoeuvres in flying. Yet at the same time it is an elementary exercise for a trainee pilot. As soon as a cadet has learnt to land

and take off solo, he is taken to the zone (an area of sky specially set aside for training purposes) and taught how to put his aircraft into a spin and recover from it. It's a very simple process. You cut the throttle so as to lose speed. Then you pull back the stick and simultaneously kick the rudder bar to full lock. After a few tries even the thickest cadet can master that. Usually the aircraft goes into a spin easily enough. But it doesn't always come out of it easily. This doesn't mean that you've created a dramatic situation worthy of novels or the cinema. It merely means that you have to go through a few more manipulations of the controls which are hardly worth mentioning. If the aircraft doesn't recover from the spin, that is a banal, run-of-the-mill occurrence: something has snapped, either in the aircraft or in the pilot.

There was a pilot in the regiment. A real one. The only real pilot in the regiment. All the rest were merely pilots in name and by their job, or if you prefer, by profession or circumstance. But this particular pilot could do things with his aircraft that no-one else in the entire air force could do. Sometimes the divisional commander would say, in a burst of sincerity, that pilots like him were one in a hundred thousand. The Pilot thought that talking was a waste of time. He lived only to fly. The rest of the time he drank and slept. From time to time he got some funny ideas into his head which resulted in his being passed over for even the most routine decorations. As long as the war lasted the divisional commander was fond of saying: I don't care what kind of shit they are on terra firma as long as they're aces in the air. And he quoted the Pilot as an example. When the war ended, everything changed. That self-same divisional commander said one day: Now they can be shits in the air as long as they're aces on terra firma. And he gave the Pilot five days in the cooler for drunkenness. He was stopped almost completely from flying. Just little five-minute training flights. The Pilot plunged into the deepest gloom and took to drinking seriously. And so he was not sent to the test-pilot training school. Instead they sent a model cadet who had top marks in military and political education and who had only joined the regiment after the end of the war. One Monday, after a very heavy Sunday night, the Pilot failed to bring his aircraft out of a spin. No-one knows what went wrong. The aircraft crashed and

nothing was left of the Pilot. At his funeral they buried a
parachute pack stuffed with blood-stained clods of earth.

> During the war, when we were being shot,
> The scale of values altered quite a lot.
> The general used to say to us in jest,
> 'Stay off the booze! But if you do your best
> And fly like aces, down here fool around.'
> But now those values are turned upside down.
> For since the war, the good old days have died.
> Put a foot wrong, they'll fall us in outside
> And drill us by the hour, right through lunch.
> The general bellows, 'Right, you rotten bunch,
> Fly as you will—be aces on the ground!'
> Ace on the ground? That's got a stupid sound.
> The hell with all your imbecility!
> Is there no end to your stupidity?
> There's only one way out, as we've been told.
> Cut throttles. Stick hard back and firmly hold.
> Rudder bar over, as far as it will go.
> Then grit your teeth, and wait, and mutter low,
> 'Go screw yourselves, you band of fucking shits.'
> And let them try to gather up the bits.

The next day Bawler applied for demobilisation. In his discharge papers, his character was summarised like this: Fails to
seek any benefit from his wartime experience, does not work
with his subordinates, has been caught red-handed in contacts
with the local population, etc. This assessment was written by
Friend. 'There's no point in getting angry,' he said. 'Everything I've said is true.' 'Yes,' said Bawler, 'with a few small
exceptions. My wartime experience was getting out of date by
the time the war ended. It went on the scrap-heap, along with
our obsolete aircraft. As far as subordinates are concerned, I
never had any, and I've got you to thank for that.' 'It's your own
fault,' said Friend. 'You shouldn't have drunk so much.'
'Maybe I shouldn't,' said Bawler, 'but you slipped me
hundred-proof spirit, straight, without giving me a bite to eat,
without telling me that the general had sent for me. Or rather,
you told me when I was already drunk. There's a word for that
kind of thing. And do you think you've gained anything by it?
You mark my words, the regiment will be disbanded anyway,

and you'll have to start all over again. You bastard!' Many years later they ran into each other in the street, but neither acknowledged the other.

> Suddenly, sometimes you stop and stare
> At a familiar figure approaching there.
> He was once your friend. Now with lowered eye
> He turns away as he passes by.

Truth-teller's interview

Double-dealer's behaviour makes me feel very angry, said Truth-teller. No Ibanskian should leave his fatherland of his own free will. It is the duty of every Ibanskian intellectual to consider the wellbeing of his people. The Ibanskian people is sick. It is criminal to abandon a sick person without trying to help him. Every . . . Duty . . . Obligation . . .

Journalist's opinion

Truth-teller's position seems strange, to say the least, and has caused anger and disappointment.

Neurasthenic's opinion

He should not be judged too severely. You must understand his situation. He is a man who has developed in isolation. He has had to write in complete secrecy so that no-one should have any idea what he was doing. The criticism to which he has had to submit has been biased and unjust. When he has been praised, the praise has taken the form of equally biased and uncritical rhapsodies. The only standard of comparison has been official literature, which is worthless, deceitful and propagandist. Western culture is virtually unknown. And moreover it is regarded in a suspicious and indeed hostile light. No factors exist to permit a scientific analysis of the situation. And in our time, without that, any serious literature cannot exist. He has had no contacts with young people. Need I go on? Truth-teller is the victim of circumstance, even though he plays the role of a prophet. That is why he claims the function of a mentor and a judge.

Reflections

Soilophagist was thinking of something else as well. When I have finished my work I shall present it to the Leader, he said.

The Leader is far from stupid. He will understand that there is something to be gained from it which may win him immortality. In principle he should have me by his side. He won't get anything done with his bunch of cretinous deputies. They sleep and dream of how to overthrow him and take his place. And what if . . . I'm going to have to think about it all very carefully. Mustn't hurry. You only need to hurry when you're trying to catch fleas. Certainly Deputy number 5 seems to have a good chance. That's the way things are going . . . That's pretty clear. Should I put it up to him? He'd grab it with everything he's got. But would he take a risk like that? If the Leader takes the bait, I'd have a good chance of becoming a Deputy myself. Almost for sure. And, once there . . . But Teacher is putting things far too sharply. I'll have to smooth off the corners. Let's see what he's scribbled down this time.

Solitude

'We must separate,' She said. 'Very well,' He replied. 'I love you but I've got a family all the same,' She said. 'I'm not reproaching you,' He said. 'My husband knows,' She said. 'These days all intellectual women have lovers, and all the men have mistresses,' He said; 'your husband knows that just as well as you do.' 'He knows that it's you,' She said. 'He says anyone you like as long as it's not that schizophrenic adventurer.' 'And informer,' He said. 'And informer,' She agreed. 'Why am I worse than anybody else?' He asked. 'He thinks that with you I'll end up behind bars,' She said, 'and he doesn't want to have to bring me food parcels. And he doesn't want the child to have to grow up without a mother.' 'That's reasonable,' He said. 'Are you sorry I'm leaving you?' She asked. 'No,' He said. 'You're all the same,' and She began to cry. 'You mustn't,' He said. 'Now go.'

You're on your own again, He said to himself. That's good. That's good. Peaceful. Peaceful. Peaceful. Everything's fine. There's no need to be angry with anyone. No need for hate. No need for jealousy. No need for gratitude. No-one is being unjust to you. Time will go by so fast you'll hardly notice. Just the blinking of an eye—and then nothing. All that counts is the present moment. Protect it. Nurture it. Live it to the full. The main thing is knowing that you're doing what you have to do, what you want to do and what you believe must be done. It doesn't matter a damn what others may think of it. That has no significance.

Teacher wants to bring in the concept of the degree of applicability of a decision. Why does he need that? Anyway that's his business. He's got something going at the moment. So be it. That's his business. Various methods of measurement can be used here. For instance—one divided by the number of people on whom the execution of a decision depends. But perhaps it would be better if . . .

Double-dealer's interview

I have no wish to save the Ibanskian people from disaster of any kind, said Double-dealer. There is nothing to save them from. No-one is threatening them except themselves. They are fed and clothed. And they are free as well. Even perhaps too free. That is not a joke. They are freer than even their own leaders think they are. And everything that has happened and is happening in Ibansk is the product of the freedom of the people and not of the oppression of the people. Quite the contrary, it is the product of oppression exerted by the people on something else, and in particular on themselves. It is the popular will that has driven out Truth-teller, not an arbitrary decision of rulers cut off from the people. The rulers have saved Truth-teller from the people. Had they not done this, the people would have torn him to shreds. The people do not like to hear the truth about themselves. They prefer lies about themselves. They know the truth without Truth-teller's help. And I was forced to leave of my own free will at the will of a free people, with only one difference—that in the end I myself wanted to leave and so for two years I was prevented from doing so since my own voluntary desire to fulfil the wishes and the will of the people was self-will. And a free people cannot allow that. They even want to fulfil their own will as regards me despite my own will. They thirst to oppress, and nothing more. It is stupid to attribute everything to the machinations of a reactionary government. The present government of Ibansk is more progressive than the people it governs. I merely fought for my own personal right to act according to my own will within the limits set by official Ibanskian law and morality.

Writer's opinion

Writer wrote a long article about Double-dealer's book, which, as he admitted in the article, he had not read and had no intention of reading. He ended the article with the following lines:

> It is slander, vile and baseless
> Falsehood with an evil gleam,
> We the people are dictators
> Incarnation of a dream.

The programme of reforms

These are just minor details, Teacher wrote in the margin of Soilophagist's manuscript against all the passages of which Soilophagist was most proud. Soilophagist was proposing to abolish the system of taxes and other deductions by simply recalculating salaries. He also proposed other measures which should in theory have led to considerable economies. We need radical ideas, wrote Teacher. This is not after all a report to a seminar in a Brotherhood school, but a scheme for governmental reform. These ideas should be developed along three main lines. The first is to reduce to a minimum the apparatus of control and of parasitic strata and organisations. Secondly, we must aim for the freedom of action of managers, together with their own accountability for the results of that action. And thirdly, subordinates must have the right to defend themselves and be given the means of doing so. In each of these directions we must bear in mind the corresponding social laws and seek to limit their effects. For instance if a certain function of a social group tends to become detached from it as a function of a particular independent group, then the number of people performing that function necessarily increases in a specific ratio which is easy enough to calculate. How should we combat this? We must decide which functions of social groups may be allowed to have an independent and separate existence and which may not. That can be done as a result of empirical observation. For example it would be rational to ordain that the direction of youth be a power function inseparable in principle from other functions of the organs of the Brotherhood. That would result in the slimming down of the ponderous apparatus of youth organisations, and thus the overall direction of youth would be improved. Strict rules could be established for functions which enjoy a separate existence. For example, one could have not only a fragmentation of certain organisations but also a redistribution of function accompanied by a centralisation of smaller organisations of similar kind in order to avoid an increase in the proportion of managers and parasites. Up to the present time the increase in the number of social groups has always tended to enlarge this proportion. So it could be stabilised. One could also introduce a compensatory rule: that the formation of new social groups should be matched by the elimination of others.

The more Soilophagist read Teacher's notes the more convinced he became that he might get himself involved (if indeed he were not already involved!) in a most unpleasant mess. I'd better get out of this before it's too late, he thought. He had recently attended a meeting of the commission on the preparation of a draft for a new constitution and he had been deeply shaken. Almost all the members of the commission, with few exceptions, were young people. Almost certainly none of them had fought in the war. Judging by their constant references to Western authors, they all knew at least two languages. Who were these people? Where were they from? Teacher claimed that they were the gilded youth, the second and third generation of the leadership class. That they had all studied in institutes for the highly privileged. That they were all editors, assistants, co-authors, commentators, consultants. Very well, say that they are. What does it matter? But what about the things they were saying? They dismissed with astonishing ease, as if of only secondary importance, things which he, Soilophagist, had turned for years deep in his heart. He had reflected on them during his years in the trenches, in military hospitals, on construction sites far away from the city of Ibansk. And they said exactly the same as Soilophagist could have said at that time. And yet there was a certain difference. Where did the contradiction lie? Was it in the tone of what they said? Was it in their off-hand approach? Did it lie in the importance they accorded to his ideas in the scheme of their ideas? Was it possible that Teacher was right and that it really was impossible to invent anything that could not be invented by dozens of other people? And that the key really lay in one's ability to select what was important, to establish necessary relationships and proportions and to identify those sensitive points, pressure on which would set the whole machine working in the desired direction? And in which direction? What would the whole social structure look like after all this? He would never be able to sort it all out without Teacher's help. And as for the kids who sit on the commission, they are nothing but happy, successful, flourishing chatterers, who had contrived to scale the highest summits. Teacher was worth all of them put together. But he was stepping completely out of line. He was becoming dangerous. The break had to be made. The time had come . . .

The most important, the fundamental thing, if society is to progress and to make significant economies, he read further in Teacher's notes, is a system which would allow subordinates to defend themselves against their superiors, citizens to defend themselves against their own power, and individuals to defend themselves against their own group, against the masses. Without such a system of self-defence, any measures designed to improve society in the desired direction are condemned to failure. This self-defence is the only true form of feed-back without which the existence and the development of a self-organising social system of the Ibanskian mould would be inconceivable. In this case feed-back does not comprise files, reports and accounts and so on—which operate on quite a different level of life (to say nothing of consistent failure)—but consists of the citizens' ability to defend their own interests in their struggles with higher authorities and with collectives.

So that's where you're trying to get to, thought Soilophagist. No, that'll never do. All this will have to be destroyed. Ideas like this could get me into really big trouble. I was quite wrong to get myself mixed up with Teacher. Quite wrong. He could wreck everything.

My own voice

'What do you think about Singer's poetry?' Journalist asked Snottyhanky. 'Poetry is untranslatable,' said Snottyhanky. 'Take me for example; I can't even be translated into Ibanskian.' 'But what language do you write in?' asked Journalist in astonishment. 'Every great poet has his own language,' said Snottyhanky. 'I have my own voice and speak in my own tongue.' 'You should hold your tongue for a bit,' said Chief. 'If you don't, you might lose your voice. Now, I've got a job for you. Go to America and show the world that we here in Ibansk have complete artistic freedom. But go easy on the fancy gear. Keep it within reason. People are beginning to talk. No more than ten fur coats, okay?'

The moment he arrived in America, Snottyhanky declaimed the following poem:

> Naught on earth can make me fear;
> Kings and gods just make me sneer.
> But there's one thing shakes me mute:
> Angles that are too acute.
> No matter where my steps I aim,
> (Whether to lecture or declaim)
> My voice I raise without demur:
> The oval is what I prefer.

Way out! cried the Americans. Brilliant! Oh, these Ibanskians, they've always got something up their sleeve. We couldn't produce anything like that now. We're all too fat and opulent. As you see, said Snottyhanky to the newsmen, I am here. And I, as everyone knows, am the most intellectual intellectual in Ibansk. When I was getting ready to come here my friend Truth-teller said to me: Snottyhanky, my old friend, he said, you just go and sing them all the truth about us, because they've got a very distorted idea of what we're really like. And my old childhood friend, Dauber . . .

'It's quite true that he is pretty bold,' said Teacher. 'Kings and gods—they're no joke, nothing like the secret police. You've got to be brave to say a thing like that.' Fellow-worker, who was very envious of Snottyhanky's world-wide fame, said that this lousy little poem ought to be rewritten thus:

> No matter whom I give away,
> Never mind whose arse I kiss,
> I must bleat the livelong day:
> Ah my oval, ah my bliss!

When he returned from America, at the request of Colleague Snottyhanky wrote a long memorandum on Singer's work. 'It's for Himself,' said Colleague. 'So be objective.' So Snottyhanky wrote that from the point of view of modern poetry, Singer was extremely mediocre, but that as a citizen he was worthy of respect and that he, Snottyhanky, believed in his sincerity and would vouch for him . . . 'We've got quite enough citizens without all these singers trampling all over us,' said Deputy number one, 'and we don't need any mediocre poets. Throw him into jail!' The Leader, who was liberally inclined, suggested a more humanitarian measure: kick him in the pants and chase him over the border! Why hang on to bad poets when we've got as many good ones as you like!

Basic principles

'Double-dealer is right,' said Chatterer. 'Truth-teller has accomplished a mighty work. Maybe the mightiest of its kind in the whole history of Ibansk. But his positive programme is laughable, and as for his role as a self-appointed pastor, it's unattractive to say the least. We must start from positive basic principles. The negative viewpoint can produce nothing except bitterness and disappointment. We must accept the following as indisputable facts. The revolution was a great blessing for the Ibanskian people. For all practical purposes the people got everything they had been dreaming of. And they got something else besides, but that's another question. The country's progress over the decades has been quite staggering. The people are free and on the whole happy. The government reflects the interests of the people. The Brotherhood is the only force capable of maintaining order in the country, of restraining to a certain degree an explosion of oppression, and of ensuring a certain measure of progress. In most cases discontent neither runs deep nor concerns essential principles. It has not yet touched the fundamental bases of the life of the people. I am prepared to accept almost everything which official doctrine and propaganda say about the Ibanskian way of life. It would be senseless to reject it all. But that is not the crux of the matter. Everything about which our official propaganda remains mute, and about which any mention in conversation is regarded as slander, is also the legitimate product of all the positive achievements of Ibanskian life. All the progress which we boast about and flaunt in every conceivable way inevitably engenders all those abominations which we keep quiet about and whose existence we deny by every method open to us. They have the self same source. The freedom of the people engenders oppres-

(546)

sion first on the individual and subsequently on the people as a whole. Collectivism engenders individualism. Fanaticism leads to cynicism and loss of faith . . . There are natural laws of social existence over which neither peoples nor governments have any power. When Double-dealer was preparing to leave, he was promised mountains of gold if he would stay. Even Leader promised his protection, and I believe, sincerely. They say he's not such a bad old stick at heart. Double-dealer tried to explain to him that it wasn't within Leader's power to keep his promise. Where could he find him able students who were attracted to learning for its own sake? How could he force them to learn for the love of knowledge, and not just to set themselves up with a nice little career? The very least that would be needed to do that would be a radical revision of society's scale of values and the possibility afforded to each individual of realising his potential. How could a new educational programme be introduced, with a different system of control of knowledge, of selection, of organisation of work, of publication, of defending theses? Who would look after all this? The same people and organisations who had created and who maintain the present system, and who had made him, Double-dealer, into an alien element in our life? You say he should have gone on fighting? He had fought for thirty years. The sum total? The complete ruin of all his efforts. In a word, Leader couldn't make head or tail of all this, flew into a fury and had Double-dealer expelled, but had it made out to be the voluntary flight of a renegade. That is progress, of course. In the past he'd have been shot. Say what you like, but the Leader follows a democratic line, quite contrary to what the Boss would have done.' 'It's horrifying,' said Dauber. 'It *is* horrifying,' said Chatterer. 'Here we are up against a kind of history in which time is measured in millennia and people in millions. Here is another plane of existence which Truth-teller never mentions. Nor the others. The Ibanskian people is living through a tragedy of unrealised possibilities: the worst tragedy a civilised people can undergo. Double-dealer is moving on this plane, and Truth-teller will never be able to understand him.'

Neurasthenic's response
But all the same, Truth-teller is hitting at the most tender, most painful spot of Ibanskian society. Its most important spot.

Right on the nerve. The fact is that the Ibanskian people is still living with the knowledge of the crime it has committed. In a little time this knowledge will fade away. One generation, and no-one will understand Truth-teller any more. But for the time being there is still an outside chance of making the people confess to its crime, and purge itself of its recent past. If that doesn't happen now, in ten or fifteen years it will be too late. Then it will never happen. And then the people will be condemned to life with a clear conscience and a criminal nature. I am afraid that confession and remorse will not come. Why? Because the events of the recent past were no chance accident, but had their roots in the essence, the fundamental nature of the Ibanskian people. Truth-teller does not understand this. And it is a good thing that he does not, said Chatterer. While there is still the slightest chance of purging the national conscience, that chance must be exploited.

Double-dealer's second interview
The Ibanskian people are condemned to drag out a happy existence under the wise leadership of their beloved government, said Double-dealer. The people are beautiful. The authorities are even better. So let's say that I am evil. But I do not want to be good like them, or happy like them. I have committed no moral or legal crime, and for this I have been justly punished. For a long time they didn't want to let me leave. And that was a good thing for me. To be granted the right to leave the country, it has to be merited. Then they told me to get out. And that, too, was good for me. But what if they hadn't let you out, Double-dealer was asked, what would you have done? It had become completely impossible for me to go on living in their marvellous society, said Double-dealer. I have no wish to struggle for changes in it. And I think it would be a waste of time. I am tired.

The twelfth hour
Early one sunny morning, Bawler, his chest covered in glittering orders and decorations, strode out on to the Ibansk station square. He was immediately arrested by the military police and charged with being improperly dressed in that he was wearing plastic buttons — a ban which had come into force while the

demobilised airmen's train was still chuffing its way towards Ibansk. At police headquarters there were hundreds held on the same charge. The well-meaning commandant ordered them to be drilled for a couple of hours and then released with his blessing. Bawler refused to do any marching, ripped off his shoulder-boards and chucked them in the rubbish bin. Many of the others followed his example. One captain unhooked his medals and orders and shoved them carelessly into his pocket. 'The whores,' said the Captain. 'Who?' asked Bawler. 'You know perfectly well who I mean,' said the Captain. They were detained until late that night. But in the end they let them go. 'There was a time when we'd have got the camps for that,' said the Captain. 'Come round to my place, it's quite near. We'll celebrate our glorious homecoming. We've done pretty well to stay alive.' 'And free, for the time being,' said Bawler.

Professional difficulties

'Our life's not all beer and skittles, either,' said Colleague. 'When we were maintaining surveillance on Moaner, do you know what that turd dreamt up? He began to wrap all his rubbish up in his drafts, spat in them, and even pissed and shat on them. That's a cultured man for you! And we had to clean all the crap off, stick the papers together and restore them to readability. And that got us a lot more angry than what he'd written in his miserable little book. And if he isn't allowed to leave for another year, he's only got himself to blame.' 'How so?' asked Dauber. 'He broke the rules of the game,' said Colleague. 'He shouldn't have given the slightest hint that he knew he was being watched. It's a job for us, you know. We don't do it for fun. We've got our professional self-respect. As far as the book goes, we've nothing against it. It's a semi-scientific book, and it won't have any success in the West. They won't understand it. It's far too intelligent a book for those fat degenerates. Nothing spectacular about it. So it won't cause any sensation.'

Points of view

'We're going a bit over the mark in our judgments of the Boss,' said Wife. 'After all, he didn't only shoot people. He did some positive things as well.' 'That's true,' said Colleague. 'There

(549)

were some dams, some expeditions, some victories.' 'That's true,' said Singer.

> We see things differently, I and you,
> From totally opposite points of view.
> For you, this bloke is a god, sublime;
> For me he's a bandit steeped in crime.
> For you he's a leader, good and wise,
> For me he's a murderer, damn his eyes.
> For me he's a thief, a louse, a turd.
> And so this argument is absurd,
> A waste of time for me to pursue,
> Speaking the truth to the likes of you.
> Why not stand me against a wall?
> Just a single sound, and that'll be all.

'You're overstepping the mark,' said Colleague. 'Now's not the time!'

A page of heroic history

The Boss was an outstanding scientist in every discipline, provided that he didn't really get to grips with any subject. Once he addressed a conference of anthropologists on the origins of man. 'Accoordin 'ter th'Ism,' he said, 'chimps started off livin' int'trees, then they gor agate runnin' around on t'greawnd, an' thi geet a wider 'orizon.' 'But they could see more from higher up,' whispered one academician to another, who in his time had had the opportunity of seeing for himself the origin of man, and knew exactly how it had happened. The academician went to jail. Then his friend. And then all the others. When the Boss was told that the academician had been joking, he replied 'Jokes is a serious bisness. An'if a joke's not serious, it's jus' laffable.'

A symposium on scatology

[This passage depends on the Russian word 'mat', for which there is no adequate English equivalent. It means 'cursing, swearing, the use of foul and abusive language, usually with a heavily sexual content'. So the cant Soviet abbreviation 'diamat'—short for 'dialectical materialism'—takes on a certain overtone; 'mat', of course, is also the last syllable of 'avtomat'—automat—slot machine, dial telephone booth etc. And it is the first syllable of 'matematika'—mathematics. And it should be borne in mind that Russian coarse language is much coarser than the usual range of English abuse. 'Fuck your mother'—'Yob tvoyu mat' is frequently used. Unhappily, the full flavour of this section may not carry through into the translation!]

For three years the forces of the avant-garde tried at the highest levels to promote the idea of a Pan-Ibanskian Symposium on the theory and practice of Ibanskian scatology. An early difficulty was that no-one could decide which faculty should host the symposium. The Board of Linguistics shuffled it off on to the Mathematical Board. They passed it on to the Philosophers, the Philosophers on to the Pedagogical Faculty, who in their turn pushed it off on to the Psychological Faculty. But the lower reaches of the linguists were desperately anxious to run the symposium, and so were the lower levels of the mathematicians, the philosophers and all the rest. And there was no possibility of agreement being reached. The Secret Police warned that doubtful characters would get involved in the symposium, and that improper conversations would take place. After the Leader's speech about the close links that existed between avant-garde science and revolutionary practice in Ism-building, his Deputy on Scientific Affairs happened to observe that it might be worth reconsidering the Symposium on Scatology. The comment was taken as a directive, and an Organising Committee was set up under Secretary's chairmanship. Within a year the Organising Committee had worked out the Symposium programme. After another year's work, it drew up a list of five hundred participants, divided into sections. The philosophical section was to cover a number of basic subjects: (1) scat and diamat; (2) the classics of the Ism on scatology; (3) scatology in the works of the classics of the Ism; (4) scatorealism as the highest stage of development of materialism before the dawn of diamat. The mathematical section was to include (1) the formalisation of the scatology of semi-structures; (2) the immersion of second-degree scathematical calculation in the theory of hydro-complex tensors of imaginary sub-space of the first order relative to parity; (3) the theory of algorithms; (4) terminal autoscats; (5) the Ibanskian concept of number. The linguistic section was to deal with (1) the structure of third degree scatalanguage; (2) the scatalanguage of cobblers in ancient Ibanskian dialect; (3) the scatalanguage of nineteenth-century Ibanskian waggoners; (4) problems of computer translation of scatalanguage into foreign languages and back again. There is no need to set out the symposium programme in detail, since it has been published.

The symposium proceeded with extraordinary vigour. It was opened by President himself. Deputy number nine delivered the welcoming address. There were representatives of friendly Brotherhoods, and foreign scientists. When Secretary delivered his report, and burst into tears of tender nostalgia as he recalled the splendid flights of abuse his grandfather used to unleash upon him as he flogged his naked arse with a leather strap, Deputy asked President if he knew what scat and diamat had in common. 'Go on, tell me,' begged President, splitting his sides with anticipated laughter. 'They are both mighty weapons in the hands of the proletariat,' said Deputy, who had learnt the joke the previous day from one of his aides. 'And what's the difference between them? Go on, what?' asked President, spraying the red cloth of the presidium table with tears of delight. 'The difference is that everyone understands scatology and pretends not to, while with diamat it's just the opposite,' said Deputy, clutching his belly as it heaved with laughter. President was taken ill, and had to be replaced by another, more progressive one. It did no good, because the progressive one turned out to be even worse than the one he replaced.

If there is one great contribution that the Ibanskian people has made to world culture, a contribution which is a direct result of its latent development, read Secretary from the report prepared for him by Thinker, it is scatology! It can truly be said to be the greatest invention mankind has produced. It is a universal super-language, in which we can communicate not only with workers throughout our own planet, but also with extra-terrestrial civilisations. It is no mere chance that our great Ibanskian poet has written:

When your telephone stays silent all day long,
When no-one even speaks to you for weeks,
When your ex-friends, an ever-growing throng
Start slandering you and kick you in the teeth;
When the future shows no tiny chink of light,
When there's no-one to help you in the least,
And when your life is just one ceaseless blight,
And you would howl like some poor stricken beast.
When your tongue withers up from lack of use,
When all men think you're guilty, if not worse,

When no-one wants to know how you're abused,
Just one thing helps—a good old-fashioned curse.
At this the audience of many thousands rose to their feet in a
stormy ovation. Even Deputy was on his feet applauding. This
was the culminating point of the unity of all the avant-garde
elements in Ibansk, and the high point of liberalism. The
decline began next day. Deputy was transferred to another, less
responsible, job.

Outrageous poems

The Period of Perplexity saw the onset, not merely of the well
known epidemic of anecdotes, but of an epidemic of outrageous
verse. It was a less significant epidemic but nevertheless one of
sufficient scale to merit a reference in this study. The authors of
these outrageous verses were not professional poets, and were
wholly unconcerned about poetic techniques. They would take
any established verse forms and models which came to hand
and produced what were ostensibly imitations and parodies of
them. But the results were not mere imitations or parodies of
the original. They were unique phenomena which should be
studied according to other parameters. As a general rule the
authors of these outrageous verses deliberately used the crudest
possible poetic methods, and in particular the most hackneyed
rhymes. And by these means they achieved remarkably striking
effects, a great deal stronger than those of the refined virtuoso
poems of the professionals. May be this was not poetry at all,
but merely a primitively rhyming form of coarse prose. But
what difference does it make what we call them? The aim of the
outrageous verses was to compress some important existential
content into small dimensions of traditional literary form. If
that aim is achieved, it makes no difference what the experts
say. It was not intended for them. The authors were not looking
for fees, prizes, or even for publication.

The outrageous poems produced an enormous effect, an
effect far greater than the classic poetry of the past. And
immeasurably greater than the verses of the best and most
talented officially recognised poets of our age. On one occasion,
a highly aesthetic group invited Snottyhanky to come to one of
their gatherings. It was very hard to persuade him to accept. In
the end he agreed only when his hosts had all chipped in to buy

him an expensive gift. The gift had to be agreed in advance. Snottyhanky recited his most successful poems, as he described them himself. He was, of course, respectfully applauded. Then an author of outrageous verses, who happened to be present, was asked if he would recite some of his work. He demurred for a long time, saying that he would be embarrassed to exhibit his scribblings in the presence of so distinguished a poet. Snottyhanky promised not to be too hard on him since he was only an amateur. So in the end the outrageous poet gave in. He read part of a poem about the Boss. There was an uneasy silence. It was quite clear to the assembled company, including Snottyhanky, that the outrageous poem about the Boss was streets ahead of all Snottyhanky's poems put together. Snottyhanky was asked what he thought. 'Not unamusing,' he said. 'A bit short on technique, of course, but there's a certain amount of thought there. Not too bad as a party piece.' The assembled company heaved a sigh of relief. Well, of course, it was tolerable for a bit of fun at a party. But from the truly poetic point of view . . . Those present were educated people. They knew perfectly well that if anything important were to come out of Ibanskian culture, it would have to come from the amateurs and the underground. And yet they were content. They had now heard a judgment passed and were able to consign the author of this illegal outrageous poem to his proper place outside the boundaries of art. Once in my army unit, one of those present said later, we were training for a weightlifting competition. A soldier came wandering along who'd never had any interest in sport at all. Someone jokingly asked him to try to lift the weights. He picked the bar up effortlessly with one hand. Our eyes almost popped out of our heads. But we calmed down later. He hadn't lifted it according to the rules.

If there had been the slightest possibility in Ibansk of publishing the outrageous poems and some objective criticisms, an interesting literary trend might have developed. But that did not happen, like so much else in Ibansk. Official poetry had a profound lack of interest in allowing the development of a dangerous competitor in the form of the outrageous poetry. And the authors of the outrageous poems didn't think for a moment of daring to try to get their pieces into the press. But the main obstacle was not that of official poetry, nor even that of the poetry authorities and the censorship. It came from the writers and their audience themselves. The audiences, who derived both pleasure and food for thought from the outrageous poems, would not have got more out of them had they been officially recognised. Nor did they wish to do so. Why go to all that trouble, they said. After all, who's the author? Just one of the lads. The same crap as we are, perhaps even worse. He drinks. And the other one, well, he'll never escape from the madhouse. The poems are brilliant, of course. But they're just our own little local provincial verses. Who'd be interested in them? After all, if you look at them from outside, perhaps they wouldn't seem so good.

The social position of the authors was not affected by the admiration provoked by their poems. No-one paid them any money for them. Their fame was limited to the narrow circle of their friends or workmates. And if the authorities got wind of who the authors were, then they could be in trouble. In the absence of any criteria for judging them, the authors attached very little importance to their poems. Many didn't even preserve them. And gradually outrageous verse got lost and forgotten. Just once in a while at some drunken party, someone would remember two or three lines. A few sighs would be heaved. He was a poet of genius, someone would say. Those were the days. And then the conversation would turn to more pressing topics—to villas, to motor cars, to ikons, to Paris, to the forthcoming elections and promotions.

The authors of the outrageous poems included some quite outstanding talents. One of them, who was quite well known in Ibanskian literary circles, wrote his poems in a big notebook. Had he followed the example of Truth-teller, Singer and Double-dealer and published in the West, he would have achieved world-wide fame in no time. But he could not make his mind up to it. He was afraid that if he published he would lose his job, or maybe worse. And he was not wholly confident that what he had written had any universal importance. And from where could that confidence come if he were not published? And time passed. Maybe years will go by, and then suddenly Ibanskian outrageous verse will become the object of the impassioned attention of world culture. People will rush to collect examples of it, in the same way that they rushed to collect old Ibanskian ikons. But will much of it last until that time? One outstanding master of the genre will die in a mental hospital. Another will perish in the struggle for improved living conditions. Yet another will have wasted his gift in writing some miserable book on official philosophy in co-authorship with some fossil of Ibanism. And no-one will cry aloud: Look out, people, you are being robbed! Remember that every talent suppressed in your neighbour means that you have one fewer festival in your own life. Remember that all that is needed to eliminate a whole new literary tendency is the elimination of some of those who were carrying it forward. And sometimes the crushing of one single man, maybe your neighbour or work-mate who has had no recognition or payment for his talents, is enough to prevent the birth of a new direction in culture.

Outrageous poetry was intimately intermixed with songs. Many of Singer's songs, for instance, which were widely known, started out as outrageous poems, or were re-writes of them.

Social systems

Social systems, wrote Teacher, belong to the category of empirical systems. They are conglomerations of a large number of empirical objects. They are localised in space and they have an adequately durable existence in time. Their elements are in an interdependent relationship. The objects and the links which comprise the system are more or less homogeneous, regular and stable.

If we consider empirical systems we must distinguish between two types of research: (1) the study of a system as a whole, so as to determine its composition; thus finding an answer to the question, what is its composition; and (2) the study of certain problems, bearing in mind the nature of the given system. The first case establishes the system's components, their inter-relation, their number, the system's spatial dimensions, its hierarchical structure, and so on. The second case determines the link between the phenomenon under study and the nature of the system on which it depends. In the second case it is the effects of the system that are being studied.

Let us consider the following example. The scientific level of the country is determined by (among other things) the number of Doctors and Bachelors of Science, the number of publications, of scientific conferences, of journals and so on. A decision to raise the level of science is taken. Among the steps to be taken, naturally, will be a decision to increase the number of Doctors and Bachelors of Science, the number of publications and so on. Money is ear-marked for this purpose. But a decision is a decision, and execution is quite another matter. If our society was in reality as it is depicted by our official propaganda and as our leaders think of it (at least officially), then the problem would be easily solved: a purely quantitative change would entail a proportionate qualitative change. But what really happens in view of the peculiarities of the system within which the decision is taken? It becomes far easier initially to be accepted as a research student, to be awarded degrees, to get work published and so on. But these new opportunities are used primarily and principally by mediocrities, cheats, careerists and other similar types who have a great facility for carving themselves large chunks of society's cake. It's true that some real scientists manage to grab a few crumbs, but in relative terms their share in the business is sharply reduced. The level of science may rise slightly, but a long way short of the level envisaged by the leadership and the propagandists. Here, perhaps, one could calculate the effect of the system in the corrections it imposes upon the predicted results.

Let us pursue the example. We see that university degrees have been devalued and for most of their holders are nothing more than useless pieces of paper. So a decision is taken to change the pay structure of scientific research workers. The new system takes into account the real value of the research. Who will be responsible for working the systems out? Will they be impartial, just, godlike creatures? No, they will be those same Doctors and Bachelors of Science who were the reason for the whole upheaval. And they will do everything in their own way, and almost nothing will change. The only people to suffer will be the most defenceless, productive and talented scientists. There are very few of them, but they are the soul and nerve of science. And as it is they who suffer, the consequences will be disastrous. All this is an example of the qualitative effect produced by the system. In such cases any reforms preserve the status quo and only damage the most highly organised and superior forms of the system. And if the leadership is really well-intentioned it should strive not towards reform but towards stability, while applying a protectionist policy towards the most eminent representatives of science and culture.

New measures taken with regard to scientific research
In the end they got round to looking at scientific research. There was a special meeting, which formulated a directive to increase, to improve and to rectify. The following practical measures were adopted: (1) An increase in the number of Doctors of Science and Senior Research Workers; (2) An improvement in the quality of training of research workers, and in the scientific and theoretical level of theses; (3) An increase in the number of articles published on immediate scientific problems, and so on. No sooner said than done. As the proverb has it, the hare hates to kick his heels. And within six months there was a hundred per cent increase in the number of research students and a ninety-nine per cent in the number of doctors. The total volume of publications rose to a hundred million tons. No point in half measures. And soon Ibansk was stuffed to the seams with science. Just one backward area, whose population had burst straight into the Ism (thanks to its semi-wild state), and which had become literate only a year earlier, and still wasn't too sure of its spelling, had more doctors of science than France and England put together.

Some genuine scientists took advantage of all the confusion to infiltrate themselves into the scientific world, and began to get too big for their boots. When this oversight was detected certain urgent measures were taken. This was the beginning of the anti-doctor campaign. It was pursued with such vigour that one might have got the impression that all Ibanskian doctors of science were ignorant boors, although the newspapers all declared with a single voice that the doctors of Ibansk were all quite splendid, except for one or two who had slipped through the net. But in fact everyone knew what the true position was. In particular all the doctors from that region of Ibansk which was so far ahead of England and France together, had all presented the same thesis, which the first candidate had copied out of a popular science pamphlet for housewives. He became President of the Regional Academy of Sciences. The press quoted the examples of a plumber who had outclassed all the doctors of technical sciences, and of a stable lad who had rubbed the noses of all the doctors of letters in the mud. It became clear that the further progress of Ibanskian science would accelerate less quickly without reforms than with.

An outrageous poem about doctors of science
Some people have the happy lot
To roam abroad by any route.
My daily journey—all I've got
Is to and from my Institute.
In drizzle, drought, in frost and heat
From now until the day I die
I shall wear out my trousers' seat
Writing rubbish for on high,
Webs of words for them to see,
Me, a learned D.Sc.
I've often thought I'll make an end,
Flush their papers down the pan.
I'll go to bed and quite intend
To hit the road, go where I can.
But when I wake, it seems absurd,
A daft idea of no avail
To waste the five degrees I've earned,
Three foreign languages as well.
It's not for that I chose to be
A useful modern D.Sc.
I've got to think about my sons
Who have to study hard so they
Will publish papers, as I've done
At the Institute one day.
And anyway it's been made clear
That antillectuals of our kind
Are not allowed to travel far.
Go abroad?—Out of your mind!
So don't imagine you'll get free—
You rotten bastard D.Sc.
It's no use trying to agitate!
You learned doctors breed like fleas,
And every other chap you meet

Has got himself a few degrees.
We've got to have some order here,
So don't you try to sneak away.
For if you do—well, never fear,
We'll come and teach you to obey.
Though you may be a learned don,
There's plenty more where you came from.

Unity

'In our country,' cried Teacher, 'the main problem is the liberation of men from serfdom.'

'Yes, yes! For we're all slaves. From top to bottom, everyone is a slave.' The customers in the Pavilion exchanged anxious glances. Their amazement stemmed not from what this drunken student was saying, for after all they themselves had said things that were even more extravagant. What was surprising was that he was shouting it all at the top of his voice and no-one had laid a finger on him. The customers looked towards the door, through which in theory the usual plainclothes secret policemen should have been appearing. But there was no sign of them. Life maintained its normal course, and the customers were alarmed and confused by this departure from normality. They're going to let him go on, and then they'll suddenly turn up, and what a going-over they'll give us then! Then in despair they began to shout themselves. Teacher's frenzied cries seemed to them to be the childish babbling of a kid who knew nothing of the world. And in the shouts of the customers terrible words could be heard: arrests, solitary confinement, denunciation, guard towers, executioners, cretins, bastards, famine . . . 'Just try to change your job,' yelled Teacher, 'or to move to another town! Try and get a hotel room. To dissent. To go abroad . . .' 'Why are you giving me all this shit,' shouted a one-armed man at the next table. 'All this crap about heroes! I know him. I've known him since the beginning of the war. Do you know how many thousands of people that bastard has ruined?' 'What a joke,' thought Bawler. 'I knew all this when I was still a child. There was a time when I thought it was a secret all of my own. Nowadays everyone talks about it. I was a long way ahead when I discovered for myself the serfdom of our daily life. Now it's become the subject of drunken ravings.

They're all on my heels. If everyone knows about it, that must mean that the essence has eluded me. I must go further. I am not going to say and do things which everyone can say and do without any particular risk.'

'The best way of making sure you don't go bald,' said Wife to Fellow-worker, who was losing his hair, 'is never to wash your hair at all.' 'But you'd get lice,' said Fellow-worker. 'Nonsense,' said Wife. 'There are lots of very effective anti-lice preparations these days. The human head has developed from a protracted biological evolution, and its normal state is to be filthy.' 'Well, who knows,' thought Fellow-worker. 'Maybe she's right. I'd better try. After all, filth is normal in our life. It's cleanliness that is a deviation. When cleanliness becomes universal, it always smacks of the regime. Cleanliness is only attractive when surrounded by filth.'

'I'm a pacifist,' said Puss, 'and I haven't the slightest interest in all your military exploits. It's better to be a peacetime private than a wartime general!' Puss always talked in aphorisms. They were formed deep down in his gut, somewhere near his appendicitis scar, and crept to the surface like worms, emerging as a total surprise for himself and for those about him. 'Every coward,' said Colleague, 'is a natural pacifist. My point of view is diametrically opposed to yours. I'd much prefer to be a peacetime general than a wartime private.'

'Man is always a slave,' said Wife. 'It's impossible to live in a society and remain free from it.' 'I am not talking about freedom from society, but about freedom in society,' said Teacher. 'Don't try and confuse the issue! We're talking about the elementary rights of man, man who is the heir to . . .' 'We are the heirs to the Boss and his victims,' Puss burst out, casting prudence to the wind, and was then so appalled by the possible consequences of what he'd said that he shat himself. 'This is very serious,' thought the Boy. 'I must write a report.'

'Look here,' shouted One-arm. 'I'll draw you a picture. See? Even a babe in arms should know what's got to be done—get away, of course. But where to? That's absolutely right! What did I tell you! It's child's play. And what's your military genius gone and done? Left us to rot here for a whole bloody week. No food. No ammunition. Why? Important reasons of strategy? Rubbish! They think with their arses, not their heads. They don't give a bugger for people. All their talk about how much they care is lies and demagogy. Their thinking is completely twisted. They always have to show each other how bloody clever they are, those misbegotten bastards. And it's us who've got to pay for their idiocy. Just look around you! Anyone who could build a marvellous mess like this must be weak in their head! Do you know how much it cost to paint those three whores on the wall? They could've built three houses for the price! And what about these columns? They only put them there to leave less room for tables, and no space to pass. So that the waitresses have got something to curse about. It's time to stop all this. That's not why we joined the Brotherhood, to let all these bastards . . .'

The thirteenth hour

Life in the cellar had become impossible. There wasn't room for Bawler to sleep on the trunk between the stove and the lavatory, so he slept on the floor. What made things worse was that in the army he'd lost the habit of living among such terrible filth and stench. 'Move in with me for a bit,' said Captain. 'Once you've learnt how to make money you can rent a place of your own. Or you can marry someone who's got an apartment. Even a minister's daughter would be glad of a lad like you.' So they set out to make some money. First they got a job unloading wagons. But the foreman kept their pay-packets and gave them a crate of apples instead. 'You just sell those,' he said, 'and you'll make three times as much.' It took them two hours to sell the apples, and they had to give the policeman on the beat almost half of what they made. What was left was barely enough for a meal, and they had to sell one of Captain's uniform jackets to raise enough for a drink. 'This doesn't pay well enough,' said Captain. Down at the flea market he noticed something, and proposed an ingenious scheme. It consisted of buying up ration cards and cashing them in, thus enabling them to buy enough bread for twenty days ahead. For this they needed holiday certificates to substantiate their need to buy ahead. And then all they had to do was to sell the bread at a profit. 'Look how it works out,' said Captain, displaying his calculations. 'That's not bad,' said Bawler. 'We could live on that.' The following day he managed to get hold of a pad of holiday certificate forms at the Faculty in exchange for a pair of almost new shoes. Captain found the knack of forging official stamps, and they were in business. They earned a great deal, but they drank a great deal more. But then they were picked up in a police raid—it turned out that there were a whole lot of bright lads who were onto exactly the same racket. They only just got out of it. They were saved by Bawler's array of medal ribbons. 'We can't go on with this,' said Bawler. 'We'll have to shut up shop, or we're both in for it. I feel as if I'm getting bogged down.' 'As you wish,' said Captain. 'You're right, of course. But then you've got some prospects. What about me, though? I didn't even finish secondary school. What if I became an agent for a children's toy factory? There's no money in that. And I've been offered a job as senior engineer in a lock factory. But that's even worse. And anyway, it's full of grafters looking for an easy touch. The ration cards were quite a nice sideline, but they'll be withdrawn soon. But I've just met some characters who've got something really big in mind. Would you like to take a chance?' 'No,' said Bawler. 'I didn't leave the army for that kind of thing.' 'At least you left of your own accord,' said Captain. 'I was chucked out. I don't know anything except how to fight wars. And I don't want to learn. I'm going to go on fighting to the end. Goodbye.'

They never met again.

An acquaintance offered Bawler quite a decent job of translating the technical literature for machines which had been captured during the war. His acquaintance found the work, Bawler did the translations and they split the profit. Then he found something even better, doing the same translations but this time for publication or for internal consumption on the same conditions but at better fees, and he began to have rather more money in his pocket. He rented a small room on the outskirts of the city. For the first time in his life he bought himself an ordinary civilian suit, a white shirt and tie. And he felt happy. By now, he said to himself, I could make someone a proposal of marriage. But who? While he was looking around he found that he'd been picked out himself. One evening at a party in the university (there were parties of this kind pretty well every week at this period) She came up to him and said: 'This is a lady's Excuse-me. May I have this dance?'

'I've dreamt about you all my life,' She said. 'Where have you been? Why have you turned up so late? I'm married, and I've got a child. I won't leave my family. I can't and I won't. Things are very agreeable the way they are. But I'm madly in love with you. I don't want other girls to keep looking at you. And you keep your eyes to yourself. You belong to me!' She brought photographs to show him. 'That's me,' She said. 'Don't I look funny? That was when I was twelve. And that one was when I was seventeen, at my school-leaving party. And that's daddy.' 'You're father's a soldier, is he?' he asked. 'Worse than that,' She laughed, 'My husband is, too. He's quite a big wheel, and getting bigger. And here we are at the seaside . . .' Can none of my dreams come true, because they're all about the past, he wondered. Am I just completely made up of nostalgia for an idealised past? People say that man is just a monkey who has lost his tail. Maybe progress just means the loss of honour, fidelity, reliability, conscience, sincerity, and firm principles. It can't be. That's not the problem. 'You've got a very tidy place here,' She said. 'Have you got someone looking after you? You can't do it all on your own. You must have somebody here apart from me. Just you watch out! I won't put up with that!' 'What are you going to do about it?' he asked. 'Complain to your husband? Or even to Daddy?' 'Don't make jokes like that,' She said. 'You mustn't joke about things like that.'

Mysticism

'To hell with the past,' said Dauber. 'It's time to think about the future. The future is an inevitable reality before which everyone is powerless.' 'That's nonsense,' said Schizophrenic. 'People are only powerless in the face of their past. It's absurd to put any hope in the future since it holds no prospects at all. If our ancestors could see what we've taken to calling the realisation of all their hopes, they'd be the first to come out in wild protests. Hopes are never realised except as minor details of some monstrous abomination. You can only base your hopes on the past. That cannot be destroyed. If you existed in the past, then you'll go on existing in the future. But the opposite is not true. The future is a mirror-image of the past, and the present, our present life, exists at the point where the future and the past meet. It's not true to believe that life passes from the past to the

(564)

future. It goes on simultaneously in both the past and the future. My theory is no more mystical than yours.' 'Your point of conjunction of the past and the future moves about in time,' said Dauber. 'No,' said Schizophrenic. 'It is time itself, and time cannot move about in time. That is absurd. There is no criterion on which to base a judgment.' 'But what about the appearance of new names in the past?' asked Dauber. 'New names in the past do not appear at the junction but deep in the past,' said Schizophrenic. 'How can you establish whether they have appeared or whether they existed already? What characterises the past is not the concept of appearance but the concept of existence. It is possible to disappear in the past but not to appear. And what's more, at the gates of the past your documents are checked and you're given a thorough search.' 'There's something really rather aesthetic about all this farrago of nonsense,' said Dauber. 'It's very easy to call it nonsense,' said Schizophrenic. 'It is the laws of language which determine the way that we think about fate. You are preoccupied with the question of immortality, but what bothers me is where to find the next fifty roubles. That is why you are a coarse materialist, while I am a refined idealist. Your problem can be resolved. Mine is pure utopia. See you!'

An intellectual's prayer
It's you I'm talking to, O God,
So don't turn a deaf ear.
Let all things happen for the good
And evil disappear.
Give posts to the ambitious ones
And pay them ten times more;
Give victory to competitors
And bonuses galore.
Give them their mugshots on each street
And medals by the row;
Let them have power, but—I entreat—
Not over us, oh no!

'It's important to us to know,' said Colleague, 'who writes all these little witticisms.' 'It's all part of the oral tradition,' said Sociologist. 'There is no specific author. Someone thinks up the basic idea, then there are others who polish it and introduce variants.' 'I don't think so,' said Colleague. 'That may be partly true, but there's a basic unity of style, subject and *weltanschauung*. How about Bawler?' 'Bawler?' said Sociologist in astonishment. 'Hardly. He's a mathematician. He'd never be able to. Fellow-worker would be a better bet.' 'You underestimate Bawler,' said Colleague. 'Fellow-worker's way out of it. It's not his style at all. And anyway we've got everything he's written, from first line to last. I've got something to ask you. About Bawler . . .' 'Very well,' said Sociologist. 'We'll have to get the linguists to work on it and the semiologists. We've got some talented lads in that line. They'll sort it out in two shakes . . .' 'That's all arranged, then,' said Colleague. 'Do what you can. And don't worry about England. The delay is no fault of yours. We'll sort it out for you as soon as we can. So long, pal.'

Scientific life

Ibanskian physicists discovered a new elementary particle. In honour of the Ism they named it the Ismatron. The Ismatron has remarkable properties which completely overturn former conceptions of matter while leaving its philosophical concepts untouched. The Ismatron has no dimensions of velocity, mass or charge. It was impossible to detect it with any instrumentation, and so it had to be discovered under the auspices of the very highest form of knowledge—the theory of the Ism. The physicists who discovered it discovered it before the deadline, and over-fulfilled their plan by one hundred per cent. The Ismatron is a unity of opposites. It constantly moves between quantity and quality, is simultaneously found and not found in one and the same place, and progresses from its inferior to its superior state by negating negation in a spiral, and regularly takes its stand beside the proletariat. Dishcloth, Ph.D., has asserted that the classics repeatedly referred to the Ismatron. The Ismatron is just as inexhaustible as the electron. When physicists in the West heard about the discovery of their Ibanskian colleagues, they declared: 'Fuck me!' and died of envy. Two intellectuals were put inside for having kept in their homes and distributed shamizdat publications.

Cultural life

That favourite child of the secret police and the Americans, Snottyhanky, returned from America with ten fur coats made of trinitrotoluol-chlorvinyl-paralon and some new poems. Two men on the beach. One is black and one white,

> But the white skin, I realise, is only skin-deep:
> I feel in my guts that they're both black as night
> And black is the way they're both going to keep.
> And my own sallow arse, well, I hide it from view:
> Things are different here in this foreign milieu.

Fellow-worker, forever jealous of Snottyhanky's pre-mortal glory, added venomously:

> Said Snottyhanky, miserable wretch,
> Giving his yellow bollicles a scratch.

Ibanskian men of culture, said Neurasthenic, excel at resolving other people's problems, particularly those which the West does not wish to solve by its own means.

The problem of self-immolation by fire

'There's a report in the Newspaper that some totally unknown but mentally abnormal citizen has tried to burn himself to death,' She said. 'The police and a group of the People's Militia courageously flung themselves on him and put him out. The malefactor was taken to . . .' 'To the police station,' He said. 'And there he was almost beaten to death.' 'How do you know?' She asked. 'It'll be reported in the next issue of shamizdat.' 'Who is this man?' She asked. 'Just a boy,' He said. 'A student. A mathematician. A very bright lad. Perfectly normal mentally. Maybe he is very impressionable and painfully honest, with an over-developed sense of justice.' 'Then why?' She asked. 'As a sign of protest against our mission of liberation,' He said. 'The poor chap,' She said. 'How he must have suffered.' 'It isn't very painful,' He said. 'Or rather it's terribly painful for the first few seconds, until the top layer of skin has been burnt off.' 'That's not what I'm talking about,' She said. 'What'll happen to him now?' 'Oh,' He said, 'they'll cure him. It's true that he's lost one eye, and the other's in a bad way. Then they'll put him to rot in a mental hospital.' 'How can they?' She said. 'Someone should do something . . .' 'They should,' He said. 'It's an

(567)

amazing world all the same. He got the petrol at an enormous price from some crook, who even made some kind of joke about suicide by fire. And the petrol was diluted. It didn't burn for long.' 'Everything's always diluted here,' She said. 'It's funny,' He said. 'A long time ago there was another boy, another mathematician, who wrote a little comic verse:

—take a gallon of petrol,
And make for the square . . .

I've forgotten the rest.' 'I just can't accept it,' said She. 'It's monstrous. How can people get to that state?' 'That depends on who it is,' He said. 'It must be that they couldn't do anything else.' 'But you mustn't get the idea that it's an easy thing to do. You need real courage to take a deliberate decision like that.' 'Oh God,' She said. 'How I wish I could do something to ease his pain.' 'That needs courage, too,' He said. 'Oh, I've just remembered another line:

Light the flame carefully . . .'

'It's nightmarish,' She said. 'Did he really strike a match?' 'I don't know,' He said. 'There's been a technological revolution these last few years. Maybe he used a lighter.'

New measures taken with regard to scientific research
A new and more progressive pay system for scientific research workers was introduced. Under this system, scientists were paid according to the number of points they scored on a scale: directors of institutes—500 points; research visit abroad—450 points; denunciation—500 points; head of section—100 points; a report submitted to higher authority—250 points; political overtime—50 points; a monograph—3 points; an article—1 point; a discovery—0.5 points, and so on. And the level of scientific work began to rise irresistibly. The most talented and productive scientists competed fiercely for the highest posts, and everyone rushed off abroad, wrote propaganda articles and denunciations. Synchrophasotrons began to sprout like mushrooms. Those who failed to amass the requisite number of points were initially sent off to help with the potato harvest and were then fired, since they were casting a shadow over an otherwise healthy collective.

The Ibanka Theatre

During this period, the Ibanka Theatre was enormously popular. Its full title was the Small Non-Academic Semi-Artistic Theatre of Truth and Comedy on the Ibanka River, named in honour of the Secret Police, etc. SNASATOTACOTIR for short. The people simply called it the Ibanka. It is still held in high regard. Later, when the Ibanskian government had stifled all the innocents and those who refused to recant, and resolved to show the world that there had never been any persecution of Ibanskian intellectuals, the Theatre, plus Artist, Snottyhanky, and an antique academician who had been a childhood friend of Isaac Newton, were promoted to the position of leading lights in the cultural world of Ibansk, thereby occasioning great jealousy to GAFATOTATOTIR (the Great Academic Fully Artistic Theatre of Truth and Tragedy on the Ibanka River, named in honour of the Brotherhood), to Writer and to the three hundred young academicians who had recently discovered the ismatron. But at this time its role was qualitatively different. It served simultaneously as the Jacomitovbin Club and the Vodkonvention of the Ibanskian intellectual movement. The soul of the Theatre was the Producer, its brain was Brother, and its conscience was Snottyhanky.

In the beginning, back in the time of the Boss, the Theatre had been a studio for the Secret Police Amateur Dramatic Society, which was allowed a great deal more freedom than other similar bodies. After the Boss had died, and his Member had been expelled from the Pantheon and buried in the wall like any rank and file head of state, the Secret Police lost the place and it became a public theatre. To a certain degree this put a limit on creative freedom, while allowing a greater degree of innovation. The Theatre blossomed and flourished with amazing speed, and became the spiritual home of the left-wing intelligentsia. The Theatre did not lose its former close links with the Secret Police, as without their support it would not have lasted a week. It would not have withstood the onslaughts of the Ministry of Culture. 'That's entirely normal in these circumstances,' said Wife. 'After all Shakespeare's theatre was dependent on the king. So was the theatre of Molière. Ibanskian ballet was born under the protection of the Emperor. Even GAFATOTATOTIR arose under the tutelage of the Chief of

(569)

Police.' 'That's a sacred truth,' Brother chimed in. 'Beaumarchais was an informer. Milton was an informer. Oscar Wilde was a pederast. Bernard Shaw was . . .' 'Every great art needs the protection of the powerful ones of this world,' said Snottyhanky. This conversation was taking place in the private box of the Head of the Secret Police, to which Snottyhanky had his own key.

The Theatre promoted, and applied, two genuinely innovatory principles. The first was that actors and sets have no part to play in the theatre. It is the director who is all important. It is a director's theatre, not an actor's. The second principle was that the content of the play is of no importance. Everything depends on how it is interpreted. For example, the Theatre staged a new interpretation of Shakespeare. Hamlet looked like a failed research student in physics-lyrics who reckoned himself a genius but who was quite incapable of writing even the most minor article for the most minor journal; he put it all down to the appalling conditions prevailing in the Danish Court, which were very similar to those in any Scientific Research Institute in Ibansk. Shakespeare himself, who on the whole approved of the production, admitted that he had never seen Hamlet in quite that light.

Students of theatre will long rack their brains in trying to discover the true secret of the Ibanka's phenomenal success. But there is no secret. Or rather, as Chatterer established, there *is* a secret, but it lies in Ibansk rather than in the Ibanka. If the Ibanka had not existed, Ibanskian intellectuals would have adopted some other, equally safe, place to congregate and to blow their minds.

This is how things actually happened. The Producer would select a play which was acceptable to the authorities, some play which exposed the evils of capitalism. He would then proceed to re-interpret it. With Brother's help, of course. And Snottyhanky, beloved of the Secret Police and the Americans, would lend a hand as well. And so the show would open. The house was always packed. Half of the audience were foreigners, another half informers, and the third everyone else. It was impossible to buy tickets at the box office, since they were all distributed to embassies and ministries. Words hurtled from the stage into the audience: Repression, Executions, Concentration Camp, Hangmen . . . Everyone knew that the references were to repression *here*, executions *here*, concentration camps *here*, *our* executioners. And the audience would greet each reference with frenzied applause. They would all rise to their feet and eye each other and the stage in delight. Everyone felt themselves to be taking part in some great and historic enterprise. And they would go home to continue their excited chatter as if they had just come from the barricades, or at the very least had given voice to some bold protest. Seeing all this, the authorities requested that all allusions to events from Ibansk's recent past should be expunged. At the present time this play, which was intended to expose the evils of capitalism, proceeds as if there were no such evils Over There. Now the audiences say: Just look—they don't have any repression Over There! But what about here? They have no concentration camps Over There! But what about here? And there is frenzied applause. And everyone goes home to discuss the self-same problems. And some members of the audience go home to consider the best excuse for jailing N. on the quiet, and to decide which members of the audience to call as experts and which as witnesses.

The essence of the Ibanka, said Chatterer, is that the company can stage an officially acceptable play about the Decembrists in a production which has been previously discussed at a special Brotherhood meeting, and backed by the highest ideological authorities—and they can still think of themselves as real Decembrists. And the audience regard the play, and the fact that they have seen it, as tantamount to participation in an uprising. It is a phenomenon wholly within the official framework of Ibanskian reality; it tries to pass itself off as being outside the framework, but at the same time it is unwilling to suffer or to be deprived of any of the comforts of life.

Unity

'You heard what old One-arm was saying,' said Teacher. 'I understand what he means. I've been in the same boat myself. But he's wrong. It wasn't a question of stupidity. It was something more serious than that. Essentially the problem was very simple. That is precisely why it was so difficult to solve. Hundreds of minds set themselves to the task, and they were never able to recognise it as an easy problem for the simple reason that hundreds of great minds cannot bend themselves to the solution of easy problems. If it is they who are examining the problem, then by definition it cannot be easy. So they seek a complex answer. And here I would cite a law which I discovered myself and which in time I shall prove conclusively: a complex solution of a simple problem is necessarily erroneous. Consider it from the point of view of all our government's actions in domestic and foreign policy. They give an impression of quite extraordinary stupidity. But it is not stupidity. These problems are very carefully considered—and by people many of whom are literate and intelligent. Yet stupidity is the effect they produce. Why? Because of the operation of my law. Why, then, cannot they approach these problems as if they were simple? That is quite another question, a social question. Here the social laws come into play. In particular, the importance or unimportance which society accords to a problem does not coincide with a gnostic assessment of its difficulty or facility. But the effect of social relationships is such that any important problem is regarded as being gnostically difficult. It has a high social rating, and therefore, in view of its social level, it has a right to a specific number of people to solve it, and moreover of solvers of a particular rank. And once a group of high-ranking solvers has been formed, the problem begins to be considered as appropriate to that level of solution. This error is inevitable as a social phenomenon. That's the heart of the matter.' 'That's a first-class analysis,' said Bawler. 'Utter nonsense,' said Colleague. 'It's simply that everyone who views a battle from outside considers himself a strategist.' 'I've taken part in this battle,' said Teacher. 'At that time I was a member of the general staff and together with other officers I proposed a simple but correct solution.' 'How did it all end?' asked Fellow-worker. 'I was transferred to the command of another unit,' said Teacher.

The State

There are various ways in which power can reproduce itself, said Slanderer. There is natural inheritance, testamentary inheritance, usurpation, elections and others. What is the position as regards the Ibanskian state? Although there are persistent attempts to present it as an elective government, it is not so in fact. Here elections are a charade which masks the complete absence of any true electoral principal. Since everyone knows what the charade means, elections become an officially constituted and habitual form of falsehood. What's the sense of an election if the electors are obliged in advance to commit themselves to one—the only one—candidate nominated from above? Nothing is essentially changed if two or three people are nominated with the choice of electing one of them. The candidate has been in every way just as much forced on the electorate. In our country elections are nothing but a demonstration of loyalty to a non-elective and self-sufficient power. Elections to institutions of the Brotherhood are equally fictitious. Although in this case passions are sometimes aroused, although conflicts sometimes flare up, although the original candidates are sometimes removed from the ballot and replaced by new ones, this is all sanctioned from above. If there is any resistance, the obstinate ones get a thorough shaking-up. And anyway those who are elected to the institutions of power have no real power of their own. Power lies in the hands only of people and institutions elected in the second round. And their pre-established nature is clear from the very beginning. For these 'second round' apparatchiks do not even have the outward appearance of having been elected. Beginning from the second stage of the power hierarchy, the ordinary citizen, including members of the Brotherhood, has no say at all in any election. Members of the Brotherhood are selected but never select themselves until they have penetrated to those cells in the power system which allow them to take part in the selection of others.

The way in which the Ibanskian system of power reproduces itself is a purely professional interchange of individual strands in a stable power fabric whose pattern has been determined once and for all. Power itself is considered in purely practical terms; it is a task, the principal task, a task par excellence, a task in the full meaning of the word, and the question of the reproduction of power is only one part of this task. There are specific power-professionals who decide exactly which people should be selected for admission to individual power-cells. The situation is in no way changed by the fact that within the selecting group there may exist various opinions and maybe even conflicts. Any social group, even one whose object is the uniting of opinion and the liquidation of conflict, takes on all the characteristics of the group as a whole, including divisions and conflicts. So here the method of reproducing power remains not an election from below but a selection from above, carried out as a routine operation.

There is a hierarchy of selection. Its highest levels are superimposed on the social and economic hierarchy in such a way that it is impossible in practice to distinguish between them. As a general rule the same people have their part to play in these distinct and separate spheres of social power. Pure power is represented by only a comparatively small group of people. But the distinction is theoretically possible if we start from the principle by which appointments are made. No director of a factory, of an institute, of a store can be appointed without the sanction of the Brotherhood organisation.

A lawless civilisation

'How can you talk about the criminality of the whole power system and even of the whole of society,' She said. 'It's ridiculous. It's simply that this society has its own system of law and morality.' 'No,' He said. 'The idea that systems of law can be interchangeable, the idea which you've just expressed, merely conceals the concept of non-legality. Every law is based on general principles. If those principles are broken, then the society cannot consider itself as based on law. Here are some examples of general legal concepts. Everyone is equal before the law, no matter where they stand in the social hierarchy. If the action of one individual does not fall outside the law (and there is a code of laws to determine this), it cannot be considered a crime and the individual cannot be brought to trial. The judicial punishment of the innocent, or of people who have committed no action which contravenes the law, is a crime. There can be no justification for crime. A crime committed against one individual may have been to the benefit of even millions of people, it still remains a crime and cannot be justified by the benefit it brings. In other words there are principles embodied in the very definition of terms like: "law", "justice", "a lawful society", and so on. But you should note that these principles are in no way concrete (for example they do not say who should be punished for what, or what form that punishment should take).

They merely deal with the formal mechanism of the law's action. In a given society the law can be good or bad. It is quite another matter to show whether any law exists at all. If there is a violation of the principles which form part of the definition of law or of justice, this means that these terms are simply not applicable to the society in question. Let us suppose that a certain A. performs some act which the authorities and the people at large disapprove of, but for which he cannot be brought to trial since the action is not a violation of the law. But nevertheless, the institutions of power bring A. to court and punish him. According to the country's code of law all the people involved in this action against A. are criminals. The authorities who allow this action to go forward are accessories after the crime, i.e. they are themselves criminals. If the people as a whole know that A. is juridically innocent and that the authorities have dealt with him not according to the law, and if they do not rise up in protest against this action of the authorities, they are also accessories to crime, and therefore also criminal. So it is quite logically possible to conceive of a situation where the people as a whole are guilty of a criminal act towards a single person.' 'That is pure semantic casuistry,' She said. 'That's the kind of casuistry on which all lawful civilisation is based.' 'What if the national interest . . .' She said. 'In that case the whole legal code is a fraud,' He said. 'And the society is itself lawless. A society which officially adopts the slogan that the interests of the people transcend those of the individual is a lawless society. And that's all there is to it.'

History yet to come

'In order to be able to assess what has passed in the life of Ibansk,' said Teacher, 'we must envisage what is going to happen in the future. And since the future is still to come we cannot permit any errors in our judgments of it. Judgments about the future must be infallible.' 'Yes,' said Chatterer, 'but they are not true all the same.' 'On the other hand,' said Teacher, 'they may be even more criminal than judgments about the past, so we must be wary at least in our suppositions.' 'That is impossible,' said Chatterer. 'Everything we say about the past in fact deals with the future. And everything we say about the future in fact deals with the present.'

(575)

Reflections

The most important thing in Ibanskian society, thought Soilophagist, is the Brotherhood. That is axiomatic; if we do not understand that, we can understand nothing. The Brotherhood is not merely the directing force and the power. It is something much more than that. That is where the problem lies. In Ibansk the Brotherhood is a society within a society, and the highest ranking society. Everything non-Brotherhood is either the social milieu of the Brotherhood as a self-sufficient society, or a lower ranking society. We are in advance of the West for the very reason that we have created a society within a society, a superior society, a super-society. And naturally superior and inferior societies must live by different laws. Yet in our country they are mixed together. And citizens must be divided into two groups which differ in principle. The children of non-Brotherhood members provide part of the reserve from which Brotherhood members can be drawn. But not all those children will qualify. One can forecast at this stage which children will in due course join the Brotherhood.

And as time goes by this will become even clearer, to the extent that the differentiation of citizens into their social ranks can be carried out by ascribing the social level of the heads of each family to every member of that family. That is a fact which cannot be contradicted, a social fact and not a biological fact. There is no racism in this. Certainly the frontiers are not absolute. Movement between one social rank and another is still possible, but on the whole we have here an essential stability. It is clear also that higher ranking members of society must have privileges over lower ranking members and must exercise power over them, as over their own colony. It will be necessary to consider as exhaustively as possible the rules of life for each of these societies and for their mutual relationships, and to inculcate these rules so thoroughly that they should be accepted by all as completely natural and indisputable. In the absence of the idea that some people are superior to others throughout society, life would lose meaning and interest. Why cannot people see this fact or recognise it? Because they're afraid? What is there to be afraid of? Analogies? Yet in time hypocrisy and the concealment of reality will produce a much worse effect.

Foolosopher delivered the philosophy lectures himself. He had had a remarkable life which had been repeatedly rehearsed in his own memoirs and in those of his colleagues. In his youth, Foolosopher had met the classics of the Ism, who had even dandled him on their knees. One of them had once patted him on the head. Another, a lady classic, had once given him a sweet when he opened the gates to the classics when they returned to Ibansk in a horse-drawn carriage. Yet another had once exchanged some precious words with a crowd in which Foolosopher was having a fine time fumbling in a number of pockets that weren't his own. Every year on the anniversary of every classic and every classic-ess, Foolosopher published his I-remember-it-as-if-it-were-yesterday recollections. They were always different, and there would have been enough to fill ten volumes. And historians were already racking their brains over how the classics had been able to develop the doctrine and fight the class struggle in view of the fact that they clearly spent thirty hours a day in Foolosopher's company. And as there were thousands of people like Foolosopher in Ibansk there could be no possible doubt about the super-genius of the classics.

The most remarkable thing of all was the abundance of indisputable documentary proof. For instance, one of the classics referred to above wrote to another that on a visit to M, M's son (a disgusting snotty-nosed brat) who had been sitting on his knee, had performed so brilliantly that he had had to send his trousers (incidentally, pre-revolutionary trousers, not any of your inferior modern products) to the cleaners (from where, incidentally, they had still not returned). After this experience the classic wrote two books—one on the need to re-organise the dry-cleaning industry, and the other on the proper upbringing of children in the spirit of the Ism. The latter was the basis of everything that was subsequently written on this subject.

Foolosopher's adventures, said Teacher, were only the beginning. It's a problem that could easily be resolved without any serious contradictions. But if you take all the houses in Ibansk in which some classic or another is said to have held forth, and if you allow for just the time that would have been needed to get from one house to another, mount the rostrum, yell out a slogan, shake a hand or two, nip into the lavatory, tear off a sheet of paper, or (since there was a shortage of paper at the time) insert a comma and so on . . . well, then, chums, you'll easily see that Einstein was sadly mistaken when he claimed that nothing could move faster than light.

After his heroic youth, Foolosopher became a highly responsible citizen. He was interrogated because of his quite extraordinary natural stupidity and near total illiteracy. But as a faithful and trusted person, he avoided being shot like the others and was made instead the director of a pig farm. Like every cretin, Foolosopher fought on a grand scale. He undertook to turn the entire district into the model pig farm of the future. Within a few years he had developed the enterprise to such a flourishing state that you would have been hard put to find a drowned cat in the area, let alone a pig. But on every wall there was a portrait of the Boss, and every shelf was weighed down with his collected works. To get rid of Foolosopher, the local government authorities sent him to the Institute of Avant-garde Professors. Foolosopher arrived at the IAP at the same time as Secretary, who turned up carrying his wooden plough across his shoulders, and Troglodyte, who had betrayed his class and who with this end in view had transferred himself to the side of the proletariat. Foolosopher got a distinction in his final IAP examinations. For his part in all the pogroms he was awarded a military decoration and became one of the leading theoreticians of Ibansk. Even Troglodyte considered Foolosopher a downright fool and once, among his friends and supporters, said that in the past Foolosopher had cast philosophy before the swine, and that now he was casting swinery before the philosophers. And so he proposed him for the Prize and later for election to the Academy.

When he had finished his lecture about the ultimate stage Foolosopher tried to persuade his audience to ask him any little question that might come to mind. 'There's nothing to be afraid of,' he said. 'I won't eat you.' 'You say that it will be to each according to his needs,' said Teacher, just for something to say. 'But would that be just? For example, Puss is a parasite, a scrounger and a fool, while Schizophrenic is hard working, undemanding and very gifted, but according to his needs Puss will ask for about a hundred times more than Schizophrenic. How can this be?' 'There'll be enough for everybody,' said Foolosopher. 'And we shall see that everything is in order.' 'Who is this "we"?' asked Teacher. 'The most intelligent and aware members of society,' said Foolosopher. 'But what if you aren't obeyed?' Teacher insisted. 'There are ways of forcing obedience,' said Foolosopher.

'It's a waste of time to argue with people like that,' said Bawler. 'It does get boring,' said Teacher. 'They give us all this drivel and expect us to take it as the most magnificent product of human thought for all time. And they want us to take a lively interest in it.' 'But they're right,' said Bawler. 'You can feed people, clothe them, find them somewhere to live, things to amuse them. But that won't resolve anything. There'll still be inequality and privilege just the same. They're obliged to find "ways of forcing obedience", and they will. Power is every-where and in everything—that's the essence of the ultimate stage.'

The fourteenth hour

He too had a family and a wife. He had a daughter. All this passed through his life in a flash and disappeared, leaving no trace on his soul. He had to go on studying and earning money. His wife too had to work. 'I'm not going to be your house-keeper,' she declared. They had to find his daughter a place in a creche, which cost them a lot in bribes. Then there was illness, medical certificates, quarrels. 'I've had enough of this,' said his wife. 'I'm not going to ruin my life for you.' And she went off to her mother with the child. When He discovered that his wife had lovers, He suffered a great deal. Not from jealousy, but for other reasons which were incomprehensible even to people like Teacher. 'It's the problem of how to rely on other people,' said Teacher in surprise. 'That's what your trouble is . . . Society as a whole stopped bothering about that kind of thing long ago. And as far as that trollop's concerned you should have broken it off long ago.' 'You're a bourgeois,' She said. 'These days every attractive woman has lovers!' And She told him the tired old story of the woman who walks with bowed head because she has a lover, and about the woman who holds her head high because she has a lover. The point of the story is that if a woman has a head, she has a lover. He looked at Her and felt Himself totally

(579)

powerless face to face with the world which He had engaged in single combat. The secret police are nothing, He thought. They're nothing but an outpost. Once you've got past them you come up against the whole strength of the army—it's the army that's invincible. The army is those who are close to you and you yourself. 'Surely you don't want me to believe that you are without sin,' She asked. 'Perhaps you're unique; or a fool, more likely. With a mind like yours you could make a fortune!' So they divorced. And He decided that the modern family, with its frivolous approach to marital infidelity and its mutual independence, was not to his taste. No more experiments of this kind, He decided. It's better alone. Not that it's easier, but it's more honest. 'I don't agree with you,' said Teacher. 'Your family,' He said, 'is the rare exception that proves the rule.'

The language of the intellectuals

In times gone by Ibanskian intellectuals used in conversation words like: my dear, my sweet, my respects, thank you, please, would you be so good as to . . . and so on. In this respect contemporary intellectuals have made great strides forward. They now use expressions like: mate, old sod, bastard, shithead, go fuck yourself, you stinker, sonofabitch, up your arse and so on. One arrogant intellectual who chose to cross the street at the wrong place, as a sign of protest, even called the policeman who rebuked him 'mate'. The policeman had meant to let the malefactor off with an on-the-spot fine, but on hearing the expression 'mate', he realised what he was up against, so he hauled the intellectual off to the police station, where he was charged with resisting arrest and sentenced to ten days. And a document was sent to his place of work where it stated in black and white that he had been drunk and disorderly in a public place. At just about this time the pan-Ibanskian campaign against drunkenness had been launched. Although the intellectual never drank at all, and his employers knew this perfectly well, he was dismissed. His article on hypersuperentrobrutto-nettophasic quasi-space in the half-dead languages was immediately dropped from the symposium in which it was about to be published. Since the intellectual had cast a shadow and caused a stain on a healthy collective, a commission was set up to study the ideo-political education of youth. The commission revealed deficiencies and certain measures were introduced to improve the situation.

But the intellectuals did not learn their lesson. An example: two typical intellectuals, A and B, meet in the street. 'Hi, pal,' A says to her. 'Why didn't you phone, you shithead?' 'I couldn't,' says B. 'C came round, the old bastard and bent my ear all night. The silly cunt's written quite a good article about the new left. By the way, could you put your hand on a couple of tickets for the Ibanka?' 'Are you off your chump?' says A. 'You don't want to watch crap like that.' 'They're not for me, you silly sod,' says B. 'I'm still in my right mind. I've got some Italians coming.' 'Fuck them for a lark,' says A. 'I can't,' says B. 'Those wankers are going to translate my book. By the way, old D rang. She wants back the money she lent me. She needs it to go abroad. She's got a trip to France, the cow.' 'What did she do to get that?' asks A. 'She had it off with that bastard E,' says B. 'They've really got it made, that lot,' says A. 'If you see her, tell her to get stuffed . . .'

History yet to come

'The future of society,' said Teacher, 'is the total Ism. How can we assign within our society the various attitudes held towards the total Ism? It's very simple. We need only to take some random individual samples: (1) believes that it is possible to construct the total Ism, not merely in an isolated country surrounded by enemies (that is easy enough), but even where the country is not so surrounded (which is infinitely more difficult); (2) believes that it is impossible; (3) does not believe that it is possible; (4) does not believe that it is impossible; (5) shouts at the top of his voice that it is possible; (6) shouts at the top of his voice that it is impossible; (7) shouts at the top of his voice that he believes it will come; (8) shouts at the top of his voice that he does not believe that . . . Thus we can list all possible attitudes of individuals to the idea of the total Ism. Then we can consider all their possible combinations. Logical contradictions can be excluded. Non-contradictions can be considered from the point of view of such social parameters as the degree of security, profitability, careerism and so on. And then the degrees of probability can be calculated. I have done all this purely theoretically and have reached the following result.

The highest degree of probability for those who are well disposed towards the total Ism lies in the following combination: (1) they sincerely do not believe that the total Ism can be built, and are delighted; (2) they shout at the top of their voices that they sincerely believe that the total Ism must be built; (3) deep in their hearts they fear that suddenly one day (whisper it low!) the Ism might build itself. The highest degree of probability for hostile forces produces the following combination: (1) they sincerely believe that the total Ism can be built and are in a panic about the possibility; (2) they shout at the top of their voices that they sincerely disbelieve that the total Ism will be built; (3) and at the bottom of their hearts they hope that the whole thing will fall apart and that humanity will get by without the total Ism.' 'If the total Ism is built one day,' said Bawler, 'then it will only be thanks to the fact that it had enemies. But your calculations are of no value for the simple reason that the total Ism will not be built: it will be proclaimed.' 'There is no way,' said Teacher, 'of constructing a theory to cope with that variation, because it is purely subjective.'

The principle of oppression

Oppression for oppression's sake, said Neurasthenic, oppression as a principle. If they have the possibility of carrying out oppression, they would prefer to do so even if that brings harm to the state and discredit to themselves. They will not exercise oppression only when they lack the capability of doing so, and in particular when a superior force is exercising pressure on them. Oppression is so much an organic part of their nature that they never regard it as oppression. Indeed, they take it as a blatant injustice towards themselves if the victims of their oppression resist them or manage to wriggle out from under their claws. This must be taken as axiomatic. There is no point in having any illusions. Oppression is not the product of their evil intentions, but a function forced on them by the conditions of their existence. Even if they suddenly were to wish to stop being oppressors they could not desist from oppression, since their lack of will to oppress could only be realised in the form of oppression, which would entail nothing more than a change in the aspect and sphere of application of oppression.

Discussion on the role of theory

'You must never disregard theory,' said Teacher. 'I'll tell you a story. The war was at its height. We were en route from east to west, heading for the front. Our train got stuck in a siding bang in the middle of the steppe. At least a hundred miles to the nearest village. There was just one little hut—the signal cabin. And we discovered that the signalman was a woman. What was she like? No matter. When there's one woman and a thousand men, it makes no difference whether she's pretty or ugly, old or young. She is simply Woman. You can imagine what was happening on the train! A thousand healthy young men who hadn't seen a woman even from a distance for more than a year. What if we take a ticket in this lottery, I said to the chap in the bunk above mine. Well, he said, you're a well enough set up lad, but your chances would be practically zero. He did a calculation, and it was true that my chance was negligible. Your sums are impeccable, I told him. But they're based on an erroneous theory about our train. You've assumed that all the thousand of us want to have it off with this woman. But in fact that isn't the case. I'd say, on the basis of certain empirical observations I've made, that a good three-quarters of the lads on the train would rather have a kip than wrangle over the very doubtful chance of spending the night with the lady. I'd reckon that the great majority of them are kids who've never had a woman in their lives. Would you agree? My neighbour agreed. Then we went over a few more points, and established that not more than ten of us would want to have a go at the woman. Subsequent events dazzlingly confirmed my theory: in fact, there were only five candidates. And none of them were what you might call ladykillers. But that's a different question. Now you have calculated the coefficient of social activity of the population of Ibansk. And you've come up with quite a large figure. But it seems to me that your theoretical bases are false. You could do the calculation on a different theoretical basis, i.e. adopting the following postulates. The only people who are socially active are members of the Brotherhood. And not all the members. The Brotherhood itself is a social organism whose active part can be determined using your methods. Try the calculation on that basis.' 'It works out the same,' said Bawler. 'The fact is that socially active people indicated by this method

(583)

are dispersed throughout society, so we have to introduce an adjustment for distance, which reduces the previous gain to zero. But how did your story end?' 'I had deduced theoretically,' said Teacher, 'that the winner in this situation would be the most patient and the most resourceful. So I took my greatcoat and set off to the cabin before nightfall. I even let my neighbour have my supper. What's up with you? the signal-woman asked when I arrived. The bosses ordered me to come, I said. Oh, well, if the bosses sent you, you'd better stay, she said. Until midnight we chatted about this and that, and then I lay down on a bench and went to sleep. Of course I didn't try anything on. For me she was a kind of decisive experiment, the proof of my theory. Towards dawn she woke me up, and I grabbed my greatcoat and dashed back to the train with every man aboard watching me. The enraged company commander (he'd been one of the competitors) shoved me in the cooler, severe régime, for absence without leave. That's how I travelled all the way to the front—in the cooler. After that the train passed through towns, where there were as many women as you wanted, and anyone who had a mind to could get his leg over. But I was in the cooler.' 'That's not a theory,' said Bawler. 'A theory's rational, and your behaviour was irrational. That defies any theory.' 'So what?' asked Teacher. 'Can't you imagine something analogous on the scale of an entire society? Let's be absolutely clear what it is that we want.' 'In these matters absolute clarity is the biggest mistake,' said Bawler. 'Here we need something totally irrational that won't fit into any theory. And that excludes any precise definition both of premises and aims. On the contrary what we need is imprecision and a lack of definition. And I think I've discovered something.' 'I hope it's not a secret,' said Teacher. 'Of course not,' said Bawler. 'I have uncovered one of the tenderest, most vulnerable parts of this society. And we must keep on bashing away at this vulnerable spot, bashing and bashing and bashing, without worrying about the consequences or about the future. Now this vulnerable point is their panic fear of publicity. We must get publicity at any price, in any form, and above all directed outside. The world must get to know what sort of people we are.'

Western perspectives

When he got back from France, Snottyhanky turned a suitcase full of perfumes and ladies' underwear into cash and went off for a month in a rest home, at the expense of the Secret Police, to relax and collect his impressions. He set them out in a poem, whose sense was expressed in some outrageous verses ascribed to Singer:

Just wait and see, for your turn's coming fast,
The happy life we'll build for you at last.
Your clapped-out bourgeois ways right off we'll strip;
If you object, we'll give your ear a clip.
Be patient then, we're on our way to you,
And we'll bring our ideals with us too.
We'll teach you what your fine new life should be.
If you don't want it . . . Well, just wait and see.
Don't build false hopes: once there, we won't withdraw
To leave you on your own with the bourgeois.
We will not let our brothers be oppressed
And lose their oil wealth, stolen by the West.

The fifteenth hour

'All the same, there are some steps they have to take,' She said. 'All the most inveterate bastards are being replaced—and what's more, by liberals and fairly decent people.' 'Just you wait,' He said. 'These decent people will show themselves for what they are in due course.' 'You shouldn't look at things like that,' She said. 'Life is lived on many levels. There are improvements in some respects.' 'There are,' He agreed. 'But the general atmosphere is still the same. There's no point in looking for sub-tropical flora on the arctic circle. The other day there was a top-level discussion of the Journal of Theoretical Problems of Chamber Pots and Ikonostases (JOTPOCPAI). They detected an ideological error in an interpretation of nose picking and arse scratching. The editor was fired. And do you know who was appointed to replace him?' 'It can't be,' said She. 'He's a monster!' 'Why,' said He. 'It's an improvement.' 'There's a rumour that . . .' She said. 'Surely that can't be true?' 'It is,' He said. 'What'll happen now,' She said. 'Things'll be better,' He said. 'Who is he?' She asked. 'That's a strange question', He replied. 'He's mad, of course.' 'It'll be interesting to see how they announce it,' She said. 'They can't keep it secret.' 'They won't try to,' He said. 'Ibanskian history has lost its innocence and has passed from a bureaucratic dream into a schizophrenic reality. It's funny. All the old forms of protest have come around again. And how! Take terror, for example. In the past people went round throwing bombs into open carriages. Now a hundred years have gone by, a century of scientific and technical advance—and what happens now? It's almost the same as using catapults against tanks. I can imagine a meeting of revolutionaries today. What are they going to discuss? Where to get hold of a petrol can and petrol of good enough quality to catch fire when they put a match to it. How to find better quality elastic for their catapults. Of course, knicker elastic's quite good, but not quite good enough. How to reconcile God with quantum mechanics for the benefit of illiterate old women who've survived by some miracle.' 'There's nothing funny about that,' She said. 'You're just being coarse about religion . . . If you'd taken the trouble to go and listen just once . . .' 'I have listened,' He said. 'And more than once. I know them all personally. They're coarse themselves. That's not the result of the good life. Success? Thinker's lectures on psychoanalysis are successful, too, but that doesn't stop him being a charlatan.' 'So what are you suggesting?' She asked. 'Clarity,' He said. 'Pitiless, prosaic clarity. No distortions. Pathological methods produce pathological results.'

On social systems

It is of no consequence for the theory of social systems whether a particular system arose naturally or whether it was artificially invented. Such a distinction is wholly absurd when applied to a society. When people say that the peculiarities of Ibanskian society derive from the fact that it is artificially conceived, they are talking absolute nonsense. Even if a society is constructed on a plan made by a single man, a large number of people are needed to serve either as building materials or as builders. And this leads to the inevitable result that social laws come into play. And those who have taken part in the realisation of the original conception will, sooner or later, begin to live by these laws. They will begin to form groups, to struggle for power and privilege and so on. When the artificial nature of Ibanskian

(586)

society is interpreted as an excess of bureaucracy, a system of bans, an ideology imposed by force, and so on, those who so interpret it are overlooking a simple and self-evident truth: that all this is not some deviation from the norm of this society, but its legitimate product, its real existence, its true nature.

Unity

'Here we are sitting around looking as if we were all together,' said Visitor, 'but in fact we all live different lives. In different worlds. Take you, for example, young man, you've never earned a penny through the sweat of your brow your entire life, yet you've already got an apartment and you can afford to spend as much in one evening in a restaurant as would feed me for a whole month. And I'm an ex-officer, with seven decorations and four wound-stripes. I've earned my living since I was fourteen. But I live in a damp cellar—a room three yards square for three people.' 'What have your military exploits and your labour record got to do with me?' asked Colleague. 'If you hadn't played the fool you'd have been a general.' 'Perhaps you can tell me what form my playing the fool took?' asked Visitor. 'You should be ashamed of yourself, being so rude to an old man,' said Wife. 'If you lived like him perhaps you'd change your tune.' 'I didn't say a thing,' said Colleague. 'I've just got bored with all this moralising. Haven't I got the right to have an apartment or a meal in a restaurant?' 'I've nothing against you, and I'm not trying to moralise,' said Visitor. 'I'm simply using an image to express a general thought.' 'All right then,' said Colleague in a rather scornful, superior tone, 'what's this general thought then?' 'Stop dodging the issue,' said Bawler. 'You know perfectly well what he's talking about. We're all drinking companions here and in some cases we were at school together. But as soon as we get outside the doors of the Pavilion we're social individuals going about our own little affairs. In here you're just one of the lads. Out there you're an activist, or rather a careerist.' 'And a scrounger,' added Teacher. 'Look here,' said Colleague, 'take it easy.' 'Or else what?' asked Teacher. 'Or else you'll organise a little pogrom like the one you ran against Double-dealer? Personally I don't give a damn for you or your pogroms, your bosses or your assistants.' 'Come on lads,' begged Wife, 'do stop it. What's the point of arguing

(587)

about silly things like this. We all know each other. There are more important things to talk about.' 'It's all the same to me,' said Colleague; 'I'm a perfectly decent chap. You know, old man, it would be better if you told us how you managed to live on so little. It wouldn't be enough to keep me in fags. I'm not used to that miserable kind of life, and I've no intention of getting used to it.' 'That's fine,' said Visitor. 'Don't get used to it whatever you do. It's a specifically Ibanskian aberration. I'm not proposing it as the norm. But if it's inevitable, you've got to adapt to it. I've got my own theory. I invented it when I was put inside for the first time.' 'What were you put inside for?' asked Teacher. 'That doesn't matter,' said Colleague. 'It was for nothing, of course. Every one of them was put inside for nothing.' 'Not all of us,' said Visitor. 'I actually had done something. I wrote to the Boss about all the disgraceful things that were going on in our unit. They said it was slander, and what's more, it was a breach of military discipline.' 'Tell us about your theory,' asked Bawler, 'but keep it short.' 'Certainly,' said Visitor. 'There is a scale of all the vital processes. It has a lower and an upper limit and specific correlations. It might seem, for example, that if you don't eat much you need to sleep more and work less. That is an error. It holds true, of course, only if the amount of food you eat remains above the vital minimum. If it does fall below this, then a man stops being a man. I would even like to bring in a law: that a man who is deliberately given less food than the minimum has the right to commit any crime against authority.' 'And who would see to it that norms like that were observed?' asked Colleague. 'Don't interrupt,' said Teacher. 'All this is fine talking, and the main problem doesn't lie there. Carry on,' he said to Visitor, 'I'm most interested in what you're saying.' 'Well,' said Visitor, 'I discovered . . .'

The State

This method of reproduction of power, said Slanderer, is fully consonant with its nature. What this power expresses and realises is not political relationships, but other social relationships—the relationships of domination and subordination. It is not political power, but oppression-power, and nothing more. And it has no other foundation. It is a self-sufficient power which has no intermediaries, no superstructures, no appendices. In our country it is not a case of power existing for the sake of society, but one in which society is allowed to exist only in as far as it is necessary and adequate for the reproduction, the operation and the ideals of power. Our society is nothing but a culture medium and an arena where the spectacle of power can be played out. For this reason the Ibanskian power system does not fulfil the function of being the intellect of society. That function is alien to it. If it ever has anything to do in this capacity, then it is only as an inevitable evil or as a weapon in the battle to gain power and to hold it. It is an anti-intellectual power. All the intellectual activity of participants in that power is expended on trying to gain a more favourable position. It is an element of purely social behaviour in a specific sphere of social life, and not an element of politics as a professional form of activity. Here we have no professional politicians. All we have are professional careerists. This power is anti-political.

The real and the illusory

I am perfectly prepared to accept, said Neurasthenic, that Truth-teller's conception is politically progressive, morally sincere and so on. But from the scientific point of view it is as bankrupt as the official point of view. Let's take for example the history of the relationships between the Boss and Demagogue. The facts appeared to be the following. The Boss put forward his plan—a singularly stupid plan. But at that time the question it raised was of secondary importance and Demagogue didn't want to make an enormous fuss about it. This was correct tactics from the point of view of the more important problems of the time. So Demagogue gave a general approval to the Boss's plan and made a few critical observations. In practice these observations meant the total destruction of the Boss's plan and proposed a radically different solution. This was apparent to everyone. And it seemed equally apparent that if Demagogue's proposals were adopted, his position would be strengthened and that of the Boss weakened. That was the way that everyone behind the scenes assessed the situation. It was said of Demagogue that he was the head, the real brain of the state. It was said of the Boss that he was a minor semi-literate intriguer. They understood everything, but failed to understand the most important thing: the fact that they were living in a new epoch in a new type of society. Now in this society, where the only thing that has any real power is what is officially included in the record, behind-the-scenes ideas, no matter how true and wise they may be, have no official existence. In other words they either have no existence at all, or their existence is a deceptive mirage. So at an official level everyone approved the Boss's plan. On an official level it was the Boss's plan, not Demagogue's, that was discussed. Demagogue had merely made a few comments. And the record showed only one of Demagogue's remarks as emanating from him. And even that was not to his advantage, as became clear the very next day. So the Boss appropriated Demagogue's plan for himself. Truth-teller is right. But it was not a theft nor a plagiarism. There was nothing wrong either juridically or morally. It all happened in full view of everyone. No-one made any protest. Was it that they were afraid? No, for the Boss at that time was not as powerful as he later became. He was only just beginning. And moreover, everyone was quite pleased that this business had the Boss's name on it. It dealt with grubby little details to which no great importance was attached at the time, and which had a strong smell of adventurism about them. And if the plan had gone forward officially as Demagogue's, this would have had no effect on the situation. He would have lost on other points and whatever the outcome might have been, the whole business of the plan would have finally turned against him in one way or another. But that is getting off the subject.

What happened next? The Boss accepted Demagogue's plan. But in what way? He began by criticising the figures which Demagogue had adduced to support his ideas. In high politics of this kind no detail is insignificant. If you come along with an idea, do us the favour of thinking it through fully in advance, or keep quiet. No one had dragged him along by the tongue, he came of his own accord. The Boss said that Demagogue had reduced the level of capital investment and postponed various crucial planning dates, and in doing so had put a brake on our real possibilities. So what did Demagogue and Co. do? They began to shout that we must know our limitations, that we must talk in terms of real possibilities, and that we should make allowances for false optimism and red tape. These cretins actually imagined that they were indeed resolving certain of the country's real problems. They failed to understand that in fact they were dealing with slogans and not with executive instructions. Slogans follow laws which are quite different from those of executive instructions. These people were trying to stay within the limits of a policy which would appeal to economic interests. Or rather, they were then pushed into that position. The Boss played his hand according to slogan rules. For this reason he gained an indisputable advantage in terms of demagogy, and he skilfully exploited the situation. Demagogue and his advisers (who had immediately betrayed him) began to look like opponents of their own plan. With his iron logic the Boss, for all to hear, derived certain conclusions from this position. If they are against, it follows that they must be in favour of our lagging behind. Who gains by seeing us lagging behind? The bourgeoisie. In other words, Demagogue's position is objectively on the side of the bourgeoisie. Therefore he is for defeat and the restoration of the old régime. And suddenly, to everyone's surprise, a minor question became the centre of attention. Why? Who wanted it to happen? No-one. The fact of the matter was simply that a struggle for power and for key positions was going on within the leadership. Whatever question was under discussion, it was this fundamental reality which was bound somehow or other to come to the surface. Moreover, the struggle was also aimed at capturing the very foundations, the moulds of power. On the one hand there was a system of power which had grown up and prospered right from the very foundation of Ibanskian society, i.e. a system of social power. On the other hand there were scraps of a political, or rather a quasi-political power, which had no real basis in the structure of society and which was still undeveloped. The presence of individuals in one camp or another was a matter of chance, their individual destiny. In particular Demagogue was the leader of the second camp only because the position of leader of the first camp was already occupied. In terms of his personal qualities he was almost as big a villain as the Boss.

There was one more side in this story which must be considered. In general the people were pleased that the Boss had given Demagogue a hiding and had saved the people from restoration. It would have been impossible to have found a better form of agitation for the Ibanskian people of that period. Truth-teller is right when he says that the whole affair was presented in propaganda terms as if there had been a genuine struggle for the fate of the country. While in reality, according to Truth-teller, all that had happened amounted to the crafty manoeuvres of a cruel and dishonest man in his struggle for personal power. But it is in fact true that a real struggle was being pursued in the land over the way of life in the future. It was a very serious and decisive struggle. But the front line of this struggle lay elsewhere and fell between quite other social forces. It is not possible to trace the front line of this struggle on a map. It passed through the souls of men, through families, through towns and villages. It was to be found at many different levels and in many different cross-sections. It was not a line, it was a struggle between states of mind. The struggle between the Boss and Demagogue was not specially invented for this purpose. It was being fought on quite a different plane. But it took on the form it did not by sheer chance but as a reflection of the general situation in the country. In accordance with the rules of the power struggle, Demagogue was obliged on some point at least to adopt a position different from that of the Boss. And whatever he may have thought or said, he was involuntarily thrust into the position of leader of one of the warring tendencies in the life of the country. And that is not a fabrication. Even if all this had been specifically dreamt up by the Boss and his entourage, it would have become a reality. Otherwise Demagogue's ace would not have been trumped.

I am not trying to justify anyone, but it is no bad thing to take account of the actual position. It is a mistake to depict Ibanskian life as if some gang of bandits had usurped power and now lorded it over a peaceful people with an arbitrary disregard for morality and law. There has been no usurpation of power. That is sheer rubbish. It is simply that a society has grown up which it is absurd to consider in the context of law and morality. And the power which has arisen naturally according to the laws of this society has grown stronger, has displayed its might, has convinced itself that it really is power, and has celebrated its triumph. In our country a drama has been played out, an analysis of which supposes a system of concepts and values quite different from that held by Truth-teller. The leadership must thank destiny for having sent them such an opponent. For a long time he has diverted the attention of a considerable and concerned part of humankind away from the most profound problems of our life.' 'You are right,' said Chatterer. 'But if we apply your conception to Truth-teller himself, then we find the following. It makes no difference what precisely he shouts about. The main thing is how loudly he shouts, and who listens to him. He shouts so loud that all the world can hear, and all the world has listened. And that is quite something. As far as science goes—it's of no consequence. To hell with science. It might as well not exist at all.'

Anecdotes

But the most important phenomenon of the spiritual life of Ibanskian society of this period became the anecdote, or more precisely the forbidden and punishable anecdote. Anecdotes were classified by appropriate specialists according to the lengths of prison sentence which could be imposed for them. The underlying principle of the anecdote can be seen from the following anecdote. One in ten Englishmen dies at sea, but that doesn't stop them from being passionate sailors. One in five Americans die in road accidents, but that doesn't stop them being passionate motorists. One in three Frenchmen dies of love, but that doesn't stop them being passionate lovers. Every other Ibanskian is an informer, but that doesn't stop Ibanskians from being passionate admirers of anti-Ibanskian anecdotes. Anecdotes sprang up in amazing numbers on subjects which it might have seemed were in principle wholly inapplicable to anecdotes or to humour of any kind. But the most striking thing about this epidemic of anecdotes was that there was nothing anecdotal about the anecdotes. They merely retold in a brief aphoristic and concentrated form events from everyday Ibanskian life. For instance, one Ibanskian asks another why musquash fur hats have disappeared from the shops. The other replies, because the musquash multiplies in an arithmetical progression, while Brotherhood workers multiply in geometrical progression, and it's a long time since there have been any purges. But that is not an anecdote, it's the simple truth. Or, an Ibanskian asks another Ibanskian, how many people were killed in the recent rail crash. Fifty, replies the Ibanskian. Oh, says the first, that means five-hundred in the old style. The incident happened shortly after the currency reform when face values of notes were altered in a ratio of ten to one. But the interesting thing is that about five hundred people really were killed in the disaster.

The dawn of the anecdote dates from the most liberal days of the period which has just passed. An anecdote, no matter how critical it may be, supposes a certain degree of optimism. As soon as optimistic illusions were replaced by the awareness of the inevitability of a gloomy future, anecdotes disappeared without any intervention by the secret police. They simply faded away on their own. The Ibanskian anecdote is a tragedy with a dash of comedy. But tragedy with no trace of comedy is infertile soil for the anecdote to grow in.

Perspectives

'Whatever's done about it,' said Soilophagist, 'sooner or later the victory of the Ism will encompass the whole world, and it will be there to stay. We never consider a whole series of factors which work in its favour with irreversible force. What are they? For example, there is the ever increasing complexity of industry. This leads in the end to the establishment of a military-bureaucratic type of régime in industry, which is the principal sphere of social activity. Then there is the climate. Yes, I really mean it, the climate. It is getting progressively more severe. So what does that mean in the final analysis? It means a restriction of freedom of movement, and a transfer of ideas towards the purely material aspects of life, and to strict rationing of everything which was previously regarded as a free gift of nature. And if the conquest of space becomes a real practical possibility, then even doubts will disappear.' 'I admit that those are powerful arguments,' said Teacher. 'But let's look at them individually. Discipline and the organisation of industry? But that has no connection with the Ism. They follow a different line which is hostile to the very nature of the Ism. The complexity of industry is a more serious matter. But it offers a real hope that the Ism will be restrained and not that it will explode uncontrollably. There is a tendency rooted deep in the Ism which leads to the stagnation of industry and turns it into an arena for a purely social drama. You're in a high position. Surely you must be aware of that?' 'I am aware of it,' said Soilophagist, 'very much so. But we are fighting against this tendency.' 'You are, I agree,' said Teacher. 'But we are talking about something else. What is the significance of this struggle —is it for the Ism or against it?' 'It is for it,' said Soilophagist, 'but by way of trying to limit its growth, if we adopt your position. That doesn't alter the matter.' 'Yes it does,' said Teacher. 'What you call the Ism is something rather different from what I call the Ism. Let's at least agree about terminology if we can't agree about our position. For you the Ism means a rational organisation of the life of society by the state. Right?' 'Right.' 'For me it is a type of society which can only develop if the people at large are genuinely steeped in social principles, whatever kind of rational organisation we foist on society. And moreover, that very organisation will be dependent on these social laws. The idea of a state-run organisation of life is one thing, its actual operation is quite another. Your conception is an empty abstraction although it may seem that you are proceeding from very convincing facts. I do not dispute that your facts are impressive. But they are not social. Let's move on: the climate and space-flight. They are serious factors. But in what? Any notable effect of the deterioration of climate on the way people live will show itself only after several centuries. And space-flights will become vitally inevitable (and note I am talking not about their use, but about their vital necessity) only even later. There are already certain social forces which are going about their business with this in mind. The principle is very simple: in a hundred years time the temperature is going to fall, and there they go publishing their illegal shamizdat! Eliminate the bastards! They're stopping us from conquering the cosmos. Be it said in passing, if anyone's thinking about the real problems of space or of temperature-drop, it's these self-same bastards and not their oppressors. What's needed is to do what needs doing!! That's what work means!! As to the Ism . . .' 'I find it very hard to argue with you,' said Soilophagist; 'I feel that to a certain degree you're right. But I feel that I'm right as well. At all events, you won't deny that the country is an enormous economic mechanism and that if it's going to survive and develop . . . we must. . . .'

Soilophagist held forth for a long time on what we must and what we absolutely need. Meanwhile Teacher sat staring glumly at a gigantic portrait of the Leader. In the end he had had enough. 'All you're doing is serving me a rehash of editorials from the newspapers,' he said. 'I'm obliged to you because I haven't read them myself for a long time. I am practising mental hygiene. Let me give you some advice. It helps, as you'll see. Take a month off reading newspapers, then have a quick look at them and your eyes will start out of your head with amazement that you could ever have read such rubbish. We shall never find common ground because you approach things as a statesman and I as a scientist. You say things like "we need" and "we must" and so on but "needs" and "musts" are not an empirical fact. Science cannot base itself on bureaucratic ideas like that. They are the principle of power, and not of science. Science starts from the fact that, for whatever reason, we have large masses of people and the complex mechanisms of their economic life. And then sets out to explain what follows from these real facts. The Ism grows as a reality from this real basis and not from the ideas of civil servants, no matter how honest or good or intelligent they may be, about how life should be organised.'

The sixteenth hour
One day after a particularly heavy drinking session, Chatterer dragged Bawler off to a lecture by Slanderer, where Chatterer intended to borrow a fiver from Double-dealer so they could buy a hair of the dog. By all accounts Double-dealer had just received a very healthy fee for something so he almost certainly had some cash. 'Anyway,' said Chatterer, 'he'll move heaven and earth to get his hands on some.' Double-dealer was wandering up and down the corridors in search of an empty lecture theatre. 'Later,' he said. And Bawler was obliged to sit and listen to what had every appearance of being some incredibly boring drivel about the laws of some society or other which was in a state of complete lawlessness. The audience was very small. There were a couple of rather stupid and plain girls who, judging by the spots on their noses, were not best pleased with the existing order. That bloke over there is clearly an informer. You can tell just by looking at him. You'd be better off staying

out of his clutches—he'd crush you to death. When everyone had sat down, the supposed informer turned out to be Slanderer himself. Well then, thought Bawler, that's all your past experience gone up in smoke. Probably because you don't need it any more. Don't need it? Hardly. It will still come in handy. In fact the informer was a pleasant looking lad whose refined features suggested a fifth-generation intellectual. There was one research student who took careful notes of Slanderer's lectures and was using them to prepare his own avant-garde thesis, without of course making any reference to his sources. There was another research student who also listened with close attention because he was working on a detailed denunciation, a task handed down by his superiors. There were two or three rather indeterminate characters, and finally Double-dealer, Slanderer's closest pupil, and some rather vague individuals with rather frightened eyes. This can't be serious, thought Bawler. Surely nothing can come of it? How little it takes for any important matter to be brought down to a level of total triviality! They only need to prohibit the use of a lecture theatre, cut off a salary, cancel an examination, and send a few idiots and informers to make even a genius seem like some do-it-yourself amateur.

Although the period of liberalism was at its height, people were still afraid of being seen at Slanderer's lectures. He was too hated a figure, and it was considered that he was a bad lecturer. And since he never referred at all to the Ism, it was assumed that he understood nothing about it. Yet there is no truth outside the Ism. Even the most progressive elements in Ibansk were convinced of this. Wife, now, was quite another matter. What erudition! She knows the classics by heart. What a profound understanding of the Ism! Nothing like Secretary or Troglodyte, not to mention Foolosopher. What daring references to Western authors! How boldly she calls us not to dismiss them at first sight but to criticise them by means of profound creative analysis, uncovering those embryonic truths which they have deformed! And they are not always wrong. There is something there worthy of attention. They do not spring up like weeds in the desert; they are branches of the great and healthy tree of knowledge. They feed like parasites on the great varieties which can only be understood fully from the point of view of the Ism.

And most important of all, Wife pleads with us to think creatively. And Wife's lectures are always packed to the roof.

When Slanderer began his lecture, for the first time in his life Bawler regretted that he had not met him earlier and had not followed the course right from the beginning.

'When the representatives of any area of culture,' said Slanderer, 'begin to express concern about its purity, this is an infallible indication that not all is well in that area. Its representatives are afraid of being unmasked.'

Social systems

A systematic approach is rational when it is concerned with the interaction of a large number of variable factors for which it would be impossible, or too difficult, to follow the action by precise methods and to establish general rules for doing so. It is only effective in the case of mass phenomena when the question is to diagnose general tendencies and the probabilities that certain events will take place. And the efficacity of the systematic approach is further limited in the following way.

The line of conduct followed by social individuals represents a certain number of social actions organised in time and space. It can be defined by the following indices: (1) its purpose; (2) its strategy; (3) its tactics. The strategy determines a large number of actions through which the aim can be achieved. The tactics establish the methods by which those actions can be performed, their sequence and their combinations, i.e. is a means of executing the strategy. For example, A has set himself a target of overthrowing B and taking his place. He chooses the following strategy: to discredit B as a person of dubious morality. He chooses the following tactics: to get B drunk at a time when he is being observed by his superiors, to get him involved with a woman so as to get his workmates gossiping. I know of a case where a man specifically hired a beautiful woman with venereal disease, got his friend and superior drunk, and left him to spend the night in his apartment with this woman. I heard about this from the man himself, who considered it one of his most successful schemes. He was a cheerful man and very good with his family. And of course he was a good member of the Brotherhood. So the systematic approach is valid for a strategy of conduct, i.e. not in the case of one individual action, but for the selection and combination of actions as elements of a strategy. It provides an orientation for conduct if one bears in mind the type of system one is dealing with. It is interesting to note that almost all careerists strive instinctively towards the systematic approach but as a general rule do not achieve it. They are only saved by the fact that all their competitors are in the same position.

Politics

Politics, said Slanderer, is the most elusive and confused subject of conversation of all social subjects. If you try to clarify it publicly you will see with what hostility your attempt is received by all the members of the talking shop. Progressives will regard you with even greater hostility than the conservatives. They are far more afraid of clarity on questions of politics than are the conservatives, since clarity would reveal their cowardice and their lack of vision for the future.

Politics is generally taken to be a question of power. That is true. But the problem of power is not always politics. When people aim to take power and try to do so, the question of power is a political question. But if power has already been taken and consolidated, then in a society of the Ibanskian type the question of power ceases to be a political question. So politics cannot be reduced to the problem of power although one of its tendencies reaches in that direction.

The word 'politics' is used in two different senses—to characterise the line of conduct followed by certain individuals, or a particular kind of social relationship. In the former case it is said of people: he supports, or he applies, and so on, such and such a policy. The line of conduct followed by a social individual (including groups of individuals right up to the level of entire countries) is the aggregate of actions carried out by the individual to achieve a specific aim. And in this process individuals are guided by certain principles. These latter can be divided into actual principles and those which are officially proclaimed. It is common knowledge that here there is no complete coincidence. What is termed 'lack of principle' is an actual principle in accordance with which any official principles can be proclaimed, depending on the circumstances. This applies to any forms of conduct of any social individuals, including conduct which brings into being a particular type of social relationships which are termed political relationships. What we refer to as 'politics' merely means this form of conduct of individuals, i.e. their conduct in political relationships.

We have already seen that relationships between social individuals can be divided into domination-subordination relationships and into relationships of co-operation (or co-subordination). Political relationships form a third type of social relationship. They take place between individuals who are in neither a domination-subordination relationship, nor in a relationship of co-operation, i.e. they take place between socially independent individuals. Thus political relationships begin with a striving for independence and end in its destruction. The struggle waged by individuals for social independence is not of itself politics. It is a struggle for the conditions under which a political life is possible, where individuals can enter into relationships on a political level. So the struggle of the opposition in Ibanskian conditions for elementary democratic liberties is not yet a political struggle, and their crimes are not political crimes. It is a struggle against power. And these are common-law crimes. In its inner life the Ibanskian state is not a political individual, for there is within it no other independent and opposing individual. There is therefore nothing surprising in the fact that the state regards opposition activity in general as a criminal activity on the same level as robbery, gangsterism, speculation and so on. Hence we see these determined efforts to present opponents as amoral persons, as speculators, as crooks, as currency smugglers and so on. All this is not the result of some Machiavellian thought; it flows directly from the nature of the society and of power and also of the opposition. Nor is the Brotherhood in Ibansk a political organisation. If it were to happen that the economic institutions became independent of the Brotherhood institutions, and if both, or at least the former, were independent of the state, then a political situation might develop.

Briefly then, individual A enters into a political relationship with individual B in the pursuit of an aim, C, if and only if A and B are independent (sovereign) as regards the achievement C, and if A is obliged to take account of B. In this instance actions undertaken by individual A towards individual B are political actions. And they may result either in agreement or in a conflict.

Do there then arise in Ibanskian society situations which can properly be described as political relationships or political actions? Of course. You all know of cases where a certain group of people who have an effective power in society disintegrates into a number of comparatively independent groups. Within the limits of their divergence and their independence they function as political forces and perform political actions. Cases are also possible where the state on the one hand and the individual on the other enter into a political relationship. But to undertake this the individual must have a very solid position in the world to avoid being crushed like a beetle. In general, however, political relationships are not characteristic of Ibanskian society. It is a society which in principle excludes political relationships and tries as best it can to prevent them. It is a non-political society, not in the sense that it has not yet reached a level of maturity where it could accept the freedom of political relationships, but in the sense that political relationships are alien to it.

A society where political relationships are habitual, and where they have an important influence on the whole social life of the country is a higher type of society. A society where political relationships dominate in the system of social relationships is a political society. Ibanskian society displays a minimum of politicisation tending towards zero. If it were to be established, which in many respects would be a sign of progress, from the point of view of the level of social organisation it would be a regression.

The lack of need for and the habit of political conduct leads to its place being occupied by non-political forms of conduct even where political conduct is necessary. So an entire system of pseudo-political actions and personalities is created.

Unity

After Visitor had explained his theory, Colleague told an anecdote. Some chap is being admitted to the Brotherhood. He's asked: Do you drink? Yes. Do you smoke? Yes. Do you chase girls? Yes. Do you spend much time in restaurants? Yes. You'll have to stop all that. Will you stop it? Yes. And will you give your life for your country? Yes of course. How can you agree to that so lightly? Well, what else have I got left to do? 'O.K., chum,' said Colleague to Visitor, 'but you don't know the first thing about life. Come on, lads, how about another bottle and then a nice shashlik.'

'Everyone has his own system of living,' said Teacher. 'Visitor's system is beautiful, but it demands unusually high spiritual qualities which are given only to a few. I've got my own: it's the system of the most advantageous vital cycles. I, like Visitor, have based it on my own experience, which is not of course as rich as his, nor as dramatic. It's at a lower level—or even two or three levels lower, but my experience is of more general use than his. When I joined the army we were taken off to the canteen. We were given a pot full of soup for eight. We divided it up. I stirred mine with my spoon a bit and then poured the lot back in the pot. The rest followed my example. Oh, what a fuss there was! Mutiny, no more no less. We were forgiven because of our youth and lack of experience. I was called in as the ringleader by the resident secret policeman and told that I would be weighed every day. If I lost weight, I'd get double rations, but if I began to put weight on I'd find myself in the cooler. So then began a hopeless battle with nature. I almost stopped eating altogether. I shared my bread among the rest of them and became everybody's favourite. And what happened? Within a month I had put on six pounds. I even gained another two in the cooler.' 'They tricked you,' said Colleague. 'No,' said Teacher, 'it wasn't that. These days I am sitting for ten hours a day, I eat like a regiment, and I've lost eight pounds in six months. The whole thing, my dear friends, is a question of feeding cycles. I've studied this question very exhaustively and I've come up with some incontestible formulae. Feeding cycles can be every twelve hours, every twenty-four hours, one a week, one a month and so on. They can even be every six months or a whole year. The cycle which is followed by the great mass of the population and which is always being recommended by doctors and propagandists has a purely social significance. It's a cycle of enslavement. By this cycle man is chained to food outlets controlled by the state—to his home, to canteens, to food shops and so on. By my calculations the degree of an individual's social freedom is inversely proportional to the duration of the cycle. I personally live by a three-months cycle. Within it I can allow myself any sort of disorganised feeding, but the whole should have a certain regularity. For example, the quantity of proteins, fats, and carbohydrates I take in ought to be roughly constant for each three-month period. The same kind of cycles apply to everything else. In sexual relations. In hygiene. In work. In leisure. Even in spiritual life. Cycles have their natural minima and maxima. For instance, the minimum of the feeding cycle depends on the speed of digestion and its maximum on the speed with which surplus energy is dissipated in the organism, given a minimal level of feeding. The minimum of the spiritual cycle is determined by the lowest threshold of creative innovation, and the maximum by the highest threshold of conservatism.'

'As far as I'm concerned,' said Snottyhanky, 'I prefer a cycle which varies according to circumstances.' 'Oh, you're a poet,' said Teacher. 'And poets don't have their own personal cycles. They follow the cycles of those who feed them.' Snottyhanky took offence and used this as an excuse to leave without paying his whack.

Nostalgia for foreign lands

They say home's best . . . But what am I to say:
My dreams are all of countries far away!
What's happened, Motherland, if in my mind
My one desire's to leave you far behind?
Oh foreign motherland—but who's to blame
If my one thought's to go and not remain:
I would all things forsake, and with good cheer,
For but one hour of living Over There.

Ibanism

Ibanism, which is often for convenience referred to as the Ism, is the theoretical basis of Soc-Ism. So Ibanism is sometimes also called Soc-Ism. Ibanism is the highest, the most fundamental, the most profound, all-embracing, omnipotent, irrefutable doctrine of society, affirmed by the whole of man's past development and confirmed by all man's future development. Such is the unshakeable dogma of Ibanskian society. When Truth-teller said that Ibanism had been imposed by force on the

(603)

Ibanskian people, and that it stopped them living, he was making a crude error. The Ibanskian people bound itself voluntarily to Ibanism and can no longer live without it. It is Ibanism which lights its way forward. There is no social problem which with the help of Ibanism cannot be resolved in the most exhaustive and uniquely correct way. Moreover, if anyone tries to resolve these problems without the help of Ibanism, then he is doomed in advance to the gravest errors, to total incomprehension, to monstrous distortion and to other similar crimes. And the least of them presents a crack through which idealism might infiltrate. A nod towards idealism is graver still, while to embrace idealism is a still worse crime. And this headlong plunge into crime only ends when, as a result of the inner logic of the struggle, the sinner openly becomes a lackey of imperialism.

In the time of the Boss this dogma was followed to the letter. All the specialists in the social sciences were selected by promotion from the ranks of the most trustworthy and loyal Ibanskians. Their duties included maintaining a total ignorance of any Western sociology, and a responsibility for ensuring that no-one found out anything about it by illegal means, such as reading books which were in the libraries but which were not recommended by the authorities. And anyway, what kind of sociology could there possibly be except Ibanism? Ibanism, after all, is sociology in the true meaning of the term! Everything else is error and distortion, and must be crushed. But it was only possible to attack those Western sociologists who had already been crushed by the classics of Ibanism—and then only if they were crushed in the orthodox fashion. Here there was a whole science of the pogrom. If there were a crushing attempt that didn't quite crush, if some aspect were missed, or if someone failed to show enough determination in the struggle, all was lost. One leading Ibanologist was shot simply because he used the phrase 'from my point of view'. Another, even more leading, got a ten-year sentence in the camps, where, incidentally he snuffed it after six months, because in demolishing his former colleague he had omitted to bring in one of the mandatory quotations from the classics, which would have been inappropriate in this case, but which was floating around in the befogged mind of the Boss at the very moment when a third leading

Ibanologist was denouncing the second. And by these means Ibanism was preserved in all its pristine purity.

All the Western sociological literature was kept in closed sections of the libraries, literally behind the armour-plated doors. Access to it needed special authority. But these precautions, as posterity showed, were superfluous. Even if it had been permitted, it would have remained unread, or at least misunderstood, owing to the ignorance of foreign languages and the generally abysmal level of illiteracy. What few social scientists there were who understood foreign languages and a smattering of the terms of Western sociology were either in the Secret Police or spent their time digging out quotations for eminent Ibanologists and the higher leadership to use in the next routine pogrom.

But even if all the social scientists had studied foreign languages, even if they had been forced to read foreign books, and maybe even to understand something of them, the situation would not have been essentially changed. This truth came to light in the Period of Perplexity, when some relaxation appeared even in the field of the social sciences. It was in this period, and not in the epoch of the Boss—when there was no such relaxation—that it became clear that the ideological monolithism of Ibanskian society was an organic phenomenon which could develop even in the absence of constraint. In the Boss's epoch the authorities feared that if the reins were slackened then Ibanism would crumble. They themselves did not believe in its all-conquering strength nor in its youth. They themselves believed it to be the product of oppression and enforcement from outside, since historically it had indeed been imported into Ibansk. The Period of Perplexity revealed that Ibanism would have survived even without oppression and that it would have prospered even without any imports from abroad. For Ibanism is the organic product of this society.

On power

We must distinguish, said Slanderer, between political power and non-political power. The former develops from political relationships. It is selective and immoveable. It presupposes opposition and publicity. It is subject to the control of public opinion and of open criticism. Political power does not exhaust all the power of society. For instance, it is impossible without the existence of an appointed administration and of all kinds of specialists and technical advisers. It is not necessarily the dominant power in society. Examples of society in which it has been and remains in secondary or even tertiary roles are well known. If it exists, it can take on itself various functions of power. But its essential and original role is to strengthen and protect the law in the country concerned. It grows up together with social relationships and with a legally based form of conduct of social individuals. Its existence without social law is unthinkable.

There is no political power in Ibanskian society. There is only non-political power disguised as political. Why is this masquerade necessary? In the first place, it is a product of history, in which this form of power was born as a political power. Secondly, this masquerade has turned out to be a convenient means for the ideological processing of the population. Thirdly, the Ibanskian authorities on the international scene have to have dealings with the political powers of other countries, and they therefore wish to appear as equal partners. If we delete countries which have political power, or reduce them to a state where Ibansk may disregard them, we shall find that all political camouflage is stripped off Ibanskian power. And the theoreticians will present their form of power as the best. It is true to say that politics here is in a state of atrophy. But that is not the highest form of social progress. On the contrary, from the social point of view it has dropped back to a lower level.

In this respect, summit meetings between the leaders of the political powers of the West and the leaders of the non-political power of Ibansk present an amusing spectacle. The former are not omnipotent, they are limited and subject to criticism. But they do have power in the matters they are discussing. If they go beyond that, they go beyond their political framework, no doubt under the pernicious influence of their interlocutor. The latter is all-powerful, unlimited in his prerogatives, and beyond the reach of criticism. But he has no real power in the matters under discussion. This may seem strange and improbable, but it is a fact. Whatever happens within the ruling group, in the given circumstances he speaks as the representative and the leader of that ruling group. And his power is defined not by juridical norms and the legal situation in the country, which do not exist, but exclusively by social relationships within the group and the position the group holds within the social relationships of the society. We have already considered what this means. The former can be trusted, since any deception would weaken his own position and the position of his brotherhood or party. The latter cannot be trusted since he is essentially irresponsible. His destiny does not depend on the meeting, or depends on it very little, for he is operating at quite a different level. One could compare this meeting with, on the one hand, an efficient but limited scientific theory, and on the other, a huge, noisy ideological structure which claims to explain everything on earth in the best way possible. They do not and cannot have any point in common, but only the appearance of contact. Certainly there are subjects on which they can reach agreement. But the essence of their relationship remains the same.

Unity

'Whisky?' offered Soilophagist, 'or brandy? I can recommend this—it's real French cognac.' 'Really?' said Teacher. 'You've got yourself very nicely set up, you know. You might tell me, as your old battalion commander, how you set about it.' 'Stop clowning, commander,' said Soilophagist. 'Could you organise us some sandwiches and coffee, and a bit of the hard stuff?' he asked his secretary when she appeared. 'We haven't seen each other for a long time. Tell me, what earth-shattering discoveries have you been making recently? It always seems to me that that's all a waste of time. You'll get nothing that way. You're starting at the wrong end. A science of control? I'm not one of that gang, as you know. Of course, there isn't any idealism or metaphysics about it, but it's still a bit early to start talking about things like that round here. This business has to be approached politically . . .' 'Just you stop this demagogy,' said Teacher. 'I've heard it dozens of times before. I came to see you as an old friend from the front line. If you can help me, do. If you can't, just say so. There's no point beating about the bush. It's not worth it. There's nothing political or ideological in this collection. Just a phone call from you would do it. It's already paged up.' 'That's the trouble,' said Soilophagist, 'nothing ideological. Why don't you stick another article in, linking all your little this's and that's with the Ism? And shove a couple of words into the other articles? A reference or two to the classics.' 'But that'd be even worse,' said Teacher. 'Then they'd have our guts for garters as revisionists. What are you so afraid of? Just think, in a year or two this'll be being shouted from the house tops. People will be making their living out of it, building careers on it. Take a chance!' 'You know me,' said Soilophagist. 'You know I don't mind taking risks. I'm not a coward. And in this case there's nothing for me to risk anyway. That's not the question . . . This conversation's getting us nowhere. Let's drop it. Let's have a drink instead. No interruptions for the next hour,' he told his secretary. 'I'm in conference.'

'We still don't know much about human nature,' said Soilophagist. 'You don't change much, commander, do you? You still knock cognac back in tumblers. Science is only just beginning to penetrate the depths of the human being. I'm convinced that the true, integral Ism will only arrive when we have learnt how to control human nature. See what we've got at the moment. You can't call that the Ism. Everyone doing their best to cheat, to steal, to inform, to do other people dirt, to dodge responsibility . . . You know, you wouldn't believe some of the things I've seen from where I've been sitting. You'd think you were dreaming.' 'The true, integral Ism has already existed,' said Teacher. 'Under the Boss. And it'll soon be back. Just at the moment you're all a bit perplexed, and you've got involved in these soul-saving confessions. But in five years or so you'll put the screws on everyone again, and you'll have your integral Ism all right. There is no other, my dear commissar. Your call for a deeper understanding of human nature is just so much rubbish. It's a false problem. I'm telling you that as a scientist, not as a reckless battalion commander whom you always had to be rescuing from scandals he'd got mixed up in. What is a man? A combination of finite qualities. If you work out the degree of probability of one particular combination or another, you can calculate the degree of probability of such and such a type of man. How else can you explain the fact that in institutions of the same kind you always find much the same percentage of arse-lickers, informers, careerists, innovators, champions of justice, geriatrics and so on? How is it that the higher the standing of the institution, the greater percentage it

(608)

has of careerists and villains, and the lower the proportion of intelligent and gifted workers? Why is it that the variations in these values fluctuate in surprisingly close correlation to the type and level of the institution? What relationship does this have with some allegedly unkown human nature? It's a myth, a fairytale for idiots. It's just an opportunity for thousands of villains to squeeze themselves into degrees, titles and high-ranking positions. The average man contains the germ of every possibility imaginable. The concrete man is merely a unit in the mathematically predictable distribution of people into groups. And do not believe that in these groups men occupy positions which are what their nature would choose. This hypothesis could only ever be envisaged if one day all people got together and were offered the chance of taking any job in society they wanted. Believe me, there wouldn't be any secretaries; you'd be just one of three hundred million heads of state.' 'You've included me in your theory,' said Soilophagist. 'Of course I have,' said Teacher. 'Usually the kind of rubbish you've been giving me comes out of the mouths of fools and riff-raff. Now you are intelligent and incontrovertibly honest. So you're a rare specimen. On balance, quite a likely person to become a minister. But for this very reason, you won't be promoted soon.'

History yet to come

As is well known, the total Ism was proclaimed under His Leadership XVIII—and for eternity. There can be no further doubt about that. The only thing now open for discussion is to what extent the historical truth has been correctly described. But to avoid pointless, purely semantic arguments, let us first define what we mean by the total Ism. Total Ibanism is a social stratum which possesses the following characteristics. Here there are not, and cannot be, any serious deficiencies. If there are any shortcomings at all, they are only minor and can be easily eradicated. On the other hand, there is no shortage of qualities. In large numbers. Great and small. But more great than small. But even more small ones. Under the Ism the good flourishes to an unheard of extent. There is a flow of spiritual and material values, a high degree of conscience and morality. The state, politics, law and other superstructures fade away, but only after such preliminary reinforcement that . . . but in general, they fade away. There is such abundance that there's nowhere to put anything. And everywhere there are slogans: From each according to his abilities, to each according to his needs. Voluntary superactivists scurry about the streets begging the super-citizens: we implore you to accept this mink coat! Please, would you like to have this pure gold lavatory? Would you do me the favour of accepting this free holiday in the South Seas! Go on, it's only for two years! If there's any decency in you, would someone take this barrel of caviar off my hands just for a favour! To make it worth your while I'll throw in this diamond necklace that used to belong to the Empress! Would anybody like the rank of Marshal and the Order of the Great Member? There are still some jobs going as President of the Academy! Anybody here like to become a great writer? There's a magnificent novel already written! Who wants . . . But the citizens had such a highly-developed conscience that all this left them completely cold. And those ultrasuperhyperconscientious people who, in intelligence, honesty, ability and other blessings were so far ahead of everything in this genre which history ever produced, had to take up this heavy cross, and for the good of the workers had to become ministers, generals, marshals, academicians and so on, they were obliged to deck themselves in gold and diamonds, to stuff themselves three times a day with the same old caviar, sturgeon, the finest cuts of meat and pineapples, and four times a day to drink those weary rounds of cognac, vermouth, and liqueurs, spend much of their time travelling to holiday resorts, going to opera and ballet, living in huge apartments, villas and houses, and in general sacrificing their precious health, time, energy and peace of mind for a thankless, exhausting and arduous labour. And the rank-and-file superconscientious Ibanskians saw all this, understood the depth of the sacrifice, and thanked them for it. Our grateful thanks, you dear, dear people! If you hadn't agreed to take on the load, we'd have had to . . . Oh, see, the poor little man, he's got to carry all those medals! What a heavy load it must be! Fancy that poor darling having to eat so much caviar! Oh, the poor dear's had to drink so much brandy! My God, my God, how they suffer for us! What martyrs they are! Just think how long he's been reading those papers! And he

reads and reads and reads! . . . He really ought to take a break.
He's bound to have someone to go and see tomorrow . . .

The seventeenth hour

'What do you mean when you use words like Ism and Capitalism?' asked Slanderer. 'The Ism is not any deviation from the
norm, or a particular form of society. It is a purely social
phenomenon, the fundamental tendency of the life of society.
Everything else is either a struggle against this tendency or
against resistance to this tendency. The progress of society
consists of a battle against its own normal state. Structures?
Certainly there is something in that. But let's take the example
of capitalism. What is it exactly? It is an anti-social eruption, a
temporary and partial victory of the creative I over the inert and
stagnant We. Now, that is a deviation from the norm. A transitional phase between two forms of social enslavement. It is a
particular form of the Ism in which the I has a slightly bigger
role than in our society; in which there are commercial and
financial relationships within the conditions of a free market
and private property—and much more besides. An Ism of the
Ibanskian variety presupposes the development of capitalism.
But in what sense? In the sense of a society capable of making
spontaneous progress and of achieving creative results. For
what purpose? So as to be able to enjoy the fruits of its creative
work. Of itself the Ism is hostile to creativity. It only allows it to
exist as a last resort, or by oversight, or because it is not able
to stifle it. Capitalism as a Western-type society developed
entirely owing to the oversight of the authorities. When the
authorities gather their strength together they will put an end to
capitalism and establish the Ism throughout the world.'
'That is terrifying,' said Bawler. 'I have thought a great deal.
I have read everything I could lay my hands on. I have
developed a whole diverse heap of theories myself. And all that
counts for nothing. I'm afraid that's the simple truth. Desperately simple. Behave as you think fit, and time will decide what
will happen and how.' 'I agree with you,' said Slanderer. 'But
one must know how to tell the truth. And that is not as simple as
it seems. No matter how careful I am, I am certain that very
soon my course of lectures will be closed down.' 'I believe you
wrote a book,' said Bawler. 'It was seized and destroyed,' said

Slanderer. 'There isn't a single copy left, not even my own. But that doesn't matter much. Now that Truth-teller's works have appeared, my book made no sense any more.'

'You are interested in practical conclusions,' said Slanderer. 'But is there any possibility at all for action, even if we accept that this kind of conclusion is possible?' 'In theory there are never any possibilities for action,' said Bawler. 'But what is the point of knowing that action is impossible if a man is nevertheless obliged to do something?'

His conversations with Slanderer developed more and more often into arguments about action. In delivering his lectures and having interminable discussions with students and anyone else who cared to join in, he was performing his action all the while considering that an action was something different—but never possessing any really clear idea of what it was. Bawler believed that Slanderer's lectures constituted an action, but for himself he sought an action of a different kind.

'One day during the war,' said Bawler, 'my plane was hit. A shell exploded right in the engine. Half of the cylinders were knocked out. I just about made it back to the airfield. All the ground staff said that the plane could never fly. Well, I had flown it despite their theories. The speed of dolphins cannot be explained theoretically, for the time being at least. But the fact of the matter is it's never been explained. And what can we say about the example of Truth-teller? Who could have foreseen his appearance theoretically? We must take a risk and do something without paying any attention to theoretical calculations.' 'But what exactly?' asked Slanderer. 'It's still difficult to say,' replied Bawler. 'But we have to be ready to seize the opportunities when they arise, and most important of all to recognise them.'

Ibanism

Despite its manifest absurdity, or perhaps because of it, Ibanism is an irrefutable truth. When Truth-teller attacked it as the source of all evil, he committed a grave error. Ibanism has never been and could never be the source of all evil, if only for the reason that it is not any ordinary source at all but the prime source. And from the prime source everything proceeds—both evil and good, and consequently nothing at all. For Ibanism itself is derived from everything.

According to the doctrine of Ibanism no-one created the world, and indeed it had no birth. It has existed throughout eternity and will go on existing throughout eternity. It develops from the lowest stage to the highest. As an exception, certain parts of the world may skip a few stages of development, provided they have the authorisation of the Ibanskian government, and that Ibansk supplies them with disinterested aid. Starting from the electron, which has inexhaustible depths, the world developed to the highest level attainable—the level of Ibanskian society. From now on the entire future development of the world can go forward only on the basis of Ibansk, through the medium of Ibansk, in line with the development of society in Ibansk. Consciousness is the highest form of our capacity for reflection which lies at the basis of existence. It is nothing more than a reflection of existence. Naturally the highest form of consciousness is the consciousness achieved by Ibanskian society, incarnated in Ibanism and in its wise leadership. Nothing higher than that can exist. This of course does not mean that everything stops there in a state of stagnation. The Ibanskian leadership creatively develops Ibanism on the basis of the experience it has derived from the practice of building the total Ism. The latest speeches of Ibanskian leaders and the latest decrees of government are the pinnacle of human consciousness at the present time. And that holds good until the next speeches and decrees.

Briefly, Truth-teller confused the form and the essence of Ibanism. The essence of Ibanism is very simple. Our society is the most perfect, the most humane, the most free, the best organised, the most . . . the best . . . the most . . . The doctrines of Ibanism are the most intelligent, the most profound, the most . . . the most . . . the most . . . of every doctrine of society in general, and of Ibanskian society in particular. If you stumble upon anything good anywhere you must know that it is much better done in Ibansk. If anywhere you discover something bad, you must know that in Ibansk this does not exist, since in Ibansk, as a matter of principle, nothing bad can exist. If anywhere you hear a wise thought, you must know that there are still wiser thoughts on the subject in the concept of Ibanism. If anywhere you observe an error, you must know that this error does not exist in the doctrines of Ibanism, since Ibanism excludes error as a matter of principle. Such, by definition, are Ibanskian society and its scientific interpretation—Ibanism.

Social systems

One of the fundamental principles of the systemic method is the principle of the homogeneity of the system. This principle means that all individuals in the system belong to one and the same class of individuals, and that all relationships between them belong to one and the same class of relationships. This principle should not be interpreted to mean that the systemic method can be applied only to systems made up of homogeneous individuals and relationships. To put it in a more concrete form, the principle means that the point of view chosen for the observation of a given empirical system must be such that from it all its individuals and relationships may be presented as homogeneous. It is not a principle which permits the selection of the subject of research, but a principle which permits the observation of any given subject. If such a viewpoint of a given system cannot be found, then the systemic method cannot be used. The second fundamental principle is the hierarchical principle, according to which all types of individuals and relationships can be defined via a number of elementary individuals and relationships in the system.

I shall illustrate these principles and their application to social systems. The individuals which comprise these systems are isolated men and women, groups of people, combinations of groups, and so on, right up to the level of entire countries. All these individuals belong to the same class of social individuals in the sense that they are all considered from the same viewpoint: as beings capable of making a conscious choice and of performing volitional acts towards other individuals. Here the hierarchical principle consists in the selection of an isolated man or woman as the elementary individual, and all groups are defined as individuals in which the directing organ and the directed body consist of isolated people or, in the case of superior groups, groups of people. To define the class of relationships it is necessary to determine the degree of dependence of certain individuals on others in the pursuit of certain aims where some individuals need the help of others in order to realise these aims. An elementary relationship can be represented in the following form. An individual A has set himself an aim C. The accomplishment of this aim depends on the free will of individual B. This latter may hinder or help, accelerate or delay the achievement of the aim, permit it or forbid it, and so on. Other corollary relationships within the system can be defined on the basis of this elementary relationship. I shall quote some examples.

For instance, an individual A depends on $B^1 \ldots B^n$ relative to aim C, where $n \geqq 2$. The individual A depends on B in pursuit of aims $C^1 \ldots C^n$. Individuals $A^1 \ldots A^n$ depend on B relative to aim C. Individual A depends on B relative to aim C, while B depends on A relative to aim D. If we introduce variables for individuals and aims it is possible to calculate a much greater number of possible combinations. In principle they can all be calculated. Social life is subject to the laws of combinatory analysis to the same extent as all other phenomena. The concrete facts of social life are merely the realisation of certain logical possibilities. Given a large enough number of repetitions, they are all realised more or less quickly, at a speed which by the same principle can be calculated *a priori*. Any suggestion that social phenomena are basically more complex than any other phenomena occurs either because it is made by people who are wholly ignorant of the field (which includes practically everyone who claims to be an expert) or because of ideological intimidation.

If A depends on B relative to C, and B depends on A relative to D, and the realisation of C or D are mutually interdependent, an exchange of services takes place. In the absence of attendant circumstances one can say that C and D are equivalent given certain evaluative criteria shared by A and B. Social oppression occurs when an individual is constrained to provide a service or to take part in an exchange of non-equivalent services. The domination-subordination relationship is based on the organisation of an act or of an oppression. In this case the principle of equivalence is not observed. The subordinate may receive a large reward for a small service or a small reward for a large service. In this case other principles come into operation. The co-operation relationship is the joint subordination of two or more socially independent individuals to the same superior. Political relationships are an exchange of services on a contractual or juridical level. In reality we have an interweaving of a vast number of social relationships and a further interweaving of social relationships with relationships of other kinds. This interweaving forms the fabric or the body of society.

The law

You are familiar with the official concept of law, said Slanderer. Its superstructure, its class nature, and so on. All that of course is laughable. But I would beg you to consider this problem seriously. Not that the conception has some hidden intellectual depth, for it does not. But it is interesting for what it can reveal from the social point of view. After all, we feel its effects on our own skins, which is why it cannot merely be considered as a product of ignorance and stupidity. The problem of the official conception of law leads us directly with no intermediate links to the problem of the very foundation of Ibanskian society.

Voices are sometimes raised demanding that the executioners who have committed crimes in Ibanskian concentration camps and the organisers of these camps should be brought to justice. From a purely human point of view I can understand this position. But it is absurd in theory and unattainable in practice. I don't want you to think that I am defending these people. I have been through this hell myself. I know very well how all this monstrous apparatus of extermination was recruited, and how it operated. But the whole horror of the situation lies in the fact that no-one can pass judgment on anybody, since the concept of judicial retribution has no meaning when applied to Ibanskian society.

Here we must deal with some rather delicate semantic problems, and so we shall not rush to conclusions. Is Ibanskian society based on the law, or is it not? It might seem that the large number of instances of lawlessness and arbitrary behaviour by the authorities would justify our speaking of it as having no basis of law. But on the other hand, it is not difficult to demonstrate that from certain points of view it is more just than a Western type of society. And then we find ourselves in a position where we want to say that on the one hand, here matters are thus, but on the other hand they are different. That, however, is not a scientific approach, which demands clarity and clearly defined concepts.

Let us examine the most fundamental concepts of law. It is clear that we must distinguish between legal standards and the way they are applied. A society may have a magnificent code of laws which enshrine every conceivable democratic freedom and human right for its citizens, but may live in practice as if any reference to democratic freedoms were regarded as a crime. You know this perfectly well from your own experience, or at least beyond the shadow of doubt from the experience of your fathers. Let us consider the matter first from the viewpoint of legal standards.

Legal standards are a particular case of standards in general. Standards in general authorise, forbid or compel something to be done or not done. Legal standards concern those actions of social individuals which have a real effect on the interests of other social individuals. This is reflected in the very fact that these standards have been adopted. Legal standards affect the freedom of action of individuals, that is to say actions which are carried out at the free will of the individuals concerned. They are established in a specific kind of text (codes) which, in principle, can be studied by every citizen. These codes are adopted by legislation and they are recognised as legal standards.

Every kind of standard is based on certain purely logical principles, which apply also to legal standards. I am not saying here that no-one can transgress these principles. On the contrary, nothing is so often transgressed as the laws of logic. I mean simply that these principles are of a logical nature and relate to every kind of standard. What concern us here are the following general principles. A standard exists if, and only if, it is accepted or derives logically from accepted standards. As far as legal standards are concerned this means that a legal standard exists if and only if it is contained in the officially accepted code of standards or is derived logically from the standards in the code. If a court is not able logically to derive a certain legal standard from standards which are known to it, then it cannot consider it a proper legal standard. There must be specialists who are able to make such deductions or discover errors in them with the same mathematical rigour as is applied to a theorem. Indeed they must be even more rigorous since they are concerned with human destiny. It is for this reason that the development of a generally accepted logical standard is a matter of primary importance.

Further, if a particular standard is not accepted, it does not follow from this that its negation should be a standard. In the case of legal standards this means that if the code omits a certain standard A, this does not indicate that its negation, i.e. not-A, is a legal standard. It follows from this that the absence of a standard prohibiting a certain action does not indicate the existence of a standard permitting it, and that the absence of a permissive standard does not indicate the existence of a prohibiting standard. A distinction must be drawn between the absence of a standard and the existence of a negation-standard. The absence of a prohibiting or permitting standard is one thing. The existence of a norm by which something is not forbidden (or, correspondingly, not permitted) is another. I have observed many cases of juridical practice where these things have been confused, and often deliberately confused.

An action is not subject to a standard evaluation unless a standard relative to it exists or can be logically deduced. For instance, until recently the Ibanskian legal code included no standard dealing with the typing of reprehensible manuscripts. And it was impossible to deduce such a standard logically because of the absence of adequate terminology in the code. So actions of this kind were not capable of legal judgment, i.e. it could not be said whether they were permitted or forbidden. Actions which are not embraced by legal standards can be permitted or forbidden, but not by law, only on another basis, for example by arbitrary decision or by custom. The persecutions suffered by shamizdat, Truth-teller, Singer and so on are unlawful actions by the authorities in as much as the actions of the persecuted individuals were not susceptible of legal evaluation.

The standards either indicate or suppose the people to whom they are addressed, i.e. the subjects of the standards. The class of these subjects can be more or less broadly defined. Certain standards may suppose one class of subjects, others another class. A standard can have meaning only when its subjects exist. If the subjects of a standard disappear, the standard itself loses its meaning or disappears itself. For example laws concerning the relationships of land-owners and peasants, or capitalists and their employees, lost their meaning and disappeared in Ibansk after the disappearance of land-owners and capitalists. But if the subjects of the standards exist, their fate must be described in other expressions. These standards can be repealed or ignored in practice. They do not disappear of their own accord. They can be destroyed, and it sometimes happen that they destroy themselves.

The standards can be divided into active and passive standards. Active standards permit or forbid certain specific subjects to perform a certain action. Passive standards permit or forbid certain subjects to do a certain act towards other subjects. They are passive as regards the latter group, but active as regards the former. For example, a superior is forbidden to use his position to exploit a subordinate in his own personal interest. From the point of view of the subordinate this is a passive standard. Standards can be further divided into rights-standards and duties-standards. The rights-standards permit individuals to perform certain actions and forbid other individuals to prevent those actions being performed. Duties-standards forbid individuals to abstain from performing certain actions. A society may have a highly developed code of citizens' obligations and take great care to see that the code is scrupulously observed, but at the same time have an underdeveloped code of rights and pay no attention to its observation. When a certain society is described as unlawful this often refers not to the total absence of a code of laws but to the specific absence of a code of rights. In this sense a society may be equipped with laws but deprived of rights. When I speak of the existence of a lawful society as a social characteristic of society as a whole, I am referring exclusively to rights-standards. Although they may be bound into the same volume as duties-standards they are of a qualitatively different nature.

Legal standards can be further divided into political and non-political. The former concern the relationship of the citizens and their groups on the one hand, and the authorities on the other, as social individuals who in the given case are mutually independent, that is to say that they concern their political relationships. The latter, the non-political standards, concern the exercise of the functions of power, relationships between citizens in daily life and so on. The first group constitute the standards of political law. It is here that we reach the crux of the matter. The well-known democratic freedoms are the essence of standards of political law. And they figure in the Ibanskian legal code. How did they come to be there? This is due in part to illusions about the Ism, and in part to propaganda and demagogy. And in part, too, they are a camouflage, a desire to look decent in the eyes of the outside world. But the main reason that they got into the Ibanskian legal code is that from the very beginning there was complete certainty that no-one would ever take it into his head to make use of these freedoms.

The impression which has been and still is presented by Ibanskian legal practice as far as political rights are concerned is common knowledge. The essence of the problem is not that good laws have been and are being broken by malefactors, but that in Ibansk the people who were capable of being subjects of political legal standards have been exterminated, and that Ibanskian society, as at present constituted, produces such citizens in infinitesimal numbers. In Ibansk the number of people who are concerned about a guarantee of their right to political activity as equal partners with the authorities is minute. The number of influential people who are concerned to see that these people should exist and should have this guarantee is even smaller. The existence of such people in no way derives from the laws of Ibanskian society. So in this society political rights have no meaning. They simply do not exist because they have neither representatives nor defenders. The appearance of a large number of people who have joined in political conflict with the Ibanskian authorities is a purely fortuitous phenomenon from the point of view of the social structure of this society. When such people have appeared they have naturally come up against a certain legal practice which has matured during the establishment of an Ibanskian society which has never seen the need for political relationships or for political rights. These people have not sprung up in the normal course of Ibanskian life, and it cannot be expected that they will reproduce themselves. Even if they achieve a certain measure of success, this will in no way indicate the establishment in society of a permanently effective institution of political rights. The authorities deal with this problem, and will go on dealing with it, not according to legal standards but on the basis of other

(620)

considerations which have nothing to do with the law.

To sum up. Ibanskian society is one which, in practice, has no effective institution of political rights. The reason is that it does not produce or reproduce on a large scale individuals capable of becoming the subjects of political law. Nor does it produce or reproduce on a large scale the conditions and people who would guarantee the functioning of political rights towards those isolated individuals who, by force of circumstances, come into political relationships with the authorities.

The number of victims who suffer from the absence of political rights in Ibansk is infinitely small. It is not true to say that the mass repressions were the consequence of this state of things. They arose from quite different causes. The arbitrary nature of authority and massive oppression do not of themselves argue a lack of political rights. The overwhelming majority of those who have suffered repression have never entered into political relationships either between themselves or with the authorities. These repressions took place outside the framework of politics. If they had happened inside that framework, we might have been able to preserve some illusions. But, alas, that is not the case. The repressions and the absence of political rights, or of a guarantee for such rights, have a common cause. They are parallel consequences of the same causes.

Of course it matters little to the victim for what reasons he is being oppressed. But it would be useful to know what we can expect of this society in the future. Maybe there will be no more massive repressions. At the moment, for example, they have to all intents and purposes ceased to exist. But this does not indicate that political rights have been established. It signifies rather an absence in the country of political life as a mass phenomenon. The few political individuals who appear from time to time are subjected to persecution not because of a bad political law, but because of the absence of any political law. They are quite simply exterminated as elements undesirable to authority. And from this point of view authority is omnipotent.

History yet to come

When the thirteenth leader was in power the official title of His Leadership was introduced. And so that each His Leadership could be distinguished at least in some particular from his predecessors and successors, leaders were given an official number, like kings in ancient times. In the case of kings this was very unjust because they were all exploiters and right-wing revisionists, but in this case everything was in perfect conformity with the true laws of history. The Boss came to be referred to as His Leadership I, the New Leader who had replaced Hog became His Leadership II, and so on. Special conferences were called to establish the dates of birth and death and reign of each of Their Leaderships, and to catalogue the measures introduced under their wise direction. It was a great achievement. Previously each succeeding leader had roundly abused his predecessor, appropriated to himself everything good that had come out of the previous reign, and attributed to his forerunner everything bad that he did himself. When they finally came to realise that the fate of their predecessor was one that they themselves would share, the leaders decided to start giving their due to their predecessors and consequently to themselves. Since every successive leader was a whole head higher than his predecessor, and made a great step forward, this innovation marked the beginning of a period of irresistible progress. The Ibanskians were moving at such a speed that they did not even notice that they had overtaken America and left her somewhere far behind. They had to turn back, as they always needed to keep an eye on America.

His Leadership XIII made an attempt to proclaim the total Ism. There was a momentous build-up to this, the greatest event in the history of mankind. But the attempt foundered. At a secret plenum of the Deputies it was declared premature. Not because, as some hostile historians were to declare later, at the time there was an almost total disappearance from Ibansk of meat, milk, eggs and other carcinogenous products, nor yet because, as other friendly historians declared later, it was still too early, but because of the very number XIII. Just at this time Ibanskian scientists discovered (thus stretching their lead over the Americans by a hundred per cent!) scientific and philosophical justification for the noxious consequences of this figure. But Chatterer held a different view. He said that His Leadership XIII was shortly to be deposed, and that the Deputies had decided to keep the honour of proclaiming the total Ism for themselves, since each of them had hopes of becoming His Leadership XIV. It was only at this moment that His Leadership XIII realised what a basic error he had made when he proposed the omission of Hog from the list of Their Leaderships. And he died of grief.

Argument with an Ibanist

'Come on, let's talk seriously,' said Ibanist. 'You know that I'm a sincere ibanist.' 'I know that,' said Teacher. 'But bear in mind that I regard sincerity as an optional form of behaviour and not as a virtue. The Boss was sincere too. And Troglodyte. And Claimant. And . . . But it doesn't matter.' 'No it doesn't,' said Ibanist. 'I agree that human history is only a tiny part of the history of life on earth. But there is something which distinguishes it from the rest of that history. What is it?' 'What distinguishes it,' said Teacher, 'is everything that has been produced by human endeavour, everything which has been created by human hand and mind and is maintained by human effort. In a word, it is human culture.'

'Very well,' said Ibanist, 'but does it have its own laws? It does. And what are they? Does it not seem to you that if we set about seeking these laws we shall always come back to those famous productive forces, productive relationships, the basis, the superstructure and so on, which you are always so sarcastic about?' 'That depends on what we are looking for and who is looking for it,' said Teacher. 'If someone is looking for manure, he'll go to the stable. But if he's looking for gold he'll go to a goldfield. I have nothing against the words which you have used, but they are purely ideological creations and not scientific concepts. Their meaning is not established by logical laws, and they do not operate according to logical laws.' 'I agree,' said Ibanist, 'they are dialectical laws. But is not dialectic . . .' 'No,' said Teacher. 'Dialectic is an ideological weapon and nothing more. Never, under any circumstances, can it be a weapon of science. It is sheer illusion to claim that it is, a grand illusion, but an illusion just the same.' 'We're getting off the subject,' said Ibanist. 'What direction do you suggest we follow? Where does your gold lie?' 'Why do you talk about "my gold"? ' asked Teacher. 'I am not looking for gold but for manure. Gold is a product of nature. But manure is a product of human history.

You are asking about the nature of the specific laws of human history. It all depends what you mean. There are laws which control human associations—sociological laws. There are laws which control human actions as a whole and particular aspects of these actions. These include rules for controlling and brutalising the masses, rules for building houses and cities, cooking chops and soup and so on. There are even rules for the conduct of arguments—which make our argument meaningless. Let's go and have a drink instead. By the way, I would like you to explain the ibanist principle which says that production relationships are relationships between people in their production process.'

Singer's first letter

When I visit a gallery with abstract art on show,
Or go into a restaurant with lots of seats to spare,
Or at shop windows stop and stare, it's not a dream, I know,
Yet I must rub my wondering eyes to prove I'm really there.
When you are feeling hungry you can eat just what you like,
Or buy whatever clothes you want, no matter how bizarre;
If you're dissatisfied you're free to say what you dislike—
Say anything you feel or think without the slightest fear.
I'm picking up a word or two of their strange foreign talk,
And constantly from dawn to dusk of every homesick day
I stammer out repeatedly that one obsessive thought:
These bastards lead a splendid life, no matter what you say.

The letter produced an ambiguous impression on the Ibanskian intellectuals. On the one hand they were envious of the fact that Singer could simply go into a brothel without anybody feeling the need to work him over for it. And the same thing went for all his trendy gear. On the other hand they pitied Singer since he had cut himself off from the sources of his creative inspiration. All the same he was an Ibanskian cultural phenomenon. In the West no-one gave a damn for him. They were interested as long as he was here in Ibansk. As long as he was persecuted. But now . . .

Humanism and the balance of forces

'The shamizdat people all got between five and seven years,' said Neurasthenic. 'How mild!' said Journalist. 'That sounds like a very humane sentence.' 'Yes,' said Neurasthenic. 'But what was it for? Even under our laws there was nothing to arrest them for, let alone try them. And they were inside for a year before the trial without being told what they were accused of.' 'But you must admit that it's progress all the same,' said Journalist. 'There was a time when they'd simply have been shot without any trial at all.' 'But where do you see your humanity?' asked Chatterer. 'The very use of the word in this context betrays your implicit acceptance that they were guilty. And what is shamizdat guilty of?' 'But they confessed their guilt,' said Journalist. 'Were you at the trial?' asked Neurasthenic. 'No,' said Journalist, 'we weren't let in.' 'And do you know the kind of little game that's been played with them all this last year?' asked Neurasthenic. 'Did they all confess or not? And where are the ones who didn't confess? Where's Bawler and all the others who got on with the job without constantly showing off to foreigners? They've been arrested too. But there hasn't been a word about them anywhere. Try reading the confessions of the "penitents" closely, even in their published form. As time goes by people will start being amazed that anyone could have been tried on charges like that. Do you think this trial has damaged Ibansk abroad?' 'Of course it has,' said Journalist. 'So why aren't the people who organised it being tried?' asked Neurasthenic.

'Deputies No. 1 and No. 5 wanted them to be shot,' said Brother, 'but the Leader and Deputies No. 2 and No. 3 insisted on a milder, more humane sentence.' 'That's a brilliant example of juridical practice,' said Neurasthenic, 'when the court had the punishment dictated to it even before the trial started.' 'It's a matter of serious policy,' said Journalist. 'Whose policy?' asked Visitor. 'A policy towards the West from whom at the moment we need to squeeze out as much as we possibly can. That's why we need to show them that we are liberal humanists.' 'So something's been gained,' said Dauber, 'and half a loaf is better than no bread.' 'That's not the point,' said Neurasthenic. 'What if our little flirtation with the West is suddenly broken off? What happens then?' 'Then humanism will be suddenly broken off as well,' said Visitor. 'Our kind of humanism is never a spontaneous advance, it's always a temporary and very guarded political move.' 'There are a great many things

(625)

that you simply don't see,' said Journalist. 'In the West people believe there is evidence of a serious split in your supreme leadership, both on foreign and domestic policies, and it looks as if the Leader's group is coming out on top, which is regarded as a good thing with some prospects for the future.' 'What kind of prospects?' said Chatterer. 'The balance of forces in the leadership is a reflection of the balance of forces in the country as a whole. The socially active population has split into two lines or groups: the suppressors (traditionalists) and the improvers (liberals). The two factions are not equally powerful. The former represent stability, the normal bases of our life. They are always the stronger. And when it appears that the improvers are coming out on top, here is what it means: the suppressors are obliged by circumstances to expel from their own circle, and to admit the existence of, a certain group of people—a group which pursues its activities completely within the framework of the regime, but gives the impression of seeking to improve it. This is allowed to go on for a short time and on a very limited scale. Very quickly the improvers realise the senselessness and impossibility of making improvements, even if they ever genuinely had any illusions on that score. And when they have achieved their own personal objectives they become even more diehard conservatives than those who originally drove them from their ranks. Incidentally, the Boss and his gang were largely from the liberal camp, but for some reason everyone keeps quiet about that. Part of the liberals were sacrificed during the purges. Who were they? That depends on the circumstances. They included the most stubborn, the most stupid, the losers, the careerists, the superfluous and so on. In principle the objective result of the liberals' action is to introduce minor correctives to preserve the regime as the situation changes. For example, it is they who authorise the growing of beards, the private ownership of a cow, the wearing of mini skirts and drainpipe trousers, a hint of abstractionism and so on. As soon as the particular aim is achieved, or the need for it ceases to exist, then the liberals disappear themselves or are destroyed.

'Imagine the sight of an army on parade. Who marches at their head? The answer's clear. But say that the situation changes, and they're no longer on parade but marching into battle. Who is now moved up to march at their head? That is clear as well. But if the matter in hand is not a battle with the enemy but some immoral task, like slaughtering a peaceful population, looting, and so on, who's going to be in front this time? That too is clear. Whoever marches in front is the one who sets the tone. The situation we have here at the moment is complicated. It's partly a parade, partly a battle, partly dirty work. Only time will tell which line will crystallise. The likeliest outcome of all is a dirty parade.

'And there's another important fact that must be borne in mind. There is a law which determines the relationship between conservatives and liberals: the strength of the liberals is inversely proportional and the strength of the conservatives directly proportional to the square of the distance between their place of action from the centre of the country and to that of the distance between their position in the hierarchy and the supreme power. The distances are calculated in the appropriate social units of measurement. For example the administration of a district is more remote from the supreme power than that of a region. Do I make myself clear? This law clarifies a phenomenon which might at first sight seem paradoxical—the inertia of liberalism at the highest levels. At the lowest levels, and on the periphery of power, the conservatives have long since crushed the liberals in places where they happened to exist, for in most places and cases they had never been heard of. And in the higher reaches the liberals still have the initiative. But their song has already been sung.'

'But your law,' said Journalist, 'applies also to conservative inertia when liberalism, which has started at the top, gradually begins to spread downwards.' 'First of all,' said Chatterer, 'we must establish precisely whether at the present time we are at the beginning of the era of liberalism or at its end.' 'I would have thought rather at the end,' said Journalist. 'And secondly,' said Chatterer, 'there is no such law. Liberalism does not grow in the milieu of the supreme leadership, nor indeed from the leadership milieu in general, but from resistance to the leadership in the population at large.' 'I understand,' said Journalist. 'Your reflections are not without interest. Have you anything you want to add?'

'The situation is made more complicated by one special

(627)

characteristic of the present-day liberals,' said Chatterer. 'Ibansk's position on the international scene has come to the foreground in every respect. At the present time we need to have trade relations with the West. And to do this we need to pay heed to their ways of conducting business and to give ourselves the appearance of being rather different from what we actually are. The initiative is not in our hands since we are the petitioners. Now the Western man in the street, who has begun to get some idea of what we are like in reality, puts pressure on his own government, which in its turn is obliged to put pressure on our government to see that domestic affairs in our country look more presentable to the West. Our liberalism is an enforced concession in trade relations with the West, and not the result of any internal evolution. Much the same goes for the enlivening of our opposition. The whole business now depends on how long and how seriously the West will go on pushing us in this direction, and on our willingness to carry on business with the West on the kind of terms that suit them. Are we capable of keeping our promises? Will they go on believing us for long? Will Western politicians keep on flirting with us, the better to sort out their little domestic problems?

'The conservatives are engendered by the internal bases of our life. Their principle is to live as though no foreign country existed. Those foreigners aren't going to lay down the law for us! We don't give a damn for those foreigners! We know what we're about! And by their own lights they're right. They are an abstraction which corresponds closely with the dominant tendency in Ibanskian society towards isolation from Western civilisations. In a word the liberal tendencies in our leadership are superficial, ephemeral and deceptive. They are also adventurous, which puts a powerful trump card in the hands of the conservatives. The liberals, too, are in favour of crushing their opponents, but at the same time they want to look like humanists in the eyes of the West.'

'You are a truly terrible man,' said Journalist. 'You leave no room for illusion or for a gamble. Yet those are things which you need in life.' 'Yet, as you see, we're going on living,' said Chatterer. 'Do you call this a life?' asked Neurasthenic. 'Amen,' said Dauber. 'Come and see what I've just done!'

Singer's second letter

When you wander in the woodlands
and the meadows of Ibansk.
Then you feel 't would make no difference
if you'd flitted Over There.
Yes, but if one day you got There
just believe you'd change your tune,
Fondly dreaming, in your exile,
that you were back safe at home,
Where they'd come and stoop and whisper,
'Welcome friend, we bid you welcome,
You have sinned, you are forgiven,
and your slate, we wipe it clean.'
Then your dream becomes a nightmare
and you wake up in a sweat,
And you'd sooner face the gallows
than go back inside Ibansk.

Similarity and dissimilarity

'Look,' said Teacher, 'here are two books. They're both collections of essays. Both on the same subject. This one is American, and this is one of ours. The first is edited and compiled by A, the second by B. They look exactly the same, superficially. But essentially? Who is A? A major scientist. Not at the very top but of considerable stature and widely known. He selected his authors himself, included an important piece of his own work, edited it himself, and got it published on his own account. I'm not saying that it's always that way Over There, I'm just taking this particular book as an example. And who is B? A complete nonentity. A parasite. He latched on to C as co-author. He has no responsibility of any kind. No published work. His function? He is head of a research department. A trusted man. High-ranking. You always need the name of someone like him on the cover so as to know whom to attack if . . . His main job is to prevent any ideological or political error slipping into the text. In the first case A's functions are essentially positive. In the second, B's functions are essentially negative. It might seem that the result adds up to much the same thing. But there is an essential difference in principle. Indeed, one might say that they are diametrically opposed. If you multiply this a million

(629)

times you see the effect on a national scale.' 'I notice,' said Bawler, 'that this collection includes an article by you.' 'What difference does that make?' asked Teacher. 'If my article had been in the American book its effect would have been immeasurably greater even if the article had been a great deal worse.' 'You should have sent it to them,' said Bawler. 'They invited me to,' said Teacher. 'I had a letter from A himself, and I wrote the article for him. But I had to wait so long for permission that the book was published without it.'

Outrageous verse

Outrageous verse is a joke spoken in earnest, but in whose serious intention no-one wants to believe. It appears without warning, bringing with it total clarity or total confusion, leaves deep traces in the soul, but can never be recollected.

'You are constantly wrapped up in your own thoughts,' She said. 'You never pay an attention to me. And that's a mistake. Look at me—I'm pretty. Men turn their heads when I pass them in the street.' 'You are too pretty,' He said.

I would have written you an ode
To praise your eyes, your lovely hair;
Too late, alas, I am betrayed,
Sold by my Friend, no time to spare.
My Colleague has prepared my case;
Interrogation's what I face.

'I like that,' She said. 'We've lost a great poet in you.' 'Yes,' He said. 'But not quite a poet. It's something else. I'm not exactly sure what it is, and I shall probably never know.'

'I'm afraid for you,' She said. 'They'll end up by putting you into a mental home.' 'They will,' He said. 'It's a nightmare,' She said. 'It's a nightmare,' He said.

Faced with such a doctors' pack
Who could fail to quake with fear?
'Now, you bastard, tell us quick
About the congress held last year.'
'Last was it, now are you sure?
Heavens, what a fool I be?'
Feebly giggling where I sit
Hugging myself in misery.

'You should record that on tape,' She said. 'It's not worth it,' He said. 'It could cause you a lot of trouble, for nothing.'

> Enough, enough, the experts yell,
> To go on trial he is unfit;
> He's loony, any fool can tell.
> Let's kill him to restore his wit.

'That's not nothing,' She said. 'Can it really be true?' 'Yes it is true,' He said. 'But there can only be a few like that,' She said. 'Even if there's only one,' He said, 'it doesn't make it any easier for him. It's not a question of numbers. Mankind becomes criminal if it consciously allows that to happen, even in one solitary case.'

> It's unimportant, then we say,
> He's but an isolated case.
> But s'posing he is quite unique
> And no-one comes to take his place?

Who can tell how many peoples have condemned themselves to stagnation and degeneration by exterminating this kind of isolated individuals. The Ibanskian people have driven themselves into an evolutionary cul-de-sac by painstakingly destroying every germ of any real or imaginary opposition.

> Don't try to scare us, we reply,
> With such a stupid little tale.
> We'll build our own new world one day,
> A world in which we must prevail.

On ideology

From the point of view of its role in society, said Chatterer, the official Ibanskian ideology has nothing in common with religion. It is absurd to compare them. The former has not replaced the latter. Religion has been wiped out, but the place which it used to occupy remains a vacuum. Ibanskian ideology grew up from different sources and for different purposes. Religion is a fact of human consciousness which exercises a real influence on people's behaviour. It is a general state of human spirituality. Official Ibanskian ideology is not a state of spirituality. It has no influence on human behaviour. It is indifferent to people's aims and actions. Tell me, who has any interest in knowing that one social formation is replaced by another once in a thousand years, that progress moves in a spiral, and so on? Ibanskian ideology is only a means towards human behaviour. It is a means of making a career, a means of enslavement, of restraint, of brutalising and so on. It does not become man's inner state, something which determines the way he acts. It is merely something that is used by certain people against others, and even here their acts are determined not by the ideology but by other factors. So it is at the very least naïve to regard the official Ibanskian ideology as the source of those evils which Truth-teller talks about. Ibanskian society does have within it in an amorphous state something which can be compared with religion in the role it plays in the life of society. But this is something which is hostile to religion and to religious consciousness. It is an anti-religion, in the proper sense of the word, which is a conscious recognition of the social laws of Existence. These are the unwritten dogmas of anti-religion: you are not a thief until you are caught; each for himself and the devil take the hindermost; attack is the best form of defence! charity begins at home; pull up the ladder, Jack, I'm on board; and so on. It's possible that, some day, some kind of circumscribed religion will be invented for Ibanskian-type societies. Possibly it will include certain elements from both official ideology and the old religions. There is a perceptible need for this, but so far it has been very slight. I am thinking about the attraction that Christianity and Buddhism have for certain people, and particularly the young.

The eighteenth hour

'Our opponents,' said Slanderer, 'only consider our existence here by comparison with life in the West. But our problems should be considered initially on an autonomous basis, quite independently of whether people in the West live well or badly. Surely our objectives cannot be reduced to an attempt to establish an imitation of the Western way of life in Ibansk? Apart from anything else there are some areas where we are ahead of them. And anyway life isn't all milk and honey in the West either. Our official propaganda exploits the fact very cleverly. So food prices have gone up? They've gone up in the West as well. Opponents of the regime have been sent to jail? The same thing happens in some Western countries. Our life does contain something universally human which can be understood without making specific comparisons, and which engenders problems specific to us!' 'That may very well be true,' said Chatterer. 'But we can't simply ignore the West. Our problems are the problems of the West carried to the limit in their Ibanskian form. You talk about problems like food price rises, bad living conditions and so on. But those are not our real problems. Our problems are things like democratic freedoms, the protection of the law for the individual, conditions in which creative activity can flourish, and so on. Whatever happens in the West, the West remains our ally in all this, and our only protection. And this is not merely because they have begun to realise that in this respect their own fate depends on us. When their governments and particular business circles have dealings with Ibansk they themselves become Ibanskoid and try to introduce an Ibanskian state of things into their own countries. There still remain in the West forces which can resist Ibanskian tendencies in the world. It is they who provide the main support for the Ibanskian opposition. You surely are not relying on our own internal forces? They are minute. They have only lasted so long because of support from the West.'

How much time we spend in talk, thought Bawler. Can that really be the only action we're capable of? But what else can we do. At all events they are right in what they say.

'They're right, of course,' said Teacher. 'But do you know what we lack? We lack movement. We're just marking time. For instance we've just been talking. What next? Nothing. In a week we'll have forgotten all about it, and we'll begin to talk about the same thing all over again. Conversations of this kind should be set down in some literary or scientific form, and then we should move ahead. We need a journal. No matter how scruffy and miserable it may be. But it must be free. And as for you, I advise you to write a book and get it published Over There, and damn the consequences. After all, you have got somewhere. You are on the brink of an important discovery. Drop everything else. Cut yourself off for a year and finish what you've begun. You know the kind of effect that it would produce! There'd be nothing they could do to you! Then you could show them! . . .'

I wonder what I would show them, thought Bawler. No, this idea doesn't appeal to me. But what should I do?

(633)

The meeting

'Ibanskians spend a large part of their time in meetings,' said Journalist. 'What are these meetings exactly?' 'They are the greatest invention of civilisation,' said Neurasthenic, 'the highest form of social democracy for individuals who are on the lowest rungs of the social hierarchy. When the total Ism is established, mankind will move into a new cycle of progress whose pinnacle will be the transformation of society into a permanent meeting. And in the stage beyond that, Society will have developed so far that it will become a permanent committee of that meeting, and finally it will become an honorary committee. What happens after that could not be foreseen even by the classics if they were alive today, and they after all were the grand masters in this game.

'The science of meetings (meetingology, let's say) has not yet come into being despite the huge amount of practical experience. But the scientific total Ism does exist, although apparently it has not yet been thought fit to proclaim it as such. It's strange, isn't it? At all events I am making a bid for meetingology. I am the founder of a new science. But unfortunately I won't be able to get any personal benefit from it. And if you betray me I'll get it in the neck.

'So where shall we begin? With a classification. It makes no real difference where we start. My newly created science of meetingology has no clear beginning. It could begin at either end. Meetings are divided into open meetings and closed meetings. Everything that happens at closed meetings is accessible to anyone who wants to know. But even people who take part in open meetings are frequently unaware of what is going on at them. Why is this? Because they spend their time reading and chatting with their neighbours. Nobody can hear anything above the noise. Or there is nothing to see or hear because the proceedings are absurd. A favourite joke among meeting-goers is to declare an open meeting closed, or a closed meeting open. And when meetings are hybrid (the first part open and the second closed) the joke moves into the area of mysticism. After the first half the chairman declares the open part closed and the closed part open. Why do dialectical logicians not use this as an example of the legitimacy of logical contradictions which reflect the actual contradictions of reality? Probably because they can find no reference to this in the prime sources. Yet it is a dazzling example, every bit as good as plus and minus in mathematics.

'A further division of meetings is into regular, periodic gatherings, and extraordinary meetings. Regular meetings are a tedious routine with the one exception where elected bodies present their reports and the meeting then proceeds to elect their replacements. On occasions like this passions are sometimes inflamed in a way very reminiscent of kitchen quarrels in communal apartments of the recent past. But all this is meaningless froth which has an effect on the destiny of only a handful of individuals and is more of a comedy than a tragedy. Extraordinary meetings are summoned to approve decisions taken by supreme authority, to express enthusiasm, to receive information and so on, and also to heap obloquy on those on whom it is directed that obloquy shall be heaped—people like Truthteller, Double-dealer, Slanderer, and so on.

'How is a meeting conducted? It all depends. Here is the procedure. A couple of weeks in advance posters appear announcing that such and such a meeting will be held on such and such a day. On the day of the meeting itself women from the very lowest level of the secret police sit themselves down at the entrance to the hall, armed with sheets of paper, and write down the names of all the participants. These women are generally always the same. This is their normal function. The primary reason for their presence is that a quorum must be established, and secondly absentees must be punished. Some people get themselves registered and then slip off quietly—but they are very few. They're mainly people who have reached a position where there is no danger of retribution, or else a position where they don't give a damn about retribution. So the meeting begins. The committee is elected. It has of course been appointed in advance. To be included in the committee is not merely an honour and a dream of the average Ibanskian, it is a sign. If an Ibanskian is elected to the committee it indicates that he is well seen by authority, and foreshadows the possibility that he might be marked for the top. And if you've been selected in the past and this time you find that you aren't, it shows that something is going wrong. And the gossip gets going, there are knowing smiles, and rumours begin to circulate. The extraordinary thing about all this is that they never get it wrong. Once, just for a joke, I started a rumour like that about Claimant. And what do you think? He was shot down in flames almost immediately. When the president invites nominations for the committee, some previously appointed grey man sticks up his hand and reads out the list he has been given. Normally about half those present are elected. All the bosses. Their most devoted lackeys. The activists. All the young hopefuls and the rising stars. Guests and observers from above. On particularly ceremonial occasions an honorary committee is appointed, including all the highest leaders in a previously established order of precedence. Then the meeting proceeds to a soporific report which is listened to by no-one, or only by a handful of individuals who know in advance that they are going to be praised or blamed. Then follow the interventions from the floor which no-one listens to either. They are made by professional orators or by people appointed in advance. The speeches they make have also been prepared in advance. Silence in the hall and animation among the audience only happen when quarrels break out. But this happens very rarely. They are even rarer than a decent thriller on Ibanskian television. Normally it is never allowed. Then a resolution is adopted. It consists of a preamble which refers to successes and failures, and the resolution itself which talks of the need to increase the successes and to eliminate the failures. The formulation and the adoption of the resolution constitute the main part of the meeting. It is here that people's destinies are decided. Say for instance that you are among those praised. That means that you'll be praised on every occasion and at every level. You've got a chance of being given a bonus. Your pay will go up. You'll get a better apartment. But if you're among those who are blamed, it's curtains. You can look forward to at least a year in the doghouse. It'll go right to the very top. Sometimes it may be over something entirely trivial, but that'll make no difference to the people at the top. All they see is the formal statement. Higher up still echoes are even wider. And you'll hardly have time to turn round before the newspapers are attacking you for your grave error. So the formulation of the resolution is a vitally important matter. It often happens that people spend hours trying to get the word Error replaced in the resolution by the word Oversight. Seen from outside it's a comedy. But in fact it's a drama.

If the first version is accepted that can mean that a man's career is blocked for a clear five years. If he gets the second version it merely means a year in purgatory, and he might get away with it altogether.

'Generally speaking there is a hierarchy of positive and negative appreciations which can be applied to each individual and group. The appreciation of the work of a group amounts to an indirect evaluation of the individuals who comprise that group. For example, it might be noted that such and such a section has permitted an error to creep in. That means that the error has been permitted by the head and by colleague A, who actually controls the section's activity. Appreciations are classified like army ranks—beginning with private soldiers and ending with generals and marshals. The proportions, too, are similar. Incidentally, this is a question which has never been fully studied—the stereotype quality of the hierarchy in every single aspect of Ibanskian life. Even funerals have their own hierarchy. Failings, for example, can be divided into oversight, negligence, underestimations, miscalculations, inadequacies, deficiencies, errors, grave errors, gross errors, unforgivable errors, catastrophic errors and so on. Merits can be divided into improvements, upsurges, revivals, achievements, successes, several successes, notable successes, considerable successes, major achievements, and so on. You have perhaps not noticed that at the meeting we attended together various people were described as Well-known, Eminent, Major, Popular, Outstanding, and so on. These are no mere literary variants. They figure in that self-same hierarchy of appreciation. We have people who are virtuoso specialists on the subject. Look, here's a leading article from the Newspaper. You may see it as empty drivel and demagogy. But for a connoisseur it is an inexhaustible mine of information. It includes dozens of explicit and implicit appreciations. The first task of any Ibanskian careerist is to learn to interpret texts of this kind which have no meaning for the casual reader. You and I may see these texts as mere hollow sounds. But for them they are a handbook for action. So here we have our own complex, highly differentiated and structured system of evaluation, inaccessible to the casual observer, but a clear and habitual guideline for interested parties. This system of evaluation has a close correspondence with our system of real values. You may see all this as terrifying and disgusting details. But for us the struggle for a five per cent pay rise, or for ten more square metres of living space, is a much more acute problem than the kind of battle which goes on elsewhere for a ministerial portfolio or for a crown.

'But I am getting off the subject. What powers does a meeting have? They are at the same time enormous and insignificant. They never go beyond the framework of the affairs and interests of a particular enterprise. And moreover they can only deal with small matters and in a manner imposed from above. We see here the same counterfeit democracy, but one which has a few real consequences, albeit at a trivial level, for people's lives. But in every way which affects the oppression of truly talented or creative people they are omnipotent. If a meeting of your own enterprise or institution brands you with the mark of shame, you are finished. And that is what usually happens unless there are counter-directives from above. For you must accept that if anyone in our society bursts through to the surface, it is only because he has protection from on high.'

History yet to come

Under His Leadership XV the hostile Western encirclement of Ibansk was completely liquidated, and Ibansk was established over the whole surface of the globe. After appropriate re-education and the rectification of their ideological errors, all surviving Western cities were renamed as Ibanskets, with corresponding serial numbers. Paris, for example, was numbered 031/5634 A. And the Parisians should feel grateful for that, because one little English burg (London or Landon, I forget exactly) was completely abolished. The trouble was that they didn't want to part with their Queen. That's a first-class example of the monstrously reactionary character of the exploiting classes of the past! They'd accepted everything, given everything in return, agreed to everything. They'd hung up all the portraits. But they didn't want to drop the Queen. It would be a pity, they said, It's a tradition, they said. At the start we dealt very gently with them. What do you want a Queen for, we said. We're all queens now. All equal. All a whole head taller. But they stuck to that same old story. Tradition, they said. It would be a shame. We're used to her. Traditions? Well, in the end we showed them what traditions were—we gave them some of our own.

At that time the moon was not yet part of Ibansk. It had remained on its own. Of course people had already visited it in the days of capitalism. Houses had been built there, and there were reserves of oxygen. Gardens had been laid out, and a goat had been raised. People were beginning to get used to the idea of living there. But they had hardly got back when Ibansk was established throughout the world. The sciences were brought together in a Pan-Ibanskian worldwide Academy of Sciences. The sciences took off with such a mighty leap that even His Leadership's route to the lavatory was calculated in a computer centre which was linked to every computer in the world. The calculation was carried out very precisely: they showed that His Leadership relieved himself exclusively within a radius of fifty metres from the WC (which, incidentally, was made of solid gold), and on one occasion he very nearly made it to the bowl itself. Every building in Ibansk was stuffed full of newly discovered elementary particles and chromosomes. Outstanding achievements were made in the field of space travel. At the present time even the Pan-Ibanskian Society for the Conquest of the Whole Universe Around the Earth (PISCWUAE) could not have found the moon in the Ibanskian heavens without the help of first-year school children. And as for going there . . . And anyway, there was no point, and for that matter no resources. 'It's of no consequence,' said His Leadership. 'Even without our disinterested help, They'll snuff it soon enough up there. They won't have anything to breathe, ha, ha, ha,' Then someone pointed out to His Leadership that one of our chaps was up there. The Leadership issued a directive ordering him to take charge. 'That's a first-class idea,' said Deputy. 'That way they'll snuff it even quicker.'

When he delivered his report to the next Congress, His Leadership declared: 'We have achieved the most outstanding success in our history in the field of foreign policy. We have eliminated foreign policy altogether. Now we can throw all our efforts into the field of domestic policy.'

Which is what they did.

> The position of a liberal intellectual
> I sip my wine and whisper low
> To the people that I know—
> Friendly forces:
> 'It's all nonsense, clear and plain,
> Where's the truth, I ask again,
> In prime sources?'
> But when I have to make a speech
> Or in the journal write a piece
> About the Ism,
> I find the quote that helps me out
> To prove without the slightest doubt
> Its great charism.
> As I chew my fillet steak
> I laugh to make my shoulders shake
> About our lot.
> The people's, and the leaders' too—
> No freedom, and our pants worn through,
> That's all we've got.
> But if I'm called on to support
> A speaker making a report
> About our riches.
> 'We lead a splendid life,' I'll swear,
> And kick those homegrown slanderers there
> Right up the breeches.

Ibanism and sociology

Relaxation did not come immediately. Although the Boss had died, there was no change for a time. Or rather the reverse. There was a brief outburst of savage cruelty. But the pendulum of Ibanskian history was already beginning to swing towards liberalism. In the initial stage the most avant-garde and educated sociologists began to refer to names hitherto unheard of in Ibanskian pogromology. Of course they continued as before to demolish Western imperialist lackeys. But the circle of demolished sociologists and demolished ideas was of much greater scope. In the second stage, this circle spread even wider. And it acquired a new characteristic. The demolition was not as crude and absurd as that handed out by the dinosaurs of the previous epoch, but much better qualified and intelligent.

Some people were not even demolished, but merely criticised in an academic if rigorous way. That's objectivism, howled the dinosaurs. But soon even they got a taste for the new style, and replaced their old advisers and research assistants with younger people who knew foreign languages. We must use the creative approach, the dinosaurs shrieked. We must develop our science and pose new problems. At the third stage certain little ideas of Western sociologists began to creep in without even being criticised. At first they were smuggled in as ideas belonging to the classics which had been distorted by bourgeois pseudo-thinkers. But progress began to have its way. References to the classics began to decline, and those ideas from Over There started to turn up in their original form in the ideologically (over)prepared Ibanskian press. Sometimes their authors were even referred to by name. Some Ists went so far as to make no reference at all to the classics, and even began to refer to Western sociologists as 'their colleagues'. The dinosaurs of Ibanism realised that the time had come for steps to be taken. But they had not got the necessary resources. And those who had the strength and the ability had not yet risen to a level which would permit them to take any steps. They were still taking examinations, joking about Ibanism and the dinosaurs, talking about progress and spending days on end chewing over out-moded ideas from the West which were regarded as the *dernier cri* in Ibansk.

At first Ibanskian sociologists never travelled to the West, and later began to go there even less frequently. During the Period of Perplexity they started to be allowed out provided that their brains had previously been so thoroughly laundered that nothing remained in them except for the most primitive Ibanist dogma. Although once they got Over There they looked like absolute fools, they derived a certain benefit from their travels. As long as the enemy swears at you and curses you, all's well. That means he's jealous of our success. But if the enemy starts to praise you, then something's gone wrong. Heaven preserve us from the praise of our enemies! So the Ibanskian sociologists did all in their power to see that their enemies did not praise them. And in this at least they scored notable triumphs.

But times changed. It became necessary to go to the West

more and more often without getting your noses rubbed in the shit. It even began to be necessary to let foreigners from the West into Ibansk and to show ourselves off to our best advantage. The dinosaurs of Ibanism learnt a dozen or so new words (words like group, behaviour, integration, stratification and so on), without understanding their meaning, and surrounded themselves with able youngsters who knew languages, could chatter along on any of the fashionable subjects, and who were employed by the Secret Police. These lads soon developed into leading specialists who could represent Ibanskian science on the world stage. They permitted themselves to go to lengths which would never have been dreamt of by even the most radical Ibanskian sociologists. Ibansk was deluged in Western social thought. There was an epidemic of sociological fever. Everyone rushed to get something out of it for themselves without ever going to the heart of the matter or digesting anything properly. Because of all this execrable professional education, incredible platitudinous stupidity, complete amorality, careerism, profiteering and so on, Western sociological thought was distorted into monstrous Ibanskian forms. Anyone who undertakes a serious study of the sociological literature of Ibansk at this period will be amazed by the picture of intellectual decay laid before his eyes. It became clear to all that sociology must be authorised, but in an officially established form under the aegis of Ibanism. So this is what was done.

So began the period of the transformation of sociology into a material force of Ibanskian society. Hundreds of groups, sections and sectors were set up. Hundreds of books were published, hundreds of meetings and symposia held. More than a thousand specialists turned up at the first Pan-Ibanskian symposium. Almost as many went off to the international congress. And there were ten times as many applications for places in the delegation. Sociology turned out to be a most convenient subject. It began to provide magnificent support for the truth of Ibanism, and an excellent demonstration of the superiority of the Ibanskian way of life over all others.

But there was another side to all this, as there is to any great historical movement. First of all, a large part of sociology consigned to oblivion some of the basic truths of the Ism, ignoring them and even making fun of them. Secondly, the

(642)

young careerists, who had started off wishing to make a contribution to science, began to aspire more to positions, degrees, titles, foreign trips, apartments and other benefits, hitherto reserved for the dinosaurs of the Ism in recognition of their long and faithful service, their stupidity and their boorishness. The dinosaurs and the mini-dinosaurs rose in revolt. 'What's all this?' they bellowed. 'They've got their foreign languages, their fashionable little articles and books, their meetings with foreigners, and now they want jobs, titles, villas and apartments! It's unfair!' Thirdly, strange though it may seem, a few real scientific works were to be found bobbing about in the murky waters of sociological charlatanism. It turned out that Ibansk was a fruitful field for sociological experiment. And even the most primitive experiments produce a noticeable effect. It was also noticed that the results of scientific sociological experiments came into conflict with the dogmas of the Ism and with official propaganda. It was this that finally brought matters to a head. One hint from on high was enough to scotch any light-hearted approach to the verities of the Ism. The young careerists swiftly turned into dinosaurs and dinosauresses. But the true scientists and their results, although there were distressingly few of them, were not transformed into anything and paid no attention to any hints. So they had to be nipped in the bud. About this time the conservatives sorted out what was going on, and realised that they could turn out all these high-sounding sociological whatsits within the framework of the Ism every bit as well as the progressives. The authorities decided that the time had come. And a purge was organised. It was led by the young careerists who pointed the finger at those who were to be liquidated. And sociology in Ibansk returned to the bosom of the Ism, but following a spiral track, enriched by new methods of phraseology, careerism and profiteering. The laws of Ibanskian society, invented a hundred years before that society came into being, remained untouched and untouchable, masters if not of life itself, at least of any discussion of life.

Social systems

In the study of empirical systems, wrote Teacher, the main problem is to construct one's analysis in such a way that it is possible to measure the properties of the system and express them quantitatively. In principle all the properties of social systems are susceptible of measurement, even such properties as the execution of orders, individual freedom, responsibility and so on. Incidentally, officially published data are a rich source of such material. The state is not able to preserve in secrecy the most important mechanisms of its social life. If certain data are no longer published, they can be replaced by others. The secret can only be preserved in the complete absence of any data at all about social life. But at what a price? At the price of a total exposure of the most basic essence of society. The more painstakingly social secrets are concealed, the more clearly they come to light.

The parameters (the measurable indices) of social systems fall into positive and negative categories. The positive parameters are those which are neither born nor maintain themselves spontaneously, or do so only to a small extent. Considerable effort is needed to create them or to preserve them. Negative parameters create and perpetuate themselves, or at least need very little encouragement. The difference between them is similar to the difference between cultivated plants and weeds. This distinction does not always coincide with the distinction between bad and good phenomena. These concepts do not imply any judgments, and particularly not moral judgments.

The parameters of social systems can be further divided into constant and variable. The former constitute the basic characteristics of the system. They include, for instance, the parameters of the systematic nature, dimensions, liability, liberty, depth, falsehood and so on. It should be possible to establish specific values for these, which are the constants of the system. This can be done empirically, but I do not rule out the validity of theoretical calculations, which, I believe, are partly of an *a priori* kind.

Every system, for instance, has a systematic constant. This is a value which reduces in a certain proportion all the positive values of the system and increases its negative values. Thus, if you have theoretically calculated that this year the harvest will be X, then the actual harvest will not exceed X/a, where a is the systematic constant ($a \geq 1$). If you plan to complete a building in Y days, it will in fact be finished in Y.a days.

The Book

It is common knowledge that the publication in the West of
Truth-teller's Book was a most important, perhaps *the* most
important event in the history of Ibansk during the Period of
Perplexity. It is indeed true that the Book made a shattering
impression in the West, and did more than any of its predecessors for the formation of Western public opinion about Ibansk.
But who knows how this Book had been written? Such a weight
of documentary and factual evidence was amassed in its preparation that any similar enterprise would have normally needed
at least three or four special institutes, with dozens, maybe
hundreds, of qualified researchers. And Truth-teller wrote it
under conditions of constant surveillance by the secret police;
every scrap of paper which he touched, even by accident, came
to serve as material evidence for anything that came into the
heads of those engaged in Truth-teller's case. And once the
Book had been written, it had to be scrupulously hidden, for
had it fallen into the hands of the secret police, it would have
been immediately destroyed, along with anyone who had taken
a hand in its preparation or its concealment. Finally it had to be
sent to the West, and all the possible ways that used to exist had
been blocked, especially for Truth-teller and members of his
family.

The most remarkable outcome of the Period of Perplexity
was the appearance of people able to solve such a major problem. When people in the West begin to talk about contributions
to Ibanskian literature, about the loss of illusions about the Ism,
about the way in which Ibanskians are beginning to recognise
. . . it makes you want to scream, and scream and scream . . .
Surely they can't be as cretinous as we are! Surely they must see
and understand something at least! After all, if there's been an
explosion, there must have been someone who made the bomb,
put in in the appropriate place, took a decision to detonate it,
and detonated it. Things don't happen of their own accord, and
even less so in conditions when the entire weight of a powerful
state is directed to seeing that this kind of thing does not
happen. Well, forget it. Let us merely accept that it was the
courageous act of one man who had resolved to speak the truth
about a time long gone by.

It is hard to say precisely when Bawler began his systematic study of materials regarding repression in the period of the Boss. By the time he finally met other people of the same kind, he could consider himself a specialist. He had long felt that this was the crux of the matter. This is the point we must start from, he thought. The present social structure of Ibansk must be brought to the eyes of the world in the most incontrovertible way possible, he thought, even in its most appalling and horrifying manifestations, including the mass repression which began in the earliest days of the state of Ibansk and which has never stopped since. We must have concrete facts, figures, documents, eyewitness testimony. On no account must this nightmare be prevented from coming to light. In those days people saw things differently, and could not suppose that words which then seemed just would later be seen as evidence of atrocious crimes. In maybe a dozen years from now our newspapers and magazines may well themselves become prohibited documents because of the terrible indictments they make of society.

And so began those interminable sessions in library archives and that digging through private papers. And Bawler became a tiny cog in the machine which was to spew a flood of paper on to the desk of the man whose fate it was to become in the next few years the greatest citizen of Ibansk.

Privileges

It is reckoned, said Slanderer, that Ibansk is governed by the principle: from each according to his ability, to each according to his labour. It cannot be said that this principle fails to operate in our society. One could indicate many sub-divisions of the life of society where it seems to operate quite openly. But is this principle, even in those cases where it seems to be in operation, a specific characteristic of Ibanskian society? Is it a general principle, or at least a dominant principle? Give me some instances where this principle appears to be applied in Ibansk, and you will see that in Western countries it operates no less frequently and just as scrupulously. But let us leave comparisons on one side, and pose the problem in the following way: what position does this principle hold within our society? I believe that from this point of view its position is of such secondary importance that it is absurd even to regard it as a principle of our society. It is officially inflated because it serves as a cover for what is the true essential principle of society, which derives from the structure of society, and which amounts to a principle of distribution in accordance with social privilege. Our society is a society of social privilege.

Social privilege is an advantage which individuals of a particular kind (and one individual in particular) have over others by virtue of their social position. Not every privilege is a social privilege. For example, people who happen to live by the sea and who make a handsome profit out of holiday-makers, enjoy an economic-geographic privilege, not a social privilege. A youth who is the son of a highly placed official has many advantages over a youth who is the son of a poor creative intellectual. The former, for instance, even if he only gets mediocre results at school, is guaranteed a place in the university or college of his choice. Or rather of his parents' choice, which will be based on considerations of where the greatest personal profit can be gained, and certainly not according to the principle of 'from each according to his ability'. Even if the intellectual's son is brilliant, it is none too easy for him to get into any institute at all, let alone into one which meets his abilities and his interests, unless his parents can pull a string ensuring that the examiners are secretly directed to give him a pass-mark.

Yet the privilege which the first young man has over the second, who may even share a desk with him at school, is not a social privilege; or rather, it is the social privilege of the father rather than of the young man himself. Thanks to these privileges of birth, the young man will acquire his own social privileges. So it can be regarded as a potential social privilege. But lack of time prevents me from going into subtleties of this kind. I shall leave it to you to establish appropriate definitions and complementary classifications.

Western societies also have their systems of privilege. For example, wealth provides an opportunity to acquire an education in accord with the individual's capacity and wishes. But not everyone is wealthy, so it is a privilege. But it is a financial privilege, not a social one. It makes no difference how that wealth has been gained. It may have been stolen, earned, inherited or be the result of social privilege. But the fact of

(647)

having money is not of itself a social privilege. Similarly, a man who has a considerable sum of money, no matter where it comes from, can, if he is a citizen of a Western state, travel abroad anywhere he likes. There again, this is a privilege, since not everyone can afford it. But it is not a social privilege. In order to travel abroad it is not enough, in our country, for the average citizen to have sufficient funds. It is one of our most important social privileges. And as a general rule, the privileged are offered such foreign travel at no cost to themselves.

There is no society without privilege. The chief of a primitive tribe, who is offered the first cut of meat from a newly killed animal, is exercising a privilege, and a very important privilege, within that society. It is important to establish what kind of privilege is typical for a given society, and what part it plays in the life of that society. Our liberals, with their demands for greater freedom of movement around the country and abroad, for greater freedom of speech, of the press, of creative work and so on, are striking at the very roots of Ibanskian society and at its system of privilege. Their wishes are the product of what they have read about the past and about the West, of all their conversations on the subject, and maybe also of what they have seen. But these ideas are alien to Ibanskian social reality.

Social privileges can be divided into official privileges, established by the law or by custom, and unofficial. These latter can be divided into those which are liable to be punished, (or at least censured), and those which are not (or almost not). But there are no strict boundaries. For example, a high salary, a decent apartment, a personal automobile, access to a special restricted food store, free rest homes and so on are legitimate privileges for highly placed officials. But the power to force your subordinates to sleep with you, to steal their ideas, to use your position to get jobs for your friends or promotion for your relatives, these are *de facto* privileges which are not legitimised. They are officially condemned. But do you know of many cases where bosses have actually suffered for exercising this kind of privilege? These privileges are just as secure as legitimate privileges. There are a great many jobs where illicit privileges are the main source of income. This is sometimes even taken officially into account when wages are being calculated, when the wage itself becomes a pure fiction. For instance, wander around the high-class residential quarters and find out how much villas cost and what their owners earn. You will discover that in a very large number of cases the owners would have had to save every penny of their salaries for decades to amass enough to buy a villa.

History yet to come

In the absence of any hostile encirclement it became markedly more difficult to construct the total Ism. For a start there was no-one left to catch up and overtake. And that being the case, there was no longer any need to hurry. There was nowhere left to borrow from, and no-one to seek aid from, no-one to steal discoveries and inventions from, no fashions to imitate, nowhere to seek refuge from the stresses of Ibanskian life or to acquire a few foreign goodies, no-one to blame all your troubles on, no-one to brag about your amazing successes to. In a word, there was no longer that beloved enemy, who had given life at least some degree of interest and meaning. No-one was left but our own people. And our own people? Just the dregs. They weren't even worth talking to about all the things closest to your heart.

There was a wish to disband the army. But what was to be done with such a vast number of well-trained and worthy officers, generals and marshals? And anyway it would be risky. You never know when suddenly! . . . No, the army mustn't be disbanded. Quite the opposite, said His Leadership, here everything should wither away, but by way of reinforcement. And he produced a quotation in his support. And who can argue against a quotation?

Of course in some ways things did get easier. There was no longer any support from outside for the opposition, and nowhere for them to flee to. The opposition as a whole had lost its meaning as there was no audience left to admire its clowning. The slanderous voices of foreign radio stations had all fallen silent. Everything became profoundly boring. On one occasion His Leadership spent an entire evening twiddling the knobs of his radio hoping to find some slanderous voice, no matter how faint and far away, and to hear some mite of truth about Ibansk. But alas there were no voices left at all. When the secret police realised this, they decided to establish on a piece of marshland where no-one wanted to live a Non-aligned Bourgeois Demo-cratic Republic (NBDR) whose area was two square yards, from whose territory slanderous broadcasts were started up and whither it was decided from time to time to expel opponents, to promote a little intrigue and sensation. His Leadership heaved a sigh of relief and delivered a speech in which he called for peaceful coexistence. 'By meanth of peathful competithon we mutht demonthtwate the incontwovertible thuperiority of our total thtwucture,' he said. 'And we mutht not theathe fwom vigilanth. We will perthitht in thtwengthening our defenthes, and we will weinforth our beloved theecret poleeth.' And so they did. And they also reinforced the frontier guards from the interior as there was no longer any exterior left.

The nineteenth hour

Who was the first to have the idea of starting up the illegal typewritten shamizdat journal? It is now quite impossible to find out. A certain informer who was present at that historic meeting reported that the idea was put forward by Bawler, who stubbornly defended it in argument with Idleader, who was tight as a newt and very uncertain what he was talking about. Another informer who was present at the same meeting reported that it was Idleader who put the idea forward, and that Bawler had knocked it to pieces like a child's toy. But in fact there had been no meeting. There had merely been an ordinary get-together with vodka, a tape recorder and the usual conver-sations about the camps and the trials. In fact there wasn't just one get-together, there were several. The informers' reports refer to several different dates. It was pure chance that Bawler turned up on one of these occasions. He had been brought along by She to meet some interesting people and listen to the music. That was the occasion when Brother, who had drunk more than he should, suggested that if all their conversations were recorded and transcribed they would make up a stupendous pamphlet. Brother took out a notebook and started jotting things down. This was a familiar habit of his and no-one paid any attention to it. 'If anything's to be printed,' Bawler said, 'it's going to have to be done properly. Indisputable facts. Documents. And we must find a way of sending it to the West.'

A few months later the first number of shamizdat appeared

and created a sensation. No-one knows who prepared it or who typed the ten copies. It spread throughout Ibansk like wildfire retyped in literally hundreds of copies. So an edition of shamizdat had been published, and nothing out of the way happened. No-one was sent to jail. But the conversations continued. Rumour attributed the edition to Idleader. He did not deny the rumours, and later he even began to believe in them. And he took affairs into his own hands. It must be acknowledged that he put things on a sound footing. Editions of shamizdat became a regular feature of Ibanskian intellectual life.

Colleague, who had at one time known Bawler personally and who had followed his scientific career with close attention, advised Instructor, who was keeping an eye on shamizdat activity, to pay particular attention to him. 'Don't forget,' he said, 'that Bawler is a gifted scientist, well known abroad in his field, and that he knows several foreign languages. He's very cool, resourceful and determined. And he is fundamentally hostile to the Ibanskian way of life.' Good God, thought Bawler, when Brother read this character assessment to him from his notebook. If only I'd been given a reference like that when I was in the forces I'd be a top-ranking test pilot by now or a cosmonaut. And the secret police wouldn't have had to bother their heads about me. My God, what a lot of cretins they are!

Paradoxes of cognition

'I think I can understand why things are going on the way they are,' said Dauber, 'but I can't take it calmly. Truth-teller's false and superficial ideas are sensationally successful and immensely effective. But true and profound ideas of people like Schizophrenic, Slanderer, and even Double-dealer have no notable success or effect. Even the people for whom they have been written receive them with a certain hostility. How can you explain that?' 'You know perfectly well yourself,' said Chatterer. 'True and profound ideas are individual, false and superficial ideas are fit for the masses. People in the mass are inclined to wander into confusion and seek sensation. They find intelligence and profundity both incomprehensible and damaging. The level of understanding is inversely proportional to the number of people seeking to understand. The effectiveness of social ideas is inversely proportional to their scientific level.

Once I happened to be present at a conversation between Truth-teller and Bawler. You remember him, that very bright lad who's been round to your place. They were talking, of course, about the purges. "I take my hat off to your exploit," said Bawler. "I recognise the enormous importance of the work you've done. I've no doubt that your book will be immensely successful, and I acknowledge that it will play a huge part in the history not only of Ibansk but of mankind in general. Yet I cannot accept your conception. Whether you like it or not, the way you present things makes it look as though a cruel and hateful government, with the help of the secret police, has for decades exterminated millions, tens of millions, of wholly innocent citizens. That is a very powerful literary device, but no more than that. I have studied this problem," Bawler continued, "for several years. The process is extremely complicated and confused. It is this very complexity which allowed the Boss and his gang to go about their dirty business with complete impunity, and even with a certain profit, both for themselves and for society. It would be naïve to suggest, for example, that immediately after the Revolution the legitimacy of the new power was acknowledged universally and opposed by no-one. Of course people opposed it, and by methods which were far from legal. You won't deny that there were many rebellions against the new power. And it would be absurd to deny the methods they used. And how many victims have the authorities destroyed from their own ranks! How many times have the executioners exterminated tens of thousands of other executioners! Yet you believe that the victims of the Boss's personal struggle were really the innocent victims of a great criminal! I repeat that the whole process was carried out on many planes and was quite extraordinarily complex. I do not want to impose my point of view on you in any way. I merely think that your ideas would gain if they were complemented by a scientific analysis of the situation, even if it were only an approximation. The book would not lose any of its effect. Quite the opposite. It would be more profound and durable. Even if its sensational impact were a little reduced, that would be a gain rather than a loss. Just think of the future. In a little time the orientation of human consciousness will change sharply. We have to be ready for that. The book must be prevented from

(652)

going out of date as long as possible . . ." And he went on and on in the same vein.' 'That's excellent,' said Dauber. 'Your Bawler is absolutely right. I agree with him in every way. I thought the same thing myself. What did Truth-teller reply?' 'Nothing,' said Chatterer, 'he only smiled. When Bawler had gone, Truth-teller said to me that that was exactly the way the secret police saw things, that in his view Bawler was working for them, a view which his many years of prison experience and intuition confirmed, and that many people believed Bawler to be an informer . . . Brother, for example. . . .' 'He's off his head,' said Dauber. 'No,' said Chatterer, 'it's simply that in this society it's impossible to sort people out rationally. It's not a question of whether he's right or not. Circumstances turn out in such a way as to confirm his irrational ideas. Don't go thinking that he's being cunning and calculating. He sincerely believes that his ideas are true down to the last full stop. It is simply that his ideas coincide with the collective madness of our society. And that is where their strength lies.'

Foreign apolitics

'He's gone abroad again,' She said. 'Ah well, it might all be for the best.' 'Of course,' He said. 'God grant him good health. Personally, I'm for.'

> Our Leader-Father, we all bellow,
> Is a simply splendid fellow.
> Always dashing overseas,
> Now to Paris, now to Nice.
> Not wasting time in consultations
> He sagely leads negotiations,
> Signs alliances with some,
> With others treaties. Oh what fun!
> And kissing other heads of state
> Will often solve the great debate.
> Some he batters, some he bribes,
> Some he cheats with hooded eyes.
> And joking with the middle classes
> He comes back home to rule the masses,
> To guide us with his steady hand
> . . . .
> That's why freedom here is banned.

(653)

The school

'I was a pupil in this school myself,' said Teacher, 'and then I taught here for a few years. I want to show you two curious things. The first is a laboratory attached to the Pedagogical Academy. They're studying new teaching methods, and experimenting. At the moment the children in the reception class are learning tensorial calculation right from the start. And this is a closed-circuit television system to observe what goes on.' 'What kind of results are they getting?' asked Bawler. 'Brilliant,' said Teacher. 'The director of the laboratory has been elected to the Academy, and his deputy has been made a corresponding member. It's being talked about all over the world. There's an idea they might be given a prize.' 'That's not what I mean,' said Bawler. 'Oh, you mean the other thing,' said Teacher. 'They're looking for a panacea that does not and cannot exist. All there can be is some kind of counterfeit which'll come in handy for reports and propaganda. Something like educational maize. The headmaster understands that perfectly well. He's an exceptional man, a complete solitary, who has no belief in any Ism. Yet at the same time he's obliged to be at the centre of stupefying Ibanskian formalism. You've no idea what the life of our headmaster is like, and still less of what life is like for a good headmaster. I don't understand how he manages to go on from year to year. But if there weren't people like him, we'd be back in the wild state in no time at all. Incidentally the director of studies flung himself out of that window not long ago. He was a war veteran, a first-class teacher and the children adored him. But he was the victim of intrigue, gossip and slander. They got him in the end. He couldn't hold out. He had broken a basic rule of our school: a teacher must be well thought of but should not stand out of the mass as anyone exceptional. Compared with him all the rest looked grey, untalented nonentities. They couldn't stand that. We're in a paradoxical situation. Official ideology preaches collectivism. But true collectivism is in reality counter-productive. It is even more alien to this society than individualism. Individualism runs counter to the bases of society and is officially punishable. Collectivism strips the mask off society. But it is officially recognised. That is why it is punished on the sly and stifled in silence, and then praised in every way.'

(654)

When they talked with the headmaster Bawler was struck by his desperate fatalism. 'So what if I am not allowed to give anyone a mark lower than C, or to exclude weak pupils, or to make them repeat a class? It doesn't matter. It's not important. What if the teachers are weak and the curriculum full of absurdities? It doesn't matter. It's not important. The laboratory? New methods? It doesn't matter. It's not important.' 'But what *is* important?' asked Bawler, and immediately realised that it was a stupid question. The headmaster shrugged his shoulders. 'First of all you tell me in precise terms what you find unsatisfactory about school education and its results,' he said, 'and then I might be able to say something sensible. Because the problem is that all official claims for the school are fictitious. And any attempt to improve things is a fiction as well. It's not true to say that the schools don't meet the demands of higher education. Higher education institutes are unable to establish with any precision what their demands are. It is a falsehood to say that the schools are lagging behind modern knowledge. In many respects modern knowledge itself is a fiction. I repeat that this isn't the problem. School isn't merely a way of preparing people to receive an education and a speciality. School is a sphere of social life which is subject to the same rules as society as a whole. It is a reflection of society with all the same characteristics and problems, which vary only in proportion to the age and the position of the citizens. If I were to take you into a classroom what would you see? Pupils? Average? Weak? Strong? Brilliant? No. That is of no importance. You would see A, who is bound to get into the Institute of International Relations. He is a miserable, grey, mendacious and thoroughly repulsive child. Yet everyone pussyfoots around him. Why? Because of his papa. And on his left sits B. He is a downright careerist and demagogue. He knows where he's going. He'll be found a job, he will always be accepted, received, transferred, posted, and so on. Need I go on? This year fifty pupils will leave our school. Are there many who could become top-ranking scientists? Two or three. And they have learnt more in school than many elderly doctors of science. They have taught themselves. The school doesn't really matter to them. Indeed the old style would have suited them better. One of them is a quite exceptionally gifted boy. But, alas, he won't get into university, and he knows it. You may say that's a great loss to science. It is. But does that depend on the school? I could tell you a great deal more, but I am afraid I am too busy at the moment. Come and see me again some time. You were in the air force, weren't you? So was I. But I was in bombers; a navigator.'

'Well?' asked Teacher. 'I am very sorry for him,' said Bawler. 'He is a real man. That's why he will never throw himself out of a window.'

Singer's interview
Somewhere far away in space,
Very close to heaven's gate,
Lives a brilliant, stupid race
In a crowded, lonely state.
Foolish yet intelligent,
Obdurate yet indolent,
Happy and unfortunate,
Majestic and despicable,
Most substantial yet devoid,
Transparent yet insoluble,
Complicated, yet a void.
Quite unable to escape
From its triumphs and disgrace,
Yet it lives at heaven's gate
This negligible, mighty race.
Gallant and yet cowardly,
Generous yet niggardly,
A servile and rebellious race,
Humble folk and yet vindictive,
Pliable yet arrogant,
Clumsy, feckless and inventive,
Hasty and yet hesitant.
Waiting for their paradise
One fine day, in the year dot.
Trusting nobody's advice—
How the people bloom and rot!
Sleepy and yet vigilant,
Kind and yet malevolent.
They're a proud yet servile lot.

(656)

Cautious yet improvident,
Thoughtful and yet talkative,
Bungling and yet competent,
Quite farsighted, yet naïve.
They'll achieve their goal tomorrow,
Heaven's gates will open wide;
They'll get drunk from joy and sorrow
When they're safe and snug inside.
Laughing happily yet tearful,
Gloomy, sad, yet not uncheerful,
Hard oppressed but also free.
Open yet inscrutable,
Militant and yet resigned,
Sated yet insatiable,
All-seeing, and yet ever blind.
Any attribute you please
Which you ever could envisage
Can at once with greatest ease
Fairly be ascribed to them.
Yet if ever you dare try
To present them with your case,
Swiftly they'll give their reply
With a punch right in the face—
This sensible, senseless,
Oppressive, defenceless,
Imperial, persecuted race.

Privileges

The principal mechanism for the distribution of things of material and spiritual value, and of everything which is of general interest to the consumer, said Slanderer, is distribution according to social privilege. The principle here is: to each according to his social position. There are of course a whole mass of circumstances which prevent this principle from being applied in its pure form and which make its operation seem obscure. These include, for example, cases where distribution is made according to work done, to cheating, to machinations, to abuse of office, to talent or to inheritance, to parasitism, and so on. But I repeat that the basis and the axis of the distribution system in our society is the system of social privilege and of distribution according to the social position of individuals. It is for this reason that the essence of our social life is a bitter struggle for an enhancement of social position and social privilege. And as there is a tendency for the various social strata to become hereditary institutions, the struggle takes on truly stupefying forms, since it concerns the fate of a whole tribe of one's children and one's children's children.

From this point of view the much propagandised concern for the well-being of the workers is just as much an ideological myth as is the principle of 'to each according to his labour'. It cannot be said that it does not exist. But what exactly is it? In part it is the professional activity of a great number of people who make their living by it, for instance construction firms, hospitals, and so on. It is absurd to think that an architect or a doctor exists for the benefit of the workers. The correct scientific formulation would be that this group of people exists thanks to the existence of this sphere of activity. Concern for the well-being of the workers is also a means by a certain category of people in their struggle for their own position and advancement. By displaying concern for the workers, leaders win themselves a reputation and keep themselves in power. But for the most part it is ideological propaganda and demagogy whose aim is to preserve the *status quo*.

One task for a scientific theory that could be constructed out of this would be to clarify the consequences inevitably deriving from the situation. In particular the main motivation for the most active part of society becomes the achievement of a high level of consumption, not as a result of personal talent or personal effort but by way of a struggle for more advantageous social positions in accordance with the laws of this struggle which have nothing to do with talent or effort. As a result, society will tend to lose its creative potential. It is my belief that this society is profoundly hostile to all aspects of creative phenomena.

The principle of distribution which I have set out is neither a manifestation of some kind of natural justice nor the result of arbitrary legislation. It is the result of the combined effect of a mass of voluntary actions, and it constantly reproduces itself and consolidates its hold on customs, laws, habits and so on. It is simply that people who hold a particular social position appropriate the largest slice of the cake which their strength permits. Everyone seeks to acquire the maximum available to him according to his position. The biggest slice at the lowest cost is the sacrosanct principle of this society, disguised as concern, generosity, kindness, justice and so on.

Thus Ibanskian society is a highly complex, differentiated and hierarchical system of privilege. A whole complex power system is called upon to preserve and reproduce this system of privilege. Ibanskian culture, for its part, creates a system of falsehood which camouflages this very prosaic life and represents it as general equality, justice and prosperity.

I have deliberately said nothing about the first part of the principle under consideration (from each according to his abilities) since it is ambiguous. If by 'abilities' it refers to the ability to make one's way in life, the principle is just. There is no need to persuade people to do that. But if it means the natural ability to produce things of spiritual and material worth, we must then assert that these are not social privileges and are permitted only to the extent that they do not jeopardise social privileges.

The price of experience

'The book is finished,' said Truth-teller. 'Now what?' 'We must hide one copy here,' said Friend, 'and send another Over There.' 'It would be better to have two copies here and two There,' said another Friend. 'Just as an insurance.' 'I'll hide one copy,' said Friend. 'And I'll hide the other,' said Brother. 'But how can we get copies out?' asked Truth-teller. Brother mentioned Bawler. 'It's true,' he said, 'that there's something about him I don't like. What do you think?' Truth-teller asked Friend. 'Our years in prison have taught us how to assess people's characters. We can't afford any mistake.' 'I've got my doubts about him too,' said Friend. 'Well that's that then,' said Truth-teller. 'But perhaps we could string him along a bit. I've got an idea,' he laughed. 'Let's type out Writer's last novel. Bawler can try and get that out!' The idea appealed to everybody. They all laughed merrily, imagining the expression on the faces of the secret police when they . . .

And so it was decided. Taking one copy of the Book, Brother rushed off to his friends in the secret police. 'It's a stupendous

Book,' he said. 'Truth-teller must be helped.' 'We'll help him,' said Colleague. 'Leave it with me so I can read it.' 'I can't,' said Brother. 'It's the only copy, and he's entrusted it to me personally.' 'Well get some photocopies made,' said Colleague. 'We'll bear the cost.' 'O.K.', said Brother. When he'd made several copies, Brother slipped one to Journalist, another to somebody else, and lost the third when he was drunk. He took the rest round to Colleague. Colleague was busy and passed Brother on to Instructor. Instructor was just off on holiday and postponed the whole matter until he got back. When he returned from holiday and began to read the Book it struck him as being a tiresome nuisance. He didn't know exactly how to approach it or how to incriminate it. And he sent the Book for an opinion to those two civilian experts Sociologist and Thinker. Sociologist, who had a very high estimation of his own highly qualified conclusions, was never in a great hurry to produce them because in delaying he could increase his fee. And he put the Book on one side with the intention of dealing with it in a month's time. He didn't even look to see who had written it. Thinker had a deep and committed hatred for Truth-teller on account of his own complete lack of talent. He leafed through the Book and wrote a short opinion in which he observed *en passant* (among a mass of meaningless sentences about world literature) that this was typical rambling on the theme of the camps. So the normal routine procedures began, in the course of which the Book somehow or other managed to slip through to the West. And only Brother, who had taken to calling repeatedly on Colleague, was able to explain to him with some passion what Truth-teller's new book was about. Colleague's son borrowed it for a night. He gathered his friends together and regaled them with this new book about the camps. 'We've really taken them for a ride,' Truth-teller said to his Friend. 'Yes,' said Friend, 'no-one can deny us that! Our prison experience has been of some use after all.'

A hymn to the meeting
'Just imagine,' He said, 'Double-dealer has had a tremendous critical drubbing at a meeting. The things that people said about him! They were mainly friends and colleagues of his

who'd known him for twenty years or more.' 'He'd have done better to have told them to stuff themselves and not go to their meeting,' She said. 'He couldn't,' He said. 'They wouldn't have given him his reference.' 'He should have told them to stuff their reference,' She said. 'Without a reference he wouldn't have been allowed to leave, or at the very least they'd have held him back for another year.' 'It's a monstrous absurdity,' She said. 'After all, what do our meetings really add up to?' 'Nothing,' He said. 'But in cases like this it is an omnipotent nothing.'

> Oh, the comradeship of meetings!
> Youthful dreams of far away.
> A girl beside you. Murmured greetings.
> Smoke-filled rooms on meeting day.
> There's the bell. The early warning.
> Some rush off to have a pee.
> They would never last the morning,
> So they seek the lavatory.
> Others dash from near and far
> To grab a sandwich from the bar.
>> Oh, the effort of a meeting!
>> Joys of early middle age.
>> Everlasting dull orating;
>> Smells of sweat my nose enrage.
> Now we're getting tired of waiting;
> People shout and start to laugh.
> Someone tries to calm the meeting.
> 'Kindly fill the chief's carafe.'
> Then a silence, which must mean
> Our fat director has been seen.
>> Oh, the torture of a meeting!
>> Bound to cause some heart attacks.
>> Hear the speaker's weary bleating
>> And the grovelling of the hacks.
> Take your seats. On your agenda
> Item One. 'Presidium.'
> Round the hall some lackey wanders—
> Ballot sheets for everyone.
> Who's elected? Never fear:
> Just the same as every year.

Oh, the boredom of a meeting!
Yawns, and now and then a snore.
Demagogy means repeating
What we've heard ten times before.
The meeting now is in a doze,
The occasional joke disturbs its rest,
And the informer notes down those
Who don't show much interest.
And the usual bunch of creeps
Clear their throats before their speech.
    Oh, the zeal we show at meetings!
    Desperate tries at exhortation:
    Give the vote they've been entreating,
    Be it praise or condemnation.
The hall awakes, for now's the time
To draw up the resolution,
And all are eager—that's no crime—
To present their own solution.
The squad of trusty party might
Makes certain that it turns out right.
    Oh, the waste of time of meetings!
    They go on throughout the years.
    We submit to annual beatings,
    So democracy endures.

'At least,' She said, 'he's well off Over There without any meetings.' 'Yes,' He said. 'But he writes that it's very boring without meetings.'

The twentieth hour

According to rumour, from the very beginning the secret police had controlled shamizdat, and fifty percent of the output was their own invention. But why, one might well ask, would the secret police behave in this way? To give themselves a long-range target? But they are capable only of point-blank aim, and then only when the victim is defenceless. There are plenty of informers everywhere. Informers' reports about the first steps of shamizdat could only be read by the secret police after the case against shamizdat had already been opened, i.e. not less than a year later. And what could they have fished up from this sea of reports and the testimonies of shamizdat members? It's nothing but a joke, an oddity. And on top of that, the secret police is a typical Ibanskian institution which works according to the general rules of official Ibanskian institutions, i.e. badly and unproductively. And the grounds of their investigation proffered much the same picture. It appears that even an opposition organisation in Ibansk can live only according to the general rules of Ibanskian society. This fact was referred to even by representatives of certain foreign embassies and foreign journalists. These organisations have imperceptibly acquired the spirit and the letter of Ibanskian institutions and citizens. Finally, all the enormous documentation amassed by the secret police was not worth tuppence in the absence of the necessary internal connection between the actions (duly verified) of the shamizdat associates and the content of their published material, while each of these two elements contained absolutely nothing which could lead to prosecution in the courts. Despite the mass of material there were no grounds for a trial. There was material in plenty for the normal practice of punishment within the system of Ibanskian society. There was enough to deal with thousands of people. But from the juridical point of view this material was completely inadequate. It would have been difficult to squeeze out of it enough to underwrite even a pathetic little trial of two or three people. Surely Idleader and his group must understand that, thought Bawler. That is their only salvation: to keep within the limits of the law, and to insist on the limits of the law. But that can only be done at a high price: at the price of confessing their guilt and recanting. But they could have got round to that. The authorities could not have disposed of everybody in the same way that they disposed of me. There would necessarily have been a trial anyway. They have made an error, the usual one. They have conceded, and justified this concession by the possibility of a trial. But this possibility would have existed even had they not made their concession. Indeed without the concession, it would have been even more certain. No, this concession was not calculated. It was a reflex, and it merely displayed weakness. Incidentally, why bring them to trial at all? They had after all done something, something real and serious. It would have been better to forgive them for their weaknesses. They are, after all, people, and Ibanskians for good measure.

The choice of viewpoint

'In the end everything depends on the choice of one's point of view,' said Soilophagist. 'That's true,' said Teacher. 'But the choice of one's point of view does not lead to the acknowledgement or the rejection of specific pre-established judgments. It can also mean the choice of phenomena to be examined. Let us take for instance the business of Knacker, Selector and Geneticist. Now, according to you, this is the way it happened. The incredibly evil and stupid Boss had an ambition to destroy agriculture and science and so decided to elevate the charlatan Knacker and to eliminate those eminent scientists Selector and Geneticist.' 'I think nothing of the kind,' said Soilophagist. 'That's a pure caricature of my point of view. I am merely saying that that is what objectively happened.' 'What do you mean "objectively"?' asked Teacher. 'Let's leave value judgments aside. Let me just give you a small chunk of reality. The Boss knew that agriculture was in a difficult position. You didn't need to be a great mind to realise that. And he knew, too, that Selector and Geneticist were major scientists. But what was their science producing at that time? Even today it can only make promises without producing any significant practical conclusions. And at that time it was reckoned that Selector's research would have an effect in twenty or thirty years time, and Geneticist's work in fifty years at the very least. And something had to be done immediately. A miracle was needed. The people were desperate for a miracle. And the only thing the government could rely on was a miracle. And suddenly this miracle came along in the shape of Knacker. A man of the people. A man who promised mountains of gleaming gold just around the corner. Was he a charlatan? Who can tell? That was the kind of thing that was being said behind the scenes and in the corridors by specialists. Nothing was said aloud. Was it that they were frightened to speak out? Yes. But not only that. They were not fully confident of their own science. They were not fully confident that this was a pseudo-science. What if he were right? What if he suddenly turned up trumps? And if rumour was anything to go by his experiments were turning out right. And what about the Boss? Because Knacker had been his choice, there could be no other option. As a social phenomenon, he came in most handily. The Boss was a tribal chief. That wasn't just *agitprop*. A tribal chief is a very specific social phenomenon in the field of power. He was a true tribal chief. At all events he felt intuitively that the main thing was to control men's minds. And no matter what Knacker actually was, he needed him as something to get things going. Knacker, the miracle worker. So he was put on a pedestal. The people believed in him, i.e. they believed that everything would be all right. It was the correct social solution to an economically insolluble problem. And the rest was the usual kind of show. Selector, Geneticist and the rest despised the regime of the Boss and the Boss himself. Indeed they were his enemies. They were a nuisance to a lot of people. They could be blamed for the famine and for the agricultural disaster. Their elimination was wholly in the spirit of the times.' 'That is pure apologetics,' said Soilophagist. 'No,' said Teacher. 'It is you who are the apologist. You say that all this squalor is a deviation from the norms of our society, and that it must be combatted by strengthening society. But I tell you that all this squalor is an entirely healthy product of our society, and that the very foundations of our society must be undermined if forces capable of resisting this squalor are ever to be produced.' 'You are a dangerous man,' said Soilophagist. 'In that case,' said Teacher, 'it's high time to denounce me.'

History yet to come

Under His Leadership XIV money was abolished. The result was that money fell into alarmingly short supply. Any miserable three-rouble note cost a fortune. And people literally fought to get their hands on foreign currency because it could be used to buy things that were more or less decent. 'Screw them all,' said one extremely conscientious Ibanskian in an interview granted to his no less conscientious drinking companion. 'At least in the past you could get your hands on a bit of cash. Now we won't even have that. They might at least have left us enough to buy fags and booze. We'd have managed without canapés if we'd had to.'

The rule of His Leadership XV saw a tremendous burgeoning of medicine. It was discovered how to prolong the lives of Their Leaderships to five hundred years, and those of their Deputies to three hundred. The scientists were given the job of finding a way of stretching the lifespan to a thousand years. 'This 'ere li'l ma'er,' said His Leadership, 'is puffickly strite forwid nowadize.' In the country at large the life expectation of the average Ibanskian, as had been established by observations from artificial satellites, was increasing at a rate of 0.0001 milliseconds per year. For achieving such an hitherto undreamt of precision a large number of research workers attached to the Academy of Sciences were awarded decorations and bonuses. 'Our science,' said the President in his speech of thanks on behalf of the fortunate award winners, 'has surged forward into world leadership thanks to this, the greatest discovery of the century. Our task now is to overtake the NBDR in the field of science as well as in everything else.'

Scales were established for diseases and for sexual potency. Depending on their rank, members of the ruling classes were exempted from diseases of certain categories and were granted certain levels of sexuality. His Leadership was exempted from all diseases, with one exception we shall refer to later, and was accorded absolute sexual potency. The same kind of thing happened with food and drink. So, starting from the level of company director, a member of the ruling classes could spend all day fornicating with up to fifty women, pouring liquor down his throat (up to a hundred bottles of one hundred star cognac), and consuming tons of food in short supply of a quality which was hard to find even in the restricted shops for the privileged. It became the fashion to stroll the streets with your flies undone and your snout smeared with red caviar. There was only one disease which offered a stubborn resistance to any kind of treatment—feeble-mindedness. Indeed, feeble-mindedness grew more prevalent among the ruling classes with rank and age, at the highest levels reaching a state where they needed a computer to work out twice two. But this was only a minor difficulty, for we were, after all, in the white heat of the scientific and technological revolution! The computers, however, could not tackle this task without external help and persistently made the same mistakes, like eighteen-year-olds who are never going to make it out of the first form. So the philosophers brought their minds to bear on the matter. With the help of references to the prime sources they demonstrated that this was not feeble-mindedness at all, but the development of a kind of super-genius which had begun in the time of the classics and which had now achieved, in the person of our well-beloved super-super-super-super-genius, His Leadership, a truly glorious heyday.

Singer's third letter
From now until I'm in my grave
I'm condemned to spend my time
Here in exile, boredom's slave,
Drinking Their weak bitter wine.
It's true there's clothes and food to spare,
And so much freedom you feel sick,
But that's all crap, I truly swear,
All dreamt up as a filthy trick.
Oh, could I only live like you,
Retaste the life where I began,
And stand for ages in a queue,
Or read about some fulfilled plan,
Or hear at meetings those abstruse
Inspiring speeches by the score,
Or be condemned, on some excuse,
To five years' jail, or maybe more!

The twenty-first hour
When shamizdat became a universal topic of conversation, and to read it became a sign of good breeding among the liberal intelligentsia, the student class, literate members of the most highly placed institutions and among the families of the supreme leadership, General presented himself to Minister and reported that he had certain evidence which led him to believe that something suspicious was happening. It appeared that the routine exchange of information with Western intelligence services had produced documents suggesting that a certain shamizdat was operating on Ibanskian soil. A bourgeois reactionary journalist (which means he is someone you can trust) had reported, in his application to visit the region of Cosmodrek, that he had handled a copy of a shamizdat publication. Minister ordered an enquiry to determine first who the organisers were, and to collect all the editions published so far. This

turned out to be not quite as easy as anticipated. Although lists of the names of the organisers and activists of shamizdat had been lying in the files, the archives, the drawers, the cupboards, the safes and the shelves of the all-powerful secret police for many years; and although they had been systematically checked and up-dated by dozens of professional employees and hundreds of voluntary informers; although every listener to foreign radio stations broadcasting in Ibanskian knew off by heart the names of every shamizdat organiser, it was nevertheless necessary to establish a special group of operatives and to implement all the rules of search and surveillance. Droves of special agents began to sneak around the streets of Ibansk by night, listening to the thunder of typewriters and searching the dustbins for pieces of carbon paper. Samples of type were taken from every typewriter, and every typist had to produce a specimen of her fist. In every office typewriters were put in locked covers for the night. In a word, a mighty work was put in hand, of which only an Ismatic society would have been capable, and which was a silent testimony to its manifest superiority over bourgeois society. And in only a few years an approximate list of shamizdat organisers was produced. By some strange misunderstanding Idleader himself was not included, but Bawler was. One day, at a party given by Sociologist, the head of the group of special agents met Idleader and told him everything. Idleader asked to see the list and made a few corrections. 'To start with,' he said, 'why aren't I here? After all, I'm the boss, the onlie begetter and the soul of the whole business. And secondly, what's Bawler doing on your list? He's a very dubious character. He's a downright villain and, in my view, an informer. Of course he is. He's certainly nothing to do with shamizdat. And he'd better not try to climb aboard the bandwagon.' In the end a list of shamizdat activists was established. They included five civilian members of the secret police, ten informers, and a few dedicated opposition members. Idleader was accepted as the undoubted mastermind. This was a great victory for the secret police, indeed the greatest in their history, since this was the first time they had had to deal with a real organisation, not a counterfeit of their own.

The business of gathering in all the copies of shamizdat publications went rather worse. Sociologist and Colleague both

(668)

had complete sets. But these were valuable exhibits in their private collections of anti-Ibanskian literature, and they were very reluctant to part with them. In theory Idleader's secretary, a secret police agent from the very inception of shamizdat, should have had a full set as well. But when the screws were put on him, it turned out that he had sold them on the black market to an attaché from a foreign embassy in exchange for foreign currency. Minister's son and General's daughter had a few individual copies. But the former said he wouldn't part with them except in exchange for a Japanese tape recorder and a complete collection of Singer's songs on tape, and the latter's price was a tourist trip to Italy. Their demands had to be met. The missing editions were bought for foreign currency in the West, or borrowed temporarily from Idleader, with a promise that they would soon be returned.

When he had scanned the material and discovered what it contained, Minister was horrified and dashed off to Leader. Leader was even more alarmed, and immediately set up an extraordinary and secret meeting, which the rest of Ibansk knew about the following day, and which the foreign radio stations reported an hour before it was convened. And what's more, the radio commentator forecast what the decision would be, and introduced an eminent lawyer, a specialist in this kind of case. The lawyer said that according to Ibanskian law, the only people who could be brought to book were the typist and a couple of girls who had often been seen when the publications were being handed out, and whom the readers could clearly identify. Leader, Minister and others listened most attentively to the foreign radio station. 'Yes,' said Leader, 'the situation is complicated. On the one hand it can't be allowed. And on the other we can't let it slip by. We're going to have to bargain with the bastards. If we put too much pressure on, they'll raise merry hell and wreck everything. It's all got to be legal.' 'That's true,' said the Deputy for ideology. 'We'll have to catch them red-handed at the scene of the crime and set up a big trial keeping very close to the rule book.' To give him his due, the Boss was a past-master at that. Minister had a good grasp of the matter and gave the appropriate instructions to General. General called in Colonel who gave Major the job of drawing up the plan of the operation.

Major, who had just had the pleasure of watching a film in fifty episodes about the brilliant work of the secret police, prepared an original plan. It was ingeniously simple and Colonel was delighted with it. Colonel recalled a few scenes from the film which Major had forgotten, incorporated some of them in the plan and took it to General. General, who had seen the film on his personal television set, which was kept in a special safe to which only he and Minister had keys, was delighted with the plan. Minister prepared the plan under his own personal direction and made a different general responsible for its execution, after reprimanding the first one for turning his work in late and ill prepared. The operation was given the code name Duplicating Machine.

Duplicating Machine envisaged the infiltration of the West by fifty well-trained agents of local origin but maintained by us. Some of them were to become major capitalists, some of them politicians, some Western secret agents, some, advisers to heads of state, and some were to be important writers and artists. The plan was also to set up in Ibansk an underground organisation made up of secret police agents which was to publish anti-Ibanskian tracts. To ensure that this group could win the necessary confidence, the leaflets were to contain nothing but the truth, and if possible genuine opponents were to be drawn in. If none came forward, Colleague was to create them artificially by refusing permission to cultural and scientific workers to go abroad, by banning the publication of inoffensive books and so on. Once the activity of this organisation became known in the West, one of the secret police agents infiltrated in the West was to come to Ibansk as a tourist, meet an agent member of the underground organisation and propose to send him a portable duplicating machine from abroad to set up a clandestine press. It would be at this point that the idea should be mooted of joining up with shamizdat and printing their publications on the underground press. Active members of shamizdat were to be associated with the organisation. Once the underground press had printed a shamizdat edition, they would all be arrested at the scene of the crime. The entire operation was to be filmed by concealed cameras which were to be installed in advance in appropriate places.

Operation Duplicating Machine was brilliantly executed

according to plan with the exception of one insignificant detail. When Idleader said there was a chance of getting hold of a portable duplicating machine and putting the publication of shamizdat works on a firm footing, Bawler said that that was a blatant provocation. But no-one paid any attention to him. Idleader said that even if it were a provocation, all the more reason for exploiting it. 'They won't do anything to us anyway, because times have changed. And anyway it'll create an enormous effect!' 'All right,' said Bawler, 'go ahead if you like. But I wash my hands of you and I won't play along with you any more.' 'You go and get the duplicating machine,' said Idleader, 'and then we'll see. It might well be that we ourselves will ask you to quit. There are rumours that you've got yourself involved in some dirty little deals on the side.'

So Bawler took some unpaid holiday and went off to a border town with two informer members of the underground press to get the duplicating machine. Everything was already prepared. But Bawler played a trick which disturbed the normal course of events. Half an hour before the appointed time, he asked a porter to bring his suitcase, (explaining how and where to find it). The porter brought the suitcase which contained the duplicating machine, and Bawler boarded the first train to come along, slipping a handsome tip to the guard. While mobs of informers were wandering round the frontier town in search of Bawler and the duplicating machine, Bawler was peacefully lying in his berth in the sleeping car of an international train, telling himself that it was really time to break with these cretins and riff-raff. They had started off flirting with revolution and had turned into the worst kind of shit.

When he got back to Ibansk, Bawler took the duplicating machine round to Idleader's apartment. Idleader was horrified. We could get years for this, he said, and had the machine taken to his secretary. His secretary took it round to the secret police depot, but there they refused to accept it because it had no way-bill. 'Do you take me for a fool?' said Idleader's secretary. He shoved the suitcase under the stairs and went off to finish the current edition of shamizdat. The secret police charged all over the place in the search for the missing duplicator, without which the whole carefully planned operation would collapse. They haven't found it to this day. But time was pressing. So

Minister shrugged his shoulders and ordered that they should be brought to trial with what evidence they had.

History yet to come

Frontiers began to be wiped out way back in the days of the Boss. But the process of wiping them out completely did not begin until the present time. Until now there'd been too much else to do. The first to go were the frontiers between the town and the country. The result was that part of the country fled into the cities and the other part stood in line for meat, eggs, sprats and other industrial products in the city shops. And it's still standing in line to this day, waiting. There'd been a promise that it would get something thrown to it sooner or later. The next frontiers to go were those between intellectual and manual labour. As a result gifted scientists began to earn almost as much as charwomen, house-painters and caretakers. This was such a mighty achievement that His Leadership delivered a special speech about it. 'We, as you might say, er, er, this . . . er . . . em . . . em . . . er . . . on the whole . . . em . . . er . . . have . . . er . . . er . . . achieved . . . er . . . as you might say . . . em . . . er . . .,' he said, '. . . er . . . em . . . whatcher-mecall'ems . . . er . . . these . . . em . . . scientists . . . after all . . . er . . . they're . . . er . . . em . . . merely people . . . er . . . like . . . er . . . .'

Finally, under the next His Leadership, work began on the elimination of the frontiers between men and women. Women were allowed to wear trousers, smoke, drink cognac, cuss, and run the country. Men were allowed to wear their hair long, cut their finger nails and occasionally change their underwear. And ultimately beards were permitted so that it became quite impossible to tell the difference between men and women by appearance. Documents had to be produced before people struck up acquaintance. But as there was a campaign just starting against bureaucratic red tape, a particularly tough problem arose: should men have bits cut off, or should women have bits stuck on? A great struggle started in which, as always, it was the general line that emerged triumphant. 'W-w-w-we,' His Leadership said in his report, 'have sh-sh-sh-shown enor-m-m-m-mous hu-m-m-m-anity, in m-m-m-aking this his-t-t-t-toric st-st-st-step.'

The monopoly of the Theatre of Life

'Just look at this,' said Neurasthenic, holding out the News-paper. 'Just read it. The Leader has received the Ambassador. The Leader has arrived in Paris. The President has arrived in Ibansk and has had talks with the Leader. Deputy has received the King. The King has visited the pig farm. A meeting has been addressed by Assistant. Deputy has been awarded a medal. The Leader has been awarded a medal. The metallur-gists have over-fulfilled their plan and sent a telegram to the Leader. The harvesters have fulfilled their plan ahead of schedule, and so on. It's exactly the same in the other news-paper, and in the third. And on the radio. And on television. And in films . . . And in . . .' 'But you shouldn't pay any attention to that,' said Journalist. 'That's just officialese.' 'If you're drowning it's not much help to spit,' said Neurasthenic. 'It's all very well not to pay attention if there were anything else. What you see in the papers isn't just formal officialese, it's our real life. What is it that makes life interesting for people like me? It is its theatrical side, its public appearances. But they've usurped all that for themselves. They have imposed their scene, their game, their theatre on all of us. They ponce around forcing us to watch all their grimaces, and they don't let us do anything ourselves. Their real social life is made up of travels, talks, meetings, speeches, decorations, resolutions and so on. They have nothing else. And they don't let us have anything else. They have transformed their grey, boring bureaucratic existence into a social theatre. And anything that is really theatrical, bright, beautiful, intriguing, they either destroy or drive into the background where it's used as the stage set for their miserable little playlets.' 'It's theatre everywhere,' said Journalist. 'In our country too.' 'That's true,' said Neuras-thenic. 'Life always has something of theatre about it. But it matters who the actors are. When the stage is full of little men without an ear, a voice, or taste, all bawling and strutting about, and the auditorium is full of real singers and connoisseurs of beauty, and the former force the latter to sit and listen to them and pretend to be pleased and show their enthusiasm, then it's a nightmare for the audience. But the situation gets still worse when there are only a few isolated people in the audience with taste or voices or a good ear and all the rest are worse than those

(673)

who are on the stage.' 'Then leave the auditorium,' said Journalist. 'And go where?' asked Neurasthenic. 'To the Other World beyond? Abroad?' 'You're laying it on thick,' said Journalist. 'By the way, yesterday I went to . . .' 'I understand,' said Neurasthenic. 'You were on the stage. But we're not allowed up there.'

> Singer's last letter
> I hope I make my meaning plain,
> My dear old friends back home:
> Life abroad is full of pain
> No matter where you roam.
> But if you wish our country well,
> If you want to set her free,
> Your moral duty, I can tell,
> Is to pack your bags and flee.
> I've meditated all the day
> As across the world I travel,
> But, friends, I see no other way
> This tangle to unravel.
> I know that you will long for home,
> But you must understand:
> That's the way to tackle Them
> If we're to save our land.

'I don't blame him,' He said. 'But that wouldn't suit me. I couldn't do that. I don't know why. But I couldn't. My place is here. Maybe it's a waste of time, but it's here. All my unfortunate ancestors are buried here. My Father died here for nothing. It is here that my Mother was tormented to death by all that crushing work day after day. My own life has been ruined for nothing. It is here that I have frozen, starved, been betrayed by my friends, ill-treated by my bosses, and all the rest of it. How could I leave all this? I cannot. It is mine. I can only exist as long as I stay here. Long ago we had to retreat. And the retreat had to be covered otherwise we'd all have been caput. There were no orders, no pleas.'

> To cover our retreat we saw
> Volunteers—first one, then more—
> Come stepping forward from the ranks.
> 'See you later, lads—and thanks.'

'See us later? Not a chance.
Best of luck when you advance.'
Then we offered them our bread:
'Might come in handy yet,' we said.
They said, 'What's the point of giving?
Keep it. Bread is for the living.'
  'I stayed with them. I don't know why. How could I have
done anything else? And I can't leave them now. Never.' 'I am
afraid,' She said.

The twenty-second hour

'So you're leaving us? asked Idleader. 'Yes,' said Bawler.
'There's no point in taking umbrage,' said Idleader. 'In our
kind of business all sorts of things can happen in the heat of the
action. You should be more patient.' 'I'm not taking umbrage,'
said Bawler. 'That's not why I'm going. You are fighting
against lawlessness, repression, dictatorship. But what about
yourselves?' 'What do you mean?' asked Idleader. 'A great
deal,' said Bawler. 'For example, take the case of the man who
committed suicide by fire.' 'But you aren't against this kind of
action,' said Idleader. 'Not if they're voluntary, individual
decisions,' said Bawler. 'But I am when they're organised. You
terrified that lad. You forced him to do what he did. I can never
forgive you for that. It was bestial cruelty worthy of the Boss.'
'We've talked about this several times before,' said Idleader. 'It
was a mistake that doesn't affect the essence of the matter.' 'The
essence of the matter reveals itself in characteristic mistakes,'
said Bawler. 'And another thing, who is shamizdat intended for
and who actually reads it? Informers. There are too many
informers here. The darling sons of our highest leaders. Little
girls who've got so much time on their hands they don't know
what to do with themselves. Brilliant young officials from the
foreign ministry. Privileged journalists and government advisers. Successful actors who haven't yet got their honorary titles.
Are there many shamizdat readers who are really sincerely and
deeply concerned about the situation in the country? Shamizdat
has become reading matter to titillate the nerves of a particular
kind of public who may pretend that they're rebels, but who in
fact are aiming if not at power itself, then at least at participation in power in conditions that suit them. Shamizdat is like a

detective story with a social tinge. And what about the turn its external orientation is taking? How were the last few numbers compiled? "We'll have to bring out editions that'll have an effect on the West," you said. On whom? What effect? There are effects and effects. There's the superficial effect of the moment. And there's the effect which grows deeper with time. Effect and sensation aren't the same thing. You've begun to drift towards sensation, towards striking attitudes, to self-advertisement, to narcissism. That doesn't suit me. I've had enough. I'm moving on.' 'Where to and who with?' asked Idleader. 'If you leave us you'll be in total isolation. Because everybody else thinks you're an informer, or at least very suspect.' 'That doesn't matter,' said Bawler. 'I am my own judge, and I'm not disturbed by what other people think. My conscience is clear.'

He had somewhere to go. But the place which he went to differed from the place he had left only in the scale of the enterprise and the degree of sensation. So there was nowhere to go, but nowhere to stay either.

Choice of a viewpoint
'The whole trouble is,' said Journalist, 'that your intelligentsia was at one time completely wiped out,' 'And then,' said Neurasthenic, 'it was reconstituted on a grandiose scale. I'm going to tell you something which may sound sacrilegious, but don't leap to conclusions. You know that I am not an apologist. Nor am I an enemy or a fighter. I am just someone who lives here. But not an apologist. So, then. Look at these new residential areas. There is a hotel. Those are office buildings. Shops. Cinemas. You see this avenue? Not bad is it?' 'Of course,' said Journalist. 'Well,' continued Neurasthenic, 'this area used to be full of churches and private houses that have all been demolished. And even more buildings of all kinds fell into ruins from the effect of time and because no-one looked after them. A whole crowd of old architects ended up in the camps! Now what effect has all this had on our contemporary architecture and on building in general? Have we lost many ancient monuments? Yes we have. Have we got our priorities wrong and do we lag behind? Yes. Have many innocent people suffered? Yes. But in principle, if all that hadn't taken place, would what you are now

looking at be any different? You don't need any proof or documentary evidence. Rely on your intuition. Just say what you think.' 'No, it wouldn't be,' said Journalist. 'But that's another question.' 'No it isn't,' said Neurasthenic. 'It's the same question, but from a different viewpoint. You've already guessed where I'm taking you. You can see exactly the same thing in the field of science, technology, painting, sculpture, military strategy, and so on—in general in every field of culture. No matter what our past had been, we would always have arrived at the same result in the end, since this result has its roots in the very foundations of our life. Maybe it would have come a little earlier. Maybe things would have been a little gayer, more interesting. But the result would have been the same. We have destroyed our past, not our future. We were able to destroy it because we were moving towards this present and we could choose to pay no heed to the past. All we have done is to clear the road to where we are today. That is an objective and dispassionate assessment, no matter what those who took part in the process may have thought. I am not setting out to justify anything or anybody. I merely want to say that our present state and the road which has led to it are not a disease, not a deformity, not an artificial malformation, but a normal, healthy, worthy state for a society of this type to be in. It would be untrue to maintain that this society arose because someone or other had been exterminated. If people were exterminated it was because this society was in the process of being born. And as far as our intellectual brothers are concerned the situation is as plain as a pikestaff. We are scruffy mongrels who think we're great danes.' 'But Ibansk has produced, and still produces, great cultural figures of worldwide reputation,' said Journalist. 'That's true,' said Neurasthenic, 'but they are mongrels too. They may be enormous, but they are still mongrels. In time we will breed mongrels next to which your great danes will look like bugs.' 'People say that mongrels are the most intelligent dogs,' said Journalist. 'That's possible,' said Neurasthenic, 'but that doesn't make them into great danes.' 'So what do you propose?' asked Journalist. 'Nothing,' said Neurasthenic. 'I am simply passing the time. If I were a great dane I would be a leading writer, a journalist, a politician, or something in that line. At all events I'd have a job, an income, and an interesting varied life. But I'm a mongrel. I talk, and that's all I do. Or I keep quiet. I may howl sometimes, but I don't bite. My masters beat me, and I just lick their hands. They kick me and chase me away. And I crawl back to them on my belly, and look at them with big servile eyes. If they throw me a bone I'll do anything my masters want out of gratitude. And as for intelligence . . . they say mongrels are the easiest to train up to circus tricks.'

History yet to come
Thousands of volumes have been written, and there are hundreds of thousands more to come, on preparations for the promulgation of the total Ism and on the procedure whereby that promulgation will be made. But nevertheless all this will only be a relative truth, approaching absolute truth like an asymptote, but never coinciding with it. So let it go on approaching. We won't interfere with it. When he announced the imminent approach of the total Ism, His Leadership XVIII said: 'Thage agagage agold drageagam agof magankagind, hagowagevager, agis agaccagomplagishaged. Fragom nagow agon agand thragoagugh agall agetagernagity, thage tagotagal agism agis agestagablagishaged agand nagow agoagur bagannager wagill bageagar thage wagords Tago agevagery Agibaganskagiagan agaccagordaging tago hagis nageageds. Nagow agevagery Agibaganskagiagan magust bage vagery cagonscagiagentagiagoagus, agor wage shagall . . .' What would happen to any Ibanskian who was not conscientious enough was familiar to everybody, for it was just as it had always been.

One fact which dates from the establishment of the total Ism is passed over in silence by all the historians although it played a most important part in the later history of Ibansk. It was decided to invite guests from abroad to witness the unveiling of the total Ism. Let them watch and learn something! We've nothing to be ashamed of! We can show them a thing or two! But then they remembered that there was no abroad any more. So they decided to invite instead beings from outer space. The beings from outer space were delighted with everything they saw. The leader of their delegation delivered a speech written for him by Thinker, and passed by Theoretician. At the banquet given in honour of the launching of the total Ism, the beings from outer space drank a great deal but, according to their custom, ate nothing at all. They stuffed their pockets with the sandwiches they were given with the intention of taking them home for their children. They were allotted two sandwiches per head. The head of the delegation of beings from outer space embraced one of the secret police men who made up fifty per cent of the guests, belched full in his face and asked: 'Do you respect me, eh?' And the secret police man, who had drunk every bit as much as the being from outer space, bellowed in reply in a voice which could be heard all over Ibansk.

Through the reeds there blew a wind,
And the trees . . .

The assembled company, unashamed of their tears, took up in chorus

Began to bend!

At this point Teacher decided not to pursue his study of Ibanskian history any further into the future.

Perspectives

'Who said that in Ibansk there was no possibility for protest, exposure and opposition?' said Neurasthenic. 'What rubbish! Everything's possible in Ibansk. Even more so than in the West.' 'You're joking, of course,' said Journalist. 'We never joke,' said Neurasthenic. 'A sense of humour is one thing we don't have. What we haven't got we haven't got. There's no point in denying it. The only thing about us,' added Neurasthenic, 'is that everything gets done in its own time, following a well established order. And that's a rule. In these circumstances, everything is possible here. It only needs a hint to our local authorities: you know it would be no bad thing . . . it might well be time to . . . and the very next day they fling out everything and everybody and set up . . . This is the way things are done. The Leader and the Deputies get together. "It's time we got to grips with this business," says the Leader. "Some shortcomings and delays have been noticed in this area. The pace is slackening. We're only in sixth position in the world protest league. And we're only tenth for civil disturbance. It's true that we have been very successful in the growth of crime. In this area we've completely trampled Europe underfoot, and we're very close behind America." So decisions are taken and practical measures proposed. And what do you think? Everything goes like clockwork.

An initiative from below is to be organized. Of course the initiators will be selected in advance, people who really deserve it, like Snottyhanky, Artist, Producer, Brother. Who knows, even Dauber's name might be mentioned. Of course he's a scandalous figure, but he's outside politics. Let him make a protest. Then everybody'll be able to see: a man's protested, he's not been arrested, and won't be arrested; he's referred to in the newspapers, promised trips abroad, and that promise might even be kept, and then he's been given some leader or other to sculpt. Yes, let them sing, or draw, or carve . . . that's allowed now. It's been decided. There's a directive. And there'll be plans to be fulfilled, fulfilled ahead of time and over-fulfilled. Some highly placed cretin will take it all seriously and work out his own personal scheme. He'll be promoted first of all to the Academy, then given a pension, and then a place in the Old Whores' cemetery.' 'But where will all this end?' asked Journalist. 'Like every campaign,' said Neurasthenic, 'in nothing. There'll be some new directive. The campaign for protest will be forgotten and it'll wither away on its own.' 'Without repression?' asked Journalist. 'That will depend on circumstances,' said Neurasthenic. 'If there's a directive . . . Except, of course, for the opponents who haven't been provided for in the plan. They'll be treated in the same way as outstanding artists and scientists who haven't been included in the plan. They'll be liquidated by every known method without any need for directives. And you Over There, you'll begin to scream about five years later that the course of history is irreversible.'

The discovery
'I have constructed a mathematical theory of Ibanskian society,' said Teacher. 'Let's drink a toast to it, and then proceed to its empirical verification. To do this we shall have to choose various kinds of example. I suggest we include this year's harvest, the space programme, and the policy of the Ibanskian government in some remote part of the world where no Ibanskian foot has trod.' 'It's an intriguing proposition,' said Bawler, 'but how are we going to get our hands on the empirical data?' 'That's dead easy,' said Teacher. 'The ideas about secrecy and confidentiality have changed a great deal. There's partial information about all these things in the Ibanskian press, and plenty of it in the foreign press.

What's secret today is the price of smoked sausage and the number of pensioners per head of population.' 'If I were head of state,' said Bawler, 'I would make you into my principal adviser on all the country's main problems. But now I must advise you to hide your theory away and show it to no-one. It's all very well to joke, but you have in fact discovered the most profound mechanism of Ibanskian society: the absence of any rigorous mechanism. By using your theory any charlatan could make flawless predictions from any premises. It's quite remarkable.'

Teacher's theory was in truth unique in science. Having tried hundreds of variants on a serious scientific level, Teacher decided that seriousness was a sign of mediocrity. And he decided to try to establish purely *a priori* links between empirically independent values. After all, he thought, what do I care about what's going on in this whorehouse? What do I want? To find a method of prediction. How I invent it is of no consequence. The main thing is that it should produce correct predictions, i.e. predictions which more or less frequently turn out to be right. So he drew up a system of postulates which made Bawler first of all fall about with laughter, and then go on to propose a decisive proof. Here are some examples of the postulates on which the theory was based: if the number of cows is multiplied by n, the number of permanent civil servants in the field of agriculture will be multiplied by 2^n; if the number of cosmonauts is multiplied by m, and the area of ground under cultivation is multiplied by k, the probability of accidents in space would increase by $\frac{m+k}{L}$ where L is the coefficient of growth of capital investment in the national liberation struggle of underdeveloped nations to free themselves from the yoke; and so on. Laughing till the tears ran down his cheeks, Bawler immediately worked out that the Period of Perplexity had ended before it started, and started after it had ended, that the reserves of liberalism of our government would last for another two years at most, and that all those inhabitants of remote places on the planet who had placed themselves under our benevolent protection, and which we find so expensive, will be told to stuff themselves in a year's time. And they threw the theory in the wastepaper basket. 'In a hundred years' time,' said Bawler, 'some young genius will rediscover all this sludge, and mankind will achieve another step forward in its spiritual development.'

'I don't give a damn for our ingenious descendant,' said Teacher. 'But I believe that I really have found the bases of the theory of Ibanskian society. And I'm not prepared to give it up. We're not joking any more. How much time do you thing we still have left? No more than a year? That's what I think too. So let's say six months at most. In other words, we've got to get everything on paper in three months. You know I put all my affairs in order. I've had enough. I can't wait any longer. I've got to get into the battle with all my strength. We are surrounded anyway. There's no other way out. Our only defence is a full-blooded, full frontal attack. Right, I'm off.'

He never reached his home.

Condemned to treatment

'I wasn't able to help Bawler,' said Brother. 'I went there. It turned out that they'd really got things sewn up. They've got a permanent commission including psychiatrists, psychologists, professional experts, people's judges, and an inspector from the High Court. The commission draws up a list of questions corresponding roughly to the level of education, the social position and the profession of the accused. The questions are formulated in such a way that any average, normal individual in the given category would be able to answer them. They're very varied. For example, what was your maternal grandfather called, what is two times two, what resolution was adopted by the March plenum, where has the Leader just visited, who is the head of the Brotherhood in Inner Pangolia, and so on. A hundred questions in all. This is the way things are done. The accused is brought in. A question is posed and they press a button. If the accused manages to answer before the bell and gets the answer right, he earns one point. If he gets the answer wrong, he gets zero. And if he doesn't manage to answer at all, he gets minus one. You think it's easy. All right, let's have a go! When did your paternal grandmother die? One, two, three . . . minus one. Your wife's patronymic? One, two, three . . . minus one! Your name? One, two, three . . . minus one! Well then? That's what it's like. And when you've got a commission of twenty people . . . On the whole the questions are compiled so that there can be no real complaint about them, yet the accused is condemned in advance to fail to answer any of them in the permitted time. And the higher the intellectual level of the accused, the easier it is to sink him with ridiculous questions. The decision as to whether the accused is normal or not is made on the basis of the number of points scored. And if he's shown not to be normal, his points indicate the category of abnormality. A refusal to answer a question is counted as minus one. By the way, Bawler scored minus one hundred. Something of a record, ha, ha, ha! To be regarded as normal you have to have at least fifty points. Between twenty-five and fifty, you are a third category mental case. Between zero and twenty-five, second category. Less than zero, first category, and less than minus fifty the highest category of all. Then the commission adopts a resolution to declare the accused normal or abnormal in such and such a category, depending on the points he's scored. If he is declared to be mentally ill the verdict is announced: to be condemned to enforced treatment of such and such a category. They put special hand-cuffs and fetters on him, and take the condemned man to the clinic to show him what prisoners in this category look like. I had a look myself at the third category. It was like a nightmare. I couldn't go on after I'd seen two of them. I couldn't stand it any more. I spent the next few days vomiting, and I still feel sick. After he's had a look at the people undergoing treatment, the condemned man is offered a last chance to sign the documents—testimony, confessions, recantations. If he signs he gets let off lightly. Either he's put in a lower category of treatment, or handed over to the ordinary courts. The next thing is the injections. That again depends on the category.' 'That's cruel,' said Wife. 'They might at least not force them to see the results of the treatment.' 'Not at all,' said Sociologist. 'If they didn't, the punishment wouldn't have any sense. The person about to be punished must know what awaits him.' 'What's the state of people who've been treated?' asked Thinker. 'Oh,' said Brother, 'they've got that well worked out. A death sentence would be child'splay compared to that. Just imagine the state of mind of a man who finds out that he's going to be killed, and stretch this state over many years. By the way, they live for a long time there. And then there's the physical suffering.' 'And what's the difference between the categories from this point of view?' asked Fellow-worker. 'It's a matter of degree,'

(683)

said Brother. 'You can't visit a first-category patient without a document signed by a Deputy. And as for the top category, no-one but the staff is allowed to see them. So you can imagine . . .'

Life begins

'What's that?' asked Chatterer. 'Oh nothing,' said Dauber. 'A piece of nonsense. I'm only doing it for the money. It's a gravestone for some fellow called Soilophagist.' 'Who's he?' asked Chatterer. 'Oh, he was quite a big wheel,' said Dauber. 'Not very old either. Our generation. He died suddenly. Heart attack. His family decided that I'd do the stone. I could name my own price! I'm becoming a fashionable undertaker.

How glorious in Ibansk to work and play,
And fashion leaders out of clay!

Have you heard the Voice?' 'No,' said Chatterer. 'Is there anything new?' 'There certainly is,' said Dauber; 'everyone's talking about it. Dancer has defected. It's a real blow! He's having a wild success Over There, and here he was only dancing minor roles. That's what shaking off the fetters can do for you. It's as if the Queen herself had kissed his feet.' 'Not bad,' said Chatterer. 'It makes sense to run away,' said Dauber. 'But I'll wait a bit longer. When they begin to kiss our arses, that'll be the time to go. Do you remember Bawler?' asked Chatterer. 'No,' said Dauber. 'There are so many people who drop in here. I can't remember them all.' 'Bawler's not just anyone,' said Chatterer. 'Anyway, what's happened to him?' asked Dauber. 'Nothing special,' said Chatterer. 'He's in a psychiatric clinic.' 'What for?' asked Dauber. 'Who knows?' said Chatterer. 'Probably because of shamizdat. Colleague comes round here doesn't he. You couldn't try . . .?' 'No,' said Dauber. 'I don't want to get mixed up with that.' 'I understand,' said Chatterer. 'It's not your problem. I went to see him. He looked awful. He keeps on talking about the real Ism. He's planning to write a book, and he asked me for paper and a pencil. The only thing is, he says he can't remember all the letters.' 'Well, who knows,' said Dauber, 'maybe that's where the real truth is to be found. By the way, I've got permission.' 'Congratulations', said Chatterer. 'For always?' 'No,' said Dauber. 'Just two years.' 'That means forever,' said Chatterer. 'I'll just get this imbecile

(684)

finished,' said Dauber, 'and then I'll begin to get myself ready to go.' 'I wish you luck,' said Chatterer. 'I'm off. See you!' 'See you,' said Dauber. 'Don't forget to write! If you can remember the letters, of course—ha, ha, ha!'

Chatterer left, and the soul left Dauber's body. And he felt light and happy. Life is only just beginning, he said. And he began to sing.

> If only you would set me free,
> I could conquer all the earth.
> I'd amaze the whole wide world,
> Carving a great masterpiece.

What incredible rubbish, he thought. What fool wrote that?

> Carving a great masterpiece
> Great master pie-e-e-ce
> Masterpie-e-e-e-ce
> Pi-e-e-e-ce
> E-e-e-e-ce
> . . . .

The penultimate hour

Even so why did they capitulate so quickly? Idleader gave them all away. Even those the secret police had never heard of. Cowardice? That's not an explanation. Principle? A wish to create the appearance of something really big? But at what a price! They're going to lose a lot in the eyes of society. They're standing in the presence of history, and they are unaware of the fact. Could it be stupidity or constraint? That's an enigma for history to solve. But there's really no mystery about it. They are simply the flesh and blood of this society. They are Ibanskians, and once you've said that you've said everything. They are ordinary, normal Ibanskians. They're just in an unusual position. No-one could have expected anything else of them. Rats live like rats, and protest like rats. They did what they could. They deserve respect. And what about you? You've still got time. Don't jump to conclusions. Maybe you're an ordinary Ibanskian as well, like them? Of course I'm an ordinary Ibanskian. But I don't want to be. And I won't be. So I shan't exist at all. That's it! Life is over.

And he felt light and happy.

Life has now written out its final line;

(685)

All that remains to add is a full stop.
Now life is done. It matters not a whit
Whether you were a hero—or a shit.
Remains now but one thought to think upon—
The job you had to do—well, is it done?
What an amazing world it is! Can it really be possible that this is
a new and higher stage in the development of society? So be it.
And I hope they're all the better without me.
The job you had to do—well, is it done?
The job you had to do—
Is it done?
Is it?
· · · · · · · ·

Coming to terms

I could come to terms with all this, said Neurasthenic. That's
impossible . . . the state's interest. This is impossible . . . the
Brotherhood's interest. This must be done because . . . That
must be done because . . . So be it. In practice my needs are
very small. But if all this were the action of a soulless, faceless
machine! If it were, everything would be accepted as a natural
necessity. But there aren't machines of that kind here. Here we
have real living people. Your colleagues, friends, comrades-in-
arms, fellow-pupils, your teachers, your students, subordinates, bosses, neighbours, relatives, children and so on. When
people blame it all on some faceless machine, as is fashionable,
they merely swallow the bait of official demagogy. There is no
machine. What there is is people. Say that you've been refused
permission to attend a congress abroad. It may well be
unreasonable. But who decided to refuse? And who went in
your place? Why was it that no good scum took the decision?
Why was it that ignorant lout who went? In fact all these
discussions about rationality, needs and so on are merely a
demagogic figure of speech for careerists, profiteers, boors,
crooks, and nonentities. So if we talk of coming to terms, of
resigning ourselves, the question must be phrased not with
what, but with whom? Must we be prepared to come to terms
with careerists, villains, dimwits, louts? It is they who set the
tone. It is they who are the masters. Must we obey them? Must
we sing their tune? Must we let them pull the strings? No, that

(686)

doesn't suit me. There are very many it doesn't suit. And we resist. But how? Take me, for instance. Say I've got to write a piece in a book whose principal author is to be Secretary. I will write it any old how. Even then there's no-one who could do it better. And all the other contributors do the same. And so another second-rate book comes out. It will be praised to the skies. There'll be first-class reviews. It'll be translated for abroad. It'll be proposed for a prize—and it'll get it. And then this book will become a new standard reference for everyone. I resist, but the result is the burgeoning of cretinism in some field of culture. Do you think that's criminal of me? It suits everybody. If I were to write a decent text I'd be shot down. So in the end my resistance adds up to coming to terms. One can try to break through, of course. There are people who do and who make it. Does that change anything? Yes. It begins to look as if this sphere of life is becoming rather more decent. Look, people say, talent is really being encouraged. Look at this brilliant work! Yet essentially it remains the same general situation, just better camouflaged. And so it becomes even harder to break through. Even those who have broken through ahead of you do everything they can to see that you don't break through yourself. So, on the whole, it makes no difference whether you've resigned yourself to it or not. No-one will even bother to ask.

Dauber's interview
When Dauber arrived in Paris the reporters asked him whom he regarded as the most significant figure in the spiritual life of Ibansk at the present time. In the past few years, said Dauber, a great many intellectuals have appeared who, it seems to me, discuss mankind's problems on quite a high level. For example, the names of Brother, Snottyhanky, Producer, Thinker, Sociologist, Wife, Moaner, Sniveller, and many others come to mind. And what do you intend to do here, the reporters asked. I want to erect an enormous statue representing the struggle between the forces of good and evil, said Dauber.

Yet life goes on
'Have you heard that . . .?' said Sociologist in a very significant tone. He was dribbling with horror, and the dribble flowed down his beard and dropped onto his new ultra-violet check

(687)

trousers with their baggy knees, which he'd bought recently abroad. 'It's a nightmare. We do everything we can, and they . . .' 'They say that . . .' said Wife, hitching up her fashionable skirt in crocodile skin, which she had had made to measure in a secret police boutique, and which was now dragging on the ground. 'I can tell you in confidence that . . .' said Puss, swelling visibly from self-importance. And he immediately shat himself, terrified by his own gossip. 'There are rumours that . . .' said Thinker, and his mighty dome came out in a sweat at the thought of the abject part which these blackguards had forced him to play in this affair. And anyway he had never shared the views of these cretins. That wasn't his style at all. 'I've heard that . . . I was talking to . . . about . . .' said Fellow-worker. And his snub nose began to quiver with excitement. 'No, no,' he added hastily. 'I don't mean that . . . I merely mean that . . .' 'How long will all this go on?' asked Neurasthenic, and answered his own question. 'A year! No more than that. All their plans will fail and then . . .' 'They've failed already,' said Brother. 'Someone told me . . . being scorched out, high and low.' 'But what if . . .?' said Wife. 'It would be a nightmare,' said Fellow-worker, and rushed to the toilet. 'Who could have thought,' said Sociologist, 'That the time would come when we would be praying that that c— should hang on to power as long as possible!' 'That'd be the best thing that could happen,' said Neurasthenic. 'Yes,' said Journalist, 'in the West it's considered that if . . .' 'Let's drink to his health,' said Fellow-worker, and burst into song:

Raise high your glasses,
Toss them back fast.
Let's hope that these asses
Sit tight to the last.
Don't let them shave us
The military way,
Or—Heaven save us!—
Lower our pay.

The assembled company took up the refrain:

Lower our p-a-a-a-a-y.

The last hour

So what remained? Nothing. Just froth. An ending for an

unwritten novel. The final formula of an unsolved equation.

Bawler noticed a car outside his house. And recognised it. It was one of theirs. Outside his front door there was a group of young men who made no attempt to conceal themselves or their intentions. He'd noticed the big one when they'd been seeing Singer off at the airport. So he couldn't go back into the house. Where then? All the routes he knew were sure to be blocked. And it was clear that he couldn't go back to Truth-teller's. And anyway, judging by their last meeting, that relationship was over. It's strange, he thought, that such a great man can be so naïve. Just like a child. I wonder why he decided to entrust the book to me? After all, he's certain that I'm an informer. Is he playing some game with me? To use the secret police to do his work for him? Ideas like that are fashionable these days. Could it be that he's taken the bait? Hardly. The likeliest thing is that he's given the job to several people, two at least, and I'm only one of them. Maybe I'm only involved to act as a diversion . . . Anyway, it doesn't affect me. It's not my problem any more. Here everyone's got some little game. But what about me? . . .

He walked to the avenue and sat down on a cold, damp bench. Where did he go from here? He began to run through the names of all his acquaintances, and he realised with horror that there was no-one he could go to. He wasn't horrified for himself—after all he was used to it. He was horrified for them. When you are not appreciated, that is not loneliness. When you are not understood, that is not loneliness. When there is no-one for you to pour you heart out to, that too is not loneliness. Loneliness is when you sit out on a street bench at night, like this, in a wet, cold, sleeping multi-million city and know that you have nowhere to go and no-one to go to. There's only one thing left to do, he decided. Leave it to chance, as always. And he began to walk. At first he just walked anywhere, and then he realised that he was walking towards the airport.

So here I am, he thought, walking mile after mile along the roadside, in the mud. A man who is no longer young, a man who is mortally tired. Why? What good will it do? Of course millions of people will get some brief entertainment from it. And that's quite something in our grey life. Is it for that? No. And afterwards how many people will be pleased that They have had it smack between the eyes and will feel like celebrating.

(689)

And how many people will say, enough's enough! It's true that only a few of them will put their decision into action. Maybe no one. But they'll say it all the same. Is it for that? No. And what a panic there'll be at the top and in the secret police! How many reprimands there'll be! What a lot of extra work it's going to make for them ! Real work, not imaginary. This will be a truly significant event and not a mere counterfeit. Is it for that? No. He had long since come to regard them not as people but as soulless natural forces. And what about the intelligentsia? My God, what a lot of talk there'll be! A sea of words, of winks, of sighs, of lamentations. Could it be for that? No. He'd known for a long time that there's nowhere you'll find as many degenerates as in the ranks of the arts and sciences. And what degenerates! Could it be for them? Heaven preserve! Of course there are among them a few people who will understand everything. But they are a drop in the ocean. On the threshold of imperceptibility. And who will recall who did all the dirty work? We are Ibanskians always and everywhere. Do people talk a great deal about humble research workers when it's the bosses who take all the credit for discoveries and get all the benefits? People do refer to them but it's just for conscience's sake. They are never mentioned individually. So what is it for? Who is it for? They're meaningless questions. Motives for action ceased to exist long ago. They served out their time and disappeared. Once upon a time he used to have an aim which pointed him in the right direction, clapped him on the shoulder and said There you are, now get on with it! and vanished. And then there was nothing left. All there was was an empty form of a man, a spectre, a shadow without a body. Such a life cannot be lived with impunity. Such a life leads inevitably to empty abstraction. So why are you walking? You are walking because you can't do anything else. That is the sum total.

Once a car stopped by him. Its occupants offered him a lift. He refused. Perhaps it was Them? But it didn't matter any more. The experiment was over. And it would not be repeated.

The prayer of the believing atheist
It's been proved by cyclotrons
And so it must be true,

The world is full of electrons
And chromosomes—not YOU.
And so you don't exist, oh God,
You're just a priestly lie;
But all the same, I pray you, God,
Exist for me—please try!
You may not be omnipotent,
Omniscient, all-blest,
Farsighted and benevolent,
Forgiving and the rest.
It's not a big request I make,
So do your best for me:
All-seeing be, for goodness' sake,
I pray you, God, please see.
Just see, that's really all I want,
Just that and nothing more.
Just keep an eye on what goes on,
On who's against, who's for.
That's all you've got to do, oh Lord,
There's nothing else to say;
All else besides can be ignored
Save what *I* do, what *They*.
I'll make concessions if you want:
If you can't watch it all,
Watch one per cent of what goes on,
Just that and nothing more.
We need someone to watch this world,
So that's why I insist
And roar and scream and rant
Oh Lord!!
Not pray—demand:
Exist!!
I whisper,
I croak:
Exist
Oh Lord!!!
I pray,
Not demand,
Exist!!!!

The end

At the airport he looked around and picked out two girls. These days, he thought, the most trustworthy people are girls, and he went over to them. 'I have a Book,' he said to them. 'It has to be sent Over There. Can you do that?' 'Yes,' they said, because they were girls. He waited until he had seen them go through the checks, and walk out onto the tarmac, where they waved to him. He didn't know that the Book had been taken off the girls, and that they'd been ordered to give the agreed signal. So that's all right, he thought. How simple it's all turned out to be! And a wave of sadness came over him, as if he had parted from the last person who was close to him, as if he had been unjustly and irreparably deceived. Nor did he know that all this no longer had any importance, since the Book was Over There already and was being prepared to reveal its terrible words to the world, the blackest and most truthful words about the brightest, most radiant fiction in the world.

The young men were waiting at the exit. They were in no hurry. The game was over. And they didn't stop him making a detour into the buffet. I could still get away, he thought. But where to? And why? Just as a matter of principle? No, chum, it's too late. I don't want any more of it, he said aloud. And he pushed aside his untouched glass and walked towards the exit. Over Ibansk the sun was rising, its rays falling on the yawning heights of the approaching Ism and encouraging the contented Ibanskian people to go about their peaceful business. Oh God, give me the strength to put in the final full stop!

III

POEM ON
BOREDOM

POEM ON BOREDOM

. . . .
. . . .
And the dead rose from their ashes
And came to the Judgment Day,
And all joy, all fear, all passion
From their souls had drained away.
And the Judge listened to them recounting,
And yawning with boredom he swore:
'You can't alter, lads, the accounting;
I tell you, that's History's law.'
The villains, they stiffened their backbones—
'Why, we can take all that you've got!'
But the meek bent their heads even lower,
Always victims—for that was their lot.
    He looked around and heaved a sigh.
    What a fool I've been, how dumb!
    It's perfectly true that the world's a sty,
    Perfectly true that men are scum.
. . . .
. . . .

(From the lavatory poem *The Last Judgment*)

The return

The studio was crammed with people. Young women of an indeterminate age and sex drifted aimlessly about among the crumbling plaster and the imperishable bronze. Some of them were so tightly crammed into their trousers that every detail of both underwear and anatomy was clearly discernible. Others were so underclad that every movement clearly revealed every detail of underwear and anatomy. 'You might think that you were in Paris,' sniggered Chatterer. 'But their underwear isn't up to much. They must have spent all they had on the exterior and didn't have enough left for underneath. You might think

(695)

they've spent the last few months almost starving and sleeping with anyone who came along for the sake of economy. No, it isn't Paris. Please God it isn't Paris.'

The informers slid around silently and invisibly, looking at everything, listening to every word. Chatterer recognised one of them and they nodded to each other. Technique's all very well, thought Chatterer, but the rank and file informer is still the foundation stone. No super-sophisticated instruments can replace human presence. But it's totally impossible to see or hear anything in a whore house like this. Yet why are all these informers around? They would only have to ask and Dauber would answer any question they wanted to put to him completely frankly. He has absolutely no secrets.

Some old acquaintances were roaming about the room plunged in thought. Thinker, Neurasthenic, Colleague, Sociologist. Brother's grimy feet were sprawled out on an equally filthy divan. Visitor had found a place for himself perched on its corner. Some newcomers were hanging about looking rather lost—Rat, Louse, Flea, Bug and Mouse. It was the first time that Chatterer had seen them here. But it was no surprise to him. There had been such changes in Ibansk and in the world at large in the last few years that it would have been more surprising had they not been here. They had crawled on to the stage of Ibansk's grey and gloomy history, partly by displacing his old acquaintances, partly by using them for their own purposes, and partly by infiltrating their circle. And all these fine folk were of course keen on the arts, and particularly on the unofficial arts, the arts which were almost persecuted,—but whose frequentation did not carry any risk of punishment or of damage to their careers. And Dauber's studio was the front line of world art. But it was a front line completely safe for visitors. No-one had been put inside for frequenting it, no-one had been demoted, nor even found his advancement blocked. It was not without reason that Assistant had Dauber's engravings hanging in his apartment. There was a rumour that even He Himself had something of the kind in his office. In a word, the studio was like any self-respecting literary or cinematic front—the bullets may whistle by but nobody ever gets killed. People do get killed, of course, but not in this place and not for this reason.

'When is all this going to end?' yelled Brother, brandishing a bottle and trying to attract the attention of the assembled company. 'Are we serfs, are we slaves, or what? In every civilised country journeys abroad for a writer or an artist are something completely normal. But for us they remain a privilege of power, of its whores and its informers, the cunts!' Some people were drinking glass after glass of instant coffee, bought in a job lot which included inedible apples and rock-hard cakes which no-one would buy. The glasses were left standing on books and drawings, and little light-brown puddles spread around them. Others were drinking brandy, also out of tumblers, and nibbling rather greenish looking salami and pastries, scattering sugary crumbs all around them. Others again were sucking at unripe, imported grapes, spitting the pips on the floor and on to newly printed etchings. Everyone was smoking, spattering themselves and their neighbours with ash, stubbing their cigarettes out on crucifixions, and throwing the fag-ends into the gaping belly of the Prophet. Thinker knocked out his pipe against the head of Orpheus. No, thought Chatterer, it is Paris after all, but Paris after its take-over by Ibansk.

A group of foreigners were working their way through the crowd towards the exit, assuring each other and those about them that they were staggered by what they had seen. They were all clutching little rolls of paper—etchings which Dauber had given them. 'What a scandal,' said Colleague to Thinker. 'They're all wealthy people. They could have afforded to buy them. And there they go, carrying away a thousand dollars' worth at least, without even blinking.' Another group of foreigners was examining a huge wooden figure which had been begun many years ago by one of Dauber's assistants, who was drunk at the time, and which had not been thrown out onto the wood pile for reasons incomprehensible even to informers and the Department of Culture. The foreigners were taking photographs of the idol, shaking their heads in amazement, and assuring each other and those about them that they too were staggered. It all looks much the same as before, thought Chatterer, but it is quite different. Why am I here? But where else would you be? Your body has returned, and you, its spirit, must return to your body. But apparently your body isn't too keen to give up its spirit.

Dauber, dressed from top to toe in foreign-made clothes and

looking a lot thinner but no younger, was carving a gigantic bust. 'Hi, there, old man,' he nodded to Chatterer, without breaking off his work and carrying on telling some tale about Paris to a bunch of girls who were hanging on every word. 'Greetings,' said Thinker to Chatterer. 'They've let you out already, have they? You got off lightly. Is Teacher still inside? We never really understood what you'd been done for. Just a stupid and silly charade. It was Bulldozer who blew it all up to help him in his career. But he's burnt out now. Haven't you heard? It's quite a story! . . .'

Occasionally the visitors wandered up to Dauber and examined, with the air of connoisseurs, the chunk of clay which bore a faint resemblence to the head of the Leader of Ibansk (Leadiban, as he had now come to be referred to), and expressed various profound judgments. 'You've really made great progress,' said Sociologist. 'That's what comes from living a few years in the West. I've only just got back from England with a delegation. I had the luck to meet . . .' 'It's staggering,' burst out Neurasthenic. 'What a monster! Leave his left eye the way it is. I had a book out recently. A good one, though I say it myself. I must give you a copy. I really managed to say something.' 'You've really managed to convey all his spiritual poverty and his petty vanity,' observed Colleague. 'I wouldn't like anyone to show me in that light. The only thing is, they'll never let you get away with it. No chance! Our leaders are all beauties by decree. So you're going to have to make the forehead a bit higher, and make the chin jut forward.' 'Come here,' shouted Brother, pouring brandy into coffee glasses. 'Drop all these bastards!'

'And what have you got to say for yourself?' Dauber asked Chatterer. 'I'm reminded of the man who once reckoned that it was impossible to write a leading article of genius,' said Chatterer. 'But where is . . .?' Chatterer looked round the studio and in a corner, piled high with boxes and scraps of discarded works, made out with some difficulty the Great Project. Dauber followed Chatterer's eyes. 'Come again another time and we'll have a talk. There are too many people about now. What's new?' he said, turning to Rat. 'Double-dealer has been killed in a car crash. It was set up by our people,' said Rat. 'I doubt it,' said Dauber. 'Over There car crashes are an everyday event. He'd been drinking a lot lately. And anyway he'd have been more useful alive to what you call Our People. As an example: if you behave like that, that's where you'll end up. Singer's committed suicide. Why? It's hard to say. He was very successful Over There as long as he stayed here. But once he was There everyone lost interest and he was completely isolated. What's Truth-teller doing? He's writing books, three at a time. One is the true history of Ibansk. The second is the falsity of the ideology of Ibanism. And the third is about where the Ibanskian people should go now, and how.' 'That's not serious work,' said Thinker. 'It shows a complete loss of a sense of reality. Why is he meddling with things that don't concern him?' 'But where is it set down what things can concern you and what cannot?' asked Visitor. 'Well, we're living in the twentieth century,' said Sociologist. 'People ought to be responsible citizens.' 'You accuse Truth-teller of not having any sense of civic responsibility?' asked Visitor. 'That's very strange.' 'I was thinking about something else,' said Sociologist. 'For instance, what kind of real history can he be talking about? It's something that doesn't exist. History is only written to distort the past in the interests of some preconceived idea. Everyone distorts it. The only important thing is the direction and the purpose of the distortion. That's an elementary truth. In my article in the Journal I wrote . . .' 'Truth-teller's attitude is clearly known,' said Dauber, raising Leadiban's forehead by another two inches. His attitude is anti-socist. And his purpose is the good of the people.' 'And what's the people?' roared Brother. 'Stuff the people! And shit on them! Come over here and have a drink!' 'It'll be just the same as the official history but turned inside out,' said Thinker. 'Truth-teller's entire philosophy consists of reversing the roles of the guards and the prisoners,' said Louse. 'But will that improve anything?' 'It'll make things worse,' said Thinker, pondering how best to approach Louse for a large and extended loan. 'And what does he know about Ibanism?' asked Dauber. 'Thinker here, for example, could refute him very easily if he wanted to. He's a specialist.' 'Hardly,' said Neurasthenic. 'He could put up a better defence than other people, but that is very dangerous, more dangerous than a refutation. You need a lot of courage for that.' 'You must be joking,' said Dauber. 'Certainly not,' said Neurasthenic.

'It's competition. A good book about Ibanism would immediately result in a high position, fame, titles, money. They'd find it easier to forgive a bad book against than a good book for.' 'He's joking of course,' giggled Rat. 'Well then?' Dauber asked Chatterer. 'Do you think he's looking better? Ha, ha! What a face I've given him! Napoleon! Ha, ha! A Roman patrician! Ha, ha ha!' 'It's not that that counts,' said Chatterer. 'Well, what does count then?' asked Dauber. 'The fact that you are sculpting Him,' said Chatterer, 'and the fact that he is being sculpted by You. That's the essence of the age.' 'It's staggering,' Chatterer heard Neurasthenic burst out as he was leaving. 'That nose! Don't do another thing with it! That's a real nose! That's a mug for you!! What a beauty!'

The return

No-one noticed the return of Chatterer. Even he did not notice that he had returned, because the way of life in the camps and here in freedom were so similar. When he had left Dauber's he decided to write a new treatise on him. But as the times for some reason were even more liberal than they had been before, it had become practically impossible to write the treatise without other people knowing about it and steps being taken. So he decided to compose it in his mind. During his time in the camps he had composed literally dozens of treatises in this way and had learnt to hold them in his head and reproduce them at will. If I could get hold of a tape recorder, he thought, I could dictate a whole book in a week simply because I've got nothing else to do. Since his meeting with Dauber he had been suffering from a mortal boredom. And he called his treatise:

THE RETURN

Initially I wanted to compose a poem about the victory of the strong man over sluggish circumstance and hostile surroundings, of a free spirit over a shackled body, of a genius over mediocrity, thought Chatterer. And it seemed that reality corresponded to this vision. The victory seemed to be self-evident. One could only dream about such a fate. Worldwide fame, recognition, the possibility of doing what one wanted to do, saying what one wanted to say, going where one wanted to go. What more could there be? But that would have been a lie. The strong man wins his victories by one course only—by becoming weaker. The genius conquers by becoming more mediocre. The free man conquers by putting fetters on himself. But whose victory would that be?

The return

Teacher came out on to the station square. The very sight of him made the passers-by pat their pockets to see if their wallets were still there. 'What a bandit,' they said. 'Just look at that face. People like that ought to be put inside! They ought to be hanged!' The policeman walked firmly up to him and demanded his papers, keeping a hand on his gun just in case. 'All in order,' he said, glancing at the documents. 'Now get the hell out of here! There are foreigners about. If they take your photograph it'll be the worse for you.' 'Go fuck yourself,' said Teacher lazily, and unhurriedly he put the documents back into order. There've really been some changes while I've been away, he thought. Just look at those skyscrapers! Just like New York! But there's still something that hasn't changed, the same bad taste, the same all-pervading drabness. Over there, for instance, they've dug the road up in the most visible place. They probably forgot to put the sewers in. And that skyscraper's being repaired already. Ibansk is still Ibansk. A province with pretentions to being a metropolis. A capital of capitals, as Leadiban put it. A remote little burg which thinks it's the centre of the universe. 'What are you doing here still?' he asked the policeman, who was getting more and more terrified. 'I told you to go fuck yourself! You can hang on to your gun. I might stay and sleep here.'

Indeed, where is there to go, he thought. I've no home to go to. His wife had immediately divorced him, as he had been told with some ceremony, and had had him deprived of his paternal rights. She had changed her apartment. Where could he get himself registered now? None of his friends was left. He came out on to deserted Claimant's Avenue. That's strange, he thought. It's still early but there's no-one about. Oh, of course, it's the match today. Our lot against the Greenland professionals. The match of the century! We need a victory of Ibanist principles in sport whatever the cost. If our lot lose somebody could well end up inside.

When he got to the Grocer's Stall, Teacher sat down on one of the empty boxes which lay scattered around, intended for some kind of fruit which could no longer be found in the shops. If my memory doesn't deceive me, Teacher thought, these boxes have been here since before I went away. So here I am, free again, he said aloud. Free! And he laughed. Beside him some-one else laughed. 'Who are you?' Teacher asked. 'No-one,' replied a voice. 'What about you?' 'I'm the same,' Teacher replied. 'Where are you from?' asked the voice. 'From the past,' Teacher replied. 'And you?' 'I'm worse,' the voice re-plied. 'I am from the future.'

'I usually live here,' said Bloke 'I've got a little corner where I can kip. It's my pad. But my Mistress is sleeping with the local Fuzz tonight. It's his turn. I could have gone off to sleep with the Speculatress, but she's sleeping with the Inspector today. There's been a lot of theft in their shop recently and they're having an inspection. So you can see the problem. Let's pop into the Pavilion for a bit and we'll think of something.'

The Ibanskian's kiss

Ibanskians have made great contributions to world culture. Radio, the samovar, little wooden dolls which fit inside each other—there's far too much to list. The Ibanskian explorer Bloke got to America on foot before Columbus—several times, in fact. Sometimes he would just grab a crust of bread and a spare pair of sandals and set off. 'Going far?' his next-door neighbours would ask. 'America,' Bloke would say. 'A proper little Christopher Columbus, isn't he!' his neighbours used to say with venom born of envy. 'Bring us back a little present. A bottle of their caca-kali. A suede jacket. Or a nylon fur coat. Ha, ha!' 'I would if I could,' said Bloke. 'It's the currency that's the problem.' And he set off, and got down to work. He went straight to the Brotherhood Bureau. 'Give me a character refer-ence,' he asked. 'Are you going far?' asked the Brother-organiser. 'To America,' said Bloke. 'A proper little Christo-pher Columbus, aren't you!' said the Brother-organiser. 'What d'you want to go there for? D'you think they can't get on without us, snottynosed lot? They'll discover America for themselves, without our help! They're not the same as us Europeans.' 'I've got a relative there,' said Bloke. 'Chingach-gook. Maybe you've heard of him. He sent me this invitation.'

'What kind of chap is he, your Chinthinmuk?' asked Brother-organiser. 'A millionaire is he? Some kind of reactionary? A racist? Works for the CIA?' 'No,' said Bloke. 'He's a chief—a Red Indian chief. All naked. Just like an Ibanskian. Can't tell them apart.' 'In that case,' said Brother-organiser, 'go and discover America!' And Bloke went. Straight to the special commission of senile pensioners. 'Tell me,' said Geriatric, 'what's the political set-up in your . . . whatd'ye call it? . . . America?' 'Savagery and barbarism,' said Bloke. 'And no family, no private property and no state.' 'You win,' said Geriatric. 'And what is the attitude of the king of a foreign power to events in the Middle East?' 'Negative,' said Bloke. 'Right again,' said Geriatric. 'And how many potatoes were harvested this year by the agricultural workers of Transibansk?' 'Twice as many,' said Bloke. 'Well done,' said Geriatric. 'You're politically well equipped. Someone who can be trusted. Off you go!' And off Bloke went. Straight to the Undertaking for National Oversight (UNO). 'So you're thinking of going to America?' said Colleague. 'Excellent. High time, too. But tell me: what did you say to your mate Blockhead in the Pavilion? And what about that story you told Sandal that night when you were pissed out of your mind? And are you aware that your Chinarsfuk has made some slighting references to the measures we've undertaken for the re-education of intellectuals who've blotted their copybook?' And Colleague pressed a button. A little window just in front of Bloke flew open and out shot an automatic snook-cocker which stamped the word REJECT on Bloke's forehead. 'Off you go,' said Colleague. 'No point coming back in less than a year. And just you remember . . .' And Bloke went off. Straight home. 'Did you get far?' asked his neighbours. 'To America,' said Bloke. 'Another one who takes himself for Christopher Columbus,' sneered his neighbours, winking at each other. 'Did you bring any presents, any little souvenirs? A bottle of coca-cola? Give us a taste—it's a long time since we had any. And how's your relative Hemingway? Haven't you brought any "anti" books back with you? We're so uneducated!' 'Just push off,' said Bloke. 'You're all putting spokes in my wheel, and while you're at it, Columbus'll be under full sail across the Atlantic and getting priority.' And he was right. After his voyage to America, Columbus visited Ibansk in the guise of a foreign tourist and met Bloke, who gave him a few addresses. The UNO agents rapidly unmasked Bloke, but it was too late. Columbus had sailed away.

Yet the Ibanskians' greatest contribution to world culture was the custom of the triple kiss. Historians consider that its worldwide spread has had as important an influence on the fate of mankind as the discovery of fire or the invention of the printing press. It is no mere coincidence that the year in which an international assembly adopted the Declaration of the Kiss became Year 1 of the new calendar. All historical events began to be dated as before or after the Ibanskian Kiss (BIK or AIK)

In the terms of the above-mentioned Declaration, the procedure of the kiss is as follows. The persons appointed to perform the kiss approach each other, their faces bearing an expression which in great Ibanskian literature is interpreted as 'Look who's here! It's ages since I last saw you! What a wonderful surprise!!!' When they have approached so far that the lower part of their stomachs are firmly pressed together, the participants in the ritual of the kiss stop and stretch out their arms at an angle of sixty degrees, palms upwards. Simultaneously they open their gobs, not so wide as to let their false teeth drop out, but wide enough to stimulate an adequate flow of saliva, and thrust their lips as far forward as possible. Then, with a sharp movement, they fling their arms about each other, the host-kisser leaning slightly to the left, while his right arm goes up across the left shoulder of the guest-kisser, while his left moves downwards to the right hip joint of the guest-kisser, while the guest-kisser bends slightly to the right, laying his left arm on the right shoulder of the host, and his right on the host's hip. In the past, kissers frequently confused the right and the left of the partner they were facing, and intertwined in such a remarkable way that it was sometimes very difficult to separate them. On some occasions oxyacetylene cutters had to be used. Then a special set of instructions was drawn up as a supplement to the Declaration and circulated to kings, presidents, chairmen, shahs and similar persons who were admitted to the levels of summit kissing. The instructions were prepared by the Association for Research and Scientific Evaluation of the Problems of Daily Life (ARSEPDL, or ARSE for short). Misunderstandings became less frequent, and there were fewer grave pathological consequences. At least they occurred only when other points of the Declaration were not observed. For example, if the navels of the two parties were not vertically aligned, then the partner's right shoulder, not his left, would be nearer to the kisser's right hand, while his left hip, not his right, would be nearer to the kisser's left hand. In such cases, the kissers would spend some time trying to catch each other as if they were playing blind man's buff, giggling merrily the while. 'Oh, Your Royal Majesty, where've you got to, fuck you! Ha, ha, ha!' 'And what about you, Your Supreme Excellency Comrade Chairman, where are you hiding? Ha, ha, ha!' In the end, the embrace would be established in strict accordance with the instructions, and each of the participants would clamp his lips to those of the other, while emitting sounds similar to the bursting of a child's balloon or the extraction of a cork from a bottle, and spattering the onlookers with saliva. They would do this three times. First from right to left, then from left to right, and then directly face to face, the noses being turned slightly to one side. During the performance the onlookers would clap their hands, put on angelic smiles, and chant 'Friend-ship! Friend-ship!'

Of course, this custom did not take on immediately. The leaders of Ibansk had to put a good deal of effort and imagination into getting it accepted. Thus, on one occasion, the Leader of Ibansk (Leadiban) was told that the king of some petty Western power, with whom Leadiban had decided to have a heart to heart talk, was not prepared to kiss. It seemed that his upbringing would not allow it. He had even laid down no kissing as a condition of the meeting. 'That's no problem,' said Leadiban. 'We've re-educated more stubborn cases than that.' And he was of course right. When the king came down the steps of his aircraft, Leadiban walked up to greet him with his hands behind his back. The king sighed with relief, and smiled. That was all Leadiban needed. He winked at the Defence Minister, a sign for the latter to thrust his huge belly covered in decorations up against the puny little kinglet, almost swamping him. The commander of the guard of honour drew his sword with such a flourish right under the nose of his majesticule and brandished it so furiously, that his majesty fled in terror into the arms of Leadiban, who grabbed him and was able to kiss him as much as he wanted. The king spent the next fortnight trying to scrub himself clean, as if he had spent a night in the cage of Ibansk Zoo's old camel, and she had spat all over him. Back home, the king's subordinates began to address him in most familiar terms and demand reforms. And the king abdicated. Briefly, Ibanskian leaders had to kiss several thousand politicians before the custom of kissing took over the world. After this, in the vocabulary of Ibanskian leaders, the old fashioned phrase, 'Just you wait, we'll show you!' was replaced by the phrase, 'Just you wait, we'll kiss you!'. A wave of student disorder in Paris was totally inexplicable to Western sociologists, but was brilliantly explained from the ibanistic point of view by Sociologist, Wife and Louse. For Colleague, the explanation was clear even before the troubles started. And he laughed condescendingly when he read Louse's article in the Journal of Directives. Under the influence of left wing forces, a café had been opened in Paris called 'The Ibanskian's Kiss', and a new perfume of the same name had been introduced. 'Just a little patience, now,' said Leadiban, 'and we'll crush them all like bedbugs.'

The return

'How've you been living while I've been away?' asked Dauber. 'No-one's been living,' said Chatterer. 'Nothing much has been happening. Just trivia. People see the recent past as the Golden Age. People like Claimant, Academician, Thinker and the rest are remembered as beacons of wisdom and liberal thought. You can imagine the kind of thing that must have crawled on to the Ibanskian stage to make those nonentities seem like titans! Rat, Flea, Louse, Bug and Mouse and rubbish like that. And they aren't the worst examples by a long chalk. In fact they're the best there are.' 'In other words,' said Dauber, giving Leadiban's twisted nose the shape of that of a Roman patrician, 'the Period of Perplexity came to nothing.' 'Why nothing?' said Chatterer. 'In fact what emerged from that period was very characteristic and quite significant. First, Ibanskian society expelled the elements which were alien to it, and reverted to its course towards a monolithic homogeneity.' 'And what about us?' said Dauber, 'don't we count?' 'You're sculpting Leadiban,' said Chatterer, 'and I'm still doing nothing at all. So we don't come into the reckoning. Secondly, the attempt of the liberals to get themselves confirmed in power ended in total failure. The liberals were either ejected from the power system, or they put on new faces, or drowned in the rising tide of mediocrity and drabness.' 'And what about the ones who *did* come to power?' asked Dauber. 'What are they like? Nothing at all? Mediocre? Dullards?' 'Something of the kind,' said Chatterer. 'But that's too superficial a way to look at it. It doesn't take account of the specification people like this have to fit. After all, the liberals weren't exactly gleaming talents. As a rule, mediocrity and stupidity aren't noteworthy social characteristics—they're normal qualities that most people share.' 'But what kind of people were they?' asked Dauber. 'Well, I'll explain it to you,' said Chatterer; 'take the example of the institute where I work. It's typical of the whole range of institutes which take an active part in determining the nature of power. And those are the only ones which should be considered here. Hairdressers, shops, factories and so on have no decisive influence on power.

'Rat was appointed our director,' continued Chatterer. 'What kind of man is he? Nothing out of the ordinary. In the past no-one would have ever dreamt he might be appointed to a senior post. And yet, just think, it took them two years to find him. But they found exactly what they wanted. An honest, efficient worker. He wasn't a careerist in the sense that he never made any concrete efforts to force his way upwards. In general, these people make their career in association with the layer they belong to, and not individually. He writes articles and books. They're very mediocre, but at least he writes them himself. And he's aware of modern science, and new ideas, and all the rest. It's all deadly dull. Never a mistake. Whatever line is demanded of him from above he's going to follow quietly, calmly, without the slightest deviation, just aiming at infinity. If they order him to brew up an artificial row, he'll brew one up. If necessary he can put on the most convincing appearance of anger. He'll turn red in the face and really blow his top. He's an extraordinary combination—calm, cold-blooded, self-controlled, psychotic, pathetic, rabble-rousing, sincere, hysterical and so on. In the time of the Boss he was trained as a real Brotherhood functionary. Then he was under a cloud for a while. But recently he's begun to make some progress. He's not a rogue—he lives modestly. A good husband and father. Well? Is that the kind of thing you want to hear?'

'Yes,' said Dauber. 'It's very interesting. Carry on!' 'His first deputy is Bug. They dug him up from under some stone. He and I were once students together. During the war he served in the military police. All the time he was studying he was always the local party organiser. A perfect product of the Boss's regime, and a devoted supporter of the Boss. He's modest, not stupid, but as grey as asphalt. He's a man of principle, and so on and so forth. The Scientific Secretary is Louse. I've known him since university days as well, when he and Bug and another of the same kind were terrorising the entire faculty. They organised all sorts of campaigns and persecutions against lots of unfortunate individuals. Then they overstepped the mark a little and had to be mildly rebuked. He's got no talent. He's honest, a hard worker, determined, sticks to his principles. In the days of the Boss he was still a child when he started his career. But then he resigned from quite an important job to study on a miserable little bursary. All that group submitted their theses when they were well past forty. Until recently they were never ever quoted anywhere, which gives you some idea of their mediocrity; they still look mediocre in our circles, which are crammed full of mediocrities.

'Under the eyes of people like that, the liberals published article after article, book after book. They took their doctorates when they were about thirty. They went to congresses, conferences, symposiums. They organised faculties, laboratories, institutes. Their names were constantly in the papers and magazines. They paraded themselves on television. In short, they were lapping up the cream. And these people were waiting. They'd been waiting for more than twenty years. They had built up enormous reserves of bitter hatred. They had learnt something. They had defended their theses. They had been published. They had risen. Never in the limelight, always on the fringes. But they had risen. And the main thing was that they realised that from the creative point of view the liberals were just as much crap as they were themselves, and sometimes even crappier. So they established definite lines of action. They were comparatively young, like the liberals. Maybe just a shade older. So they're here for a good long time.' 'So it's a restoration of the Boss's regime?' asked Dauber. 'Why a restoration?' said Chatterer. 'It's a normalisation.' 'So what can we expect?' asked Dauber. 'Nothing,' said Chatterer. 'Anything you like. They don't know themselves. That doesn't depend on them or on us.'

'But there has been some progress all the same,' said Dauber. 'You yourself admit that they are sincere and honest people, and not unprincipled hooligans and careerists like Claimant.' 'Don't forget that we're in Ibansk,' said Chatterer. 'Here every nightmare begins with a sickly honesty and hypertrophied principles. And all honest and high principled figures end up as petty villains of boundless vanity. And all the lighter periods we have lived through (and there haven't been so many!) have begun with petty villainy.' 'And they end, you believe, in . . .' Dauber broke in. 'No,' said Chatterer. 'They end in nothing. They have no continuation. Nightmares have other sources, quite independent of these. It became clear in the end that the liberals were neither talented nor honest, despite their pretensions to both. The people who have replaced them . . . what shall I call them? . . . not conservatives, not reactionaries, that'd be inaccurate . . . let's say the stabilisers . . . the stabilisers are playing the same kind of dirty tricks as the liberals used to play, but the stabilisers are doing it deliberately, as a matter of principle, and that's why dirty tricks are the normal thing these days. They correspond completely to law and practice.'

Détente

This was the beginning of a fierce struggle for détente which reached an immediate climax. The warring camps exchanged the customary Ibanskian triple kiss. The Ibanskians exchanged a few dissident intellectuals with dubious backgrounds for one and a half million tons of cabbage soup from America. The democratisation of Ibanskian society reached its zenith. The Ibanskian authorities authorised the erection over Hog's tomb of a gravestone in black and white marble. The interweaving and the blending of the black and the white symbolised the struggle between good and evil in the complex character of Hog, who, even in the opinion of the Boss, had been a man of low and primitive cunning, a small-time crook. The authorities also permitted a handful of wholly unknown artists to exhibit their nasty little daubs on a rubbish tip, having previously organised the breaking up of the exhibition with the help of the enthusiastic masses. 'Just look,' screeched the progressive forces of the West. 'What did we tell you! The Ibanskians are getting it right! They have triumphed!' 'Just wait a bit,' said the conservative forces. 'History could repeat itself.' 'Nonsense,' screeched the progressive forces. 'History is repeating itself, but the first time as a tragedy, and the second time as a farce. And there's nothing to be frightened of in a farce. You can't put history into reverse. Times have changed.' 'What an utter misinterpretation!' said Double-dealer. 'History does repeat itself, but the first time as a tragedy, the second time as a catastrophe.' But no-one paid any attention to Double-dealer. No-one listened to him at all since everyone had forgotten about him. 'The fate of Western civilisation is being decided in Ibansk,' said Truth-teller. 'The problems of Ibansk are not exotica or an entertaining side-show, they are your problems here in the West, and in the end you must come to understand that!' But even Truth-teller was not heeded. Even he had been forgotten. And no-one wanted to understand what he was saying. 'Remember the lessons of the past,' said Truth-teller. 'Who were the first victims of the Boss's regime?' 'Enough!' screamed the progressive forces. 'More than enough! Don't forget the justification of history! You mustn't exaggerate! See how well the Ibanskians are living today! After all, facts are facts! . . .' 'But the Boss's regime is a fact as well,' said Double-dealer. 'It is a fact of the present day, not of the past. It is not a dream, it is reality. Words are powerless,' said Double-dealer. 'It's not a question of blind delusion. If people were to know precisely where their actions were leading them they would still not desist from those actions. They perform these actions regardless of what they know; they merely follow the laws of mass behaviour, perhaps presenting them in a different verbal form. It is absurd to try to tell a man who is falling from a cliff that his fall will have unpleasant consequences for him. Yet, knowing this, it is impossible to keep silent.'

The return

In the Pavilion Bloke and Teacher immediately found themselves the centre of a warm and friendly crowd. They all knew Bloke. And Teacher had come back from Thence, and this produced a greater impression than if he had come back from outer-space. Thence, as everyone knew, no-one returns. And yet, suddenly, here was this miracle before their very eyes. At first no-one believed it. They scrutinised his documents. Then they shook their heads and said that no doubt one day Teacher would have to pay for his good fortune. Then they sang songs, thieves' songs of course.

> Mottle-faced drunkard soaked in gin,
> A year or two more and that's your lot.
> Baby-faced pilot with maiden's skin
> Drawing your flight plan and radar plot.
> Your song has been sung to the very end,
> For you can't tell life what to do, that's plain.
> In the dawn sky see the flare ascend—
> Scramble, chaps! Into your planes again!
> Not a dream, no grief, no family ties.
> The vomit stench that fills the bar.
> The pilot wheels high up in the sky
> And strafes the ground below him far.
> A moment of time is a tedious age,
> The world's end comes in a filthy bar.
> The aircraft circle to return,
> But the lead-plane falls like a blazing star.
> The trace of life is a bruised black eye;
> No-one wants to hear what you've got to tell
> As you lie there bleeding until you die,
> Your engine wrecked by an enemy shell.

They stayed in the Pavilion until closing time, stretching it by another half-hour while the cleaners scrubbed the floor. Then they moved off to the Bar. 'Recently,' said Teacher, 'I have found myself thinking only about the past. I can't think about anything else. It's terrible. And I can't find any peace because it seems that I have been living someone else's life, not my own. It's as if some idiot director has made me play a part which is not mine. And it's too late to change my role.' 'I understand what you mean,' said Bloke. 'The same kind of thing happens to me. I feel myself unjustly condemned to an infinity of grey stupidity, to an eternal vulgarity. A lieutenant, with his blood pouring from him, has at least a touch of the romantic about him. But what if we said:

(711)

The scientist pouring out streams of piss,
The poet brought down by a volley of snot?'
'That's nearer to the truth,' said Teacher. 'We have given our
whole life to the conquest of inner freedom. And we have
conquered. But what can we do with it? One might say that we
know everything, understand everything, that we are not constrained by any prejudices. But what now? More years? I don't
want to start living again.' 'Here's our house,' said Bloke,
prising a sheet of plywood from the wall of the Bar and squeezing through. 'A separate apartment—the dream of every Ibanskian! Crawl in! We'll manage here for tonight, and tomorrow
we'll think of something.' 'I think we'd better move in with the
Speculatress. She's quite a girl! And kind and resourceful with
it. You'll be like a pig in clover. That's, of course, if she gets
away with this inspection.'

And so it was that Teacher had a roof over his head for his
first night at liberty. And he dreamed a dream. He dreamed
that he really was at liberty.

A great victory

The very first day after the Ibanskian Kiss (IK), without any
declaration of war the Great Global Kissing (GGK) began.
No-one knew why. Only after it had ended, and when peace
broke out without any declaration of peace, did it emerge that
the hostile forces had wanted to reverse the course of history.
But the Ibanskians outkissed everybody and covered themselves with eternal glory. From which it followed that, in their
view of course, the GGK had been just. It was a further confirmation of the truth of Ibanism, that most scientific of sciences
in accordance with which every event in preceding centuries
had taken place. The Leader of Ibansk (Leadiban) was awarded
ten thousand of the highest decorations, and accorded the
supreme military title of Corporalissimus. His Deputies were
awarded five thousand medals each and the rank of Lance-
corporalissimus. And so on down, right to the worthless Bloke
who ended the GGK as a hopeless buck private and received no
medals at all. He was delighted by this, as it could have been a
great deal worse. The only thing he asked of higher authority in
the person of the local Fuzz was that he should be left in peace.

In return for a comparatively modest reward (two bottles a week) the Fuzz met him half way and allowed Bloke to do nothing.

The GGK was the biggest the world had ever seen. And it was the last. 'Now the war is over we can really piss in their faces,' said Leadiban, crawling out of the cellar from where he had directed operations. And he ordered the Academy of Sciences to prepare for him a twenty-four-hour-long speech to be delivered on the occasion of the Great Victory. To help in the delivery of this speech by Leadiban the inventive and creative scientists made a Robot, a perfect facsimile of Leadiban himself. To avoid any misunderstandings, Robot-Leadiban was locked up in a cupboard, from where a monstrous and pestilential odour soon began to emanate. When the cupboard was opened it was discovered that the Robot had shat its pants in the most natural way possible. This was the only proof that he was the real Leadiban, and the Leadiban who at the time was wandering round Ibansk issuing lunatic directives was the Robot. Leadiban appropriated all measures taken by his *doppelgänger* and was extremely proud of them. 'There will be no more GGK,' said Leadiban. 'There is no-one left to kiss, and no-one left to do the kissing. So we shall increase our military might not by a hundred per cent, as had been planned, but by two hundred per cent. We shall conscript everyone without exception. From henceforth we shall give highest marks to those who can miss the target using the most sophisticated infra-wretched sights. Target practice: that's the ticket! We now have great military experience and we are tempered in war.' For the great scientific value of his speech, Leadiban was granted the supreme scientific title of Einsteinissimus. His Deputies were awarded the title of Newtonissimus, and so on right down to the illiterate and worthless Bloke, who was left with no degrees or titles at all, and was delighted because he was left in peace.

During the GGK, Ibansk and its total population were wiped from the face of the earth. But the Ibanskians were in no way disturbed and founded a new city on the site of the old one, but this time a little higher up, on stilts, as it had become dangerous to live at ground-level because of the industrial waste which had completely polluted the environment, and household rubbish.

The surface of the land was turned into a rubbish tip and the Ibanskians from time to time organised specially authorised expeditions to search for raw materials and food. Since no-one bothered the Ibanskians any more, they swiftly re-established everything that used to exist, and even some things which had never existed. In particular, in their haste, they published a harmful little book by Slanderer. But they caught themselves in time, a feat for which Leadiban was awarded the highest artistic title of Picassissimus. The Deputies were awarded the title of Leonardodavissimus. And so it went on, right down to the worthless Bloke, who was completely indifferent about what might happen to art, and who was delighted to be left in peace. Slanderer was sent to jail, and Leadiban was awarded the highest detective title of Agathachristissimus. In a few words, the Ibanskians had launched themselves on a path of vigorous progress. They developed so fast and so far that, well ahead of their projections they achieved the supreme degree of Socism or of Total Socism—Madogism. They were not so much delighted by this as astonished that they had somehow or other managed to get there. 'Who'd ever have thought that we'd make it,' Leadiban said in a drunken conversation with his old enemy the Chief Theoretician. 'Be it said between enemies, no-one ever believed in this nonsense. And now look: It's been achieved!' 'To be perfectly honest,' said Chief Theoretician, 'I never believed in it either. We're not as idiotic as all these lousy little intellectuals think we are, not daft enough to believe in that kind of rubbish. I still don't understand how it happened myself. Surely it can't mean that Ibanism is really right?! Now that really would be a laugh! Ah well, the hell with theory. Here we go. The time has come to inaugurate this madogism. They're out there waiting for us.'

Bloke

Bloke spent most of his time hanging about near the Grocer's Stall, scraping together by honest or dishonest means enough cash to keep himself in drink and to pay off the Fuzz. When he had got drunk in the handiest Bar he rolled off to his lair, the little room belonging to Mistress, singing obscene songs at the top of his voice.

> A victory over all our foes!
> Hooray! But not so fast—
> Now we've eliminated those
> We're on our own at last.

A poet laureate, who had come down to the level of the people with the aim of becoming their guide and mentor, scornfully curled his thin and envious lips, the lips of the ravaged and impotent homosexual he was. In his view this was not art. But Bloke didn't give a damn for the opinion of this favourite of UNO and youth, as he himself categorically rejected any connection with art. And he carried on bellowing out his obscenities.

> From now on, who will take the rap
> For shortages of grain?
> Who will help us close the gap
> When our space programme fails again?

The poet couldn't stand this and rushed off to lay a complaint. Bloke was slung inside. In the lock-up he found a rusty nail and with it directly below a portrait of Leadiban he wrote this eulogy:

> Our democratic paradise
> To growth is now inclined.
> You may flee where'er you list
> And speak what's on your mind.

But there was nowhere for him to flee to, as Ibansk was everywhere. It stretched out to the site of Paris, to the site of New York, and even to the site of London.

> I'd like to flee. But this I know:
> By now there's nowhere left to go.

And there was nothing left to say, since everything had already been said—and with no result.

> And there's lots I'd like to say,
> But words don't mean a thing today.

'I can't judge its poetic qualities,' said the Warder, 'but it's all right as far as content goes.' It was later established that Bloke was the only and the last Ibanskian to have a zero level of political consciousness. 'How can this be?' the UNO agents chorused in amazement. 'An Ibanskian who has no medals, no degrees and no titles? It's impossible!' And Bloke was sent home to be kept in reserve for the subsequent progress of social and political consciousness.

(715)

The return

'It's very difficult Over There if you don't speak the language,'
said Dauber. 'I really don't understand it! You learn a foreign
language for ten years in school, then in an institute, and then
with private teachers. And it does no good at all. How can you
explain that?'

'There are various explanations,' said Chatterer.

We study foreign tongues at home
    From cradle to the tomb,
But the results, I freely own,
    Are not what you'd assume.
We stammer, stutter, er and um,
    And pretty soon, I reckon,
Back to Ibanskian we've come
    And dropped 'parler' and 'sprechen'.
So why, I wonder, what's the cause,
    That 'neath all this lies hidden?
I'm pretty sure that it's because
    Foreign travel is forbidden.
A chap from here, once Over There—
    No matter if he stutter—
Will be exposed to poisoned air
    In every breath They utter.
How can this be, when we've got faith
    In our superior theory?
Does socism have no firm base?
    Here is a valid query.
My boss explained it all to me,
    'It isn't for our sake,
But think how awful it would be
    If the Western world should shake.
Speaking strictly *entre nous*,
    Now listen calmly please,
It's not just cussedness that you
    Can't get an exit visa.
For if you talked to them out there,
    They'd take a resolution,
They'd shout and stamp and loudly swear
    And have a revolution.'
'Well then, what's wrong with that?' I cry,

'That's not an awful plight.
   It merely to my simple eye
   Confirms our theory's right.'
'There's nothing personal, you know,
   No arbitrary tricks.
The reason why you cannot go
   Is serious politics.
You've got to think and use your brain
   It's really not outrageous:
If the West went down the drain,
   Then who'd be left to aid us?
The Chinese, yes, our former friends,
   Would come—the thought appals—
And twist things round to suit their ends
   And have us by the balls.
So that's the way the matter stands,
   Empirically shown:
If you learn tongues of foreign lands
   You'll learn them here at home.'
   'Do these problems still really exist?' asked Dauber. 'Of
course they do,' said Chatterer. 'They are eternal. When there's
no abroad any more the world will be divided into regions, and
artificial barriers to movement and communication will be
erected. It is one of the most fundamental social laws. The
individual must be restricted in every respect. Otherwise such a
huge society could not exist. All this talk about communication
in the twentieth century is empty nonsense. It is anti-
demagogy, but demagogy just the same. When did you last see a
cell from an individual's backside set off on a tourist trip or
emigrate into his right cerebral hemisphere?' 'That's beside the
point,' said Dauber. 'Very well then,' said Chatterer. 'And how
often do brain cells from one free individual trot off to the brain
of another? We're living with the ideals of the past. In fact we're
moving towards the formation of extremely complex and gigantic autonomous social mechanisms which permit no freedom
and no interchangeability of parts. Just look what I've been
reading: even the Hottentots are building a steel plant and a
sewing-machine factory, setting up an academy of sciences and
developing a space programme. And without a visa they aren't
even allowed now to climb a tree for bananas.' 'So the story

(717)

goes,' said Dauber. 'There's nothing like that in the West.' 'They're lagging behind,' said Chatterer, 'in every respect. Go on, read a bit more: in the people's Republic of Tibangolia an exhibition of painting and sculpture has been opened. They had one and a half times as many sculptures on view as there are in all the galleries in Paris put together, and twice as many paintings as in New York, including the suburbs. There you are! And you talk to me about the West! They're shortly to open a school for super-gifted children here. A hundred thousand places. That's a scale for you! There's been a directive to raise our level and rub the West's nose in it. They might even ask you to go Over There and give them a course of lectures on the marriage between sculpture, architecture and politics.'

Sub-Ibansk

Well before the GGK a vast network of subterranean passages was established beneath Ibansk. There were tens of thousands of subway stations alone, to say nothing of cesspools and rubbish dumps! There were anti-kiss-raid shelters, with everything necessary to sustain the life of large numbers of people for long periods. The population engaged in this subterranean economy would have been enough on its own to form a state of considerable size. In his speech awarding a decoration to the sewage system, Leadiban said that the night-soil men alone could provide enough personnel to maintain the apparatus of government and staff all the scientific institutes of any Western state. First-class scientific research institutes were set up to study the subterranean economy. The underground dwellers were provided with pleasant residential areas, rest homes, sports grounds, all underground of course. The majority of underground workers grew so accustomed to the subterranean way of life that they felt uncomfortable when they were driven upstairs to take part in processions, receptions and farewell ceremonies. So when the war began and Ibansk was wiped from the face of the earth, and the exits to the surface were blocked with the debris, the underground dwellers went on for a long time as if nothing had happened. They were even happy in the beginning that they were being left in peace. No-one came bothering them with commissions, inspections, competitions, demonstrations and other great social activities. Later, legends began to be told about this period as of a mythical golden age. When young people heard these legends they just laughed. No meetings? No visits? No competitions? Not even any arrests? That's just old wives' tales! Tell it to the marines! . . .

When the war was over and its worst consequences erased and when Ibansk could be reconstructed on the surface of the land, (Super-Ibansk), they remembered subterranean Ibansk. It was the general opinion that everybody there had died. The efforts of the scientists to make contact with the subterranean civilisation were not crowned with success and it was agreed that Sub-Ibansk had ceased to exist. But the subterraneans had held out. They weren't Ibanskians for nothing. They had preserved and strengthened all the achievements of Socism. Since they lived in total darkness they had no need to write or read books, paint pictures or strike poses in theatres, films or on television. Thanks to this they had constructed Madogism much earlier than in Super-Ibansk. Their joy at this was so powerful that the earth trembled, and here and there in Super-Ibansk a few buildings fell down. But the scientists regarded this as a sure sign that inter-atomic processes were taking place in the centre of the earth.

The Shithouse

A matter of first priority in Ibansk was the reconstruction of that most ancient monument of Ibanskian culture, the Shithouse. At the opening ceremony Leadiban delivered himself of a twelve-hour speech. His entire audience fell asleep. Bloke, who'd been invited as one who had taken part in the building of the original Shithouse, took advantage of this. From his torn pocket he produced a rusty twelve-inch nail which was allegedly from that first Shithouse, and on the plastic wall of the new Shithouse he scratched the words of a folk song of the distant future:

> I tried to clear my intestine
> But first they made me stand in line
> With the builders of socism.
> They ordered me to shout 'Hooray!
> Life's getting better every day!'
> And show no cynicism.

For years I've had to heave and push,
What I need's a colonic flush
To avert a cataclysm.
But first I'm ordered to attend
A course of lectures which defend
The essence of the Ism.
I died and then began to rot;
I should be buried in my plot
For the sake of hygienism.
But first I had to do a test
On the laws and nature of—you've guessed—
The essence of the Ism.
If I had my time again
I'd see it wouldn't be the same,
Enough of cretinism.
Some senna pods, some castor oil,
And pull the flush, a flush right royal,
On the ideas of the Ism.

'That is not art,' said Bug, wiping Leadiban's arse with a
progressive editorial from the Journal which had been specially
written for this purpose. 'He's taken no account of the latest
scientific achievements,' said Thinker, who was standing
beside Claimant in the guard of honour around Leadiban's
arsehole. The liberal and astute Wife picked up the nail and
above the seditious verses scraped her favourite Ibanskian
four-letter word.

Madogism
'Madogism is the ultimate degree of socism, or total socism,'
said Leadiban on the eve of the inauguration of madogism in a
speech on the occasion of his decoration with the Highest Medal
for his services to progress. 'It can be distinguished from the
inferior stages of socism in the following way. In the inferior
stages each individual labours according to his abilities, and
receives a reward in accordance with what he has done. As the
phrase had it at that time, according to his labour. At the same
time, such a level of awareness is reached that each individual
knows precisely what abilities he has and which he has not, and
never tries to slip beyond the constraints of those abilities.
Society has methods powerful enough to prevent an individual

from working beyond his ability or trespassing on the abilities of others, and of convincing him that he has got what he deserves. Since everything exists in abundance, the individuals are quite happy and await the arrival of the ultimate stage. At the ultimate stage individuals go on contributing according to their ability but get back what they need rather than what they deserve. At this point awareness develops to such a monstrously high level that even in his dreams every individual remembers what needs he is entitled to and which he is not. And society develops yet more powerful methods to maintain individual consciousness at this supreme level. There's no other way. Otherwise everything would be pillaged in the blinking of an eye. The people! You know the people! You have to keep a firm eye on them! Since we have more than enough of everything, all needs are satisfied and . . . That is the essence of the matter. Many sceptics believe that men will become so content that they will need nothing better, and that from then on there will be no further need for progress. Progress will stop. Yet we can't do without progress. The theory does not permit it. It is here that we can see the gravest hazard of madogism—there will be such an abundance that there will be no further need for progress. Our enemies are particularly hysterical about this precise and central point of our scientific madogism. Ah ha, they cry. They will have everything in abundance. Everyone will be happy and content. But what happens then? Stagnation? No, we tell them, calmly and firmly. Progress will go on. It must. That is what the theory and the classics teach us. So what will happen then? Even to that question we have a precise and scientific reply. Then we shall see a struggle between the good and the even better. The even better will conquer the good. And society will continue its vigorous march forward.'

Leadiban's predictions were brilliantly fulfilled. As soon as the age of madogism dawned, progress moved ahead at an even swifter tempo. Something good, or even very good, had only to appear for something even better to get to grips with it in the struggle which the even better always won. For instance potatoes that were just about tolerable appeared. And immediately the even better launched itself into the struggle. The ealier potatoes disappeared altogether. And while the victors were being planted they were eliminated by even better potatoes, and so it went on. And in a comparatively short period madogism had not merely moved but galloped from its first stage to its second. It is now generally acknowledged that the first stage lasted from the inauguration of madogism until the unmasking of a group of enemies of madogism in the queue for thingammyjigs outside the Grocer's Stall at the corner of Boss Avenue and Victors' Avenue. The second stage began immediately after this and is still going on. It will soon end, for our beloved and brilliant Leadiban has insisted on the preparation of a concrete plan of transfer to the third stage and the fixing of a suitable date, which is to be Leadiban's next birthday. The first stage of madogism is characterised, as everyone knows, by the fact that it saw the emergence of a new and higher form of social community—the queue. At this stage there were still material interests underlying the queue. At the second stage, since those who had been awaiting thingammyjigs in the first stage had disappeared altogether, the queue acquired the attributes of the highest possible form of human community, being based on a high form of consciousness in which the mere notion of needs satisfied becomes equivalent to the actual satisfaction of those needs.

The return

'Why did you come back?' asked Chatterer. 'It's a long story,' said Dauber. 'You see, I never had any conflicts of principle with the authorities. My conflicts were with my own professional milieu. I overcame those. But Over There I found myself in a different milieu, and there too I gradually began to feel another conflict coming on. I felt that I would need at least ten years to win that one. And I don't have those ten years.' 'But what about your Great Project?' asked Chatterer. 'You see, as long as we're here, they regard us as being in the front line. But when we go There, we fall back into the rear-guard, and their interest in us changes. As far as my Project is concerned, it's not so simple. While I was here I had more propositions than I knew what to do with. When I went There they all disappeared in a puff of smoke. So I shall do it here.' 'But in the meantime you're sculpting Leadiban,' queried Chatterer. 'What else can I do?' replied Dauber. 'It's a matter of money. And apart from that, it's not as if I'm doing a deal with my conscience. I am making a real work of art. You've got to admit that Raphael painted the Pope, Goya painted the King, Praxiteles made a bust of Pericles, Delacroix painted Napoleon. I can see nothing wrong in that.' 'Are you suggesting that the Pope, the King of Spain, Napoleon and Leadiban are all birds of the same feather?' asked Chatterer. 'But he is a Leader,' said Dauber. 'The head of state.' 'That's not the question,' said Chatterer. 'The question is what mechanism pushes an individual to the summit of power, and what kind of individual is he apart from the power he wields, and what is the moral and psychological climate of that power. Leadiban can be painted or sculpted; but if it's to be a work of art, it must be a caricature.' 'That's what I'm doing,' said Dauber. 'See for yourself!' 'I can see,' said Chatterer, 'but I am afraid that no-one will notice that it is—especially the generations to come. No matter what kind of masterpiece you produce, it will be regarded as grovelling flattery just the same.' 'You're wrong,' said Dauber. 'If your principles were to be strictly observed it would be impossible to work at all. And how would I live?' 'As far as money goes, you could sculpt academicians,' said Chatterer. 'You've had offers and you've turned them down. Why? Because they've got a different kind of face? Ridiculous! Academicians have mugs every bit as ugly as Leadiban's. That's not the point. A portrait of Leadiban is just more publicity. Dauber has made a bust of Leadiban himself! Art transcends politics! And so on and so forth. You've got no problem of How To Live. All you have is a subjective ambition to live your life in a certain way.' 'You're too hard,' said Dauber. 'We are only people after all.' 'Yes, but we claim to be gods,' said Chatterer. 'We're not people. We are lice, or rats. If you want to be a man you must be a God. And to become a God you must become a Man.' 'Words! Words!' exclaimed Dauber. 'You take a trip Over There and look at all our little discussions from outside. You'll see how ridiculous and insignificant they are.' 'If my memory doesn't deceive me,' said Chatterer, 'we never claimed that they had any special importance, or indeed truth. All we claimed was sincerity. They seem insignificant to you since you believe they're insincere. But I cannot go Over There and observe all this from the outside. I am your spirit, and the spirit cannot emigrate. I am condemned to sincerity over trivia.' 'There is a lot that we shall have to talk out again from the start,' said Dauber. 'You know, the centuries will pass and our descendants will have quite a different impression of our epoch. Which means . . .' 'Which means,' said Chatterer, 'that it will be their life and not ours. We must live this life! There will be no other.' 'Words, words, words!' said Dauber. 'I'll never convince you. You must see and experience for yourself everything I have seen and experienced these last few years.'

The return

'Let's keep Speculatress as a last resort,' said Teacher. 'First let's go round to all my old friends, if the word still has any meaning. There must surely be some survivors of the past?' 'I doubt it,' said Bloke. 'They may ransack the past, but they do their best to forget it. And since in this society everybody is a friend there are no friends here at all. The only relationship which has the slightest resemblance to what friendship used to be is that with drinking partners. But that is condemned by the higher morality which has become enshrined in the law.'

Bloke's pessimistic predictions turned out to be true. One friend said he had left on a business trip. Another said that he was on holiday. A third said that he'd never heard of any 'Teacher'. A fourth . . . At every step they were stopped by policemen, self-appointed vigilantes, children serving as police volunteers, pensioners serving as part-time police, and even by dogs. 'What extraordinary vigilance,' said Teacher. 'These animals hold us up for the very reason that we're completely harmless and defenceless. If we were real thieves or began to rape and pillage in full view, not one of these swine would stop to help the victim.' 'We'll have to change our skin,' said Bloke. 'Let's slip in here. One of my old drinking companions, Sandal, lives here. He can probably let us have the right kind of clothes.'

'Hi,' said Sandal. 'You look a right beauty,' he said to Teacher. 'What is it, a fancy-dress ball? Oh, you're from Thence! Surely not! People say no-one ever comes back from Thence. Come in. Just cast your eyes on my apartment! Separate, believe it or not! Two rooms! It's a dream! It's a co-operative apartment, of course. You've got to make money where you can, and we're up to our necks in debt. But it's separate all the same! Oh, we sure had to rush about to find this place! Clothes you want, is it? You must be joking, lads! Just look at what I'm wearing! We could lend you a TV set if you like. Just look at that beauty. Latest model. Dawn of madogism, that's what it's called. A technological miracle. Receives all one hundred channels. Beautiful colour. Stereo. Make yourselves at home. Here you are, the chairs are self-adjusting.' They switched to Channel 1. Leadiban was presenting a medal to a tree under which he had once crapped during the war. The local inhabitants had taken great care of the little pile and had kept it fresh until now. There was even a little cloud of steam rising from it. Leadiban was deeply moved. Now he was going to embrace everybody . . . And then a speech, which would go on for a couple of hours. Channel 2. Leadiban delivering a speech. Channel 3 . . . By the way, you can switch directly to Channel 10. Ten, so be it . . . Leadiban taking off from the airport . . . Guard of honour . . . Leadiban returning home . . . Embraces . . . Guard of honour . . . Speech . . . Channel 33. Hero of labour. He has managed to grow thingammyjigs twice the size . . . What's this? Channel 47. Results of the competition . . . 69 . . . the political education channel . . . 71, hockey. 95 . . . football . . . What do you think of that? It's a nightmare, isn't it!' 'Why don't you sling this crap out of the window?' asked Teacher. 'Come off it,' said Sandal. 'It costs a fortune.' 'So why did you buy it?' asked Teacher. 'Everybody buys them,' replied Sandal. 'And then there's my wife, and my mother-in-law and my son. And just once in a while they put on something decent. Cartoons about animals. And sometimes there are quite good thrillers, mainly old ones from abroad. Apart from that, of course, it's the most god-awful rubbish. There's nothing to watch at all. It makes you sick. And yet you can't not watch. It's so boring. There's nowhere to go anyway. Just think, a hundred channels!!! Marvellous colour and a perfect picture. And what do they show? An endless flow of high-quality crap! Progress! What progress? Progress of culture? Which is better—technically superb reproduction of crap, or bad reproduction of real works of art? A hundred channels and almost no information about real life. Lies from beginning to end, or rubbish. And most of all, their idiotic poncing about. Speeches. Parades. Congresses. Presentations.

Congratulations. My God, will it never end? And what's happened to real life?' 'Alas,' said Teacher, 'I can tell you this as a
specialist: this *is* real life. And there is no other. They only allow
you what you call real culture so as to ensure for themselves
what they see as real life. So switch off this crap. Let them get
on with their posturing without our help.' 'It's hardly worth it,'
said Sandal. 'They might as well get on with their clowning.
Whatever else, it's better than nothing.' And he switched to
Channel 100. Leadiban was delivering a speech in honour of the
award of the Higher Medal to the Lower Medal for outstanding
services. He was speaking without notes. 'Just look at that,'
said Sandal. 'No notes! That's something new!' 'Rubbish,' said
Bloke. 'What they do these days is to shove a micro-receiver in
his ear and atomic powered micro-motors in his tongue. A radio
announcer records the speech on tape. Then they only need to
press a button on a control panel, and, whether he likes it or
not, Leadiban begins to deliver a speech. You can see he's
pissed out of his mind and sound asleep.' 'That sounds like a
good scheme,' said Sandal. 'There's no denying the progress
that science and technology have made. They're our only hope.'
'That's nothing,' said Bloke. 'Just recently an amazing brain-
receiver has been invented. It's implanted in the brain. And any
time now all Ibanskians, without exception, will find themselves hearing and seeing—yes, seeing!—anything the
authorities want. And there's no switching off! That's real
progress for you!'

After this visit they went off to the Pavilion and then on to see
Mistress. 'That'll give us someone to sleep with,' said Bloke.
'And they'll be able to rustle up some clothes for us.'

Madogism

Although from the very beginning the Ibanskians knew that
madogism was a tissue of lies, they never for a moment doubted
that sooner or later it would come to fruition. The founder of
Ibanist realist literature, Vermin, expressed these longings of
the people in these marvellous verses:

> We thought the day would soon be reached
> To dream of which had been decreed:
> According to his gifts, from each;
> To each according to his need.

(726)

The founder died on the eve of the inauguration of madogism, with his last breath confessing to his latest under-age wife that madogism was pure delirious schizophrenia. His country estate was divided into a hundred allotments and handed out to young prize-winning writers, who, in an access of gratitude, seized the banner of Ibanist realism as it fell from the tenacious claws of the founder, and published a joint statement:

Ibanskian! Believe! That dawn will break,
The dawn of happiness—our goal.
And madogism will awake,
Not incomplete, but full and whole.

The Ibanskians knew precisely when madogism's arrival would be announced, and rehearsed repeatedly, under the direction of the specialist instructors, how they were to behave at this moment, the most solemn moment in the whole past and future history of mankind. They even knew where to find the sandwiches which had been prepared for them and which they were to eat as they wished. And they even put distinguishing marks on their sandwiches to avoid any confusion. But despite all these preparations they were completely petrified when one day, at dawn, millions of loudspeakers roared full blast to the entire universe:

Hey, Ibanskians! Rise! Awake!
The cock has long since crowed!
Get your clothes on, for God's sake!
Madogism's on the road!

That was the voice of Leadiban beginning his famous speech. The speech had been prepared by all the workers of Ibansk, with the exception of Bloke, over the last hundred years and each of them had contributed his ha'pennyworth. Bloke had declined to help prepare the speech, adducing the heavy burdens of his life as a political activist. He had just been appointed head of a methodological seminar in a chemistry institute, without being relieved, as he had been promised, of his responsibilities as cultural organiser to a group of rogues and spivs in a furniture shop. 'Mothers and daughters!' bayed Leadiban, 'grandmothers and granddaughters! Fathers and sons! Grandfathers and grandsons! Brothers and sisters! Men and women! My friends, I am talking to you! At last has dawned . . .' And you go and . . . thought Bloke, and rushed into the nearest bar

(727)

to get his sandwich and his regulation portion of ersatz de-alcoholised vodka. But his way was blocked by a group of giants from the People's Militia. 'Where do you think you're going?' said one, driving his enormous fist into Bloke's puny rib-cage. 'I just thought I'd stop in for a drink,' groaned Bloke, without a great deal of hope. 'What's happened to your consciousness?' said another, driving his knee into Bloke's puny arse. 'You could do with rinsing your dirty mouth out for a start. The drink ration won't be issued until after Leadiban's speech, and then only if you've got tickets. And bring your own bottle, you idiot.' 'All I want is a drink,' muttered Bloke, as he wandered around the rubbish tip. He had not been issued with any tickets as his consciousness had not risen to the level of total Ibanism. He had no idea where these tickets were to be found. I'll have to go and see Speculatress, he thought. 'Psst! darlin', come here,' a cleaner in a grocer's shop whispered to him. 'Wotcha want? Only three roubles for a weeny bottle.' 'Three for that?' said Bloke angrily. 'For three roubles I could get a half-litre . . .' 'That was before,' the cleaner whispered maliciously. 'Now we're at the higher stage. 's gone up ter five now . . .' There was no avoiding it, and Bloke handed over his last five roubles. He drained the bottle, cheered up and went off to listen to the speech, intoning a song which his imagination had dredged up from somewhere:

> I'd like a drink. Some grub to eat,
> And then a girl to screw.
> Ideas? I just don't give a shit—
> They leave me cold, they do.

As he turned into Victors' Avenue he was stopped by patrols who insisted on seeing his consciousness disc. Bloke groped through his pockets and managed to find a circular piece of metal about the size of a commemorative medal, which depicted the cerebral hemispheres and bore the figure zero, which indicated the lowest level of consciousness. 'How can he be at liberty with a number like that?' said the patrol leader. 'It's very odd. Must be a mistake.' So Bloke was taken off to the police station. On the way he carried on singing:

> From the shithouse to the bar,
> From th'apartment to the tip,

Towards the ideal, from near and far,
The people surge in comradeship.
When Bloke had been flung into his cell he took his rusty nail from his pocket and on the wall, already scrawled over with various oaths, he wrote these words:

The new order is a perfect fit
To those most high ideals.
You've got talent? Shut your lip!
Got needs? Well, cool your heels.

The following day he was released with his level of consciousness increased to one point. I'm beginning to make a career, thought Bloke. This could well end badly.

There was no light in the room. The door was locked. That's interesting, thought Bloke, I wonder where the bird's flown to. He groped around among the breadcrumbs, spent matches and scraps of paper which filled his ragged pocket and brought out his key. He quietly inserted it in the lock and turned it twice clockwise, then twice anti-clockwise and finally twice back again. This was a wily protection against thieves who had proliferated incredibly in Ibansk on the eve of the inauguration of the highest stage of socism. In the tiny room the local Fuzz was lying on the bed with Mistress, without his trousers but still wearing his boots and holding his whistle between his teeth. Bloke crept over to Fuzz's jacket, took a three-rouble note from his pocket and went off to the Pavilion. Just for a joke he left a note for Mistress saying, Here you are with this . . . . , while down at the shop they're giving away thingammyjigs! How was he to know that this joke was to change the entire course of Ibanskian history and divert it in a direction which was very far from that predicted by the classics.

Progress

When the whole world had become Ibansk, Leadiban began to feel bored. He had nowhere to go visiting. He was tired of handing out medals, and anyway it was almost humiliating for him, Corporalissimus, Supreme Commander of All the Armed and Disarmed Forces of the Galaxy, to go off to some stinking little hole far away to hand out these bits of meaningless cardboard. There was no-one really worth kissing. He hated kissing his Deputies. Although it was laid down in the Statutes, and he respected the Statutes, it was sickening just the same. He knew these Deputies like his own skin. He'd been one himself. All they ever thought about was how to overthrow him and take his place. A worthless crew! What were they fit for? Nothing but wagging their tongues and lolling about on presidiums . . . Ah, those were the good days, the days before, before . . . Guards of honour! The applause of the masses groaning under the yoke of Colonialism!

Fervent handshakes. Kisses. Meetings.
Fond embraces. Speeches. Greetings.
Waving banners. Crowds applauding.
Tears at parting. Most rewarding.

Could that all be over? No! We must not have a nihilistic attitude to the past. There were good things in the past as well. Take the Boss, for example. Now he . . . And Leadiban summoned his Deputies, Assistants, Insistants, Inspectors, Collectors, Injectors and Ejectors and so on, right down to the most junior advisers. And he issued a directive.

Soon Ibansk was divided into geometrically identical regions all of the same size. Each region was conceived so that it was like Ibansk as a whole. The only difference was that at the head of each region was placed a Leadibanlet, as the supreme power in Ibansk and all the former system of government remained unchanged. This new division and the new regional system of power was closely associated with the old forms, but acted as if there were no power apart from itself. Relations were established between the regions like those which had existed in the past between sovereign states. Frontier guards and customs posts were established. Visas were introduced. And now Ibanskians were able to go from one region to another just as freely as they used (before) to go abroad.

Now as Leadiban travelled about the regions people began to greet him as if he was arriving in some sovereign state abroad, whose people adored him devotedly and wished to follow in his footsteps and be united with him. In the regional capitals special shops were established where foreign tat could be bought for hard currency. Leadiban, his Deputies and UNO agents were able to acquire this tat without hard currency as if they had indeed travelled abroad. Leadiban's visits to a region became national holidays. On these occasions the Ibanskians were obliged to drop their work and hurry to their appointed place to greet the great man. In recompense they had the right to buy one salami sandwich each.

Leadiban conceived a particular affection for the lavatory region. There a permanent guard of honour was established. And the inhabitants of the region mounted a twenty-four hour watch on the sides of the roads along which proceeded the super-armoured cars of Leadiban's motorcade. No-one ever knew which car carried the real Leadiban, as the Robot Leadibans sitting in the other cars looked identical. The only thing that they could not do was what the real Leadiban did in the lavatory. As he sat in the lavatory, Leadiban, apart from doing what the robots could not do, spent his time in reading speeches. Leadiban's Lavatory speeches were greatly loved by the people and were published in editions of such fabulous size that they began to clutter up the streets. Then they began to be sold as a make-weight to every kind of goods—a tendency reinforced by obliging the citizens to join study groups to learn the speeches and to take examinations about them.

After this Leadiban became a great deal more cheerful. Life had taken on a new interest and meaning. When he saw with his own eyes the rejoicing of the populace, tears streamed down his cheeks into his liquor glass, and he would say: 'It is not for nothing that we have poured out our blood by the barrelful on the barricades.'

The return

'You're wrong,' said Dauber. 'Just remember the business of Hog's gravestone. Was it a success? It was. Did I preserve my dignity? I did. And this is the same kind of case. Whatever you say, Leadiban is at the head of a progressive movement. His foreign policy is a great step forward. And it's a very sensible step.' '*His* policy?' said Chatterer in astonishment. 'All right, let's say that it is his. Even if it weren't, this step was forced on him by circumstance. And actions that are forced on you cannot be described as wise or stupid or good or evil. They are forced and that's that. Anyway, that's not the problem. You talk about success, but you have to make a distinction between real success and illusory success. If you want to measure them, you have to use a different formula for each. The value of the former is equivalent to a certain fundamental constant of personality divided by the coefficient of popularity and fame which must be greater than one, and the value of the latter is equivalent to this constant multiplied by the same coefficient. Although that may be commonplace, it is the truth. Go ahead and sculpt Leadiban. There's nothing wrong in that in principle. But can it be said to represent progress in your creative development?'

Our children are our future
'The school sent for me today,' said Sandal. 'It seems that my daughter has been writing verse. And what verse! Not to put too fine a point on it, anti-Ibanskian verse! They told me to do something about it. But what can I do?' 'What has your daughter got to say about it?' asked Bloke. 'She says it wasn't her,' said Sandal. ' "All right then," she says, "let them prove that it was me." Here, just read it. This one's about the anniversary of Writer's death:'

You died before your time, you cur,
Your death was somewhat premature.
Our need has never been so great
To hear you, kiss-arse, perorate.
These are strange times. The Ibanskian land
Has no strong, firm, controlling hand,
Despite the people's wish and will.
We live as one great family. Still,
We none of us get on too well,
But make our lives a merry hell.
Rebellious words are now expressed.
Awake then, poet! Get you dressed!
Declaim, denounce, your lips unseal!
As in the past, sing once again
Of one whose name will yet remain,
Of one whom time cannot conceal.
(translated from Assish)

'Oh,' said Teacher. 'That's something to think about! And what's this "Assish"?' 'I don't know,' said Sandal. 'It's some kind of language they've invented. The headmaster kept on trying to discover what it meant. I said, jokingly, that it was probably something to do with Buddhism. That put him into an even greater panic.' 'I remember,' said Teacher, 'that when I

(732)

was at school we played at constitutions. It's the game that all the grown-ups were playing at the time. We used to draw up our own constitution and we issued our own money. Just for safety's sake we wrote on the notes: Nothing can be bought with this money. There was a tremendous row about it at school. Incidentally, that poem can be interpreted in a completely orthodox way.' 'That's what I said to the headmaster,' said Sandal, 'but he said "we're not that stupid!" The thing that alarms me most of all about the poem is that it's impossible to tell when it's joking and when it's serious, that there's no frontier between the comic and the terrifying. Just look at that! Here we are, racking our brains about the most complex problems of existence without finding any solutions. Yet for our children all our deepest problems lie on the surface. They simply don't see them as problems. You might think that the education of a person here is a development of his ability not to understand the obvious. I'm prepared to come to terms with everything. But when I consider the swamp that our children are going to have to cross, I go out of my mind with despair. Recently I went to see Scientist. And of course we began to poke fun at the authorities. And his seven-year-old son interrupted. "You can't talk like that about our leaders," he said. Scientist explained to him that this gentleman was only joking, that in fact he really loves our leaders. That surely can't be historical necessity as well? And another thing. The grandfather of one of the boys in their class died. Snuffed it, as they say. A very meritorious grandfather. He ought to have been buried in the Old Whores' Cemetery, but for some reason or other permission wasn't given. And what a row there was about it in the family!'

> At twenty he became a copper,
> Always moaning, good and proper,
> 'Why can't I get enough good food?'
> This thought became his ruling passion:
> 'If I'm promoted, if I'm good,
> I'll get a supplementary ration.
> But we don't get such approbation;
> I've tried everything, I fear,
> So must we die of cruel starvation
> While They've got kasha up to here?'

At forty his promotion came,
But he still grumbled, just the same.
'I'd like a villa—that's my right.'
The thought kept running through his mind:
'When they say yes, I'll get a site
In some village, unconfined.
I've got no chance? It isn't fair!
It means we are some lower sort
Who've got to breathe polluted air
While They have their seaside resort.'
At sixty, when retirement came,
His false teeth clicking, just the same,
He moaned, 'I want a burial plot
Beside the great—that's my desire.
These last five years I've done a lot
To try to get it passed up higher.
I'll never see the day, you think?
So all my life's consumed in work.
I can lie anywhere to stink—
Even here, They pick up every perk.'
'Don't tell me all their heads are crammed full of that kind of
stuff,' said Bloke. 'Why not?' said Sandal. 'They're not blind.
There's no hiding anything from them if they want to see it.
Take her, for instance. She'll be leaving school soon. And then
what? I could use my position and my connections like
everyone else. But she said that if I do she'll leave home. And
she would, too. I know her. And for an intellectual's daughter
to get into an institute without a helping hand! . . . But just say
she gets in anyway. What difference will that make? She wants
to be an art historian, and we all know what that means here.
And she knows it too. Read the rest; that predicts everything!
It's about the birth of my son.'

So you've arrived? And you think you've done well?
You think that life's the pleasantest invention?
I tell you this, young man: our life is hell;
Evil's the rule, and good has no dimension.
And life on earth, what's more, is very brief;
You'll hardly have had time to take a breath
Before you realise that it's time to leave
Back to the Nothing and the Nowhere—death.

There's no god—but there's still a Judgment Day;
Your useless life will prove that in the end.
Nothing that happens to you, sad or gay,
Can save you from yourself, my foolish friend.
Even in death you'll find no consolation,
And far too late you'll realise for sure
That there's no end to earthly tribulation:
Eternity means suffering evermore.

'That's not bad,' said Teacher. 'What for us is the product of long reflection is a mere starting point for our children.' 'That's a pity,' said Bloke. 'Our descendants will not be able to appreciate our wisdom.' 'No matter,' said Teacher. 'After all, our ancestors will give us our due.'

The queue

Shortly before the inauguration of madogism a Greengrocer's Shop was built at the corner of Boss Avenue and Victors' Avenue. Since there were neither fruit nor vegetables to be had, the Shop was boarded up with rough-hewn planks and soon became an unofficial latrine for all the local drunks and hooligans, who had become so insolent that it was to all intents and purposes impossible to avoid the introduction of madogism. So those critics who regarded the inauguration of madogism as unnecessary and premature could not have been more wrong. Incidentally, when the principal critic was stripped and beaten round his critical head in the area of the Shop, he radically changed his opinion. 'Let them have their madogism, the scum,' he said as he left the police station and subsequently the hospital. 'That's exactly what they deserve!' 'So you've finally got the point,' said the Fuzz. 'It's never too late. And since they'd begun to think of themselves as the masters . . .' Because of the fetid stench which emanated from the Shop, the Ibanskians avoided it by using a side street, for they had not yet had time to rid themselves of the survivals of the inferior stage of the Ism (Infism).

No-one knows how the rumour started that the Shop was going to begin selling thingammyjigs. Yet that very evening, outside the Shop there began to form a

By the morning the queue had grown to five hundred people. And by mid-day, when the rumour was almost confirmed, it had passed the thousand-mark. Lists were drawn up. There was a roll-call every hour on the hour. The queuers started having their numbers drawn on their foreheads. But the result of this was the appearance of a multitude of impostors bearing forged numbers. So they began to write the numbers on their left buttocks. This was to have an enormous educative importance, as it obliged many citizens to change their underwear for the first time in ages. Blockhead joined the queue with the number 3957. It was then that he saw Bloke and Teacher sitting on a couple of empty crates sharing a small bottle of vodka.

A.R.S.E.

Beyond any doubt, the most accomplished scientific research establishment in Ibansk was ARSE. It had been established not according to the last word in science and technology, but according to the word which was still in preparation for many centuries in the future. It was founded by Ibanist-futurologists.

Ten one-hundred storey blocks made of tetracycline and trichlorethylene, which formed, as it were, a single indivisible unit. One hundred million workers, including ten thousand Academicians, twenty thousand Corresponding Members, fifty thousand Co-Researcher Members, one hundred thousand Co-Debaucher Members, five hundred thousand First-Rank Sages (Firasas), and so on. It's true that there was at first something of a scuffle in the entrance hall where passes were checked and pockets searched (these bastards'll take anything they can carry!), but the mathematicians took charge. They began to push two or three workers through at a time, and the congestion eased. The main thing was the total automation of the whole complex of research and activity. A graph of the individual biological processes of each worker was taken, and they were all fed into the Computer which occupied nine blocks of the ten which formed the institute. Bio-detectors were installed throughout, which were able to determine the absence or the presence of any given worker on the premises of ARSE, his particular location and his movements through the building. All each individual worker had to do was to arrive in the morning at the given time and take his place on a conveyor belt, which with a speed close to that of light, rushed him into the interior of the building. Once there, a system of elevators delivered him to his place of work. He would find on his desk special sheets of paper which, after a certain length of time, were transferred to special reading and analysing equipment. These converted the sheets into columns of figures and fed them into the Computer. The Computer checked the quality of the work and gave it a mark. The results were then passed to the Totalising Computer, and then to the Evaluative-Outpayer. Thus it went on from day to day. Twice a month the workers went to the Outpaying Department where they were given (again automatically) what they had earned (this was the case before madogism; after the introduction of madogism certain amendments were introduced, about which more later): their wages, bonuses, medals, degrees, titles, punishments. It is interesting to note that even at that time consciousness had achieved such a level, and science had probed so deeply into the secrets of matter, that there was strict observation of the principle that the higher the position the greater the reward, and the lower the position the more severe the punishment.

Everything went very well. Unqualified Junior Researcher (UNJURES) Blockhead received, as was laid down, merely a few pennies, won no bonuses, but in compensation was awarded dozens of rebukes. And suddenly one day the Computer announced that Blockhead had earned more than the Director of ARSE himself. The institute was petrified in astonishment. The news of this event was all over Ibansk in a flash. Can it be, the Ibanskians whispered to each other, that in Ibansk a genius has appeared who has no degrees, no titles, no rank and no position? Surely not! How could such a genius not be the Director? And he's not even a Firasa! Impossible! There were some who said that there had once been a time when this sort of thing happened fairly often . . . Take Dauber, for example. He was never one of the bosses! Oh yes he was, said other, better informed Ibanskians. Dauber was the head of the Central Department for Sculpture in Shit!

The return

'Intelligentsia . . . intelligentsia . . .' grumbled Dauber. 'I'm the intelligentsia. And so's that Shithead from the Department of Culture. And you're the intelligentsia, and Rat as well, and Colleague. So what is the intelligentsia? No, I've no personal ambition to count myself among their ranks.' 'Even though you swear like a trooper and garble foreign words and scientific terms, you're an intellectual just the same,' said Chatterer. 'You are a refined intellectual. And Shithead is not an intellectual.' 'What is he then?' asked Dauber. 'An official, a civil servant,' said Chatterer. 'Rat's not an intellectual either, even though he has published a dozen books. He's a clerk. But I'm an intellectual, although I've published nothing.' 'So what is an intellectual?' asked Dauber. 'Let's try and define the concept! I think that's putting it scientifically enough?' 'No,' said Chatterer. 'In this case it's not a definition of the concept we need but to delimit a specific social phenomenon within the general social milieu, and to mark it off from other kinds of social phenomena. This is not a definition, but quite a different kind of operation. It is similar to what chemists do when they isolate a certain substance from a compound of other substances or from some more complex structure.

'What we need here,' Chatterer continued, 'is not the classification of people according to social categories. We need rather to isolate a certain substance or a fabric of society which is associated with the word "intelligentsia". Of course there are people who are characteristic representatives of this substance. You, for example, or Truth-teller, Singer, Double-dealer, Slanderer, Schizophrenic. Neurasthenic too, in parts. Visitor absolutely. Even Producer, even Brother. There are whole groups of people who form part of the intelligentsia without any doubt at all. They're people who put forward new ideas and who lay down new paths in the field of mankind's spiritual culture. But the great mass of people form part of the substance only to a certain extent. For example, true connoisseurs of music, poetry, science in its more spiritual forms and so on. They form the medium without which the artist, the writer, the actor or the scientist could not exist. It is impossible here to draw clear boundaries. An official can sometimes fulfil the function of an intellectual. Even policemen, militiamen, prison guards, informers and so on are, to a certain extent, part of the intelligentsia. A given society can be defined equally by its intellectuality—which can even be measured. How? This is the key to our problem. The level of education of a society does not indicate its intellectual level. Education and intellect are closely linked, but they are not one and the same thing. In modern conditions a highly educated society of low intellect is perfectly possible. How can I say this? By comparison with the intellectual level of past societies and of the countries about us, for instance. But that is a separate problem. What matters to us is that they are not one and the same thing. We have ample numbers of highly educated scientists, officials, artists, writers and so on, who are totally without intellect and who are deeply hostile to it. In one way education and intellect are enemies. Education is static. Intellect is dynamic. The former gathers in the fruits, the latter ploughs the soil and sows the seed. Do you see what I'm getting at? The intellectual level of a society cannot be defined by the number of engineers, doctors of science, professors, writers, artists and so on, either in absolute or relative terms. In Ibansk there are hundreds of thousands of such people, even millions. But it remains a society of a low intellectual level. Neither is the number of books published, the number of exhibitions, cinemas, films produced, theatres, studios and so on an indication of the intellectual level of society. They are pointers, but to other characteristics of society. An intellectual society is a society which is capable of objective self-knowledge, and of withstanding blind and elemental tendencies which exist within it. It is a society which is capable of spiritual self-improvement and progress. It can pursue this course by any means in any form. The intellectual principle can manifest itself in art, which is the most usual way. But not the only one. It can manifest itself also in science. The birth and development of certain ideas in physics, mathematics, biology and so on have more than once shown quite powerfully the intellectual nature of a society. The same goes for morals and religion. It can even be seen in fashions in clothing or furniture. Even in the way people make love. Here there are no strictly defined frontiers or categories of people. This is why the intellectual principle is very closely connected with considerations of morality, law, creativity, conscience, and so on. An intellectual society is, in a word, one which has the ability to recognise its own essence, an essence which expresses itself in its spiritual creativity and is defended by a specific social milieu. This is why an intellectual society can be defined (and measured) by the number and scale of the people who form it, by the number and scale of the ideas and creative results they produce, by the degree of their influence on society, and by the degree of their continuity and their durability. Consider all the spheres of our cultural life and count up the phenomena of this kind, and you'll see how intellectually impoverished we are. We have almost nothing. Folk song and dance ensembles? Ballet? None of that is a reflection of the specific social problems of our times. It is art. But it is an art which camouflages the essence of our society and diverts attention from it. It is apologetics. The intelligentsia, by their very function in society, are critical and given to opposition. Those are their inherent traits. No apologia can be intellectual. So you will come across periods when art flourishes while intellect goes bankrupt. The same thing happens in science. The intellectual, as a social individual, is a person professionally engaged in some area of intellectual activity. You are an intellectual. But Artist is not. He is a careerist and a scrounger who has simply chosen art as his field of endeavour. He is an artist, but not an intellectual. Truth-teller is an intellectual to the highest degree, although it cannot be said that he is a highly educated man, that in any general sense he has had a good social upbringing, that he is a good conversationalist and so on. The lads who were chased away from the Rubbish Tip by the bulldozers are also intellectuals, although in your opinion they were only mediocre artists. They are intellectuals by their social position and their social role. It makes no difference whether or not this role was forced upon them. All roles of this kind are always imposed on people in our country. People do not go into opposition of their own free will. They are driven there by circumstances.

'The intelligentsia is the most difficult element of the social fabric to form, and it is the easiest to destroy. And once it is destroyed, it is incredibly difficult to revive. It needs constant protection. There is no need even to attack it to destroy it. Simply deny it protection, and society will see to its destruction. The world in which the intellectuals move, their colleagues, their friends and in particular pseudo-intellectual circles, all hate the genuine intelligentsia because they would like to be considered the true intellectuals themselves. These circles are powerful, and therefore pitiless. Does it take much to kill off an intelligentsia? It takes nothing. A silence here. A cutback there. A couple of words in the right place. A rumour started, and so on. In our country we've got the techniques off to perfection. There's no need to learn them. They simply come into people's minds. And the authorities either close their eyes to all this or encourage it, because an intellectual is a man who speaks the truth about society as a whole, including the authorities.'

'That's evident,' said Dauber. 'That's all been evident for ages. But when it's all wrapped up in pitiless formulae it becomes unbearably tedious and depressing.'

The queue

The management of the Shop occupied a tiny little ten-storey building on Hog Square, although offices of such importance had a right to their own forty-storey block at the very least. There were only about five hundred employees, although down at the ministry people had been saying for ages that it was high time to double the staff. The director was tearing his hair out to increase his staff by a mere hundred, and to build an additional four or five floors. But all his efforts came to nothing against the unsurmountable wall of bureaucracy and red tape. It would take some extraordinary circumstances to get things moving.

The rumours that the Shop was going to sell thingammyjigs came as a complete surprise to the management. Thingammyjigs had disappeared from sale long before the arrival of madogism. Not only ordinary Ibanskians, but even expert thingammyjigologists had completely forgotten what they were. Later, when the radio and television stations began to get millions of letters asking for explanations, they usually produced two experts: one explained how thingammyjig was drunk, and the other, how it was chewed. All the same, the director immediately realised the benefits he could derive from these rumours. They were those very extraordinary circumstances he had dreamt about ever since his youth. My hour has come, he thought. There'll be a queue. People will pay attention to me at last. They'll put me in a forty-storey . . . No, in a fifty-storey building. I'll get ten times the staff. They'll give me the rank of First Rank Assistant (Firaas). I'll be elected to the Academy. I'll get a medal. Then I'll be transferred to the ministry as a deputy. And then, who can tell? Minister! And the director urgently summoned to his office the Brother-organiser, the union-organiser, the youth-organiser, the wall-newspaper editor, the sports organiser, the personnel manager, the secret police-organiser and the heads of departments—in short, the entire management. The meeting lasted a full twenty-four hours. It was resolved to approach the minister with a request to be allowed to show initiative. But the rumours had already reached the ministry and had been judged. The cumbersome and normally sluggish bureaucratic machine on this occasion showed remarkable agility. The minister had an immediate meeting with his First Rank Deputy (Firadep), who had an entrée to UNO, and had a long talk with him. At a general meeting of the management of the Shop it was decided to launch a competition with the management of the Book Kiosk, where a queue had also begun to form as there was a rumour that a subscription list was going to be opened for the works of the old writers who had died before the Great Victory. The Academy of Sciences resolved to hold an all-Ibanskian conference on the actual theoretical problems of thingammyjigology. The illuminated advertising panel on the Ministry of Food and Drink building displayed some lines written by the poet Bug.

Thingams are useful for old and for young.
Myjigs are useful for healthy and sick.
They're cheap and they're tasty and highly nutritious.
Hurry and buy them—or you're for the nick.

By the way, said the director of the Shop, it'll soon be the fiftieth anniversary of our foundation. It's a good round figure. It'd do no harm to get some mentions in the press. We'll have to draw up lists of staff to be awarded medals.

And who are you?

Then they went to the Pavilion. There were three of them this time. On the way they decided to introduce themselves. 'I'm a physicist,' said Blockhead. 'In that case, I'm a lyricist,' said Teacher (alluding to a once hotly-debated distinction of talents). 'And I'm a combination of opposites,' said Bloke. 'I'm No-one.' 'That can't be,' said Blockhead. 'Oh, yes, it can,' said Teacher. Bloke just shrugged his shoulders.

A physicist? Why not? That's quite OK.
Indeed one could say, most respectable.
A lyricist? Well, all right in its way;
Not quite so vital, but acceptable.
I could discover some new vital particle,
Work out some theorem, solve a hard equation,
Write it all out in a long learned article—
Or dig for ore (that's if I found occasion).
Or what of sport—I might score a few goals,
Or heave up weights until the audience cheers.
But ere performing any of these roles,
You've got to get into the highest spheres.
You'll find no plain man living in these parts;
They're all embodiments of some hope or plan,
And even among pimps and drunks and tarts,
Plain Ivan's an extraordinary man.
Yet I'm a Nobody, I am the exception,
The simple, passé, ordinary type,
Two-headed sheep, that's me—a strange confection,
An old survival, for extinction ripe.

'That's clear,' said Blockhead. 'But how did you survive? There hasn't been anyone like you left in Ibansk since the Great Victory.' 'I've been preserved as an Awful Example,' said Bloke. 'It's high politics. It's all beyond simple-minded souls like us.'

Sandal came in. 'I've been to see the Management,' he said. 'They need some loaders. But they wouldn't take you. You've not got the right education. And anyway, there's a law that in food distribution they can't hire anyone with a criminal record. They demand absolute honesty.' 'I suppose that's why ninety per cent of all workers in trade have at least two convictions,' said Blockhead.

The problem

The story of Blockhead revealed an irritating contradiction between the subjective idea an individual has of himself and his objective position in society. Just think, here's some UNJURES who imagines he's ten heads higher than Firasa, whose social position is ten times higher than his! Blockhead's example proved infectious. Not only Blockhead himself, but other employees of ARSE began to think that Blockhead was if not ten heads higher, at least one head higher, than the director, Rat. Things reached the point where Rat himself deep in his heart began to feel something similar, stopped sleeping peacefully at nights or at work, was always worried, and began to put on weight to a catastrophic degree. And that was in the most refined intellectual milieu of Ibansk, at its very brain centre—ARSE! You can imagine how much worse things were elsewhere! There was a nocturnal meeting of EPSPO. 'They'll have to be put inside,' said Leadiban. 'They'll have to be put inside,' said the Firadeps. 'They'll have to be put inside,' said the Secradeps. Although no official decision was taken, lists were gradually drawn up of individuals who had attracted attention to themselves for their exaggerated self-assessments. Blockhead was brought to UNO. But that made things even worse. Then the scientists were assembled, and the problem was put to them. 'Dig around in your idealistic and metaphysical chromosomes,' said Leadiban. 'You might find some kind of button or spring down there. Something you can press, and that's that. One, two, and hey presto! And none of your little quirks and conceits this time. Is that clear? I want regular reports! ARSE will be responsible for supervising the research.' Blockhead was released—after all, someone had to do the work! But he was asked to keep his genius to himself. Blockhead promised to think about it. Bloke was waiting for him in the lobby. And they went off to the Pavilion.

> By courtesy of the Brotherhood
> We've reached our great ideal,
> But there's one detail that we should
> Get right quite soon, we feel.
> We haven't tried quite hard enough
> To prevent the situation
> Where the brains that people have
> Aren't fitted to their station.
> The boss may have a tiny wit,
> But the problem really starts
> When those beneath the stupid shit

Are gifted men of parts.
The higher up the scale you rise,
The brighter you should be, we know;
We tried out every wild surmise
To find out why it isn't so.
To make life easier to live
And ease our rulers' pains
We've got to find out how to give
The bosses better brains.

The return

It's not the attacks that are frightening, said Chatterer. Persecution amounts to official recognition. It's the deliberate indifference to everything you do. And the more important your work is, and the better its results, the greater the indifference becomes. I'm not talking about indifference as a mere lack of interest, but an active indifference. That's something positive. It's a specifically Ibanskian phenomenon. This indifference can be expressed clearly or in vague terms, it can be sharply defined or have blurred edges, it can be explicit or implicit. It can even be measured. The degree of indifference! There's something to think about! Have you ever come across that kind of reasoning Over There in the West? Or in analyses of the past? This is something new. This is a specific form of conduct by people representing the attitudes of society towards a given individual. Let's say you have an exhibition of your work, and Stinker has one too. Yours is something brilliant. His is nothing but mediocre rubbish. But when the exhibitions are reviewed in the press, you are both written down to the same level—that's one degree of indifference towards you. Or they might devote more space and enthusiasm to his exhibition—that's a higher degree. They might say nothing at all about you—a still higher degree. Or you might both be praised, and you even a little more than him. That is still a certain degree of indifference, since everyone knows that your work is a hundred times better. And no-one will protest about these reviews. There might even be displeasure if anything good is said about your work. One point on which there is total agreement: your work must be made to seem quite unexceptional. They are even prepared to praise a nonentity to the skies to demonstrate their indifference to your work. Their aim is to distort judgments and divert public attention to trivia. And this does not merely affect cultural life. It affects every important aspect of our life. Have you seen today's Newspaper? They've published a kind of moral and legal code as a basis for general discussion. It's presented as the summit of morality and law. And what's more, as a kind of synthesising summit, ending the age old divorce between the two. The code lists possible breaches of its provisions, which it claims happen only rarely. To eliminate them altogether, a scale of penalties is proposed. For instance, if you don't give up your seat to an old woman—it's a fine. For the second offence, ten days forced labour. If someone sneezes and you don't say 'Bless you'—a fine. If you step on someone's foot and don't apologise, a fine again. If you don't intervene on behalf of someone who's being insulted—two weeks' solitary. Just read it. It's a strange document. The most important aspects of human activity have no juridical guarantee, but this very elaborate code is drawn up to cover all this stupid triviality. And it's taken ten years for ARSE to turn out this drivel! But there is another aspect which shows what dim cretins they are. The very fact that the document has been published makes it obvious that the way people actually behave in their daily life is very far from ideal. And because they're afraid to touch the deep underlying causes, they try to save the situation by attacking the fringes. And since there is no force capable of making even the slightest allusion to the real magnitude of the problem, all these silly, nonsensical trivia are taken seriously. If you take a detached view, it's a nightmare. But there aren't any detached observers. And if any appear on the scene, they are eliminated. By the same method.

The queue

'What's this queue for?' the Girl asked Blockhead, early one morning. She wasn't asking with any particular purpose. Just from boredom, and to show her self-assurance. 'That's a naïve question,' said Blockhead. 'So naïve I'm at a loss for an answer at this moment. Let's postpone the conversation to this evening. Here's my telephone number and address. Come and see me and we'll talk about queues and queuing. It's an interesting subject.'

(746)

'The queue is a fiction of existence which comes into being in complete accordance with the laws of real existence, but with the same consequences—that it produces no result at all,' said that inveterate drunkard Bloke in an interview with Speculatress from the hardware shop. At this moment he was lolling on some empty packing cases near the Greengrocer's Shop, in which neighbourhood he operated to secure both his material and his spiritual livelihood; and he was writing some coarse words on the door of the Shop, closed forever by an imposing padlock. Speculatress was being extremely flirtatious towards Bloke, raising her skirt so that he could glimpse not only her improbably fat thighs, fit to madden the entire Ibanskian intelligentsia (who currently expressed a fashionable preference for thin, bony women), but also a new slip acquired from abroad, which was adorned with little bells and pornographic pictures. She was trying to kill two birds with one stone. First, she was engaged in the seduction of Bloke. She had stopped fancying him a long while since, but she still dreamt of dragging him away from Mistress at all costs. 'The end justifies the means,' she said to the Fuzz, who had promised, at the price of a phial of Parisian perfume, to compromise Mistress, or at least to put her inside for a couple of weeks for hooliganism. And during that time . . . And secondly, Speculatress was certain that Bloke would tell Mistress about the slip, and that she would ask him to get her one the same. A woman is a woman after all, even under socism. Particularly an old bag like her.

Bloke felt the slip with the air of a connoisseur, and patted Speculatress's fat thighs, but without showing any particular interest. 'A queue,' he said, 'is normal existence transplanted into the cranium of a schizophrenic, where it becomes monstrously distorted.' 'You're a fool,' said Speculatress, 'even if you do know how to read! A queue is the stage on which speculators, crooks, parasites, leaders, laureates, distinguished pensioners and the rest of that shitty crowd play our their social spectacles. I know this business inside out. I know them all like the back of my hand. Just ask that trollop over there what she had to do for her mink coat, or her toreador pants, or her crutchless knickers just in case she's in a hurry. Or her three-piece suite. . . .' 'How do you know she's got crutchless knickers?' asked Bloke with quickened interest. 'That's a novelty.' 'I can tell just from looking at her,' said Speculatress. 'That's psychology for you.'

'The queue is a semi-structure,' said Rat, so loudly that every Ibanskian on Boss Avenue and Victors' Avenue could hear. He had been lusting after Speculatress for a long time, and he wanted to impress her. 'I,' he continued, paying no attention to the fact that no-one was paying any attention to him, 'in my course of lectures at the Higher Prophylactic Academy (HPA), start from precisely this hypothesis . . .'

'That's interesting,' said Blockhead, late that evening, as he examined the crutchless knickers. 'What's that for?' 'I don't know,' said the Girl. 'It's the fashion at the moment. A girl friend got them for me.' 'Phew,' said Blockhead when he heard the price she'd had to pay for them. 'But d'you know what next year's Paris fashion's going to be? No knickers at all. And they'll cost you a fortune. Far more than we can afford. But I fancy you, and I'll willingly make you a present of a pair.'

'The queue is the highest form of social communion, expressed in deeds, not words, an absolute social equality between individuals,' said Leadiban in a speech prepared for him by the entire collective of ARSE for the centenary of the Shop.

The return

'You know yourself,' said Dauber, 'how little money Ibanskian tourists are allowed when they go abroad. Just a few coppers. And naturally they try to use them as rationally as possible—buying clothes. Well, what else can they do! You say yourself that the shops are full of shoes, but buying a pair is out of the question. So you can see their problem. Now in N., for instance, there's a public lavatory near the art gallery. But it costs you money to get in there. It's enough to make you sick. So our tourists went to pee behind the statue of Apollo round the corner. And just imagine, the statue got such a soaking it fell to bits. It turned out that it wasn't the original, but a recent copy. So the Ibanskians made an important contribution to world culture. It may seem strange, but I've had the chance of looking at us from outside, from Over There, and I have observed that the progress of civilisation passes via Ibansk. You can't get away from it!'

'Ibansk,' said Chatterer 'is a dead-end civilisation. Like an ant-hill.' 'But there is some progress even in an anthill,' said Dauber. 'It's just that we don't notice it.' 'What kind of progress is it that passes unnoticed?' asked Chatterer. 'Progress only has any meaning if its participants are aware of it. And even if the ants are making progress, are they aware of it themselves?' 'You said yourself that everything needs time,' said Dauber. 'Decades will go by, centuries, millennia, but in the end there'll be some change in Ibansk.' 'Maybe you're right,' said Chatterer. 'But what difference can that make to us? What difference can it make to our economy if the average temperature in Ibansk falls by five degrees in a million years time? You don't imagine that tomorrow people are going to rush to start making warmer clothes?' 'But what makes you so sure that we're a dead-end civilisation?' asked Dauber. 'Is your only basis your personal observation of a few people over a short period?' 'What other can there be?' asked Chatterer. 'Would you prefer me to wait until we've amassed observations of millions of people over thousands of generations? And anyway that wouldn't add an atom of knowledge to what can be seen by any half-way intelligent man who takes the trouble to think along these lines. We aren't talking about transforming things, but about understanding them. And understanding is always a solo operation. We've discussed the subject many times. It isn't merely the observation of the facts of our life. It's an analysis of the whole system of life, a theory constructed according to scientific laws and confirmed by a huge number of facts. You've been surprised more than once in your life by the terrifying accuracy of Schizophrenic's predictions. Yet now it seems as if everything's been forgotten . . . But what about the activity of people like Truth-teller, Double-dealer, Singer, your friend Bawler,' said Dauber. 'And who else did you mention? Teacher . . . Me . . . Can I be classed with them?' . . . 'That's much too limited a group,' said Chatterer. 'Far too cloying an environment. Their efforts have about as much effect as chucking a handful of peas in an ocean of oil. And when individuals of this kind form a group, the only result is the formation of new social circles which live by the same laws as the mass, in other words we get a few new puddles of oil.' 'How can you go on living if you feel like that?' asked Dauber. 'Something's got to be done!' 'We are doing something,' said Chatterer. 'You're sculpting Leadiban. And I . . . I am justifying my actions. Together we are greasing the edges of the little cracks through which we might eventually be able to crawl out of our cul-de-sac. That is the duty of ant-Dauber and ant-Chatterer in this beautiful, perfect, wise, rational anthill.' 'What about space-flight?' asked Dauber. 'That has the same role,' replied Chatterer. 'When ants transfer their anthill to a new site they reproduce their former social structure down to the last detail.' 'I can't believe it,' said Dauber. 'There must be a way out somewhere! There must!' 'No,' said Chatterer. 'But why not, why not?' asked Dauber. 'I don't want to go over it all again,' said Chatterer. 'But if you insist, I can tell you in two words. It is precisely because Ibansk is the way out of all the difficulties of mankind's past history. Or at least the result of attempts to find the way out.'

The celebration

The guests at the party to mark Bloke's release included Blockhead and Girl, Fuzz and Speculatress, Sandal and Teacher. They talked and ate and drank, and as the evening wore on they began to sing songs. And then they asked Teacher to sing them something about the war.

I take my guitar and I pluck at a string.
Shall I sing? Well, I will if you wish.
But what kind of song would you like me to sing?
About war? Very well, here it is.
The memory's as clear as if it were last week:
These young girls asked us round for the night,
But the drink that they served still makes me feel sick
And one poor sod dropped dead outright.
One night my gunner and I got so pissed
We were pie-eyed the following day;
We crawled to the plane on our hands and our knees,
And took off in the opposite way.
And once we were flying from X back to base,
My crew'd sold my 'chute for some booze,
And so I'd not notice they'd stuffed up the case
With some rags and an old pair of shoes.
It's the war that we asked for—the blood and the glory—
You shot down the Huns, you yourself nearly died;

Tell us all about that. I've forgotten that story. Remember it then. No, I've not even tried.

'But the queue goes on growing all the time,' said Speculatress. 'Where will it ever end?' 'It'll end in nothing,' said Fuzz. 'I'll come along, blow my whistle, and they'll all scram.' 'I doubt it,' said Blockhead. 'This is something serious.' 'I want to come with you,' said the Girl to Teacher. 'Why?' asked Teacher. 'Blockhead is young and I am old.' 'You were young too, once,' said the Girl. 'I love you as you are, a man from the past.' And they left.

'Tell me something about the past,' said the Girl. 'Very well,' said Teacher, 'I will.'

Legend about myself

At the passing-out parade from the School, the officer-cadets were read an order appointing them to their commissions—as subalterns of course. 'The hardest part is getting a start,' said Gelding. 'In forty or fifty years we'll be generals, if of course we behave ourselves and make our beds properly.' 'There's a war on,' said Burdock, 'and promotion will come faster. There's one lad from the School who's only two or three years older than us, and he's a colonel already.' 'Yes,' said Teacher, 'but he's a little white hen that never laid astray.' 'Even so, it's still quicker,' said Burdock, 'if you don't get killed, of course.' 'If you get killed you go straight to heaven,' said Gelding. 'There's just been a directive,' said Intellectual: 'All fighter pilots, no matter what their merits or their sins, are to be regarded as saints during their life time, although only junior saints of course. So you'll have to start from the bottom, even in paradise.' 'Yes, but at least there won't be any political education courses in heaven,' said Gelding. 'Oh yes there will,' said Teacher. 'There are political education courses everywhere these days. We set them the example and every good example is contagious.' 'Stop all this drivel,' said Deviationist. 'Don't forget that informers become officers as well.'

The cadets were issued with their uniforms. They were only other-ranks' uniforms and made of cotton, but at least they were new. And they got artificial-leather boots. The first thing the lads had to do was to narrow the tops of their boots, take in the enormous trousers which had been designed to fit any

Ibanskian citizen, whatever his size, and shorten their tunics. 'Now we look like real officers,' said Teacher, rocking with laughter. 'Real Hussars! We look like a circus act. We certainly wouldn't need any make-up.' Then they got their pistols, and their pay, which was just as miserly as their rank. But it was the first pay they had ever received and it felt like a gift from heaven. Never in their lives had they had in their hands such a bundle of cash, with which they could afford to buy a whole litre of vile smelling illicit hooch. As soon as they were released, they rushed off to their favourite spots to turn this heaven-sent hard currency into liquid assets—after all, there was nothing else to do with it. They went out under the eyes of the sentries, the orderlies and the sergeants. Quite lawfully. They went out in their narrowed plastic boots and their shortened tunics with their new stripes on the left cuff, with their coarse canvas holsters weighed down with real pistols and spare magazines bouncing on their hips.

Soon shooting was heard in the village. No-one paid any particular attention to it. Everyone knew that it was end of term at the Flying School. And everyone knew as well that with these pistols, however real, it was impossible to hit even the garrison catering officer at more than three paces, even if the pistol were in sober hands. The garrison duty officer warned the patrols to leave the pilots alone, to avoid the tragi-comic incidents which had resulted on the previous occasion. On that occasion a drunken pilot had disarmed three of the patrol, stripped them naked, locked them in a hangar and pawned their uniforms for more drink. 'Yes, they're shooting all right, the bastards,' said the School Director. 'Sixty-five . . . sixty-six . . . they won't stop until they've got through all their ammunition. Sixty-seven . . .'

By morning all the newly fledged officers had returned to barracks safe and sound, partly under their own steam and partly with the help of their comrades and the aboriginal population. Burdock had lost his greatcoat some time in the night, and Deviationist had an enormous bruise below his left eye. 'Oh,' said Gelding, 'it looks as if you've tried to rape a black-smith.'

'Women are very hard to understand,' said Deviationist, as they walked back to the airfield. 'She invited me in herself and provided the drink. She wouldn't take any money from me for the vodka. She was even insulted when I offered. She put the light out herself, got her clothes off, got into bed and dragged me in with her. And when I tried to do something about it, she said that she was a decent girl, and thumped me in the face. Then when I dressed and got ready to go, she burst into tears and begged me to stay.' 'So what did you do?' asked Teacher, 'you surely didn't leave without having it off?' 'Of course I did,' said Deviationist. 'Well you're a fool,' said Teacher. 'She probably spent her last pennies on that vodka. She wanted it. And you! . . . Women are strange creatures, chum! You've got to know how to handle them.'

'These pistols are only for show,' said Gelding. 'Deviationist and I decided to try them out. We went off to a bit of waste ground and saw a cat sitting there about ten paces away. It just looked at us and then turned its back on us in complete disdain. You could tell it wasn't the first time. The old tabby was used to it. So we fired off all thirty-two rounds at it without a single hit.' 'It's a pity about my greatcoat,' said Burdock. 'I can't imagine where it could have gone. I laid it out on the ground and it may have moved a yard or two in the heat of the action. And afterwards I looked everywhere for it. Surely the bitch couldn't have nicked it?' 'Of course she did,' said Intellectual. 'Just count yourself lucky that she left you your pants and your boots.' 'But I didn't take them off,' said Burdock. 'That makes no difference,' said Intellectual. 'Where women are concerned you've got to be ready for the unexpected. Women are subtle creatures.' Subtle, my arse, thought Burdock, remembering the thud his bird had made as she fell flat on her back. Oh what a fool I am! She must've buried my greatcoat in the mud with the weight of her hundred-pound bum!! . . .

When the squadron took off, one aircraft's engine failed, and it crashed on a railway line. When they landed at the next airfield it turned out that it was Burdock. 'Every cloud has a silver lining,' said Gelding. 'At least he doesn't have to worry about his greatcoat any more.'

The queue
By the evening the queue had divided of its own accord into groups of ten, a hundred or a thousand. A decurion was placed

at the head of each ten. A management collective was selected: a Brother-organiser, a union organiser, youth organiser, cultural organiser, a PT organiser, an insurance delegate, a liaison-officer for relations with the army and UNO, a representative of the mutual assistance fund, and so on—more than forty people for each group of ten. At the head of each hundred a centurion was appointed with two deputies, one for political affairs and one for liaison with UNO. Every hundred had an elected Brotherhood bureau of forty people, a trade union bureau of seventy, and a number of other social organisations which added up to more than five hundred people for every hundred. Special councils were organised for young specialists, for the care of pensioners, for aid to nations engaged in the class struggle, for aid to developing countries, and to oversee the international chess organisation. At the head of every thousand . . . But there is an excellent description of the organisational structure of thousand groups in Ibanov's three-volume work *The Development of the Queue in the Primary Stage of Queueology in Conditions of Madogism*. The power structure of the thousand group was calculated at ARSE with the help of the Computer.

At an extraordinary meeting of EPSPOSVKBI (Extreme Presidium of the Supreme Principal Office, etc.) Firadep proposed the establishment of the State Committee for the Queue at the Shop (SCQATS). He was supported by a number of Secradeps and Firasas, who immediately divined which way the wind was blowing. Leadiban was tempted to oppose the idea, but when he recalled that he could gain a further medal and another speech from it he agreed. But it was too late. The Firadeps, who had already had more than enough of Leadiban, combined to remove him and elected a new one. It wasn't the one who had made the proposal, but another, the most stupid, the most insipid and the most insignificant of them all. 'That idiot's not capable of anything,' they said among themselves. 'So we . . .' But as with the last Leadiban, they had gravely miscalculated. This new insipid and stupid Leadiban immediately had a speech prepared for him to deliver on the anniversary of the Shop, a speech in celebration of the newly-created SCQATS, a speech for . . . and he made it very plain that if things went wrong he wouldn't hesitate to make an arrest or two. 'I am not the fool the you take me for,' he said. 'I'm no more a fool than you are!'

Finally an agent of UNO was attached to each group of ten, and the masses used their own initiative to appoint two informers for every member of the Queue. UNO established a special department headed by that old UNOist, Colleague.

Sub-Ibansk

'I'm prepared to bet,' said Teacher, 'that if people have survived under the ground they will have developed a civilisation which is an exact copy of ours.' 'Why do you think that?' asked the Girl. 'After all, they can't see anything down there, and there's nothing for them to eat or to wear.' 'Nonsense,' said Teacher. 'They've kept their sense of touch, and that's a very good substitute for sight. As far as food and clothes are concerned, there's no shortage. First of all, they've got hordes of rats at their disposal, and they've probably taken up rat breeding. Then there are the sewers and the rubbish tips . . .' 'You can't mean . . .' stammered the Girl. 'Indeed I do,' said Teacher. 'I would even guess that they call them the food mines. You see, before the war, the Ibanskians ate far too much, and more than half of what they ate was never digested. That was established even then. When Hog promised to build madogism in ten years he was relying very heavily on the rationalisation of food supplies (his proposal was to cut them by fifty per cent), and on the recycling of waste (it was proposed, for instance, that ten different kinds of sausage could be made from primary excrement), so the subterraneans have almost unlimited food sources. They need no living quarters since they're constantly under cover. And as for clothes, it's as warm there as it is in Africa. It's by far the best place to build madogism! The main thing is, you can't see a thing down there. You could pass off any old rubbish as madogism, and they would believe you.'

'You describe this underground life as if you'd been there yourself,' said the Girl. 'Okay, let's say they eat our shit. But at least they have real equality, not like here.' 'Alas,' said Teacher, 'that's something they have even less of than we have because the degree of equality depends on the general wealth of society. And we are somewhat richer than they are.' 'But how can they have any inequality?' asked the Girl. 'In every way,' said

Teacher. 'For example, rat-tail stew might be a privilege for the highest leadership. That may be trivial. What is more important is something quite different, the dependence of their social structure on ours. From this point of view their civilisation is derived from ours. They must have observed that the contents of various sewage pipes differ in their calorific value, the number of vitamins they supply, and so on—or at least they differ in flavour. And gradually their society will have developed a hierarchy based on that of sewage effluents. This hierarchy will have become a tradition. Since they live in complete darkness they have grown used to keeping their eyes closed. And that is very convenient for those in power.' 'What if a subterranean expedition were organised?' said the Girl. 'What for?' asked Teacher. 'We could open their eyes to their own life,' said the Girl. 'Nonsense,' said Teacher. 'First because they wouldn't see anything anyway. And secondly, because there's no-one people hate worse than those who tell them the truth about themselves. They would eat us along with the rats.'

The return
'Do you think that Truth-teller's intention to unmask Ibanism is doomed to failure?' asked Dauber. 'Certainly,' said Chatterer. 'Unmasking can only strengthen it.' 'How do you explain the extra-ordinary vitality of Ibanism?' asked Dauber, sticking a lump of clay on to Leadiban's twisted chin, making him look a bit like some great thinker. 'History never follows the predicted course. Science refutes Ibanism at every step, and everyone mocks at it. Yet it grows from strength to strength. It's almost supernatural!' 'Ibanism's strength doesn't lie in its intelligence, its clairvoyance or its scientific nature,' said Chatterer. 'It is strong because it and it alone exists. Name me a single doctrine which makes so many claims on human souls and which has been so insistently, obstinately and profoundly drummed into those souls. Religion? Christianity, Islam, Buddhism . . .? Sure, they're serious enough. But they are are for the old, the trendy and the snobs. Other problems, a different spiritual basis and other purposes have given rise to them. They are not concerned with the principal problems of today's man-in-the-street. But Ibanism takes a special interest in these problems. People don't give a damn for all your scientific niceties, and

(756)

they certainly don't understand them. What matters to them is Ibanism's generally optimistic orientation. History definitely embraces a tendency to progress. Even if people know that it will take decades, or even centuries, to produce a real improvement in living conditions, their awareness of such a remote prospect, however far it may be beyond their own reach, still brightens their existence. It is better to know that working people like you will be able to spend their holidays in southern resorts, even though it won't happen for another hundred years, than to think it will never happen. The fact is that the huge mass of people regard the promises of Ibanism as real promises. That's the nub of the matter. But what does religion offer? Or science? You know the theory of Schizophrenic and Slanderer. It is infinitely closer to the truth than Ibansim. But what does it offer, and to whom? All it does is to give a few isolated individuals a certain intellectual satisfaction and sense of direction. And moreover, a huge number of writers, artists, scientists, actors and so on work for the cause of Ibansim without being aware of it, or even with the ambition of over-throwing it. Who? You, for example. And Truth-teller. And Double-dealer.' 'What about Slanderer and Schizophrenic?' asked Dauber. 'Those two? No,' said Chatterer. 'But they have been destroyed by a general effort. They have been nipped in the bud.'

Hymn to the Queue

Who's the last?
I'm next to go.
What are they selling?
I don't know.
Who're you shoving?
Bloody fool!
What's the hold up?
Just keep cool.
No more thingammyjigs,
That's the crunch;
And, what's more,
We're closed for lunch.
Got more coming?
Keep your hair

(757)

On, and come back
This time next year.
If you want to eat or drink or buy some clothes,
Pay the bills for light or heat, or perhaps the rent,
Time is precious, so be quick and join the queue,
Ask who's last and stand behind him, that's the way.
Don't try stepping out of place—you'll have them screaming:
'Hey, In-tell-ect-ual! Just you keep your bleeding place!'

I curse you, queue, and often wonder
What stone did you creep out from under?
I am your life, the queue replies,
Without me, not a step you move,
Without me, no-one sells or buys,
Without me, nothing you can do.
You stand there dreaming: oh if you
Could find a way to dodge the queue.
If you were a cripple . . . or Armenian,
Maybe foreign . . . perhaps Ruthenian,
A pensioner of a special class,
A policeman, even—a pretty pass.
Oh queue, you're so long! I can't wait any more!
Who invented you, tell me, you miserable whore?
I am eternal, whispers the queue;
The fact you're here means that you are mine.
Wait and wait, as you've got to do,
Wait and wait, till the end of time.
You wait and you wait. No sign of the end.
Like it or not, you wait in pain,
You sigh, you curse, you fall silent again,
Wondering if anything will remain.
Oh queue, oh queue, how much more time?
When will you end, you hateful swine?
I'm your fate, says the queue in derision,
You must suffer me every day.
For I'm the perfection of the Ism.
I am your life, your truth and your way.

An opposition is needed
'Reports are coming in of a general feeling among the grass
roots,' whispered Assistant into Leadiban's open mouth, 'that

we are departing from the principles of Ibanism. In theory we should be engaged in the struggle between the new and the old. We've got the new. But where is the old? Say that we have a struggle between the good and the even better, between the new and the newest. We've got the even better. But we have nothing good. We've got the newest, but nothing new.' 'That'll never do,' Leadiban roared down Assistant's throat. 'Find the guilty men! And punish them!' Leadiban's wise directive was passed down to ARSE. The director of ARSE called in his deputies. His deputies called in the departmental heads. The departmental heads called in the section heads. The section heads called in the sub-section heads. The sub-section heads called in their senior staff. The senior staff called in their qualified junior staff, who called in their unqualified junior staff. From among these latter the most sloppy and hopeless were selected. 'We want your conclusions,' they were told, 'and we want them soon.' The sloppy and hopeless junior staff sat down at their desks, ordered the worst books on the subject, and copied out everything they needed. And within five years, after countless re-writings, discussions, re-drafts, re-redrafts, re-editing, corrections, additions, and other highly scientific operations, a vast document left ARSE and began to move upwards. It said roughly this: Who is guilty of everything? The intellectuals. But not all intellectuals. There are some intellectuals who are on our side. So these are not really intellectuals at all, but people who have come up from the masses, who are their flesh and blood. These people serve us, are devoted to us, fawn upon us. But there are also intellectuals who are not on our side. Or, more exactly, they pretend to be on our side but this pretence is only for a term. You only have to put a little pressure on them for them to start spouting all manner of little foreign words. Among these intellectuals who are essentially not on our side we must seek out those who are not on our side to such an extent that they cannot even wriggle out of the consequences. It must be made clear to everyone that they are full-blooded counter-revolutionaries, slanderers, traitors, drunkards, homosexuals, drug-addicts, currency speculators. It must be made plain that they are in Their pay, and that they are getting currency from Over There. It would be advisable to choose the most stupid, for they are easier to criticise, and also the weakest, for they confess and recant the most readily to crimes they have not committed.

Assistant, and therefore Leadiban himself, liked the document. 'Just see how far they've gone, the bastards,' he said to Counsellor. 'They must be excised as an example to the others. But we must take care how we strike. Everyone must think that we are showing true humanity. Is that clear?' 'That's clear,' said Counsellor, and gave the appropriate orders to UNO. 'That's very clear,' said Colleague. 'So in accordance with Leadiban's directive we have to create a group of oppositionist intellectuals who are intelligent and truthful critics of our society, who will not compromise with us, and who will not confess or recant. Otherwise their punishment will not frighten anybody, and no-one will believe us, for these days there is no place for magnanimity. There is no need any longer to put on a charade. The opposition must always be brave and intelligent. Then it can be easily refuted and demolished. It is apologetics which must be stupid and cowardly. That makes it unassailable. The opposition must be connected with the Queue. There aren't going to be any thingammyjigs, even if people discover what they are and gather in a rich harvest. They will either rot in the fields or be stolen. So someone will have to take the responsibility for that. As far as the composition of the group goes, that presents no problem at all. Bloke, Blockhead, Teacher, Sandal, Mistress, Speculatress, the Girl. Throw in a dozen or so criminals and infiltrate the lot with a couple of dozen agents and provocateurs. Tack on five or six foreigners and fifty or so people chosen at random from the Queue. Link them all with criminal elements from the remote past and the near future. Get a little correspondence going with Truth-teller. Slip them a couple of typists. Give them a duplicator. Oh, my word! We're going to have a real party! No, we'd better trim that down a bit, just in case they get too enthusiastic and organise a genuine *coup d'état*! You've got to expect anything of a gang like that. A *coup d'état* mightn't be a bad idea! But that's for later. Who'll be the leader? Bloke? Teacher? No way! That'd be going too far. I think it had better be me.'

The return

'Quite a large number of people were aware of Slanderer's and Schizophrenic's works,' said Dauber, 'and most of them were scientists. But they weren't particularly interested in them. Why would that be? It must mean that the works were only superficially serious. If they had been really serious, they would have produced some kind of effect.' 'You're wrong,' said Chatterer. 'Monstrously, offensively wrong. They did arouse interest. That is why their authors were so speedily and unanimously eliminated, and why no-one ever mentions their names. And the works themselves were pillaged by everyone. And then their ideas spread. Today they're being chewed over in the most widely varying circles without anyone ever thinking about where they came from.' 'But people aren't obliged always to go back to prime sources,' said Dauber. 'Of course not,' said Chatterer, 'and that's a point they take great care to remember. But we're getting off the subject. There were such prime sources, and you know them perfectly well. And yet you talk to me about a lack of effect. It's true that there was no public effect. But this is an example of the action of a law defined by Schizophrenic himself: The deeper and more serious social ideas are, the less they are seen to penetrate into human consciousness. They penetrate less quickly and less widely than superficial or circumstantial ideas. And even when a serious author wins recognition, he wins it initially for the superficial or secondary aspects of his ideas. And here this is reinforced by the fact that a creative Ibanskian has to overcome the resistance of authority of all kinds, the resistance of his professional peers and the resistance of the general tradition of habits of thought and judgment. All these factors are so intertwined that it is not possible in a concrete situation to determine which factors are operating and in what proportions. And here we observe one very pernicious phenomenon. As a man overcomes these resistances he gradually assumes an ever closer resemblance to that society's Mr Average. If he fails to do so, he will not be able to penetrate the fissures in the obstacles he faces. It may seem to the man that he has preserved his creative individuality and is bringing his ideals to fruition; but in fact he is increasingly conforming to the standard.' 'Still, there are people who do overcome resistance while preserving their Ego,' said Dauber. 'No,' said Chatterer. 'Those who preserve their Ego are not penetrating the fissures. They either perish or remain confronting the obstacles without appearing on the visible stage of history.'

The legend

When they had taxied their aircraft in the pilots went off to the canteen. 'Who'd have thought that Burdock would be the first victim in our group,' said Deviationist. 'It's fate,' said Teacher.

> Your next intoxication, Fate being blind,
> Predict you never will;
> Nor which girl's pants you'll rip off her behind
> To give the lass a fill.

'That's not bad,' said Deviationist.

> And so, as 'twas in days gone by,
> Life ne'er attains perfection.

'Too true,' said Teacher.

> And you have got a big black eye.
> Me—total satisfaction.

'That depends on the consequences,' said Deviationist.

> You can't do any deals with Fate,
> So try to be less hasty;
> Total satisfaction's great,
> But gonorrhea's nasty.

For a moment Teacher was nonplussed. The eyes of the assembled company glowed with satisfaction. 'One-nil to . . .' Gelding began to say, but he wasn't allowed to finish.

> I'm not frightened of VD,
> And I shall not repent;
> I've had some women fucking me,
> And held their tits—oh glory be,
> You'd go quite mad if you could see!

Teacher noticed a pretty young girl who had stuck her head out of the canteen to look at the young pilots, and concluded:

> And now I'll try again.

Deviationist followed Teacher's glance and gave a thumbs up sign.

> You're right! I willingly concede,
> It's daft to fight one's fate.
> Their tits, you say? Well, I give in,
> Just take me with you, mate.

'One-nil to Teacher,' said Gelding. 'If you've no objection I'll join you.' When the pilots went into the canteen the entire female kitchen staff crammed themselves into the window of the serving hatch. 'That lad'll turn into a real man,' said Biddy, the motherly cook, nodding towards Deviationist. She was a mature woman who knew the score. 'I like the thin one better,' said Waitress, a raw beginner, pointing to Teacher. It was evident from the look in her eyes that she was available and that Teacher could count on her today. Teacher raised two fingers. Waitress understood and winked knowingly. 'Some snot-noses have all the luck,' said Chief. 'That little tart has no respect for age or rank or medals. Where's the justice of it? I am only just thirty. I'm a major. I've got all this fruit salad on my chest. What's more, I've been to university. Yet I have to seek the favours of old bottle-washers. Come on, you lads! Anyone want that old bag? Right then, put her down for me.' These snotty-nosed kids, he thought, they've no idea what a real woman's like. He only made one trifling mistake: he had forgotten that a real woman must know what a real man is like. At all events, a real woman knows that real men don't play hockey, football or politics. Real men don't play at all.

Extra-terrestial civilization

Late one night the caretaker in charge of the reception hall and forecourt of the Committee for the Redistribution of Academic Publications (CRAP), was coming back from the Pavilion where he and the night-watchman from the Committee for the Unification of Nonsensical Trivia (CUNT) had drunk the profit on the sale of fifty tons of pulp, to wit, the complete works of the old Leadiban. The caretaker was completely stoned and collapsed in the yard in front of the headquarters building, his left ear pressed firmly against a sewer manhole cover. When he came to in the morning he heard suspicious sounds coming from the sewer, as if someone were walking about down there, talking and scratching the walls. There must be someone down there, thought Caretaker. Perhaps the intellectuals again, drawing things! Any minute now they'll start writing verses and singing them! So Caretaker reported it all to Fuzz. 'Must be the drink,' said Fuzz. And he reported Caretaker for disciplinary proceedings. Matters might have rested there had it not been for the CUNT night-watchman. When he left Caretaker, the night-watchman set off towards his garret and on the way fell into a hole which had been dug at the time of the old Leader in front of the CUNT building for some important purpose and later forgotten, so the hole could not be filled in again without special permission. And anyway there were no funds available for the purpose. As he fell, the night-watchman broke his neck—in the literal sense. When he was dragged out of the hole, a week later, he murmured that there was someone in the hole, and then died. Thanks to this tragic event the post of night-watchman became vacant and Caretaker's statement was followed up. UNO agents installed bugging devices everywhere and were forced to acknowledge that something highly suspicious was going on beneath Ibansk. But no-one could sort out what it was. The Academy was brought in. After many decades of scrupulous investigation, using the most sophisticated computers, QUIM I (Quintessential Universal Intellect of Madogism) the Pan-Ibanskian Institute for the Study of Space and Peoples Out There (PISSPOT) came to the conclusion that such a pattern of sound could not be emitted by any conscious, let alone any living, body. The results of the research were published in fifty volumes and sold very well. Whatever you say, the self-satisfied Ibanskians said to each other, we Ibanskians are the only intelligent life in the universe. For their outstanding scientific discoveries in the field of extra-terrestrial communication, the scientists (at least those who merited it) were given bonuses and awarded decorations. Everything might have ended here. Once again Ibanskian science would have covered itself with imperishable glory and written another deathless page in the history of world science, had it not been for Blockhead. As he glanced through the first volume of the PISSPOT report, before he threw it into the dustbin, on the very first page and in the very first second Blockhead deciphered a series of familiar expressions: 'Fuck your mother', 'Up your arse', 'Up yours too', and so on. Blockhead's discovery was so convincing and self-evident that there was no way of ignoring it. Had it not been immediately acknowledged, by the following day every schoolboy in Ibansk would have been claiming it as his own. There was an immediate meeting of the Scientific Committee of ARSE, where the director himself presented a report about his discovery. There could no longer be any doubt at all. Within a few moments Ibanskian radio and television announced an imminent extraordinary meeting of the Plenum of Academic Power (PAP), at which Leadiban himself was to deliver a special statement. And immediately the Ibanskians heard the voice of Leadiban himself, trembling with emotion: 'Citizens of Ibansk! Brothers and sisters! Mothers and daughters! Fathers and children! Swineherds and Shepherdesses! Gangsters and philanthropists! It is I who speak to you, friends! Today for us all, is a Great Festival. Only under our wise leadership could our glorious scientists, supported as they are by the popular masses, have discovered a subterranean civilisation of intelligent beings! I call upon you to remain calm! Our people are accustomed to difficulties and privations! I am certain that this further test which has fallen to your lot will be accomplished with honour! Be on your guard! If you notice anywhere the appearance of any intellectuals, you must take exceptional steps . . .' Leadiban's speech was heard and fully grasped. Bloke was hauled off to the police station. Blockhead was arrested at work but immediately released. His collective stood warranty for him. Bloke was also released in view of certain long-term plans. When they were at liberty again they set off to the Pavilion. On the way they picked up Teacher, who had just taken over the vacant position of CUNT night-watchman.

Our children are our future

'Just listen to this,' said Sandal. 'That little bitch keeps on churning out poem after poem. What makes a thing like this happen in the family of a grey, mediocre, rank-and-file civil servant?'

> Chingachgook is known no more;
> The Iron Mask is gone,
> And D'Artagnan, through memory's door,
> His foil no longer drawn.
> Athos, Porthos and Aramis
> All gone beyond recall;
> The Musketeers now lie in peace,
> Their swirling cloaks a pall.
> Shakespeare's kings no longer show,
> Henry Four and Five.
> Quentin Durward, Ivanhoe,
> They too no longer thrive.
> So who is left to fill my mind?
> What heroes have we now?

What fantasies, what myths define
The dreams that soothe my brow?
The shepherd guardian of his sheep?
The miner seeking ore?
The idiot spaceman probing deep?
The scribe of Ism's law?
The scientist who's in control?
The bright resourceful spy?
The footballer who scores a goal?
Must we on them rely?
Alas, there is no other choice.
The fairy tale has died,
Their heroes vanished, stilled their voice,
There's nothing left beside.

'That's first class,' said Bloke. 'Let's drink to our children!
They'll sort out everything, just as well as we will, without our
help.' 'What do you think?' Sandal asked Teacher. 'I feel very
sad,' said Teacher. 'Listen, I'll sing you a song.'

I close my eyes: pain grips my soul,
All living things to obliterate.
I see bright armour, cloth of gold,
The clash of swords, the king in state.
Some talk of modern-day romance,
Which I'm quite ready to forget,
And hold my breath, and backward glance:
The cavalry's sabres are flashing yet.
They've taught me this is all a lie;
But what is life if dull and grey?
People must dream, or else they die,
Believe in legends, or decay.
But palaces and swords have passed,
Princesses, sorcerers are no more.
Our myths are full of modern man,
Objective life—oh, what a bore!
Our myths are full of bathroom suites,
The sordid, grey intrigues of power,
The press's fawning sick deceits,
Life's hopeless drabness, hour on hour.
Open your eyes—what's left for you?
Your fairy tale in fragments lies,

An awful nightmare that's come true—
The world unmasked before your eyes.
'That was written long ago by a fifteen-year-old boy.' 'So let's drink to our sons and daughters who come up with things that their fathers and mothers keep quiet about,' said Bloke.

Genius

At first, Blockhead went religiously day after day to his ARSE, sat at his desk for the prescribed time, and conscientiously covered the requisite number of pages per day. And although he made considerable progress in his own field of science (which he understood) this had an adverse rather than a beneficial effect on his position and his pay, i.e. on the index of his needs. Initially he paid no attention to this. He was young, and fond of science. But later, as he saw the social position and the consumption of his inept fellows rising constantly, Blockhead began to ponder. And he became tired of scientific work for no return. During this period of spiritual crisis, he would come into ARSE, sit at his desk and spend hours doing nothing, feeding blank page after blank page into the computer. And to his enormous surprise at the end of the month he found that his indices were the same, even showing a slight tendency to rise. The he decided to experiment. For months he wrote not a single line. For months he transcribed chapters from textbooks. For months he wrote downright rubbish. And finally he achieved the optimum result. His indices began to show a marked increase. The bosses began to clap him on the shoulder, and sometimes to hold him up as an example. Then Blockhead came up with a simple idea whose realization lifted him into the category of genius. He invented a bio-substitute, a simple device which produced bio-currents identical to his own. Now when he came to work, Blockhead simply left his bio-substitute on his desk, switched on an automatic supply of pages torn from the first book to come to hand—mainly school textbooks—for feeding into the computer, and went off about his own affairs. He returned in the evening to register his departure on the automatic counter. And his bio-substitute went on working round the clock. Since the Ersatz-Blockhead went on working after all the other workers had left, his pay, calculated on the approved formula, kept going up, so that after three months Blockhead was earning more than the director, and had passed through ten levels of promotion. Ibansk was thrown into panic. Blockhead was summoned to UNO, where he was told either to put a limit on his genius, or else . . . In a word, an ordinary research worker could not be more intelligent than the director and the deputies, or still less earn more than they did. Blockhead promised to set things to rights, and did so. He proposed an extremely simple method of re-calculating the over-production of a worker (if it involved earnings greater than those of the director or the deputies) in such a way that the higher authorities profited from it in proportion to their grade. The immediate result was that the computer restored Blockhead to his proper place in the Ibanskian scientific hierarchy. The staff of ARSE laughed when they saw Blockhead's time sheet. That's your genius for you! He's worth no more than we are! And they went back happily to their desks. The director, however, was elected a Super-Academician, and his deputies were promoted to Academic-Researchers. They all received medals. Blockhead was reprimanded. At first he took to drink in despair. But when he had run out of cash to drink with, he went into mass production of bio-substitutes which he sold initially to reliable friends, then to anyone who wanted one, but via trustworthy intermediaries, and finally to anyone who wanted to buy with no intermediaries at all. Soon Ibansk was in the grip of a new fashion for bio-substitutes. The government resolved to set up the biggest bio-substitute factory in the world, polluting three rivers and four lakes in the process. Thanks to this, Ibanskians were able to stand peacefully in queues, attend meetings, and travel to the other end of Ibansk to earn a beggarly salary. And science made such a prodigious leap forward that it became quite impossible to catch up with it, or even more so to move into its front line. 'But why bother to try to catch up?' said Chief Theoretician. 'There's no need. Let it move forward on its own. That's what science is for, to be ahead of its time. Our task is to encourage it and to find it industrial applications.' So Ibansk started to build the world's biggest Complex for the Construction of Institutes Making Major Scientific Discoveries (CCIMMSD) on the pattern of ARSE. And soon institutes of that pattern began to flourish in all the cities in the world. The production of bio-substitutes soared to one hundred times the level of 1913.

The organisation of the opposition
'Well, here we are, lads,' said Colleague, tapping a thick file with his finger-nail. 'You're all in our hands. There's no point in trying to deny it. So you may as well come clean. You're beginning openly to express your discontent with our society, to spread truths which are slanderous and damaging to our society, to call for improvements and so on. You don't need me to tell you that'. 'But we're perfectly happy', said Bloke. 'Everyone is quite happy,' said Colleague. 'But not with everything. Have you got an apartment? No. Veneered furniture? A suede jacket? Brandy? Girls? . . . There you are then! There really isn't anything to be happy about! You're unhappy, beyond a shadow of a doubt. You can't possibly be happy.' But Bloke insisted:

A private apartment? That's everyone's dream.
But I've got a mattress where I lay my head.
A handsome suede jacket? The *crème de la crème*;
But my tattered old anorak does me instead.
You talk about cognac? A five-star hotel?
A rare fillet steak? It sounds better than stew,
And yet even though I don't live quite that well,
I still manage for something to drink and to chew.
Soft lights and sweet music? A girl in my bed?
I freely agree that's attractive enough.
But I'm not such a fool, let it clearly be said,
And I manage to find enough birds to stuff.
You say 'All very fine but that's far too low-class'?
Well, you can't fool me with sheer nonsense like that.
Have it off in a doorway, or out in the grass,
Or drink hooch from the bottle—*then* tell me what's what.

'Very well,' said Colleague, 'you and I will have a private talk afterwards. But what about you?' he said to Teacher. 'You used to be a professor! Might have made it into the Academy! Won a prize! What are you so happy about? Do you want to die just as you are, a nobody?' 'That's my dream,' said Teacher.

Let me die *sans* rank or title. Answer this, though,
    first of all.

(769)

Just how many Leadibans now are immured
within the Wall?
How many Deputies, Directors?
First Assistants or Inspectors?
Secretaries, Counsellors?
High Court Judges, Chancellors?
The world is one vast grey mosaic of the
gravestones of the great.
I'll be unique throughout the planet—I'll have
'No-one' on my slate.
I'll have no titles, decorations,
No high rank or commendations,
No obituary, no citation,
Nor words as to my avocation,
And in years far in the future, folk will view my
tomb in awe:
'He must have been a skilful fellow, to stay
No-one and no more.
They never made him a Director,
Deputy or Chief Inspector.
Not like the others. I declare,
He must be someone very rare.
His colleagues must have overlooked him, his
bosses failed to see the light.
They must have got it in the neck for such an awful
oversight.
And if they did, it's very proper,
They should have come a dreadful cropper.
Nowadays, to say the least,
No-one can our force resist.'
'And furthermore,' said Blockhead, 'we don't know any
truth which slanders our society. We don't know any truth at
all.' 'Just leave that to me,' said Colleague. 'I'll pass you docu-
ments to give everyone the creeps. Figures! Locations! Names!
The lot! Well, what do you say? Agreed?' 'But we'll be
punished for that,' said the Girl. 'Of course you will,' said
Colleague. 'And how!' 'And tortured?' asked Speculatress. 'Of
course,' said Colleague. 'You might even be permanently crip-
pled.' 'Well, that changes everything,' said Sandal. 'Yes, in that
case everything makes sense,' sighed Mistress. 'But will society

be the better for it?' asked Speculatress. 'It'll be the worse,' replied Colleague. 'Well then,' said Bloke, turning to Blockhead and Teacher. 'Shall we take a chance on it?' 'Let's give it a try,' they replied. 'But bear in mind,' said Bloke to Colleague, 'we're completely disinterested; we'd rather be taken on part-time.' 'Well, thank you very much, lads,' said Colleague. 'Part-time's difficult to arrange, but I'll fix it. Talk it over among yourselves, and I'll go and get you your documentation. We've got everything ready for you. You're to produce an underground newspaper, and we've set the first ten numbers up for you to give you a start. And there are some leaflets. By the way, do you know what Leadiban's last trip abroad cost the state? Oh, you're just children! Ten times that! Close on a billion! And do you know how much the Leadibanlet of the eleventh region has fiddled for himself? What kids you are! A hundred times more than that! Five billion! That's what! And you say you're happy, that you don't know, that you don't want. If we told you the whole truth!!! . . .'

Later the opposition set off for the Pavilion, where Teacher put forward a draft programme for discussion. Roaring with laughter, the members of the opposition went their various ways, while Teacher and Bloke decided to continue the discussion in Teacher's garret. Here they were joined by Colleague who had brought his own bottle along.

Oh, fuck their politics! Up their arses!
Let's split this bottle! Fetch the glasses!
'You know, lads, you can be straight with me,' said Colleague when he'd had a few. 'I'm not one of those. People say you've a nice little business in nice little girls. Set me up with a couple for tonight.' So they took him off to the Slopwoman, and Colleague was very happy with her.

To each his own anxieties

Bloke, Blockhead and Teacher started drinking Teacher's first pay packet at crack of dawn. They got into a fruitless argument about which was better—to have healthy false teeth or rotting ones of your own. 'It's better to have healthy ones of your own,' said Blockhead. 'You're a perfectionist,' said Bloke. 'It's better to have healthy ones whosoever they are.' 'Some kind or other,' said Teacher, 'as long as you can chew.' And he told how a

group he was with had once by mistake been told to unload a
lorry-load of sausage. The sausage was as hard as rock. They
were allowed to eat as much as they liked, but were forbidden to
take any away with them. And he reduced his finger nails and
his gums to a mass of bleeding pulp, but he wasn't able to eat so
much as an ounce. He wept with rage. He begged a young
friend of his with whom he always shared his last crumb to bite a
bit off and chew it for him, but the lad told him to fuck off.
Blockhead said he'd read something of the kind somewhere.

Sandal came along and hurried to catch up with their drinking. Then he produced a grimy sheet of paper from a school
exercise book. 'Just listen to what that little bitch has been up to
now,' he said, more with pride than with irritation. An epitaph
for her living father!

> He married twice, like most men of his sort,
> Ate tons of carbohydrates in his time,
> Went short. Survived. He never faced a court.
> He must have drunk a cellar of bad wine.
> Kept clear of all political debate.
> Throughout his life he never went abroad.
> He slept around, although no reprobate.
> A full time job, plus fighting in the War.
> One third part of his life he spent in bed.
> A quarter of it on a crowded bus.
> He wasted years in meetings, need be said,
> The rest in queues, like all the rest of us.
> For all his efforts, service to the cause,
> For the millions of useless jobs he did
> He got what's recommended by the laws—
> Some thanks, his wage, paid leave when merited.
> He got the luxury of a two-roomed flat—
> The dream of everyone. He had to share
> The kitchen and the toilet. After that,
> When taken ill, to hospital he went.
> They treated him the best way that they knew.
> Not like They do. It didn't cost a cent.
> But he died. Prematurely, too.

Blockhead said that our free medical service was just a sham.
'How can anyone say it's free when you've had a sum deducted
from your wages whether you're ill or not?' 'Rubbish,' said

Bloke. 'By the way,' he asked Sandal, 'what kind of teeth have you got?' Sandal replied that alas, his were false, but they ached. 'That reminds me of the old pre-war story of the sea captain who caught syphilis from an inflatable rubber woman.' 'You weren't born before the war,' said Bloke, 'so it's no use talking as if you were. You'd do better to order another round. And we'll drink to our children who follow in the footsteps of our parents.'

> So what? There's nothing left to say.
> I'm on the same road too.
> I'll snuff it, also, one fine day,
> There's nothing else to do.

'That's all very true,' said Teacher. 'Just a little longer and the same thing'll happen to you as happened to all the other sandaloids.'

> A grievous loss we here must mourn,
> Our brother we're bemoaning.
> He's now gone from us to that bourne
> From which there's no returning.
> On orders from above they came
> Their last respects to pay,
> Although they didn't give a damn
> That he had passed away.
> Pretending sorrow in his sighs
> The speaker falsely whined
> That despite his sad demise
> His work remained behind.
> The orators all took their turn
> And when they'd had their say,
> They gathered up his funeral urn
> And shoved it in the clay.
> Thus knowing what his comrades thought,
> To whom should he make his report?

At this point a puppy came trotting up to them wagging his tail which he had omitted to have docked. He had a little beard, very like that of an intellectual who desperately wanted to be persecuted for his progressive ideas and outstanding talent, but who was completely ignored owing to his lack of either. 'There was a time,' said Teacher, taking the puppy on his lap and giving him a piece of his salami sandwich, 'when every dog in

Ibansk was a pure-blooded mongrel. But look at these fantastic mixtures you see running around the streets these days. Take this one for example. He looks like the fruit of a chance union between some highly refined aristocratic lapdog and the scruffiest dustbin-foraging cur. Yet what a beauty he is! And so intelligent. I wouldn't be in the least surprised if he suddenly began to point out the fallacies in the ideas of Truth-teller or Double-dealer. No, whatever you say, progress marches on. Our children will go further than we have managed. So let's drink to our children—our future.' 'Woof, woof,' said the puppy. They christened him Intellectual, and he decided to stay with them for good.

They left the Pavilion and wandered off aimlessly. On the way they picked up Fuzz, dropped in on Mistress, phoned the Girl and then set off to see Speculatress. They argued for a long time about what they should drink to, and as usual failed to reach any conclusion. 'Here in Ibansk,' said Teacher, 'we can only achieve unity of opinion and action in the complete absence of any general platform, or when we are totally indifferent to the subject.'

They had a little whip-round. The women prepared some revolting snacks. After the first glass Sandal returned to his subject.

> Monte Cristo never lived. And Ivanhoe's false too.
> D'Artagnan never served the queen. And Robin
>   Hood's not true.
> But Crusoe lived, the papers say; they're right
>   there, it would seem,
> But if it's true, his life, for sure, was one
>   nightmarish dream.
> Of any hero that you choose, the same thing can be
>   said.
> And yet an aircraft's not a steed, a sten-gun's not a
>   blade.
> Preserve the past? A useless deed!
> For no-one can it aid.
> An aircraft cannot be a steed,
> A sten-gun's not a blade.

'I suspect,' said Blockhead, 'that you write these verses yourself and attribute them to your daughter.' 'Nonsense,' said

Sandal. 'If I could write verse like that, I'd take jolly good care not to.' 'Adults can't think like that,' said Teacher. 'Adults these days are all dreadfully intelligent and well educated, and for verse you need a certain degree of stupidity and ignorance.'

'Do you remember that little old house in the courtyard of ARSE?' said Speculatress. 'It's been demolished.' 'That's progress,' said Bloke. 'That's not the point,' said Speculatress. 'There were two old women living there—they must have been getting on for a hundred. One of them had been paralysed for the last thirty years. The other was quite frisky for her age. Anyway, they refused to move out. The militia had to be called. Do you know why they didn't want to move? It turned out that the paralysed one had died more than twenty years earlier, and the other one had embalmed her, so she could go on drawing both pensions. And she did it so well apparently that the old woman's been there all these years looking as if she were alive.' 'Well done, the old woman,' said Bloke. 'Poor old thing,' said Sandal. 'Now she'll have to pay back twenty years' pension.' 'They'll never manage to get it out of her,' said Blockhead. 'She'll die. And where could she lay her hands on so much money? Her pension'll be terribly low. Won't keep her in fags—and not a chance of buying a drink.' 'Far from it,' said Teacher. 'They'll put her in a home for specially privileged pensioners and look after her as if she were the apple of their eye. They've got to get her secret of embalming out of her! So we can keep our leaders for future generations to marvel at. The scientific methods of embalming are totally useless, as you know. The leaders rot. They don't last more than a year. But this old woman's method—she's kept the corpse looking so fresh it could've got up on a platform any time.' 'They've taken the dead woman off to the Embalming Institute,' said Speculatress, 'and the one who's alive's been taken to UNO. But she won't confess. She's afraid they'll put her inside.' 'Well, they have, to all intents and purposes,' said the Girl. 'And she'll die soon anyway. What's she got to worry about?' 'It's habit,' said Teacher. 'Here even prisoners are afraid of being put inside. And the dying as well.'

Mistress whispered something to Speculatress and heaved a sigh. 'Don't worry,' said Speculatress. 'I'll fix you up.' 'There's a new contraceptive come out,' said the Girl. 'A new one!' said Mistress. 'We haven't even tried the old ones yet.' 'It's most effective,' said Bloke. 'Women only conceive one time out of two, and only then if the man gets right in there. You can only get it on special prescription with three official stamps, or else from under the counter at ten times the proper price. The authorities can have as many as they want. They even supply them to their bitches. But for you and me—no way!' 'Ridiculous!' said Blockhead. 'They only cost a couple of coppers. What a relief it'd be to people!' 'It's not ridiculous,' said Teacher. 'It's wise policy. The less free people are in their actions, the more fettered they feel, and the more fearful they are.' 'What's politics got to do with it?' asked Sandal. 'What if medicines like that didn't exist at all?' 'Then only a natural need would subsist,' said Teacher. 'People don't become psychopaths simply because a body may fall to the ground. But once you invent some way of stopping such falls, make the antidote a privilege and spread the word around, just wait and see what that leads to.' 'Don't worry,' said Speculatress. 'I'll get you a sackful of the stuff.' 'I'm not worrying,' said the Girl. 'It's just a matter of principle.'

'They've launched a campaign at ARSE,' said Blockhead, 'against a really important scientist.' 'It looked as if campaigns were going out of fashion,' said Sandal. 'Why do you say that?' asked Teacher; 'there's always a campaign going on against someone. It's only the style of pogrom that changes. In the past people used to bawl and shout but now it's low key, quiet, almost imperceptible. Pogroms used to be a pleasure reserved for the authorities, but now they let the rank and file join in. Persecution now means not being protected.' 'You're behind the times,' said Blockhead, 'these days persecution means being protected but not so much so as to avoid being persecuted. The scientist they are after at the moment, the one I mentioned, is even openly praised. Sometimes they hand out such enormous bonuses to him that any fool can see he's finished. To judge by the breadth of his ideas and his ability, he stands in no need of protection. If there were any justice, he should have been given his own institute long ago, elected to the Academy and the rest. Yet he's barely got to head of section.'

'Don't make me cry!' said Speculatress sarcastically. 'How dreadful—not to be elected to the Academy! The people don't even have anything like as much as your unrecognised genius. The main thing is that the people should be happy, the happier the better. That's the whole secret of history.' 'She's right, you know,' said Sandal. 'The number of contented people isn't of the slightest importance,' said Teacher. 'When you come down to it, you can make people feel happy by force, or with drugs. That's not the problem. The problem is to recognise the rational criteria for forming judgments. What matters is the degree of conscious happiness, not some vague feeling of contentment for reasons one isn't even aware of.' 'We've been given the job of writing a new speech for Leadiban,' said Sandal. 'Not just any old speech, but one that is to give a profound scientific analysis of all aspects of social life. And I'm the one they've seconded from my section again, the bastards.'

'If we were to tell anyone the kind of things we've been discussing,' said Blockhead, 'they'd never believe us.' 'And with reason,' said Bloke. 'People never talk among themselves about what they say they've been discussing; they always talk about what they won't admit to having discussed.'

'When's the wedding?' asked Speculatress. 'It's off,' said Fuzz. 'That bitch doesn't give a damn for me as a person. She thinks that I've got no future.' 'It's absurd to seek essential personal qualities in a social individual,' said Teacher. 'A man is his social position, and no more than that. There was a second lieutenant in our unit who wanted to get married. But he wanted his future wife to love him for himself and not for his elevated rank. So he carefully concealed his high position from applicants for the role of spouse. In the end he found what he was looking for and married her. But once he asked his wife whether she knew that he was a second lieutenant, and not just anybody. "Of course," his wife replied, "it's written all over your face that that's the best you could hope for."' 'So what?' said Fuzz. 'So nothing,' said Teacher. 'The idiot tried to shoot himself, but he missed and hit the regimental commander's dog. After that his military service became a nightmare.'

'There's an article in the Newspaper,' said Mistress, 'that they're soon going to open a school for gifted children. They're going to take them from the age of two and develop their genius by every method they can. What'll happen?' 'Nothing,' said Sandal. 'All it means is that from the age of two they're going to keep a close watch on our children to avoid any new Truth-teller (God forbid!), Dauber, Double-dealer, and so on.' 'Where's this school going to be?' asked Speculatress. 'I ought to tell my sister about it. Her son is a right little pest. He scribbles all over the wallpaper and scratches the furniture. You wouldn't try helping us to get him a place, guv'nor? We'd make it worth your while.' 'I'm fed up with always being leeched on,' said Fuzz. 'Now then, cut the chatter! Clear off home, the lot of you. My shift's over.' 'As a person you're O.K.' said Specula-tress. 'But as a copper you're a right bastard.' 'Now then belt up and fuck off,' said Fuzz. 'Or else . . .' 'Just keep talking about democracy,' said Blockhead. 'When the most democratic cop-per in Ibansk starts waving his fists about if he's asked a simple question, it really is time to pack up,' said Teacher. 'I've got to be up at the crack of dawn because we're starting the Pan-Ibanskian Symposium of Night-watchmen. Firadep 5 is pres-enting the report. I've got to be there as part of the applauding multitude. There's been a list drawn up! . . .'

When they had gone their separate ways, two youths jostled Speculatress, thumped her in the face and grabbed her hand-bag. 'Help! Thieves!' Speculatress screamed after the lads got away. Fuzz, who could hear the cries for help perfectly well, didn't even turn round. Go screw yourself, he thought, I'm off duty. And he hastened his steps. 'There's someone else being mugged,' said Blockhead, who had heard the shouts as well. 'There was a very bad case here a few days ago . . .' 'Crimes like that are just survivals of the past,' said Sandal . . . 'The bas-tards,' said Speculatress. 'They might at least have raped me . . .'

The return
'Well, what's new?' asked Dauber. 'Nothing,' said Chatterer. 'Nothing's happening. Everyone seems to have disappeared. There's no-one to talk to and nothing to talk about. How are things with you?' 'Nothing much to report,' said Dauber. 'I've been doing a bit of sculpting. Do you want to see?' 'No,' said Chatterer. 'Well, that's life,' said Dauber. 'It's not life,' said Chatterer. 'We are not living. It's other people who are alive. It's their life. We've been dropped from it long ago. It's only by pure generosity that we're being allowed to live out our lives. Or

by indifference.' 'You ought to get out of here,' said Dauber. 'But that wouldn't change anything now,' said Chatterer. 'We've all lost the game already.' 'But why?' asked Dauber. 'After all, you said yourself that my game was unloseable.' 'That's the very reason why we've lost,' said Chatterer. 'We got distracted by our victories. We failed to notice our own death. Do you remember the end of the war? The war was over but in many places there were still little individual battles going on. There were battles but no war any more. What's happening to us are the last little battles of a war which is already over.'

The legend

While they were eating, someone nicked Teacher's parachute. 'That's just what you need,' said Chief. 'That'll teach you to look after your things. A parachute's something you've got to keep under your eyes.' 'That'd mean you'd have to lug it about with you everywhere,' said Gelding. 'It'd be a bit inconvenient!' 'That's no problem,' said Chief. 'You could just sew it to your trousers.' 'So what do I do now?' asked Teacher, 'report it to the police?' 'I wouldn't,' said Chief. And he looked thoughtfully at a squadron of dive-bombers which were coming in to land. 'I get you,' said Teacher. 'You keep an eye open for me,' he said to Deviationist and Intellectual. Within an hour Teacher was back with two parachutes. 'What's the other one for?' asked Deviationist. 'Don't be naïve,' said Teacher. 'It's a spare.' And he hid his trophies deep in the tail section of his fuselage. 'A parachute's a real fortune,' said Gelding. 'Just think how many handkerchiefs, blouses and knickers the women'll be able to make out of it!' 'We can live it up for a bit,' said Teacher. 'We'll get some real leather boots, broad belts and proper leather holsters. At least we'll look a bit like officers. And we'll drink the rest.' 'It'd be better the other way round,' said Gelding. 'Drink the lot first, and buy boots with the change.'

After supper Teacher and Deviationist got hold of a bottle of vile smelling hooch and went off to Waitress's home. She had asked a friend along as well, a thin and rather ugly girl. Teacher sniggered behind his hand. 'Watch out,' he whispered to Deviationist, 'take care not to break any bones!' Deviationist gave Teacher such a look that Teacher stopped feeling witty. They had a snack and discovered a rusty old gramophone and a couple of records so worn they were hardly playable. They drank a little and ate less, but smoked immense quantities of coarse tobacco. Deviationist, who wasn't used to it, felt rather ill. Then they danced a bit. Then a half-ruined guitar turned up from somewhere. While Teacher was tuning it Deviationist discussed literature with the ugly girl. 'All set,' said Teacher.

> The bitter wine you pour me, love,
> Won't get you anywhere.
> I've girls a-plenty, Heavens above!
> But my true love's the air.

And an immense, incomprehensible sadness from the huge world outside descended into the tiny, dimly-lit attic with its creaking floor. And the girls pressed themselves more closely against the boys, who seemed to them to be mighty, handsome knights from some marvellous fairy story. And their wide, unblinking eyes gazed somewhere far off into the distance where they imagined they glimpsed some inaccessible, elusive happiness.

> My heart will heed the engine's roar,
> Over town and village soar,
> For our life, like a curving furrow,
> Is here today and there tomorrow.

And it no longer mattered that your boots were made of plastic, that your frock was one of your mother's altered cast-offs. It didn't matter that the guitar only had three strings, that you played it badly, that you had no voice, and that the hooch smelt of petrol. You were a knight. And you were a beautiful princess.

> Today I kiss my fair-haired lass,
> Tomorrow, a brunette.
> And then? Only the devil, alas,
> Can tell which one I'll get.

And the boys knew that nothing of that was true. And the girls believed nothing of that was true. But all the same it seemed to be true. That it might come true one day. Please, God, let it be true.

> I won't be back. Don't wait around.
> I'll be some other place.

Maybe I'll crash into the ground—
'twill be my last embrace.

At midnight they went home, or rather to their dugout.
'Some evening that was!' said Teacher. 'And it was all your
fault. If I'd known, I'd never have taken you. What a time to
start philosophising! And look who with! There I am, digging
you in the ribs, winking at you, hinting. And you go all starry-
eyed! Let me finish! You can talk as much as you want with the
political commissar. He reads the Short Course five times a day.
But that's not what women are for.' 'Pack it in,' said Deviationist. 'Don't spoil a good day. They're still children. That's not
what they mean. They still need fairy tales. They liked being
with us. Maybe it was the happiest day of their lives.'

'Hey, you two,' they heard Chief's voice. 'What are you
doing wandering about out there? Get into the dugout, the pair
of you!' Chief was sitting on the bench between two enormous
women. One of them was Biddy. 'Who are you bossing about?'
she said. 'Get out yourself!' 'Shut your face,' Teacher said to
Chief. 'Or else we'll have your pants off and give you a thrashing, with these girls looking on. You wouldn't fancy that.' Chief
said he wasn't going to stand for that, and he'd have them court
martialled. Deviationist grabbed Chief by the throat. Chief
went for his pistol. 'Take your hands off that pop-gun,' said
Deviationist, 'or you'll end up with your teeth in the back of
your neck.' Chief beat a hasty retreat. And the lads went off
home with Biddy and her friend. Biddy had such a powerful
grip on Deviationist's hand that he couldn't have got away even
if he'd wanted to. And Teacher needed no persuading. He
roared with laughter, slapping the Woman on her mighty arse.

Where are you, swiftly fleeting night?
Where are you, oh those eyes so bright?
Where are you, youthful innocence?

The queue

'Say that this represents all the goods available for consumption
by society,' said Blockhead, drawing a big circle in chalk on the
asphalt. 'The best part of it, the part which is in shortest supply,
goes into the system of outlets reserved for the privileged. So
this part doesn't come into the queue system. The rest, in
principle, is for everybody else. But is this so in actual fact? You

(781)

know perfectly well that a large part of this remainder, and its best part, is distributed among the second-rank authorities. There's no law about it, but it's a custom which is religiously observed by those responsible for distribution. And they are subordinate to those second-rank authorities. So, as you see, the circle is much reduced. Then another large part goes off to various kinds of special regions and special undertakings. There again it is divided among the hierarchy, but it has to be deducted from the initial circle. From what remains, the lion's share is distributed from hand to hand, by the black market or in return for bribes. And finally of what remains for the real queue to line up for, a good deal is stolen and never gets to the queuers. And all that's left for us is a small share, and the worst. So that is why we are standing here, waiting for our miserable crumbs.'

'But it would seem a lot simpler,' said Sandal, 'to make people work instead of standing around in queues. There'd be more goods and shorter queues. And standing in queues is more tiring than working.' 'Just you try,' said Blockhead. 'You'll see what happens. It's been tried before more than once by enthusiasts. First of all no-one yet knows what thingammyjigs are. So special research studies are ordered. But what can they study, since there aren't any thingammyjigs to study? They have to use models. Fortunately the theory of models has grown to a monstrous scale. But before you make your models, you have to have a theory. So they'll have to develop a conceptual mathematical scheme. There'll be conferences and congresses and so on. Institutes will be founded. If the thing's going to be done at all, it had better be done on a grand scale. We always think big. And until a dozen or so layabouts have become academicians, fifty or so corresponding members, a couple of hundred research members, a thousand or so doctors of science, and so on, and until everyone who can lay their hands on a bonus have got it in their pockets, there's no chance of production beginning. Grandiose plans for the production of thingammyjig harvesters have to be prepared. The structure of thingammyjig chromosomes will have to be studied. Tons of books have to be written . . . Everything you can imagine will be turned out, except of course thingammyjigs. But say that thingammyjig production does get under way. Who is going to sow them? Who's going to cultivate them? Who's going to harvest them? Where will they be stored? How will they be stored? How will they be delivered? Who's going to be responsible for it all? A million insoluble problems will be set. It's far simpler to do nothing at all. More peaceful. And anyway, people are busy—they're standing in a queue. They even stand in a line during their leisure hours. And if there weren't any more queues, people would begin to think! They'd begin to demand a better type of leisure-time activity. And when all that begins to happen, malcontents begin to appear.'

The encounter

At last the long awaited encounter took place. The buildings around the manhole were adorned with slogans and portraits of the leaders of the Brotherhood and the Government. The manhole itself was banked in fresh artificial flowers specially reared for this purpose by the geneticists of the war veterans co-operative 'UNI-BLOOM'. The combined bands of the Army and the Secret Police filled the entire length of Boss Avenue. The guard of honour was lined up along Victors' Avenue. Bullet-proof cars arrived bearing the leaders of the Brotherhood and the Government, who were depicted in the portraits. They arrived in the order in which the portraits were displayed from left to right, and arranged themselves on a dais separated from the mass of the people by bullet-proof glass. The massed bands brayed out the anthem. The commander of the guard of honour went through some complex sabre evolutions and marched off at double-time to report to Leadiban. Caretaker, with the help of the new Night-watchman from CUNT, ceremonially raised the manhole cover, securing it with a metal hook. An incredible stench wafted from the manhole and swiftly engulfed the whole of Ibansk. The Ibanskians were mute and stupefied. Then, one after another, the sub-Ibanskian delegation began to crawl out of the hole. Their appearance astonished the Ibanskians. They were prepared for anything. For centuries they had been taught that intelligent beings from extra-terrestrial civilizations might have incredible, fantastic forms. For example, they might look like octopuses or jellyfish. Or even . . . But suffice it to say that the Ibanskians were ready for anything except this. From the manhole emerged naked . . . Ibanskians, but with empty eye-sockets crammed with filth. They were quite incredibly grimy and stinking and covered in woodlice, worms, fleas, bugs, and every other kind of vermin which, far from trying to remove, they protected tenderly from any possible external contact. The last to crawl out was the Leader of the sub-Ibanskian delegation (Lesidel), who sneezed three times, farted three times, and then got on to all fours. The members of the sub-Ibanskian delegation froze to attention and sang the sub-Ibanskian national anthem, which in some way recalled the old Ibanskian anthem: 'The wind blew through the reeds and the trees began to bend!' The encounter of the two Great Civilizations had taken place.

The draft opposition programme
The revolution? That we shan't achieve.
It's no use asking us to agitate.
Foregoing it may make your stomachs heave,
But suffering it—that's not to contemplate!
Don't look to us to make life any better.
The most you'll get—and only when you squeeze—
Is some quite meaningless and idle mutter,
Mere frothing, take it any way you please.
We'll write your nonsense down as holy writ—
You *are* the bosses, so we quite agree.
We'll seal our lips if you desire it,
Or stick to falsehoods—anything you say.
Or if you wish, we'll stretch out in our room,
Our feet and heads well wrapped to keep us warm,
Lose ourselves in our well-upholstered womb,
Forget the world in idleness and calm.
Our hands caressing richly polished wood,
We'll switch on the TV if you desire,
Though boredom makes us ready to expire,
That speech uplifting won't be understood,
Your flickering faces slowly fade away.
We shan't even live our lives out to the end.
Inter us in some far off place, we pray,
Lest anyone should dig us up again.
Oh please do not disturb us once we've died.
No busts or photographs should mark our grave;
The very most we want's some dignified

But humble epitaph: 'Their lives they gave
Not to disease or violence unconfined,
Nor yet old age, which so much life devours.
They died of boredom, the ordinary kind,
While at the very summit of their powers.'
  Bloke presented this draft opposition programme to Colleague. But he just put it in a drawer, without even reading it. 'I haven't time at the moment,' he said. 'I'm not ready for you. Come in again some other time.' And Colleague plunged back into Agent's report.

Agent's report

Agent reported that the sub-Ibanskians had different kinds of stenches, and their social hierarchy could be determined by a classification of their various stinks. But if a graph of the odours emitted by the sub-Ibanskians were established in accordance with their frequency and intensity, one could see from the stench curve that there was one exception in the sub-Ibanskian delegation. The ugliest sub-Ibanskian, Runt, who held the lowest post in the delegation, had a stench of the very highest rank. In all probability he was the actual head of the delegation, and Lesidel was only a figurehead. Like Firadep 39 in our delegation. We'll have to sort out the key to this Runt, thought Colleague. Any real contact between civilizations must begin with the recruitment of special agents. If these rats have managed to build madogism as well, we'll have to keep our eye on them. They've probably already recruited someone. Who? Serasa 1979 has just bought his old woman a fur coat. I wonder where the loot came from? And what about his villa? Yes, there's something fishy going on here.

The return

'These days unlimited horizons are opening up for monumental sculpture,' said Dauber, in an interview with the correspondent of sub-Ibanskian television. 'Our remarkable scientists have invented a material which is to all intents and purposes everlasting, light, easily worked and readily available. It's called, snotoplast. You ask how it's made. You take ordinary snot which is produced in abundance by our literature, our film industry, our television, our press and other cultural activity in our society, and it is exposed to super-ultra-sound. This produces a highly fluid plasma which can assume any shape. So it is perfectly possible to make a sculpture half a mile high covering an area comparable with that supposedly once occupied by the legendary country of Italy. Incidentally, the rumours that traces of this mythical land have been discovered turned out to be false. In fact no Michelangelo ever actually existed. What was it we were talking about? Oh yes, . . . but snotoplast has one shortcoming. If our sculptors litter the entire earth with statues of leaders, heroes and sportsmen, then there'll be no possibility of getting rid of them. So this lays increased demands on our artists. What am I working on? I am sculpting a bust of Leadiban. Yes, I intend to make it a hundred times bigger, and to replace this red porphyry with modern snotoplast.' 'Splendid,' said the interviewer from sub-Ibanskian television. 'Our sculptors use turdotron for their busts and statues of our leaders. This is shit which has gone through two, three or more processes of refinement. It is quite remarkably strong, and wonderfully plastic. For instance, if you take a piece of turdotron 3 in your hands it tries of its own accord to take on the form of a leader—and so accurately that the leader immediately tries to mount a platform to make a speech. And would you believe it, he can carry on about any subject without even a scrap of paper.'

Dauber made the correspondent a present of a dozen etchings and a few bronze sculptures. The correspondent promised that the next time he came he would bring Dauber a couple of tons of turdotron 5 to try out. There really are some ingenious people about, thought Dauber. That's technology for you! And yet we go on working with any old material. Marble. Bronze. Gold. Only the other day I bought a couple of antique gold lavatory bowls from some drunk. It was a waste of five roubles. Old-fashioned stuff.

The legend

The morning after, Teacher described the qualities of the Woman in such graphic terms that Gelding rushed off into the lavatory and stayed there rather a long time. He returned looking tired but relieved. A new poem appeared on the wall of the dugout:

I clutch my cock until in pain;
To overcome my body's lust
I want a real live cunt again,
A really well upholstered bust.
I'll grab some randy little whore,
Fling her down and try my luck;
Up her skirt and down her drawers,
Then I'll have a proper f—.

'That's very striking,' said Intellectual. 'Lyricism of the most modern kind, and completely in accord with the spirit of this age of scientific and technological revolution.'

At lunch Deviationist and Teacher each received an extra bowl of kasha. 'What's all this about?' asked Deviationist. 'Shut up and eat,' said Teacher. 'It's a reward for honest toil.'

Chief wrote a report in which he named Biddy and Woman as witnesses, and demanded their written confirmation of the incident. 'What a bastard he is,' said Biddy, 'and him a fighting man.' And she refused to sign. Chief said that, as a matter of principle, he would get Biddy court-martialled. 'You know where you can shove your bloody court-martial,' said Biddy. 'I could find a better use for your piece of paper!'

Waitress slipped a note into Teacher's hand. 'Come again today,' it said. 'We just couldn't do it the very first time. We're expecting you.'

Biddy caught Deviationist in the corridor. 'If you go off to those two randy little tarts,' she hissed angrily, 'we'll confirm Chief's report.' 'Oh ho!' said Teacher. 'Blackmail already. Fine. We'll go and see the two old bags tonight. In the first place I fancy Woman, and secondly these girls have to learn their lesson. It'd do them no harm to spend tonight wondering what's happened to us, and then tomorrow they'll be like putty in our hands.'

The bomber pilots raised hell about the parachutes and accused the fighter pilots. It looked as if there was going to be a big brawl. The commandant called in Chief, read his report, advised him to use it as toilet paper and ordered him to put a stop to all this. Chief tried to stammer out something about the weather being unsafe for flying (it had started to snow), the commandant merely laughed. 'Very good, Sir,' said Chief. And within an hour the fighter squadron was taxi-ing out to take off.

(787)

As soon as they were out of sight of the airfield, Chief waggled his wings and led the squadron down to hedge-hopping level. The fighters flew barely above the ground, chopping bushes and the dry grass with their propellers, raising waves on the ponds, forcing chance passers-by to fling themselves into the mud, and a few old nags to gallop wildly away. People often think that the great romance of flying lies in looping the loop, rolls, altitude, long-distance flights and so on. But this is a basic mistake, a prejudice. There is nothing finer in flying than hedge-hopping, which is even more enjoyable in places where it's forbidden, and even better at a height lower than the permitted minimum. Below you, to right and left, and even sometimes above you, but anyway very close to you, the ground whirls by at terrifying speed—houses, people, cows, dogs, ponds, bushes . . . —everything which you have grown up with. It is your familiar world, yet passing by in a whirlwind like some unattainable fairy tale. So close and at the same time so inaccessible. Just as grey as ever. Yet unbelievably beautiful. It flashes by and disappears for ever . . . and you long to bring your aircraft closer and closer to the earth . . . closer . . . closer . . . Teacher didn't even notice that Snotnose, flying just behind him, had hit some hillock or some telegraph pole or other . . .

When they landed at the reserve airfield another machine was missing as well. And the mechanics discovered bits of human arm and skull in Calf's radiator. 'The joke's over,' said Gelding. 'Chief'll be demoted now. And Calf will be sentenced to death, commuted to service in the penal battalion. And that'll be the end of him. But it's nothing to do with us. We've got our life ahead of us.'

> Your next intoxication, Fate being blind,
> Predict you never . . .

The queue
An extraordinary meeting of EPSPOSVKBI was held to consider the approaching anniversary of the Queue. It was decided to set up an anniversary commission under a Seradep. The commission was to prepare a plan of action and put it forward for confirmation. The plan was to include ceremonial meetings, public rejoicing, amateur concerts, and decorations. The pro-

gress of preparations for the anniversary was to be widely reported in the press. There was some discussion of who should be selected to deliver the speech. The difficulty was that according to Ibanskian law the person who delivers the speech becomes its author, although he doesn't actually write the speech himself. And he gets a fee for his television delivery of the speech, for its publication in all the newspapers, for its publication in individual pamphlets and in collected works which, of course, include the speech. And of course he gets the glory. So the question of who is to deliver a speech is one of great importance for the Ibanskian leadership. The Ibanskians have learnt how to establish the true social status of their leaders, and their prospects, from the number of speeches delivered, the subject of the speeches and the time and place of their delivery. On this occasion Leadiban decided to give his Deputies the chance of delivering the speech. A bitter quarrel broke out. In the end the victory was shared by two claimants—Firadep 17 and Firadep 39., 'It's my turn,' yelled Firadep 17. 'But what about equality?' bellowed Firadep 39. 'You've already got fifteen volumes of collected works, and I've only got seven! And I'm older than you!' Agents of UNO had to be brought in, and they decided that the speech would be delivered by Firadep 17. 'It is our duty to keep the workers happy,' said Leadiban. And he suggested that the speech should include the announcement that this year a super harvest of thingammyjigs was expected.

Biological difficulties

Immediately certain unforeseen biological barriers were detected. Since the Ibanskians emitted rather less powerful stenches than the sub-Ibanskians, the sub-Ibanskians decided that the Ibanskians were intellectually inferior to them, and the Ibanskians decided that they were superior to the sub-Ibanskians. And each of the delegations therefore wanted to have its way. For this reason the sub-Ibanskians began to stink to such an extent that the head of the Ibanskian delegation, Firadep 17, had an apoplectic fit and had to be hurriedly replaced by Firadep 39. All the members of the Ibanskian delegation had to wear gas masks. Thanks to this, the Ibanskian delegation derived a certain benefit, and foreign journalists were now able to distinguish them from the sub-Ibanskians. The problem then arose of how to proceed further. ARSE was instructed to produce some constructive proposals. Rat called in Blockhead. 'It's easy,' said Blockhead. 'Let our lot pretend that we are a shade more stupid than they.' In sub-Ibansk, in their turn, a special meeting of the supreme defecutive ordered its delegation to pretend that the sub-Ibanskians were a shade more stupid than the Ibanskians. So the difficulties were ironed out. But then a new obstacle was detected: the language barrier.

Legend

Teacher made up his bed and, of course, flopped on to it in his dirty boots. And on the wall of the dugout he read the following:

If the pox you've never caught,
You've not lived as people ought.
What is pox? It's honestly
The mark of male maturity.
It shows you know your way about,
A virile chap, without a doubt.
It ne'er attacks, so I've been told,
The very young or very old.
To catch the pox was not my aim;
I got infected just the same,
Like you. And him. And him as well,
And thousands others, I can tell.
One fine day I had a piss.
Ouch! Is it pox? I'm sure it is.
I yelled aloud in awful pain:
Lads, the pox has struck again!
Help, help! I cried, till someone came,
My prick is bursting into flame.
What an attack! The pain's extensive,
And treatment can be quite expensive,
For if you want to keep it quiet
And need medicine, you must buy it;
It costs two greatcoats, plus your gaiters,
Loaves of bread, sacks of potatoes.

So if you want it stopped in time,
You must lead a life of crime.
To prison I don't want to go,
So I called on the M.O.
Beneath the poem someone had added:
But the M.O. won't treat the pox
Before he's notified the cops.
That's not bad, thought Teacher. And he read another poem
written alongside, but in different handwriting:
'Get on parade!' the sergeant cries.
'Fall in and form a square.
Dress by the right! Now stand at ease.
'shun! And no talking there!
Three paces forward march! You, yes!
'bout turn! And face your front.
Your bedspace is a filthy mess,
Your boots are too, you cunt!
Every shot you've fired has missed,
You march like a baboon.
You've lots more faults that I can't list,
Disgrace to the platoon!
Politically you're quite inept,
And you've gone AWOL twice.
When on guard duty you have slept.
Your hair is full of lice.
Take off your badges! Your belt, too!
Don't stand there open-jawed.
You've had your fun, but now you're through,
And here's the final straw:
You thieved a greatcoat from your friend,
And now you face a court.'
But me? Believe me, I don't mind:
The fact that I've been caught
Means no-one's going to fire at me,
And I won't see the enemy.
'That's very strange,' said Teacher aloud. 'And what shall I
write? There's plenty of space.' Gelding came in. 'Go and get
your parachute,' he said. 'I've got a buyer. He's offering a
bucket of hooch and two pairs of boots. They're not chrome, of
course, but they are real leather, not plastic. And we can drink

the profit of the plastic boots afterwards. Let's have a ball! By the way, I've met a couple of girls. Very dishy. They've asked us round this evening.'

The return

'What a life we live here,' said Dauber. 'I've got out of the habit of it. And it all seems totally absurd. It's the way people work here! Two or three years to turn out a bust of some hero or other, a statesman or an actor. A gravestone. If it's a life-size statue of a leader, that's accounted a great coup. A few illustrations for some lousy little book. One canvas in a regional exhibition. A portrait shown in the club. Medals and titles for anything you like, but not for any real contribution to art. And as for reviews, or books on the history of art, that's not even worth talking about. It's brain-addling boredom. I'm sure it wasn't like that ten years ago.' 'It was,' said Chatterer. 'It was always like that. But at that time there was Hope and Illusion. That's all vanished now. All that's left is absolute grey monotony. It's exactly the same in my field. Take a bright young man who's beginning his career in science. What's he got to look forward to? At best the same thing that the most mediocre of mediocrities can expect. Just look here, in the Journal. Two books are reviewed. You might think that you'd be able to tell from the reviews which book is the better. No. In this case the bad book has got a first-class review. But the other, which is quite good, has got a very restrained notice. But it could have been different. If the author of the average book had had a higher rank he'd have got a better review. But a third book was published at the same time as these two. It was a really good one. It got through by accident. And there are no reviews of it at all, nor will there be. And if one does appear through some extraordinary circumstance, it'll be even more half-hearted than the one on the average book. The author of the good book isn't even being considered for a doctorate. I know him. He simply won't be allowed to defend his thesis. The author of the bad book has already defended his successfully and been proposed for the Academy. And the author of the average book is waiting for his turn to come round. That's not out of the ordinary. It's typical. We lack any moral principles or traditions under which some influential group of people would give priority to any really worthwhile and talented creative products. And since that's the way it is, the number of people who have any hope of being judged by any fair assessment of their creative abilities is declining all the time. There are only a few isolated individuals who are able to withstand this situation. And they don't create the climate. They either perish or get the hell out of it. As a result, all judgments are distorted. The categories which were developed for the assessment of truly talented and hard-working creative people are being applied to worthless rubbish as if it were true art or true science. It is the triumph of mediocrity. And an official system of falsehood has been established to cover all this up. In a word, the place of genuine normal creativity has been usurped by a worthless imitation. The sum total is mortal boredom. Sometimes certain groups of people are, for a time, led astray with regard to certain cultural phenomena. But either they are quickly undeceived or they don't affect the general atmosphere of mediocrity and monotony. And life comes to be measured in decades. Decades must pass before a creative person can amass the very minimum he needs to show that he has really accomplished anything. Here one could produce mathematically precise formulae permitting us to forecast the prospects of any individual.' 'But you don't need them,' said Dauber. 'Even without them everything is clear from the very start. Think what I can expect over the next five years. In cash it's far more than I need. But from the creative point of view it's about five minutes' work. And from the point of view of its technical execution it's fiendishly difficult, because . . . you know yourself how things work here.'

Teacher's objection

When he'd read Bloke's draft programme, Teacher agreed in principle but with some objections.

According to the latest scientific data
Our Ibanskians cannot die of boredom now or later.
Anyone who thinks they can must drop his mad
    persistence,
For boredom is our very life, the essence of existence.
We're no poets: we apply the very strictest laws.
We are boredom when we work, and boredom when
    we pause;

We're boredom in our family life, or in our love's
    embraces,
We're boredom in the endless queue in which we take
    our places.
We're bored at a lecture,
We're bored with creation,
There's even the torture
Of bored contestation.
We're bored when we're lying,
We're bored when we're critical,
Oh, the tedium trying
Of boredom political!
Who are we? The product of history past,
We're the practice and theory of *ennui* to the last.
Bored to eternity,
Yawning for ages,
Bored uniformity
Laid down by sages.
Scientists tell us
It's proved beyond doubt
That dying of boredom
Is the only way out.

'That's a first-class basis for schism,' said Blockhead. 'The
time's ripe. Every serious political movement begins with
schism and then a clearly defined split. But just let's make sure
that we split into two equal halves and draw lots for which half.
And then, because of our action, history will end up in a
complete dead-end. That'll be a laugh!' 'Dead-ends don't exist
because of schisms,' said Teacher. 'If we split down the middle
there'll be those ahead and those behind. Just think, a schism
between the behind-chiks and the before-chiks.' 'How about
bums and busts?' said Mistress. 'Oh ho!' said Bloke. 'If the
women are coming out into the political arena, that'll mean
trouble!' 'True enough,' said Sandal. 'The Pavilion's going to
shut soon for an inventory.'

The queue
Firadep's anniversary speech made a shattering impression.
Although everyone knew that his promises were all empty, they
began to prepare their shopping bags. There was a spontaneous

initiative of the workers to devote a Saturday to voluntary labour, cleaning and repairing the thingammyjig stores, but it turned out that there were no stores to repair. So the workers resolved to give up a Sunday to voluntary labour to prepare the wasteground on which the thingammyjig stores were to be built. But the wasteground was already cleared. So the workers resolved to give up a Monday to voluntary labour to scatter rubbish all over it. But where was the rubbish to be found? So the workers had to break up and destroy everything they could find, and for this they organised a voluntary labour Tuesday, Wednesday, Thursday, and Friday. And they created such a mess that everyone had to be called on to give up a Saturday to clear . . . The factories closed down for a time, and the offices closed down until autumn.

Linguistic difficulties

Long before the date of the encounter, linguists, mathematicians, psychologists, logicians, and so on and so on had been working jointly on the preparation of a Great Universal Language (GUL) suitable for communication between the Ibanskians and any other civilizations. In their work on GUL the Ibanskian scientists started from the extreme hypothesis that there would be nothing in common between the Ibanskian language and that of the representatives of sub-Ibanskian culture. It was demonstrated with some precision that languages for every other case could be deduced on an analagous principle from GUL. The basis of GUL was formed from the multiplication table, Pythagoras' theorem and Newton's binomial theorem, which had been statistically shown to be the most constant invariants of all human knowledge. Blockhead's idea of basing GUL on the most ancient linguistic forms of Ibanskian obscenity and blasphemy was rejected as being revisionist and mechanistic. This rejection was erroneous, as it was on this very basis that the first subterranean civilization was discovered and the first contacts with it made.

But when it came to the point of negotiations, it became clear that there was no known scientific method of finding a correlation between GUL and the sub-Ibanskian language. It turned out that this language was grammatically very similar to Ibanskian, and there were even many mutually similar words. But that was as far as it went. The sub-Ibanskian language included words for which there were no equivalents in Ibanskian, and in Ibanskian there were words with no equivalents in sub-Ibanskian. And there were no methods to determine what they meant. After several years of failed attempts, the two delegations were still unable to begin negotiations. The sub-Ibanskians crawled back into their sewer and the Ibanskians crawled back into their luxurious super-Ibanskian apartments. It seemed that no communication could result, and the Ibanskian government had already broached a plan to fill in the pit and cement over the manhole covers. But the problem resolved itself. Blockhead, Bloke, Caretaker and Night-watchman were discussing the subject in the Pavilion. 'It's a ridiculous problem,' said Night-watchman. 'There's no point in beginning with this idiotic multiplication table, which isn't really understood by any of our academicians in mathematics, logic or philosophy (although there's nothing really mysterious about it)! They ought to start from conversation on social topics. After all, social topics tend to be the same everywhere.' 'You're absolutely right,' said Blockhead. And he rapidly rehearsed the entire sub-Ibanskian lexicon which had anything to do with the structure of society. An informer who had overheard all this drunken babbling reported it to Colleague. The drinking companions were arrested. 'Here's some paper,' said Colleague. 'By morning I want a complete Ibanskian-sub-Ibanskian-Ibanskian dictionary, or else.' The very next day Firadep 39 was knocking on the manhole cover to summon the sub-Ibanskian delegation to the negotiating table.

The legend
After half the parachute had gone in booze, Teacher came to know true love. His love was great, but the girl was insignificant. Not that it mattered. They sat there side by side in silence, experiencing something which Teacher had never felt before or since. Not far away, Gelding was grappling on the ground with his girl and swearing the most fervent oaths that he would marry her very soon. 'You're all the same,' whispered the girl. 'You always begin with promises and then you disappear like the morning dew.' At dawn they returned to the dugout, Gelding's knees covered in earth; he was fully intending to marry

(796)

and experience married bliss, no matter how briefly, and
Teacher fully intended to fill up the empty space on the wall
above his bed. Teacher managed to fulfil his intention. Gelding
did not.

Let me address this simple, modest, private little prayer
Not to the devil, nor to God—just to Some-one out there.
Be good to me, stretch out your hand, and make this moment
    last.
And afterwards? Well, what you will, just once this time is past.
But Some-one answered from above—his voice was very stern:
My friend, your prayer distresses me. You've really got to learn
That I can't do that kind of thing, as you quite well should
    know,
Not even with a drink or two, this kind of thing won't go.
I could this barracks, if you wish, for some great palace trade,
I could promote you—say the word—into a higher grade.
Even harder things than that I'll give, like genuine leather
    boots,
Or trousers that will hold their crease, or neatly fitting suits.
If I order it you'll become the hero of the nation,
The cloak of fame will fall on you, even a decoration.
I can show you many ways to start a revolution,
Or how to win a Nobel Prize, or head an institution.
And at a pinch, you always could my great benevolence feel
By suffering, at my behest, for some profound ideal.
But what you ask me to perform is quite beyond my power—
I'd have to have the go-ahead from authorities much higher.
Silent he fell; and Heaven's Voice died away.
The Special Branch is not beneath his sway.

Mutual understanding

'We have built madogism,' said Firadep 39, in his speech
opening the negotiations. The sub-Ibanskians clutched their
sides and roared with laughter, emitting a quite intolerable
stench against which even gas masks were ineffective. 'They've
built madogism,' gasped Lesidel, doubled up with laughter.
'Just look at these idiots, lads! Ha, ha, ha!! We built madogism
ages ago. In time immemorial. Before the dawn of history. We
didn't even need to build it, because we never had anything
else. We had madogism right from the start. Just you come and

visit us! You'll see straightaway that we have no truck with morality or democracy or culture. We've no time for that kind of frivolity. We simply don't need them. None of us. It's true that our legends have some allusions to a disturbed time which only lasted a few years. Intellectuals appeared. They sculpted some bizarre statues out of clay, sang dirty songs and demanded that they should be allowed to go abroad. But we caught up with them very quickly.' 'What did you do with them?' asked Firadep 39. Lesidel was amazed by such an absurd question. 'We ate them, of course,' he snorted, bursting with laughter. 'What do you do with your intellectuals?' 'We simply don't protect them,' said Firadep 39. 'And they eliminate themselves. Even before they appear.'

In the evening there was a banquet in honour of the sub-Ibanskian delegation. At first the sub-Ibanskians felt ill at ease and a little unhappy, although the tables were laden with food of a kind which the Ibanskians knew only from old books. But then the sub-Ibanskians went off to the lavatory en masse and stuffed themselves to such a degree that they had to be put into special sewage disposal tankers and carted off to the manhole. All the newspapers carried the text of a joint communiqué which reported that the meeting had been held in an atmosphere of cordiality and good will, that it had been wholly constructive, and that the parties had achieved a perfect mutual understanding.

Runt was denounced in the act of trying to rape a protesting fox-terrier belonging to Firasa 739. He had no alternative but to agree to co-operate with UNO.

The agents' reports

A highly experienced agent, who knew fifty foreign languages and how to hold his knife and fork, who had been infiltrated into the Queue right at the start, despatched a Most Secret report to Colleague. The report was so heavily enciphered that it could not be decoded even by the ARSE computers. So Blockhead was sent for. He instantly read off the following text; 'Some isolated manifestations of contentment have been observed in the Queue. There are rumours of the formation of an opposition group to defend the existing system.' The report interested Colleague, and he immediately despatched to the

Shop area fifty agents, all with bachelor's or doctor's degrees, to try to establish whether or not there was any substance to these rumours. The agents, once they had improved their life-style and published at least one book and a dozen articles each, reported that the rumours had no foundation whatsoever. The agents never actually appeared anywhere near the Shop. They were afraid that they would be stripped. So it's all lies, Colleague decided.

The return

'You allege,' Dauber said, 'that our society is not only lawless but amoral. I cannot agree with that. A society without morality cannot exist. Even gangsters have their own morality. Totalitarian régimes of the past also had a morality of their own. So we can talk of a society with bad morals, but a society with no morals at all . . . Forgive me for saying so, but that's downright rubbish.' 'But what do you call morality?' asked Chatterer. 'Is it just a code of rules of behaviour? We hear a lot of talk about the moral code these days. But such conversations are symptomatic. They reflect the fact that society contains no morality as a socially significant factor, as a real element in its life, and that it tries to pass something else off as morality. No rules of morality exist. Morality itself is merely a way of behaving. In extreme cases it is itself the only rule. The problem is that the word "morality" is ambiguous to say the least. In one sense it is a code of specific rules of behaviour. And in this sense we can speak of the "morality" of gangsters, gangs of rapists, and so on. But in the other sense it means something different in principle. When I speak of morality, I am considering exclusively this second meaning. If you want to use the word "morality" in the former sense, do so. But then we have to introduce a second term for the other concept. Let's call it "conscience". In that case our society becomes moral in your sense (although it's true that the question as to whether that morality is good or bad remains unresolved), but in my sense it is totally devoid of conscience.

'Morality-conscience concerns the voluntary actions of some people towards others. And those who perform the actions know whether their actions will do other people good or ill, and in what proportion. An action is moral if its author is free to choose whether to perform it or not, and if it does not cause harm to others. A higher degree of morality is achieved if the action causes good to others. So degrees of morality can be measured. More complex situations arise if a man is forced to do harm to another and he chooses the course which will cause least damage; if a man causes himself harm by doing good to another, and so on. It is a simple logical task to consider all possible situations of this kind. One can judge the degree of a man's morality by the percentage and weight of his moral actions related to all his actions taken together. And as you can see for yourself, there is no place here for codes of conduct. This is a different kind of phenomenon.

'The tendency to perform amoral actions (in the sense of actions lacking in conscience) is one of the laws of society. So what is it that forces people into moral actions? They are, after all, voluntary actions. People choose to perform them of their own free will, and even to their own detriment. There are two questions here. The first is where it all springs from, and the second is what sustains it. The origin is a chance result, a mutation. And the free will of the individual concerned. As far as the maintenance of the action is concerned, it can happen like this. If moral actions are performed *en masse*, the advantage of behaviour of this kind becomes apparent to society as a whole. It results in a great economy of resources, of energy and so on. An amoral society wastes a huge amount of energy because of its very lack of a high enough level of morality. But a certain accumulation is needed before such actions can become truly massive. What is needed to produce this accumulation? The only thing which is able to help towards this end is publicity, a judgment of actions as moral or amoral, an opportunity to unmask and denounce at least part of people's concealed behaviour. In the past this function was performed by the fear of God. But nowadays, people do not want to have God in their souls. In others words, if they want a moral society, they must be prepared to fight for the birth, the preservation, the strengthening, the transmission of a God exterior to them, for the means of submitting some part, however insignificant, of human actions, to public judgment. We have still not fully realised the enormous role played in this respect by two of the most important events of recent decades—Hog's secret speech and Truth-teller's Book. If you want to know my view, Hog played the part of John the Baptist, and Truth-teller that of the Saviour. I'm not joking. They began (although whether this was their intention or not is a different question) the whole enterprise of the moral improvement of our society.'

'And what does the future hold in store?' asked Dauber. 'Everything depends on how this heritage will be handed down to succeeding generations, and on the capacity of individuals to make sacrifices along the road,' said Chatterer. 'Society can only stay on this road through suffering and sacrifice. There is no other way.' 'And what is my place in all this?' asked Dauber. 'You are outside it,' replied Chatterer. 'You paint and sculpt the battle of good and evil. But your battle of good and evil is being fought on an intellectual plane, not at the very foundations of life itself. It involves neither renunciation nor self sacrifice, without which moral-conscience is unthinkable. I am convinced that at the price of enormous sacrifices society will re-establish the heights of past morality on a new basis, and make further progress ahead. It is a great pity I realised this too late. Like you, I have remained outside the living, or the organic, thread of history.'

The legend

Tell me why soldiers have nothing to say
When their martial achievements are praised.
Or why they mutter and mumble when they
Find that questions of warfare are raised?
I know that a war is no picnic, that's true,
But hunger and suffering and cold,
But there must be some respites, if only a few,
And some tales of high deeds to be told.
Yes there are. And especially if warm and well fed,
You sit there back safe at H.Q.
And at the cost of the unnumbered dead
All the medals get pinned onto you.
Yes, it's fine if you're posted well back in the rear
And you can't hear the guns' distant roar.
But for all of the millions who're fighting up here,
War's a mortal, ineffable bore.
Assaults and attacks are all right for some,
For the papers, the cinema reel;

For the rest, it's awaiting the end that must come,
It's the soul's wound which never will heal.
So the answer's quite simple. The dead never speak,
And the villains take all of their glory.
The survivors—well, no-one endeavours to seek
Them out, or discover their story.
The leaders, who feel no remorse for past crime,
Go on plotting the science of war,
And those who romanticise warfare in rhyme,
Well, they're wrong. For it's one deadly bore.
That is why . . .

The congress of the defeated

'It would be interesting to bring them all together,' said Teacher. 'To organize a symposium or a conference or a congress. Just imagine! The Pan-Ibanskian Congress of Cracked Skulls!' 'It wouldn't be hard to arrange,' said Bloke. 'Just open another half litre and you'll find them all appearing. Even Hog'll show up with his trendy progressive gravestone.' 'Maybe he'll even give a speech,' said Blockhead. 'Yes, one composed by Claimant, Thinker, Sociologist and the rest,' said Sandal. 'They're pastmasters at the art.' 'The main theme of the speech,' said Teacher, 'would be something like this. We have achieved remarkable defeats. Our defeats would have been even more remarkable had we not been hampered by reactionary forces in the persons of Truth-teller, Double-dealer, Slanderer, Singer and others of that ilk. We exerted every effort to destroy these reactionary forces, and we would have achieved our purpose, had it not been for . . .' 'And then,' said Bloke, 'they would adopt an Appeal to Posterity.'

The liberals' appeal to posterity

Hey, you youngsters! Snotty-faces! We're your ancestors,
    that's who!
Come on, tidy up our leavings. Come on, slobs, it's up to you!
We're Ibanskians bold and bright,
Of the Left we're the far right,
Practised in naïvety,
Skilled in inactivity,
Honest in our cynicism,

Passive in our dynamism,
Individuals in the mass,
And progressive as a class.
We'd shake hands with anyone, no matter what his post.
We'd scrounge and grab at any chance, to gain the very most.
We were prepared to think about the failings of our time,
But we got beaten round the head and came back into line.
We'd have done a great deal more if we had had a chance,
But the old men slapped us down and made us dance their
    dance,
And forced us into viciousness and vile abomination,
Without allowing us to show our liberal inclination.
We're Ibanskians bold and deft,
Of the Right we're the far left,
Practised in naïvety,
Bold in our passivity,
Honest in our cynicism,
Powerless in our activism,
Individuals in the mass,
And progressive as a class.

An exchange of experience

After an exchange of views on the structures of their respective
societies, the parties turned to economic matters. 'How do you
manage without money?' asked Firadep 39. 'It's very simple,'
replied Lesidel. 'We have nothing to buy with money. As your
classics used to say, before you get involved in philosophy,
people have to have food, drink and clothing, and so on. We
have no need for housing—we live under cover naturally all the
time. We don't want clothes—in fact we positively dislike
them. People are made to wear them as a punishment. We've
got ample food supplies. We live surrounded by food. We can't
get away from it. Certain delicacies (rats' tails, for instance,
what ambrosia!) are awarded for special services to the state. So
almost all our time is leisure. And we use it to bring our creative
ability to a peak of fulfilment. Whoever is capable of anything,
he does it to the full! You should hear our Fartovsky! The
melodies he produces would take your breath away! What
notes! Compared with him your Chaliapins and Carusos are
pathetic! . . . Forgiven me, we seem to be getting off the

subject. And what about you? How do you get on without money, if it isn't a secret?' 'In various ways,' said Firadep 39. 'In some undertakings, the management, in association with the Brotherhood and Trade Union officials, confirm the consumer needs of their various workers in accordance with the directive, and in the firm's shop each employee can take according to his needs. In other cases tokens are handed out, very like the old money in appearance but playing quite a different role. They are used to establish the consumer needs of each individual. And there are mixed methods. It's true that speculators and crooks sometimes try to re-establish the monetary system, but we can cope with that all right. How? By stopping the production of goods which are the object of speculation.' 'That is very clever,' said Lesidel.

Then Firadep referred to the fact that the Ibanskian government was extremely interested in raising a loan from the Sub-Ibanskians for the improvement of agriculture and the reconstruction of industry. Runt let it be known that he intended to raise the question of most favoured nation status. He had already begun to establish a widespread network of agents in Sub-Ibansk to suborn foreign businessmen and local leftists. And the businessmen had begun to insist on the establishment of economic relations. They had been promised that a crap processing plant would be built on mutually disadvantageous terms.

The legend

The snow fell damp into the foxholes, lashed our faces, filled our eyes.

The lecturer in his sheepskin jacket praised the future to the skies,

Talked of 'exploits', 'sacrifices', made an hour's 'inspired oration',

Told us, from his sheet of paper, who'd been heroes of the nation.

Then he ended and departed. Now's the time, the captain said.

Some of us swore muffled curses. Others yelled Hooray instead.

When we'd taken our objective, first we buried those who'd died,

Then lay waiting in the snowstorm, huddled freezing side by
    side.
But the lecturer—our friend—*he* didn't suffer, never fear!
When the medals were awarded, he got chestfuls, and to spare.
He kept his name in the headlines, his face gawped from every
    page;
He became a great commander ere he got to middle age.
I don't care. No odds to me. So let him play the hero part.
But I sometimes sit and wonder, how did all this nonsense start?
Is there any rhyme or reason in the way that things turn out,
For he is a yellow coward, fool, informer, layabout.

The queue

The Ibanskian Statistical Planning Bureau (Istaplan) published
data to show progress in the production of thingammyjigs for
the preceding year. As always, production targets were one
hundred per cent overfulfilled long before the stated date. The
agricultural workers of Transibansk had distinguished themselves particularly. They would have harvested thingammyjigs
all round the clock if they had known where they had planted
what they had never planted, and if what had not grown had
really turned out to be thingammyjigs. A large group of what
the newspapers came to call the 'gatherers of grey, crimson-
speckled gold' were given medals. The Queue was enlarged and
reinforced by the cadres of control. 'Now our Queue has raised
itself to a new level,' said Leadiban, in a speech on no particular
occasion.' In the past we queued up out of sheer materialist
interest. Today our motives are purely spiritual. In the past the
living queue was dominant. Today our workers have opportunities on occasion to leave the queue to go about their business if they first warn the person behind that they intend to
return. So, we see here a transition from the living queue to the
half dead queue. We're discussing the draft of a new law which
would allow members of the same family to take each other's
places in the queue on the preliminary submission of an application form giving their home and work addresses and a character
reference certified by the Controlling Triangle. There were
some proposals to organize a waiting list for permission to join
the Queue. But we consider that this would be premature. In
our view we should first authorize citizens to join a waiting list

for the right to join a waiting list to join the waiting list to join the Queue.'

The return

'Yesterday I went to a banquet at Sociologist's,' said Neurasthenic. 'It was very strange. Of course everyone tore Truthteller, Double-dealer, Singer and the rest to bits. Very cautiously, of course, as befits intellectuals, using formulae like: You have to admit, but even so . . . or, They are thus and so, but you have to admit that . . .' 'Alas,' said Dauber, 'there's a touch of truth in that. After all, it is quite true that . . .' 'That is immoral,' said Chatterer. 'It is immoral to try to find fault with people of that kind, even if they do actually have shortcomings. You've been in the front line and you know what a sacrilege it is to recall that a man who has given his life to save yours sometimes wet his bed or had blue funks. A great deal of what you have, you have thanks to people like that. It is thanks to them that you were able to go Over There and to come back again. It is thanks to them that you can now calmly reflect on the most effective path for your creative development to follow.' 'It's not quite like that,' said Dauber. 'It's due in part to my own efforts, too.' 'That's true,' said Chatterer. 'But people talk about you in much the same way as about them.' 'Even worse,' said Neurasthenic, 'because in your case there aren't even any "buts".' 'So you can see that here we have a general rule, not an individual case,' said Chatterer. As Singer once said:

> He spoke the truth aloud with pride
> And looked you in the eye;
> And yet you turned your gaze aside
> And heaved a sneering sigh.
> I said, 'Oh him, he's full of guile,
> An expert in sensation.'
> 'Informer, too,' you said with bile
> And righteous indignation.
> 'He's very trivial,' one says,
> Another says, 'Naïve'.
> 'He doesn't understand our ways,
> Nor grasp what we believe.'
> 'And what about his fine ideas,
> Essentially absurd?'

'He's told some lies too, it appears.
He's known to break his word.'
All right, then, He's a zero;
We'll shun Him as befits:
Till He's proclaimed a hero,
Let no-one call us shits.

The opposition gets down to work
'I've got ideal conditions for creative work,' said Teacher. 'I'm
alone. My job only takes up a couple of hours a day, or even less.
I've got as much paper as I need, and any reference book I want.
In the end even all the secret documents reach me. It's my job to
burn them. I've got no preconceptions, no dependence on set
ideas. I'm completely free. So what should be easier than to sit
down, advance hypotheses, and develop concepts? But ever
since I was released, I haven't written a single line. I've even
stopped looking at secret documents. It was interesting at first,
forbidden fruit after all. But eventually I realised that it was all
as drab and tedious as everything that is published officially,
and there was nothing secret in them anyway. All there is is an
empty, meaningless pretence of secrecy. The documents were
no use at all for any serious scientific study. When I was Inside,
I used to think that as soon as I was set free I would begin to
work night and day to catch up with lost time. That was sheer
nonsense, just the despairing vanity of a corpse determined to
relive his past life. First, anything I might have written would
never have been published. Secondly, if it had been published
no-one would have read it. And thirdly, if anyone did read it
they wouldn't be able to understand it, and everything would
be distorted, plagiarised and vilified.' 'If you'd been Leadiban,
your scribblings would have gone down in history,' said Blockhead. 'Never,' said Teacher. 'Leadiban is barred from thinking
in this kind of way, and even from signing things which other
people have written. Not that there's any need for him to be
barred. Such is the way people rise to become Leadiban, that
there's no chance of their thinking at all. I could set out a
detailed programme of social reform which would operate in
favour of those in power but which would improve the lot of the
others at the same time. It's not very complicated. You don't
need to be a genius to work out a system of sensible rationalization.

(807)

But I'm not going to. It'd be a waste of time. There is no need for rationalization here. Indeed, it's something they couldn't care less about. Do you find that strange? No. It's the instinct of self-preservation. Any rationalization would make social relationships more transparent, and that's exactly what they want to avoid. They only feel normal in conditions of misty confusion, where no-one can understand anything. It is in their essential nature to spend their time shuffling the cards, for they play by the methods (not the rules!) of some entirely fictitious game. They fear reformers even more than opponents. Note well that they have made us into an opposition group, not a group of rationalizers. An opposition is something easier to combat. It's clear that opposition has no future. Rationalization appears to have a future because it fits in with official propaganda. Incidentally, the best way of distinguishing between propaganda and sincere intentions is to try to put the slogans of propaganda into practice.' Speculatress came running in. 'Hey!' she said, 'you lot! Have you forgotten it's pay day at UNO? Let's get going! We've got a place in the queue.'

The legend
The captain's voice was low and hoarse,
His words, though, had a mighty force:
We're in a bloody mess!
The casualty list is long,
We're quite cut off. Don't get me wrong,
We must break out, no less.
They promise us that we can have apartments as of right,
And building sites for country homes will soon be handed out.
Some seats in the Academy? They're getting rather tight.
But we've got four that you can have without the slightest
    doubt.
Of course we haven't got the right to force you to accept.
You've got to make the choice yourselves, so think about it
    well,
Reflect upon it thoroughly, you know what to expect,
And once you've made your choice, that's it, although it may be
    hell.
But some of you must here stay back
To face the enemy's attack;

(808)

Decide as best you can.
Then, like our half-destroyed platoon,
The entire institute quite soon
Stepped forward as one man.

The return

'I'm prepared to agree with you,' said Dauber. 'But in that case you'll have to acknowledge that I was right about the Gravestone. You've said yourself that Hog's report was one of the most significant events in the development of our society.' 'We constantly confuse two different questions,' said Chatterer. 'The development of an artist is one thing, the development of the society he lives in is quite another. If you want to make progress in the second way you should be sculpting Truthteller, not Leadiban. Hog's report cannot be repeated. And all the rest has nothing to do with the moral progress or the development of the anti-social principle. You don't want to sculpt Truth-teller. It seems to you that he and you are on the same scale, since as an artist you are as great as he is, and may be even greater. You are a genius. But you're an Ibanskian just the same. You're an Ibanskian genius. As for Truth-teller, even if we accept that he's a mediocre artist, he is god. Even if he is an Ibanskian god. Even if he's a godling, a godlet, a demigod. Whatever he is, he has brought a fragment of God into our society.' 'That'll do,' said Dauber. 'The hell with the lot of them—truth-tellers, hogs, leadibans, gods, demigods, and the rest. I'm fed-up to the back teeth with this country. I'll finish Leadiban . . . can't just drop it like that . . . almost finished . . . see for yourself . . . not coming on too badly . . . pity to chuck it in . . . I'll finish Leadiban, and then get the hell out of this Ibanskian murk. It's an insult to one's humanity to go on living here, no matter what one's ideas and intentions are.'

The end of the problem

As was to be expected, a sensational discovery was made at ARSE. It was the discovery of the millennium, as Leadiban put it. The ARSE team invented Vitamin Z-1974 which could be used for:

Turning Mogul into Gogol,
Turning Gogol into Hegel,

(809)

Making Baabel out of Babel,
Turning a Chair into a Table,
Lyricist to Physicist,
Hedonist to Platonist,
Making toffee out of turds,
And elephants to fly like birds.

In a word, they could make anyone they liked from any individual and then turn him into anybody else. And this could all be done in a matter of minutes. Two or three injections, and it's all over. So now we can have as many physicists, lyricists, charwomen, Chinamen, diplomats, alcoholics, hooligans, lawyers, inventors, geniuses, generals, friends, cyberneticists, delegates, enemies, and so on, and so on as we like said Leadiban. And in case of need, we can transfer any man from any job to any other, just the time it takes for a couple of injections. But in these new conditions the directing role of the Brotherhood and UNO becomes even more important. We cannot make all our citizens into physicists, no matter how much some people may find this desirable. It's still too early. If society were to consist entirely of physicists, there would be no-one left to rule the state, to fight alcoholism and crime, to sculpt busts of the leaders, and to take charge of political education. And who would protect our frontiers and unmask spies and saboteurs? We need not only physicists, but lyricists as well. And diplomats. And charwomen. And cooks. And women. Yes, yes, indeed we need women. Even though our scientists have discovered how to create the rising generation from the industrial effluents which in the past used to pollute the atmosphere, and men therefore have no more need for women, women still play a huge part in the cultural and economic life of our country. We even need enemies and malcontents so that our all-conquering doctrine should become progressively more refined in the continuing struggle with them, and so that everyone should see with their own eyes the superiority of our social system above all others. But it's not just any old enemies we need, nor in any random quantity. We must observe rigorous proportions and dosages. As the proverb has it,

Every woman's always needed
Papa's words are always heeded.

Today we have overcome all the problems and difficulties of

growth. Now we shall throw all our strength into the battle for thingammyjigs. The time has come! . . . But we must in all matters retain our sense of proportion and not overdo it, otherwise we might end up like the recently departed Firadep 17. He suffered from nocturnal enuresis and tried to get himself cured by hypnosis. The cure was so effective that he couldn't pass water even during the day. The result was that he died of a cerebral urinorrhage. So we have to engage ourselves in a nationwide struggle against the excessive consumption of thingammyjigs. As the proverb has it:

> If after meals you keep on eating
> Your guts will take an awful beating.

The legend

Why have you stayed, and not fled with the rest?
I shrugged and shook my head, I felt depressed.
I long have fought for this my motherland,
For her I've lain and shivered in the frost,
For her I've starved when no food came to hand,
Here I grew up. I'm hers at any cost.
I weep, but not a maudlin drunkard's tears;
They're tender recollection I can't hide
Of all the love I've given her down the years,
My only love, my own grey land, my bride.
Bereft of wife and babes one can survive;
To leave one's land's a thought I can't endure.
Better by far be buried here alive
And feed her —be it only as manure.

The exchange of experience

'Our system of government,' said Lesidel, 'has gone through a considerable period of evolution. We can distinguish three schematic stages. The first stage consisted of crushing everyone who came to hand, and crushing them in such a way that everyone else could see and feel that their turn would soon come. The second stage also consisted of crushing people, but selectively, in such a way that everyone thought that all we were doing was consolidating our achievements and re-educating those who had fallen into error. This was known as the humane democratic period. This experiment was not successful, as

ill-intentioned elements imagined that we were actually humane and democrats, and began to behave in such a way that we had to return temporarily to the first stage. The third stage consists of making sure that there is no-one to crush. This is the most rational period and it is still in operation. It combines within itself the best qualities of the first and the second stages. Since no-one is being crushed, power reveals its deeply humane and democratic nature. And since everyone understands that with the support of the masses we shall not allow the development of a situation where steps have to be taken, it is evident that we are the only true power. We have even introduced a clause into the constitution according to which every sub-Ibanskian has the right to criticise the actions of the authorities, and that anyone who tries to prevent him from doing so is punishable by law. And this clause is religiously observed.'
'You mean there are people who criticise you?' asked Firadep. 'Come off it!' replied Lesidel. 'That's the last thing anyone would think of doing. All it means is that the representatives of authority have never yet been brought to book for repressing criticism of their actions or for prosecuting those who criticise.'

The return
'Soon it will all be over,' said Dauber. 'Why should we act towards each other against our conscience! Tell me quite honestly: What was it that induced you to take the path you've chosen?' 'Once upon a time,' said Chatterer, 'I was surprised by the disparity between official propaganda about our way of life, and life itself. And I wanted to discover whether or not this was a law of our life, and if so, why. And as the years passed, this wish became stronger and stronger. And the more I understood the question, the stronger grew this desire. That's all.' 'And did you discover it?' asked Dauber. 'I did,' said Chatterer. 'How is this law to be explained then?' asked Dauber. 'There is no explanation,' said Chatterer. 'It is a false problem. The assertion which defines this law can be deduced like a theorem from Schizophrenic's most fundamental propositions. There can be no other basis or explanation. In general, if one seeks explanations and fundamentals in cases like this, it just shows how little one has grasped the heart of the problem.' 'So?' asked Dauber. 'So that's that,' said Chatterer. 'I discovered what I wanted to

discover. I discovered more than I wanted to discover. I discovered everything. And now I want to learn nothing more. I am bored.' 'With everything?' asked Dauber. 'What about the electron? Knowledge of the electron, surely, is inexhaustible?' 'Knowledge of the electron is not knowledge,' said Chatterer. 'Science offers no more knowledge since it became common gossip. At best, science can offer faith but a false and amoral faith. But more often than not it leads us into error.' 'Doesn't it strike you that your motive for living was somewhat egoistic?' asked Dauber. 'No,' said Chatterer. 'Among the laws of our life which I discovered there are these: When people go about shouting at the top of their voices that they are only thinking of the good of the people, they are thinking mainly, or entirely, about their own good; when people shout that they are ready to sacrifice themselves, in fact they are trying to get their hands on everything they can. And so on and so forth. In brief, I knew everything from the very beginning. And now at the end of my life I am convinced that, sadly, I was right.' 'What about me?' asked Dauber. 'You? You've not known anything from the start.' said Chatterer, 'and you will never know.' 'But I listen to you,' replied Dauber; 'I understand, I agree, I see a lot for myself.' 'That means nothing,' said Chatterer. 'All this is just reflected in you. It is not born, nor does it live within you.' 'So, what does live within me?' asked Dauber. 'Something quite different,' said Chatterer, 'a creative force, which is blind, involuntary and disincarnate. From the moment I realised, I began to grow bored. Now there is nothing left for me to do. And soon you will have performed everything which was contained in your creative force, and you too will become bored. Boredom is not merely an absence of joy, of gaiety and so on. Boredom is something positive. It is born, it grows, and it matures. It is the inevitable product of our way of life.'

The end of the legend
'Nothing further happened,' said Teacher. 'There was just interminable meditation.' 'Where did this meditation lead you?' asked the Girl. 'To the realisation that we think too much, and do too little. We think a great deal because we do not know how to act, do not want to act, and have no opportunity to act. And therefore we think a great deal, substituting real action

with fictitious action.' 'Why is this?' asked the Girl. 'Because we are what we are,' said Teacher. 'We want to be like that, and so we are like that.' 'Surely it can't be as simple as that?' asked the Girl. 'Yes,' said Teacher, 'it really is as complicated as that.' 'People say that imaginary actions give as much satisfaction as real actions,' said the Girl. 'So what difference does it make if things happen mentally and not physically.' 'That's all very well in principle,' said Teacher. 'But there is a minor quantitative difference. The satisfaction one gets from imagining being promoted to generalissimus is no greater than the satisfaction one gets from an actual promotion to corporal. If you imagine making love with Venus, your pleasure from that will be no greater than the pleasure you get from a night spent with some ignorant bottle-washer on her old-age pension.'

'Well, what next?' asked the Girl. 'There'll be progress,' said Teacher. 'Our scientists will discover how to free people from pain, from the fear of death, from envy, from hurt feelings. Just a couple of injections at birth and a cloudless future is guaranteed.' 'What a beautiful thought,' said the Girl. 'I wish I could be born then!' 'You're wrong,' said Teacher. 'You only have to go to the psychiatric hospital and they'll show you as many varieties of these men of the future as you like. Life without the fear of death and other disagreeable feelings is deprived of any kind of human content. And on top of that, a man who does not have these feelings, but who still has his reason, constitutes a threat of violence and murder on such a scale that the nightmares of our recent past will look like child's play in comparison.' 'Stop frightening me,' said the Girl. 'I'm doing nothing of the kind,' said Teacher. 'Unfortunately, it won't be frightening at all. Even now, no-one is frightened by it.'

Today there's no more pain. Our doubts are past.
The fear of death has left our heart and soul.
Not animals now, not even plants we're classed—
Just cogs in a machine blind men control.

A plan for a coup d'état
'The time is ripe for a coup,' said Colleague. 'Here are the facts. Leadiban has been awarded ten tons of medals. He has made ten thousand journeys. He has delivered a hundred volumes of speeches. He has done a million foolish things. His Firadeps are

bursting with envy. Just a little longer and they'll begin to peg out without having managed to flaunt themselves on the stage of history in leading roles.' 'I agree,' said the Director of UNO 'But who shall we replace him with?' 'There are one hundred and ninety-seven pretenders with any chance,' said Colleague. 'A mere handful this time.' 'Yes,' said the Director. 'That's what makes things more complicated.' 'Very well,' said Colleague. 'We'll have to bring the Seradeps in as well. That'll treble the number of pretenders.' 'Fine,' said Director. 'And the new Leadiban will be the most useless candidate with the least chance. As always.' 'Perhaps you yourself,' Colleague began to stutter. 'Are you out of your mind?' bellowed Director. 'I've got the best chance of anybody. I'm candidate No. 1, as always. Can you think of a single instance when the best placed pretender has come to power? Well? Now let's have your plan for the coup!' 'Very good, Sir,' said Colleague. 'The first thing, take control of the Pavilion, and then the Shithouse. Simultaneously we surround the Shop and cut off the telephone. We get Fuzz drunk. And all this must be done without anyone noticing any coup. Just an ordinary drunken orgy! As for the masses, the masses will follow us. We'll put out a slogan: Thingammyjigs for All! No queues! What about that, then? The classics would have been green with envy. Then we liquidate the opposition group. We just need a trial or two. We can make them responsible for whatever goes wrong.' 'Good,' said Director. 'Go ahead. When the coup is over, report to me. Wait a moment! When's it going to be?' 'Today's too late, and tomorrow's too early,' said Colleague. 'So . . .

The return

And Dauber dreamed a dream. He dreamt that from the early hours his new studio on Victors' Avenue began to fill up with officials from the Ministry of Culture, UNO agents, the directors of the Department of Culture, representatives of the Directing Council of the Visual Arts, inspectors from the private office of Chief Theoretician, journalists, artists, writers, women, girls, informers, friends, acquaintances and foreigners. The new studio was large and there was no crush. The monumental sculptures made from the new everlasting material, snotoplast, looked much smaller and the crowd much thinner. The largest number of foreigners were sub-Ibanskians, since by now they were the only foreigners possible. Some American and French Ibanskians had tried to slip in, but hadn't been given visas. Who are you kidding? You've done enough travelling—now just stay put. The sub-Ibanskians pretended to like everything very much. But between themselves they said that their Hack, whom they had recently devoured because he had abandoned the principles of the sub-Ibanskian Ism, was a much better sculptor. And the materials he used were much stronger— Turdotron 3. His little statuettes had proved too much even for the atomic hammers specially imported from Ibansk. That's real quality work for you!

'Stand by,' ordered the Television Director. 'Action!' And with a resolute gesture, Dauber removed the dirty, tattered cloth which veiled his new work. The assembled company caught their breath in astonishment and froze into attitudes of enthusiastic admiration. Before their eyes, sculpted from an even more eternally durable material, five times refined Turdotron, they saw Leadiban's magnificent head, his curls cascading over his wise and powerful brow. His straight, strong, ancient Roman nose expressed serenity and confidence in the rightness of his actions. His jutting, modern German jaw revealed his indomitable spirit. His soft, ancient Greek lips were of a feminine cast and spoke of the extreme goodness and kindness of this, the greatest statesman of the age. 'It's amazing,' exclaimed Neurasthenic. 'I don't mean the likeness, which is perfect of course. But with what depth and precision you've been able to show the spiritual essence of this man who is the personification of our age.' 'Yes,' said Thinker. 'When they see this, our descendants will say of our times: "Alas, the Golden Age of mankind is now long past." '

> The law that governs history
> Is rigid, firm and fast:
> The one authentic Golden Age
> Is always in the past.
> There's no point trying to refute
> This cast-iron rigid law;
> Just learn to live with it, and thus
> Some useful lessons draw.
> Reforms are useless, only wait,

One day not far ahead,
A Golden Age our kids will see
In this cruel age of lead.

'Well?' Dauber asked Chatterer. 'We each die in our own way,' said Chatterer. 'Some are killed violently. Others are killed without noticing it. And yet others kill themselves. I have nothing more to do here. It is time. I engendered this schizophrenic world. And I shall destroy it, and I shall destroy it according to the laws of this world itself. I shall destroy myself.' 'What a nightmare,' thought Dauber. And he tried to waken himself. But he could not. There was no waking from this nightmare. And then he saw clearly, but it was too late.

I sit and draw, not caring, without thought,
In unbelief at what my senses tell.
I feel, not hear, a voice behind me yell:
You'd be no loss! Fuck off! We know your sort!
No loss indeed, if all you feel is pain,
When you are alien to each and all
And walk a tightrope and you fear to fall.
Through trackless bog there's no sure way to tread,
No foothold in the treacherous swamp ahead
In which . . . as countless moments in the past . . .
Discussion's useless, agreements do not last.
Creative urges—they're just youth's delusion,
Real work is pain—and pain is no illusion.
True inspiration is waiting for the end,
One premise against which none can contend.
So which way now? What way must I behave?
What thread must be snapped through? What is my goal?
Freedom's the step from prison to the grave,
And deathlessness, the worm that gnaws my soul.

The death of a genius is not an episode but the essence of this society—that was his last thought.

In the morning a gang of workmen turned up at the studio. They collected up the empty bottles and with the money they got for them bought a half-litre, which they drank on the spot from the bottle on empty stomachs. The studio was demolished. On its site there rose up the magnificent buildings of the Institute for the Discovery of Talent in the Embryo. The Ibanskians were rewarded. Some were given medals, some

(817)

villas, some sandwiches, some only a brass farthing. The junior research workers were sent to gather in the rotting potato harvest. The trusted informers went off to an international congress. The hand of fraternal aid was proferred to the inhabitants of Roachland. There was a formal protest. A friendly visit. Universal compulsory super-higher-education was introduced, which showed everyone else where to get off. An anniversary was celebrated. A resolution was passed calling for everything to move to a new, higher stage. Shortcomings were eliminated. A war was started against corruption and drunkenness. People lined up in a queue and waited for it to get round to their turn. In a speech to mark these successes, Leadiban said: 'At the present time Ibansk lives according to the laws of beauty. One needs only to see the appearance of an Ibanskian,' he exclaimed, exposing every detail of his mighty mug on the television screens. 'Not only have we produced a new and superior type of human society, but a new and superior type of human faceology.' Snottyhanky, the pensioners' favourite poet, replied to Leadiban's speech with a new poem:

See here the ultimate Ibanskian shit!
In him all is explained.
Such beauty in this world nor in the next
Can never be attained.

It's a good time, thought Theoretician, to start shoving people inside, etc., etc., etc., etc.

Oh, fuck ....
....
....your mother!

The exchange of experience

'Crime has disappeared here,' said Firadep. 'We never had any,' said Lesidel. 'How come?' asked Firadep in astonishment. 'It's very simple,' said Lesidel. 'We never had any concept of crime.' 'But surely there must be occasions when your individuals behave in a way that demands punishment,' said Firadep doggedly. 'Oh, that's what you mean,' said Lesidel. 'We've got as much of that as you like. But why call them criminals? Real criminals are always very good at escaping retribution, and the people who get punished are usually perfectly innocent and are only punished because they can't get out of it. That's why we didn't feel the need to introduce a concept of crime. And how do you manage to avoid crime?' 'It's very simple,' said Firadep. 'We destroy the criminals before they manage to commit their crime. Preventive medicine!' 'That's excellent,' said Lesidel. 'We shall have to try to apply your remarkable method.'

Lesidel then went on to talk about the system of punishment employed in sub-Ibansk. The Ibanskians were particularly interested in the corrective ring. This was a closed ring-shaped corridor. The man under sentence was given food at a specific time, and to get his next meal he had to complete the number of circuits to which he'd been sentenced. He had to do this without interruption throughout the entire length of his sentence. For instance, a criminal might be sentenced to 10/5. That meant that for ten years he had to complete five circuits in order to get his food. Five circuits in Ibanskian measure was thirty miles. The sub-Ibanskians had no death penalty, which had been replaced by the very humane punishment of 100/100. 'And who passes sentence?' asked Firadep. 'The people,' said Lesidel. Firadep revealed the high level of perfection achieved by Ibanskian jurisprudence. Everything was automated and done by computers. The judges had been replaced by scientists who programmed the computers. 'What is the severest punishment you have? asked Lesidel. Firadep explained that it was reading aloud under the control of a computer the complete works of all the Leadibans, starting from Leadiban I. 'It's a very humane punishment as all those sentenced to it die of mortal boredom before they've even got through the speeches of Leadiban I.' But Lesidel did not understand this punishment. The sub-Ibanskians did not know what reading meant, and writing even less so. It is true that Firadep failed to point out that the condemned man was given food only when he had finished the reading of a complete volume.

The opposition at work

The members of the opposition group took their places in the longest queue, at the window from which the lowest ranks of UNO received their pay-packets. They joined the line which included civilian informers, secret agents, lower ranking spies, revolutionaries, liberals, progressives, and so on, who were either hourly paid or part-time. A rather shorter queue waited alongside. In it, Teacher spotted Sociologist, Thinker, Wife and others he knew. But they showed no sign of recognising him. As a general rule there was a principle that was observed rigorously in the UNO pay office: HERE NO-ONE KNOWS ANY ONE. And when Bloke tried to address some familiar remark to Blockhead, the other replied that he was not accustomed to such coarse approaches from people he did not know. Bloke began to sulk. In the shortest queue, which was intended for people who had the right not to queue, stood Colleague. And everyone was bored.

Summit meetings

Later, naturally, there were summit meetings. First the Leader of sub-Ibansk (Leasubib) visited Ibansk, then Leadiban visited sub-Ibansk. It's true that in the course of his visit, Leadiban was so thoroughly impregnated with the stench of sub-Ibansk that he had to be replaced by a new one. And who do you think his successor was? Firadep 39! And not 17, as had been supposed previously. The new Leadiban cooled things down rather but there was no longer any possibility of stopping the march of history. The new Leadiban, in practical terms, continued his predecessor's policies, although he stank a good deal less.

During the exchange of visits by Leasubib and the old Leadiban a number of treaties were concluded. The principal one was a non-aggression pact according to which the two contracting parties promised not to attack each other, for the time being. In consequence the General Staffs of the two great powers immediately proceeded to rearmament and drew up contingency plans for mobilisation and operations to be conducted in the forthcoming war. It became difficult to walk freely on the streets of Ibansk because the pavements were so crammed by sub-Ibanskian spies. As far as Sub-Ibansk was concerned, the large number of sensational trials which had taken place there recently bore eloquent witness to the fact that the sub-Ibanskians could no longer rely even on their own Leasubib.

Then there was a treaty of mutual aid and comfort in their struggle against the common enemy. The Ibanskians began to supply the sub-Ibanskians with tanks and aircraft, receiving in return from the sub-Ibanskians stench-laden gases and putrefying bacteria. Thanks to this selfless and disinterested aid, both armies were rapidly reinforced. At the beginning of the summer a sub-Ibanskian reconnaisance aircraft of unknown construction was shot down in Ibanskian air space. The aircraft flew without fuel, without a pilot and without cameras, but managed nevertheless to take photographs of all the secrets. Had it not been for the vigilance of UNO the affair might have ended badly long before the projected deadline.

A further treaty dealt with economic co-operation. The Ibanskians began to export to sub-Ibansk agricultural machinery, looms and other industrial equipment. The sub-Ibanskians exported food stuffs. The Ibanskian leaders were particularly interested in thingammyjigs. Although no-one knew what they were, the sub-Ibanskians promised to supply the Ibanskians with large quantities of thingammyjigs at rock-bottom prices. It's true that in exchange they demanded from the Ibanskians deerskin caps, automobiles of the new popular Ibana make, and three million souvenir dolls. The Ibanskians contracted to supply and build a camera and cine camera factory for sub-Ibansk. The sub-Ibanskians embarked on the construction of a major urine pipeline which was to pass right through the earth and come out in the very centre of Ibansk. The Ibanskians began to build an industrial complex for the processing of thingammyjigs, for which the sub-Ibanskians were contracted to supply the most sophisticated machinery. In all, trade agreements were reached on 93,715,371 types of product. The Ibanskians made the sub-Ibanskians a substantial loan to help them overcome inflation. And the sub-Ibanskians promised to apply most favoured nation treatment in their trade relations with Ibansk.

Finally, joint research programmes were initiated into outer space and into the electron which, as everyone knows, is also inexhaustible. And within a year the sub-Ibanskians went into orbit.

One further agreement, which was not reported in the press, was also made. This concerned joint action against the intelligentsia, but its content still remains unknown.

Clear frontiers were established, with all the attributes frontiers normally involve, (passports, visas, customs, excise duties and so on).

It became fashionable to go about naked, to be swarming with lice, to eat excrement and to emit a stench appropriate to one's social position.

'The situation is very encouraging,' said Leasubib, shortly before he was accused of corruption and eaten. 'Our policy of détente with sub-Ibansk has produced brilliant results,' said Leadiban, shortly before he was accused of liberalism and deposed.

The sub-Ibanskians came across only one difficulty in their relations with the Ibanskian leaders: the latter all looked the same and the sub-Ibanskians repeatedly confused them, which led to embarrassing incidents.

The return

Throughout my life, Chatterer said to himself, there has been one thought which I have constantly affirmed: we desperately need a public opinion which is guaranteed by law, and which as a result could be the beginning of the moral progress of society. Here in Ibansk real life goes on under the form of deals and settlements behind the scenes. Everything that appears on the surface is nothing but deceptive froth. That is why our masters are men-fleas, men-rats. And they force us to watch their flea-rat performance. If there is no expression of public opinion, society will perish in the end by suffocating in an enormous rathole. That may be a commonplace, but there is no alternative. But then everything is commonplace here. All our complexities are terrifyingly commonplace. They're compensations for the absence of any real complexity.

The collapse of the coup d'état

As in any good spy thriller, the ingenious plan for the coup d'état fell apart over minor details. They weren't able to get the Fuzz drunk because he had been completely sozzled since dawn. The Pavilion had been closed the day before for an inventory, as the manager had been fiddling too much. The telephone had been vandalised the previous year. The pretenders to the position of the new Leadiban turned out to be so identically mediocre that the most stupid of them could not be detected even by the ARSE computers. Colleague cursed the Ibanskian structure of society, drank vodka and tried in vain to find at least one member of the opposition group, for he hated drinking alone.

The return

Early one morning Chatterer went to the Undertaker's and took his place in the queue. The queue moved forward amazingly slowly. Although a good twenty or thirty clerks were hanging about the office doing nothing, the funeral documentation was being filled in by just one peevish little man who hated every-thing alive. He argued over every tiny detail, forcing his clients to fill in their forms as many as four times. No more than one in ten of those who were waiting received their voucher for the crematorium and the columbarium. 'What a nightmare it all is,' said an extremely old intellectual-looking woman who was standing in front of Chatterer; 'it's the fifth time I've had to queue here. Just look. This is the first batch of forms. He corrected them. Then I went round all the offices again, filled the forms in and had them stamped as he told me to. Then I brought them back here. They were still wrong. He altered them to what I'd had in the first place. And now it's the fifth time. My God! You can't even die and get buried without all this humiliating procedure. I told him that one day I'd simply die here in the queue. And do you know what he said? "You'll get fined," he said. "Or ten days in jail." Me, with fifty years of honest work behind me! What *is* the answer?' 'It's very simple,' said Chatterer. 'You just have to work out every possible var-iant of the way the forms could be filled in and bring all the variants back at the same time. There are only about ten million possible variants. A mere nothing.'

When Chatterer's turn drew near the Funeral Director turned up. 'The office is closed.' All the staff went into a meeting to discuss preparations for the next festival, and their competitive challenge to the neighbouring Undertaker's. The peevish little man proposed that the number of deaths should be trebled, and the number of cremations increased ten-fold. The meeting received the proposal with tumultuous applause. When the office re-opened the peevish little man became even more ferociously vigilant in checking the documents, which had cost his clients so much hard labour to prepare. I'd be willing to bet, thought Chatterer, that he and his family live in a tiny room in a communal apartment, that he gets paid a pittance, that he still hasn't been able to get his youngest into a creche for the second year running, and that when his wife gets home from work she has to hang about in queues for food, trying to find the cheapest things. And he pours out all the hatred for his miserable existence on his defenceless fellow men. And here in the office he is the king and the god. Here he is omnipotent.

But it turned out that Chatterer was in luck, for the first time in his life. And the last, he thought. After he had rejected the documents of the twenty people ahead of Chatterer, the man decided to have a breather. He even addressed Chatterer politely, something he did only once a year, as an extreme exception. 'It looks as if it's all in order,' said the peevish man. 'Your reference isn't in exactly the prescribed form, but it'll do. We aren't bureaucrats. Why bother with red tape. But how is it that you've been given a pass for the crematorium if you haven't even reached pensionable age? You need special circumstances for that. Incurable illness, is it?' 'Yes,' said Chatterer. 'Mortal boredom.' 'Ah,' said the peevish little man. 'That's quite another thing. Here's your voucher for the crematorium and this one's for the columbarium. Right. Take care of yourself. Next!'

Chatterer left the office tranquil and at peace. According to the law, he now had the right to three days in which to make his farewells to his family and friends and to put his worldly affairs in order, i.e. to destroy or otherwise dispose of all of his possessions and hand his room over to the manager of the block. But after three days, at a precise time, he had to report to the crematorium, and . . . take his place in the queue to be incinerated. According to the Ibanskian classification of queues, this queue was referred to as 'live'. In the entire period since the law on death had been adopted in Ibansk, there had never been a single instance of a person who sincerely wanted to recognise the inevitability of his death failing to turn up at his crematorium at the appointed hour. In Ibansk, free-will governs even death itself.

The end of the opposition

'It seems to be well matured,' said Leadiban, drinking down his words with a glass of sub-Ibanskian hooch. 'God, it's strong! That's the genuine article you get from abroad.' 'All the same, our Ibanodka is something else again,' said Firadep 21. 'Certainly it's mature,' said Firadep 11, although he hadn't the faintest idea what being mature meant. Leadiban himself didn't know. It was in this that lay the entire wisdom of drivelectic. 'It's well matured,' bellowed the inferior masses, and began to take initiatives approved at the top. In order to accelerate the arrival of what was mature (no-one had the slightest doubt that it had matured), it was decided on an initiative from below and with the approval of those at the top—they later changed places, and then changed back again, thus forming a monolithic unity—in a word it was decided to introduce an austerity programme. 'Food is far too cheap,' said Miss Backscratcher. 'That's true,' said Leadiban. And to meet the wishes of the workers, food prices were increased. 'We eat far too much meat,' said Arselicker. 'That's true,' said Leadiban. And meat disappeared from the shops; this was meat which they had been wanting to sell for a year but without success because it had disappeared the previous year. 'We're stuffing ourselves with too much butter,' said Harvester. 'That's very true,' said Leadiban, and . . . Soon a certain disparity was observed between too high a standard of living and a certain difficulty in satisfying it. 'We'll have to admit honestly,' said Leadiban, 'that we're pushing ahead too fast. We must . . .' In a few words it was resolved, at the request of the intelligentsia, to reduce the numbers of lower ranking hourly-paid and part-time workers. And so the opposition lost their jobs. The newspapers printed articles explaining that thanks to these wise measures the standard of living of the workers had risen sharply. The opposition was forgotten about, in the same way as people forgot to fill in the pit beneath the windows of the house where Chatterer lived. 'It's nothing to worry about,' said Teacher. 'Now I'll have even more free time for creative work.' 'The distinguishing feature of our society,' said Leadiban, in his speech to mark the imminent approach of the second stage of madogism, 'is its irresistible dynamism. We're moving forward well ahead of our arses.'

The return

'One good friend of mine spent his entire life in a desperate search for the key that would solve all our problems,' said Teacher. 'Did he find it?' asked Blockhead. 'No,' said Teacher, 'he never did, even though it was in his hands all the time.' 'And have you found it?' asked Bloke. 'Yes, I have,' said Teacher. 'It is public opinion, guaranteed by law, which as a result could be the foundation of the moral development of society.' 'You are asking too much,' said Bloke. 'Who's going to give you that? No-one,' said Teacher. 'People are going to have to invent it for themselves. At any price. Otherwise it'll be the end of everything.' 'How banal all that is,' said Blockhead. 'Yes, indeed,' said Teacher. 'And what can you suggest that's out of the ordinary? Nothing. The appalling banality of our problems engenders a psychologically complex compensation. How boring!'

The end of the queue

The site for the construction of the biggest Thingammyjig Processing Plant in the world (TPP) was designated in the most remote part of Ibansk, as far as possible from any centre of population or means of communication. The most boggy area possible was selected and a gigantic chimney erected. Foreign machinery was brought in and promptly sank in the bog, as was only proper, since we can do very well ourselves without the exploitation of backward peoples. Then a test well was sunk, followed by the first bore hole. 'When we build the TPP,' the pioneers said to a television reporter, 'no-one will ever believe that this site was once a desolate marsh. Here, for instance, you can see where our fifth tractor sank with all its crew. Not bad, eh! Romantic!' And the pioneers, keeping off the mosquitoes with cigarette smoke and the smell of vodka, burst into their favourite song, performed in rather hoarse voices:

Let mosquitoes and gnats bite as hard as they're able,
Let's live in the woods, an old log for a table.
For together with all these old lags out of prison
We're building the ultimate stage of the Ism.

The plant had been planned in such a way that its various effluents poisoned what remained of the environment, which no-one needed anyway. Its main effect was to suffocate the fish in the neighbouring lake, which slightly lowered the output of caviar and fur for the state's benefit. The extermination of the fish was made a major priority. 'Let us put all our strength behind TPP,' declared Leadiban in his speech on the occasion of the presentation of awards to the area where soon the multi-storey apartment blocks were to reach up to the polar sky. Preliminary calculations showed that ten million volunteers would be needed for the construction work. There was a general meeting of the Queue, at which all the queuers resolved to emigrate to the TPP along with the Shop and the Pavilion. Bloke, Blockhead, Teacher and others were also grabbed and voluntarily made to join the volunteers. 'That's the end,' said Bloke, digging himself a slit trench. 'Yes,' said Teacher, sucking a filthy looking rusk between his toothless gums. 'It's the beginning.'

A documentary film on the life of the TPP-ites was shown on television in several episodes. It was clear from the film that every TPP-ite had his own five-room apartment, a car, a master's or a doctor's degree, a deerskin hat, a jar of red caviar, a jar of black caviar, a whole smoked sausage, as much shashlik as he wanted, and a beautiful young wife with a coloratura soprano voice. 'They're getting above themselves, those bastards,' said Leadiban to a group of Firadeps. 'We'll have to transfer part of these supplementary rations away from TPP . . .'

Then it was decided to hold a cross-country running championship against the Sub-Ibanskians. All cash and materials were placed at the disposal of the Extraordinary Committee for the Organisation of Long-Distance Running Championships, including a Steeplechase Course. (ECOLDRCISC). And everyone forgot about TPP, which was handled over to UNO to look after for their own purposes. 'It's not a camp, it's a rest home,' said Colleague, as he signed the budget for the construction of walls, wire fences, and homes for the guards. 'We'll have to distribute passes for visits there very fairly between various organisations. It's high time!'

The end of the return

The Apartment Block Committee gave Chatterer a document on which he had to collect the signatures of a large number of organisations certifying that he owed them nothing. There was the regional library, the kindergarten, the dispensary, the mutual aid fund, the pensioners' committee and so on. Three days was barely long enough to get round them all. When he had handed in the form and the key to his room to the Block Manager, and had received in exchange a document declaring that he had no debts in the world, Chatterer set off for the crematorium. He had an hour to spare, so he did not hurry. He wanted to walk along Victors' Avenue, but he was turned away by the volunteer militia. The entire avenue was jammed with the queue waiting for thingammyjigs. Lucky people, thought Chatterer. They've still something left to hope for.

Let's tot up the balance sheet, Chatterer said to himself. Just a summary of accounts. But a vital one. What is the foundation of the foundations of human existence? Alas, the answer is a commonplace. It's been clear from the very start. Why did I have to live my life through to be sure of it? I don't know. I know only one thing: truth is the foundation of any truly human existence. The truth about oneself. The truth about others. The battle for truth and against it is the most ferocious and profound battle fought in society. And from now on the level of development of society, from the point of view of its humanity, will be defined by the degree of truth it allows. This is the first, the most primitive of evaluations. When people achieve a certain minimum level of truthfulness, they will advance other criteria. But everything begins from there.

Not far from the crematorium, Chatterer met Colleague. When Colleague discovered where Chatterer was heading for, he offered to get him in without having to queue, in memory of their long friendship which had stood the test of the years. And he did indeed manage to jump the queue, for he had other long-standing connections which still operated despite the passage of time.

Above the entrance to the cremation chamber, Chatterer read these words quoted from Leadiban's speech delivered on the occasion of the adoption of the Law on Death: REMEMBER! NO-ONE AND NOTHING IS FORCING YOU TO TAKE THIS STEP! He did not know that over the exit from the chamber there was a quotation from the last clause of the Directive on Death: AS YOU LEAVE, TAKE THE URN CONTAINING YOUR ASHES WITH

YOU! But that was no longer of any importance. And a last
thought came into his mind:
It was clear from the earliest days of my youth
That the years would go by without leaving a trace,
But it's rather annoying, to tell you the truth,
That there will not be a Last Judgment to face.
The departed will never rise up from their graves,
And their souls won't return, seeking mouldering flesh,
To learn if they're damned, or if they have been saved.
That there will be nothing, I freely confess
I think it's a shame. It'd be rather fun
For a moment or two to rise up from the dead
In the splendour of Heaven, to gaze on the One
In the seat of his Judgment, in fear and in dread,
And hear his voice calling: Speak now, come, we're ready!
One lie, you poor bastard, and you'll be unmasked;
Tell us all that you've done—but we know it already.
Be honest then. Honest, Lord? That's quite a task!
Consult your own ledgers. They're far more complete,
They'd show you my sins are just run of the mill.
I admit I've not always protected the weak;
I admit that I've frequently done people ill.
I admit that I've compromised, been less than frank,
I've informed on my friends—sometimes when I've been
    forced;
I've licked arses to get an improvement in rank,
I've broken my promise and shown no remorse.
I've lied on my own, and I've slandered in chorus,
I've put in the tune to the demagogues' lines.
I've consorted with scoundrels, although I deplored it,
I've tippled with crooks of all classes and kinds
So you see, Lord Almighty, my life has been pure.
If you want to reward me, I've got a request.
Perhaps I could ask you—or rather implore—
To order that I should now cease to exist.
I'm told that the dead feel no pain and no fear;
Their conscience is clear, for all that that's worth,
But their main advantage—they can't see or hear
How the living are treating each other on earth.
    And he ceased to exist. And that was the end of everything.